Great
SHORT
STORIES
OF THE
WORLD

Great
SHORT
STORIES
OF THE
WORLD

30 Classic Tales by
Ambrose Bierce, Leo Tolstoy,
Arthur Conan Doyle,
O. Henry, Anton Chekhov
and Many Others

EDITED BY LOIS HILL

AVENEL BOOKS
NEW YORK

First published in 1991 by Avenel Books, distributed by Outlet
Book Company, Inc., a Random House Company, 225 Park
Avenue South, New York, New York 10003.

Printed and bound in the United States of America

Library of Congress Cataloging-in-Publication Data
Great short stories of the world : 30 classic tales/by Ambrose
Bierce . . . [et al.] : edited by Lois Hill.
p.   cm.
ISBN 0-517-05448-5
1. Short stories.   2. Short stories—Translations into English.
3. Short stories, English—Translations from foreign languages.
I. Bierce, Ambrose, 1842–1914?   II. Hill, Lois.
PN6120.2.G74   1991
808.83′1—dc20   90-1245
                                                                    CIP

8   7   6   5   4   3   2   1

CONTENTS

INTRODUCTION

What the sage poets taught by th' heav'nly muse,
Storied of old in high immortal verse,
Of dire chimeras and enchanted isles,
And rifted rocks whose entrance leads to hell.
                                        —Milton

For everyone who enjoys superb storytelling, this anthology of thirty classic tales by some of the world's greatest writers will bring hours of reading pleasure and entertainment.

The word "story" comes from the ancient Greek word *historia,* meaning a small tale or an account of a single incident—and in a broader sense, the rich and brilliant tapestry of history. In 800 B.C., the date generally used for the period when Homer's great oral epics *The Iliad* and *The Odyssey* were first recorded in writing, storytelling and history were completely intertwined. As written literature evolved throughout the centuries, history separated itself from literature. Literature itself became endowed with a higher purpose than mere fiction, and those practicing the art of the literary short story often wrote miniature masterpieces. The short story is now recognized as one of the most difficult genres to perfect in the literary field.

Great Short Stories of the World presents a selection of these masterpieces drawn from the works of famous authors, both European and American, who lived and wrote during the past one hundred and fifty years. Many of these timeless and immortal tales rank among the greatest works of short literature.

Here is Washington Irving's classic tale of Rip Van Winkle's well-timed awakening from a twenty-year nap; Edgar Allan Poe's "The Murders in the Rue Morgue," one of the very first locked room mysteries and a brilliant analysis of an impossible crime; Nathaniel Hawthorne's "The Great Stone Face," where an old Indian prophecy comes to life in a sleepy little valley; and Hjalmar Hjorth Boyesen's "Good-for-Nothing," who finally finds his niche in life.

Ambrose Bierce's "The Damned Thing" undertakes an investigation into the impossible; O. Henry's tough tale of "The Phonograph and the Graft" occurs in an unsuspecting Latin American village. Booth Tarkington's "Mrs. Protheroe" assumes full charge of a silver-tongued young senator; Nikolai Teleshov's "The Duel" twists a matter of honor into an insurmountable obligation. "The Hanging at La Piroche" by Alexandre Dumas fils begins in 1498, on a lonely road that winds along the coast of Brittany; Anton Chekhov's "A Work of Art" describes what a modest doctor might do when presented with an ornate candelabrum made from the statues of two nude female figures.

In Arthur Conan Doyle's "Scandal in Bohemia," Sherlock Holmes and Dr. Watson undertake one of their more secretive investigations; while Jean August Strindberg's "Love and Bread" observes that not everyone is provided with gratuitous partridges and strawberries. If you are truly tired of life, forty pounds will buy a chance for death in Robert Louis Stevenson's "The Suicide Club." Théophile Gautier's magnificent "The Mummy's Foot" suggests that the charming little limb of Princess Hermonth is best *not* used as a paperweight; something completely unexpected lies within the darkness of Robert Louis Stevenson's "The Sire of Malétroit's Door". Finally, Leo Tolstoy's "The Long Exile" opens in the city of Vladímir where a young merchant named Aksénof is living an ordinary life, until one day . . .

Whether you're looking for tales of mystery, intrigue, the intricacies of human relationships, a hint of the supernatural, scandal, honor, history, politics, or simply justice, *Great Short Stories of the World* provides a treasure trove of some of the brightest gems in literature.

LOIS HILL

New York
1991

RIP VAN WINKLE

Washington Irving

Whoever has made a voyage up the Hudson must remember the Kaatskill Mountains. They are a dismembered branch of the great Appalachian family, and are seen away to the west of the river, swelling up to a noble height, and lording it over the surrounding country. Every change of season, every change of weather, indeed every hour of the day, produces some change in the magical hues and shapes of these mountains; and they are regarded by all the good wives, far and near, as perfect barometers. When the weather is fair and settled, they are clothed in blue and purple, and print their bold outlines on the clear evening sky; but sometimes, when the rest of the landscape is cloudless, they will gather a hood of gray vapors about their summits, which, in the last rays of the setting sun, will glow and light up like a crown of glory.

At the foot of these fairy mountains, the voyager may have descried the light smoke curling up from a village whose shingle roofs gleam among the trees, just where the blue tints of the upland melt away into the fresh green of the nearer landscape. It is a little village of great antiquity, having been founded by some of the Dutch colonists, in the early times of the province, just about the beginning of the government of the good Peter Stuyvesant (may he rest in peace!), and there were some of the houses of the original settlers standing within a few years, built of small yellow bricks brought from Holland, having latticed windows and gable fronts, surmounted with weathercocks.

In that same village, and in one of these very houses (which, to tell the precise truth, was sadly time-worn and weather-beaten), there lived many years since, while the country was yet a province of Great Britain, a simple, good-natured fellow, of the name of Rip Van Winkle. He was a descendant of the Van Winkles who figured so gallantly in the chivalrous days of Peter

1

Stuyvesant, and accompanied him to the siege of Fort Christina. He inherited, however, but little of the martial character of his ancestors. I have observed that he was a simple, good-natured man; he was moreover a kind neighbor, and an obedient henpecked husband. Indeed, to the latter circumstance might be owing that meekness of spirit which gained him such universal popularity; for those men are most apt to be obsequious and conciliating abroad who are under the discipline of shrews at home. Their tempers, doubtless, are rendered pliant and malleable in the fiery furnace of domestic tribulation, and a curtain lecture is worth all the sermons in the world for teaching the virtues of patience and long-suffering. A termagant wife may, therefore, in some respects, be considered a tolerable blessing; and if so, Rip Van Winkle was thrice blessed.

Certain it is that he was a great favorite among all the good wives of the village, who, as usual with the amiable sex, took his part in all family squabbles, and never failed, whenever they talked those matters over in their evening gossipings, to lay all the blame on Dame Van Winkle. The children of the village, too, would shout with joy whenever he approached. He assisted at their sports, made their playthings, taught them to fly kites and shoot marbles, and told them long stories of ghosts, witches, and Indians. Whenever he went dodging about the village, he was surrounded by a troop of them hanging on his skirts, clambering on his back, and playing a thousand tricks on him with impunity; and not a dog would bark at him throughout the neighborhood.

The great error in Rip's composition was an insuperable aversion to all kinds of profitable labor. It could not be from the want of assiduity or perseverance; for he would sit on a wet rock, with a rod as long and heavy as a Tartar's lance, and fish all day without a murmur, even though he should not be encouraged by a single nibble. He would carry a fowling-piece on his shoulder, for hours together, trudging through woods and swamps, and up hill and down dale, to shoot a few squirrels or wild pigeons. He would never refuse to assist a neighbor even in the roughest toil, and was a foremost man at all country frolics for husking Indian corn, or building stone fences. The women of the village, too, used to employ him to run their errands, and to do such little odd jobs as their less obliging husbands would not do for them; in a word, Rip was ready to attend to anybody's business but his own; but as to doing family duty, and keeping his farm in order, he found it impossible.

In fact, he declared it was of no use to work on his farm; it was the most pestilent little piece of ground in the whole country; everything about it went wrong, and would go wrong in spite of him. His fences were continually falling to pieces; his cow would either go astray, or get among the cabbages; weeds were sure to grow quicker in his fields than anywhere else; the rain always made a point of setting in just as he had some outdoor work to do; so that though his patrimonial estate had dwindled away under his management, acre by acre, until there was little more left than a mere patch of Indian corn and potatoes, yet it was the worst conditioned farm in the neighborhood.

His children, too, were as ragged and wild as if they belonged to nobody. His son Rip, an urchin begotten in his own likeness, promised to inherit the habits with the old clothes of his father. He was generally seen trooping like a colt at his mother's heels, equipped in a pair of his father's cast-off galligaskins, which he had much ado to hold up with one hand, as a fine lady does her train in bad weather.

Rip Van Winkle, however, was one of those happy mortals, of foolish, well-oiled dispositions, who take the world easy, eat white bread or brown, whichever can be got with least thought or trouble, and would rather starve on a penny than work for a pound. If left to himself, he would have whistled life away, in perfect contentment; but his wife kept continually dinning in his ears about his idleness, his carelessness, and the ruin he was bringing on his family.

Morning, noon, and night, her tongue was incessantly going, and everything he said or did was sure to produce a torrent of household eloquence. Rip had but one way of replying to all lectures of the kind, and that, by frequent use, had grown into a habit. He shrugged his shoulders, shook his head, cast up his eyes, but said nothing. This however, always provoked a fresh volley from his wife, so that he was fain to draw off his forces, and take to the outside of the house—the only side which, in truth, belongs to a henpecked husband.

Rip's sole domestic adherent was his dog Wolf, who was as much henpecked as his master; for Dame Van Winkle regarded them as companions in idleness, and even looked upon Wolf with an evil eye, as the cause of his master's going so often astray. True it is, in all points of spirit befitting an honorable dog, he was as courageous an animal as ever scoured the woods—but what courage can withstand the ever-during and all-besetting terrors of a woman's tongue? The moment Wolf entered the house, his crest fell, his tail drooped to the ground, or curled between his legs, he sneaked about with a gallows air, casting many a sidelong glance at Dame Van Winkle, and at the least flourish of a broomstick or ladle, he would fly to the door with yelping precipitation.

Times grew worse and worse with Rip Van Winkle, as years of matrimony rolled on: a tart temper never mellows with age, and a sharp tongue is the only edge tool that grows keener with constant use. For a long while he used to console himself, when driven from home, by frequenting a kind of perpetual club of the sages, philosophers, and other idle personages of the village, which held its sessions on a bench before a small inn, designated by a rubicund portrait of his Majesty George the Third. Here they used to sit in the shade, of a long lazy summer's day, talking listlessly over village gossip, or telling endless sleepy stories about nothing. But it would have been worth any statesman's money to have heard the profound discussions which sometimes took place, when by chance an old newspaper fell into their hands, from some passing traveler. How solemnly they would listen to the contents, as drawled out by Derrick Van Bummel, the schoolmaster, a dapper learned little man, who was not to be daunted by the most gigantic word in the dictionary; and how sagely they would deliberate upon public events some months after they had taken place.

The opinions of this junto were completely controlled by Nicholas Vedder, a patriarch of the village, and landlord of the inn, at the door of which he took his seat from morning till night, just moving sufficiently to avoid the sun, and keep in the shade of a large tree; so that the neighbors could tell the hour by his movements as accurately as by a sun-dial. It is true, he was rarely heard to speak, but smoked his pipe incessantly. His adherents, however (for every great man has his adherents), perfectly understood him, and knew how to gather his opinions. When anything that was read or related displeased him, he was observed to smoke his pipe vehemently, and to send forth short, frequent, and angry puffs; but when pleased, he would inhale the smoke slowly and tranquilly, and emit it in light and placid clouds, and sometimes taking the pipe from his mouth, and letting the fragrant vapor curl about his nose, would gravely nod his head in token of perfect approbation.

From even this stronghold the unlucky Rip was at length routed by his termagant wife, who would suddenly break in upon the tranquillity of the assemblage, and call the members all to naught; nor was that august personage, Nicholas Vedder himself, sacred from the daring tongue of this terrible virago, who charged him outright with encouraging her husband in habits of idleness.

Poor Rip was at last reduced almost to despair, and his only alternative to escape from the labor of the farm and the clamor of his wife was to take gun in hand, and stroll away into the woods. Here he would sometimes seat himself at the foot of a tree, and share the contents of his wallet with Wolf, with whom he sympathized as a fellow-sufferer in persecution. "Poor Wolf," he would say, "thy mistress leads thee a dog's life of it; but never mind, my lad, while I live thou shalt never want a friend to stand by thee!" Wolf would wag his tail, look wistfully in his master's face, and if dogs can feel pity, I verily believe he reciprocated the sentiment with all his heart.

In a long ramble of the kind, on a fine autumnal day, Rip had unconsciously scrambled to one of the highest parts of the Kaatskill Mountains. He was after his favorite sport of squirrel-shooting, and the still solitudes had echoed and re-echoed with the reports of his gun. Panting and fatigued, he threw himself, late in the afternoon, on a green knoll covered with mountain herbage, that crowned the brow of a precipice. From an opening between the trees, he could overlook all the lower country for many a mile of rich woodland. He saw at a distance the lordly Hudson, far, far below him, moving on its silent but majestic course, with the reflection of a purple cloud, or the sail of a lagging bark, here and there sleeping on its glassy bosom, and at last losing itself in the blue highlands.

On the other side he looked down into a deep mountain glen, wild, lonely, and shagged, the bottom filled with fragments from the impending cliffs, and scarcely lighted by the reflected rays of the setting sun. For some time Rip lay musing on this scene; evening was gradually advancing; the mountains began to throw their long blue shadows over the valleys; he saw that it would be dark long before he could reach the village; and he heaved a heavy sigh when he thought of encountering the terrors of Dame Van Winkle.

As he was about to descend he heard a voice from a distance hallooing, "Rip Van Winkle! Rip Van Winkle!" He looked around, but could see nothing but a crow winging its solitary flight across the mountain. He thought his fancy must have deceived him, and turned again to descend, when he heard the same cry ring through the still evening air, "Rip Van Winkle! Rip Van Winkle!"—at the same time Wolf bristled up his back, and giving a low growl, skulked to his master's side, looking fearfully down into the glen. Rip now felt a vague apprehension stealing over him: he looked anxiously in the same direction, and perceived a strange figure slowly toiling up the rocks and bending under the weight of something he carried on his back. He was surprised to see any human being in this lonely and unfrequented place, but supposing it to be some one of the neighborhood in need of his assistance, he hastened down to yield it.

On nearer approach, he was still more surprised at the singularity of the stranger's appearance. He was a short square-built old fellow, with thick bushy hair, and a grizzled beard. His dress was of the antique Dutch fashion —a cloth jerkin strapped round the waist—several pairs of breeches, the outer one of ample volume, decorated with rows of buttons down the sides, and bunches at the knees. He bore on his shoulders a stout keg, that seemed full of liquor, and made signs for Rip to approach and assist him with the load. Though rather shy and distrustful of this new acquaintance, Rip complied with his usual alacrity, and mutually relieving each other, they clambered up a narrow gully, apparently the dry bed of a mountain torrent. As they ascended, Rip every now and then heard long rolling peals, like distant thunder, that seemed to issue out of a deep ravine or rather cleft between lofty rocks, toward which their rugged path conducted. He paused for an instant, but supposing it to be the muttering of one of those transient thundershowers which often take place in mountain heights, he proceeded. Passing through the ravine, they came to a hollow, like a small amphitheatre, surrounded by perpendicular precipices, over the brinks of which impending trees shot their branches, so that you only caught glimpses of the azure sky, and the bright evening cloud. During the whole time, Rip and his companion had labored on in silence; for though the former marveled greatly what could be the object of carrying a keg of liquor up this wild mountain, yet there was something strange and incomprehensible about the unknown, that inspired awe and checked familiarity.

On entering the amphitheatre new objects of wonder presented themselves. On a level spot in the centre was a company of odd-looking personages playing at nine-pins. They were dressed in a quaint outlandish fashion: some wore short doublets, others jerkins, with long knives in their belts, and most of them had enormous breeches, of similar style with that of the guide's. Their visages, too, were peculiar: one had a large head, broad face, and small piggish eyes; the face of another seemed to consist entirely of nose, and was surmounted by a white sugar-loaf hat, set off with a little red cock's tail. They all had beards, of various shapes and colors. There was one who seemed to be the commander. He was a stout old gentleman, with a weather-beaten countenance; he wore a laced doublet, broad belt and hanger, high-crowned hat and feather, red stockings, and high-heeled shoes, with roses in them. The whole group reminded Rip of the figures in an old Flemish painting, in the parlor of Dominie Van Schaick, the village parson, and which had been brought over from Holland at the time of the settlement.

What seemed particularly odd to Rip was, that though these folks were evidently amusing themselves, yet they maintained the gravest faces, the most mysterious silence, and were, withal, the most melancholy party of pleasure he had ever witnessed. Nothing interrupted the stillness of the scene but the noise of the balls, which, whenever they were rolled, echoed along the mountains like rumbling peals of thunder.

As Rip and his companion approached them, they suddenly desisted from their play, and stared at him with such a fixed statue-like gaze, and such strange, uncouth, lack-lustre countenances, that his heart turned within him, and his knees smote together. His companion now emptied the contents of the keg into large flagons, and made signs to him to wait upon the company. He obeyed with fear and trembling; they quaffed the liquor in profound silence, and then returned to their game.

By degrees, Rip's awe and apprehension subsided. He even ventured, when no eye was fixed upon him, to taste the beverage, which he found had much of the flavor of excellent Hollands. He was naturally a thirsty soul, and was soon tempted to repeat the draught. One taste provoked another, and he reiterated his visits to the flagon so often that at length his senses were overpowered, his eyes swam in his head, his head gradually declined, and he fell into a deep sleep.

On waking, he found himself on the green knoll from whence he had first seen the old man of the glen. He rubbed his eyes—it was a bright sunny morning. The birds were hopping and twittering among the bushes, and the eagle was wheeling aloft, and breasting the pure mountain breeze. "Surely," thought Rip, "I have not slept here all night." He recalled the occurrences before he fell asleep. The strange man with the keg of liquor—the mountain ravine—the wild retreat among the rocks—the wobegone party at nine-pins —the flagon—"Oh, that wicked flagon!" thought Rip—"what excuse shall I make to Dame Van Winkle?"

He looked round for his gun, but in place of the clean well-oiled fowling piece, he found an old firelock lying by him, the barrel incrusted with rust, the lock falling off, and the stock worm-eaten. He now suspected that the grave roisterers of the mountain had put a trick upon him, and having dosed him with liquor, had robbed him of his gun. Wolf, too, had disappeared, but he might have strayed away after a squirrel or partridge. He whistled after him, and shouted his name, but all in vain; the echoes repeated his whistle and shout, but no dog was to be seen.

He determined to revisit the scene of the last evening's gambol, and if he met with any of the party, to demand his dog and gun. As he rose to walk, he found himself stiff in the joints and wanting in his usual activity. "These mountain beds do not agree with me," thought Rip, "and if this frolic should lay me up with a fit of rheumatism, I shall have a blessed time with Dame Van Winkle." With some difficulty he got down into the glen; he found the gully up which he and his companion had ascended the preceding evening; but to his astonishment a mountain stream was foaming down it, leaping from rock to rock, and filling the glen with babbling murmurs. He, however, made shift to scramble up its sides, working his toilsome way through thickets of birch, sassafras, and witch-hazel; and sometimes tripped up or entangled by the wild grape vines that twisted their coils and tendrils from tree to tree, and spread a kind of network in his path.

At length he reached to where the ravine had opened through the cliffs to the amphitheatre; but no traces of such opening remained. The rocks presented a high impenetrable wall, over which the torrent came tumbling in a sheet of feathery foam, and fell into a broad, deep basin, black from the shadows of the surrounding forest. Here, then, poor Rip was brought to a stand. He again called and whistled after his dog; he was only answered by the cawing of a flock of idle crows, sporting high in air about a dry tree that overhung a sunny precipice; and who, secure in their elevation, seemed to look down and scoff at the poor man's perplexities. What was to be done? The morning was passing away, and Rip felt famished for want of his breakfast. He grieved to give up his dog and gun; he dreaded to meet his wife; but it would not do to starve among the mountains. He shook his head, shouldered the rusty firelock, and, with a heart full of trouble and anxiety, turned his steps homeward.

As he approached the village he met a number of people, but none whom he knew, which somewhat surprised him, for he had thought himself acquainted with every one in the country round. Their dress, too, was of a different fashion from that to which he was accustomed. They all stared at him with equal marks of surprise, and whenever they cast eyes upon him, invariably stroked their chins. The constant recurrence of this gesture induced Rip, involuntarily, to do the same, when, to his astonishment, he found his beard had grown a foot long!

He had now entered the skirts of the village. A troop of strange children ran at his heels, hooting after him, and pointing at his gray beard. The dogs, too, not one of which he recognized for an old acquaintance, barked at him as he passed. The very village was altered: it was larger and more populous. There were rows of houses which he had never seen before, and those which had been his familiar haunts had disappeared. Strange names were over the doors—strange faces at the windows—everything was strange. His mind now misgave him; he began to doubt whether both he and the world around him were not bewitched. Surely this was his native village, which he left but a day before. There stood the Kaatskill Mountains—there ran the silver Hudson at a distance—there was every hill and dale precisely as it had always been—Rip was sorely perplexed—"That flagon last night," thought he, "has addled my poor head sadly!"

It was with some difficulty that he found the way to his own house, which he approached with silent awe, expecting every moment to hear the shrill voice of Dame Van Winkle. He found the house gone to decay—the roof fallen in, the windows shattered, and the doors off the hinges. A half-starved dog, that looked like Wolf, was skulking about it. Rip called him by name, but the cur snarled, showed his teeth, and passed on. This was an unkind cut indeed. "My very dog," sighed poor Rip, "has forgotten me!"

He entered the house, which, to tell the truth, Dame Van Winkle had always kept in neat order. It was empty, forlorn, and apparently abandoned. This desolateness overcame all his connubial fears—he called loudly for his wife and children—the lonely chambers rang for a moment with his voice, and then all again was silence.

He now hurried forth, and hastened to his old resort, the village inn—but it too was gone. A large rickety wooden building stood in its place, with great gaping windows, some of them broken, and mended with old hats and petticoats, and over the door was painted, "The Union Hotel, by Jonathan Doolittle." Instead of the great tree that used to shelter the quiet little Dutch inn of yore, there now was reared a tall naked pole, with something on the top that looked like a red nightcap, and from it was fluttering a flag, on which was a singular assemblage of stars and stripes—all this was strange and incomprehensible. He recognized on the sign, however, the ruby face of King George, under which he had smoked so many a peaceful pipe, but even this was singularly metamorphosed. The red coat was changed for one of blue and buff, a sword was held in the hand instead of a sceptre, the head was decorated with a cocked hat, and underneath was painted in large characters GENERAL WASHINGTON.

There was, as usual, a crowd of folk about the door, but none that Rip recollected. The very character of the people seemed changed. There was a busy, bustling, disputatious tone about it, instead of the accustomed phlegm and drowsy tranquillity. He looked in vain for the sage Nicholas Vedder, with his broad face, double chin, and fair, long pipe, uttering clouds of tobacco smoke, instead of idle speeches; or Van Bummel, the schoolmaster, doling forth the contents of an ancient newspaper. In place of these, a lean bilious-looking fellow, with his pockets full of handbills, was haranguing vehemently about rights of citizens—election—members of Congress—liberty—Bunker Hill—heroes of seventy-six—and other words, that were a perfect Babylonish jargon to the bewildered Van Winkle.

The appearance of Rip, with his long, grizzled beard, his rusty fowling-piece, his uncouth dress, and the army of women and children that had gathered at his heels, soon attracted the attention of the tavern politicians.

They crowded round him, eyeing him from head to foot, with great curiosity. The orator bustled up to him, and drawing him partly aside, inquired "on which side he voted?" Rip stared in vacant stupidity. Another short but busy little fellow pulled him by the arm, and rising on tiptoe, inquired in his ear, "whether he was Federal or Democrat." Rip was equally at a loss to comprehend the question; when a knowing, self-important old gentleman, in a sharp cocked hat, made his way through the crowd, putting them to the right and left with his elbows as he passed, and planting himself before Van Winkle, with one arm a-kimbo, the other resting on his cane, his keen eyes and sharp hat penetrating, as it were, into his very soul, demanded in an austere tone, "what brought him to the election with a gun on his shoulder, and a mob at his heels, and whether he meant to breed a riot in the village?"

"Alas! gentlemen," cried Rip, somewhat dismayed, "I am a poor, quiet man, a native of the place, and a loyal subject of the King, God bless him!"

Here a general shout burst forth from the bystanders:

"A tory! a tory! a spy! a refugee! hustle him! away with him!"

It was with great difficulty that the self-important man in the cocked hat restored order; and having assumed a tenfold austerity of brow, demanded again of the unknown culprit what he came there for, and whom he was seeking. The poor man humbly assured him that he meant no harm, but merely came there in search of some of his neighbors, who used to keep about the tavern.

"Well—who are they?—name them."

Rip bethought himself a moment and inquired, "Where's Nicholas Vedder?"

There was silence for a little while, when an old man replied, in a thin, piping voice, "Nicholas Vedder? why, he is dead and gone these eighteen years! There was a wooden tombstone in the churchyard that used to tell all about him, but that's rotten and gone too."

"Where's Brom Dutcher?"

"Oh, he went off to the army in the beginning of the war; some say he was killed at the storming of Stony Point—others say he was drowned in the squall, at the foot of Anthony's Nose. I don't know—he never came back again."

"Where's Van Bummel, the schoolmaster?"

"He went off to the wars, too; was a great militia general, and is now in Congress."

Rip's heart died away at hearing of these sad changes in his home and friends, and finding himself thus alone in the world. Every answer puzzled him, too, by treating of such enormous lapses of time, and of matters which he could not understand: war—Congress—Stony Point!—he had no courage to ask after any more friends, but cried out in despair, "Does nobody here know Rip Van Winkle?"

"Oh, Rip Van Winkle!" exclaimed two or three. "Oh, to be sure! that's Rip Van Winkle yonder, leaning against the tree."

Rip looked, and beheld a precise counterpart of himself as he went up the mountain; apparently as lazy, and certainly as ragged. The poor fellow was now completely confounded. He doubted his own identity, and whether he was himself or another man. In the midst of his bewilderment, the man in the cocked hat demanded who he was, and what was his name?

"God knows," exclaimed he at his wits' end; "I'm not myself—I'm somebody else—that's me yonder—no—that's somebody else, got into my shoes—I was myself last night, but I fell asleep on the mountain, and they've changed my gun, and everything's changed, and I'm changed, and I can't tell what's my name, or who I am!"

The bystanders began now to look at each other, nod, wink significantly, and tap their fingers against their foreheads. There was a whisper, also, about securing the gun, and keeping the old fellow from doing mischief; at the very suggestion of which the self-important man with the cocked hat retired with some precipitation. At this critical moment a fresh, comely woman passed through the throng to get a peep at the gray-bearded man. She had a chubby child in her arms, which, frightened at his looks, began to cry. "Hush, Rip," cried she, "hush, you little fool; the old man won't hurt you." The name of the child, the air of the mother, the tone of her voice, all awakened a train of recollections in his mind.

"What is your name, my good woman?" asked he.

"Judith Gardenier."

"And your father's name?"

"Ah, poor man, his name was Rip Van Winkle; it's twenty years since he went away from home with his gun, and never has been heard of since—his dog came home without him; but whether he shot himself, or was carried away by the Indians, nobody can tell. I was then but a little girl."

Rip had but one question more to ask; but he put it with a faltering voice: "Where's your mother?"

Oh, she too had died but a short time since: she broke a blood-vessel in a fit of passion at a New England pedler.

There was a drop of comfort, at least, in this intelligence. The honest man could contain himself no longer. He caught his daughter and her child in his arms. "I am your father!" cried he—"Young Rip Van Winkle once—old Rip Van Winkle now!—Does nobody know poor Rip Van Winkle?"

All stood amazed, until an old woman, tottering out from among the crowd, put her hand to her brow, and peering under it in his face for a moment, exclaimed, "Sure enough! it is Rip Van Winkle—it is himself. Welcome home again, old neighbor! Why, where have you been these twenty long years?"

Rip's story was soon told, for the whole twenty years had been to him but as one night. The neighbors stared when they heard it; some were seen to wink at each other, and put their tongues in their cheeks; and the self-important man in the cocked hat, who, when the alarm was over, had returned to the field, screwed down the corners of his mouth, and shook his head—upon which there was a general shaking of the head throughout the assemblage.

It was determined, however, to take the opinion of old Peter Vanderdonk, who was seen slowly advancing up the road. He was a descendant of the historian of that name, who wrote one of the earliest accounts of the province. Peter was the most ancient inhabitant of the village, and well versed in all the wonderful events and traditions of the neighborhood. He recollected Rip at once, and corroborated his story in the most satisfactory manner. He assured the company that it was a fact, handed down from his ancestor, the historian, that the Kaatskill Mountains had always been haunted by strange beings. That it was affirmed that the great Hendrik Hudson, the first discoverer of the river and country, kept a kind of vigil there every twenty years, with his crew of the "Half-moon," being permitted in this way to revisit the scenes of his enterprise, and keep a guardian eye upon the river and the great city called by his name. That his father had once seen them in their old Dutch dresses playing at nine-pins in a hollow of the mountain; and that he himself had heard, one summer afternoon, the sound of their balls, like distant peals of thunder.

To make a long story short, the company broke up, and returned to the more important concerns of the election. Rip's daughter took him home to live with her; she had a snug, well-furnished house, and a stout, cheery farmer for a husband, whom Rip recollected for one of the urchins that used to climb upon his back. As to Rip's son and heir, who was the ditto of himself, seen leaning against the tree, he was employed to work on the farm; but evinced a hereditary disposition to attend to anything else but his business.

Rip now resumed his old walks and habits; he soon found many of his former cronies, though all rather the worse for the wear and tear of time; and preferred making friends among the rising generation, with whom he soon grew into great favor.

Having nothing to do at home, and being arrived at that happy age when a man can do nothing with impunity, he took his place once more on the bench, at the inn door, and was reverenced as one of the patriarchs of the village, and a chronicle of the old times "before the war." It was some time before he could get into the regular track of gossip, or could be made to comprehend the strange events that had taken place during his torpor. How that there been a revolutionary war—that the country had thrown off the yoke of old England—and that, instead of being a subject of his majesty George the Third, he was now a free citizen of the United States. Rip, in fact, was no politician; the changes of states and empires made but little impression on him; but there was one species of despotism under which he had long groaned, and that was—petticoat government. Happily, that was at an end; he had got his neck out of the yoke of matrimony, and could go in and out whenever he pleased, without dreading the tyranny of Dame Van Winkle. Whenever her name was mentioned, however, he shook his head, shrugged his shoulders, and cast up his eyes; which might pass either for an expression of resignation to his fate, or joy at his deliverance.

He used to tell his story to every stranger that arrived at Mr. Doolittle's hotel. He was observed, at first, to vary on some points every time he told it, which was doubtless owing to his having so recently awaked. It at last settled down precisely to the tale I have related, and not a man, woman, or child in the neighborhood but knew it by heart. Some always pretended to doubt the reality of it, and insisted that Rip had been out of his head, and that this was one point on which he always remained flighty. The old Dutch inhabitants, however, almost universally gave it full credit. Even to this day, they never hear a thunderstorm of a summer afternoon about the Kaatskill but they say Hendrik Hudson and his crew are at their game of nine-pins; and it is a common wish of all henpecked husbands in the neighborhood, when life hangs heavy on their hands, that they might have a quieting draught out of Rip Van Winkle's flagon.

THE MURDERS IN THE RUE MORGUE

Edgar Allan Poe

What song the Syrens sang, or what name Achilles assumed when he hid himself among women, although puzzling questions, are not beyond all conjecture.

—*Sir Thomas Browne.*

The mental features discoursed of as the analytical are, in themselves, but little susceptible of analysis. We appreciate them only in their effects. We know of them, among other things, that they are always to their possessor, when inordinately possessed, a source of the liveliest enjoyment. As the strong man exults in his physical ability, delighting in such exercises as call his muscles into action, so glories the analyst in that moral activity which disentangles. He derives pleasure from even the most trivial occupations bringing his talent into play. He is fond of enigmas, of conundrums, hieroglyphics; exhibiting in his solutions of each a degree of acumen which appears to the ordinary apprehension preternatural. His results, brought about by the very soul and essence of method, have, in truth, the whole air of intuition.

The faculty of resolution is possibly much invigorated by mathematical study, and especially by that highest branch of it which, unjustly, and merely on account of its retrograde operations, has been called, as if par excellence, analysis. Yet to calculate is not in itself to analyze. A chess-player, for example, does the one, without effort at the other. It follows that the game of chess, in its effects upon mental character, is greatly misunderstood. I am not now writing a treatise, but simply prefacing a somewhat peculiar narrative by observations very much at random; I will, therefore, take occasion to assert that the higher powers of the reflective intellect are more decidedly and more usefully tasked by the unostentatious game of draughts than by all the elaborate frivolity of chess. In this latter, where the pieces have different and bizarre motions, with various and variable values, what is only complex is mistaken (a not unusual error) for what is profound. The attention is here called powerfully into play. If it flag for an instant, an oversight is committed, resulting in injury or defeat. The possible moves being not only manifold, but involute, the chances of such oversights are multiplied; and in nine cases out of ten, it is the more concentrative rather than the more acute player who conquers. In draughts, on the contrary, where the moves are unique and have but little variation, the probabilities of inadvertence are diminished, and the mere attention being left comparatively unemployed, what advantages are obtained by either party are obtained by superior acumen. To be less abstract, let us suppose a game of draughts where the pieces are reduced to four kings, and where, of course, no oversight is to be expected. It is obvious that here the victory can be decided (the players being at all equal) only by some recherché movement, the result of some strong exertion of the intellect. Deprived of ordinary resources the analyst throws himself into the spirit of his opponent, identifies himself therewith, and not infrequently sees thus, at a glance, the sole methods (sometimes indeed absurdly simple ones) by which he may seduce into error or hurry into miscalculation.

Whist has long been known for its influence upon what is termed the calculating power; and men of the highest order of intellect have been known to take an apparently unaccountable delight in it, while eschewing chess as frivolous. Beyond doubt there is nothing of a similar nature so greatly tasking the faculty of analysis. The best chess player in Christendom may be little more than the best player of chess; but proficiency in whist implies capacity for success in all those more important undertakings where mind struggles with mind. When I say proficiency, I mean that perfection in the game which includes a comprehension of all the sources whence legitimate advantage may be derived. These are not only manifold, but multiform, and lie frequently among recesses of thought altogether inaccessible to the ordinary understanding. To observe attentively is to remember distinctly; and, so far, the concentrative chess-player will do very well at whist; while the rules of Hoyle (themselves based upon the mere mechanism of the game) are sufficiently and generally comprehensible. Thus to have a retentive memory, and proceed by "the book," are points commonly regarded as the sum total of good playing. But it is in matters beyond the limits of mere rule that the skill of the analyst is evinced. He makes, in silence, a host of observations and inferences. So, perhaps, do his companions; and the difference in the extent of the information obtained lies not so much in the validity of the inference as in the quality of the observation. The necessary knowledge is that of what to observe. Our player confines himself not at all; nor, because the game is the object, does he reject deductions from things external to the game. He examines the countenance of his partner, comparing it carefully with that of each of his opponents. He considers the mode of assorting the cards in each hand; often counting trump by trump, and honor by honor, through the glances bestowed by their holders upon each. He notes every variation of face as the play progresses, gathering a fund of thought from the differences in the expression of certainty, of surprise, of triumph, or chagrin. From the manner of gathering up a trick he judges whether the person taking it can make another in the suit. He recognizes what is played through feint, by the manner with which it is thrown upon the table. A casual or inadvertent word; the accidental dropping or turning of a card, with the accompanying anxiety or carelessness in regard to its concealment; the counting of the tricks, with the order of their arrangement; embarrassment, hesitation, eagerness, or trepidation—all afford, to his apparently intuitive perception, indications of the true state of affairs. The first two or three rounds having been played, he is in full possession of the contents of each hand, and thenceforward puts down his cards with as absolute a precision of purpose as if the rest of the party had turned outward the faces of their own.

The analytical power should not be confounded with simple ingenuity; for while the analyst is necessarily ingenious, the ingenious man is often remarkably incapable of analysis. The constructive or combining power, by which ingenuity is usually manifested, and to which the phrenologists (I believe erroneously) have assigned a separate organ, supposing it a primitive faculty, has been so frequently seen in those whose intellect bordered otherwise upon idiocy, as to have attracted general observation among writers on morals. Between ingenuity and the analytic ability there exists a difference far greater, indeed, than that between the fancy and the imagination, but of a character very strictly analogous. It will be found, in fact, that the ingenious are always fanciful, and the truly imaginative never otherwise than analytic.

The narrative which follows will appear to the reader somewhat in the light of a commentary upon the propositions just advanced.

Residing in Paris during the spring and part of the summer of 18—, I there became acquainted with a Monsieur C. Auguste Dupin. This young gentleman was of an excellent, indeed of an illustrious family, but, by a variety of untoward events, had been reduced to such poverty that the energy of his character succumbed beneath it, and he ceased to bestir himself in the world, or to care for the retrieval of his fortunes. By courtesy of his creditors, there still remained in his possession a small remnant of his patrimony; and, upon the income arising from this, he managed, by means of a rigorous economy, to procure the necessaries of life, without troubling himself about its superfluities. Books, indeed, were his sole luxuries.

Our first meeting was at an obscure library in the Rue Montmartre, where the accident of our both being in search of the same very rare and very remarkable volume brought us into closer communion. We saw each other again and again. I was deeply interested in the little family history which he detailed to me with all the candor which a Frenchman indulges whenever mere self is the theme. I was astonished, too, at the vast extent of his reading;

and, above all, I felt my soul enkindled within me by the wild fervor and the vivid freshness of his imagination. Seeking in Paris the objects I then sought, I felt that the society of such a man would be to me a treasure beyond price; and this feeling I frankly confided to him. It was at length arranged that we should live together during my stay in the city; and as my worldly circumstances were somewhat less embarrassed than his own, I was permitted to be at the expense of renting, and furnishing in a style which suited the rather fantastic gloom of our common temper, a time-eaten and grotesque mansion, long deserted through superstitions into which we did not inquire, and tottering to its fall in a retired and desolate portion of the Faubourg St. Germain.

Had the routine of our life at this place been known to the world, we should have been regarded as madmen—although, perhaps, as madmen of a harmless nature. Our seclusion was perfect. We admitted no visitors. Indeed, the locality of our retirement had been carefully kept a secret from my own former associates; and it had been many years since Dupin had ceased to know or be known in Paris. We existed within ourselves alone.

It was a freak of fancy in my friend (for what else shall I call it?) to be enamored of the night for her own sake; and into this bizarrerie, as into all his others, I quietly fell, giving myself up to his wild whims with a perfect abandon. The sable divinity would not herself dwell with us always; but we could counterfeit her presence. At the first dawn of the morning we closed all the massy shutters of our old building; lighted a couple of tapers which, strongly perfumed, threw out only the ghastliest and feeblest of rays. By the aid of these we then busied our souls in dreams—reading, writing, or conversing, until warned by the clock of the advent of the true Darkness. Then we sallied forth into the streets, arm in arm, continuing the topics of the day, or roaming far and wide until a late hour, seeking, amid the wild lights and shadows of the populous city, that infinity of mental excitement which quiet observation can afford.

At such times I could not help remarking and admiring (although from his rich ideality I had been prepared to expect it) a peculiar analytic ability in Dupin. He seemed, too, to take an eager delight in its exercise—if not exactly in its display—and did not hesitate to confess the pleasure thus derived. He boasted to me with a low, chuckling laugh, that most men, in respect to himself, wore windows in their bosoms, and was wont to follow up such assertions by direct and very startling proofs of his intimate knowledge of my own. His manner at these moments was frigid and abstract; his eyes were vacant in expression; while his voice, usually a rich tenor, rose into a treble which would have sounded petulant but for the deliberateness and entire distinctness of the enunciation. Observing him in these moods, I often dwelt meditatively upon the old philosophy of the Bi-Part Soul, and amused myself with the fancy of a double Dupin—the creative and the resolvent.

Let it not be supposed, from what I have just said, that I am detailing any mystery, or penning any romance. What I have described in the Frenchman was merely the result of an excited, or perhaps of a diseased intelligence. But of the character of his remarks at the periods in question an example will best convey the idea.

We were strolling one night down a long dirty street, in the vicinity of the Palais Royal. Being both, apparently, occupied with thought, neither of us had spoken a syllable for fifteen minutes at least. All at once Dupin broke forth with these words:

"He is a very little fellow, that's true, and would do better for the Théâtre des Variétés."

"There can be no doubt of that," I replied, unwittingly, and not at first observing (so much had I been absorbed in reflection) the extraordinary manner in which the speaker had chimed in with my meditations. In an instant afterward I recollected myself, and my astonishment was profound.

"Dupin," said I, gravely, "this is beyond my comprehension. I do not hesitate to say that I am amazed, and can scarcely credit my senses. How was it possible you should know I was thinking of—?" Here I paused, to ascertain beyond a doubt whether he really knew of whom I thought.

"—of Chantilly," said he; "why do you pause? You were remarking to yourself that his diminutive figure unfitted him for tragedy."

That was precisely what had formed the subject of my reflections. Chantilly was a quondam cobbler of the Rue St. Denis, who, becoming stage-mad, had attempted the rôle of Xerxes, in Crébillon's tragedy so called, and been notoriously pasquinaded for his pains.

"Tell me, for Heaven's sake," I exclaimed, "the method—if method there is —by which you have been enabled to fathom my soul in this matter." In fact, I was even more startled than I would have been willing to express.

"It was the fruiterer," replied my friend, "who brought you to the conclusion that the mender of soles was not of sufficient height for Xerxes *et id genus omne.*"

"The fruiterer!—you astonish me—I know no fruiterer whomsoever."

"The man who ran up against you as we entered the street—it may have been fifteen minutes ago."

I now remembered that, in fact, a fruiterer, carrying upon his head a large basket of apples, had nearly thrown me down, by accident, as we passed from the Rue C— into the thoroughfare where we stood; but what this had to do with Chantilly I could not possibly understand.

There was not a particle of charlatanerie about Dupin. "I will explain," he said, "and that you may comprehend all clearly, we will first retrace the course of your meditations, from the moment in which I spoke to you until that of the rencontre with the fruiterer in question. The larger links of the chain run thus—Chantilly, Orion, Dr. Nichols, Epicurus, Stereotomy, the street stones, the fruiterer."

There are few persons who have not, at some period of their lives, amused themselves in retracing the steps by which particular conclusions of their own minds have been attained. The occupation is often full of interest; and he who attempts it for the first time is astonished by the apparently illimitable distance and incoherence between the starting-point and the goal. What, then, must have been my amazement when I heard the Frenchman speak what he had just spoken, and when I could not help acknowledging that he had spoken the truth. He continued:

"We had been talking of horses, if I remember aright, just before leaving the Rue C—. This was the last subject we discussed. As we crossed into this street, a fruiterer, with a large basket upon his head, brushing quickly past us, thrust you upon a pile of paving-stones collected at a spot where the causeway is undergoing repair. You stepped upon one of the loose fragments, slipped, slightly strained your ankle, appeared vexed or sulky, muttered a few words, turned to look at the pile, and then proceeded in silence. I was not particularly attentive to what you did; but observation has become with me, of late, a species of necessity.

"You kept your eyes upon the ground—glancing, with a petulant expression, at the holes and ruts in the pavement (so that I saw you were still thinking of the stones), until we reached the little alley called Lamartine, which has been paved, by way of experiment, with the overlapping and riveted blocks. Here your countenance brightened up, and, perceiving your lips move, I could not doubt that you murmured the word 'stereotomy,' a term very affectedly applied to this species of pavement. I knew that you could not say to yourself 'stereotomy' without being brought to think of atomies, and thus of the theories of Epicurus; and since, when we discussed this subject not very long ago, I mentioned to you how singularly, yet with how little notice, the vague guesses of that noble Greek had met with confirmation in the late nebular cosmogony, I felt that you could not avoid casting your eyes upward to the great nebula in Orion, and I certainly expected that you would do so. You did look up; and I was now assured that I had correctly followed your steps. But in that bitter tirade upon Chantilly, which appeared in yesterday's 'Musée,' the satirist, making some disgraceful allusions to the cobbler's change of name upon assuming the buskin, quoted a Latin line about which we have often conversed. I mean the line

Perdidit antiquum litera prima sonum.

I had told you that this was in reference to Orion, formerly written Urion; and, from certain pungencies connected with this explanation, I was aware that you could not have forgotten it. It was clear, therefore, that you would not fail to combine the two ideas of Orion and Chantilly. That you did combine them I saw by the character of the smile which passed over your lips. You thought of the poor cobbler's immolation. So far, you had been stooping in your gait; but now I saw you draw yourself up to your full height. I was then sure that you reflected upon the diminutive figure of Chantilly. At this point I interrupted your meditations to remark that as, in fact, he was a very little fellow—that Chantilly—he would do better at the Théâtre des Variétés."

Not long after this, we were looking over an evening edition of the "Gazette des Tribunaux," when the following paragraphs arrested our attention.

"Extraordinary Murders.—This morning, about three o'clock, the inhabitants of the Quartier St. Roch were roused from sleep by a succession of terrific shrieks, issuing, apparently, from the fourth story of a house in the Rue Morgue, known to be in the sole occupancy of one Madame L'Espanaye, and her daughter, Mademoiselle Camille L'Espanaye. After some delay, occasioned by a fruitless attempt to procure admission in the usual manner, the gateway was broken in with a crowbar, and eight or ten of the neighbors entered, accompanied by two gendarmes. By this time the cries had ceased; but, as the party rushed up the first flight of stairs, two or more rough voices, in angry contention, were distinguished, and seemed to proceed from the upper part of the house. As the second landing was reached, these sounds, also, had ceased, and everything remained perfectly quiet. The party spread themselves, and hurried from room to room. Upon arriving at a large back chamber in the fourth story (the door of which, being found locked, with the key inside, was forced open), a spectacle presented itself which struck every one present not less with horror than with astonishment.

"The apartment was in the wildest disorder—the furniture broken and thrown about in all directions. There was only one bedstead; and from this the bed had been removed, and thrown into the middle of the floor. On a chair lay a razor, besmeared with blood. On the hearth were two or three long and thick tresses of gray human hair, also dabbled with blood, and seeming to have been pulled out by the roots. Upon the floor were found four Napoleons, an earring of topaz, three large silver spoons, three smaller of métal d'Alger, and two bags, containing nearly four thousand francs in gold. The drawers of a bureau, which stood in one corner, were open, and had been, apparently, rifled, although many articles still remained in them. A small iron safe was discovered under the bed (not under the bedstead). It was open, with the key still in the door. It had no contents beyond a few old letters, and other papers of little consequence.

"Of Madame L'Espanaye no traces were here seen; but an unusual quantity of soot being observed in the fireplace, a search was made in the chimney, and (horrible to relate!) the corpse of the daughter, head downward, was dragged therefrom; it having been thus forced up the narrow aperture for a considerable distance. The body was quite warm. Upon examining it, many excoriations were perceived, no doubt occasioned by the violence with which it had been thrust up and disengaged. Upon the face were many severe scratches, and, upon the throat, dark bruises, and deep indentations of finger nails, as if the deceased had been throttled to death.

"After a thorough investigation of every portion of the house without further discovery, the party made its way into a small paved yard in the rear of the building, where lay the corpse of the old lady, with her throat so entirely cut that, upon an attempt to raise her, the head fell off. The body, as well as the head, was fearfully mutilated—the former so much so as scarcely to retain any semblance of humanity.

"To this horrible mystery there is not as yet, we believe, the slightest clew."

The next day's paper had these additional particulars:

"The Tragedy in the Rue Morgue.—Many individuals have been examined in relation to this most extraordinary and frightful affair" [the word 'affaire' has not yet, in France, that levity of import which it conveys with us], "but nothing whatever has transpired to throw light upon it. We give below all the material testimony elicited.

"Pauline Dubourg, laundress, deposes that she has known both the deceased for three years, having worked for them during that period. The old lady and her daughter seemed on good terms—very affectionate toward each other. They were excellent pay. Could not speak in regard to their mode or means of living. Believed that Madame L. told fortunes for a living. Was reputed to have money put by. Never met any person in the house when she called for the clothes or took them home. Was sure that they had no servant in employ. There appeared to be no furniture in any part of the building except in the fourth story.

"Pierre Moreau, tobacconist, deposes that he has been in the habit of selling small quantities of tobacco and snuff to Madame L'Espanaye for nearly four years. Was born in the neighborhood, and has always resided there. The deceased and her daughter had occupied the house in which the corpses were found, for more than six years. It was formerly occupied by a jeweler, who under-let the upper rooms to various persons. The house was the property of Madame L. She became dissatisfied with the abuse of the premises by her tenant, and moved into them herself, refusing to let any portion. The old lady was childish. Witness had seen the daughter some five or six times during the six years. The two lived an exceedingly retired life—were reputed to have money. Had heard it said among the neighbors that Madame L. told fortunes —did not believe it. Had never seen any person enter the door except the old lady and her daughter, a porter once or twice, and a physician some eight or ten times.

"Many other persons, neighbors, gave evidence to the same effect. No one was spoken of as frequenting the house. It was not known whether there were any living connections of Madame L. and her daughter. The shutters of the front windows were seldom opened. Those in the rear were always closed, with the exception of the large back room, fourth story. The house was a good house—not very old.

"Isidore Musèt, gendarme, deposes that he was called to the house about three o'clock in the morning, and found some twenty or thirty persons at the gateway, endeavoring to gain admittance. Forced it open, at length, with a bayonet—not with a crow-bar. Had but little difficulty in getting it open, on account of its being a double or folding gate, and bolted neither at bottom nor top. The shrieks were continued until the gate was forced—and then suddenly ceased. They seemed to be screams of some person (or persons) in great

agony—were loud and drawn out, not short and quick. Witness led the way upstairs. Upon reaching the first landing, heard two voices in loud and angry contention—the one a gruff voice, the other much shriller—a very strange voice. Could distinguish some words of the former, which was that of a Frenchman. Was positive that it was not a woman's voice. Could distinguish the words 'sacré' and 'diable.' The shrill voice was that of a foreigner. Could not be sure whether it was the voice of a man or of a woman. Could not make out what was said, but believed the language to be Spanish. The state of the room and of the bodies was described by this witness as we described them yesterday.

"*Henri Duval,* a neighbor, and by trade a silversmith, deposes that he was one of the party who first entered the house. Corroborates the testimony of Musèt in general. As soon as they forced an entrance, they reclosed the door, to keep out the crowd, which collected very fast, notwithstanding the lateness of the hour. The shrill voice, this witness thinks, was that of an Italian. Was certain it was not French. Could not be sure it was a man's voice. It might have been a woman's. Was not acquainted with the Italian language. Could not distinguish the words, but was convinced by the intonation that the speaker was an Italian. Knew Madame L. and her daughter. Had conversed with both frequently. Was sure that the shrill voice was not that of either of the deceased.

"*—Odenheimer, restaurateur.*—This witness volunteered his testimony. Not speaking French, was examined through an interpreter. Is a native of Amsterdam. Was passing the house at the time of the shrieks. They lasted for several minutes—probably ten. They were long and loud—very awful and distressing. Was one of those who entered the building. Corroborated the previous evidence in every respect but one. Was sure that the shrill voice was that of a man—of a Frenchman. Could not distinguish the words uttered. They were loud and quick—unequal—spoken apparently in fear as well as in anger. The voice was harsh—not so much shrill as harsh. Could not call it a shrill voice. The gruff voice said repeatedly, 'sacré,' 'diable,' and once 'mon Dieu.'

"*Jules Mignaud,* banker, of the firm of Mignaud et Fils, Rue Deloraine. Is the elder Mignaud. Madame L'Espanaye had some property. Had opened an account with his banking house in the spring of the year (eight years previously). Made frequent deposits in small sums. Had checked for nothing until the third day before her death, when she took out in person the sum of 4,000 francs. This sum was paid in gold, and a clerk sent home with the money.

"*Adolphe Le Bon,* clerk to Mignaud et Fils, deposes that on the day in question, about noon, he accompanied Madame L'Espanaye to her residence with the 4,000 francs, put up in two bags. Upon the door being opened, Mademoiselle L. appeared and took from his hands one of the bags, while the old lady relieved him of the other. He then bowed and departed. Did not see any person in the street at the time. It is a by-street—very lonely.

"*William Bird,* tailor, deposes that he was one of the party who entered the house. Is an Englishman. Has lived in Paris two years. Was one of the first to ascend the stairs. Heard the voices in contention. The gruff voice was that of a Frenchman. Could make out several words, but can not now remember all. Heard distinctly *'sacré'* and *'mon Dieu.'* There was a sound at the moment as if of several persons struggling—a scraping and scuffling sound. The shrill voice was very loud—louder than the gruff one. Is sure that it was not the voice of an Englishman. Appeared to be that of a German. Might have been a woman's voice. Does not understand German.

"Four of the above-named witnesses being recalled, deposed that the door of the chamber in which was found the body of Mademoiselle L. was locked on the inside when the party reached it. Everything was perfectly silent—no groans or noises of any kind. Upon forcing the door no person was seen. The windows, both of the back and front room, were down and firmly fastened from within. A door between the two rooms was closed but not locked. The door leading from the front room into the passage was locked, with the key on the inside. A small room in the front of the house, on the fourth story, at the head of the passage, was open, the door being ajar. This room was crowded with old beds, boxes, and so forth. These were carefully removed and searched. There was not an inch of any portion of the house which was not carefully searched. Sweeps were sent up and down the chimneys. The house was a four-story one, with garrets (*mansardes*). A trap-door on the roof was nailed down very securely—did not appear to have been opened for years. The time elapsing between the hearing of the voices in contention and the breaking open of the room door was variously stated by the witnesses. Some made it as short as three minutes—some as long as five. The door was opened with difficulty.

"*Alfonzo Garco,* undertaker, deposes that he resides in the Rue Morgue. Is a native of Spain. Was one of the party who entered the house. Did not proceed upstairs. Is nervous, and was apprehensive of the consequences of agitation. Heard the voices in contention. The gruff voice was that of a Frenchman. Could not distinguish what was said. The shrill voice was that of an Englishman—is sure of this. Does not understand the English language, but judges by the intonation.

"*Alfonzo Garcio,* undertaker, deposes that he was among the first to ascend the stairs. Heard the voices in question. The gruff voice was that of a Frenchman. Distinguished several words. The speaker appeared to be expostulating. Could not make out the words of the shrill voice. Spoke quick and unevenly. Thinks it the voice of a Russian. Corroborates the general testimony. Is an Italian. Never conversed with a native of Russia.

"Several witnesses, recalled, here testified that the chimneys of all the rooms on the fourth story were too narrow to admit the passage of a human being. By 'sweeps,' were meant cylindrical sweeping-brushes, such as are employed by those who clean chimneys. These brushes were passed up and down every flue in the house. There is no back passage by which any one could have descended while the party proceeded upstairs. The body of Mademoiselle L'Espanaye was so firmly wedged in the chimney that it could not be got down until four or five of the party united their strength.

"*Paul Dumas,* physician, deposes that he was called to view the bodies about daybreak. They were both then lying on the sacking of the bedstead in the chamber where Mademoiselle L. was found. The corpse of the young lady was much bruised and excoriated. The fact that it had been thrust up the chimney would sufficiently account for these appearances. The throat was greatly chafed. There were several deep scratches just below the chin, together with a series of livid spots which were evidently the impression of fingers. The face was fearfully discolored, and the eyeballs protruded. The tongue had been partially bitten through. A large bruise was discovered upon the pit of the stomach, produced, apparently, by the pressure of a knee. In the opinion of M. Dumas, Mademoiselle L'Espanaye had been throttled to death by some person or persons unknown. The corpse of the mother was horribly mutilated. All the bones of the right leg and arm were more or less shattered. The left tibia much splintered, as well as all the ribs of the left side. Whole body dreadfully bruised and discolored. It was not possible to say how the injuries had been inflicted. A heavy club of wood, or a broad bar of iron—a chair—any large, heavy and obtuse weapon—would have produced such results, if wielded by the hands of a very powerful man. No woman could have inflicted the blows with any weapon. The head of the deceased, when seen by witness, was entirely separated from the body, and was also greatly shattered. The throat had evidently been cut with some very sharp instrument—probably with a razor.

"*Alexandre Étienne,* surgeon, was called with M. Dumas to view the bodies. Corroborated the testimony and the opinions of M. Dumas.

"Nothing further of importance was elicited, although several other persons were examined. A murder so mysterious, and so perplexing in all its particulars, was never before committed in Paris—if indeed a murder has been committed at all. The police are entirely at fault—an unusual occurrence in affairs of this nature. There is not, however, the shadow of a clew apparent."

The evening edition of the paper stated that the greatest excitement still continued in the Quartier St. Roch—that the premises in question had been carefully researched, and fresh examinations of witnesses instituted, but all to no purpose. A postscript, however, mentioned that Adolphe Le Bon had been arrested and imprisoned—although nothing appeared to criminate him beyond the facts already detailed.

Dupin seemed singularly interested in the progress of this affair—at least so I judged from his manner, for he made no comments. It was only after the announcement that Le Bon had been imprisoned that he asked me my opinion respecting the murders.

I could merely agree with all Paris in considering them an insoluble mystery.

"We must not judge of the means," said Dupin, "by this shell of an examination. The Parisian police, so much extolled for acumen, are cunning, but no more. There is no method in their proceedings, beyond the method of the moment. They make a vast parade of measures; but, not unfrequently, these are so ill-adapted to the objects proposed, as to put us in mind of Monsieur Jourdain's calling for his robe-de-chambre—*pour mieux entendre la musique.* The results attained by them are not unfrequently surprising, but, for the most part, are brought about by simple diligence and activity. When these qualities are unavailing, their schemes fail. Vidocq, for example, was a good guesser, and a persevering man. But, without educated thought, he erred continually by the very intensity of his investigations. He impaired his vision by holding the object too close. He might see, perhaps, one or two points with unusual clearness, but in so doing he, necessarily, lost sight of the matter as a whole. Thus there is such a thing as being too profound. Truth is not always in a well. In fact, as regards the more important knowledge, I do believe that she is invariably superficial. The depth lies in the valleys where we seek her, and not upon the mountaintops where she is found. The modes and sources of this kind of error are well typified in the contemplation of the heavenly bodies. To look at a star by glances—to view it in a sidelong way, by turning toward it the exterior portions of the retina (more susceptible of feeble impressions of light than the interior), is to behold the star distinctly—is to have the best appreciation of its lustre—a lustre which grows dim just in proportion as we turn our vision fully upon it. A greater number of rays actually fall upon the eye in the latter case, but in the former there is the more refined capacity for comprehension. By undue profundity we perplex and enfeeble thought; and it is possible to make even Venus herself vanish from the firmament by a scrutiny too sustained, too concentrated, or too direct.

"As for these murders, let us enter into some examinations for ourselves, before we make up an opinion respecting them. An inquiry will afford us amusement" [I thought this an odd term, so applied, but said nothing], "and besides, Le Bon once rendered me a service for which I am not ungrateful. We will go and see the premises with our own eyes. I know G——, the Prefect of Police, and shall have no difficulty in obtaining the necessary permission."

The permission was obtained, and we proceeded at once to the Rue Morgue. This is one of those miserable thoroughfares which intervene between the Rue Richelieu and the Rue St. Roch. It was late in the afternoon when we reached it, as this quarter is at a great distance from that in which we resided. The house was readily found; for there were still many persons gazing up at the closed shutters, with an objectless curiosity, from the opposite side of the way. It was an ordinary Parisian house, with a gateway, on one side of which was a glazed watch-box, with a sliding panel in the window, indicating a *loge de concierge.* Before going in we walked up the street, turned down an alley, and then, again turning, passed in the rear of the building—Dupin, meanwhile, examining the whole neighborhood, as well as the house, with a minuteness of attention for which I could see no possible object.

Retracing our steps we came again to the front of the dwelling, rang, and, having shown our credentials, were admitted by the agents in charge. We went upstairs—into the chamber where the body of Mademoiselle L'Espanaye had been found, and where both the deceased still lay. The disorders of the room had, as usual, been suffered to exist. I saw nothing beyond what had been stated in the "Gazette des Tribunaux." Dupin scrutinized everything—not excepting the bodies of the victims. We then went into the other rooms, and into the yard; a gendarme accompanying us throughout. The examination occupied us until dark, when we took our departure. On our way home my companion stepped in for a moment at the office of one of the daily papers.

I have said that the whims of my friend were manifold, and that *Je les ménagais:*—for this phrase there is no English equivalent. It was his humor, now, to decline all conversation on the subject of the murder, until about noon the next day. He then asked me, suddenly, if I had observed anything peculiar at the scene of the atrocity.

There was something in his manner of emphasizing the word "peculiar" which caused me to shudder without knowing why.

"No, nothing peculiar," I said; "nothing more, at least, than we both saw stated in the paper."

"The 'Gazette,'" he replied, "has not entered, I fear, into the unusual horror of the thing. But dismiss the idle opinions of this print. It appears to me that this mystery is considered insoluble, for the very reason which should cause it to be regarded as easy of solution—I mean for the *outré* character of its features. The police are confounded by the seeming absence of motive—not for the murder itself—but for the atrocity of the murder. They are puzzled, too, by the seeming impossibility of reconciling the voices heard in contention, with the facts that no one was discovered upstairs but the assassinated Mademoiselle L'Espanaye, and that there were no means of egress without the notice of the party ascending. The wild disorder of the room; the corpse thrust, with the head downward, up the chimney; the frightful mutilation of the body of the old lady; these considerations, with those just mentioned, and others which I need not mention, have sufficed to paralyze the powers, by putting completely at fault the boasted acumen, of the government agents. They have fallen into the gross but common error of confounding the unusual with the abstruse. But it is by these deviations from the plane of the ordinary that reason feels its way, if at all, in its search for the true. In investigations such as we are now pursuing, it should not be so much asked 'what has occurred?' as 'what has occurred that has never occurred before?' In fact, the facility with which I shall arrive, or have arrived, at the solution of this mystery, is in the direct ratio of its apparent insolubility in the eyes of the police."

I stared at the speaker in mute astonishment.

"I am now awaiting," continued he, looking toward the door of our apartment—"I am now awaiting a person who, although perhaps not the perpetrator of these butcheries, must have been in some measure implicated in their perpetration. Of the worst portion of the crimes committed, it is probable that he is innocent. I hope that I am right in this supposition; for upon it I build my expectation of reading the entire riddle. I look for the man here—in this room—every moment. It is true that he may not arrive; but the probability is that he will. Should he come, it will be necessary to detain him. Here are pistols; and we both know how to use them.

I took the pistols, scarcely knowing what I did, or believing what I heard, while Dupin went on, very much as if in a soliloquy. I have already spoken of his abstract manner at such times. His discourse was addressed to myself; but his voice, although by no means loud, had that intonation which is commonly employed in speaking to some one at a great distance. His eyes, vacant in expression, regarded only the wall.

"That the voices heard in contention," he said, "by the party upon the stairs, were not the voices of the women themselves, was fully proved by the evidence. This relieves us of all doubt upon the question whether the old lady could have first destroyed the daughter, and afterward have committed suicide. I speak of this point chiefly for the sake of method; for the strength of Madame L'Espanaye would have been utterly unequal to the task of thrusting her daughter's corpse up the chimney as it was found; and the nature of the wounds upon her own person entirely precludes the idea of self-destruction. Murder, then, has been committed by some third party; and the voices of this third party were those heard in contention. Let me now advert—not to the whole testimony respecting these voices—but to what was peculiar in that testimony. Did you observe anything peculiar about it?"

I remarked that, while all the witnesses agreed in supposing the gruff voice to be that of a Frenchman, there was much disagreement in regard to the shrill, or, as one individual termed it, the harsh voice.

"That was the evidence itself," said Dupin, "but it was not the peculiarity of the evidence. You have observed nothing distinctive. Yet there was something to be observed. The witnesses, as you remark, agreed about the gruff voice; they were here unanimous. But in regard to the shrill voice, the peculiarity is—not that they disagreed—but that, while an Italian, an Englishman, a Spaniard, a Hollander, and a Frenchman attempted to describe it, each one spoke of it as that of a foreigner. Each is sure that it was not the voice of one of his own countrymen. Each likens it—not to the voice of an individual of any nation with whose language he is conversant—but the converse. The Frenchman supposes it the voice of a Spaniard, and 'might have distinguished some words had he been acquainted with the Spanish.' The Dutchman maintains it to have been that of a Frenchman; but we find it stated that 'not understanding French this witness was examined through an interpreter.' The Englishman thinks it the voice of a German, and 'does not understand German.' The Spaniard 'is sure' that it was that of an Englishman, but 'judges by the intonation' altogether, 'as he has no knowledge of the English.' The Italian believes it the voice of a Russian, but 'has never conversed with a native of Russia.' A second Frenchman differs, moreover, with the first, and is positive that the voice was that of an Italian; but, not being cognizant of that tongue, is, like the Spaniard, 'convinced by the intonation.' Now, how strangely unusual must that voice have really been, about which such testimony as this could have been elicited!—in whose tones, even, denizens of the five great divisions of Europe could recognize nothing familiar! You will say that it might have been the voice of an Asiatic—of an African. Neither Asiatics nor Africans abound in Paris; but, without denying the inference, I will now merely call your attention to three points. The voice is termed by one witness 'harsh rather than shrill.' It is represented by two others to have been 'quick and unequal.' No words—no sounds resembling words—were by any witness mentioned as distinguishable.

"I know not," continued Dupin, "what impression I may have made, so far, upon your own understanding; but I do not hesitate to say that legitimate deductions even from this portion of the testimony—the portion respecting the gruff and shrill voices—are in themselves sufficient to engender a suspicion which should give direction to all further progress in the investigation of the mystery. I said 'legitimate deductions'; but my meaning is not thus fully expressed. I designed to imply that the deductions are the sole proper ones, and that the suspicion arises inevitably from them as the single result. What the suspicion is, however, I will not say just yet. I merely wish you to bear in mind that, with myself, it was sufficiently forcible to give a definite form—to my inquiries in the chamber.

"Let us now transport ourselves, in fancy, to this chamber. What shall we first seek here? The means of egress employed by the murderers. It is not too much to say that neither of us believes in preternatural events. Madame and Mademoiselle L'Espanaye were not destroyed by spirits. The doers of the deed were material and escaped materially. Then how? Fortunately there is but one mode of reasoning upon the point, and that mode must lead us to a definite decision. Let us examine, each by each, the possible means of egress. It is clear that the assassins were in the room where Mademoiselle L'Espanaye was found, or at least in the room adjoining, when the party ascended the stairs. It is then only from these two apartments that we have to seek issues. The police have laid bare the floors, the ceiling, and the masonry of the walls, in every direction. No secret issues could have escaped their vigilance. But, not trusting to their eyes, I examined with my own. There were, then, no secret issues. Both doors leading from the rooms into the passage were securely locked, with the keys inside. Let us turn to the chimneys. These, although of ordinary width for some eight or ten feet above the hearths, will not admit, throughout their extent, the body of a large cat. The impossibility of egress, by means already stated, being thus absolute, we are reduced to the windows. Through those of the front room no one could have escaped without notice from the crowd in the street. The murderers must have passed, then, through those of the back room. Now, brought to this conclusion in so unequivocal a manner as we are, it is not our part, as reasoners, to reject it on account of apparent impossibilities. It is only left for us to prove that these apparent 'impossibilities' are, in reality, not such.

"There are two windows in the chamber. One of them is unobstructed by furniture, and is wholly visible. The lower portion of the other is hidden from view by the head of the unwieldy bedstead which is thrust close up against it. The former was found securely fastened from within. It resisted the utmost force of those who endeavored to raise it. A large gimlet-hole had been pierced in its frame to the left, and a very stout nail was found fitted therein, nearly to the head.

"Upon examining the other window, a similar nail was seen similarly fitted in it; and a vigorous attempt to raise this sash failed also. The police were now entirely satisfied that egress had not been in these directions. And, therefore, it was thought a matter of supererogation to withdraw the nails and open the windows.

"My own examination was somewhat more particular, and was so for the reason I have just given—because here it was, I knew, that all apparent impossibilities must be proved to be not such in reality.

"I proceeded to think thus—*a posteriori.* The murderers did escape from one of these windows. This being so, they could not have refastened the sashes from the inside, as they were found fastened; the consideration which put a stop, through its obviousness, to the scrutiny of the police in this quarter. Yet the sashes were fastened. They must then have the power of fastening themselves. There was no escape from this conclusion. I stepped to the unobstructed casement, withdrew the nail with some difficulty, and attempted to raise the sash. It resisted all my efforts, as I had anticipated. A concealed spring must, I now knew, exist; and this corroboration of my idea convinced me that my premises, at least, were correct, however mysterious still appeared the circumstances attending the nails. A careful search soon brought to light the hidden spring. I pressed it, and, satisfied with the discovery, forbore to upraise the sash.

"I now replaced the nail and regarded it attentively. A person passing out through this window might have reclosed it, and the spring would have caught—but the nail could not have been replaced. The conclusion was plain, and again narrowed in the field of my investigations. The assassins must have escaped through the other window. Supposing, then, the springs upon each sash to be the same, as was probable, there must be found a difference between the nails, or at least between the modes of their fixture. Getting upon the sacking of the bedstead, I looked over the head-board minutely at the second casement. Passing my hand down behind the board, I readily discovered and pressed the spring, which was, as I had supposed, identical in character with its neighbor. I now looked at the nail. It was as stout as the other, and apparently fitted in the same manner—driven in nearly up to the head.

"You will say that I was puzzled; but, if you think so, you must have misunderstood the nature of the inductions. To use a sporting phrase, I had not been once 'at fault.' The scent had never for an instant been lost. There was no flaw in any link of the chain. I had traced the secret to its ultimate result—and that result was the nail. It had, I say, in every respect, the appearance of its fellow in the other window; but this fact was an absolute nullity (conclusive as it might seem to be) when compared with the consideration that here, at this point, terminated the clew. 'There must be something wrong,' I said, 'about the nail.' I touched it; and the head, with about a quarter of an inch of the shank, came off in my fingers. The rest of the shank was in the gimlet-hole where it had been broken off. The fracture was an old one (for its edges were incrusted with rust), and had apparently been accomplished by the blow of a hammer, which had partially imbedded, in the top of the bottom sash, the head portion of the nail. I now carefully replaced this head portion in the indentation whence I had taken it, and the resemblance to a perfect nail was complete—the fissure was invisible. Pressing the spring, I gently raised the sash for a few inches; the head went up with it, remaining firm in its bed. I closed the window, and the semblance of the whole nail was again perfect.

"This riddle, so far, was now unriddled. The assassin had escaped through the window which looked upon the bed. Dropping of its own accord upon his exit (or perhaps purposely closed), it had become fastened by the spring, and it was the retention of this spring which had been mistaken by the police for that of the nail—further inquiry being thus considered unnecessary.

"The next question is that of the mode of descent. Upon this point I had been satisfied in my walk with you around the building. About five feet and a half from the casement in question there runs a lightning-rod. From this rod it would have been impossible for any one to reach the window itself, to say nothing of entering it. I observed, however, that the shutters of the fourth story were of the peculiar kind called by Parisian carpenters *ferrades*—a kind rarely employed at the present day, but frequently seen upon very old mansions at Lyons and Bordeaux. They are in the form of an ordinary door (a single, not a folding door), except that the lower half is latticed or worked in open trellis—thus affording an excellent hold for the hands. In the present instance these shutters are fully three feet and a half broad. When we saw them from the rear of the house, they were both about half open—that is to say, they stood off at right angles from the wall. It is probable that the police, as well as myself, examined the back of the tenement; but, if so, in looking at these *ferrades* in the line of their breadth (as they must have done), they did not perceive this great breadth itself, or, at all events, failed to take it into due consideration. In fact, having once satisfied themselves that no egress could have been made in this quarter, they would naturally bestow here a very cursory examination. It was clear to me, however, that the shutter belonging to the window at the head of the bed, would, if swung fully back to the wall, reach to within two feet of the lightning-rod. It was also evident that, by exertion of a very unusual degree of activity and courage, an entrance into the window, from the rod, might have been thus effected. By reaching to the distance of two feet and a half (we now suppose the shutter open to its whole extent) a robber might have taken a firm grasp upon the trellis-work. Letting go, then, his hold upon the rod, placing his feet securely against the wall, and springing boldly from it, he might have swung the shutter so as to close it, and, if we imagine the window open at the time, might even have swung himself into the room.

"I wish you to bear especially in mind that I have spoken of a very unusual degree of activity as requisite to success in so hazardous and so difficult a feat. It is my design to show you first, that the thing might possibly have been accomplished; but, secondly and chiefly, I wish to impress upon your understanding the very extraordinary, the almost preternatural character of that agility which could have accomplished it.

"You will say, no doubt, using the language of the law, that 'to make out my case,' I should rather undervalue than insist upon a full estimation of the activity required in this matter. This may be the practice in law, but it is not the usage of reason. My ultimate object is only the truth. My immediate purpose is to lead you to place in juxtaposition that very unusual activity of which I have just spoken, with that very peculiar shrill (or harsh) and unequal voice, about whose nationality no two persons could be found to agree, and in whose utterance no syllabification could be detected."

At these words a vague and half-formed conception of the meaning of Dupin flitted over my mind. I seemed to be upon the verge of comprehension, without power to comprehend—as men, at times, find themselves upon the brink of remembrance, without being able, in the end, to remember. My friend went on with his discourse.

"You will see," he said, "that I have shifted the question from the mode of egress to that of ingress. It was my design to convey the idea that both were effected in the same manner, at the same point. Let us now revert to the interior of the room. Let us survey the appearances here. The drawers of the bureau, it is said, have been rifled, although many articles of apparel still remained within them. The conclusion here is absurd. It is a mere guess—a very silly one—and no more. How are we to know that the articles found in the drawers were not all that these drawers had originally contained? Madame L'Espanaye and her daughter lived an exceedingly retired life—saw no company—seldom went out—had little use for numerous changes of habiliment. Those found were at least of as good quality as any likely to be possessed by these ladies. If a thief had taken any, why did he not take the best— why did he not take all? In a word, why did he abandon four thousand francs in gold to incumber himself with a bundle of linen? The gold was abandoned. Nearly the whole sum mentioned by Monsieur Mignaud, the banker, was discovered, in bags, upon the floor. I wish you, therefore, to discard from your thoughts the blundering idea of motive, engendered in the brains of the police by that portion of the evidence which speaks of money delivered at the door of the house. Coincidences ten times as remarkable as this (the delivery of the money, and murder committed within three days upon the party receiving it), happen to all of us every hour of our lives, without attracting even momentary notice. Coincidences, in general, are great stumbling-blocks in the way of that class of thinkers who have been educated to know nothing of the theory of probabilities—that theory to which the most glorious objects of human research are indebted for the most glorious of illustrations. In the present instance, had the gold been gone, the fact of its delivery three days before would have formed something more than a coincidence. It would have been corroborative of this idea of motive. But, under the real circumstances of the case, if we are to suppose gold the motive of this outrage, we must also imagine the perpetrator so vacillating an idiot as to have abandoned his gold and his motive together.

"Keeping now steadily in mind the points to which I have drawn your attention—that peculiar voice, that unusual agility, and that startling absence of motive in a murder so singularly atrocious as this—let us glance at the butchery itself. Here is a woman strangled to death by manual strength, and thrust up a chimney head downward. Ordinary assassins employ no such mode of murder as this. Least of all do they thus dispose of the murdered. In the manner of thrusting the corpse up the chimney, you will admit that there was something excessively *outré* —something altogether irreconcilable with our common notions of human action, even when we suppose the actors the most depraved of men. Think, too, how great must have been that strength which could have thrust the body up such an aperture so forcibly that the united vigor of several persons was found barely sufficient to drag it down!

"Turn, now, to other indications of the employment of a vigor most marvelous. On the hearth were thick tresses—very thick tresses—of gray human hair. These had been torn out by the roots. You are aware of the great force necessary in tearing thus from the head even twenty or thirty hairs together. You saw the locks in question as well as myself. Their roots (a hideous sight) were clotted with fragments of the flesh of the scalp—sure token of the prodigious power which had been exerted in uprooting perhaps half a million of hairs at a time. The throat of the old lady was not merely cut, but the head absolutely severed from the body: the instrument was a mere razor. I wish you also to look at the brutal ferocity of these deeds. Of the bruises upon the body of Madame L'Espanaye I do not speak. Monsieur Dumas, and his worthy coadjutor Monsieur Étienne, have pronounced that they were inflicted by some obtuse instrument; and so far these gentlemen are very correct. The obtuse instrument was clearly the stone pavement in the yard, upon which the victim had fallen from the window which looked in upon the bed. This idea, however simple it may now seem, escaped the police for the same reason that the breadth of the shutters escaped them—because, by the affair of the nails, their perceptions had been hermetically sealed against the possibility of the windows having ever been opened at all.

"If now, in addition to all these things, you have properly reflected upon the odd disorder of the chamber, we have gone so far as to combine the ideas of an agility astounding, a strength superhuman, a ferocity brutal, a butchery without motive, a grotesquerie in horror absolutely alien from humanity, and a voice foreign in tone to the ears of men of many nations, and devoid of all distinct or intelligible syllabification. What result, then, has ensued? What impression have I made upon your fancy?"

I felt a creeping of the flesh as Dupin asked me the question. "A madman," I said, "has done this deed—some raving maniac, escaped from a neighboring *Maison de Santé.*"

"In some respects," he replied, "your idea is not irrelevant. But the voices of madmen, even in their wildest paroxysms, are never found to tally with that peculiar voice heard upon the stairs. Madmen are of some nation, and their language, however incoherent in its words, has always the coherence of syllabification. Besides, the hair of a madman is not such as I now hold in my hand. I disentangled this little tuft from the rigidly clutched fingers of Madame L'Espanaye. Tell me what you can make of it."

"Dupin!" I said, completely unnerved; "this hair is most unusual—this is no human hair."

"I have not asserted that it is," said he; "but, before we decide this point, I wish you to glance at the little sketch I have here traced upon this paper. It is a fac-simile drawing of what has been described in one portion of the testimony as 'dark bruises and deep indentations of finger nails' upon the throat of Mademoiselle L'Espanaye, and in another (by Messrs. Dumas and Étienne) as a 'series of livid spots, evidently the impression of fingers.'

"You will perceive," continued my friend, spreading out the paper upon the table before us, "that this drawing gives the idea of a firm and fixed hold. There is no *slipping* apparent. Each finger has retained—possibly until the death of the victim—the fearful grasp by which it originally imbedded itself. Attempt, now, to place all your fingers, at the same time, in the respective impressions as you see them."

I made the attempt in vain.

"We are possibly not giving this matter a fair trial," he said. "The paper is spread out upon a plane surface; but the human throat is cylindrical. Here is a billet of wood, the circumference of which is about that of the throat. Wrap the drawing around it, and try the experiment again."

I did so; but the difficulty was even more obvious than before. "This," I said, "is the mark of no human hand."

"Read now," replied Dupin, "this passage from Cuvier."

It was a minute anatomical and generally descriptive account of the large fulvous Orang-Outang of the East Indian Islands. The gigantic stature, the prodigious strength and activity, the wild ferocity, and the imitative propensities of these mammalia are sufficiently well know to all. I understood the full horrors of the murder at once.

"The description of the digits," said I, as I made an end of the reading, "is in exact accordance with this drawing. I see that no animal but an Orang-Outang, of the species here mentioned, could have impressed the indentations as you have traced them. This tuft of tawny hair, too, is identical in character with that of the beast of Cuvier. But I can not possibly comprehend the particulars of this frightful mystery. Besides, there were two voices heard in contention, and one of them was unquestionably the voice of a Frenchman."

"True; and you will remember an expression attributed almost unanimously, by the evidence, to this voice—the expression, 'mon Dieu!' This, under the circumstances, has been justly characterized by one of the witnesses (Montani, the confectioner) as an expression of remonstrance or expostulation. Upon these two words, therefore, I have mainly built my hopes of a full solution of the riddle. A Frenchman was cognizant of the murder. It is possible—indeed it is far more than probable—that he was innocent of all participation in the bloody transactions which took place. The Orang-Outang may have escaped from him. He may have traced it to the chamber; but, under the agitating circumstances which ensued, he could never have recaptured it. It is still at large. I will not pursue these guesses—for I have no right to call them more—since the shades of reflection upon which they are based are scarcely of sufficient depth to be appreciable by my own intellect, and since I could not pretend to make them intelligible to the understanding of another. We will call them guesses, then, and speak of them as such. If the Frenchman in question is indeed, as I suppose, innocent of this atrocity, this advertisement, which I left last night, upon our return home, at the office of 'Le Monde' (a paper devoted to the shipping interest, and much sought by sailors), will bring him to our residence."

He handed me a paper, and I read thus:

CAUGHT—In the Bois de Boulogne, early in the morning of the —inst. (morning of the murder), a very large, tawny Orang-Outang of the Bornese species. The owner (who is ascertained to be a sailor, belonging to a Maltese vessel) may have the animal again, upon identifying it satisfactorily, and paying a few charges arising from its capture and keeping. Call at No.—Rue—, Faubourg St. Germain—au troisième.

"How was it possible," I asked, "that you should know the man to be a sailor, and belonging to a Maltese vessel?"

"I do not know it," said Dupin. "I am not sure of it. Here, however, is a small piece of ribbon, which from its form, and from its greasy appearance, has evidently been used in tying the hair in one of those long queues of which sailors are so fond. Moreover, this knot is one which few besides sailors can tie, and it is peculiar to the Maltese. I picked the ribbon up at the foot of the lightning-rod. It could not have belonged to either of the deceased. Now if, after all, I am wrong in my induction from this ribbon, that the Frenchman was a sailor belonging to a Maltese vessel, still I can have done no harm in saying what I did in the advertisement. If I am in error, he will merely suppose that I have been misled by some circumstance into which he will not take the trouble to inquire. But if I am right, a great point is gained. Cognizant although innocent of the murder, the Frenchman will naturally hesitate about replying to the advertisement—about demanding the Orang-Outang. He will reason thus:—'I am innocent; I am poor; my Orang-Outang is of great value—to one in my circumstances a fortune of itself—why should I lose it through idle apprehensions of danger? Here it is, within my grasp. It was found in the Bois de Boulogne—at a vast distance from the scene of that butchery. How can it ever be suspected that a brute beast should have done the deed? The police are at fault—they have failed to procure the slightest clew. Should they even trace the animal, it would be impossible to prove me cognizant of the murder, or to implicate me in guilt on account of that cognizance. Above all, I am known. The advertiser designates me as the possessor of the beast. I am not sure to what limit his knowledge may extend. Should I avoid claiming a property of so great value, which it is known that I possess, I will render the animal at least liable to suspicion. It is not my policy to attract attention either to myself or to the beast. I will answer the advertisement, get the Orang-Outang, and keep it close until this matter has blown over.' "

At this moment we heard a step upon the stairs.

"Be ready," said Dupin, "with your pistols, but neither use them nor show them until at a signal from myself."

The front door of the house had been left open, and the visitor had entered, without ringing, and advanced several steps upon the staircase. Now, however, he seemed to hesitate. Presently we heard him descending. Dupin was moving quickly to the door, when we again heard him coming up. He did not turn back a second time, but stepped up with decision, and rapped at the door.

"Come in," said Dupin, in a cheerful and hearty tone.

A man entered. He was a sailor, evidently—a tall, stout, and muscular-looking person, with a certain dare-devil expression of countenance, not altogether unprepossessing. His face, greatly sunburned, was more than half hidden by whisker and mustachio. He had with him a huge oaken cudgel, but appeared to be otherwise unarmed. He bowed awkwardly, and bade us "good-evening," in French accents, which, although somewhat Neufchatel-ish, were still sufficiently indicative of a Parisian origin.

"Sit down, my friend," said Dupin. "I suppose you have called about the Orang-Outang. Upon my word, I almost envy you the possession of him; a remarkably fine, and no doubt a very valuable, animal. How old do you suppose him to be?"

The sailor drew a long breath, with the air of a man relieved of some intolerable burden, and then replied, in an assured tone:

"I have no way of telling—but he can't be more than four or five years old. Have you got him here?"

"Oh, no; we had no conveniences for keeping him here. He is at a livery stable in the Rue Dubourg, just by. You can get him in the morning. Of course you are prepared to identify the property?"

"To be sure I am, sir."

"I shall be sorry to part with him," said Dupin.

"I don't mean that you should be at all this trouble for nothing, sir," said the man. "Couldn't expect it. Am very willing to pay a reward for the finding of the animal—that is to say, anything in reason."

"Well," replied my friend, "that is all very fair, to be sure. Let me think!— what should I have? Oh! I will tell you. My reward shall be this. You shall give me all the information in your power about these murders in the Rue Morgue."

Dupin said the last words in a very low tone, and very quietly. Just as quietly, too, he walked toward the door, locked it, and put the key in his pocket. He then drew a pistol from his bosom and placed it upon the table.

The sailor's face flushed up as if he were struggling with suffocation. He started to his feet and grasped his cudgel; but the next moment he fell back into his seat, trembling violently, and with the countenance of death itself. He spoke not a word. I pitied him.

"My friend," said Dupin, in a kind tone, "you are alarming yourself unnec- essarily—you are indeed. We mean you no harm whatever. I pledge you the honor of a gentleman, and of a Frenchman, that we intend you no injury. I perfectly well know that you are innocent of the atrocities in the Rue Morgue. It will not do, however, to deny that you are in some measure implicated in them. From what I have already said, you must know that I have had means of information about this matter—means of which you could never have dreamed. Now, the thing stands thus. You have done nothing which you could have avoided—nothing, certainly, which renders you culpable. You were not even guilty of robbery, when you might have robbed with impunity. You have nothing to conceal. You have no reason for concealment. On the other hand, you are bound by every principle of honor to confess all you know. An innocent man is now imprisoned, charged with that crime of which you can point out the perpetrator."

The sailor had recovered his presence of mind, in a great measure, while Dupin uttered these words; but his boldness of bearing was all gone.

"So help me God!" said he, after a brief pause, "I *will* tell you all I know about this affair;—but I do not expect you to believe one half I say—I would be a fool indeed if I did. Still, I *am* innocent, and I will make a clean breast, if I die for it."

What he stated was, in substance, this. He had lately made a voyage to the Indian Archipelago. A party, of which he formed one, landed at Borneo, and passed into the interior on an excursion of pleasure. Himself and a companion had captured the Orang-Outang. This companion dying, the animal fell into his own exclusive possession. After great trouble, occasioned by the intracta- ble ferocity of his captive during the home voyage, he at length succeeded in lodging it safely at his own residence in Paris, where, not to attract toward himself the unpleasant curiosity of his neighbors, he kept it carefully secluded, until such time as it should recover from a wound in the foot, received from a splinter on board ship.

Returning home from some sailor's frolic on the night, or rather in the morning, of the murder, he found the beast occupying his own bedroom, into which it had broken from a closet adjoining, where it had been, as was thought, securely confined. Razor in hand, and fully lathered, it was sitting before a looking-glass, attempting the operation of shaving, in which it had no doubt previously watched its master through the keyhole of the closet. Terrified at the sight of so dangerous a weapon in the possession of an animal so ferocious, and so well able to use it, the man, for some moments, was at a loss what to do. He had been accustomed, however, to quiet the creature, even in its fiercest moods, by the use of a whip, and to this he now resorted. Upon sight of it, the Orang-Outang sprang at once through the door of the chamber, down the stairs, and thence, through a window, unfortunately open, into the street.

The Frenchman followed in despair; the ape, razor still in hand, occasionally stopping to look back and gesticulate at his pursuer, until the latter had nearly come up with it. It then again made off. In this manner the chase continued for a long time. The streets were profoundly quiet, as it was nearly three o'clock in the morning. In passing down an alley in the rear of the Rue Morgue, the fugitive's attention was arrested by a light gleaming from the open window of Madame L'Espanaye's chamber, in the fourth story of her house. Rushing to the building, it perceived the lightning-rod, clambered up with inconceivable agility, grasped the shutter, which was thrown fully back against the wall, and, by its means, swung itself directly upon the headboard of the bed. The whole feat did not occupy a minute. The shutter was kicked open again by the Orang-Outang as it entered the room.

The sailor, in the meantime, was both rejoiced and perplexed. He had strong hopes of now recapturing the brute, as it could scarcely escape from the trap into which it had ventured, except by the rod, where it might be intercepted as it came down. On the other hand, there was much cause for anxiety as to what it might do in the house. This latter reflection urged the man still to follow the fugitive. A lightning-rod is ascended without difficulty, especially by a sailor; but, when he had arrived as high as the window, which lay far to his left, his career was stopped; the most that he could accomplish was to reach over so as to obtain a glimpse of the interior of the room. At this glimpse he nearly fell from his hold through excess of horror. Now it was that those hideous shrieks arose upon the night, which had startled from slumber the inmates of the Rue Morgue. Madame L'Espanaye and her daughter, habited in their night clothes, had apparently been occupied in arranging some papers in the iron chest already mentioned, which had been wheeled into the middle of the room. It was open, and its contents lay beside it on the floor. The victims must have been sitting with their backs toward the window; and, from the time elapsing between the ingress of the beast and the screams, it seems probable that it was not immediately perceived.

As the sailor looked in, the gigantic animal had seized Madame L'Espanaye by the hair (which was loose, as she had been combing it), and was flourishing the razor about her face, in imitation of the motions of a barber. The daughter lay prostrate and motionless; she had swooned. The screams and struggles of the old lady (during which the hair was torn from her head) had the effect of changing the probably pacific purposes of the Orang-Outang into those of wrath. With one determined sweep of its muscular arm it nearly severed her head from her body. The sight of blood inflamed its anger into frenzy. Gnashing its teeth, and flashing fire from its eyes, it flew upon the body of the girl and imbedded its fearful talons in her throat, retaining its grasp until she expired. Its wandering and wild glances fell at this moment upon the head of the bed, over which the face of its master, rigid with horror, was just discernible. The fury of the beast, who no doubt bore still in mind the dreaded whip, was instantly converted into fear. Conscious of having deserved punishment, it seemed desirous of concealing its bloody deeds, and skipped about the chamber in an agony of nervous agitation; throwing down and breaking the furniture as it moved, and dragging the bed from the bedstead. In conclusion, it seized first the corpse of the daughter, and thrust it up the chimney, as it was found; then that of the old lady, which it hurled through the window headlong.

As the ape approached the casement with its mutilated burden, the sailor shrank aghast to the rod, and, rather gliding than clambering down it, hurried at once home—dreading the consequences of the butchery, and gladly abandoning, in his terror, all solicitude about the fate of the Orang-Outang. The words heard by the party upon the staircase were the Frenchman's exclamations of horror and affright, commingled with the fiendish jabberings of the brute.

I have scarcely anything to add. The Orang-Outang must have escaped from the chamber, by the rod, just before the breaking of the door. It must have closed the window as it passed through it. It was subsequently caught by the owner himself, who obtained for it a very large sum at the Jardin des Plantes. Le Bon was instantly released, upon our narration of the circumstances (with some comments from Dupin) at the bureau of the Prefect of Police. This functionary, however well disposed to my friend, could not altogether conceal his chagrin at the turn which affairs had taken, and was fain to indulge in a sarcasm or two about the propriety of every person minding his own business.

"Let him talk," said Dupin, who had not thought it necessary to reply. "Let him discourse; it will ease his conscience. I am satisfied with having defeated him in his own castle. Nevertheless, that he failed in the solution of this mystery is by no means that matter for wonder which he supposes it; for, in truth, our friend the Prefect is somewhat too cunning to be profound. In his wisdom is no *stamen.* It is all head and no body, like the pictures of the Goddess Laverna—or, at best, all head and shoulders, like a codfish. But he is a good creature after all. I like him especially for one masterstroke of cant, by which he has attained his reputation for ingenuity; I mean the way he has *'de nier ce qui est, et d'expliquer ce qui n'est pas.' "*[1]

---

[1] ". . . of denying what exists, and of explicating what does not exist."
[Rousseau—"Nouvelle Heloïse"]

THE
GREAT STONE FACE

Nathaniel Hawthorne

One afternoon, when the sun was going down, a mother and her little boy sat at the door of their cottage, talking about the Great Stone Face. They had but to lift their eyes, and there it was plainly to be seen, though miles away, with the sunshine brightening all its features.

And what was the Great Stone Face?

Embosomed among a family of lofty mountains, there was a valley so spacious that it contained many thousand inhabitants. Some of these good people dwelt in log-huts, with the black forests all around them on the steep and difficult hillsides. Others had their homes in comfortable farmhouses, and cultivated the rich soil on the gentle slopes or level surfaces of the valley. Others, again, were congregated into populous villages, where some wild, highland rivulet, tumbling down from its birthplace in the upper mountain region, had been caught and tamed by human cunning, and compelled to turn the machinery of cotton factories. The inhabitants of this valley, in short, were numerous, and of many modes of life. But all of them, grown people and children, had a kind of familiarity with the Great Stone Face, although some possessed the gift of distinguishing this grand natural phenomenon more perfectly than many of their neighbors.

The Great Stone Face, then, was a work of Nature in her mood of majestic playfulness, formed on the perpendicular side of a mountain by some immense rocks, which had been thrown together in such a position as, when viewed at a proper distance, precisely to resemble the features of the human countenance. It seemed as if an enormous giant, or a Titan, had sculptured his own likeness on the precipice. There was the broad arch of the forehead, a hundred feet in height; the nose, with its long bridge; and the vast lips, which, if they could have spoken, would have rolled their thunder accents from one end of the valley to the other. True it is, that if the spectator approached too near he lost the outline of the gigantic visage, and could discern only a heap of ponderous and gigantic rocks, piled in chaotic ruin one upon another. Retracing his steps, however, the wondrous features would again be seen; and the further he withdrew from them, the more like a human face, with all its original divinity intact, did they appear; until, as it grew dim in the distance, with the clouds and glorified vapor of the mountains clustering about it, the Great Stone Face seemed positively to be alive.

It was a happy lot for children to grow up to manhood or womanhood with the Great Stone Face before their eyes, for all the features were noble, and the expression was at once grand and sweet, as if it were the glow of a vast, warm heart, that embraced all mankind in its affections, and had room for more. It was an education only to look at it. According to the belief of many people, the valley owed much of its fertility to this benign aspect that was continually beaming over it, and infusing its tenderness into the sunshine.

As we began with saying, a mother and her little boy sat at their cottage door, gazing at the Great Stone Face, and talking about it. The child's name was Ernest.

"Mother," said he, while the Titanic visage smiled on him, "I wish that it could speak, for it looks so very kindly that its voice must needs be pleasant. If I were to see a man with such a face, I should love him dearly."

"If an old prophecy should come to pass," answered his mother, "we may see a man, some time or other, with exactly such a face as that."

"What prophecy do you mean, dear mother," eagerly inquired Ernest. "Pray tell me all about it!"

So his mother told him a story that her own mother had told to her, when she herself was younger than little Ernest; a story, not of things that were past, but of what was yet to come; a story, nevertheless, so very old that even the Indians, who formerly inhabited this valley, had heard it from their forefathers, to whom, as they affirmed, it had been murmured by the mountain streams, and whispered by the wind among the tree-tops. The purport was that, at some future day, a child should be born hereabouts who was destined to become the greatest and noblest personage of his time, and whose countenance, in manhood, should bear an exact resemblance to the Great Stone Face. Not a few old-fashioned people, and young ones likewise, in the ardor of their hopes, still cherished in enduring faith in this old prophecy. But others, who had seen more of the world, had watched and waited till they were weary, and had beheld no man with such a face, nor any man that proved to be much greater or nobler than his neighbors, concluded it to be nothing but an idle tale. At all events, the great man of the prophecy had not yet appeared.

"Oh, mother, dear mother!" cried Ernest, clapping his hands above his head, "I do hope that I shall live to see him!"

His mother was an affectionate and thoughtful woman, and felt that it was wisest not to discourage the generous hopes of her little boy. So she only said to him, "Perhaps you may."

And Ernest never forgot the story that his mother told him. It was always in his mind, whenever he looked upon the Great Stone Face. He spent his childhood in the log-cottage where he was born, and was dutiful to his mother, and helpful to her in many things, assisting her much with his little hands, and more with his loving heart. In this manner, from a happy yet often pensive child, he grew up to be a mild, quiet, unobtrusive boy, and sun-browned with labor in the fields, but with more intelligence brightening his aspect than is seen in many lads who have been taught at famous schools. Yet Ernest had had no teacher, save only that the Great Stone Face became one to him. When the toil of the day was over, he would gaze at it for hours, until he began to imagine that those vast features recognized him and gave him a smile of kindness and encouragement, responsive to his own look of veneration. We must not take upon us to affirm that this was a mistake, although the Face may have looked no more kindly at Ernest than at all the world besides. But the secret was that the boy's tender and confiding simplicity discerned what other people could not see; and thus the love, meant for all, became his peculiar portion.

About this time there went a rumor throughout the valley that the great man, foretold from ages long ago, who was to bear a resemblance to the Great Stone Face had appeared at last. It seems that, many years before, a young man had migrated from the valley and settled at a distant seaport, where, after getting together a little money, he had set up as a shopkeeper. His name—but I could never learn whether it was his real one, or a nickname that had grown out of his habits and success in life—was Gathergold. Being shrewd and active, and endowed by Providence with that inscrutable faculty which develops itself in what the world calls luck, he became an exceedingly rich merchant, and owner of a whole fleet of bulky-bottomed ships. All the countries of the globe appeared to join hands for the mere purpose of adding heap after heap to the mountainous accumulation of this one man's wealth. The cold regions of the north, almost within the gloom and shadow of the Arctic Circle, sent him their tribute in the shape of furs; hot Africa sifted for him the golden sands of her rivers, and gathered up the ivory tusks of her great elephants out of the forests; the East came bringing him the rich shawls, and spices, and teas, and the effulgence of diamonds, and the gleaming purity of large pearls. The ocean, not to be behindhand with the earth, yielded up her mighty whales, that Mr. Gathergold might sell their oil, and make a profit on it. Be the original commodity what it might, it was gold within his grasp. It might be said of him, as of Midas in the fable, that whatever he touched with his finger immediately glistened, and grew yellow, and was changed at once into sterling metal, or, which suited him still better, into piles of coin. And when Mr. Gathergold had become so very rich that it would have taken him a hundred years only to count his wealth, he bethought himself of his native valley, and resolved to go back thither, and end his days where he was born. With this purpose in view, he sent a skilful architect to build him such a palace as should be fit for a man of his vast wealth to live in.

As I have said above, it had already been rumored in the valley that Mr. Gathergold had turned out to be the prophetic personage so long and vainly looked for, and that his visage was the perfect and undeniable similitude of the Great Stone Face. People were the more ready to believe that this must needs be the fact when they beheld the splendid edifice that rose, as if by enchantment, on the site of his father's old weather-beaten farmhouse. The exterior was of marble, so dazzlingly white that it seemed as though the whole structure might melt away in the sunshine, like those humbler ones which Mr. Gathergold, in his young playdays, before his fingers were gifted with the touch of transmutation, had been accustomed to build of snow. It had a richly ornamental portico, supported by tall pillars, beneath which was a lofty door, studded with silver knobs, and made of a kind of variegated wood that had been brought from beyond the sea. The windows, from the floor to the ceiling of each stately apartment, were composed, respectively, of but one enormous pane of glass, so transparently pure that it was said to be a finer medium than even the vacant atmosphere. Hardly anybody had been permitted to see the interior of this palace; but it was reported, and with good semblance of truth, to be far more gorgeous than the outside, insomuch that whatever was iron or brass in other houses was silver or gold in this; and Mr. Gathergold's bedchamber, especially, made such a glittering appearance that no ordinary man would have been able to close his eyes there.

In due time, the mansion was finished; next came the upholsterers, with magnificent furniture; then, a whole troop of black and white servants, the harbingers of Mr. Gathergold, who, in his own majestic person, was expected to arrive at sunset. Our friend Ernest, meanwhile, had been deeply stirred by the idea that the great man, the noble man, the man of prophecy, after so many ages of delay, was at length to be made manifest to his native valley. He knew, boy as he was, that there were a thousand ways in which Mr. Gathergold, with his vast wealth, might transform himself into an angel of beneficence, and assume a control over human affairs as wide and benignant as the smile of the Great Stone Face. Full of faith and hope, Ernest doubted not that what the people said was true, and that now he was to behold the living likeness of those wondrous features on the mountain-side. While the boy was still gazing up the valley, and fancying, as he always did, that the Great Stone Face returned his gaze and looked kindly at him, the rumbling of wheels was heard, approaching swiftly along the winding road.

"Here he comes!" cried a group of people who were assembled to witness the arrival. "Here comes the great Mr. Gathergold!"

A carriage, drawn by four horses, dashed round the turn of the road. Within it, thrust partly out of the window, appeared the physiognomy of the old man, with a skin as yellow as if his own Midas hand had transmuted it. He had a low forehead, small, sharp eyes, puckered about with innumerable wrinkles, and very thin lips, which he made still thinner by pressing them forcibly together.

"The very image of the Great Stone Face!" shouted the people. "Sure enough, the old prophecy is true; and here we have the great man come at last!"

And, what greatly perplexed Ernest, they seemed actually to believe that here was the likeness which they spoke of. By the roadside there chanced to be an old beggar-woman and two little beggar-children, stragglers from some far-off region, who, as the carriage rolled onward, held out their hands and lifted up their doleful voices, most piteously beseeching charity. A yellow claw—the very same that had clawed together so much wealth—poked itself out of the coach-window, and dropped some copper coins upon the ground; so that, though the great man's name seems to have been Gathergold, he might just as suitably have been nicknamed Scattercopper. Still, nevertheless, with an earnest shout, the people bellowed: "He is the very image of the Great Stone Face!"

But Ernest turned sadly from the wrinkled shrewdness of that sordid visage, and gazed up the valley, where, amid a gathering mist, gilded by the last sunbeams, he could still distinguish those glorious features which had impressed themselves into his soul. Their aspect cheered him. What did the benign lips seem to say?

"He will come! Fear not, Ernest; the man will come!"

The years went on, and Ernest ceased to be a boy. He had grown to be a young man now. He attracted little notice from the other inhabitants of the valley; for they saw nothing remarkable in his way of life, save that, when the labor of the day was over, he still loved to go apart and gaze and meditate upon the Great Stone Face. According to their idea of the matter, it was a folly, indeed, but pardonable, inasmuch as Ernest was industrious, kind, and neighborly, and neglected no duty for the sake of indulging this idle habit. They knew not that the Great Stone Face had become a teacher to him and that the sentiment which was expressed in it would enlarge the young man's heart, and fill it with wider and deeper sympathies than other hearts. They knew not that thence would come a better wisdom than could be learned from books, and a better life than could be molded on the defaced example of other human lives. Neither did Ernest know that the thoughts and affections which came to him so naturally, in the fields and at the fireside, and wherever he communed with himself, were of a higher tone than those which all men shared with him. A simple soul—simple as when his mother first taught him the old prophecy—he beheld the marvelous features beaming adown the valley, and still wondered that their human counterpart was so long in making his appearance.

By this time poor Mr. Gathergold was dead and buried; and the oddest part of the matter was, that his wealth, which was the body and spirit of his existence, had disappeared before his death, leaving nothing of him but a living skeleton, covered over with a wrinkled, yellow skin. Since the melting away of his gold, it had been very generally conceded that there was no such striking resemblance, after all, betwixt the ignoble features of the ruined merchant and that majestic face upon the mountain-side. So the people ceased to honor him during his lifetime, and quietly consigned him to forgetfulness after his decease. Once in a while, it is true, his memory was brought up in connection with the magnificent palace which he had built, and which had long ago been turned into a hotel for the accommodation of strangers, multitudes of whom came, every summer, to visit that famous natural curiosity, the Great Stone Face. Thus, Mr. Gathergold being discredited and thrown into the shade, the man of prophecy was yet to come.

It so happened that a native born son of the valley, many years before, had enlisted as a soldier, and, after a great deal of hard fighting, had now become an illustrious commander. Whatever he may be called in history, he was known in camps and on the battlefield under the nickname of Old Blood-and-Thunder. This war-worn veteran, being now infirm with age and wounds, and weary of the turmoil of a military life, and of the roll of the drum and the clangor of the trumpet, that had so long been ringing in his ears, had lately signified a purpose of returning to his native valley, hoping to find repose where he remembered to have left it. The inhabitants, his old neighbors and their grown-up children, were resolved to welcome the renowned warrior with a salute of cannon and a public dinner; and all the more enthusiastically, it being affirmed that now, at last, the likeness of the Great Stone Face had actually appeared. An aid-de-camp of Old Blood-and-Thunder, traveling through the valley, was said to have been struck with the resemblance. Moreover, the schoolmates and early acquaintances of the general were ready to testify, on oath, that, to the best of their recollection, the aforesaid general had been exceedingly like the majestic image, even when a boy, only that the idea had never occurred to them at that period. Great, therefore, was the excitement throughout the valley; and many people, who had never once thought of glancing at the Great Stone Face for years before, now spent their time in gazing at it, for the sake of knowing exactly how General Blood-and-Thunder looked.

On the day of the great festival, Ernest, with all the other people of the valley, left their work, and proceeded to the spot where the sylvan banquet was prepared. As he approached, the loud voice of the Rev. Dr. Battleblast was heard, beseeching a blessing on the good things set before them, and on the distinguished friend of peace in whose honor they were assembled. The tables were arranged in a cleared space of the woods, shut in by the surrounding trees, except where a vista opened eastward, and afforded a distant view of the Great Stone Face. Over the general's chair, which was a relic from the home of Washington, there was an arch of verdant boughs, with the laurel profusely intermixed, and surmounted by his country's banner, beneath which he had won his victories. Our friend Ernest raised himself on his tiptoes, in hopes to get a glimpse of the celebrated guest; but there was a mighty crowd about the tables anxious to hear the toasts and speeches, and to catch any word that might fall from the general in reply; and a volunteer company, doing duty as a guard, pricked ruthlessly with their bayonets at any particularly quiet person among the throng. So Ernest, being of an unobtrusive character, was thrust quite into the background, where he could see no more of Old Blood-and-Thunder's physiognomy than if it had been still blazing on the battlefield. To console himself, he turned toward the Great Stone Face, which, like a faithful and long-remembered friend, looked back and smiled upon him through the vista of the forest. Meantime, however, he could overhear the remarks of various individuals, who were comparing the features of the hero with the face on the distant mountain-side.

" 'Tis the same face, to a hair!" cried one man.

"Wonderfully like, that's a fact!" responded another.

"Like! why, I call it Old Blood-and-Thunder himself, in a monstrous looking-glass!" cried a third. "And why not? He's the greatest man of this or any other age, beyond a doubt."

And then all three of the speakers gave a great shout, which communicated electricity to the crowd, and called forth a roar from a thousand voices that went reverberating for miles among the mountains, until you might have supposed that the Great Stone Face had poured its thunder-breath into the cry. All these comments, and this vast enthusiasm, served the more to interest our friend; nor did he think of questioning that now, at length, the mountain-visage had found its human counterpart. It is true, Ernest had imagined that this long-looked-for personage would appear in the character of a man of peace, uttering wisdom, and doing good, and making people happy. But, taking an habitual breadth of view, with all his simplicity, he contended that Providence should choose its own method of blessing mankind, and could conceive that this great end might be effected even by a warrior should inscrutable wisdom see fit to order matters so.

"The general! the general!" was now the cry. "Hush! silence! Old Blood-and-Thunder's going to make a speech."

Even so; for, the cloth being removed, the general's health had been drunk amid shouts of applause, and he now stood upon his feet to thank the company. Ernest saw him. There he was, over the shoulders of the crowd, from the two glittering epaulets and embroidered collar upward, beneath the arch of green boughs with intertwined laurel, and the banner drooping as if to shade his brow! And there, too, visible in the same glance, through the vista of the forest, appeared the Great Stone Face! And was there, indeed, such a resemblance as the crowd had testified? Alas, Ernest could not recognize it! He beheld a war-worn and weather-beaten countenance, full of energy, and expressive of an iron will; but the gentle wisdom, the deep, broad, tender sympathies, were altogether wanting in Old Blood-and-Thunder's visage; and even if the Great Stone Face had assumed his look of stern command, the milder traits would still have tempered it.

"This is not the man of prophecy," sighed Ernest to himself, as he made his way out of the throng. "And must the world wait longer yet?"

The mists had congregated about the distant mountain-side, and there were seen the grand and awful features of the Great Stone Face, awful but benignant, as if a mighty angel were sitting among the hills, and enrobing himself in a cloud-vesture of gold and purple. As he looked, Ernest could hardly believe but that a smile beamed over the whole visage, with a radiance still brightening, although without motion of the lips. It was probably the effect of the western sunshine, melting through the thinly diffused vapors that had swept between him and the object that he gazed at. But—as it always did— the aspect of his marvelous friend made Ernest as hopeful as if he had never hoped in vain.

"Fear not, Ernest," said his heart, even as if the Great Face were whispering to him—"fear not, Ernest; he will come."

More years sped swiftly and tranquilly away. Ernest still dwelt in his native valley, and was now a man of middle age. By imperceptible degrees, he had become known among the people. Now, as heretofore, he labored for his bread, and was the same simple-hearted man that he had always been. But he had thought and felt so much, he had given so many of the best hours of his life to unworldly hopes for some great good to mankind, that it seemed as though he had been talking with the angels, and had imbibed a portion of their wisdom unawares. It was visible in the calm and well-considered beneficence of his daily life, the quiet stream of which had made a wide green margin all along its course. Not a day passed by that the world was not the better because this man, humble as he was, had lived. He never stepped aside from his own path, yet would always reach a blessing to his neighbor. Almost involuntarily, too, he had become a preacher. The pure and high simplicity of his thought, which, as one of its manifestations, took shape in the good deeds that dropped silently from his hand, flowed also forth in speech. He uttered truths that wrought upon and molded the lives of those who heard him. His auditors, it may be, never suspected that Ernest, their own neighbor and familiar friend, was more than an ordinary man; least of all did Ernest himself suspect it; but, inevitably as the murmur of a rivulet, came thoughts out of his mouth that no other human lips had spoken.

When the people's minds had had a little time to cool, they were ready enough to acknowledge their mistake in imagining a similarity between General Blood-and-Thunder's truculent physiognomy and the benign visage on the mountain-side. But now, again, there were reports and many paragraphs in the newspapers, affirming that the likeness of the Great Stone Face had appeared upon the broad shoulders of a certain eminent statesman. He, like Mr. Gathergold and Old Blood-and-Thunder, was a native of the valley, but had left it in his early days, and taken up the trades of law and politics. Instead of the rich man's wealth and the warrior's sword, he had but a tongue, and it was mightier than both together. So wonderfully eloquent was he that whatever he might choose to say, his auditors had no choice but to believe him; wrong looked like right and right like wrong; for when it pleased him he could make a kind of illuminated fog with his mere breath and obscure the natural daylight with it. His tongue, indeed, was a magic instrument: sometimes it rumbled like the thunder; sometimes it warbled like the sweetest music. It was the blast of war—the song of peace; and it seemed to have a heart in it, when there was no such matter. In good truth, he was a wondrous man; and when his tongue had acquired him all other imaginable success—when it had been heard in halls of state, and in the courts of princes and potentates—after it had made him known all over the world, even as a voice crying from shore to shore—it finally persuaded his countrymen to select him for the Presidency. Before this time—indeed, as soon as he began to grow celebrated—his admirers had found out the resemblance between him and the Great Stone Face; and so much were they struck by it that throughout the country this distinguished gentleman was known by the name of Old Stony Phiz. The phrase was considered as giving a highly favorable aspect to his political prospects; for, as is likewise the case with the Popedom, nobody ever becomes President without taking a name other than his own.

While his friends were doing their best to make him President, Old Stony Phiz, as he was called, set out on a visit to the valley where he was born. Of course, he had no other object than to shake hands with his fellow-citizens, and neither thought nor cared about any effect which his progress through the country might have upon the election. Magnificent preparations were made to receive the illustrious statesman; a cavalcade of horsemen set forth to meet him at the boundary line of the State, and all the people left their business and gathered along the wayside to see him pass. Among these was Ernest. Though more than once disappointed, as we have seen, he had such a hopeful and confiding nature that he was always ready to believe in whatever seemed beautiful and good. He kept his heart continually open, and thus was sure to catch the blessing from on high when it should come. So now again, as buoyantly as ever, he went forth to behold the likeness of the Great Stone Face.

The cavalcade came prancing along the road, with a great clattering of hoofs and a mighty cloud of dust, which rose up so dense and high that the visage of the mountain-side was completely hidden from Ernest's eyes. All the great men of the neighborhood were there on horseback; militia officers in uniform; the member of Congress; the sheriff of the county; the editors of newspapers; and many a farmer, too, had mounted his patient steed, with his Sunday coat upon his back. It really was a very brilliant spectacle, especially as there were numerous banners flaunting over the cavalcade, on some of which were gorgeous portraits of the illustrious statesman and the Great Stone Face, smiling familiarly at one another, like two brothers. If the pictures were to be trusted, the mutual resemblance, it must be confessed, was marvelous. We must not forget to mention that there was a band of music, which made the echoes of the mountains ring and reverberate with the loud triumph of its strains; so that airy and soul-thrilling melodies broke out among all the heights and hollows, as if every nook of his native valley had found a voice to welcome the distinguished guest. But the grandest effect was when the far-off mountain precipice flung back the music; for then the Great Stone Face itself seemed to be swelling the triumphant chorus, in acknowledgment that, at length, the man of prophecy was come.

All this while the people were throwing up their hats and shouting, with enthusiasm so contagious that the heart of Ernest kindled up, and he likewise threw up his hat, and shouted, as loudly as the loudest, "Huzza for the great man! Huzza for Old Stony Phiz!" But as yet he had not seen him.

"Here he is, now!" cried those who stood near Ernest. "There! There! Look at Old Stony Phiz and then at the Old Man of the Mountain, and see if they are not as like as two twin-brothers!"

In the midst of all this gallant array came an open barouche, drawn by four white horses; and in the barouche, with his massive head uncovered, sat the illustrious statesman, Old Stony Phiz himself.

"Confess it," said one of Ernest's neighbors to him, "the Great Stone Face has met its match at last!"

Now, it must be owned that, at his first glimpse of the countenance which was bowing and smiling from the barouche, Ernest did fancy that there was a resemblance between it and the old familiar face upon the mountain-side. The brow, with its massive depth and loftiness, and all the other features, indeed, were boldly and strongly hewn as if in emulation of a more than heroic, of a Titanic, model. But the sublimity and stateliness, the grand expression of a divine sympathy, that illuminated the mountain visage and etherealized its ponderous granite substance into spirit, might here be sought in vain. Something had been originally left out, or had departed. And therefore the marvelously gifted statesman had always a weary gloom in the deep caverns of his eyes, as of a child that has outgrown its playthings or a man of mighty faculties and little aims, whose life, with all its high performances, was vague and empty, because no high purpose had endowed it with reality.

Still Ernest's neighbor was thrusting his elbow into his side, and pressing him for an answer.

"Confess! confess! Is not he the very picture of your Old Man of the Mountain?"

"No!" said Ernest, bluntly, "I see little or no likeness."

"Then so much the worse for the Great Stone Face!" answered his neighbor.

But Ernest turned away, melancholy, and almost despondent: for this was the saddest of his disappointments, to behold a man who might have fulfilled the prophecy and had not willed to do so. Meantime, the cavalcade, the banners, the music, and the barouches swept past him, with the vociferous crowd in the rear, leaving the dust to settle down, and the Great Stone Face to be revealed again.

"Lo, here I am, Ernest!" the benign lips seemed to say. "I have waited longer than thou, and am not yet weary. Fear not; the man will come."

The years hurried onward, treading in their haste on one another's heels. And now they began to bring white hairs, and scatter them over the head of

Ernest; they made reverend wrinkles across his forehead and furrows in his cheeks. He was an aged man. But not in vain had he grown old: more than the white hairs on his head were the sage thoughts in his mind; his wrinkles and furrows were inscriptions that Time had graved, and in which he had written legends of wisdom that had been tested by the tenor of a life. And Ernest had ceased to be obscure. Unsought for, undesired, had come the fame which so many seek, and made him known in the great world, beyond the limits of the valley in which he had dwelt so quietly. College professors, and even the active men of cities, came from far to see and converse with Ernest; for the report had gone abroad that this simple husbandman had ideas unlike those of other men, not gained from books, but of a higher tone—a tranquil and familiar majesty, as if he had been talking with the angels as his daily friends. Whether it were sage, statesman, or philanthropist, Ernest received these visitors with the gentle sincerity that had characterized him from boyhood, and spoke freely with them of whatever came uppermost, or lay deepest in his heart or their own. While they talked together, his face would kindle, unawares, and shine upon them, as with a mild evening light. Pensive with the fulness of such discourse, his guests took leave and went their way; and passing up the valley, paused to look at the Great Stone Face, imagining that they had seen its likeness in a human countenance, but could not remember where.

While Ernest had been growing up and growing old, a bountiful Providence had granted a new poet to this earth. He, likewise, was a native of the valley, but had spent the greater part of his life at a distance from that romantic region, pouring out his sweet music amid the bustle and din of cities. Often, however, did the mountains which had been familiar to him in his childhood lift their snowy peaks into the clear atmosphere of his poetry. Neither was the Great Stone Face forgotten, for the poet had celebrated it in an ode, which was grand enough to have been uttered by its own majestic lips. This man of genius, we may say, had come down from heaven with wonderful endowments. If he sang of a mountain, the eyes of all mankind beheld a mightier grandeur reposing on its breast, or soaring to its summit, than had before been seen there. If his theme were a lovely lake, a celestial smile had now been thrown over it, to gleam forever on its surface. If it were the vast old sea, even the deep immensity of its dread bosom seemed to swell the higher, as if moved by the emotions of the song. Thus the world assumed another and a better aspect from the hour that the poet blessed it with his happy eyes. The Creator had bestowed him, as the last best touch to his own handiwork. Creation was not finished till the poet came to interpret, and so complete it.

The effect was no less high and beautiful when his human brethren were the subject of his verse. The man or woman, sordid with the common dust of life, who crossed his daily path, and the little child who played in it, were glorified if he beheld them in his mood of poetic faith. He showed the golden links of the great chain that intertwined them with an angelic kindred; he brought out the hidden traits of a celestial birth that made them worthy of such kin. Some, indeed, there were who thought to show the soundness of their judgment by affirming that all the beauty and dignity of the natural world existed only in the poet's fancy. Let such men speak for themselves, who undoubtedly appear to have been spawned forth by Nature with a contemptuous bitterness; she having plastered them up out of her refuse stuff, after all the swine were made. As respects all things else, the poet's ideal was the truest truth.

The songs of this poet found their way to Ernest. He read them after his customary toil, seated on the bench before his cottage door, where for such a length of time he had filled his repose with thought by gazing at the Great Stone Face. And now as he read stanzas that caused the soul to thrill, he lifted his eyes to the vast countenance beaming on him so benignantly.

"Oh, majestic friend," he murmured, addressing the Great Stone Face, "is not this man worthy to resemble thee?"

The Face seemed to smile, but answered not a word.

Now it happened that the poet, though he dwelt so far away, had not only heard of Ernest, but had meditated much upon his character, until he deemed nothing so desirable as to meet this man, whose untaught wisdom walked hand in hand with the noble simplicity of his life. One summer morning, therefore, he took passage by the railroad, and, in the decline of the afternoon, alighted from the cars at no great distance from Ernest's cottage. The great hotel, which had formerly been the palace of Mr. Gathergold, was close at hand, but the poet, with his carpetbag on his arm, inquired at once where Ernest dwelt, and was resolved to be accepted as his guest.

Approaching the door, he there found the good old man, holding a volume in his hand, which alternately he read, and then, with a finger between the leaves, looked lovingly at the Great Stone Face.

"Good-evening," said the poet. "Can you give a traveler a night's lodging?"

"Willingly," answered Ernest; and then he added, smiling, "Methinks I never saw the Great Stone Face look so hospitably at a stranger."

The poet sat down on the bench beside him, and he and Ernest talked together. Often had the poet held intercourse with the wittiest and the wisest, but never before with a man like Ernest, whose thoughts and feelings gushed up with such a natural freedom, and who made great truths so familiar by his simple utterance of them. Angels, as had been so often said, seemed to have wrought with him at his labor in the fields; angels seemed to have sat with him by the fireside; and, dwelling with angels as friend with friends, he had imbibed the sublimity of their ideas, and imbued it with the sweet and lowly charm of household words. So thought the poet. And Ernest, on the other hand, was moved and agitated by the living images which the poet flung out of his mind, and which peopled all the air about the cottage door with shapes of beauty, both gay and pensive. The sympathies of these two men instructed them with a profounder sense than either could have attained alone. Their minds accorded into one strain, and made delightful music which neither of them could have claimed as all his own, nor distinguished his own share from the other's. They led one another, as it were, into a high pavilion of their thoughts, so remote, and hitherto so dim, that they had never entered it before, and so beautiful that they desired to be there always.

As Ernest listened to the poet, he imagined that the Great Stone Face was bending forward to listen too. He gazed earnestly into the poet's glowing eyes.

"Who are you, my strangely gifted guest?" he said.

The poet laid his finger on the volume that Ernest had been reading.

"You have read these poems," said he. "You know me, then—for I wrote them."

Again, and still more earnestly than before, Ernest examined the poet's features; then turned toward the Great Stone Face; then back, with an uncertain aspect, to his guest. But his countenance fell; he shook his head and sighed.

"Wherefore are you sad?" inquired the poet.

"Because," replied Ernest, "all through life I have awaited the fulfilment of a prophecy; and, when I read these poems, I hoped that it might be fulfilled in you."

"You hoped," answered the poet, faintly smiling, "to find in me the likeness of the Great Stone Face. And you are disappointed, as formerly with Mr. Gathergold, and Old Blood-and-Thunder, and Old Stony Phiz. Yes, Ernest, it is my doom. You must add my name to the illustrious three, and record another failure of your hopes. For—in shame and sadness do I speak it, Ernest—I am not worthy to be typified by yonder benign and majestic image."

"And why?" asked Ernest. He pointed to the volume. "Are not those thoughts divine?"

"They have a strain of the Divinity," replied the poet. "You can hear in them the far-off echo of a heavenly song. But my life, dear Ernest, has not corresponded with my thought. I have had grand dreams, but they have been only dreams, because I have lived—and that, too, by my own choice—among poor and mean realities. Sometimes even—shall I dare to say it?—I lack faith in the grandeur, the beauty, and the goodness, which my own works are said to have made more evident in nature and in human life. Why, then, pure seeker of the good, shouldst thou hope to find me in yonder image of the divine?"

The poet spoke sadly, and his eyes were dim with tears. So, likewise, were those of Ernest.

At the hour of sunset, as had long been his frequent custom, Ernest was to discourse to an assemblage of the neighboring inhabitants in the open air. He and the poet, arm in arm, still talking together as they went along, proceeded to the spot. It was a small nook among the hills, with a gray precipice behind, the stern front of which was relieved by the pleasant foliage of many creeping plants that made a tapestry for the naked rock, by hanging their festoons from all its rugged angles. At a small elevation above the ground, set in a rich framework of verdure, there appeared a niche, spacious enough to admit a human figure, with freedom for such gestures as spontaneously accompany earnest thought and genuine emotion. Into this natural pulpit Ernest ascended, and threw a look of familiar kindness around upon his audience. They stood, or sat, or reclined upon the grass, as seemed good to each, with the departing sunshine falling obliquely over them, and mingling its subdued cheerfulness with the solemnity of a grove of ancient trees, beneath and amid the boughs of which the golden rays were constrained to pass. In another direction was seen the Great Stone Face, with the same cheer, combined with the same solemnity, in its benignant aspect.

Ernest began to speak, giving to the people of what was in his heart and mind. His words had power, because they accorded with his thoughts; and his thoughts had reality and depth, because they harmonized with the life which he had always lived. It was not mere breath that this preacher uttered; they were the words of life, because a life of good deeds and holy love was melted into them. Pearls, pure and rich, had been dissolved into this precious draught. The poet, as he listened, felt that the being and character of Ernest were a nobler strain of poetry than he had ever written. His eyes glistening with tears, he gazed reverentially at the venerable man, and said within himself that never was there an aspect so worthy of a prophet and a sage as that mild, sweet, thoughtful countenance, with the glory of white hair diffused about it. At a distance, but distinctly to be seen, high up in the golden light of the setting sun, appeared the Great Stone Face, with hoary mists around it, like the white hairs around the brow of Ernest.

At that moment, in sympathy with a thought which he was about to utter, the face of Ernest assumed a grandeur of expression so imbued with benevolence that the poet, by an irresistible impulse, threw his arms aloft, and shouted:

"Behold! Behold! Ernest is himself the likeness of the Great Stone Face!"

Then all the people looked, and saw that what the deep-sighted poet said was true. The prophecy was fulfilled. But Ernest, having finished, took the poet's arm, and walked slowly homeward, still hoping that some wiser and better man than himself would by and by appear, bearing a resemblance to the Great Stone Face.

MY TERMINAL MORAINE

Frank R. Stockton

A man's birth is generally considered the most important event of his existence, but I truly think that what I am about to relate was more important to
me than my entrance into this world; because, had not these things happened,
I am of the opinion that my life would have been of no value to me and my
birth a misfortune.

My father, Joshua Cuthbert, died soon after I came to my majority, leaving
me what he had considered a comfortable property. This consisted of a large
house and some forty acres of land, nearly the whole of which lay upon a
bluff, which upon three sides descended to a little valley, through which ran a
gentle stream. I had no brothers or sisters. My mother died when I was a boy,
and I, Walter Cuthbert, was left the sole representative of my immediate
family.

My estate had been a comfortable one to my father, because his income
from the practice of his profession as a physician enabled him to keep it up
and provide satisfactorily for himself and me. I had no profession and but a
very small income, the result of a few investments my father had made. Left
to myself, I felt no inducement to take up any profession or business. My
wants were simple, and for a few years I lived without experiencing any
inconvenience from the economies which I was obliged to practice. My
books, my dog, my gun and my rod made life pass very pleasantly to me, and
the subject of an increase of income never disturbed my mind.

But as time passed on the paternal home began to present an air of neglect
and even dilapidation, which occasionally attracted my attention and caused,
as I incidentally discovered, a great deal of unfavorable comment among my

53

neighbors, who thought that I should go to work and at least earn money enough to put the house and grounds in a condition which should not be unworthy the memory of the good Dr. Cuthbert. In fact, I began to be looked upon as a shiftless young man; and, now and then, I found a person old enough and bold enough to tell me so.

But, instead of endeavoring to find some suitable occupation by which I might better my condition and improve my estate, I fell in love, which, in the opinion of my neighbors, was the very worst thing that could have happened to me at this time. I lived in a thrifty region, and for a man who could not support himself to think of taking upon him the support of a wife, especially such a wife as Agnes Havelot would be, was considered more than folly and looked upon as a crime. Everybody knew that I was in love with Miss Havelot, for I went to court her as boldly as I went to fish or shoot. There was a good deal of talk about it, and this finally came to the ears of Mr. Havelot, my lady's father, who, thereupon, promptly ordered her to have no more to do with me.

The Havelot estate, which adjoined mine, was a very large one, containing hundreds and hundreds of acres; and the Havelots were rich, rich enough to frighten any poor young man of marrying intent. But I did not appreciate the fact that I was a poor young man. I had never troubled my head about money as it regarded myself, and I now did not trouble my head about it as it regarded Agnes. I loved her, I hoped she loved me, and all other considerations were thrown aside. Mr. Havelot, however, was a man of a different way of thinking.

It was a little time before I became convinced that the decision of Agnes's father, that there should be no communication between that dear girl and myself, really meant anything. I had never been subjected to restrictions, and I did not understand how people of spirit could submit to them; but I was made to understand it when Mr. Havelot, finding me wandering about his grounds, very forcibly assured me that if I should make my appearance there again, or if he discovered any attempt on my part to communicate with his daughter in any way, he would send her from home. He concluded the very brief interview by stating that if I had any real regard for his daughter's happiness I would cease attentions which would meet with the most decided disapprobation from her only surviving parent and which would result in exiling her from home. I begged for one more interview with Miss Havelot, and if it had been granted I should have assured her of the state of my affections, no matter if there were reasons to suppose that I would never see her again; but her father very sternly forbade anything of the kind, and I went away crushed.

It was a very hard case, for if I played the part of a bold lover and tried to see Agnes without regard to the wicked orders of her father, I should certainly be discovered; and then it would be not only myself, but the poor girl, who would suffer. So I determined that I would submit to the Havelot decree. No matter if I never saw her again, never heard the sound of her voice, it would be better to have her near me, to have her breathe the same air, cast up her eyes at the same sky, listen to the same birds, that I breathed, looked at and listened to, than to have her far away, probably in Kentucky, where I knew she had relatives, and where the grass was blue and the sky probably green, or at any rate would appear so to her if in the least degree she felt as I did in regard to the ties of home and the affinities between the sexes.

I now found myself in a most doleful and even desperate condition of mind. There was nothing in the world which I could have for which I cared. Hunting, fishing, and the rambles through woods and fields that had once been so delightful to me now became tasks which I seldom undertook. The only occupation in which I felt the slightest interest was that of sitting in a tower of my house with a telescope, endeavoring to see my Agnes on some portion of her father's grounds; but, although I diligently directed my glass at the slightest stretch of lawn or bit of path which I could discern through openings in the foliage, I never caught sight of her. I knew, however, by means of daily questions addressed to my cook, whose daughter was a servant in the Havelot house, that Agnes was yet at home. For that reason I remained at home. Otherwise, I should have become a wanderer.

About a month after I had fallen into this most unhappy state an old friend came to see me. We had been school-fellows, but he differed from me in almost every respect. He was full of ambition and energy, and, although he was but a few years older than myself, he had already made a name in the world. He was a geologist, earnest and enthusiastic in his studies and his investigations. He told me frankly that the object of his visit was twofold. In the first place, he wanted to see me, and, secondly, he wanted to make some geological examinations on my grounds, which were situated, as he informed me, upon a terminal moraine, a formation which he had not yet had an opportunity of practically investigating.

I had not known that I lived on a moraine, and now that I knew it, I did not care. But Tom Burton glowed with high spirits and lively zeal as he told me how the great bluff on which my house stood, together with the other hills and wooded terraces which stretched away from it along the side of the valley, had been formed by the minute fragments of rock and soil, which, during ages and ages, had been gradually pushed down from the mountains by a great glacier which once occupied the country to the northeast of my house. "Why, Walter, my boy," he cried, "if I had not read it all in the books I should have known for myself, as soon as I came here, that there had once been a glacier up there, and as it gradually moved to the southwest it had made this country what it is. Have you a stream down there in that dell which I see lies at right angles with the valley and opens into it?"

"No," said I; "I wish there were one. The only stream we have flows along the valley and not on my property."

Without waiting for me Tom ran down into my dell, pushed his way through the underbrush to its upper end, and before long came back flushed with heat and enthusiasm.

"Well, sir," he said, "that dell was once the bed of a glacial stream, and you may as well clear it out and plant corn there if you want to, for there never will be another stream flowing through it until there is another glacier out in the country beyond. And now I want you to let me dig about here. I want to find out what sort of stuff the glacier brought down from the mountains. I will hire a man and will promise you to fill up all the holes I make."

I had no objection to my friend's digging as much as he pleased, and for three days he busied himself in getting samples of the soil of my estate. Sometimes I went out and looked at him, and gradually a little of his earnest ardor infused itself into me, and with some show of interest I looked into the holes he had made and glanced over the mineral specimens he showed me.

"Well, Walter," said he, when he took leave of me, "I am very sorry that I did not discover that the glacier had raked out the bed of a gold mine from the mountains up there and brought it down to you, or at any rate, some valuable iron ore. But I am obliged to say it did not do anything of the sort. But I can tell you one thing it brought you, and, although it is not of any great commercial value, I should think you could make good use of it here on your place. You have one of the finest deposits of gravel on this bluff that I have met with, and if you were to take out a lot of it and spread it over your driveways and paths, it would make it a great deal pleasanter for you to go about here in bad weather and would wonderfully improve your property. Good roads always give an idea of thrift and prosperity." And then he went away with a valise nearly full of mineral specimens which he assured me were very interesting.

My interest in geological formations died away as soon as Tom Burton had departed, but what he said about making gravel roads giving the place an air of thrift and prosperity had its effect upon my mind. It struck me that it would be a very good thing if people in the neighborhood, especially the Havelots, were to perceive on my place some evidences of thrift and prosperity. Most palpable evidences of unthrift and inpecuniosity had cut me off from Agnes, and why might it not be that some signs of improved circumstances would remove, to a degree at least, the restrictions which had been placed between us? This was but a very little thing upon which to build hopes; but ever since men and women have loved they have built grand hopes upon very slight foundations. I determined to put my roadways in order.

My efforts in this direction were really evidence of anything but thriftiness, for I could not in the least afford to make my drives and walks resemble the smooth and beautiful roads which wound over the Havelot estate, although to do this was my intention, and I set about the work without loss of time. I took up this occupation with so much earnestness that it seriously interfered with my observations from the tower.

I hired two men and set them to work to dig a gravel-pit. They made excavations at several places, and very soon found what they declared to be a very fine quality of road-gravel. I ordered them to dig on until they had taken out what they believed to be enough to cover all my roads. When this had been done, I would have it properly spread and rolled. As this promised to be a very good job, the men went to work in fine spirits and evidently made up their minds that the improvements I desired would require a vast deal of gravel.

When they had dug a hole so deep that it became difficult to throw up the gravel from the bottom, I suggested that they should dig at some other place. But to this they objected, declaring that the gravel was getting better and better, and it would be well to go on down as long as the quality continued to be so good. So, at last, they put a ladder into the pit, one man carrying the gravel up in a hod, while the other dug it; and when they had gone down so deep that this was no longer practicable, they rigged up a derrick and windlass and drew up the gravel in a bucket.

Had I been of a more practical turn of mind I might have perceived that this method of working made the job a very long and, consequently, to the laborers, a profitable one; but no such idea entered into my head, and not noticing whether they were bringing up sand or gravel I allowed them to proceed.

One morning I went out to the spot where the excavation was being made and found that the men had built a fire on the ground near the opening of the pit, and that one of them was bending over it warming himself. As the month was July this naturally surprised me, and I inquired the reason for so strange a performance.

"Upon my soul," said the man, who was rubbing his hands over the blaze, "I do not wonder you are surprised, but it's so cold down at the bottom of that pit that me fingers is almost frosted; and we haven't struck any wather neither, which couldn't be expected, of course, a-diggin' down into the hill like this."

I looked into the hole and found it was very deep. "I think it would be better to stop digging here," said I, "and try some other place."

"I wouldn't do that just now," said the other man, who was preparing to go down in the bucket; "to be sure, it's a good deal more like a well than a gravel-pit, but it's bigger at the top than at the bottom, and there's no danger of its cavin' in, and now that we've got everything rigged up all right, it would be a pity to make a change yet awhile."

So I let them go on; but the next day when I went out again I found that they had come to the conclusion that it was time to give up digging in that hole. They both declared that it almost froze their feet to stand on the ground where they worked at the bottom of the excavation. The slow business of drawing up the gravel by means of a bucket and windlass was, therefore, reluctantly given up. The men now went to work to dig outward from this pit toward the edge of the bluff which overlooked my little dell, and gradually made a wide trench, which they deepened until—and I am afraid to say how long they worked before this was done—they could walk to the original pit from the level of the dell. They then deepened the inner end of the trench, wheeling out the gravel in barrows, until they had made an inclined pathway from the dell to the bottom of the pit. The wheeling now became difficult, and the men soon declared that they were sure that they had quite gravel enough.

When they made this announcement, and I had gone into some financial calculations, I found that I would be obliged to put an end to my operations, at least for the present, for my available funds were gone, or would be when I had paid what I owed for the work. The men were very much disappointed by the sudden ending of this good job, but they departed, and I was left to gaze upon a vast amount of gravel, of which, for the present at least, I could not afford to make the slightest use.

The mental despondency which had been somewhat lightened during my excavating operations now returned, and I became rather more gloomy and downcast than before. My cook declared that it was of no use to prepare meals which I never ate, and suggested that it would save money if I discharged her. As I had not paid her anything for a long time, I did not see how this would benefit me.

Wandering about one day with my hat pulled down over my eyes and my hands thrust deep into my pockets, I strolled into the dell and stood before the wide trench which led to the pit in which I had foolishly sunk the money which should have supported me for months. I entered this dismal passage and walked slowly and carefully down the incline until I reached the bottom of the original pit, where I had never been before. I stood here looking up and around me and wondering how men could bring themselves to dig down into such dreary depths simply for the sake of a few dollars a week, when I involuntarily began to stamp my feet. They were very cold, although I had not been there more than a minute. I wondered at this and took up some of the loose gravel in my hand. It was quite dry, but it chilled my fingers. I did not understand it, and I did not try to, but walked up the trench and around into the dell, thinking of Agnes.

I was very fond of milk, which, indeed, was almost the only food I now cared for, and I was consequently much disappointed at my noonday meal when I found that the milk had soured and was not fit to drink.

"You see, sir," said Susan, "ice is very scarce and dear, and we can not afford to buy much of it. There was no freezin' weather last winter, and the price has gone up as high as the thermometer, sir, and so, between the two of 'em, I can't keep things from spoilin'."

The idea now came to me that if Susan would take the milk, and anything else she wished to keep cool in this hot weather, to the bottom of the gravel-pit, she would find the temperature there cold enough to preserve them without ice, and I told her so.

The next morning Susan came to me with a pleased countenance and said, "I put the butter and the milk in that pit last night, and the butter's just as hard and the milk's as sweet as if it had been kept in an ice-house. But the place is as cold as an ice-house, sir, and unless I am mistaken, there's ice in it. Anyway, what do you call that?" And she took from a little basket a piece of grayish ice as large as my fist. "When I found it was so cold down there, sir," she said, "I thought I would dig a little myself and see what made it so; and I took a fire-shovel and hatchet, and, when I had scraped away some of the gravel, I came to something hard and chopped off this piece of it, which is real ice, sir, or I know nothing about it. Perhaps there used to be an ice-house there, and you might get some of it if you dug, though why anybody should put it down so deep and then cover it up, I'm sure I don't know. But as long as there's any there, I think we should get it out, even if there's only a little of it; for I can not take everything down to that pit, and we might as well have it in the refrigerator."

This seemed to me like very good sense, and if I had had a man I should have ordered him to go down to the pit and dig up any lumps of ice he might find and bring them to the house. But I had no man, and I therefore became impressed with the opinion that if I did not want to drink sour milk for the rest of the summer, it might be a good thing for me to go down there and dig out some of the ice myself. So with pickaxe and shovel I went to the bottom of the pit and set myself to work.

A few inches below the surface I found that my shovel struck something hard, and, clearing away the gravel from this for two or three square feet, I looked down upon a solid mass of ice. It was dirty and begrimed, but it was truly ice. With my pick I detached some large pieces of it. These, with some discomfort, I carried out into the dell where Susan might come with her basket and get them.

For several days Susan and I took out ice from the pit, and then I thought that perhaps Tom Burton might feel some interest in this frozen deposit in my terminal moraine, and so I wrote to him about it. He did not answer my letter, but instead arrived himself the next afternoon.

"Ice at the bottom of a gravel-pit," said he, "is a thing I never heard of. Will you lend me a spade and a pickaxe?"

When Tom came out of that pit—it was too cold a place for me to go with him and watch his proceedings—I saw him come running toward the house.

"Walter," he shouted, "we must hire all the men we can find and dig, dig, dig. If I am not mistaken something has happened on your place that is wonderful almost beyond belief. But we must not stop to talk. We must dig, dig, dig; dig all day and dig all night. Don't think of the cost. I'll attend to that. I'll get the money. What we must do is to find men and set them to work."

"What's the matter?" said I. "What has happened?"

"I haven't time to talk about it now; besides I don't want to, for fear that I should find that I am mistaken. But get on your hat, my dear fellow, and let's go over to the town for men."

The next day there were eight men working under the direction of my friend Burton, and although they did not work at night as he wished them to do, they labored steadfastly for ten days or more before Tom was ready to announce what it was he had hoped to discover, and whether or not he had found it. For a day or two I watched the workmen from time to time, but after that I kept away, preferring to await the result of my friend's operations. He evidently expected to find something worth having, and whether he was successful or not, it suited me better to know the truth all at once and not by degrees.

On the morning of the eleventh day Tom came into the room where I was reading and sat down near me. His face was pale, his eyes glittering. "Old friend," said he, and as he spoke I noticed that his voice was a little husky, although it was plain enough that his emotion was not occasioned by bad fortune—"my good old friend, I have found out what made the bottom of your gravel-pit so uncomfortably cold. You need not doubt what I am going to tell you, for my excavations have been complete and thorough enough to make me sure of what I say. Don't you remember that I told you that ages ago there was a vast glacier in the country which stretches from here to the mountains? Well, sir, the foot of that glacier must have reached further this way than is generally supposed. At any rate a portion of it did extend in this direction as far as this bit of the world which is now yours. This end or spur of the glacier, nearly a quarter of a mile in width, I should say, and pushing before it a portion of the terminal moraine on which you live, came slowly toward the valley until suddenly it detached itself from the main glacier and disappeared from sight. That is to say, my boy"—and as he spoke Tom sprang to his feet, too excited to sit any longer—"it descended to the bowels of the earth, at least for a considerable distance in that direction. Now you want to know how this happened. Well, I'll tell you. In this part of the country there are scattered about here and there great caves. Geologists know one or two of them, and it is certain that there are others undiscovered. Well, sir, your glacier spur discovered one of them, and when it had lain over the top of it for an age or two, and had grown bigger and bigger, and heavier and heavier, it at last burst through the rock roof of the cave, snapping itself from the rest of the glacier and falling in one vast mass to the bottom of the subterranean abyss. Walter, it is there now. The rest of the glacier came steadily down; the moraines were forced before it; they covered up this glacier spur, this broken fragment, and by the time the climate changed and the average of temperature rose above that of the glacial period, this vast sunken mass of ice was packed away below the surface of the earth, out of the reach of the action of friction, or heat, or moisture, or anything else which might destroy it. And through all the long procession of centuries that broken end of the glacier has been lying in your terminal moraine. It is there now. It is yours, Walter Cuthbert. It is an ice-mine. It is wealth, and so far as I can make out, it is nearly all upon your land. To you is the possession, but to me is the glory of the discovery. A bit of the glacial period kept in a cave for us! It is too wonderful to believe! Walter, have you any brandy?"

It may well be supposed that by this time I was thoroughly awakened to the importance and the amazing character of my friend's discovery, and I hurried with him to the scene of operations. There he explained everything and showed me how, by digging away a portion of the face of the bluff, he had found that this vast fragment of the glacier, which had been so miraculously preserved, ended in an irregularly perpendicular wall, which extended downward he knew not how far, and the edge of it on its upper side had been touched by my workmen in digging their pit. "It was the gradual melting of the upper end of this glacier," said Tom, "probably more elevated than the lower end, that made your dell. I wondered why the depression did not extend further up toward the spot where the foot of the glacier was supposed to have been. This end of the fragment, being sunk in deeper and afterward covered up more completely, probably never melted at all."

"It is amazing—astounding," said I; "but what of it, now that we have found it?"

"What of it?" cried Tom, and his whole form trembled as he spoke. "You have here a source of wealth, of opulence which shall endure for the rest of your days. Here at your very door, where it can be taken out and transported with the least possible trouble, is ice enough to supply the town, the county, yes, I might say, the State, for hundreds of years. No, sir, I can not go in to supper. I can not eat. I leave to you the business and practical part of this affair. I go to report upon its scientific features."

"Agnes," I exclaimed, as I walked to the house with my hands clasped and my eyes raised to the sky, "the glacial period has given thee to me!"

This did not immediately follow, although I went that very night to Mr. Havelot and declared to him that I was now rich enough to marry his daughter. He laughed at me in a manner which was very annoying, and made certain remarks which indicated that he thought it probable that it was not the roof of the cave, but my mind, which had given way under the influence of undue pressure.

The contemptuous manner in which I had been received aroused within me a very unusual state of mind. While talking to Mr. Havelot I heard not far away in some part of the house a voice singing. It was the voice of Agnes, and I believed she sang so that I could hear her. But as her sweet tones reached my ear there came to me at the same time the harsh, contemptuous words of her father. I left the house determined to crush that man to the earth beneath a superincumbent mass of ice—or the evidence of the results of the ownership of such a mass—which would make him groan and weep as he apologized to me for his scornful and disrespectful utterances and at the same time offered me the hand of his daughter.

When the discovery of the ice-mine, as it grew to be called, became generally known, my grounds were crowded by sightseers, and reporters of newspapers were more plentiful than squirrels. But the latter were referred to Burton, who would gladly talk to them as long as they could afford to listen, and I felt myself at last compelled to shut my gates to the first.

I had offers of capital to develop this novel source of wealth, and I accepted enough of this assistance to enable me to begin operations on a moderate scale. It was considered wise not to uncover any portion of the glacier spur, but to construct an inclined shaft down to its wall-like end and from this tunnel into the great mass. Immediately the leading ice company of the neighboring town contracted with me for all the ice I could furnish, and the floodgates of affluence began slowly to rise.

The earliest, and certainly one of the greatest, benefits which came to me from this bequest from the unhistoric past was the new energy and vigor with which my mind and body were now infused. My old, careless method of life and my recent melancholy, despairing mood were gone, and I now began to employ myself upon the main object of my life with an energy and enthusiasm almost equal to that of my friend, Tom Burton. This present object of my life was to prepare my home for Agnes.

The great piles of gravel which my men had dug from the well-like pit were spread upon the roadways and rolled smooth and hard; my lawn was mowed; my flower-beds and borders put in order; useless bushes and undergrowth cut out and cleared away; my outbuildings were repaired and the grounds around my house rapidly assumed their old appearance of neatness and beauty.

Ice was very scarce that summer, and, as the wagons wound away from the opening of the shaft which led down to the glacier, carrying their loads to the nearest railway station, so money came to me; not in large sums at first, for preparations had not yet been perfected for taking out the ice in great quantities, but enough to enable me to go on with my work as rapidly as I could plan it. I set about renovating and brightening and newly furnishing my house. Whatever I thought that Agnes would like I bought and put into it. I tried to put myself in her place as I selected the paper-hangings and the materials with which to cover the furniture.

Sometimes, while thus employed selecting ornaments or useful articles for my house, and using as far as was possible the taste and judgment of another instead of my own, the idea came to me that perhaps Agnes had never heard of my miraculous good fortune. Certainly her father would not be likely to inform her, and perhaps she still thought of me, if she thought at all, as the poor young man from whom she had been obliged to part because he was poor.

But whether she knew that I was growing rich, or whether she thought I was becoming poorer and poorer, I thought only of the day when I could go to her father and tell him that I was able to take his daughter and place her in a home as beautiful as that in which she now lived, and maintain her with all the comforts and luxuries which he could give her.

One day I asked my faithful cook, who also acted as my housekeeper and general supervisor, to assist me in making out a list of china which I intended to purchase.

"Are you thinking of buying china, sir?" she asked. "We have now quite as much as we really need."

"Oh, yes," said I, "I shall get complete sets of everything that can be required for a properly furnished household."

Susan gave a little sigh. "You are spendin' a lot of money, sir, and some of it for things that a single gentleman would be likely not to care very much about; and if you was to take it into your head to travel and stay away for a year or two, there's a good many things you've bought that would look shabby when you come back, no matter how careful I might be in dustin' 'em and keepin' 'em covered."

"But I have no idea of traveling," said I. "There's no place so pleasant as this to me."

Susan was silent for a few moments, and then she said: "I know very well why you are doing all this, and I feel it my bounden duty to say to you that there's a chance of its bein' no use. I do not speak without good reason, and I would not do it if I didn't think that it might make trouble lighter to you when it comes."

"What are you talking about, Susan; what do you mean?"

"Well, sir, this is what I mean: It was only last night that my daughter Jane was in Mr. Havelot's dining-room after dinner was over, and Mr. Havelot and a friend of his were sitting there, smoking their cigars and drinking their coffee. She went in and come out again as she was busy takin' away the dishes, and they paid no attention to her, but went on talkin' without knowing, most likely, she was there. Mr. Havelot and the gentleman were talkin' about you, and Jane she heard Mr. Havelot say as plain as anything, and she said she couldn't be mistaken, that even if your nonsensical ice-mine proved to be worth anything, he would never let his daughter marry an ice-man. He spoke most disrespectful of ice-men, sir, and said that it would make him sick to have a son-in-law whose business it was to sell ice to butchers, and hotels, and grog-shops, and pork-packers, and all that sort of people, and that he would as soon have his daughter marry the man who supplied a hotel with sausages as the one who supplied it with ice to keep those sausages from spoiling. You see, sir, Mr. Havelot lives on his property as his father did before him, and he is a very proud man, with a heart as hard and cold as that ice down under your land; and it's borne in on me very strong, sir, that it would be a bad thing for you to keep on thinkin' that you are gettin' this house all ready to bring Miss Havelot to when you have married her. For if Mr. Havelot keeps on livin', which there's every chance of his doin', it may be many a weary year before you get Miss Agnes, if you ever get her. And havin' said that, sir, I say no more, and I would not have said this much if I hadn't felt it my bounden duty to your father's son to warn him that most likely he was workin' for what he might never get, and so keep him from breakin' his heart when he found out the truth all of a sudden."

With that Susan left me, without offering any assistance in making out a list of china. This was a terrible story; but, after all, it was founded only upon servants' gossip. In this country, even proud, rich men like Mr. Havelot did not have such absurd ideas regarding the source of wealth. Money is money, and whether it is derived from the ordinary products of the earth, from which came much of Mr. Havelot's revenue, or from an extraordinary project such as my glacier spur, it truly could not matter so far as concerned the standing in society of its possessor. What utter absurdity was this which Susan had told me! If I were to go to Mr. Havelot and tell him that I would not marry his daughter because he supplied brewers and bakers with the products of his fields, would he not consider me an idiot? I determined to pay no attention to the idle tale. But alas! determinations of that sort are often of little avail. I did pay attention to it, and my spirits drooped.

The tunnel into the glacier spur had now attained considerable length, and the ice in the interior was found to be of a much finer quality than that first met with, which was of a grayish hue and somewhat inclined to crumble. When the workmen reached a grade of ice as good as they could expect, they began to enlarge the tunnel into a chamber, and from this they proposed to extend tunnels in various directions after the fashion of a coal-mine. The ice was hauled out on sledges through the tunnel and then carried up a wooden railway to the mouth of the shaft.

It was comparatively easy to walk down the shaft and enter the tunnel, and when it happened that the men were not at work I allowed visitors to go down and view this wonderful ice-cavern. The walls of the chamber appeared semi-transparent, and the light of the candles or lanterns gave the whole scene a weird and beautiful aspect. It was almost possible to imagine one's self surrounded by limpid waters, which might at any moment rush upon him and ingulf him.

Every day or two Tom Burton came with a party of scientific visitors, and had I chosen to stop the work of taking out ice, admitted the public and charged a price for admission, I might have made almost as much money as I at that time derived from the sale of the ice. But such a method of profit was repugnant to me.

For several days after Susan's communication to me I worked on in my various operations, endeavoring to banish from my mind the idle nonsense she had spoken of; but one of its effects upon me was to make me feel that I ought not to allow hopes so important to rest upon uncertainties. So I determined that as soon as my house and grounds should be in a condition with which I should for the time be satisfied, I would go boldly to Mr. Havelot, and, casting out of my recollection everything that Susan had said, invite him to visit me and see for himself the results of the discovery of which he had spoken with such derisive contempt. This would be a straightforward and business-like answer to his foolish objections to me, and I believed that in his heart the old gentleman would properly appreciate my action.

About this time there came to my place Aaron Boyce, an elderly farmer of the neighborhood, and, finding me outside, he seized the opportunity to have a chat with me.

"I tell you what it is, Mr. Cuthbert," said he, "the people in this neighborhood hasn't give you credit for what's in you. The way you have fixed up this place, and the short time you have took to do it, is enough to show us now what sort of a man you are; and I tell you, sir, we're proud of you for a neighbor. I don't believe there's another gentleman in this county of your age that could have done what you have done in so short a time. I expect now you will be thinking of getting married and startin' housekeepin' in a regular fashion. That comes just as natural as to set hens in the spring. By the way, have you heard that old Mr. Havelot's thinkin' of goin' abroad? I didn't believe he would ever do that again, because he's gettin' pretty well on in years, but old men will do queer things as well as young ones."

"Going abroad!" I cried. "Does he intend to take his daughter with him?"

Mr. Aaron Boyce smiled grimly. He was a great old gossip, and he had already obtained the information he wanted. "Yes," he said, "I've heard it was on her account he's going. She's been kind of weakly lately, they tell me, and hasn't took to her food, and the doctors has said that what she wants is a sea voyage and a change to foreign parts."

Going abroad! Foreign parts! This was more terrible than anything I had imagined. I would go to Mr. Havelot that very evening, the only time which I would be certain to find him at home, and talk to him in a way which would be sure to bring him to his senses, if he had any. And if I should find that he had no sense of propriety or justice, no sense of his duty to his fellow-man and to his offspring, then I would begin a bold fight for Agnes, a fight which I would not give up until, with her own lips, she told me that it would be useless. I would follow her to Kentucky, to Europe, to the uttermost ends of the earth. I could do it now. The frozen deposits in my terminal moraine would furnish me with the means. I walked away and left the old farmer standing grinning. No doubt my improvements and renovations had been the subject of gossip in the neighborhood, and he had come over to see if he could find out anything definite in regard to the object of them. He had succeeded, but he had done more: he had nerved me to instantly begin the conquest of Agnes, whether by diplomacy or war.

I was so anxious to begin this conquest that I could scarcely wait for the evening to come. At the noon hour, when the ice-works were deserted, I walked down the shaft and into the ice-chamber to see what had been done since my last visit. I decided to insist that operations upon a larger scale should be immediately begun, in order that I might have plenty of money with which to carry on my contemplated campaign. Whether it was one of peace or war, I should want all the money I could get.

I took with me a lantern and went around the chamber, which was now twenty-five or thirty feet in diameter, examining the new inroads which had been made upon its walls. There was a tunnel commenced opposite the one by which the chamber was entered, but it had not been opened more than a dozen feet, and it seemed to me that the men had not been working with any very great energy. I wanted to see a continuous stream of ice-blocks from that chamber to the mouth of the shaft.

While grumbling thus I heard behind me a sudden noise like thunder and the crashing of walls, and, turning quickly, I saw that a portion of the roof of the chamber had fallen in. Nor had it ceased to fall. As I gazed, several great masses of ice came down from above and piled themselves upon that which had already fallen.

Startled and frightened, I sprang toward the opening of the entrance tunnel; but, alas! I found that that was the point where the roof had given way, and between me and the outer world was a wall of solid ice through which it would be as impossible for me to break as if it were a barrier of rock. With the quick instinct which comes to men in danger I glanced about to see if the workmen had left their tools; but there were none. They had been taken outside. Then I stood and gazed stupidly at the mass of fallen ice, which, even as I looked upon it, was cracking and snapping, pressed down by the weight above it, and forming itself into an impervious barrier without crevice or open seam.

Then I madly shouted. But of what avail were shouts down there in the depths of the earth? I soon ceased this useless expenditure of strength, and, with my lantern in my hand, began to walk around the chamber, throwing the light upon the walls and the roof. I became impressed with the fear that the whole cavity might cave in at once and bury me here in a tomb of ice. But I saw no cracks, nor any sign of further disaster. But why think of anything more? Was not this enough? For, before that ice-barrier could be cleared away, would I not freeze to death?

I now continued to walk, not because I expected to find anything or do anything, but simply to keep myself warm by action. As long as I could move about I believed that there was no immediate danger of succumbing to the intense cold; for, when a young man, traveling in Switzerland, I had been in the cave of a glacier, and it was not cold enough to prevent some old women from sitting there to play the zither for the sake of a few coppers from visitors. I could not expect to be able to continue walking until I should be rescued, and if I sat down, or by chance slept from exhaustion, I must perish.

The more I thought of it, the more sure I became that in any case I must perish. A man in a block of ice could have no chance of life. And Agnes! Oh, Heavens! what demon of the ice had leagued with old Havelot to shut me up in this frozen prison? For a long time I continued to walk, beat my body with my arms and stamp my feet. The instinct of life was strong within me. I would live as long as I could, and think of Agnes. When I should be frozen I could not think of her.

Sometimes I stopped and listened. I was sure I could hear noises, but I could not tell whether they were above me or not. In the centre of the ice-barrier, about four feet from the ground, was a vast block of the frozen substance which was unusually clear and seemed to have nothing on the other side of it; for through it I could see flickers of light, as though people were going about with lanterns. It was quite certain that the accident had been discovered; for, had not the thundering noise been heard by persons outside, the workmen would have seen what had happened as soon as they came into the tunnel to begin their afternoon operations.

At first I wondered why they did not set to work with a will and cut away this barrier and let me out. But there suddenly came to my mind a reason for this lack of energy which was more chilling than the glistening walls around me: Why should they suppose that I was in the ice-chamber? I was not in the habit of coming here very often, but I was in the habit of wandering off by myself at all hours of the day. This thought made me feel that I might as well lie down on the floor of this awful cave and die at once. The workmen might think it unsafe to mine any further in this part of the glacier, and begin operations at some other point. I did sit down for a moment, and then I rose involuntarily and began my weary round. Suddenly I thought of looking at my watch. It was nearly five o'clock. I had been more than four hours in that dreadful place, and I did not believe that I could continue to exercise my limbs very much longer. The lights I had seen had ceased. It was quite plain that the workmen had no idea that any one was imprisoned in the cave.

But soon after I had come to this conclusion I saw through the clear block of ice a speck of light, and it became stronger and stronger, until I believed it to be close to the other side of the block. There it remained stationary; but there seemed to be other points of light which moved about in a strange way, and near it. Now I stood by the block watching. When my feet became very cold, I stamped them; but there I stood fascinated, for what I saw was truly surprising. A large coal of fire appeared on the other side of the block; then it suddenly vanished and was succeeded by another coal. This disappeared, and another took its place, each one seeming to come nearer and nearer to me. Again and again did these coals appear. They reached the centre of the block; they approached my side of it. At last one was so near to me that I thought it was about to break through, but it vanished. Then there came a few quick thuds and the end of a piece of iron protruded from the block. This was withdrawn, and through the aperture there came a voice which said: "Mr. Cuthbert, are you in there?" It was the voice of Agnes!

Weak and cold as I was, fire and energy rushed through me at these words. "Yes," I exclaimed, my mouth to the hole; "Agnes, is that you?"

"Wait a minute," came from the other side of the aperture. "I must make it bigger. I must keep it from closing up."

Again came the coals of fire, running backward and forward through the long hole in the block of ice. I could see now what they were. They were irons used by plumbers for melting solder and that sort of thing, and Agnes was probably heating them in a little furnace outside, and withdrawing them as fast as they cooled. It was not long before the aperture was very much enlarged; and then there came grating through it a long tin tube nearly two inches in diameter, which almost, but not quite, reached my side of the block.

Now came again the voice of Agnes: "Oh, Mr. Cuthbert, are you truly there? Are you crushed? Are you wounded? Are you nearly frozen? Are you starved? Tell me quickly if you are yet safe."

Had I stood in a palace padded with the softest silk and filled with spicy odors from a thousand rose gardens, I could not have been better satisfied with my surroundings than I was at that moment. Agnes was not two feet away! She was telling me that she cared for me! In a very few words I assured her that I was uninjured. Then I was on the point of telling her I loved her, for I believed that not a moment should be lost in making this avowal. I could not die without her knowing that. But the appearance of a mass of paper at the other end of the tube prevented the expression of my sentiments. This was slowly pushed on until I could reach it. Then there came the words: "Mr. Cuthbert, these are sandwiches. Eat them immediately and walk about while you are doing it. You must keep yourself warm until the men get to you."

Obedient to the slightest wish of this dear creature, I went twice around the cave, devouring the sandwiches as I walked. They were the most delicious food that I had ever tasted. They were given to me by Agnes. I came back to the opening. I could not immediately begin my avowal. I must ask a question first. "Can they get to me?" I inquired. "Is anybody trying to do that? Are they working there by you? I do not hear them at all."

"Oh, no," she answered; they are not working here. They are on top of the bluff, trying to dig down to you. They were afraid to meddle with the ice here for fear that more of it might come down and crush you and the men, too. Oh, there has been a dreadful excitement since it was found that you were in there!"

"How could they know I was here?" I asked.

"It was your old Susan who first thought of it. She saw you walking toward the shaft about noon, and then she remembered that she had not seen you again; and when they came into the tunnel here they found one of the lanterns gone and the big stick you generally carry lying where the lantern had been. Then it was known that you must be inside. Oh, then there was an awful time! The foreman of the ice-men examined everything, and said they must dig down to you from above. He put his men to work; but they could do very little, for they had hardly any spades. Then they sent into town for help and over to the new park for the Italians working there. From the way these men set to work you might have thought that they would dig away the whole bluff in about five minutes; but they didn't. Nobody seemed to know what to do, or how to get to work; and the hole they made when they did begin was filled up with men almost as fast as they even threw out the stones and gravel. I don't believe anything would have been done properly if your friend, Mr. Burton, hadn't happened to come with two scientific gentlemen, and since that he has been directing everything. You can't think what a splendid fellow he is! I fairly adored him when I saw him giving his orders and making everybody skip around in the right way."

"Tom is a very good man," said I; "but it is his business to direct that sort of work, and it is not surprising that he knows how to do it. But, Agnes, they may never get down to me, and we do not know that this roof may not cave in upon me at any moment; and before this or anything else happens I want to tell you—"

"Mr. Cuthbert," said Agnes, "is there plenty of oil in your lantern? It would be dreadful if it were to go out and leave you there in the dark. I thought of that and brought you a little bottle of kerosene so that you can fill it. I am going to push the bottle through now, if you please." And with this a large phial, cork end foremost, came slowly through the tube, propelled by one of the soldering irons. Then came Agnes's voice: "Please fill your lantern immediately, because if it goes out you can not find it in the dark; and then walk several times around the cave, for you have been standing still too long already."

I obeyed these injunctions, but in two or three minutes was again at the end of the tube. "Agnes," said I, "how did you happen to come here? Did you contrive in your own mind this method of communicating with me?"

"Oh, yes; I did," she said. "Everybody said that this mass of ice must not be meddled with, but I knew very well it would not hurt it to make a hole through it."

"But how did you happen to be here?" I asked.

"Oh, I ran over as soon as I heard of the accident. Everybody ran here. The whole neighborhood is on top of the bluff; but nobody wanted to come into the tunnel, because they were afraid that more of it might fall in. So I was able to work here all by myself, and I am very glad of it. I saw the soldering iron and the little furnace outside of your house where the plumbers had been using them, and I brought them here myself. Then I thought that a simple hole through the ice might soon freeze up again, and if you were alive inside I could not do anything to help you; and so I ran home and got my diploma case, that had had one end melted out of it, and I brought that to stick in the hole. I'm so glad that it is long enough, or almost."

"Oh, Agnes," I cried, "you thought of all this for me?"

"Why, of course, Mr. Cuthbert," she answered, before I had a chance to say anything more. "You were in great danger of perishing before the men got to you, and nobody seemed to think of any way to give you immediate relief. And don't you think that a collegiate education is a good thing for girls—at least, that it was for me?"

"Agnes," I exclaimed, "please let me speak. I want to tell you, I must tell you—"

But the voice of Agnes was clearer than mine and it overpowered my words. "Mr. Cuthbert," she said, "we can not both speak through this tube at the same time in opposite directions. I have here a bottle of water for you, but I am very much afraid it will not go through the diploma case."

"Oh, I don't want any water," I said. "I can eat ice if I am thirsty. What I want is to tell you—"

"Mr. Cuthbert," said she, "you must not eat that ice. Water that was frozen countless ages ago may be very different from the water of modern times, and might not agree with you. Don't touch it, please. I am going to push the bottle through if I can. I tried to think of everything that you might need and brought them all at once; because, if I could not keep the hole open, I wanted to get them to you without losing a minute."

Now the bottle came slowly through. It was a small beer-bottle, I think, and several times I was afraid it was going to stick fast and cut off communication between me and the outer world—that is to say, between me and

Agnes. But at last the cork and the neck appeared, and I pulled it through. I did not drink any of it, but immediately applied my mouth to the tube.

"Agnes," I said, "my dear Agnes, really you must not prevent me from speaking. I can not delay another minute. This is an awful position for me to be in, and as you don't seem to realize—"

"But I do realize, Mr. Cuthbert, that if you don't walk about you will certainly freeze before you can be rescued. Between every two or three words you want to take at least one turn around that place. How dreadful it would be if you were suddenly to become benumbed and stiff! Everybody is thinking of that. The best diggers that Mr. Burton had were three colored men; but after they had gone down nothing like as deep as a well, they came up frightened and said they would not dig another shovelful for the whole world. Perhaps you don't know it, but there's a story about the neighborhood that the negro hell is under your property. You know many of the colored people expect to be everlastingly punished with ice and not with fire—"

"Agnes," I interrupted, "I am punished with ice and fire both. Please let me tell you—"

"I was going on to say, Mr. Cuthbert," she interrupted, "that when the Italians heard why the colored men had come out of the hole they would not go in either, for they are just as afraid of everlasting ice as the negroes are, and were sure that if the bottom came out of that hole they would fall into a frozen lower world. So there was nothing to do but to send for paupers, and they are working now. You know paupers have to do what they are told without regard to their beliefs. They got a dozen of them from the poorhouse. Somebody said they just threw them into the hole. Now I must stop talking, for it is time for you to walk around again. Would you like another sandwich?"

"Agnes," said I, endeavoring to speak calmly, "all I want is to be able to tell you—"

"And when you walk, Mr. Cuthbert, you had better keep around the edge of the chamber, for there is no knowing when they may come through. Mr. Burton and the foreman of the ice-men measured the bluff so that they say the hole they are making is exactly over the middle of the chamber you are in, and if you walk around the edge the pieces may not fall on you."

"If you don't listen to me, Agnes," I said, "I'll go and sit anywhere, everywhere, where death may come to me quickest. Your coldness is worse than the coldness of the cave. I can not bear it."

"But, Mr. Cuthbert," said Agnes, speaking, I thought, with some agitation, "I have been listening to you, and what more can you possibly have to say? If there is anything you want, let me know. I will run and get it for you."

"There is no need that you should go away to get what I want," I said. "It is there with you. It is you."

"Mr. Cuthbert," said Agnes, in a very low voice, but so distinctly that I could hear every word, "don't you think it would be better for you to give your whole mind to keeping yourself warm and strong? For if you let yourself get benumbed you may sink down and freeze."

"Agnes," I said, "I will not move from this little hole until I have told you that I love you, that I have no reason to care for life or rescue unless you return my love, unless you are willing to be mine. Speak quickly to me, Agnes, because I may not be rescued and may never know whether my love for you is returned or not."

At this moment there was a tremendous crash behind me, and, turning, I saw a mass of broken ice upon the floor of the cave, with a cloud of dust and smaller fragments still falling. And then with a great scratching and scraping, and a howl loud enough to waken the echoes of all the lower regions, down came a red-headed, drunken shoemaker. I can not say that he was drunk at that moment, but I knew the man the moment I saw his carroty poll, and it was drink which had sent him to the poorhouse.

But the sprawling and howling cobbler did not reach the floor. A rope had been fastened around his waist to prevent a fall in case the bottom of the pit should suddenly give way, and he hung dangling in mid air with white face and distended eyes, cursing and swearing and vociferously entreating to be pulled up. But before he received any answer from above, or I could speak to him, there came through the hole in the roof of the cave a shower of stones and gravel, and with them a frantic Italian, his legs and arms outspread, his face wild with terror.

Just as he appeared in view he grasped the rope of the cobbler, and, though in a moment he came down heavily upon the floor of the chamber, this broke his fall, and he did not appear to be hurt. Instantly he crouched low and almost upon all fours, and began to run around the chamber, keeping close to the walls and screaming, I suppose to his saints, to preserve him from the torments of the frozen damned.

In the midst of this hubbub came the voice of Agnes through the hole: "Oh, Mr. Cuthbert, what has happened? Are you alive?"

I was so disappointed by the appearance of these wretched interlopers at the moment it was about to be decided whether my life—should it last for years, or but for a few minutes—was to be black or bright, and I was so shaken and startled by the manner of their entry upon the scene, that I could not immediately shape the words necessary to inform Agnes what had happened. But, collecting my faculties, I was about to speak, when suddenly, with the force of the hind leg of a mule, I was pushed away from the aperture, and the demoniac Italian clapped his great mouth to the end of the tube and roared through it a volume of oaths and supplications. I attempted to thrust aside the wretched being, but I might as well have tried to move the ice barrier itself. He had perceived that some one outside was talking to me, and in his frenzy he was imploring that some one should let him out.

While still endeavoring to move the man, I was seized by the arm, and turning, beheld the pallid face of the shoemaker. They had let him down so that he reached the floor. He tried to fall on his knees before me, but the rope was so short that he was able to go only part of the way down, and presented a most ludicrous appearance, with his toes scraping the icy floor and his arms thrown out as if he were paddling like a tadpole. "Oh, have mercy upon me, sir," he said, "and help me get out of this dreadful place. If you go to the hole and call up it's you, they will pull me up; but if they get you out first they will never think of me. I am a poor pauper, sir, but I never did nothin' to be packed in ice before I am dead."

Noticing that the Italian had left the end of the aperture in the block of ice, and that he was now shouting up the open shaft, I ran to the channel of communication which my Agnes had opened for me, and called through it; but the dear girl had gone.

The end of a ladder now appeared at the opening in the roof, and this was let down until it reached the floor. I started toward it, but before I had gone half the distance the frightened shoemaker and the maniac Italian sprang upon it, and, with shrieks and oaths, began a maddening fight for possession of the ladder. They might quickly have gone up one after the other, but each had no thought but to be first; and as one seized the rounds he was pulled away by the other, until I feared the ladder would be torn to pieces. The shoemaker finally pushed his way up a little distance, when the Italian sprang upon his back, endeavoring to climb over him; and so on they went up the shaft, fighting, swearing, kicking, scratching, shaking and wrenching the ladder, which had been tied to another one in order to increase its length, so that it was in danger of breaking, and tearing at each other in a fashion which made it wonderful that they did not both tumble headlong downward. They went on up, so completely filling the shaft with their struggling forms and their wild cries that I could not see or hear anything, and was afraid, in fact, to look up toward the outer air.

As I was afterward informed, the Italian, who had slipped into the hole by accident, ran away like a frightened hare the moment he got his feet on firm ground, and the shoemaker sat down and swooned. By this performance he obtained from a benevolent bystander a drink of whiskey, the first he had had since he was committed to the poorhouse.

But a voice soon came down the shaft calling to me. I recognized it as that of Tom Burton, and replied that I was safe, and that I was coming up the ladder. But in my attempt to climb, I found that I was unable to do so. Chilled and stiffened by the cold and weakened by fatigue and excitement, I believe I never should have been able to leave that ice chamber if my faithful friend had not come down the ladder and vigorously assisted me to reach the outer air.

Seated on the ground, my back against a great oak tree, I was quickly surrounded by a crowd of my neighbors, the workmen and the people who had been drawn to the spot by the news of the strange accident, to gaze at me as if I were some unknown being excavated from the bowels of the earth. I was sipping some brandy and water which Burton had handed me, when Aaron Boyce pushed himself in front of me.

"Well, sir," he said, "I am mighty glad you got out of that scrape. I'm bound to say I didn't expect you would. I have been sure all along that it wasn't right to meddle with things that go agin Nature, and I haven't any doubt that you'll see that for yourself and fill up all them tunnels and shafts you've made. The ice that comes on ponds and rivers was good enough for our forefathers, and it ought to be good enough for us. And as for this cold stuff you find in your gravel-pit, I don't believe it's ice at all; and if it is, like as not it's made of some sort of pizen stuff that freezes easier than water. For everybody knows that water don't freeze in a well, and if it don't do that, why should it do it in any kind of a hole in the ground? So perhaps it's just as well that you did git shut up there, sir, and find out for yourself what a dangerous thing it is to fool with Nature and try to git ice from the bottom of the ground instead of the top of the water."

This speech made me angry, for I knew that old Boyce was a man who was always glad to get hold of anything which had gone wrong and try to make it worse; but I was too weak to answer him.

This, however, would not have been necessary, for Tom Burton turned upon him. "Idiot," said he, "if that is your way of thinking you might as well say that if a well caves in you should never again dig for water, or that nobody should have a cellar under his house for fear that the house should fall into it. There's no more danger of the ice beneath us ever giving way again than there is that this bluff should crumble under our feet. That break in the roof of the ice tunnel was caused by my digging away the face of the bluff very near that spot. The high temperature of the outer air weakened the ice, and it fell. But down here, under this ground and secure from the influences of the heat of the outer air, the mass of ice is more solid than rock. We will build a brick arch over the place where the accident happened, and then there will not be a safer mine on this continent than this ice-mine will be."

This was a wise and diplomatic speech from Burton, and it proved to be of great service to me; for the men who had been taking out ice had been a good deal frightened by the fall of the tunnel, and when it was proved that what Burton had said in regard to the cause of the weakening of the ice was entirely correct, they became willing to go to work again.

I now began to feel stronger and better, and, rising to my feet, I glanced here and there into the crowd, hoping to catch a sight of Agnes. But I was not very much surprised at not seeing her, because she would naturally shrink from forcing herself into the midst of this motley company; but I felt that I must go and look for her without the loss of a minute, for if she should return to her father's house I might not be able to see her again.

On the outskirts of the crowd I met Susan, who was almost overpowered with joy at seeing me safe again. I shook her by the hand, but, without replying to her warm-hearted protestations of thankfulness and delight, I asked her if she had seen Miss Havelot.

"Miss Agnes!" she exclaimed. "Why, no sir; I expect she's at home; and if she did come here with the rest of the neighbors I didn't see her; for when I found out what had happened, sir, I was so weak that I sat down in the kitchen all of a lump, and have just had strength enough to come out."

"Oh, I know she was here," I cried; "I am sure of that, and I do hope she's not gone home again."

"Know she was here!" exclaimed Susan. "Why, how on earth could you know that?"

I did not reply that it was not on the earth but under it, that I became aware of the fact, but hurried toward the Havelot house, hoping to overtake Agnes if she had gone that way. But I did not see her, and suddenly a startling idea struck me, and I turned and ran home as fast as I could go. When I reached my grounds I went directly to the mouth of the shaft. There was nobody there, for the crowd was collected into a solid mass on the top of the bluff, listening to a lecture from Tom Burton, who deemed it well to promote the growth of interest and healthy opinion in regard to his wonderful discovery and my valuable possession. I hurried down the shaft, and near the end of it, just before it joined the ice tunnel, I beheld Agnes sitting upon the wooden track. She was not unconscious, for as I approached she slightly turned her head. I sprang toward her; I knelt beside her; I took her in my arms. "Oh, Agnes, dearest Agnes," I cried, "what is the matter? What has happened to you? Has a piece of ice fallen upon you? Have you slipped and hurt yourself?"

She turned her beautiful eyes up toward me and for a moment did not speak. Then she said: "And they got you out? And you are in your right mind?"

"Right mind!" I exclaimed. "I have never been out of my mind. What are you thinking of?"

"Oh, you must have been," she said, "when you screamed at me in that horrible way. I was so frightened that I fell back, and I must have fainted."

Tremulous as I was with love and anxiety, I could not help laughing. "Oh, my dear Agnes, I did not scream at you. That was a crazed Italian who fell through the hole that they dug." Then I told her what had happened.

She heaved a gentle sigh. "I am so glad to hear that," she said. "There was one thing that I was thinking about just before you came and which gave me a little bit of comfort; the words and yells I heard were dreadfully oniony, and somehow or other I could not connect that sort of thing with you."

It now struck me that during this conversation I had been holding my dear girl in my arms, and she had not shown the slightest sign of resistance or disapprobation. This made my heart beat high.

"Oh, Agnes," I said, "I truly believe you love me or you would not have been here, you would not have done for me all that you did. Why did you not answer me when I spoke to you through that wall of ice, through the hole your dear love had made in it? Why, when I was in such a terrible situation, not knowing whether I was to die or live, did you not comfort my heart with one sweet word?"

"Oh, Walter," she answered, "it wasn't at all necessary for you to say all that you did say, for I had suspected it before, and as soon as you began to call me Agnes I knew, of course, how you felt about it. And, besides, it really was necessary that you should move about to keep yourself from freezing. But the great reason for my not encouraging you to go on talking in that way was that I was afraid people might come into the tunnel, and as, of course, you would not know that they were there, you would go on making love to me through my diploma case, and you know I should have perished with shame if I had had to stand there with that old Mr. Boyce, and I don't know who else, listening to your words, which were very sweet to me, Walter, but which would have sounded awfully funny to them."

When she said that my words had been sweet to her I dropped the consideration of all other subjects.

When, about ten minutes afterward, we came out of the shaft we were met by Susan.

"Bless my soul and body, Mr. Cuthbert!" she exclaimed. "Did you find that young lady down there in the centre of the earth? It seems to me as if everything that you want comes to you out of the ground. But I have been looking for you to tell you that Mr. Havelot has been here after his daughter, and I'm sure if he had known where she was, he would have been scared out of his wits."

"Father here!" exclaimed Agnes. "Where is he now?"

"I think he has gone home, miss. Indeed I'm sure of it; for my daughter Jennie, who was over here the same as all the other people in the county, I truly believe told him—and I was proud she had the spirit to speak up that way to him—that your heart was almost broke when you heard about Mr. Cuthbert being shut up in the ice, and that most likely you was in your own room a-cryin' your eyes out. When he heard that he stood lookin' all around the place, and he asked me if he might go in the house; and when I told him he was most welcome, he went in. I offered to show him about, which he said was no use, that he had been there often enough; and he went everywhere, I truly believe, except in the garret and the cellar. And after he got through with that he went out to the barn and then walked home."

"I must go to him immediately," said Agnes.

"But not alone," said I. And together we walked through the woods, over the little field and across the Havelot lawn to the house. We were told that the old gentleman was in his library, and together we entered the room. Mr. Havelot was sitting by a table on which were lying several open volumes of an encyclopedia. When he turned and saw us, he closed his book, pushed back his chair and took off his spectacles. "Upon my word, sir," he cried; "and so the first thing you do after they pull you out of the earth is to come here and break my commands."

"I came on the invitation of your daughter, sir."

"And what right has she to invite you, I'd like to know?"

"She has every right, for to her I owe my existence."

"What rabid nonsense!" exclaimed the old gentleman. "People don't owe their existence to the silly creatures they fall in love with."

"I assure you I am correct, sir." And then I related to him what his daughter had done, and how through her angelic agency my rescuers had found me a living being instead of a frozen corpse.

"Stuff!" said Mr. Havelot. "People can live in a temperature of thirty-two degrees above zero all winter. Out in Minnesota they think that's hot. And you gave him victuals and drink through your diploma case! Well, miss, I told you that if you tried to roast chestnuts in that diploma case the bottom would come out."

"But you see, father," said Agnes, earnestly, "the reason I did that was because when I roasted them in anything shallow they popped into the fire, but they could not jump out of the diploma case."

"Well, something else seems to have jumped out of it," said the old gentleman, "and something with which I am not satisfied. I have been looking over these books, sir, and have read the articles on ice, glaciers and caves, and I find no record of anything in the whole history of the world which in the least resembles the cock-and-bull story I am told about the butt-end of a glacier which tumbled into a cave in your ground, and has been lying there through all the geological ages, and the eras of formation, and periods of animate existence down to the days of Noah, and Moses, and Methuselah, and Rameses II, and Alexander the Great, and Martin Luther, and John Wesley, to this day, for you to dig out and sell to the Williamstown Ice Co."

"But that's what happened, sir," said I.

"And besides, father," added Agnes, "the gold and silver that people take out of mines may have been in the ground as long as that ice has been."

"Bosh!" said Mr. Havelot. "The cases are not at all similar. It is simply impossible that a piece of a glacier should have fallen into a cave and been preserved in that way. The temperature of caves is always above the freezing-point, and that ice would have melted a million years before you were born."

"But, father," said Agnes, "the temperature of caves filled with ice must be very much lower than that of common caves."

"And apart from that," I added, "the ice is still there, sir."

"That doesn't make the slightest difference," he replied. "It's against all reason and common-sense that such a thing could have happened. Even if there ever was a glacier in this part of the country and if the lower portion of it did stick out over an immense hole in the ground, that protruding end would never have broken off and tumbled in. Glaciers are too thick and massive for that."

"But the glacier is there, sir," said I, "in spite of your own reasoning."

"And then again," continued the old gentleman, "if there had been a cave and a projecting spur the ice would have gradually melted and dripped into the cave, and we would have had a lake and not an ice-mine. It is an absurdity."

"But it's there, notwithstanding," said I.

"And you can not subvert facts, you know, father," added Agnes.

"Confound facts!" he cried. "I base my arguments on sober, cool-headed reason; and there's nothing that can withstand reason. The thing's impossible and, therefore, it has never happened. I went over to your place, sir, when I heard of the accident, for the misfortunes of my neighbors interest me, no matter what may be my opinion of them, and when I found that you had been extricated from your ridiculous predicament, I went through your house, and I was pleased to find it in as good or better condition than I had known it in the days of your respected father. I was glad to see the improvement in your circumstances; but when I am told, sir, that your apparent prosperity rests upon such an absurdity as a glacier in a gravel hill, I can but smile with contempt, sir."

I was getting a little tired of this. "But the glacier is there, sir," I said, "and I am taking out ice every day, and have reason to believe that I can continue to take it out for the rest of my life. With such facts as these before me, I am bound to say, sir, that I don't care in the least about reason."

"And I am here, father," said Agnes, coming close to me, "and here I want to continue for the rest of my days."

The old gentleman looked at her. "And, I suppose," he said, "that you, too, don't in the least care about reason?"

"Not a bit," said Agnes.

"Well," said Mr. Havelot, rising, "I have done all I can to make you two listen to reason, and I can do no more. I despair of making sensible human beings of you, and so you might as well go on acting like a couple of ninny-hammers."

"Do ninny-hammers marry and settle on the property adjoining yours, sir?" I asked.

"Yes, I suppose they do," he said. "And when the aboriginal ice-house, or whatever the ridiculous thing is that they have discovered, gives out, I suppose that they can come to a reasonable man and ask him for a little money to buy bread and butter."

Two years have passed, and Agnes and the glacier are still mine; great blocks of ice now flow in almost a continuous stream from the mine to the railroad station, and in a smaller but quite as continuous stream an income flows in upon Agnes and me; and from one of the experimental excavations made by Tom Burton on the bluff comes a stream of ice-cold water running in a sparkling brook a-down my dell. On fine mornings before I am up, I am credibly informed that Aaron Boyce may generally be found, in season and out of season, endeavoring to catch the trout with which I am trying to stock that ice-cold stream. The diploma case, which I caused to be carefully removed from the ice-barrier which had imprisoned me, now hangs in my study and holds our marriage certificate.

Near the line-fence which separates his property from mine, Mr. Havelot has sunk a wide shaft. "If the glacier spur under your land was a quarter of a mile wide," he says to me, "it was probably at least a half a mile long; and if that were the case, the upper end of it extends into my place, and I may be able to strike it." He has a good deal of money, this worthy Mr. Havelot, but he would be very glad to increase his riches, whether they are based upon sound reason or ridiculous facts. As for Agnes and myself, no facts or any reason could make us happier than our ardent love and our frigid fortune.

THE INDIAN'S HAND

Lorimer Stoddard

The men had driven away. Their carts and horses disappeared behind the roll of the low hills. They appeared now and then, like boats on the crest of a wave, further each time. And their laughter and singing and shouts grew fainter as the bushes hid them from sight.

The women and children remained, with two old men to protect them. They might have gone too, the hunters said. "What harm could come in the broad daylight?—the bears and panthers were far away. They'd be back by night, with only two carts to fill."

Then Jim, the crack shot of the settlement, said, "We'll drive home the bears in the carts."

The children shouted and danced as they thought of the sport to come, of the hunters' return with their game, of the bonfires they always built.

One pale woman clung to her husband's arm. "But the Indians!" she said.

That made the men all laugh. "Indians!" they cried; "why, there've been none here for twenty years! We drove them away, down there"—pointing across the plain—"to a hotter place than this, where the sand burns their feet and they ride for days for water."

The pale woman murmured, "Ah, but they returned."

"Yes," cried her big husband, whose brown beard covered his chest, "and burned two cabins. Small harm they did, the curs!"

"Hush," said the pale woman, pressing her husband's arm; and the men around were quiet, pretending to fix their saddles, as they glanced at another woman, dressed in black, who turned and went into her house.

"I forgot her boy," said the bearded man, as he gravely picked up his gun.

They started off in the morning cool, toward the mountains where the trees grew. And the long shadows lessened as the sun crept up the sky.

The woman in black stood silent by her door. No one bade her good-by. The other women went back to their houses to work. The children played in the dust; clouds rose as they shouted and ran. A day's freedom lay before them.

But the woman in black still stood by her door, like a spectre in the sunshine, her thin hands clasped together as she gazed away over the plain toward Mexico.

Her face was parched and drawn, as if the sun from the sand had burned into the bone. Her eyes alone seemed to live; they were hard and bright.

Her house was a little away from the rest, on the crest of a hill facing the desert plain.

She had heard the words of the bearded man: "Small harm the Indians did." Had he forgotten her boy? How could he forget, while she was there to remind them of the dead? Near her house was a small rock roughly marked. The rude letters "Will, gone, '69," she had cut on it with her own hands. It marked the last place where her boy had played. She remembered how she went away softly—so he should not cry to follow her—without a word, without a kiss.

Here her hands beat the side of the house.

"Oh, to have that kiss now and die!" But she had gone, unthinking, up the road where the pale woman lived, then a rosy-cheeked happy bride, not a widow like herself. They laughed and discussed the newcomers at the settlement. It was a holiday, for the men were away over the hills, cutting down trees to build their houses with.

As they talked there idly, they heard what they thought was the shrill bark of dogs running up the hill. Startled, they went to the window. Round the curve of the road came horses wildly galloping, and upon their backs—Here the pale woman shrieked and fled. They were Indians, beating their horses with their bare legs, their black hair streaming in the wind.

Like a flash, she had bolted the door and barred the shutters as they galloped up. She turned then. Through the open back door she saw the women run screaming up the hill, their children in their arms.

Their children! Where was hers? She stopped as if turned to stone, then undid the door.

They dragged her out by the wrists, by the hair. She fought with them stronger than ten men. But there were twenty; she was alone. The little street was empty. They strangled her, beat down her face, dragged her upon a horse, and, with her crosswise on the saddle, galloped up and down, as they fired the cabins and the sheds. Her hands were shackled, and her eyes blind with blood, but she thought only of her child. "Where could he be?"

There were gunshots. Down the hills like mad came the white men for their wives and children.

Then the Indians turned back toward the plain. They rode past her house.

There, where she had left him, stood the child, dazed with surprise. She held out her arms tied together and called to him to come.

"Fool! fool!" Here the woman in black struck her temples with her hands. "Fool!" Why had she not galloped by and never noticed him?

But she begged, caught at the horse's head, struggled to get to him; and the Indian stopped for a moment in his flight and caught up the child and went on.

Then the thought came to her of the end of that ride—what was to come—after. And she tried to drop the boy, to let him slide gently to the ground; but the Indian held them fast.

Behind, nearer, came the following men, louder the guns. The horse she was on snorted, staggered under the weight of the three, and as they reached the plain the child was torn from her, she was pushed away. But she rose and staggered after them amid the blinding dust. They must take her too. Sobbing, she called to them as she stumbled on. Many times she fell. Then she could go no more.

That was all. Her story ended there, with the thundering of horses' hoofs and the taste of dust in her mouth. They found her there unconscious. Her friends tended her. When she came back to life she asked no questions but left her neighbor's house and came to her door, where she was standing now, and gazed away over the sand where *he* had gone, down toward Mexico.

The years went by, and she was still alone in the house where *two* should have been. And now far off she saw the dust blowing in a long, rolling, pinkish line. But the dust blew so often, and nothing came of it—not even the Indians.

The boy she knew was dead, but they—his murderers—remained, somewhere.

If she could have one now in her power!

The woman in black pondered, as she had so many times, how she should torture him. No pain could be too horrible. She looked at the fire in the stove, and piled on the logs—the logs that were brought with such trouble from the mountains where the trees grew. She could not make it hot enough. She dropped on her knees and watched the iron grow red. And the letters of the maker's name stamped on it grew distinct, and the word "Congress," half defaced, and the figures "64." Ah, those letters! she could have kissed the spot, for her child had touched it. Charmed by the glow, when left alone, he laid his baby hand flat on it, and burned deep into the palm were those letters, "S S, 64."

She would know him among a million by that mark.

But he was dead. The Indians remained.

The woman in black stood up. Why should she not go to them? There were pools in the plain where she could drink. That would be enough.

The men were away; the women were at work. Who could stop her?

She put on her bonnet and started off down the hill through the green bushes. The air was still crisp, though the sun was hot.

The desert must have an end. She would keep on to Mexico. She walked quickly, and her dress grew gray with dust, and the air scorching, as she reached the plain. But she kept on, and only looked back once at the house on the hill, and at the window where the pale woman sat.

The dust choked her, and she stumbled, and the sole of one shoe came half off, and slapped, and banged, and delayed her as she walked. She tore it off and went on, but the sand cut and burned her so that she sat down and wept, and wanted to go back for her other pair, the ones she wore on Sundays. The hill, though, looked so distant that she wearily got up and went on, on, till she could go no more, and crept under the shadow of a rock. There was no water near. Her throat was parched, and her temples beat wildly. She must go back and start again, strengthened, fortified. She would start tomorrow, or at night, when the cool would let her get too far to return.

By slow degrees she dragged herself up the hill. The pale woman came out of her house, and nodded, but the woman in black did not smile in return. She closed her door, and went up to her bed, and fell on it, and slept, amid the buzzing of the flies and the fitful flapping of the window-shade in the breeze.

The pale woman sighed and glanced across the plain. The roll of blowing dust was larger, and more regular, and nearer. The woman shuddered as she watched it creep slowly along behind the sand mounds. "It always blows," she said to herself, "but not like that, so steadily, so even." She strained her eyes, but there was only dust to be seen. Then she thought of a telescope that belonged to the minister's wife, who came from a seaport town, and ran to fetch it. The two women came out with it together, the minister's wife laughing at her friend, she was such a timid thing!

But the pale woman was paler than ever, and trembled so she could not steady it. The laughing one looked through it, and laughed no more.

"I see a head over the mound there," she said.

The pale woman shrieked.

"They are miles away. We may have time."

"For what?"

"To get away."

"They may be friends—"

"They are Indians! White men would not live through that sand. We must go to the woods. Help me. Warn the women. Gather the children. Come."

She rushed into her house. The other still stood and looked.

The dust cloud was a little nearer. In a moment all was wild confusion, names were called, but not loudly, girls sobbed, some carried their little treasures, mothers held their children. All gathered together, hidden from the plain by a house.

The pale woman led out her father, then ran to her neighbor's door. She opened it, and called clearly, but softly, "Mary, Mary." There was no answer. The woman in black, on her bed, slept on. Her neighbor hesitated, then hurried after the others, as they ran up the low hills toward the mountains, where their men had gone.

The dust cloud grew nearer. Now and then a head could be seen. But all was as still as the grave. The woman in black slept heavily and dreamed that revenge had come at last—that in her hand she held an Indian's head.

The window-shade flapped loudly, and she woke with an apprehension crushing her. She went to the window and looked out. There was no blowing dust upon the plains, and the street was empty. The doors of the houses stood open; a shawl lay in the middle of the road. The woman leaned out and looked toward the woods.

She saw on the crest of a hill the white skirts of the flying women, and then, below, down the road, her ears sharpened, her heart tightening, she heard the soft, regular thumping of horses' feet.

Then she *knew*.

She sat on the edge of the bed. This was what she had waited for! Was it her turn now?—or theirs again?

She could kill *one*.

Where was her gun?

She had loaned it to the men.

But her axe—that was below.

As she started for it, there was a burst of war cries.

She ran down the narrow stairs, and took the axe from its place on the wall.

They were passing her door. The room grew lighter. She turned. One stood in the open doorway, black against the sunshine. She set her teeth hard, hid the axe behind her skirts, watched him motionless.

He stretched out his hand clawlike, and laughed, his eyes gleaming, as catlike he moved nearer. A terror seized her: with a hoarse cry, she sprang up the stairs, flinging down a chair as he followed panting.

Quickly she climbed up the ladder to the loft, threw down the trapdoor, fell on it, bolted it, waited. All was still. Outside she heard the distant yells. She stooped noiselessly and put her ear upon the floor. There was soft breathing underneath, and through a crack in the floor she saw an eye peering up at her.

She stood a long time, motionless, axe in hand, ready.

Her back was to the bolt, but suddenly she *felt* that there was something there. She turned softly. A slim brown hand was almost through a crevice in the floor.

She raised her axe. The slender fingers touched the bolt and gently drew it back.

Then with the force of all her hatred fell the axe upon the wrist. The hand sprang up at her. With a howl of agony the creature fell bumping beneath.

Then all again was still.

Her face was wet and warm with the spattered blood.

Outside she heard the crackling of a burning house, then gunshots far away, and distant shouts. On tiptoe she went to the garret window, and peeped round its edge. Over the hills, quite near, she saw the men returning. One house was blazing—the minister's. The Indians were retreating. Near her door, grazing, stood a riderless horse. *She* knew its owner. As they rode past, they caught at it, but were stopped by a shout from her door. An Indian rushed out, handsome, young, holding aloft a bare right arm without a hand. In his language he shrieked to them for revenge, pointing up with his red wrist to the attic where she stood.

The eyes of the woman shot fire. She leaned far out and shook her fist from the garret window.

"One Indian at least!"

She hurled the axe at them. It fell far short. They fired as they passed, but none hit her. Nearer came the men.

The wounded man leaped to his horse and with a curse rode on. The woman laughed as he passed beneath, then sat down in the dusky loft with a red pool at her feet.

Shortly the men returned. Some went by down the hill, after the Indians. Others put out the fire. All was confusion, bustle, shouts.

Then the women and the children came and added to the din, and the men who had followed returned. But the woman in black sat alone in the loft, till she heard the crowd at her door below, and the voice of the pale woman say:

"Where is Mary?"

She rose and lifted the trap-door—it was unbolted—and went down.

The pale woman came to her, but she pushed her aside, and wiped her face with her sleeve.

"Are they killed? any of them?" she said. Her friend answered, "No, Mary, not one." "No harm this time," said the bearded man. "Except my house, it is burned," said the minister's wife. "We'll soon have another."

"I don't mean *you!*" cried the woman in black. "I mean them—red devils. Have you got any?—killed any? *You*"—this to Jim, who never missed a shot —"you"—this to the bearded man—"have *you* killed any?"

And the men answered, "No."

And one man said, "Their horses were faster than ours."

"Not one!" The woman in black drew herself up proudly. "Yes, one; better than killed. Wait." The women shrunk from her as she darted up the stair. They looked at each other wonderingly. The woman returned with something in her grasp. She flung it on the table. "It is an Indian's hand. His arm will shrivel to the bone. They will leave him some day to die in the sand." The women shuddered and drew back; the men crowded round, but they did not touch the hand.

"Are you afraid?" said the woman in black. "Afraid of that thing!"

She bent back the fingers and looked in it with a smile of contempt. Her face took an ashen hue: the hand struck the table edge and fell upon the floor. She seemed to be trying to think for a second, then she gave one awful cry, and leaned her face against the wall, with her hands hanging at her side.

The pale woman tried to go to her, but her husband drew her back, and, with a silent crowd around, slowly picked up the hand.

For a second he hesitated, then did as she had done, but gently. He bent back the fingers of the severed hand and read its history written there, "S S, 64," in white letters on the palm.

He remembered then how, twenty years ago, when she brought the child to him, he had tied its little hand in cooling salve.

It was larger now.

The whisper went around, "It is her boy's hand," and they crept toward the door.

The pale woman took a flower from her dress, one she had put there hours before, and placed it in the brown fingers on the table and went out.

The woman did not stir from the wall. "Leave the hand," she said.

"It is there," and the bearded man closed the door gently behind him.

The woman in black turned. Her hard eyes were dim now. She took the hand from the table and undid her dress and placed it in her breast, and went to the window, and watched, far off, a cloud of dust made golden by the sun, as it rolled away across the plain, down toward Mexico.

A GOOD-FOR-NOTHING

Hjalmar Hjorth Boyesen

I

Ralph Grim was born a gentleman. He had the misfortune of coming into the world some ten years later than might reasonably have been expected. Colonel Grim and his lady had celebrated twelve anniversaries of their wedding-day, and had given up all hopes of ever having a son and heir, when this late comer startled them by his unexpected appearance. The only previous addition to the family had been a daughter, and she was then ten summers old.

Ralph was a very feeble child, and could only with great difficulty be persuaded to retain his hold of the slender thread which bound him to existence. He was rubbed with whiskey, and wrapped in cotton, and given mare's milk to drink, and God knows what not, and the Colonel swore a round oath of paternal delight when at last the infant stopped gasping in that distressing way and began to breathe like other human beings. The mother, who, in spite of her anxiety for the child's life, had found time to plot for him a career of future magnificence, now suddenly set him apart for literature, because that was the easiest road to fame, and disposed of him in marriage to one of the most distinguished families of the land. She cautiously suggested this to her husband when he came to take his seat at her bedside; but to her utter astonishment she found that he had been indulging a similar train of thought, and had already destined the infant prodigy for the army. She, however, could not give up her predilection for literature, and the Colonel, who could not bear to be contradicted in his own house, as he used to say, was getting every minute louder and more flushed, when, happily, the doctor's arrival interrupted the dispute.

As Ralph grew up from infancy to childhood, he began to give decided

87

promise of future distinction. He was fond of sitting down in a corner and sucking his thumb, which his mother interpreted as the sign of that brooding disposition peculiar to poets and men of lofty genius. At the age of five, he had become sole master in the house. He slapped his sister Hilda in the face, or pulled her hair, when she hesitated to obey him, tyrannized over his nurse, and sternly refused to go to bed in spite of his mother's entreaties. On such occasions, the Colonel would hide his face behind his newspaper, and chuckle with delight; it was evident that nature had intended his son for a great military commander. As soon as Ralph himself was old enough to have any thoughts about his future destiny, he made up his mind that he would like to be a pirate. A few months later, having contracted an immoderate taste for candy, he contented himself with the comparatively humble position of a baker; but when he had read "Robinson Crusoe" he manifested a strong desire to go to sea in the hope of being wrecked on some desolate island. The parents spent long evenings gravely discussing these indications of uncommon genius, and each interpreted them in his or her own way.

"He is not like any other child I ever knew," said the mother.

"To be sure," responded the father, earnestly. "He is a most extraordinary child. I was a very remarkable child too, even if I do say it myself; but, as far as I remember, I never aspired to being wrecked on an uninhabited island."

The Colonel probably spoke the truth; but he forgot to take into account that he had never read "Robinson Crusoe."

Of Ralph's school-days there is but little to report, for, to tell the truth, he did not fancy going to school, as the discipline annoyed him. The day after his having entered the gymnasium, which was to prepare him for the Military Academy, the principal saw him waiting at the gate after his class had been dismissed. He approached him, and asked why he did not go home with the rest.

"I am waiting for the servant to carry my books," was the boy's answer.

"Give me your books," said the teacher.

Ralph reluctantly obeyed. That day the Colonel was not a little surprised to see his son marching up the street, and every now and then glancing behind him with a look of discomfort at the principal, who was following quietly in his train, carrying a parcel of school-books. Colonel Grim and his wife, divining the teacher's intention, agreed that it was a great outrage, but they did not mention the matter to Ralph. Henceforth, however, the boy refused to be accompanied by his servant. A week later he was impudent to the teacher of gymnastics, who whipped him in return. The Colonel's rage knew no bounds; he rode in great haste to the gymnasium, reviled the teacher for presuming to chastise *his* son, and committed the boy to the care of a private tutor.

At the age of sixteen, Ralph went to the capital with the intention of entering the Military Academy. He was a tall, handsome youth, slender of stature, and carried himself as erect as a candle. He had a light, clear complexion of almost feminine delicacy; blond, curly hair, which he always kept carefully brushed; a low forehead, and a straight, finely modeled nose. There was an expression of extreme sensitiveness about the nostrils, and a look of indolence in the dark-blue eyes. But the *ensemble* of his features was pleasing, his dress irreproachable, and his manners bore no trace of the awkward self-consciousness peculiar to his age. Immediately on his arrival in the capital he hired a suite of rooms in the aristocratic part of the city, and furnished them rather expensively, but in excellent taste. From a bosom friend, whom he met by accident in the restaurant's pavilion in the park, he learned that a pair of antlers, a stuffed eagle, or falcon, and a couple of swords, were indispensable to a well-appointed apartment. He accordingly bought these articles at a curiosity shop. During the first weeks of his residence in the city he made some feeble efforts to perfect himself in mathematics, in which he suspected he was somewhat deficient. But when the same officious friend laughed at him, and called him "green," he determined to trust to fortune, and henceforth devoted himself the more assiduously to the French ballet, where he had already made some interesting acquaintances.

The time for the examination came; the French ballet did not prove a good preparation; Ralph failed. It quite shook him for the time, and he felt humiliated. He had not the courage to tell his father; so he lingered on from day to day, sat vacantly gazing out of his window, and tried vainly to interest himself in the busy bustle down on the street. It provoked him that everybody else should be so light-hearted, when he was, or at least fancied himself, in trouble. The parlor grew intolerable; he sought refuge in his bedroom. There he sat one evening (it was the third day after the examination), and stared out upon the gray stone walls which on all sides inclosed the narrow courtyard. The round stupid face of the moon stood tranquilly dozing like a great Limburger cheese suspended under the sky.

Ralph, at least, could think of a no more fitting simile. But the bright-eyed young girl in the window hard by sent a longing look up to the same moon, and thought of her distant home on the fjords, where the glaciers stood like hoary giants, and caught the yellow moonbeams on their glittering shields of snow. She had been reading "Ivanhoe" all the afternoon, until the twilight had overtaken her quite unaware, and now she suddenly remembered that she had forgotten to write her German exercise. She lifted her face and saw a pair of sad, vacant eyes gazing at her from the next window in the angle of the court. She was a little startled at first, but in the next moment she thought of her German exercise and took heart.

"Do you know German?" she said; then immediately repented that she had said it.

"I do," was the answer.

She took up her apron and began to twist it with an air of embarrassment. "I didn't mean anything," she whispered, at last. "I only wanted to know."

"You are very kind."

That answer roused her; he was evidently making sport of her.

"Well, then, if you do, you may write my exercise for me. I have marked the place in the book."

And she flung her book over to the window, and he caught it on the edge of the sill, just as it was falling.

"You are a very strange girl," he remarked, turning over the leaves of the book, although it was too dark to read. "How old are you?"

"I shall be fourteen six weeks before Christmas," answered she, frankly.

"Then I excuse you."

"No, indeed," cried she, vehemently. "You needn't excuse me at all. If you don't want to write my exercise, you may send the book back again. I am very sorry I spoke to you, and I shall never do it again."

"But you will not get the book back again without the exercise," replied he, quietly. "Good-night."

The girl stood long looking after him, hoping that he would return. Then, with a great burst of repentance, she hid her face in her lap, and began to cry.

"Oh, dear, I didn't mean to be rude," she sobbed. "But it was Ivanhoe and Rebecca who upset me."

The next morning she was up before daylight, and waited for two long hours in great suspense before the curtain of his window was raised. He greeted her politely; threw a hasty glance around the court to see if he was observed, and then tossed her book dexterously over into her hands.

"I have pinned the written exercise to the fly-leaf," he said. "You will probably have time to copy it before breakfast."

"I am ever so much obliged to you," she managed to stammer.

He looked so tall and handsome, and grown-up, and her remorse stuck in her throat, and threatened to choke her. She had taken him for a boy as he sat there in his window the evening before.

"By the way, what is your name?" he asked, carelessly, as he turned to go.

"Bertha."

"Well, my dear Bertha, I am happy to have made your acquaintance."

And he again made her a polite bow, and entered his parlor.

"How provokingly familiar he is," thought she; "but no one can deny that he is handsome."

The bright roguish face of the young girl haunted Ralph during the whole next week. He had been in love at least ten times before, of course; but, like most boys, with young ladies far older than himself. He found himself frequently glancing over to her window in the hope of catching another glimpse of her face; but the curtain was always drawn down, and Bertha remained invisible. During the second week, however, she relented, and they had many a pleasant chat together. He now volunteered to write all her exercises, and she made no objections. He learned that she was the daughter of a well-to-do peasant in the sea-districts of Norway (and it gave him quite a shock to hear it), and that she was going to school in the city, and boarded with an old lady who kept a *pension* in the house adjoining the one in which he lived.

One day in the autumn Ralph was surprised by the sudden arrival of his father, and the fact of his failure in the examination could no longer be kept a secret. The old Colonel flared up at once when Ralph made his confession; the large veins upon his forehead swelled; he grew coppery-red in his face, and stormed up and down the floor, until his son became seriously alarmed; but, to his great relief, he was soon made aware that his father's wrath was not turned against him personally, but against the officials of the Military Academy who had rejected him. The Colonel took it as insult to his own good name and irreproachable standing as an officer; he promptly refused any other explanation, and vainly racked his brain to remember if any youthful folly of his could possibly have made him enemies among the teachers of the Academy. He at last felt satisfied that it was envy of his own greatness and rapid advancement which had induced the rascals to take vengeance on his son. Ralph reluctantly followed his father back to the country town where the latter was stationed, and the fair-haired Bertha vanished from his horizon. His mother's wish now prevailed, and he began, in his own easy way, to prepare himself for the University. He had little taste for Cicero, and still less for Virgil, but with the use of a "pony" he soon gained sufficient knowledge of these authors to be able to talk in a sort of patronizing way about them, to the great delight of his fond parents. He took quite a fancy, however, to the ode in Horace ending with the lines:

> Dulce ridentem,
> Dulce loquentem,
> Lalagen amabo.

And in his thought he substituted for Lalage the fair-haired Bertha, quite regardless of the requirements of the metre.

To make a long story short, three years later Ralph returned to the capital, and, after having worn out several tutors, actually succeeded in entering the University.

The first year of college life is a happy time to every young man, and Ralph enjoyed its processions, its parliamentary gatherings, and its leisure, as well as the rest. He was certainly not the man to be sentimental over the loss of a young girl whom, moreover, he had only known for a few weeks. Nevertheless, he thought of her at odd times, but not enough to disturb his pleasure. The standing of his family, his own handsome appearance, and his immaculate linen opened to him the best houses of the city, and he became a great favorite in society. At lectures he was seldom seen, but more frequently in the theatres, where he used to come in during the middle of the first act, take his station in front of the orchestra box, and eye, through his lorgnette, by turns, the actresses and the ladies of the parquet.

II

Two months passed, and then came the great annual ball which the students give at the opening of the second semester. Ralph was a man of importance that evening; first, because he belonged to a great family; secondly, because he was the handsomest man of his year. He wore a large golden star on his breast (for his fellow-students had made him a Knight of the Golden Boar) and a badge of colored ribbons in his buttonhole.

The ball was a brilliant affair, and everybody was in excellent spirits, especially the ladies. Ralph danced incessantly, twirled his soft mustache, and uttered amiable platitudes. It was toward midnight, just as the company was moving out to supper, that he caught the glance of a pair of dark-blue eyes, which suddenly drove the blood to his cheeks and hastened the beating of his heart. But when he looked once more the dark-blue eyes were gone, and his unruly heart went on hammering against his side. He laid his hand on his breast and glanced furtively at his fair neighbor, but she looked happy and unconcerned, for the flavor of the ice cream was delicious. It seemed an endless meal, but, when it was done, Ralph rose, led his partner back to the ballroom, and hastily excused himself. His glance wandered round the wide hall, seeking the well-remembered eyes once more, and, at length, finding them in a remote corner, half hid behind a moving wall of promenaders. In another moment he was at Bertha's side.

"You must have been purposely hiding yourself, Miss Bertha," said he, when the usual greetings were exchanged. "I have not caught a glimpse of you all this evening, until a few moments ago."

"But I have seen you all the while," answered the girl, frankly. "I knew you at once as I entered the hall."

"If I had but known that you were here," resumed Ralph, as it were invisibly expanding with an agreeable sense of dignity, "I assure you you would have been the very first one I should have sought."

She raised her large grave eyes to his, as if questioning his sincerity; but she made no answer.

"Good gracious!" thought Ralph. "She takes things terribly in earnest."

"You look so serious, Miss Bertha," said he, after a moment's pause. "I remember you as a bright-eyed, flaxen-haired little girl, who threw her German exercise-book to me across the yard, and whose merry laughter still rings pleasantly in my memory. I confess I don't find it quite easy to identify this grave young lady with my merry friend of three years ago."

"In other words, you are disappointed at not finding me the same as I used to be."

"No, not exactly that; but—"

Ralph paused and looked puzzled. There was something in the earnestness of her manner which made a facetious compliment seem grossly inappropriate, and in the moment no other escape suggested itself.

"But what?" demanded Bertha, mercilessly.

"Have you ever lost an old friend?" asked he, abruptly.

"Yes; how so?"

"Then," answered he, while his features lighted up with a happy inspiration—"then you will appreciate my situation. I fondly cherished my old picture of you in my memory. Now I have lost it, and I can not help regretting the loss. I do not mean, however, to imply that this new acquaintance—this second edition of yourself, so to speak—will prove less interesting."

She again sent him a grave, questioning look, and began to gaze intently upon the stone in her bracelet.

"I suppose you will laugh at me," began she, while a sudden blush flitted over her countenance. "But this is my first ball, and I feel as if I had rushed into a whirlpool, from which I have, since the first rash plunge was made, been vainly trying to escape. I feel so dreadfully forlorn. I hardly know anybody here except my cousin, who invited me, and I hardly think I know him either."

"Well, since you are irredeemably committed," replied Ralph, as the music, after some prefatory flourishes, broke into the delicious rhythm of a Strauss waltz, "then it is no use struggling against fate. Come, let us make the plunge together. Misery loves company."

He offered her his arm, and she rose, somewhat hesitatingly, and followed.

"I am afraid," she whispered, as they fell into line with the procession that was moving down the long hall, "that you have asked me to dance merely because I said I felt forlorn. If that is the case, I should prefer to be led back to my seat."

"What a base imputation!" cried Ralph.

There was something so charmingly *naïve* in this self-depreciation—something so altogether novel in his experience, and, he could not help adding, just a little bit countrified. His spirits rose; he began to relish keenly his position as an experienced man of the world, and, in the agreeable glow of patronage and conscious superiority, chatted with hearty *abandon* with his little rustic beauty.

"If your dancing is as perfect as your German exercises were," said she, laughing, as they swung out upon the floor, "then I promise myself a good deal of pleasure from our meeting."

"Never fear," answered he, quickly reversing his step, and whirling with many a capricious turn away among the thronging couples.

When Ralph drove home in his carriage toward morning he briefly summed up his impressions of Bertha in the following adjectives: intelligent, delightfully unsophisticated, a little bit verdant, but devilish pretty.

Some weeks later Colonel Grim received an appointment at the fortress of Aggershuus, and immediately took up his residence in the capital. He saw that his son cut a fine figure in the highest circles of society, and expressed his gratification in the most emphatic terms. If he had known, however, that Ralph was in the habit of visiting, with alarming regularity, at the house of a plebeian merchant in a somewhat obscure street, he would, no doubt, have been more chary of his praise. But the Colonel suspected nothing, and it was well for the peace of the family that he did not. It may have been cowardice in

Ralph that he never mentioned Bertha's name to his family or to his aristo-cratic acquaintances; for, to be candid, he himself felt ashamed of the power she exerted over him, and by turns pitied and ridiculed himself for pursuing so inglorious a conquest. Nevertheless it wounded his egotism that she never showed any surprise at seeing him, that she received him with a certain frank unceremoniousness, which, however, was very becoming to her; that she in-variably went on with her work heedless of his presence, and in everything treated him as if she had been his equal. She persisted in talking with him in a half sisterly fashion about his studies and his future career, warned him with great solicitude against some of his reprobate friends, of whose merry adven-tures he had told her; and if he ventured to compliment her on her beauty or her accomplishments, she would look up gravely from her sewing, or answer him in a way which seemed to banish the idea of love-making into the land of the impossible. He was constantly tormented by the suspicion that she se-cretly disapproved of him, and that from a mere moral interest in his welfare she was conscientiously laboring to make him a better man. Day after day he parted from her feeling humiliated, faint-hearted, and secretly indignant both at himself and her, and day after day he returned only to renew the same experience. At last it became too intolerable, he could endure it no longer. Let it make or break, certainty, at all risks, was at least preferable to this sicken-ing suspense. That he loved her, he could no longer doubt; let his parents foam and fret as much as they pleased; for once he was going to stand on his own legs. And in the end, he thought, they would have to yield, for they had no son but him.

Bertha was going to return to her home on the sea-coast in a week. Ralph stood in the little low-ceiled parlor, as she imagined, to bid her good-by. They had been speaking of her father, her brothers, and the farm, and she had expressed the wish that if he ever should come to that part of the country he might pay them a visit. Her words had kindled a vague hope in his breast, but in their very frankness and friendly regard there was something which slew the hope they had begotten. He held her hand in his, and her large confiding eyes shone with an emotion which was beautiful, but was yet not love.

"If you were but a peasant born like myself," said she, in a voice which sounded almost tender, "then I should like to talk to you as I would to my own brother; but—"

"No, not brother, Bertha," cried he, with sudden vehemence; "I love you better than I ever loved any earthly being, and if you knew how firmly this love has clutched at the roots of my heart, you would perhaps—you would at least not look so reproachfully at me."

She dropped his hand, and stood for a moment silent.

"I am sorry that it should have come to this, Mr. Grim," said she, visibly struggling for calmness. "And I am perhaps more to blame than you."

"Blame," muttered he, "why are you to blame?"

"Because I do not love you; although I sometimes feared that this might come. But then again I persuaded myself that it could not be so."

He took a step toward the door, laid his hand on the knob, and gazed down before him.

"Bertha," began he, slowly, raising his head, "you have always disapproved of me, you have despised me in your heart, but you thought you would be doing a good work if you succeeded in making a man of me."

"You use strong language," answered she, hesitatingly; "but there is truth in what you say."

Again there was a long pause, in which the ticking of the old parlor clock grew louder and louder.

"Then," he broke out at last, "tell me before we part if I can do nothing to gain—I will not say your love—but only your regard? What would you do if you were in my place?"

"My advice you will hardly heed, and I do not even know that it would be well if you did. But if I were a man in your position, I should break with my whole past, start out into the world where nobody knew me, and where I should be dependent only upon my own strength, and there I would conquer a place for myself, if it were only for the satisfaction of knowing that I was really a man. Here cushions are sewed under your arms, a hundred invisible threads bind you to a life of idleness and vanity, everybody is ready to carry you on his hands, the road is smoothed for you, every stone carefully moved out of your path, and you will probably go to your grave without having ever harbored one earnest thought, without having done one manly deed."

Ralph stood transfixed, gazing at her with open mouth; he felt a kind of stupid fright, as if some one had suddenly seized him by the shoulders and shaken him violently. He tried vainly to remove his eyes from Bertha. She held him as by a powerful spell. He saw that her face was lighted with an altogether new beauty; he noticed the deep glow upon her cheek, the brilliancy of her eye, the slight quiver of her lip. But he saw all this as one sees things in a half-trance, without attempting to account for them; the door between his soul and his senses was closed.

"I know that I have been bold in speaking to you in this way," she said at last, seating herself in a chair at the window. "But it was yourself who asked me. And I have felt all the time that I should have to tell you this before we parted."

"And," answered he, making a strong effort to appear calm, "if I follow your advice, will you allow me to see you once more before you go?"

"I shall remain here another week, and shall, during that time, always be ready to receive you."

"Thank you. Good-by."

"Good-by."

Ralph carefully avoided all the fashionable thoroughfares; he felt degraded before himself, and he had an idea that every man could read his humiliation in his countenance. Now he walked on quickly, striking the sidewalk with his heels; now, again, he fell into an uneasy, reckless saunter, according as the changing moods inspired defiance of his sentence, or a qualified surrender.

And, as he walked on, the bitterness grew within him, and he piteously reviled himself for having allowed himself to be made a fool of by "that little country goose," when he was well aware that there were hundreds of women of the best families of the land who would feel honored at receiving his attentions. But this sort of reasoning he knew to be both weak and contemptible, and his better self soon rose in loud rebellion.

"After all," he muttered, "in the main thing she was right. I am a miserable good-for-nothing, a hothouse plant, a poor stick, and if I were a woman myself, I don't think I should waste my affections on a man of that calibre."

Then he unconsciously fell to analyzing Bertha's character, wondering vaguely that a person who moved so timidly in social life, appearing so diffident, from an ever-present fear of blundering against the established forms of etiquette, could judge so quickly, and with such a merciless certainty, whenever a moral question, a question of right and wrong, was at issue. And, pursuing the same train of thought, he contrasted her with himself, who moved in the highest spheres of society as in his native element, heedless of moral scruples, and conscious of no loftier motive for his actions than the immediate pleasure of the moment.

As Ralph turned the corner of a street, he heard himself hailed from the other sidewalk by a chorus of merry voices.

"Ah, my dear Baroness," cried a young man, springing across the street and grasping Ralph's hand (all his student friends called him the Baroness), in the name of this illustrious company, allow me to salute you. But why the deuce—what is the matter with you? If you have the *Katzenjammer,* soda-water is the thing. Come along—it's my treat!"

The students instantly thronged around Ralph, who stood distractedly swinging his cane and smiling idiotically.

"I am not quite well," said he; "leave me alone."

"No, to be sure, you don't look well," cried a jolly youth, against whom Bertha had frequently warned him; "but a glass of sherry will soon restore you. It would be highly immoral to leave you in this condition without taking care of you."

Ralph again vainly tried to remonstrate; but the end was, that he reluctantly followed.

He had always been a conspicuous figure in the student world; but that night he astonished his friends by his eloquence, his reckless humor, and his capacity for drinking. He made a speech for "Woman," which bristled with wit, cynicism, and sarcastic epigrams. One young man, named Vinter, who was engaged, undertook to protest against his sweeping condemnation, and declared that Ralph, who was a universal favorite among the ladies, ought to be the last to revile them.

"If," he went on, "the Baroness should propose to six well-known ladies here in this city whom I could mention, I would wager six Johannisbergers, and an equal amount of champagne, that every one of them would accept him."

The others loudly applauded this proposal, and Ralph accepted the wager. The letters were written on the spot, and immediately despatched. Toward morning, the merry carousal broke up, and Ralph was conducted in triumph to his home.

III

Two days later, Ralph again knocked on Bertha's door. He looked paler than usual, almost haggard; his immaculate linen was a little crumpled, and he carried no cane; his lips were tightly compressed, and his face wore an air of desperate resolution.

"It is done," he said, as he seated himself opposite her. "I am going."

"Going!" cried she, startled at his unusual appearance. "How, where?"

"To America. I sail to-night. I have followed your advice, you see. I have cut off the last bridge behind me."

"But, Ralph," she exclaimed, in a voice of alarm. "Something dreadful must have happened. Tell me quick; I must know it."

"No; nothing dreadful," muttered he, smiling bitterly. "I have made a little scandal, that is all. My father told me to-day to go to the devil, if I chose, and my mother gave me five hundred dollars to help me along on the way. If you wish to know, here is the explanation."

And he pulled from his pocket six perfumed and carefully folded notes, and threw them into her lap.

"Do you wish me to read them?" she asked, with growing surprise.

"Certainly. Why not?"

She hastily opened one note after the other, and read.

"But, Ralph," she cried, springing up from her seat, while her eyes flamed with indignation, "what does this mean? What have you done?"

"I didn't think it needed any explanation," replied he, with feigned indifference. "I proposed to them all, and, you see, they all accepted me. I received all these letters to-day. I only wished to know whether the whole world regarded me as such a worthless scamp as you told me I was."

She did not answer, but sat mutely staring at him, fiercely crumpling a rose-colored note in her hand. He began to feel uncomfortable under her gaze, and threw himself about uneasily in his chair.

"Well," said he, at length, rising, "I suppose there is nothing more. Good-by."

"One moment, Mr. Grim," demanded she, sternly. "Since I have already said so much, and you have obligingly revealed to me a new side of your character, I claim the right to correct the opinion I expressed of you at our last meeting."

"I am all attention."

"I did think, Mr. Grim," began she, breathing hard, and steadying herself against the table at which she stood, "that you were a very selfish man—an embodiment of selfishness, absolute and supreme, but I did not believe that you were wicked."

"And what convinced you that I was selfish, if I may ask?"

"What convinced me?" repeated she, in a tone of inexpressible contempt. "When did you ever act from any generous regard for others? What good did you ever do to anybody?"

"You might ask, with equal justice, what good I ever did to myself."

"In a certain sense, yes; because to gratify a mere momentary wish is hardly doing one's self good."

"Then I have, at all events, followed the Biblical precept, and treated my neighbor very much as I treat myself."

"I did think," continued Bertha, without heeding the remark, "that you were at bottom kindhearted, but too hopelessly well-bred ever to commit an act of any decided complexion, either good or bad. Now I see that I have misjudged you, and that you are capable of outraging the most sacred feelings of a woman's heart in mere wantonness, or for the sake of satisfying a base curiosity, which never could have entered the mind of an upright and generous man."

The hard, benumbed look in Ralph's face thawed in the warmth of her presence, and her words, though stern, touched a secret spring in his heart. He made two or three vain attempts to speak, then suddenly broke down, and cried:

"Bertha, Bertha, even if you scorn me, have patience with me, and listen."

And he told her, in rapid, broken sentences, how his love for her had grown from day to day, until he could no longer master it; and how, in an unguarded moment, when his pride rose in fierce conflict against his love, he had done this reckless deed of which he was now heartily ashamed. The fervor of his words touched her, for she felt that they were sincere. Large mute tears trembled in her eyelashes as she sat gazing tenderly at him, and in the depth of her soul the wish awoke that she might have been able to return this great and strong love of his; for she felt that in this love lay the germ of a new, of a stronger and better man. She noticed, with a half-regretful pleasure, his handsome figure, his delicately shaped hands, and the noble cast of his features; an overwhelming pity for him rose within her, and she began to reproach herself for having spoken so harshly, and, as she now thought, so unjustly. Perhaps he read in her eyes the unspoken wish. He seized her hand, and his words fell with a warm and alluring cadence upon her ear.

"I shall not see you for a long time to come, Bertha," said he, "but if at the end of five or six years your hand is still free, and I return another man—a man to whom you could safely intrust your happiness—would you then listen to what I may have to say to you? For I promise, by all that we both hold sacred—"

"No, no," interrupted she, hastily. "Promise nothing. It would be unjust to yourself, and perhaps also to me; for a sacred promise is a terrible thing,

Ralph. Let us both remain free; and, if you return and still love me, then come, and I shall receive you and listen to you. And even if you have outgrown your love, which is, indeed, more probable, come still to visit me wherever I may be, and we shall meet as friends and rejoice in the meeting."

"You know best," he murmured. "Let it be as you have said."

He arose, took her face between his hands, gazed long and tenderly into her eyes, pressed a kiss upon her forehead, and hastened away.

That night Ralph boarded the steamer for Hull, and three weeks later landed in New York.

IV

The first three months of Ralph's sojourn in America were spent in vain attempts to obtain a situation. Day after day he walked down Broadway, calling at various places of business, and night after night he returned to his cheerless room with a faint heart and declining spirits. It was, after all, a more serious thing than he had imagined, to cut the cable which binds one to the land of one's birth. There a hundred subtile influences, the existence of which no one suspects until the moment they are withdrawn, unite to keep one in the straight path of rectitude, or at least of external respectability; and Ralph's life had been all in society; the opinion of his fellowmen had been the one force to which he implicitly deferred, and the conscience by which he had been wont to test his actions had been nothing but the aggregate judgment of his friends. To such a man the isolation and the utter irresponsibility of a life among strangers was tenfold more dangerous; and Ralph found, to his horror, that his character contained innumerable latent possibilities which the easy-going life in his home probably never would have revealed to him. It often cut him to the quick, when, on entering an office in his daily search for employment, he was met by hostile or suspicious glances, or when, as it occasionally happened, the door was slammed in his face, as if he were a vagabond or an impostor. Then the wolf was often roused within him, and he felt a momentary wild desire to become what the people here evidently believed him to be. Many a night he sauntered irresolutely about the gambling places in obscure streets, and the glare of light, the rude shouts and clamors in the same moment repelled and attracted him. If he went to the devil, who would care? His father had himself pointed out the way to him; and nobody could blame him if he followed the advice. But then again a memory emerged from that chamber of his soul which still he held sacred; and Bertha's deep-blue eyes gazed upon him with their earnest look of tender warning and regret.

When the summer was half gone, Ralph had gained many a hard victory over himself, and learned many a useful lesson; and at length he swallowed his pride, divested himself of his fine clothes, and accepted a position as assistant gardener at a villa on the Hudson. And as he stood perspiring with a spade in his hand, and a cheap broad-brimmed straw hat on his head, he often took a grim pleasure in picturing to himself how his aristocratic friends at home would receive him if he should introduce himself to them in this new costume.

"After all, it was only my position they cared for," he reflected, bitterly; "without my father's name what would I be to them?"

Then, again, there was a certain satisfaction in knowing that, for his present situation, humble as it was, he was indebted to nobody but himself; and the thought that Bertha's eyes, if they could have seen him now, would have dwelt upon him with pleasure and approbation, went far to console him for his aching back, his sunburned face, and his swollen and blistered hands.

One day, as Ralph was raking the gravel-walks in the garden, his employer's daughter, a young lady of seventeen, came out and spoke to him. His culture and refinement of manner struck her with wonder, and she asked him to tell her his history; but then he suddenly grew very grave, and she forbore pressing him. From that time she attached a kind of romantic interest to him, and finally induced her father to obtain him a situation that would be more to his taste. And, before winter came, Ralph saw the dawn of a new future glimmering before him. He had wrestled bravely with fate, and had once more gained a victory. He began the career in which success and distinction awaited him as proofreader on a newspaper in the city. He had fortunately been familiar with the English language before he left home, and by the strength of his will he conquered all difficulties. At the end of two years he became attached to the editorial staff; new ambitious hopes, hitherto foreign to his mind, awoke within him; and with joyous tumult of heart he saw life opening its wide vistas before him, and he labored on manfully to repair the losses of the past, and to prepare himself for greater usefulness in times to come. He felt in himself a stronger and fuller manhood, as if the great arteries of the vast universal world-life pulsed in his own being. The drowsy, indolent existence at home appeared like a dull remote dream from which he had awaked, and he blessed the destiny which, by its very sternness, had mercifully saved him; he blessed her, too, who, from the very want of love for him, had, perhaps, made him worthier of love.

The years flew rapidly. Society had flung its doors open to him, and what was more, he had found some warm friends, in whose houses he could come and go at pleasure. He enjoyed keenly the privilege of daily association with high-minded and refined women; their eager activity of intellect stimulated him, their exquisite ethereal grace and their delicately chiseled beauty satisfied his aesthetic cravings, and the responsive vivacity of their nature prepared him ever new surprises. He felt a strange fascination in the presence of these women, and the conviction grew upon him that their type of womanhood was superior to any he had hitherto known. And by way of refuting his own argument, he would draw from his pocketbook the photograph of Bertha, which had a secret compartment there all to itself, and, gazing tenderly at it, would eagerly defend her against the disparaging reflections which the involuntary comparison had provoked. And still, how could he help seeing that her features, though well molded, lacked animation; that her eye, with its deep, trustful glance, was not brilliant, and that the calm earnestness of her face, when compared with the bright, intellectual beauty of his present friends, appeared pale and simple, like a violet in a bouquet of vividly colored roses? It gave him a quick pang, when, at times, he was forced to admit this; nevertheless, it was the truth.

After six years of residence in America, Ralph had gained a very high reputation as a journalist of rare culture and ability, and in 1867 he was sent to the World's Exhibition in Paris, as correspondent of the paper on which he had during all these years been employed. What wonder, then, that he started for Europe a few weeks before his presence was needed in the imperial city, and that he steered his course directly toward the fjord valley where Bertha had her home? It was she who had bidden him Godspeed when he fled from the land of his birth, and she, too, should receive his first greeting on his return.

V

The sun had fortified itself behind a citadel of flaming clouds, and the upper forest region shone with a strange ethereal glow, while the lower plains were wrapped in shadow; but the shadow itself had a strong suffusion of color. The mountain peaks rose cold and blue in the distance.

Ralph, having inquired his way of the boatman who had landed him at the pier, walked rapidly along the beach, with a small valise in his hand, and a light summer overcoat flung over his shoulder. Many half-thoughts grazed his mind, and ere the first had taken shape, the second and the third came and chased it away. And still they all in some fashion had reference to Bertha; for in a misty, abstract way, she filled his whole mind; but for some indefinable reason, he was afraid to give free rein to the sentiment which lurked in the remoter corners of his soul.

Onward he hastened, while his heart throbbed with the quickening tempo of mingled expectation and fear. Now and then one of those chill gusts of air, which seem to be careering about aimlessly in the atmosphere during early summer, would strike into his face, and recall him to a keener self-consciousness.

Ralph concluded, from his increasing agitation, that he must be very near Bertha's home. He stopped and looked around him. He saw a large maple at the roadside, some thirty steps from where he was standing, and the girl who was sitting under it, resting her head in her hand and gazing out over the sea, he recognized in an instant to be Bertha. He sprang up on the road, not crossing, however, her line of vision, and approached her noiselessly from behind.

"Bertha," he whispered.

She gave a little joyous cry, sprang up, and made a gesture as if to throw herself in his arms; then suddenly checked herself, blushed crimson, and moved a step backward.

"You came so suddenly," she murmured.

"But, Bertha," cried he (and the full bass of his voice rang through her very soul), "have I gone into exile and waited these many years for so cold a welcome?"

"You have changed so much, Ralph," she answered, with that old grave smile which he knew so well, and stretched out both her hands toward him. "And I have thought of you so much since you went away, and blamed myself because I had judged you so harshly, and wondered that you could listen to me so patiently, and never bear me any malice for what I said."

"If you had said a word less," declared Ralph, seating himself at her side on the greensward, "or if you had varnished it over with politeness, then you would probably have failed to produce any effect and I should not have been burdened with that heavy debt of gratitude which I now owe you. I was a pretty thick-skinned animal in those days, Bertha. You said the right word at the right moment; you gave me a bold and a good piece of advice, which my own ingenuity would never have suggested to me. I will not thank you, because, in so grave a case as this, spoken thanks sound like a mere mockery. Whatever I am, Bertha, and whatever I may hope to be, I owe it all to that hour."

She listened with rapture to the manly assurance of his voice; her eyes dwelt with unspeakable joy upon his strong, bronzed features, his full thick blond beard, and the vigorous proportions of his frame. Many and many a time during his absence had she wondered how he would look if he ever came back, and with that minute conscientiousness which, as it were, pervaded her whole character, she had held herself responsible before God for his fate, prayed for him, and trembled lest evil powers should gain the ascendency over his soul.

On their way to the house they talked together of many things, but in a guarded, cautious fashion, and without the cheerful abandonment of former years. They both, as it were, groped their way carefully in each other's minds, and each vaguely felt that there was something in the other's thought which it was not well to touch unbidden. Bertha saw that all her fears for him had been groundless, and his very appearance lifted the whole weight of responsibility from her breast; and still, did she rejoice at her deliverance from her burden? Ah, no; in this moment she knew that that which she had foolishly cherished as the best and noblest part of herself had been but a selfish need of her own heart. She feared that she had only taken that interest in him which one feels in a thing of one's own making, and now, when she saw that he had risen quite above her; that he was free and strong, and could have no more need of her, she had, instead of generous pleasure at his success, but a painful sense of emptiness, as if something very dear had been taken from her.

Ralph, too, was loth to analyze the impression his old love made upon him. His feelings were of so complex a nature, he was anxious to keep his more magnanimous impulses active, and he strove hard to convince himself that she was still the same to him as she had been before they had ever parted. But, alas! though the heart be warm and generous, the eye is a merciless critic. And the man who had moved on the wide arena of the world, whose mind had housed the large thoughts of this century, and expanded with its invigorating breath—was he to blame because he had unconsciously out-grown his old provincial self, and could no more judge by its standards?

Bertha's father was a peasant, but he had, by his lumber trade, acquired what in Norway was called a very handsome fortune. He received his guest with dignified reserve, and Ralph thought he detected in his eyes a lurking look of distrust. "I know your errand," that look seemed to say, "but you had better give it up at once. It will be of no use for you to try."

And after supper, as Ralph and Bertha sat talking confidingly with each other at the window, he sent his daughter a quick, sharp glance, and then, without ceremony, commanded her to go to bed. Ralph's heart gave a great thump within him; not because he feared the old man, but because his words, as well as his glances, revealed to him the sad history of these long, patient years. He doubted no longer that the love which he had once so ardently desired was his at last; and he made a silent vow that, come what might, he would remain faithful.

As he came down to breakfast the next morning, he found Bertha sitting at the window, engaged in hemming what appeared to be a rough kitchen towel. She bent eagerly over her work, and only a vivid flush upon her cheek told him that she had noticed his coming. He took a chair, seated himself opposite her, and bade her "good-morning." She raised her head, and showed him a sweet, troubled countenance, which the early sunlight illumined with a high spiritual beauty. It reminded him forcibly of those pale, sweet-faced saints of Fra Angelico, with whom the frail flesh seems ever on the point of yielding to the ardent aspirations of the spirit. And still even in this moment he could not prevent his eyes from observing that one side of her forefinger was rough from sewing, and that the whiteness of her arm, which the loose sleeves displayed, contrasted strongly with the browned and sunburned complexion of her hands.

After breakfast they again walked together on the beach, and Ralph, hav-ing once formed his resolution, now talked freely of the New World—of his sphere of activity there; of his friends and of his plans for the future; and she listened to him with a mild, perplexed look in her eyes, as if trying vainly to follow the flight of his thoughts. And he wondered, with secret dismay, whether she was still the same strong, brave-hearted girl whom he had once accounted almost bold; whether the life in this narrow valley, amid a hundred petty and depressing cares, had not cramped her spiritual growth, and narrowed the sphere of her thought. Or was she still the same, and was it only he who had changed? At last he gave utterance to his wonder, and she answered him in those grave, earnest tones which seemed in themselves to be half a refutation of his doubts.

"It was easy for me to give you daring advice then, Ralph," she said. "Like most school-girls, I thought that life was a great and glorious thing, and that happiness was a fruit which hung within reach of every hand. Now I have lived for six years trying single-handed to relieve the want and suffering of the needy people with whom I come in contact, and their squalor and wretchedness have sickened me, and, what is still worse, I feel that all I can do is as a drop in the ocean, and, after all, amounts to nothing. I know I am no longer the same reckless girl who, with the very best intention, sent you wandering through the wide world; and I thank God that it proved to be for your good, although the whole now appears quite incredible to me. My thoughts have moved so long within the narrow circle of these mountains that they have lost their youthful elasticity, and can no more rise above them."

Ralph detected, in the midst of her despondency, a spark of her former fire, and grew eloquent in his endeavors to persuade her that she was unjust to herself, and that there was but a wider sphere of life needed to develop all the latent powers of her rich nature.

At the dinner-table, her father again sat eying his guest with that same cold look of distrust and suspicion. And when the meal was at an end, he rose abruptly and called his daughter into another room. Presently Ralph heard his angry voice resounding through the house, interrupted now and then by a woman's sobs, and a subdued, passionate pleading. When Bertha again entered the room, her eyes were very red, and he saw that she had been weeping. She threw a shawl over her shoulders, beckoned to him with her hand, and he arose and followed her. She led the way silently until they reached a thick copse of birch and alder near the strand. She dropped down upon a bench between two trees, and he took his seat at her side.

"Ralph," began she, with a visible effort, "I hardly know what to say to you; but there is something which I must tell you—my father wishes you to leave us at once."

"And *you,* Bertha?"

"Well—yes—I wish it too."

She saw the painful shock which her words gave him, and she strove hard to speak. Her lips trembled, her eyes became suffused with tears, which grew and grew, but never fell; she could not utter a word.

"Well, Bertha," answered he, with a little quiver in his voice, "if you, too, wish me to go, I shall not tarry. Good-by."

He rose quickly, and, with averted face, held out his hand to her; but as she made no motion to grasp the hand, he began distractedly to button his coat, and moved slowly away.

"Ralph."

He turned sharply, and, before he knew it, she lay sobbing upon his breast.

"Ralph," she murmured, while the tears almost choked her words, "I could not have you leave me thus. It is hard enough—it is hard enough—"

"What is hard, beloved?"

She raised her head abruptly, and turned upon him a gaze full of hope and doubt, and sweet perplexity.

"Ah, no, you do not love me," she whispered, sadly.

"Why should I come to seek you, after these many years, dearest, if I did not wish to make you my wife before God and men? Why should I—"

"Ah, yes, I know," she interrupted him with a fresh fit of weeping, "you are too good and honest to wish to throw me away, now when you have seen how my soul has hungered for the sight of you these many years, how even now I cling to you with a despairing clutch. But you can not disguise yourself, Ralph, and I saw from the first moment that you loved me no more."

"Do not be such an unreasonable child," he remonstrated, feebly. "I do not love you with the wild, irrational passion of former years; but I have the tenderest regard for you, and my heart warms at the sight of your sweet face, and I shall do all in my power to make you as happy as any man can make you who—"

"Who does not love me," she finished.

A sudden shudder seemed to shake her whole frame, and she drew herself more tightly up to him.

"Ah, no," she continued, after a while, sinking back upon her seat. "It is a hopeless thing to compel a reluctant heart. I will accept no sacrifice from you. You owe me nothing, for you have acted toward me honestly and uprightly, and I shall be a stronger or—at least—a better woman for what you gave me —and—for what you could not give me, even though you would."

"But, Bertha," exclaimed he, looking mournfully at her, "it is not true when you say that I owe you nothing. Six years ago, when first I wooed you, you could not return my love, and you sent me out into the world, and even refused to accept any pledge or promise for the future."

"And you returned," she responded, "a man, such as my hope had pictured you; but, while I had almost been standing still, you had outgrown me and outgrown your old self, and, with your old self, outgrown its love for me, for your love was not of your new self, but of the old. Alas! it is a sad tale, but it is true."

She spoke gravely now, and with a steadier voice, but her eyes hung upon his face with an eager look of expectation, as if yearning to detect there some gleam of hope, some contradiction of the dismal truth. He read that look aright and it pierced him like a sharp sword. He made a brave effort to respond to its appeal, but his features seemed hard as stone, and he could only cry out against his destiny, and bewail his misfortune and hers.

Toward evening, Ralph was sitting in an open boat, listening to the measured oar-strokes of the boatmen who were rowing him out to the nearest stopping-place of the steamer. The mountains lifted their great placid heads up among the sun-bathed clouds, and the fjord opened its cool depths as if to make room for their vast reflections. Ralph felt as if he were floating in the midst of the blue infinite space, and, with the strength which this feeling inspired, he tried to face boldly the thought from which he had but a moment ago shrunk as from something hopelessly sad and perplexing.

And in that hour he looked fearlessly into the gulf which separates the New World from the Old. He had hoped to bridge it; but, alas! it can not be bridged.

THE DAMNED THING

Ambrose Bierce

I

By the light of a tallow candle, which had been placed on one end of a rough table, a man was reading something written in a book. It was an old account book, greatly worn; and the writing was not, apparently, very legible, for the man sometimes held the page close to the flame of the candle to get a stronger light upon it. The shadow of the book would then throw into obscurity a half of the room, darkening a number of faces and figures; for besides the reader, eight other men were present. Seven of them sat against the rough log walls, silent and motionless, and, the room being small, not very far from the table. By extending an arm any one of them could have touched the eighth man, who lay on the table, face upward, partly covered by a sheet, his arms at his sides. He was dead.

The man with the book was not reading aloud, and no one spoke; all seemed to be waiting for something to occur; the dead man only was without expectation. From the blank darkness outside came in, through the aperture that served for a window, all the ever unfamiliar noises of night in the wilderness—the long, nameless note of a distant coyote; the stilly pulsing thrill of tireless insects in trees; strange cries of night birds, so different from those of the birds of day; the drone of great blundering beetles, and all that mysterious chorus of small sounds that seem always to have been but half heard when they have suddenly ceased, as if conscious of an indiscretion. But nothing of all this was noted in that company; its members were not overmuch addicted to idle interest in matters of no practical importance; that was obvious in every line of their rugged faces—obvious even in the dim light of the single candle. They were evidently men of the vicinity—farmers and woodmen.

The person reading was a trifle different; one would have said of him that
he was of the world, worldly, albeit there was that in his attire which attested
a certain fellowship with the organisms of his environment. His coat would
hardly have passed muster in San Francisco: his footgear was not of urban
origin, and the hat that lay by him on the floor (he was the only one uncovered) was such that if one had considered it as an article of mere personal
adornment he would have missed its meaning. In countenance the man was
rather prepossessing, with just a hint of sternness; though that he may have
assumed or cultivated, as appropriate to one in authority. For he was a coroner. It was by virtue of his office that he had possession of the book in which
he was reading; it had been found among the dead man's effects—in his cabin,
where the inquest was now taking place.

When the coroner had finished reading he put the book into his breast
pocket. At that moment the door was pushed open and a young man entered.
He, clearly, was not of mountain birth and breeding: he was clad as those
who dwell in cities. His clothing was dusty, however, as from travel. He had,
in fact, been riding hard to attend the inquest.

The coroner nodded; no one else greeted him.

"We have waited for you," said the coroner. "It is necessary to have done
with this business to-night."

The young man smiled. "I am sorry to have kept you," he said. "I went
away, not to evade your summons, but to post to my newspaper an account of
what I suppose I am called back to relate."

The coroner smiled.

"The account that you posted to your newspaper," he said, "differs probably from that which you will give here under oath."

"That," replied the other, rather hotly and with a visible flush, "is as you
choose. I used manifold paper and have a copy of what I sent. It was not
written as news, for it is incredible, but as fiction. It may go as a part of my
testimony under oath."

"But you say it is incredible."

"That is nothing to you, sir, if I also swear that it is true."

The coroner was apparently not greatly affected by the young man's manifest resentment. He was silent for some moments, his eyes upon the floor. The
men about the sides of the cabin talked in whispers, but seldom withdrew
their gaze from the face of the corpse. Presently the coroner lifted his eyes
and said: "We will resume the inquest."

The men removed their hats. The witness was sworn.

"What is your name?" the coroner asked.

"William Harker."

"Age?"

"Twenty-seven."

"You knew the deceased, Hugh Morgan?"

"Yes."

"You were with him when he died?"

"Near him."

"How did that happen—your presence, I mean?"

"I was visiting him at this place to shoot and fish. A part of my purpose, however, was to study him, and his odd, solitary way of life. He seemed a good model for a character in fiction. I sometimes write stories."

"I sometimes read them."

"Thank you."

"Stories in general—not yours."

Some of the jurors laughed. Against a sombre background humor shows high lights. Soldiers in the intervals of battle laugh easily, and a jest in the death chamber conquers by surprise.

"Relate the circumstances of this man's death," said the coroner. "You may use any notes or memoranda that you please."

The witness understood. Pulling a manuscript from his breast pocket he held it near the candle, and turning the leaves until he found the passage that he wanted, began to read.

II

". . . The sun had hardly risen when we left the house. We were looking for quail, each with a shotgun, but we had only one dog. Morgan said that our best ground was beyond a certain ridge that he pointed out, and we crossed it by a trail through the *chaparral*. On the other side was comparatively level ground, thickly covered with wild oats. As we emerged from the *chaparral*, Morgan was but a few yards in advance. Suddenly, we heard, at a little distance to our right, and partly in front, a noise as of some animal thrashing about in the bushes, which we could see were violently agitated.

" 'We've started a deer,' I said. 'I wish we had brought a rifle.'

"Morgan, who had stopped and was intently watching the agitated *chaparral,* said nothing, but had cocked both barrels of his gun, and was holding it in readiness to aim. I thought him a trifle excited, which surprised me, for he had a reputation for exceptional coolness, even in moments of sudden and imminent peril.

" 'O, come!' I said. 'You are not going to fill up a deer with quail-shot, are you?'

"Still he did not reply; but, catching a sight of his face as he turned it slightly toward me, I was struck by the pallor of it. Then I understood that we had serious business on hand, and my first conjecture was that we had 'jumped' a grizzly. I advanced to Morgan's side, cocking my piece as I moved.

"The bushes were now quiet, and the sounds had ceased, but Morgan was as attentive to the place as before.

" 'What is it? What the devil is it?' I asked.

" 'That Damned Thing!' he replied, without turning his head. His voice was husky and unnatural. He trembled visibly.

"I was about to speak further, when I observed the wild oats near the place of the disturbance moving in the most inexplicable way. I can hardly describe it. It seemed as if stirred by a streak of wind, which not only bent it, but pressed it down—crushed it so that it did not rise, and this movement was slowly prolonging itself directly toward us.

"Nothing that I had ever seen had affected me so strangely as this unfamiliar and unaccountable phenomenon, yet I am unable to recall any sense of fear. I remember—and tell it here because, singularly enough, I recollected it then—that once, in looking carelessly out of an open window, I momentarily mistook a small tree close at hand for one of a group of larger trees at a little distance away. It looked the same size as the others, but, being more distinctly and sharply defined in mass and detail, seemed out of harmony with them. It was a mere falsification of the law of aerial perspective, but it startled, almost terrified me. We so rely upon the orderly operation of familiar natural laws that any seeming suspension of them is noted as a menace to our safety, a warning of unthinkable calamity. So now the apparently causeless movement of the herbage, and the slow, undeviating approach of the line of disturbance were distinctly disquieting. My companion appeared actually frightened, and I could hardly credit my senses when I saw him suddenly throw his gun to his shoulders and fire both barrels at the agitated grass! Before the smoke of the discharge had cleared away I heard a loud savage cry —a scream like that of a wild animal—and, flinging his gun upon the ground, Morgan sprang away and ran swiftly from the spot. At the same instant I was thrown violently to the ground by the impact of something unseen in the smoke—some soft, heavy substance that seemed thrown against me with great force.

"Before I could get upon my feet and recover my gun, which seemed to have been struck from my hands, I heard Morgan crying out as if in mortal agony, and mingling with his cries were such hoarse savage sounds as one hears from fighting dogs. Inexpressibly terrified, I struggled to my feet and looked in the direction of Morgan's retreat; and may heaven in mercy spare me from another sight like that! At a distance of less than thirty yards was my friend, down upon one knee, his head thrown back at a frightful angle, hatless, his long hair in disorder and his whole body in violent movement from side to side, backward and forward. His right arm was lifted and seemed to lack the hand—at least, I could see none. The other arm was invisible. At times, as my memory now reports this extraordinary scene, I could discern but a part of his body; it was as if he had been partly blotted out—I can not otherwise express it—then a shifting of his position would bring it all into view again.

"All this must have occurred within a few seconds, yet in that time Morgan assumed all the postures of a determined wrestler vanquished by superior weight and strength. I saw nothing but him, and him not always distinctly.

During the entire incident his shouts and curses were heard, as if through an enveloping uproar of such sounds of rage and fury as I had never heard from the throat of man or brute!

"For a moment only I stood irresolute, then, throwing down my gun, I ran forward to my friend's assistance. I had a vague belief that he was suffering from a fit or some form of convulsion. Before I could reach his side he was down and quiet. All sounds had ceased, but, with a feeling of such terror as even these awful events had not inspired, I now saw the same mysterious movement of the wild oats prolonging itself from the trampled area about the prostrate man toward the edge of a wood. It was only when it had reached the wood that I was able to withdraw my eyes and look at my companion. He was dead."

III

The coroner rose from his seat and stood beside the dead man. Lifting an edge of the sheet he pulled it away, exposing the entire body, altogether naked and showing in the candle light a clay-like yellow. It had, however, broad maculations of bluish-black, obviously caused by extravasated blood from contusions. The chest and sides looked as if they had been beaten with a bludgeon. There were dreadful lacerations; the skin was torn in strips and shreds.

The coroner moved round to the end of the table and undid a silk handkerchief, which had been passed under the chin and knotted on the top of the head. When the handkerchief was drawn away it exposed what had been the throat. Some of the jurors who had risen to get a better view repented their curiosity, and turned away their faces. Witness Harker went to the open window and leaned out across the sill, faint and sick. Dropping the handkerchief upon the dead man's neck, the coroner stepped to an angle of the room, and from a pile of clothing produced one garment after another, each of which he held up a moment for inspection. All were torn, and stiff with blood. The jurors did not make a closer inspection. They seemed rather uninterested. They had, in truth, seen all this before; the only thing that was new to them being Harker's testimony.

"Gentlemen," the coroner said, "we have no more evidence, I think. Your duty has been already explained to you; if there is nothing you wish to ask you may go outside and consider your verdict."

The foreman rose—a tall, bearded man of sixty, coarsely clad.

"I should like to ask one question, Mr. Coroner," he said. "What asylum did this yer last witness escape from?"

"Mr. Harker," said the coroner, gravely and tranquilly, "from what asylum did you last escape?"

Harker flushed crimson again, but said nothing, and the seven jurors rose and solemnly filed out of the cabin.

"If you have done insulting me, sir," said Harker, as soon as he and the officer were left alone with the dead man, "I suppose I am at liberty to go?"

"Yes."

Harker started to leave, but paused, with his hand on the door latch. The habit of his profession was strong in him—stronger than his sense of personal dignity. He turned about and said:

"The book that you have there—I recognize it as Morgan's diary. You seemed greatly interested in it; you read in it while I was testifying. May I see it? The public would like—"

"The book will cut no figure in this matter," replied the official, slipping it into his coat pocket; "all the entries in it were made before the writer's death."

As Harker passed out of the house the jury reentered and stood about the table on which the now covered corpse showed under the sheet with sharp definition. The foreman seated himself near the candle, produced from his breast pocket a pencil and scrap of paper, and wrote rather laboriously the following verdict, which with various degrees of effort all signed:

"We, the jury, do find that the remains come to their death at the hands of a mountain lion, but some of us thinks, all the same, they had fits."

IV

In the diary of the late Hugh Morgan are certain interesting entries having, possibly, a scientific value as suggestions. At the inquest upon his body the book was not put in evidence; possibly the coroner thought it not worth while to confuse the jury. The date of the first of the entries mentioned can not be ascertained; the upper part of the leaf is torn away; the part of the entry remaining is as follows:

". . . would run in a half circle, keeping his head turned always toward the centre and again he would stand still, barking furiously. At last he ran away into the brush as fast as he could go. I thought at first that he had gone mad, but on returning to the house found no other alteration in his manner than what was obviously due to fear of punishment.

"Can a dog see with his nose? Do odors impress some olfactory centre with images of the thing emitting them? . . .

"Sept. 2.—Looking at the stars last night as they rose above the crest of the ridge east of the house, I observed them successively disappear—from left to right. Each was eclipsed but an instant, and only a few at the same time, but along the entire length of the ridge all that were within a degree or two of the crest were blotted out. It was as if something had passed along between me and them; but I could not see it, and the stars were not thick enough to define its outline. Ugh! I don't like this. . . ."

Several weeks' entries are missing, three leaves being torn from the book.

"Sept. 27.—It has been about here again—I find evidences of its presence every day. I watched again all of last night in the same cover, gun in hand, double-charged with buckshot. In the morning the fresh footprints were there, as before. Yet I would have sworn that I did not sleep—indeed, I hardly sleep at all. It is terrible, insupportable! If these amazing experiences are real I shall go mad; if they are fanciful I am mad already.

"Oct. 3.—I shall not go—it shall not drive me away. No, this is *my* house, *my* land. God hates a coward. . . .

"Oct. 5.—I can stand it no longer; I have invited Harker to pass a few weeks with me—he has a level head. I can judge from his manner if he thinks me mad.

"Oct. 7.—I have the solution of the problem; it came to me last night— suddenly, as by revelation. How simple—how terribly simple!

"There are sounds that we can not hear. At either end of the scale are notes that stir no chord of that imperfect instrument, the human ear. They are too high or too grave. I have observed a flock of blackbirds occupying an entire treetop—the tops of several trees—and all in full song. Suddenly—in a moment—at absolutely the same instant—all spring into the air and fly away. How? They could not all see one another—whole treetops intervened. At no point could a leader have been visible to all. There must have been a signal of warning or command, high and shrill above the din, but by me unheard. I have observed, too, the same simultaneous flight when all were silent, among not only blackbirds, but other birds—quail, for example, widely separated by bushes—even on opposite sides of a hill.

"It is known to seamen that a school of whales basking or sporting on the surface of the ocean, miles apart, with the convexity of the earth between them, will sometimes dive at the same instant—all gone out of sight in a moment. The signal has been sounded—too grave for the ear of the sailor at the masthead and his comrades on the deck—who nevertheless feel its vibrations in the ship as the stones of a cathedral are stirred by the bass of the organ.

"As with sounds, so with colors. At each end of the solar spectrum the chemist can detect the presence of what are known as 'actinic' rays. They represent colors—integral colors in the composition of light—which we are unable to discern. The human eye is an imperfect instrument; its range is but a few octaves of the real 'chromatic scale.' I am not mad; there are colors that we can not see.

"And, God help me! the Damned Thing is of such a color!"

THE PHONOGRAPH
AND THE GRAFT

O. Henry

I looked in at the engine-room of the Bloomfield-Cater Mfg. Co. (Ltd.), for the engineer was Kirksy, and there was a golden half-hour between the time he shut down steam and washed up that I coveted. For Kirksy was an improvisatore, and he told stories from the inside outward, finely leaving his spoken words and his theme to adjust themselves as best they might.

I found Kirksy resting, with his pipe lighted, smut-faced and blue overalled.

" 'Tis a fair afternoon," I said, "but bids to be colder."

"Did I ever tell you," began Kirksy honorably, "about the time Henry Horsecollar and me took a phonograph to South America?" and I felt ashamed of my subterfuge, and dropped into the wooden chair he kicked toward me.

"Henry was a quarter-breed, quarter-back Cherokee, educated East in the idioms of football and West in contraband whiskey, and a gentleman, same as you or me. He was easy and romping in his ways; a man about six foot, with a kind of rubber-tire movement. Yes, he was a little man about five foot five, or five foot eleven. He was what you would call a medium tall man of average smallness. Henry had quit college once, and the Muscogee jail three times— once for introducing, and twice for selling, whiskey in the Territories. Henry Horsecollar never let any cigar stores come up and stand behind him. He didn't belong to that tribe of Indians.

"Henry and me met at Texarkana, and figured out this phonograph scheme. He had $360 which came to him out of a land allotment in the reservation. I had run down from Little Rock on account of a distressful

115

scene I had witnessed on the street there. A man stood on a box and passed around some gold watches, screw case, stem-winders, Elgin movement, very elegant. Twenty bucks they cost you over the counter. At three dollars the crowd fought for the tickers. The man happened to find a valise full of them handy, and he passed them out like putting hot biscuits on a plate. The backs were hard to unscrew, but the crowd put its ear to the case, and they ticked mollifying and agreeable. Three of those watches were genuine tickers; but the rest, they were only kickers. Hey? Why, empty cases with one of them horny black bugs that fly around electric lights in 'em. Them bugs kick off minutes and seconds industrious and beautiful. The man I was speaking of cleaned up $288, and went away, because he knew that when it came time to wind watches in Little Rock an entomologist would be needed, and he wasn't one.

"So, as I say, Henry had $360 and I had $288. The phonograph idea was Henry's, but I took to it freely, being fond of machinery of all kinds.

" 'The Latin races,' says Henry, explaining easy in his idioms he learned at college, 'are peculiarly adapted to be victims of the phonograph. They possess the artistic temperament. They yearn for music and color and gayety. They give up wampum to the hand-organ man or the four-legged chicken when they're months behind with the grocery and the breadfruit tree.'

" 'Then,' says I, 'we'll export canned music to the Latins; but I'm mindful of Mr. Julius Caesar's account of 'em where he says, *"Omnia Gallia in tres partes divisa est,"* which is the same as to say, "We will need all of our gall in devising means to tree them parties." I hated to make a show of education, but I was disinclined to be overdone in syntax by a mere Indian, to whom we owe nothing except the land on which the United States is situated.

"We bought a fine phonograph in Texarkana—one of the best make—and half a trunkful of records. We packed up, and took the T. and P. for New Orleans. From that celebrated centre of molasses and disfranchised coon songs we took a steamer for—yes, I think it was South America or Mexico—I am full of inability to divulge the location of it—'tis on the rural delivery route, 'tis colored yellow on the map, and branded with the literature of cigar boxes.

"We landed on a smiling coast at a town they denounced by the name, as near as I can recollect, of Sore-toe-kangaroo. 'Twas a palatable enough place to look at. The houses were clean and white, sticking about among the scenery like hard-boiled eggs served with lettuce. There was a block of skyscraper mountains in the suburbs, and they kept pretty quiet, like they were laying one finger on their lips and watching the town. And the sea was remarking "Sh-sh-sh!" on the beach; and now and then a ripe cocoanut would fall kerblip in the sand, and that was all there was doing. Yes, I judge that town was considerably on the quiet. I judge that after Gabriel quits blowing his horn, and the car starts, with Philadelphia swinging to the last strap, and Pine Gulley, Arkansas, hanging on to the hind rail, Sore-toe-kangaroo will wake up and ask if anybody spoke.

"The captain went ashore with us, and offered to conduct what he seemed to like to call the obsequies. He introduced Henry and me to the United States Consul, and a roan man, the head of the Department of Mercenary and Licentious Dispositions, the way it read upon his sign.

" 'I touch here again a week from to-day,' says the captain.

" 'By that time,' we told him, 'we'll be amassing wealth in the interior towns with our galvanized prima donna and correct imitations of Sousa's band excavating a march from a tin mine.'

" 'Ye'll not,' says the captain. 'Ye'll be hypnotized. Any gentleman in the audience who kindly steps upon the stage and looks this country in the eye will be converted to the hypothesis that he's but a fly in the Elgin creamery. Ye'll be standing knee deep in the surf waiting for me, and your machine for making Hamburger steak out of the hitherto respected art of music will be playing "There's no place like home." '

"Henry skinned a twenty off his roll, and received from the Bureau of Mercenary Dispositions a paper bearing a red seal and a dialect story, and no change.

"Then we got the consul full of red wine, and struck him for a horoscope. He was a thin, youngish kind of man, I should say past fifty, sort of French-Irish in his affections, and puffed up with disconsolation. Yes, he was a flattened kind of a man, in whom drink lay stagnant, inclined to corpulence and misery. Yes, I think he was a kind of Dutchman, being very sad and genial in his ways.

" 'The marvelous invention,' he says, 'entitled the phonograph, has never before invaded these shores. The people have never heard it. They would not believe it if they should. Simple-hearted children of nature, progress has never condemned them to accept the work of a can-opener as an overture, and ragtime might incite them to a bloody revolution. But you can try the experiment. The best chance you have is that the populace may not wake up when you play. There's two ways,' says the consul, 'they may take it. They may become inebriated with attention, like an Atlanta colonel listening to "Marching through Georgia," or they will get excited and transpose the key of the music with an axe and yourselves into a dungeon. In the latter case,' says the consul, 'I'll do my duty by cabling to the State Department, and I'll wrap the Stars and Stripes around you when you come to be shot, and threaten them with the vengeance of the greatest gold export and financial reserve nation on earth. The flag is full of bullet holes now,' says the consul, 'made in that way. Twice before,' says the consul, 'I have cabled our Government for a couple of gunboats to protect American citizens. The first time the Department sent me a pair of gum boots. The other time was when a man named Pease was going to be executed here. They referred that appeal to the Secretary of Agriculture. Let us now disturb the señor behind the bar for a subsequence of the red wine.'

"Thus soliloquized the consul of Sore-toe-kangaroo to me and Henry Horsecollar.

"But, notwithstanding, we hired a room that afternoon in the Calle de los Angeles, the main street that runs along the shore, and put our trunks there. 'Twas a good-sized room, dark and cheerful, but small. 'Twas on a various street, diversified by houses and conservatory plants. The peasantry of the city passed to and fro on the fine pasturage between the sidewalks. 'Twas, for the world, like an opera chorus when the Royal Kafoozlum is about to enter.

"We were rubbing the dust off the machine and getting fixed to start business the next day when a big, fine-looking white man in white clothes stopped at the door and looked in. We extended the invitations, and he walked inside and sized us up. He was chewing a long cigar, and wrinkling his eyes, meditative, like a girl trying to decide which dress to wear to the party.

" 'New York?' he says to me finally.

" 'Originally, and from time to time,' I says, 'Hasn't it rubbed off yet?'

" 'It's simple,' says he, 'when you know how. It's the fit of the vest. They don't cut vests right anywhere else. Coats, maybe, but not vests.'

"The white man looks at Henry Horsecollar and hesitates.

" 'Injun,' says Henry; 'tame Injun.'

" 'Mellinger,' says the man—'Homer P. Mellinger. Boys, you're confiscated. You're babes in the wood without a chaperon or referee, and it's my duty to start you going. I'll knock out the props and launch you proper in the pellucid waters of Sore-toe-kangaroo. You'll have to be christened, and if you'll come with me I'll break a bottle of wine across your bows, according to Hoyle.'

"Well, for two days Homer P. Mellinger did the honors. That man cut ice in Sore-toe-kangaroo. He was it. He was the Royal Kafoozlum. If me and Henry was babes in the wood, he was a Robin Redbreast from the topmost bough. Him and me and Henry Horsecollar locked arms and toted that phonograph around and had wassail and diversions. Everywhere we found doors open we went in and set the machine going, and Mellinger called upon the people to observe the artful music and his lifelong friends, the two Señors Americanos. The opera chorus was agitated with esteem, and followed us from house to house. There was *vino tinto* and *vino blanco* to drink with every tune. The aborigines had acquirements of a pleasant thing in the way of drinks that gums itself to the recollection. They chop off the end of a green cocoanut, and pour in on the liquor of it French brandy and gin. We had them and other things.

"Mine and Henry's money was counterfeit. Everything was on Homer P. Mellinger. That man could find rolls of bills in his clothes where Hermann the Wizard couldn't have conjured out an omelette. He could have founded universities and had enough left to buy the colored vote of his country. Henry and me wondered what his graft was. One evening he told us.

" 'Boys,' says he, 'I've deceived you. Instead of a painted butterfly, I'm the hardest worked man in this country. Ten years ago I landed on its shores, and two years ago on the point of its jaw. Yes, I reckon I can get the decision over this ginger-cake commonwealth at the end of any round I choose. I'll confide in you because you are my countrymen and guests, even if you have committed an assault upon my adopted shores with the worst system of noises ever set to music.

" 'My job is private secretary to the President of this Republic, and my duties are running it. I'm not headlined in the bills, but I'm the mustard in the salad dressing. There isn't a law goes before Congress, there isn't a concession granted, there isn't an import duty levied, but what H. P. Mellinger he cooks and seasons it. In the front office I fill the President's inkstand and search visiting statesmen for dynamite; in the back room I dictate the policy of the government. You'd never guess how I got the pull. It's the only graft of its kind in the world. I'll put you wise. You remember the topliner in the old copy-books—"Honesty is the best policy." That's it. I'm the only honest man in this republic. The government knows it; the people know it; the boodlers know it; the foreign investors know it. I make the government keep its faith. If a man is promised a job he gets it. If outside capital buys a concession they get the goods. I run a monopoly of square dealing here. There's no competition. If Colonel Diogenes were to flash his lantern in this precinct he'd have my address inside of two minutes. There isn't big money in it, but it's a sure thing, and lets a man sleep of nights.'

"Thus Homer P. Mellinger made oration to me and Henry Horsecollar in Sore-toe-kangaroo. And, later, he divested himself of this remark:

" 'Boys, I'm to hold a *soirée* this evening with a gang of leading citizens, and I want your assistance. You bring the musical corn sheller and give the affair the outside appearance of a function. There's important business on hand, but it mustn't show. I can talk to you people. I've been pained for years on account of not having anybody to blow off and brag to. I get homesick sometimes, and I'd swap the entire perquisites of office for just one hour to have a stein and a caviare sandwich somewhere on Thirty-fourth Street, and stand and watch the street cars go by, and smell the peanut roaster at old Giuseppe's fruit stand.'

" 'Yes,' said I, 'there's fine caviare at Billy Renfrow's café, corner of Thirty-fourth and—'

" 'God knows it,' interrupts Mellinger, 'and if you'd told me you knew Billy Renfrow I'd have invented tons of ways of making you happy. Billy was my side kicker in New York. That is a man who never knew what crooked was. Here I am working Honesty for a graft, but that man loses money on it. *Carrambos!* I get sick at times of this country. Everything's rotten. From the Executive down to the coffee pickers, they're plotting to down each other and skin their friends. If a mule driver takes off his hat to an official, that man figures it out that he's a popular idol, and sets his pegs to stir up a revolution and upset the administration. It's one of my little chores as private secretary to smell out these revolutions and affix the kibosh before they break out and scratch the paint off the government property. That's why I'm down here now in this mildewed coast town. The Governor of the district and his crew are plotting to uprise. I've got every one of their names, and they're invited to listen to the phonograph tonight, compliments of H. P. M. That's the way I'll get them in a bunch, and things are on the programme to happen to them.'

"We three were sitting at table in the cantina of the Purified Saints. Mellinger poured out wine, and was looking some worried; I was thinking.

" 'They're a sharp crowd,' he says, kind of fretful. 'They're capitalized by a foreign syndicate after rubber, and they're loaded to the muzzle for bribing. I'm sick,' goes on Mellinger, 'of comic opera. I want to smell East River and wear suspenders again. At times I feel like throwing up my job, but I'm d—n fool enough to be sort of proud of it. "There's Mellinger," they say here, *"Por Dios!* you can't touch him with a million." I'd like to take that record back and show it to Billy Renfrow some day; and that tightens my grip whenever I see a fat thing that I could corral just by winking one eye—and losing my graft. By—! they can't monkey with me. They know it. What money I get I make honest and spend it. Some day I'll make a pile and go back and eat caviare with Billy. Tonight I'll show you how to handle a bunch of corruptionists. I'll show them what Mellinger, private secretary, means when you spell it with the cotton and tissue paper off.'

"Mellinger appears shaky, and breaks his glass against the neck of the bottle.

"I says to myself, 'White man, if I'm not mistaken there's been a bait laid out where the tail of your eye could see it.'

"That night, according to arrangements, me and Henry took the phonograph to a room in a 'dobe house in a dirty side street, where the grass was knee high. 'Twas a long room, lighted with smoky oil lamps. There was plenty of chairs and a table at the back end. We set the phonograph on the table. Mellinger was there, walking up and down disturbed in his predicaments. He chewed cigars and spat 'em out, and he bit the thumb nail of his left hand.

"By and by the invitations to the musicale came sliding in by pairs and threes and spade flushes. Their color was of a diversity, running from a three-days' smoked meerschaum to a patent-leather polish. They were as polite as wax, being devastated with enjoyments to give Señor Mellinger the good evenings. I understood their Spanish talk—I ran a pumping engine two years in a Mexican silver mine, and had it pat—but I never let on.

"Maybe fifty of 'em had come, and was seated, when in slid the king bee, the Governor of the district. Mellinger met him at the door and escorted him to the grand stand. When I saw that Latin man I knew that Mellinger, private secretary, had all the dances on his card taken. That was a big, squashy man the color of a rubber overshoe, and he had an eye like a head waiter's.

"Mellinger explained, fluent, in the Castilian idioms, that his soul was disconcerted with joy at introducing to his respected friends America's greatest invention, the wonder of the age. Henry got the cue and run on an elegant brass-band record and the festivities became initiated. The Governor man had a bit of English under his hat, and when the music was choked off he says:

" 'Ver-r-ree fine. Gr-r-r-r-racias, the American gentleemen, the so es-plendeed moosic as to playee.'

"The table was a long one, and Henry and me sat at the end of it next the wall. The Governor sat at the other end. Homer P. Mellinger stood at the side of it. I was just wondering how Mellinger was going to handle his crowd, when the home talent suddenly opened the services.

"That Governor man was suitable for uprisings and policies. I judge he was a ready kind of man, who took his own time. Yes, he was full of attentions and immediateness. He leaned his hands on the table and imposed his face toward the secretary man.

" 'Do the American Señors understand Spanish?' he asks in his native accents.

" 'They do not,' says Mellinger.

" 'Then, listen,' goes on the Latin man, prompt. 'The musics are of suffi-cient prettiness, but not of necessity. Let us speak of business. I well know why we are here, since I observe my compatriots. You had a whisper yester-day, Señor Mellinger, of our proposals. To-night we will speak out. We know that you stand in the President's favor, and we know your influence. The government will be changed. We know the worth of your services. We esteem your friendship and aid so much that'—Mellinger raises his hand, but the Governor man bottles him up. 'Do not speak until I have done.'

"The Governor man then draws a package wrapped in paper from his pocket, and lays it on the table by Mellinger's hand.

" 'In that you will find one hundred thousand dollars in money of your country. You can do nothing against us, but you can be worth that for us. Go back to the capital and obey our instructions. Take that money now. We trust you. You will find with it a paper giving in detail the work you will be expected to do for us. Do not have the unwiseness to refuse.'

"The Governor man paused, with his eyes fixed on Mellinger, full of ex-pressions and observances. I looked at Mellinger, and was glad Billy Renfrow couldn't see him then. The sweat was popping out on his forehead, and he stood dumb, tapping the little package with the ends of his fingers. The Colorado maduro gang was after his graft. He had only to change his politics, and stuff six figures in his inside pocket.

"Henry whispers to me and wants the pause in the programme interpreted. I whisper back: 'H. P. is up against a bribe, senator's size, and the coons have got him going.' I saw Mellinger's hand moving closer to the package. 'He's weakening,' I whispered to Henry. 'We'll remind him,' says Henry, 'of the peanut roaster on Thirty-fourth Street, New York.'

"Henry stooped and got a record from the basketful we'd brought, slid it in the phonograph, and started her off. It was a cornet solo, very neat and beautiful, and the name of it was 'Home, Sweet Home.' Not one of them fifty odd men in the room moved while it was playing, and the Governor man kept his eyes steady on Mellinger. I saw Mellinger's head go up little by little, and his hand came creeping away from the package. Not until the last note sounded did anybody stir. And then Homer P. Mellinger takes up the bundle of boodle and slams it in the Governor man's face.

" 'That's my answer,' says Mellinger, private secretary, 'and there'll be another in the morning. I have proofs of conspiracy against every man of you. The show is over, gentlemen.'

" 'There's one more act,' puts in the Governor man. 'You are a servant, I believe, employed by the President to copy letters and answer raps at the door. I am Governor here. Señors, I call upon you in the name of the cause to seize this man.'

"That brindled gang of conspirators shoved back their chairs and advanced in force. I could see where Mellinger had made a mistake in massing his enemy so as to make a grand-stand play. I think he made another one, too; but we can pass that, Mellinger's idea of a graft and mine being different, according to estimations and points of view.

"There was only one window and door in that room, and they were in the front end. Here was fifty odd Latin men coming in a bunch to obstruct the legislation of Mellinger. You may say there were three of us, for me and Henry, simultaneous, declared New York City and the Cherokee Nation in sympathy with the weaker party.

"Then it was that Henry Horsecollar rose to a point of disorder and intervened, showing, admirable, the advantages of education as applied to the American Indian's natural intellect and native refinement. He stood up and smoothed back his hair on each side with his hands as you have seen little girls do when they play.

" 'Get behind me, both of you,' says Henry.

" 'What is it to be?' I asked.

" 'I'm going to buck centre,' says Henry, in his football idioms. 'There isn't a tackle in the lot of them. Keep close behind me and rush the game.'

"That cultured Red Man exhaled an arrangement of sounds with his mouth that caused the Latin aggregation to pause, with thoughtfulness and hesitations. The matter of his proclamation seemed to be a co-operation of the Cherokee college yell with the Carlisle war-whoop. He went at the chocolate team like the flip of a little boy's nigger shooter. His right elbow laid out the Governor man on the gridiron, and he made a lane the length of the crowd that a woman could have carried a step-ladder through without striking anything. All me and Mellinger had to do was to follow.

"In five minutes we were out of that street and at the military headquarters, where Mellinger had things his own way.

"The next day Mellinger takes me and Henry to one side and begins to shed tens and twenties.

" 'I want to buy that phonograph,' he says. 'I liked that last tune it played. Now, you boys better go back home, for they'll give you trouble here before I get the screws put on 'em. If you happen to ever see Billy Renfrow again, tell him I'm coming back to New York as soon as I can make a stake—honest.'

" 'This is more money,' says I, 'than the machine is worth.'

" ' 'Tis government expense money,' says Mellinger, 'and the government's getting the tune grinder cheap.'

"Henry and I knew that pretty well, but we never let Homer P. Mellinger know that we had seen how near he came to losing his graft.

"We laid low until the day the steamer came back. When we saw the captain's boat on the beach me and Henry went down and stood in the edge of the water. The captain grinned when he saw us.

" 'I told you you'd be waiting,' he says. 'Where's the Hamburger machine?'

" 'It stays behind,' I says, 'to play "Home, Sweet Home." '

" 'I told you so,' says the captain again. 'Climb in the boat.'

" 'And that,' said Kirksy, 'is the way me and Henry Horsecollar introduced the phonograph in that Latin country along about the vicinity of South America.'

"To Make a Hoosier Holiday"

George Ade

If you will take a map of the State of Indiana and follow with your pencil one of the many railway lines radiating from Indianapolis, you will find, if you are extremely diligent in your search, a black speck marked "Musselwhite." It is not an asterisk, meaning a county seat—simply a speck on the enameled surface. Furthermore, it is one of many specks. A map which shows all of the towns of the Musselwhite kind looks like a platter of caviare—a mere scramble of dark globules, each the same as the others.

As a matter of fact, Musselwhite seemed one of a thousand to the sleepy travelers in the parlor cars. Lying back on their upholstered griddles, slowly baking to a crisp, they would be aroused by a succession of jolts and grinds and would look out with torpid interest at a brindle-colored "depot," a few brick stores ornately faced with cornices of galvanized iron, a straggling row of frame houses, prigged out with scallops and protuberant bay windows, a few alert horses at the hitch-rack and a few somnolent Americans punctuated along the platform. Then the train would laboriously push this panorama into the background and whisk away into the cornfields, and the travelers would never again think of Musselwhite. Certainly they would never think of it as a hotbed of politics, an arena of social strivings, a Mecca for the remote farmhand and a headquarters for religious effort. Yet Musselwhite was all of these —and more.

The town had two wings of the Protestant faith, but they did not always flap in unison. They were united in the single belief that the Catholic congregation at the other end of town was intent on some dark plan to capture the government and blow up the public school system.

The Zion Methodist Church stood across the street from the Campbellite structure. Each had a high wooden steeple and a clangorous bell. Zion Church had an undersized pipe-organ which had to be pumped from behind. The Campbellites had merely an overgrown cottage organ, but they put in a cornet to help out—this in the face of a protest from the conservative element that true religion did not harmonize with any "brass-band trimmings."

In the Campbellite Church the rostrum was movable, and underneath was a baptismal pool wherein the newly converted were publicly immersed. Whenever there was to be a Sunday night "baptizing" at the Campbellite Church, the attendance was overflowing. The Methodists could offer no ceremony to compare with that of a bold descent into the cold plunge, but every winter they had a "protracted meeting" which kept the church lighted and warmed for seven nights in the week. During this "revival" period the Campbellites were in partial eclipse.

It must not be assumed that there was any petty rivalry between the two flocks. It was the strong and healthy competition between two laborers in the vineyard, each striving to pick the larger bunch of grapes. If the Zion Church gave a mush-and-milk sociable, it was only natural that the Campbellites, in their endeavor to retain a hold on the friendly sympathies of Musselwhite, should almost immediately make announcement of a rummage party or an old people's concert. The Campbellites had their Sunday-school in the morning, preceding the regular service, and the Methodists had theirs in the afternoon. The attendance records and missionary collections were zealously compared. Unusual inducements were offered to the growing youth of Musselwhite to memorize the golden text and fight manfully for the large blue card which was the reward for unbroken attendance. In Musselwhite, as in many other communities, there were parents who believed in permitting the children to attend two religious services every Sunday, thereby establishing a good general average for the family, even if the parents remained at home to read the Sunday papers. The children found no fault with this arrangement. The morning Sunday-school was a sort of full-dress rehearsal for the afternoon service, to which the children flocked in confident possession of those hidden meanings of the Scripture which can always be elucidated by a hardware merchant who wears dark clothes once a week.

At Christmas time the "scholars" found themselves in a quandary. Each church had exercises Christmas Eve. A child can not be in two places at the same time, no matter how busy his effort or how earnest his intention. And so it came about that the congregation offering the more spectacular entertainment and the larger portion of mixed candy drew the majority of the lambkins. The rivalry between the Methodists and the Campbellites touched perihelion on Christmas Eve. An ordinary Christmas tree studded with tapers, festooned with popcorn, and heavy with presents no longer satisfied the junior population, for it had been pampered and fed upon novelty. The children demanded a low-comedy Santa Claus in a fur coat. They had to be given star parts in cantatas, or else be permitted to speak "pieces" in costume. One year the Campbellites varied the programme by having a scenic chimney-corner erected back of the pulpit. There was an open fireplace glowing with imitation coals. In front of the fireplace was a row of stockings, some of which were of most mirth-provoking length and capacity, for the sense of humor was rampant in Musselwhite. A murmur of impatient and restless curiosity rather interfered with the recitations and responsive readings which opened the programme. It rose to a tiptoe of eager anticipation when Mr. Eugene Robinson, the Superintendent of the Sunday-school, arose and, after a few felicitous remarks, which called forth hysterical laughter, read a telegram from Kriss Kringle saying that he would arrive in Musselwhite at 8:30 sharp. Almost immediately there was heard the jingle of sleighbells. The older and more sophisticated boys identified the tone as coming from a strand of bells owned by Henry Boardman, who kept the livery barn, but the minds of the younger brood were singularly free from all doubt and questioning. A distinct "Whoa!" was heard, and then the Saint, swaddled in furs and with a most prodigious growth of cotton whiskers, came right out through the fireplace with his pack on his back and asked in a loud voice, "Is this the town of Musselwhite?" His shaggy coat was sifted with snow, in spite of the fact that the night was rather warm and muggy, and his whole appearance tallied so accurately with the pictures in the books that the illusion was most convincing until "Tad" Saulsbury, aged twelve, piped in a loud voice: "I know who it is. It's Jake Francis."

His mother moved swiftly down the aisle and "churned" him into silence, after which the distribution of presents proceeded with triumphant hilarity.

It was generally conceded that the Campbellite chimney-corner entertainment rather laid over and topped and threw into the shade any other Christmas doings that had been witnessed in Musselwhite. That is why the Methodists were spurred to unusual effort one year later, and that is why "Doc" Silverton, Sam Woodson, and Orville Hufty, as a special committee on arrangements, met in the doctor's office one evening in November to devise ways and means.

"They're goin' to give another chimney-corner show," said "Doc" Silverton. "We've got to do something to offset it. I claim that the Christmas tree is played out. Since they've started shippin' in these evergreen trees from Chicago, a good many people have their own trees right at home. We can't very well take up the chimney-corner idee. It's too much like trailin' along behind the Campbellites and takin' their dust."

"We've got to give 'em something new and different," said Orville Hufty. "I sent and got a book that's supposed to tell how to get up shows for Christmas, but it's all about singin' songs and speakin' pieces, and we know by experience that such things don't ketch the crowd here in Musselwhite."

"I've been thinkin'," said Sam Woodson, very slowly, "that we might do this: Go to the Campbellites and segest that we take turn about in givin' exhibitions. That is, if they hold off this year, we'll give them a clear field next year."

"Not much!" exclaimed "Doc" Silverton, with great decision. "That'd look like a clean back-down. Don't give 'em anything to crow about. Let's beat 'em at their own game. We can do it if you'll help me on a little scheme that I've been layin' awake nights and thinkin' about. Don't laugh when I tell you what it is. It's nothin' more or less than a weddin'."

"You mean to have somebody get married on Christmas Eve?" asked Mr. Hufty, looking at him coldly.

"That's it exactly," replied "Doc" with a grin of enthusiasm.

"What's gettin' married got to do with Christmas?" asked Sam Woodson.

"People get married every day," added Mr. Hufty.

"Not the people that I'm thinkin' about," said "Doc," leaning back and looking at them serenely. "Can you imagine what kind of a crowd we'll have in that church if we advertise that old 'Baz' Leonard is goin' to get married to Miss Wheatley?"

The other two committeemen gazed at "Doc" in sheer amazement, stunned by the audacity of his suggestion. "Baz" Leonard and Miss Wheatley! It took several moments for them to grasp the Napoleonic immensity of the proposition.

"Well, I'll be jiggered!" said Mr. Hufty. "How did you come to think of anything like that?"

"Is 'Baz' goin' to marry her?" asked Sam Woodson.

"He is," replied "Doc," "but he don't know it—yet. I'm bankin' on the fact that he won't overlook a chance to show off in public, and that Miss Wheatley is about due to get married to some one."

"I think you'd be doin' her a favor if you picked out somebody besides 'Baz,' " suggested the cold and unresponsive Woodson.

" 'Baz' is the man," said "Doc" firmly. "If we've got a public character in this town it's 'Baz' Leonard. If there's a woman in town that's supposed to be out of the marryin' class, it's Miss Wheatley. Her gettin' married to any one would be about the biggest piece of news you could spring on Musselwhite. But gettin' married to 'Baz' Leonard! Say! They won't have a handful of people at their chimney-corner show. And you can bet they'll never keep Jake Francis over there to play Santa Claus. Any time that old 'Baz' gets married again, Jake'll want to be there to see it."

"I don't see how you're goin' to work it in on a Christmas Eve exhibition," said Woodson, but even as he spoke he chuckled reflectively, and it was evident that the beautiful possibilities of the plan were beginning to ramify his understanding.

"Simplest thing in the world," said "Doc." "We announce that we're goin' to give Miss Wheatley a Christmas present."

"You'd better postpone the show till April 1," suggested Mr. Hufty, and then all three committeemen leaned back in their chairs, exchanged glances, and roared with laughter. It was evident that no vote would be necessary.

"I've thought it all out," continued "Doc." "We can have the regular entertainment, then the distribution of presents. We'll have Santy Claus bring in the marriage license and present it to 'Baz.' Then we'll lead the happy couple to the altar, and after Brother King has done a scientific job of splicin', we'll give them their combination Christmas and weddin' presents. The different Sunday-school classes can chip in and buy presents for them. They'll be glad to do it."

"It sounds all right, but can we talk 'em into it?" asked Mr. Hufty. " 'Baz' has fooled around her a little, but I never thought he wanted to marry her."

"I'll guarantee to have him on hand when the time comes," said "Doc" confidently. "I want you two fellows to have the women go after Miss Wheatley. We must take it for granted that they're already engaged. Have the women go over and congratulate her, and then convince her that if she has a church weddin' she'll get a raft of presents. It's the third and last call with her, and I don't think we'll have to use blinkers or a curb bit."

And so, next day, there began the strangest campaign that ever Cupid waged by Proxy. Rumor—strong, persistent, undeniable—had it that "Baz" Leonard and Miss Beulah Wheatley were to become as one, indivisible. "United in the holy bonds of wedlock" is the way it was put by the editor of the "Courier."

Unless you, indulgent reader, have lived in a Musselwhite, you can not fully comprehend how convulsing was the excitement that laid hold upon the whole township when the story went jumping from house to house, across farm lots, over ditches, through the deep woods, until it was gleefully discussed around the lamplight as far away as Antioch and Burdett's Grove. For "Baz" Leonard was a man who had posed in the fierce light of publicity for many years. In Rome he would have been a senator. In Musselwhite he was a constable. As a war veteran, as a member of the Volunteer Fire Department, as a confirmed juror, as custodian of a bass drum, as judge of elections, as something-or-other, he contrived to be where the common run of mortals had to look at him and rather admire his self-possession and dignified bearing. To be in the foreground of activities, to be in some way connected with every event which partook of the ceremonial, this was the one gnawing ambition of Ballantyne Leonard. His front name, by some system of abbreviation known only to small towns, had been condensed to "Baz." His wife had died soon after the war. He lived in a small frame house, more thoroughly covered by mortgage than by paint. A pension and the occasional fee coming to a constable provided him with the essentials of life—tobacco and one or two other items less important. As a factor in the business life of Musselwhite he was a comparative cipher, but at public functions he shone. Take it on the Fourth of July. On a borrowed horse, with a tri-colored sash once around his waist and once over the shoulder, he led the parade. On election nights he read the returns. The job of pumping the organ in the Zion Church he refused because he could not perform his duties in view of the congregation. Every winter, when the Methodist revival had stirred the town to a high-strung fervor, he walked up the main aisle and joined the church, becoming for a few nights the nucleus of a shouting jubilation. Every summer he attended a soldiers' reunion, drank to the memory of blood-stained battlefields, and was let out of the church as a backslider. If a traveling magician or hypnotist requested "some one from the audience to kindly step upon the stage," "Baz" was always the first to respond. The happiness of his life came from now and then being on a pedestal. "Doc" Silverton knew what he was talking about when he said that on Christmas Eve he would have his man on hand, ready to be married.

As for Miss Beulah Wheatley, she was a small, prim, and exceedingly antique maiden lady who looked out at the world through a pair of bull's-eye spectacles. Those whose memories extended back far enough testified that, as a girl, she had been "not bad lookin'," and they could account for her having been marooned all these years only on the cruel theory that some marry and some don't. Miss Wheatley was a pocket edition of Joan of Arc when it came to church activities, her efforts being concentrated on foreign missionary work. She was a landmark of Zion. "Doc" Silverton once calculated that she had embroidered twenty-seven pairs of slippers for the coming and going preachers. It was known that she owned the house in which she lived, and it was vaguely rumored that she had money invested. In Musselwhite, flitting about like a lonesome and unmated bird among the satisfied and well-fed domestic pigeons, she was a pathetic joke. People respected her because she was pious and a good housekeeper, but likewise they poked fun at her, for the "old maid" is always a fair target.

No two people in Musselwhite were more surprised by the announced engagement than Mr. "Baz" Leonard and Miss Beulah Wheatley. "Baz" met the first congratulations with good nature, his only sensation being one of gratification that the public should be interested in his private affairs. Later on, when his denials were pooh-poohed into silence, and he was given positive proof that Miss Wheatley had been up to Babcock's store, picking out dress goods, he became alarmed. Even this alarm was tempered by the joy of being the most-talked-about man in Musselwhite, and "Doc" Silverton never lost faith. At the first opportunity he called "Baz" into the office and gave him a long and violent handshaking. It's somethin' you ought to have done years ago, "Baz," he said, leading his visitor over to an operating chair. "She's a fine woman, and she's got a little property, and I don't see that you could do better."

"I'd like to know how them reports got started," said "Baz." "I ain't seen Miss Wheatley for goin' on six weeks, and when I did see her we didn't talk about nothin' except them Plymouth Rock chickens she bought from—"

"That's all right, 'Baz,' " said "Doc," patting him on the shoulder. "You kept it quiet as long as you could, but Miss Wheatley's a woman, you know, and she was so proud of gettin' you away from all these widows around town, you can't blame her for braggin' a little. Now that it's all settled, we're going to give you the biggest weddin' that was ever seen in this neck of the woods."

Thereupon he outlined the plans for Christmas Eve, minimizing the fact that Miss Wheatley would be a party to the exercises, and enlarging upon the glory that would come to the groom. He told how the organ would thunder, how the church would be jammed, how the infant class would strew flowers in the pathway of the hero, and "Baz," listening, was lost.

In the meantime Mrs. Woodson and Mrs. Hufty had been working on Miss Wheatley. They did not falsify to her, but they led her to believe that Mr. Leonard had said many things that were really said by "Doc" Silverton, and they did it in such a way that the feminine conscience did not suffer a single pang. Miss Wheatley gathered, from the nature of their conversation, that they were the emissaries of the would-be groom. Certainly their assurances were emphatic, and she, as if in a dream, permitted herself to be measured for a wedding gown.

And so Miss Wheatley and "Baz" Leonard were engaged, and neither had spoken to the other a word that was even remotely suggestive of matrimony. "Doc" Silverton, past-master at politics and all manner of deep scheming, "clinched" the matter by giving a supper at the Commercial Hotel. "Baz" was present and Miss Wheatley was present and many witnesses were present. When the pie had been served, "Doc" arose and made a speech of congratulation to the couple. He referred to the undying splendor of Mr. Leonard's war record, his long and honorable career as a public servant, and the high esteem in which he was held by the beautiful little city of Musselwhite. It was meet and proper, said "Doc," that such a man should choose for his companion and helpmate an estimable lady whose light had never been hidden under a bushel, etc.

"Baz" and Miss Wheatley looked at each other across the celery tops, bewildered, but lacking the moral courage to arise and protest. They were being carried along on a wave of popular enthusiasm. It seemed exhilarating to Miss Wheatley. "Baz" wore an air of melancholy doubt, especially after the supper at the Commercial Hotel, when he had been given the privilege of taking a long, hard, and critical look at Miss Wheatley in her best clothes.

Word came to the committee that the groom was weakening. "Baz" had been meditating and gazing upon two pictures. One was pleasant—he at the church with a yellow rose in his coat and hundreds of people looking at him. The other was a long-drawn vista of straight and narrow matrimony under the supervision of a small but determined woman.

"I guess we'll have to call it off," he said, as he met "Doc" Silverton in front of the post-office, and he looked across the street in a guilty and shame-faced manner.

"You can't call it off," said "Doc." "You've announced your engagement in the presence of witnesses and we've fixed up the whole programme."

"I didn't announce it—you did."

"Well, you were present, and silence gives consent. If you try to back out now she can sue you for breach of promise."

"What'll she git?"

"I'm surprised at you, 'Baz'—after all that your friends have done for you in this thing."

"Baz" studied a display of Christmas goods in a window and rubbed his chin reflectively. Finally he said, "I ain't got any clothes that's fit to wear."

"Doc" hesitated. The committee had not undertaken to outfit the bridegroom. But he knew that the failure of his pet enterprise would fill the town with Campbellite hilarity, so he said, "We'll see that you get a new suit."

Christmas Eve came. It found Musselwhite keyed up to the highest pitch of glad expectation. Every aspiring comic in the town had exhausted his stock of inventive humor in thinking up presents to give to "Baz" and Miss Wheatley. From cardboard mottoes of satirical character to a nickel-plated kitchen stove, the gifts, large and small, were waiting behind the pulpit of the Zion Church. As many people as could elbow their way into the seats and aisles and corners of the church were waiting. Miss Wheatley, all in white, with smelling salts, also six married women to give her courage, waited in the pastor's study. And down the street, in a small frame house, a grizzled veteran, who had faced death on many fields of carnage, lay back on his bed and told a despairing committee that he was ill, even to the point of death, and that there could be no wedding. He had put on the new black suit. The black bow tie had been carefully balanced by Sam Woodson. "Baz" with the dull horror of impending calamity numbing his resolution, had even combed his hair, and then, when Mr. Hufty looked at his watch and said, "It's about time to start," "Baz" had been stricken.

"Where does it seem to hurt you?" asked Sam Woodson.

"All over," said "Baz," looking steadfastly at the ceiling. "I'm as weak as a kitten."

"Your pulse is all right," said "Doc" Silverton, "and you've got a good color. Was Freeman Wheatley over to see you to-day?"

"Baz" rolled over and looked at the wall, and then answered hesitatingly, "Yes, I seen him for a little while."

"What did he say to you?"

"He said she didn't have as much property as most people think, and that no livin' man could get along with her."

"I thought you was slick enough to see through Freeman Wheatley," said Mr. Hufty. "He wants to sidetrack this thing so he'll come into her property."

"This is no time for foolin'," said "Doc" Silverton, arising and rolling up his sleeves. "There's nothin' the matter with 'Baz' except he's a little overheated by the pleasure of this gladsome occasion. I'll bleed him and cool him off a little and he'll be all O.K."

Saying which he produced a pocket surgical case and took out a long, glittering knife.

"Don't you go to cuttin' into me," said "Baz," sitting up in the bed.

"Then you quit this tomfoolin' and come along with us," said "Doc" sternly. "We ain't got a minute to spare."

"Baz" thereupon showed immediate improvement. With a deep sigh he stood up and they bundled him into his overcoat.

The moonlit street was quite deserted. It seemed that every one in town was waiting at the church. "Doc" Silverton walked ahead with the silent victim. Behind, Mr. Hufty and Sam Woodson executed quiet dance steps in the snow, indicative of their joy.

In front of the Gridley house "Baz" stopped. "I need a drink of water," he said. "I think it'd brace me up."

"You can get one at the church," said "Doc."

"I'd rather step in to the Gridley well here. It's the best water in town."

The committee waited at the front gate. "Baz" disappeared around the corner of the house and they heard the dry clanking of the iron pump and the splatter of water, and then there was silence and a pause, but no "Baz" appeared.

"Mebbe he's slipped out the back way," suggested Mr. Hufty in a frightened whisper, and the committee ran for the pump. The Gridley back yard lay quiet in the moonlight and there was neither sound nor sight of bridegroom.

"He couldn't get away so soon," said "Doc." "I don't see any tracks in the snow."

"D'you s'pose—" began Sam Woodson, looking upward, and then he pointed to where Mr. "Baz" Leonard sat in the high crotch of a cherry tree.

"This is a put-up job," said Mr. Leonard. "I'm just gettin' on to it."

" 'Baz,' you're actin' like a child," began Mr. Hufty. "Come on, now; they're waitin' for you."

"Let him stay up there and freeze," said "Doc." "I'm done with him. I didn't think an old soldier would be afraid to face a crowd of people."

"I ain't afraid," said "Baz," shifting his position. "I've had the cards stacked on me, that's all."

"Go over to the church, Sam," said "Doc" Silverton, after an awkward pause. "Tell the whole crowd to come over here and take a look at the bridegroom that's gone to roost like a chicken." Sam started.

"Don't you bring no crowd here," shouted "Baz" as he began to descend. "This is the lowest trick that was ever put up on a human bein'."

Thus ended his resistance. They led him like a lamb to the slaughter.

People in Musselwhite said it was the making of "Baz" Leonard. For years after that he walked a chalk mark and his habits seemed to improve, for he was afraid to attend a soldiers' reunion. He should have been happy, for he lived in a cottage that was spick and span, and had a capable woman to tell him what to do at every turn. And yet there were times when, at Sunday morning services, he would look across at "Doc" Silverton with a reproachful light in his eyes, as if to say, "You did this to me."

THE LOTUS EATERS

Virginia Tracy

And leaves me to starve," said Estella, cutting off a leg of the chicken and throwing it to the nearest dog. "Leaves me to starve in the gutter, and leaves Regina, his own flesh and blood—look at that child, Kate, look at her! What sort of a brute could desert a child like that? Was her mother's comfort, yes, she was!—leaves Regina without a rag to her back." She absent-mindedly put a piece of chicken into her mouth, and leaned her elbows on the table.

"I really don't know what we shall do about the rent," said Mrs. Donnelly. "When he came for it this morning he told Barbara he'd be back this afternoon, and it's a hot day for anybody to be out, let alone a fat fellow like him. You can't put off the landlord himself like you can an agent, anyway. I could pay ten dollars on account next Saturday night. If he won't take that, or your alimony doesn't come, I don't know what'll become of us."

"I'm sure I don't know either," said Estella. "It seems such a nuisance to move. Speak for it, then?"—"Woof! Woof!" said Dooley, the fatter of the Scotch terriers.—"I thought we were going to be so happy here, too, when we first came. He seemed such a nice, unassuming sort of man."

Tony, who was washing the household linen in the kitchen, put his head through the doorway. It was a lordly little black head, and belonged to a young fellow of a slender middle height, motions extraordinarily light and free, and blue, humorous, inquisitive, confidential eyes. Said he: "I beg your pardon, Estella, but the big dishpan—has it gone to heaven?"

"It's out on the fire-escape," replied Estella, "with gasoline in it. I put all the old gloves I could find into gasoline this morning, so that if any of us should happen to get an engagement, they'd have clean gloves, anyway."

Tony withdrew. He had not looked at Estella, but at Barbara, the Beauty, who sat in the window-sill, and who continued to look neither at him nor at

135

Estella, nor at the riot of the dogs and the chicken-bones and Regina upon the uncarpeted floor, but across the shining roof-tops to the Palisades.

The mistress of this Harlem flat was Mrs. Estella Baker. Mr. Baker was divorced. He was a prosperous person, and paid a considerable alimony, with which he was not always sufficiently prompt. With Mrs. Baker lived her infant daughter, Regina Rosalys, and her younger sister, Barbara Floyd. Also she had as summer boarders Mr. Anthony Regnault, a young actor who seldom happened to be out of work, Mr. Fred Donnelly, not much older, who seldom happened to be in it, and Mrs. Kate Donnelly, an elderly typewriter, who had married a brother Donnelly, deceased. All the boarders paid far more than their board, when they had it, and nothing at all when they had not. At the present moment, they had been some time through lunch without having as yet cleared away its remains, and Estella and Mrs. Donnelly, whose employer was away on his own vacation, had been regaling the company with accounts of the Russian coronation, which they read from the newspapers that strewed the room. Fred Donnelly, who was busy pinning the edge of his tie over a spot he had just discovered on his shirt-front, gloomily commented upon Estella's last remark: "I guess it'll be a long enough day before any of us get an engagement!"

"You forget Tony!" said his sister-in-law.

"I ain't ever let to," Fred responded with some savagery. "I—can't you stop gorging on those papers a minute? They're two months old!"

"That makes 'em all the lovelier," replied Estella. "Tony threw them off the kitchen shelf this morning, and I felt so good to read it all over again. You feel sure, then, that it's all true."

"Tony's generous with his old newspapers. That's because he's signed for a job. But he don't begin till November. November—Lord! you can't believe there's ever going to be such a month."

"Oh, we may all be working by then," cried Estella, in her voice of tragic fire. "You can't tell. You don't suppose we're going to go on like this, do you?"

"Not if we don't pay the rent, we ain't," said Fred. "We'll have fifteen dollars the week after next, Barbara and me, if we pose for those kinetoscope things. But we owe all that now, in little bills."

"That reminds me, Tony," Estella called, "I wish you could get both the tablecloths ironed by to-night," 'cause you can't do it to-morrow. No; they're going to shut the gas off to-night; we had a notice from 'em yesterday."

"Well, this fellow was just right," declared Mrs. Donnelly, glaring up from her newspaper; "this one that refused to kiss the Czarina's hand. It's a nasty, silly thing to do. They'll never catch me doing it."

"Nor me, I'm afraid," said Tony, reappearing with a bucket that brimmed wet tablecloths. He paused for a moment in the doorway, and leaned there, exceedingly comfortable and cool. Indeed, on this mid-summer afternoon, when the unshaded dining-room appeared altogether huddled and tousled and hot, there was in the look of this very competent amateur laundryman something so tranquil, so airy and sylvan, that it might have suggested a beneficent gentleman-dryad but for the absurd great pipe which was hanging out of his mouth. "I'll take these up to the roof now, Estella; I've just hung out the smaller pieces. We can't tell but that later Barbara'll help me take them down. But I do hope, Estella, that the next flat we appropriate will have a coal range. If we are to have no fire to iron with to-morrow, how shall we cook?"

"I suppose we'll have to go out to our meals. I've got my wedding-ring yet. He can force me to part with that, Tommy Baker can, but he can't force me to let our child starve."

"That must be very disenchanting for Tommy." Tony answered. "But I think I'll leap out with a chair or two before it comes to our eating up your wedding-ring, Estella."

Regina Rosalys, who was at that moment recuperating from her wrestling matches with the dogs, said suddenly: "Anny Bobs gah go ring."

"No, no, darling. Poor Auntie Barbara hasn't got any ring at all. You lost Auntie Barbara's little blue ring down the stationary washstand, don't you remember?"

"No, no, Anny Bobs gah go ring, big go ring"; Regina's fat little hands formed an oblong about the size of cucumber. "Big," she persisted, nodding.

"She means that Indian bracelet," said Estella. Tony looked anxiously and a little fearfully at Barbara, and forgot to joke. At that moment the doorbell rang. Tony leaned back into the kitchen and pressed the little electric button which opened the street door.

"Oh!" cried Estella, "that's the expressman with my money now." She rose and ran into the hall.

There was a waiting silence. Tony continued to lean in the doorway and look at the girl in the window-seat. She had gray eyes of a miraculous, deep clearness, but she kept these turned away in a far-off quiet, profound enough to strike cold upon a suitor's heart. Tony had to content himself with the faint bright color in the oval of her cheek; the pale rose of her faded and shrunken cotton blouse stopped in a little drawn circle at her throat; the throat itself was very white and regal-looking under the piled fairness of Barbara's brown hair. One hand dropped, motionless, against her old gray skirt, and Tony smiled to it wistfully. It was a modest smile, under a trick of audacity. Tony was three-and-twenty, and all women had done their best to spoil him, except Barbara, who had remained silent the summer through before his love. By the community before which so much of it had, perforce, to be carried on, the love-making was encouragingly ignored, but the community was beginning to get restless, because from the lady it received no confidence. The summer was sunning itself away, and still Barbara rested, whether or not to be wooed, passive, idle, enigmatic, lovely; and still prayerfully, and with deft derision, Tony continued publicly to woo her. Now, though he could not catch her glance, his eyes spoke declarations twenty times a minute, and formally proposed to her. They besought, commanded, laughed at her, adored her. Suddenly, when there seemed least hope, she turned round and looked at him. It was a very steadfast, searching look, and Tony tingled and rejoiced to meet it. He lifted his head happily, with a singular pride, and at the little motion the girl put her hand sharply to her throat and turned away.

"He's a long time coming upstairs," said Fred.

At that moment Estella ran back into the hall of the flat and closed the door with the effect of a subdued cyclone.

"It's not the expressman!" she called, in a shrieking whisper. "The top of his head looks like the milkman, and his bill's due." Tony laughed aloud.

"Tell him to come again," suggested Kate Donnelly, still fortified by immersion in the coronation glories.

"Told him that last time," said Fred.

"Oh, well, maybe he wasn't coming here," said Estella, listening a moment, and continued, "maybe it was only the janitor, after all. Once before the alimony didn't come, and then it turned out the expressman had brought it two or three times, only the downstairs bell didn't ring, so to-day I asked the janitor to ring the bell every time he went past, so I'd feel quite easy."

The upstairs bell unkindly rang.

"Ssh!" hissed Estella; "pretend we're out."

"Is he to suppose the downstairs door was opened by a spook?" Tony whispered.

"Well, you needn't talk. You did it." She came back into the dining-room, and sat down with infinite non-rustling precautions. "I'm sure I'd like to pay him as well as anybody. Indeed, nobody has the horror of debt I've got. I tremble with it when I wake in the night. It's born in me. I don't know why, but I can't pay what I haven't got, not if I was to coin my blood for it." The bell rang again. "Well, he can just tire himself out at that," Estella added. "I should think he'd know we'd have opened it before if we'd wanted him."

Tony's eyes overran with laughter. Regina threw herself into Barbara's lap, and Barbara put her face into the black mop of Regina's curls, and began to whisper a story to her.

"I wish I was out of the whole business," muttered Fred: "out of the profession, I mean. I wish I knew another durned thing to do. I had a chance to be a dentist once, but I was too good for it then. When that old aunt of mine in Ireland dies, I bet I take my share of what she leaves and buy an interest in a business. And when you're all down on your luck, you can come to me, people, and I'll help you out."

"My share in that pneumatic tire'll be worth thousands of dollars by then," said Mrs. Donnelly, refolding her newspaper. "They've got a backer for it now who's going to put it right on the market. Will Knowles says there's a fortune in it, and he's an inventor."

"I was thinking the other day it would be nice to invent something," replied Estella; "but I never get mine finished, somehow."

The enemy without gave a final knock and ring, and departed. He was pursued downstairs by the barks of the terriers and the shrieks of Regina, who at that moment rushed, all three, into each other's arms.

"Look here," said Fred; "are you sure it wasn't Mr. Bates come for the rent? He told Barbara he'd be here at three o'clock."

"Mercy! Look out of the window, Barbara, and see who it was." Barbara leaned out and down, watching.

"Well, I vow!" said Mrs. Donnelly. "Do you know what those Gostioffs, or whatever their name is, have been doing? The Czar said everybody could make their crowns out of silver-gilt, because some of 'em are as poor as church mice, and those Gostioffs have been over to Paris and had theirs made out of solid gold!"

"Who told you?"

"It's in the paper. And he's just come of age, a while ago, and paid all his debts."

"Seems rather an excessive person," Tony commented.

Mrs. Donnelly made a little clucking noise to her newspaper: "Tsu! Tsu!— well, poor boy, he does all he can."

"Who?" demanded Fred.

"The Emperor of all the Russias," answered Tony, laughing from under his eyelashes at Kate. "Kate's very partial to him. I sometimes feel quite piqued."

"Well, I don't care. He's a very good man; he wants—"

"They say," remarked Estella dreamily, "that she's got a gold typewriter set with diamonds."

"It was the milkman," announced Barbara, drawing in her head.

Estella had picked up an illustrated weekly, and she now passed it with a tender smile to Mrs. Donnelly. "Wouldn't Barbara look sweet fixed just the way the Czarina is? Those pearl ropes—I'll bet they're yards long—they're just the sort of thing that suits Barbara."

Mrs. Donnelly gravely regarded the Czarina's likeness. "She looks very handsome," she said. "I hope she'll be happy. She's got a kind of a sad look. I knew a girl once, a nice, pretty girl as could be; she looked something like our Barbara, too, only Barbara's the handsomest of the lot—had something that same look at her wedding, and before the very first year was out he had run off to Canada with a pot of money—he was a partner in a wholesale bicycle business—and another woman, and she, poor thing, had to take in boarders."

Estella sat up, clutched her floating yellow dressing-sack about her neck, and with the other hand shoved back the toppling mass of her black hair. "Well!" she cried, "I'd like to know what you mean by that, Kate Donnelly! I didn't think I should ever be insulted at my own lunchtable by people talking as if it were a disgrace to take boarders! You ought to honor me for it, or any other honest way of making my living. I've got my fatherless child to support, and I'm proud of it, and as God is my witness, I think a woman can be a lady, no matter how little money she has. And if you mean to insinuate anything against Tom Baker, I can tell you that whatever my troubles with my husband may have been—and I think you might have had more consideration for

Regina than to mention a woman—there never was a breath against his honesty, and he never quarreled with but one of his employers in his life that would bring men he knew home drunk to sleep in the office, and that diamond bracelet I gave him to get the doctor's bill on once when he was out of work, he went and got out and gave it back to me as soon as I got my divorce!" There was a glass pitcher full of lemonade on the table. Estella helped herself to a long drink, and added: "And even so, I shouldn't call you exactly boarders, anyway."

Mrs. Donnelly arose in trembling majesty and took her hat off the mantelpiece. "I'll send you my address, Estella Baker," she said, "as soon as I get one. And you can send your bill in when you like. I wouldn't speak to a dog as you've spoken to me, and I wouldn't take it from you if you were the Queen of England. And as for calling us boarders, I should think you wouldn't, with Tony working like a black slave, and Fred putting off the butcher, and me paying regular every Saturday. I wouldn't have stayed here to have my ears deafened the way you screech, Estella Baker, for anybody but Tony, that was the sweetest child I ever saw when I used to go on as extra in the Amazon marches at his father's theatre, before that sneaking hound of a Gillespie got it away from him—though I've worked hard here to help you, and glad to do it, as you well know. I hope, when I'm gone—"

"Before you go, Kate, dear," said Tony, putting his pipe on the mantelpiece, "we'd better clear the table, or I fear Barbara will be forced to work."

Barbara rose hurriedly, but like a creature moving in a sleep, and Mrs. Donnelly snatched up a plate with one hand, and with the other pushed the young girl back into the window-seat. "Stay where you are," said she, and strode majestically into the kitchen. Her brother-in-law, who had not bestowed so much as a glance upon the previous debate, now lifted a newspaper in his turn. "There's a cut of the Felix house," he said. "Down below, you know, on Riverside Drive, the white stone place. Good print, isn't it? I wish I'd gone in for photography when I had that chance three years ago."

"I never thought I'd much care about having that house," said Estella. "The windows come so low down, I'd always be afraid Regina would fall out. Still, of course, you could put wires across them."

"Forgot the tablecloths," cried Tony, running in and snatching up the bucket. "None of you thought of them, of course—loafers! If I have a sunstroke on the roof, say I died true." Tony peered into the pitcher of lemonade as he passed it. "Oof! Little drops of lemon. Nothing more spirited for the laborer, the poor laborer, Mrs. Tommy?" At the hall door—"I will return to you, Barbara," he said to the back of that young lady's head, and vanished.

"Tony gone pok?" asked Regina.

"I wonder," said Estella, "if Tony's written those words for Barbara to sing Sunday night?"

"Anny Bobs ta Rina pok?" Regina persisted.

"No, no," said Estella, "Auntie Barbara can't take Regina to the park now; it's too hot."

"Too hot?"

"Yes; too hot. Make Auntie sick. Poor Auntie."

"Poo Anny; Anny Bobs ta Rina pok?"

"No; now, Regina, you're naughty."

Regina puffed out an under-lip and nodded: "Rina awn do finey aws," said she plaintively.

"Oh, Regina, why don't you learn to talk plainer. Oo bid dirl, ess oo is, oo bid dirl! You mostly know what she says, Fred."

"She said, 'Regina wants to go on the flying-horses.' "

"Oh, darling, mamma hasn't any money for that.—No, indeed, Barbara, carfare and everything!—You can go on the flying horses when mamma gets an engagement. Here—here's a nickel. You can play with that."

Regina turned the nickel over and over in the creases of her little warm hand, and Fred returned to his former statement—"I guess it'll be a long day before any of us gets an engagement."

"I'll bet you anything you like," cried Estella, "that I'll be starring in my own play before the year's out. That play's bound to succeed, because it speaks right to people's hearts. I wrote every word of it out of my own soul. There isn't a word in it without a throb, and yet the comedy interest's good, too. I think Barbara'll be quite sweet in that. She's a little tall for comedy, but then—. You know Sam Tannehill? He says it's the greatest play that's been written in America since 'The Banker's Daughter.' "

Mrs. Donnelly, who had been going to and from the kitchen with the dishes, now swept away the tablecloth, and Estella, still clutching the lemonade, and waving the butter-knife, leaned back to give her free play. She concluded, "He asked me why I didn't let Olga Nethersole have it."

"Well, dearie," said Mrs. Donnelly, "why don't you? I'm sure you deserve a little luck."

"Well," said Estella, "I guess not. Nobody'll ever play that part but me. There's plenty of managers would be glad to take the play, and put their own old stars into it; night and day I'm afraid some one will steal my ideas. If I could only get a good part in New York and show people just once what I could do, there'd be plenty of managers ready to back me in my play afterward!"

Fred yawned. "Estella," said he, "when you do get an engagement you quarrel with the stage-manager and come home."

Estella planted her elbows on the table. "That's because they've got such old fuss-budgets of stage-managers. I guess after I've sat up all night wearing myself to pieces studying my art, I'm not going to be dictated to by those ignorant things. It was mean of that old Dawkins, though, to fight with me, when I'd had my pink crêpe dress made for their old piece, and I hadn't even got it paid for yet. Wasn't that a sweet dress, Kate? I wore my real coral and gold belt with it that Tommy gave me while we were married. He always said he did like me to look nice, Tommy did. I've got plenty of clothes to take an engagement if I could only get one. I wish the dogs hadn't broken Whopper, and I'd ask her when we any of us were going to get anything."

"We always ask her that, and she always lies. We'd better ask her when the alimony's coming."

Estella looked at the pieces of the broken planchette which were scattered over the floor. "They looked so cunning breaking it up, and Tony would name her that," she added, with apparent irrelevance. "Hand me the cards, Fred, and let me see if I can see anything."

As she shuffled the pack her mind went back to the pink crêpe.

"If she likes to fix it over I'll let Barbara wear that dress to Mrs. Wade's Sunday night, and I can take her blue waist; you know, Kate, that one you made out of the old pair of sleeves."

She looked cordially at Barbara, but the girl did not answer, nor turn her head.

"She's dreaming," said Fred. "Love's young dream, Barbara? Estella, do you see a dark man?"

"Let her be," pleaded Mrs. Donnelly; "maybe she is really thinking about Tony."

"You make me tired, Kate," said the fraternal Fred; "you bet Tony can do his own love-making. You bet he can look after himself. I wonder," he added in a half-voice, "if she says things to him, though, when they're alone. He keeps on so.

"You never can tell," Estella sighed.

"She might be very glad to have the chance of him!" Mrs. Donnelly almost cried aloud.

"I guess my sister doesn't need to be glad of anybody, Kate Donnelly, and he's very unsettled and extravagant; I've always heard so."

"Oh, rot!" said Fred, getting in ahead of his sister-in-law. "What of it? He's only a boy, and most of the year he's more money than he knows what to do with. I don't know why it should be worse for him to throw gold dollars around than for anybody else to do it."

"Slander loves a shining mark," said Mrs. Donnelly, sententiously.

Fred laughed. "Well there's nothing so very shining about Tony, except a first-class job in the future. But, of course, he's lucky to have that, at his age; and I daresay it is his luck and his good looks and those kid ways of his starts those notions. He's really a corking fellow. Tony is, and straight, as far as I know. But if he buys a girl a pair of gloves—and I don't say he doesn't like a pretty girl—there's as much cackle as if another man had bought her Fifth Avenue. And he's too easy-tempered; he lets stories get around about him, things that matter. Look at that old gander last week at Reilly's—said it was Mrs. Rexal who got him that part with Rexal, and—you know what people say."

"Oh!" said Barbara, "it's all cowardly. It's a lie." ("Why, she's awake after all," laughed Fred.) She turned in upon them from the window, and her live voice broke into the room with its curious little throaty richness. "I—I don't deceive myself about Tony. I daresay he's wild, I daresay he's unreliable, but we must all know that he was never—base." Her face flushed and paled, her hands clinched in her lap. "We're unsteady and extravagant ourselves, Estella, and what should we have done this summer: who would have given us any pleasure, who would have helped us, who would have worked for us, what should we have done here without Tony? I remember all the time, even if we're only a caprice of his, even if he doesn't mean a word he says, we are his debtors a thousand, thousand times."

The hall door opened, and they heard Tony banging the bucket and whistling "My girl's a high-born lady," as he went into his own room.

"My dear! my dear!" Estella warned her.

"That's right, Barbara," said Fred. "I tell you the truth, I didn't think you had so much sense. There's nothing the matter with Tony except a first-class appetite for being happy. Look at him all this summer—till his next season's manager puts a stop to it—goes and makes a darned jockey of himself, for ten dollars a week, riding their plug steeplechasers in a backwoods melodrama. Does anybody say a word for him about that? Why, no! You'd think they all did it! But he went to dinner at the Waldorf last night with a fellow I know that had made some money at Brighton, and a couple of girls, and I'll bet you everybody on Broadway's talking about it."

"At the Waldorf? Is that where he was?" cried Barbara. "Last night!" She leaned forward and stared at Fred intently. Something in her accent recalled to the assemblage their own last night's dinner; the little hot untidy dining-room, and the scramble in getting the dishes washed up, and the fact that the ice had given out. Only Estella remembered for the first time that Barbara had dressed her hair elaborately yesterday afternoon, and had tried to press out her white lace waist, and had scorched it. She remembered in the same flash that the morning before Tony had praised the stately habit of dressing for dinner. She pushed away the cards, and in her turn looked at Barbara, as Barbara was looking at Fred.

"Was *that* where he was?" said the girl again.

"I'm sure he had every right to be!" cried Kate.

"I'm sure we should be the last to question that right," Barbara said.

" 'Feathered like a peacock, just as gay,' " sang Tony's whistle, clipped suddenly by the sound of splashing water.

"That boy's got his head under the faucet again!" exclaimed Mrs. Donnelly. "He'll give himself neuralgia."

"Why, Barbara!" Estella cried; "yesterday was—"

"Oh, yes," she moved her hands helplessly in her lap; "I was twenty yesterday."

"Oh, dearie! I'm so sorry! I never thought of it."

"Tony never knew of it," said Kate.

"Why, no," Barbara replied; "why should he?"

"Here he comes now," said Fred.

He came in as radiant with idleness as he had lately been with work, and very fresh from his encounter with the faucet, whose drops were still shining, bright and cold, in his black hair. There was what Estella called a diván at one side of the room; Tony composed himself upon its cushions with a fan and a glass of lemonade, and lounged there, staring at the ceiling like a contented child. He found a considerable diversion in teaching himself to drink without changing his attitude, and while he was acquiring this art, the talk tried to jerk itself past his interruption. Everybody had been a little startled by Barbara's outbreak, everybody felt that Fred would better have kept his knowledge to himself, and a little uneasy bewilderment, as at a treachery to Tony, shadowed more lively interests and quieted the long talk. They looked rather gravely at the profile view which was once more accorded them of Barbara's head.

"What's the matter, Estella?" asked Tony, glancing at the newspapers. "Aren't there any murders?" At the continued silence he lifted his head. "Hello! What's the scandal?"

"You are!" said Estella. "The idea of you being around here, anyhow, and me with a sister that's just twenty!"

"There has to be somebody to watch Fred," said Tony.

"It's Fred's been giving you away. Oh, he didn't mean to! But he says you throw your money around."

"He wants to show you what a beautiful nature I have," said the accused. He looked lovingly at Fred, because he had black murder in his heart. He looked with anxious stealth at Barbara, but Barbara seemed not to notice.

"He says people say things about you," Estella continued.

"Slander loves a shining mark," repeated Mrs. Donnelly, with solemn emphasis.

"Nice Kate!" said Tony. He went and sat down on the floor by her chair, and stroked her hand. "Good Kate! Pretty Kate!"

"I'm sure," continued Mrs. Donnelly, pretending to push him off, "nobody could be a better boy around the house than he is. Could they, now, could they? I bet you'd all want him back fast enough if he went away! I've known him since he was no bigger than that," measuring about the height of a footstool, "and never saw a cross word come out of his mouth, and I can tell you, if this never having a cent is hard on us, he's had more money to throw away when he was a child on a rocking-horse than would pay this miserable old rent time and again, and not a complaint out of him."

"Good Tony!" said that gentleman. He added in a tone of profound conviction, "Noble Tony."

Estella studied him with her chin in her hand. "Yes," she said, "you're a very sweet boy. But—you're Irish."

"I once had a father, Mrs. Baker, and he was French."

"Well, goodness, that only makes it worse!"

"Oh, dear!" said Tony drowsily, "where French and Irish meet and make a mixture that is not discreet. That's for you, Barbara, who love the poets!" He opened his eyes and stared sadly at his hostess. "It's inelegant to display such a prejudice against the foreign, dear Estella."

"I hope you've written those new verses to Gus Fenwicke's song, since you're so smart; Barbara won't have time to learn them for Sunday night, Tony Regnault, if you've put them off again, and she won't sing the old ones. Mr. Fenwicke's going to be there to hear her Sunday, and he's going to sing himself."

"Dear me, how unnecessary of him," said Tony. He went back to the couch where his banjo lay, and began to touch an air upon it as he spoke the lines. Certainly, he looked at Barbara.

> "The sleeping princes quiet lay
> And dreamed the empty years away,
> Her love delayed;
> And princes came and princes went,
> And mighty kings magnificent
> As they above her beauty bent
> Were all afraid, afraid.

> "And no man knew what word would wake,
> Nor for what fortune's golden sake,
> Or deed of love,
> That shining princess would arise,
> Unveil the kindness of her eyes
> And stretch the hand that he would prize
> All worlds above, above.

> "A beggar at the palace gate
> Had a light heart to tempt his fate
> And entered in;
> He wished no other joy but this,
> And this for death he would not miss:
> He touched her sweet mouth with a kiss—
> She waked for him, for him!"

"Oh!" cried Mrs. Donnelly, "isn't that lovely!"

"That last line doesn't rhyme, Tony," said Estella, with severity.

"Will you sing it, Barbara?" Tony asked.

"Thank you," she said. "It is very charming. You were very kind to write it. But I don't think I shall sing it. I don't think I shall sing at all."

Said Tony: "That pink thing you have on is very becoming to you, my own."

"You mustn't call Barbara that, Tony!" cried Estella. "It doesn't sound well. I can't have it."

"Not even when it isn't true?" Tony pleaded. "Not even to please Barbara?

If you'll move over a little, Barbara, I'll sit by you a minute." He secured to himself a part of the window seat, and remained there, swinging his heels and playing "Daisy" on the banjo. Barbara's slim young stateliness, aided by her trailing skirts, made her look almost as tall as he, and far more resolute. She seemed to him, as he studied her out of the corner of an eye, to be very pale and very tragically sweet.

"I'm glad, Estella," he said, "that you are beginning to awaken to a sense of your responsibilities about us. We shall be almost grown up in a minute. 'These pretty babes went hand in hand'—you remember what happened to *their* wicked guardian, Mrs. Baker, after the robin-redbreasts had covered them with leaves? I am afraid Barbara would be rather long for robin-redbreasts; she would keep them busy."

Estella smiled disdainfully. "You look like a yard of pump-water, the both of you," said she.

"The each of us, Estella. And it's still incorrect to be cross with my physique—Napoleon was once slender. Barbara's, to be sure," lifting Barbara's lovely wrist between his thumb and finger, and critically regarding it—"Barbara's, to be sure, is no great shakes."

She did not smile, she did not even withdraw her hand. Tony laid it carefully in her lap. "Cheer up, Anny Bobs!" he whispered.

At this moment the entire apartment was filled with the roar of Regina's rage. "Mahmu a my nicky. Mahmu a my nicky."

"What?" said every one; "what is it?"

"Mahmu a my nicky! A my nicky! Bah Mahmu!"

Fred was stooping over Regina. "Mohammed ate my nickel," he translated. Mohammed was the older terrier.

"A my nicky," assented Regina.

"Ate her nickel? Heavens, swallowed it! It'll kill him!" Estella fell on her knees and glared down the throat of Mohammed, who wagged his tail feebly.

"Bah Mahmu!" cried Regina, beating the air and howling lustily. "A my nicky! Mahmu a my nicky!"

"Do you think it'll kill him?" persisted Estella; "was Stella's old boy? Did want doctor?"

"Wa my nicky!" entreated Regina.

"It seems to me extremely forehanded of him," said Tony to Regina. "You know you nearly ate it yourself."

Regina stopped crying and stared at him. She began slowly to smile and dimple, and presently extended a hand. "Nicky," said she.

Tony laid a copper on her palm. "Penny," he said; "not nicky. 'Nough."

Regina went over to Estella and pulled her arm. "Mah-ma, nicky."

Estella closed Mohammed's mouth with her fingers and kissed his nose. "Him eat nickels?" she inquired.

"No, I haven't got another nickel for you, Regina, I haven't got— Oh, don't cry. Here, you can have my pearl heart. And here," reaching for a clean napkin and a blue pencil from a crowded trunk-lid at her back, "we'll make a rag dolly, shall we?"

Tony leaped upon her, and wrenched the napkin from her grasp. "I would never wish to interfere with any of your little diversions, Estella," said he, returning in triumph to his seat, "but it is I who wash the linen."

"Oh, Lord, oh, Lord, oh, Lord!" yawned Fred. "What a deadly drag it is! I wonder shall I ever work again?"

"I wonder," said Estella, "why it's always us who can't get parts? We can all act."

"Well, said Fred, "we could if we were let. But the question now is—Mr. Bates told Barbara he'd be here after that blamed rent at three o'clock, and it's about that now; what are we going to tell him?"

"If I could only get a backer for my play," began Estella. "Oh, I wish you'd stop fooling with that banjo, Tony, you put me out so!"

"Say, look here, Tony!" cried Fred, "since you've got a job coming to you —I know it isn't the proper thing, but—couldn't you get something in advance from your management?"

"Oh!" cried Mrs. Donnelly, "and start out in debt, and be all the season getting even!"

Tony looked hopefully at Barbara, but Barbara positively frowned.

"Unh-unh!" said Tony, shaking his head at Fred; "nev-er bor-row from the man-age-ment. If you do, you'll nev-er save a cent;"—he struck a discreet tinkle from the banjo, and added: "In the mean-time, who will pay the rent?"

"Without turning her head round to the company, Barbara said: "I daresay we shan't have to pay the rent at all, if I marry Mr. Bates."

They were too surprised to speak, but as they gradually recovered their breath, they turned and stared at her; all but Tony, who went on touching the banjo and looking at it carefully. Estella leaned forward and knocked on the table with the handle of the butterknife. "What do you mean by that?" she said.

Barbara put up one hand and smoothed her back hair with deliberate fingers. "When I went into the hall this morning to see if I couldn't inveigle him to go away"—Tony lifted his head quickly and angrily, and frowned from Barbara to Estella—"as I was asked to do," Barbara continued, "he asked me if I would marry him. Or, rather, he asked me to think about it. He is coming back at three to—to help us think about it. He wants to speak to you, Estella."

"Well, I'm not going to have anything to do with it!" Estella cried. "And you needn't frown at me, Tony Regnault, for I was taking the curling irons out of the gas-range that very minute, or I would have gone out to him myself. Nobody shall ever say I forced her into it. I wouldn't wreck the life of my own sister, not if he was to pay me for it in diamonds! But God knows, Tony, what's to become of her, the way things are; for even if ever she can make up her mind, and marry you, you're all alike, you actors; I wouldn't trust a girl's heart to the best of you, though it's true Jim Folso did take care

of his mother till the day she died—I know that myself—sent her ten dollars
a week year out and in; he's had to borrow it from Tommy many a time. No,
sir, she'll have to decide it for her own self, Barbara will."

And at this moment, as though by special arrangement with a dramatic
deity, there was a ring at the front door.

"It needn't be he, you know," said Estella, confronting a circle of stricken
faces.

But it was he. Fred went to the door and ushered in a large, plump, blond
gentleman in the elder middle years. He had his coat on his arm and his hat
in his hand, and he was mopping his face and forehead with a huge clean
handkerchief.

"Good-day, all," said he. "No, don't trouble yourself for me, ma'am," to
Estella, who had risen, mute and regal, and was schooling herself to the
manner of a dowager empress. He accepted a chair, however, and looked
around with simple confidence upon the company. "It is hot! When you come
to my time of life, you feel the stairs."

"You'll have a glass of lemonade, Mr. Bates," said Tony. He brought a
glassful and his own fan to the landlord, and the two men looked at each
other as the glass changed hands.

"Thank you," said Mr. Bates, "I don't object."

An embarrassed silence followed these civilities. Tony had cuddled on to
the couch again with his inevitable banjo, and the terriers had come forward,
and were sniffing at Mr. Bates's legs. Dooley drew back suddenly and showed
his teeth; Mohammed instantly broke into a volley of shrill yelps.

"Knows I'm the landlord," tactfully remarked Mr. Bates, setting down his
glass, and smiling jovially around. He snapped his fingers at Dooley, "Nice
boy, good fellow." The dogs thrust their bodies back and their heads forward,
and continued to grumble and to growl. "Well, I guess from what Miss Barbara told me this morning, you didn't want to see me to-day."

"I'll be frank with you, Mr. Bates," said Estella. "My allowance hasn't
come yet. God is my witness, I expected it the day before yesterday. Though
why I should expect it from a man that forsakes his own child, and that I
never would have married if I hadn't been infatuated with him—a girl's
infatuation, Mr. Bates, you know what that is—I don't know. But I was so
sure it would come to-day, while that lace sale was on at Root & Stump's. I
thought of dressing to be ready right after lunch—didn't I, Barbara? But it
hasn't come. I'm sure you're the last man, Mr. Bates, that would want me to
take the bread out of my child's mouth."

"Must be a pretty mean man," said Mr. Bates; "won't spend money to
keep his own little girl. But you know, Mrs. Baker, I know people talk,
especially the Irish, but owners have to make their property pay, someways."

"Oh, well," said Estella, "after all, this isn't a flat you could really expect
much rent for. If I'd had my money this month, there's a lot of things I'd
have spoken to you about. We haven't any awnings, for one thing, and it
makes the place like a bake-oven, and it makes it look like a tenement;

though, for that matter, there isn't a tenement but what has awnings. And that woman in the flat over us, you'll have to speak to her. She says insulting things about my dogs, down the airshaft. Yes, she does; she means to insult me, because I told her she ought to be ashamed to let her parrot use such language. I couldn't let Regina listen to it, Mr. Bates, indeed I couldn't. And the storeroom leaks, or a pipe's burst in it, or something, and I shan't pay my rent at all if my Saratoga trunk is damaged, for there's a lot of wardrobe in it and things no money could replace. My white satin—I only wore it two weeks—is in there, and my husband's miniature's in that trunk. I shouldn't like to see that damaged."

"Well, well," said Mr. Bates, heartlessly putting the miniature of Mr. Baker to one side: "I guess you know it isn't altogether about the rent I came. I guess maybe Miss Barbara's told you about what I said to her this morning. No, ma'am; no, gent'men, don't go. I know it's not the usual thing, but you've always seemed sort of like a family here, and I know you'll all talk about it when I'm gone, so might's well have it now. And I'm counting that maybe you'll kind of help me out. I'm not supposing"—he turned a pair of patient eyes on Barbara, and the tame, kindly lovingness in them seemed at once to shield and to caress her—"I'm not supposing Miss Barbara's what's called in love with me. 'Twouldn't be natural, but I think she might like me if she came to know me and gave me a fair show. Especially when she knows more o' the way people get along than she does now; she'd see how different I'd treat her from the way a lot of men do that have got wives and don't know how to use 'em. I always thought this was a kind of rough world for women, and I'd like to do what's really right by one of them."

Nobody answered, but Tony lifted a long grave look to his.

"And so I thought," continued Mr. Bates, "that some of you who haven't such fancy ideas as it's natural enough she's got, would speak to her, and tell her that if—if you don't see something as pretty as you'd like, it's best to take something that's all wool."

He was greatly pleased at this flower of speech, and looked up quickly and brightly at Barbara, and Barbara smiled. She had a slow smile of infinite possibilities, and Mr. Bates looked at it a little before he proceeded: "I've got money; a couple of hundred thousand, one way and another, and more making—and I've got health and good habits, and the store I set by her, you wouldn't believe it. Well, I guess she's kind of notiony and high-spirited, and I don't seem much to her, but I'm relying you'll tell her those are things make life comfortable and worth having just the same; and I should think you, Mrs. Baker, that's had your own troubles in your time, would feel kind o' scared to have anything so pretty and so kind of high-headed and proud around like this."

"God is my witness, Mr. Bates—" began Estella, leaning forward.

"Not," hurriedly continued the suitor, "not as I've got anything to say against your profession. Those that like it—why let 'em, I say. But it ain't the life for a woman, is it? Now, is it? Nor, I shouldn't think myself, for a man either. I don't mean any disrespect, but it does seem to me a lady like Miss Barbara's got something more coming to her than this, and what's more," he added, meditatively, "it seems like it don't pay."

Tony, who was leaning on his knees, with his chin in his hands, lifted his guileless eyes, and said sweetly: "It's only fair to the profession, Mr. Bates, to tell you that we are not its most victorious exponents."

"Likely, likely," admitted Mr. Bates, a little mystified. "But we can keep a woman out of it, Mr. Reeno, and take her clean away from all this stage business."

"You don't think," inquired Tony—this was the only base advantage Tony took—"you don't think she ought to have anything to say about it herself— the being taken clean away from all this stage business?"

"Not when she's got a man to look after her," said Mr. Bates, "and to give her a comfortable home."

"Oh!" admitted Tony, and confided a twinkle to the flooring.

"Well, my dear," said Estella, "it's a very great responsibility for me, and I don't want to urge you. But if I'd married Mr. Fettercamp when he wanted me to, we'd all be rolling in our own carriages this minute. There was his sister married an Italian prince, and she wasn't a circumstance to Barbara. She's dead now, poor girl, but she married him. But, no, I would have Tommy Baker because I loved him—indeed, I did, Barbara Floyd, I loved him madly—but there's no use marrying for love when you can't even be sure he'll send you your alimony right. And because I wrecked my life, Barbara, I'd like to see you marry somebody worthy. I'd say the same if it was Regina. Regina—Regina Baker, don't you put that penny in your mouth. Come here —come here to mama."

Regina advanced slowly, and Estella gathered the curls out of her warm little neck and face, and hastily polished off her face with a handkerchief. "Don't you know Mr. Bates, darling? What do nice little girls say to gentlemen?"

Regina ducked her head, made an unintelligible sound and extended her hand.

"How-de-do, miss," said Mr. Bates, shaking the hand. "I'm sorry I didn't think to bring you some candy. Better luck next time, eh? Why, why, you mustn't begin to cry, little girl. Don't you want to be friends with me?" Regina nodded. "Don't you want to grow up and have a pony to ride and learn the piano?"

"Awn go finey aws," said Regina.

"She wants to go on the flying horses," translated the patient Fred. "Merry-go-round, you know."

"And so she shall!" assented Mr. Bates.

Regina glowed with joy. "An Anny Bobs?"

"And Auntie Barbara?" Mr. Bates repeated after Fred; "why, yes, indeed."

Regina, in a kind of vacuous triumph, smiled around the room and had an inspiration. "An Tony?"

"Why," responded Mr. Bates hesitatingly, "maybe he wouldn't want to."

A perfect torrent of joyous sounds intended to be affirmative burst from Regina's lips. In the vigor of her confidence she flung herself upon the legs of Mr. Bates and beat his knees. "Oh, yef! As time, as time, aw lone, Rina an Anny Bobs an Tony go finey aws, go roun an roun an roun, an Tony caw go ring!"

There was a suspicion of thickness in the voice of the translator: "Once, last time, nobody else happened to be there. Tony and Barbara rode, too, and Tony caught the gold ring; you know, with those little blunt swords."

"Why, he's a very clever young man," Mr. Bates affably replied.

Regina smote his knees and shrieked with joy. "Oh, yef!" she repeated, "an Anny Bobs gah go ring."

"You said it was Mr. Tony caught the gold ring, little girl."

"That's what she means to say," said Fred.

"No! no!" Regina passionately insisted. "Anny Bobs *gah* go ring! Anny Bobs gah go ring *now!* Rina fine it."

"Well, well, Regina," Estella interrupted, "Mr. Bates can't talk to you all day!"

"I paid it her as a reward of merit. I assure you, I gave the man a dime for it," said Tony, softly, with a little blush.

Mr. Bates passed over the insignificance of Tony's shabby boyhood with the good temper of a potentate. "Well," said he, giving his face a final wipe, "I guess I've said what I laid out to. I didn't come here to talk soft. That part of it's just my business, and hers—if she'll have it." He got up and took his hat and went over to Barbara. "Miss Barbara," he said, "if you can make out to like me—like me well enough to have me—you'll never regret it." He held out his hand, and Barbara gave him hers with her long boyish clasp. Kate followed him to the door, and let him out.

An unpleasant silence settled upon the company. Its members were suddenly set face to face with decision and responsibility; they were crowded and jostled and made to feel strange and ill at ease, here in the dilapidated cheer of their own home, by the encroaching wisdom of other worlds. Barbara continued to sit idly in the blinding sunshine like a person passive before the issue of events, and indifferent to it. The fierce light seemed to set her apart from counsel and from tenderness, and to blare aloud her beauty.

Estella, after two or three clearings of her throat, inquired with a kind of trembling pomp: "And what do you think about it yourself, my dear?"

Barbara rose and came slowly to the table. She stood stroking the edge of it with her hand, and finally she said: "I'll tell you what I think. I think that if I were married to Mr. Bates I shouldn't have to run out into the hall to ogle landlords to cheat them out of their rent. I think I shouldn't have to pretend to be out when the milkman comes, nor wheedle the butcher, nor have the gas turned off. I shouldn't have to walk out of a filthy mess like this"—Estella gasped—"dressed as if I were going to a beauty show, because I wanted work, and into offices where I should be looked over as if I were a horse. I think I shouldn't owe every stitch I wear and everything I put into my mouth to my sister's divorced husband. That's what I think. I think I should be looked out for and taken care of and kept away from hurt, as other women are!"

Estella began: "Well, of all the—"

"And I think," continued Barbara, her voice rising to a hysteric pitch, "that my husband would be respected everywhere, and would work for me and be true and good, and not depend for his pleasures upon a friend's getting some money, and taking him out to dinner with girls—"

"Oh! oh! Barbara!" cried Fred.

"It was such a good dinner, Barbara!" said Tony. Unquestionably, his smile was coming back.

The dogs at the same moment began to quarrel over a bone, and their voices rose in ear-splitting dispute. Estella cuffed one of them, and the other carried the bone into the sitting-room, from whence issued ecstatic lickings and crunchings.

In the comparative pause Mrs. Donnelly's tearful indignation burst upon Barbara:

"We all know what you mean by that last, Barbara Floyd," she cried. "And I guess there are other people besides you in this house that are sick and tired of being poor, and the fuss there is about meals, and that have spent all their money on you, and whose fathers were rich and famous, and thought nothing of living at Delmonico's before ever you were born. If the butcher is swindled out of his meat, I don't see but you eat your share of it. If you think it's messy here, why don't you get up and clean it? Tony's scrubbed the kitchen while you've been lolling there, and you wouldn't know how to cook anything but a boiled egg and a pickle to this day if it wasn't for Tony. You're a bad, ungrateful girl, Barbara Floyd, and Tony—"

Estella pitched her voice above the voices of Mrs. Donnelly and the dogs: "Don't you try to bully my sister, Kate Donnelly, she—"

Tony struck the table sharply with his hand. "Come, Barbara," he said. "We must get the washing down now." He held the door open for her, and without looking round she went past him into the hall.

At the head of the top flight of stairs there was a door with a heavy sliding weight, and Tony, who had run upstairs in advance, pushed it open, and with a wave of the hand, like a lavish host, welcomed Barbara to the great, shining roof. It was very wide and hot, and silent, and little airs that the sidewalk never knew drifted over its cornices. Said Tony: "To where, beyond the voices, there is peace."

Barbara stepped out fearlessly between the glare of the red roofs and the glare of the blue and golden sky. With a happy breath, she turned her unshielded face up to the light. This stretch of gleaming tin had long been their private garden, and they had known it in many kinds of weather.

"Oh, Tony!" she said, in a little soft, fluttered, laughing voice, "we needn't bother about the washing yet, need we?"

"Come," said Tony. "I've found a place where we can see the river. I found it for us this morning. Mustn't tell!"

"No," she said, and put her hand out to him, like a child. "Show me."

Behind its newer and broader substitute an old chimney rose out of the roof's western bulwark, from which it parted company a few feet above the ground in an angle of crumbling brick and mortar. Tony jumped into the niche of this angle and held down a hand to Barbara. "Step up and I'll lift you," he directed. She was beside him in an instant, and found herself breast-high above the parapet, which served as an elbow rest. It was too broad to let them see straight down into the common, cluttered street, and beyond the shops and the low buildings over the way stumbled the vine-smothered huts of squatters; past a bit of leafy, broken ground the wide green of market gardens was dotted with the gold of sunflowers and the scarlet of geraniums, a single close-shorn lawn was banked with the white and the mystic blue of hydrangeas. Further yet, between the shimmer of poplars and the frown of purple hills, the river flashed and drifted.

"It's good here," said Tony.

Barbara stretched her arm across the parapet as though she stretched it into the coolness of fresh water. "There's a yacht—a white one, watch! Going down the river! Let's pretend it's going straight to sea, Tony—what fun! Across the sea."

"We're going with it, you know. Just ourselves, of course, and a telescope, maybe, and plenty of honey wrapped up in a five-pound note. All the little fishes will come and beg us for the honey, and you'll give it to them out of your hands till I shall be jealous. It isn't nice to be jealous. I wouldn't let even a little fish suffer it, if I were you, Barbara. Why, Barbara? what foolishness you talk! And you don't even hear me!"

"I wish I could see all this from my own window," she said.

"Ah, but you can't. I had to show it to you, Barbara. It was quite easy to find, but you know you never found it." The little rosy ruffle of Barbara's sleeve lay on the rough edge of the parapet, and Tony bent his head and kissed it. "I was sure you'd like it here. Be good," he said.

The voices of some children singing ring games on a near fire-escape rose with an accent of their own natures to the two truants on the housetop. Otherwise they seemed the only living souls in a universe made up of two expanses: below them, the wide, sparkling, burning roofs, with one distant fringe of leaves and waters, and above, the radiant, hot blue, luminous and quivering, and scarcely tinged by the white clouds which slowly sailed across it and banked themselves on the horizon into palaces and temples. Toward the west, where the sun blazed in a spendor that even the eyes of lovers dared not meet, the heavens were almost white—not in pallor, but effulgence, the light incarnate. Small, lazy breezes floated through the sunshine, and brushed, fresh and sweet, against their faces.

"Barbara," said Tony, leaning forward and catching her by both wrists, "where did Regina find my ring?"

She was startled both by the suddenness of his attack and by the strength of his hold, and straining back upon his grasp she remained alert and silent, like a deer. He waited a moment, but she continued passionately quiet, passionately studious of his face. In the pause, the voices of the children arose with a new clearness:

> "And on his breast he wore a Star,
> Pointing to the East and West."

"Barbara!"

"Hush!" she insisted. Her breath was fluttering on her lips, and her eyes shining into his:

> "Go choose your East, go choose your West,
> Go choose the one that you love best."

"You kept that ring!" he said. "You kept it—because of me!" Almost as he spoke she had leaped down and away from him, and was running across the roof.

He caught up with her on the low platform of wooden slats amid the flutter of the wet linens. "Help me take these in," she called to him. "Estella will be angry." She was struggling with the clothespins, and their fingers met over a row of pillow-slips.

"They're not dry yet. Listen, I—"

"There's a breeze come up. It will dry them in a minute." She was moving further and further away.

"Why, see, my sweet, you don't know what you're saying! I want to tell you—"

"Oh," she cried, pausing oppressedly, "what does everybody tell me? That you are idle, that you are extravagant, that you—that you—that girls—"

"Barbara," he said, "though they follow me in their thousands and their ten thousands, though their dead bodies strew my pathway, I will be blind to them. I love you, Barbara."

She retreated again, making as though to reach the door, and he stood still in a sudden bitterness, with a little wound in the dignity of his love. The next instant he was startled to see her, who was so light and true of step, stumble and lose her footing on a broken slat and sink down in a heap with her hands over her face.

He ran up and bent over her without touching her. "Oh, my dear!" he asked; "what is it? Are you hurt? Or were you angry? Would you like me to go away? What is it?"

She lifted her face to his and put her arms around his neck.

"I was thinking of you," she said.

Half an hour later, as they still sat on the platform, the roof rang with their names, and from under their damp canopy of tablecloths and towels they perceived Estella in the doorway.

"Come on!" she called. "Why, whatever's kept you? Come on! The alimony's come, and we're all going to Coney Island for dinner!"

"Don't be so noisy, Estella," said Tony. "We're engaged."

"Really? Really, Barbara? Well, I'm glad of it. Yes, Regina," she called over her shoulder, "come up. Mama's here. Well, I'm very glad. And I'll have my white satin cleaned for her as soon as I can. How jolly we're going out to dinner! Like a party for you, Barbara."

"Splendid!" said Tony. "The alimony-baked meats did coldly furnish forth the marriage tables."

He sprang up and handed Barbara to her feet. There fell to the ground something Barbara had been showing Tony—a slender ribbon, as long as a watch-chain, and, dangling from its end, a great, clumsy, ridiculous gilt ring. Regina, who came staggering through the doorway, fell upon this latter object with a shriek of joyous recognition. "Anny Bobs gah go ring!" she cried. "Rina awn go finey aws, go finey aws, go roun an roun an roun!"

OUT OF THE STORM

Mulloy Finnegan

Chuggins, Nevada, was having one of its three-day winds. Rain started in, too, and blew with everything else. Tin cans went tumbling over one another down Golden Street, gathering up beer-bottles as they went along, the swishing rain driving everything loose before it.

At the upper end of Golden Street—and then back up the slope a bit—in her little dry-goods box of a house, made from several boxes, dry-goods and otherwise, Phil Martin's wife lay listening to the clattering procession, and wondering where all the tin cans came from. The little house itself rocked like a ship at sea, and, but for the friendly shoulder of the hill it leaned against, might have joined in the mad procession, as some of its scattered neighbors, less fortunately anchored, occasionally did.

Phil Martin's wife raised herself on an elbow and tried to look out through the rain-splashed window beside her bed. A little dog came from somewhere and tried to look out, too.

"No, Monk," she said. "He is not coming yet!"

She shaded her eyes with her hand, to keep out the bleary streaks of light that reached up at her, from down-town, through the wet darkness—the better to see in another direction, at right angles with them; only darting back when a sudden flash of lightning obliterated them entirely, illuminating the surrounding mountains and making them quiver in the bellowing thunder that followed.

All at once she spied a tiny light—like a faraway star. It was what she was looking for. She knew it came from the lantern carried by her husband on his way home from the Bonnie Bell mine, where he was working on the night shift.

157

"Here he comes now!" she said, springing from the bed and stepping into the felt slippers beside it.

"Row, row, row!" said the little dog, who was still very young, scratching at the door to be let out to meet his master.

"Not yet," said his mistress, shaking her head and its long brown braid, and throwing a warm wrapper over her night-dress. "He's not near enough yet."

Then she turned up the wick in the coal-oil lamp, and busied herself making things comfortable.

She put some wood and paper in the sheet-iron stove, and soon had a lively fire, which roared with the wind in the polished stovepipe that ran straight up through the low ceiling. When she had the coffee-pot on, she drew up the one comfortable armchair. She placed across it some flannel pajamas, and, in front of it, a pair of warm slippers.

"Let's see," she said, trying to think of something else. "He'll be pretty hungry when he comes in out of that storm. Let's cook him some ham and eggs."

She talked to the dog—a little black fellow with a white cross on his chest.

He had retreated from the door, at her bidding, and was playing with one of the slippers before the fire, never so intent on the pastime that his ears did not prick at attention for a sound of his master's approaching footstep.

"Gr-r-r! Woof!"

He dropped the slipper and bounded for the door, but his mistress finished breaking the eggs in a bowl and covering them over with a saucer before she answered his imperative demand to open it.

Hardly had she slipped the bolt than the door flew back against her, and a man's form came in with it out of the night and the storm.

"Down, Monk!" she commanded.

The dog was making great leaps at the stranger, who, although he slammed the door quickly behind him, in the face of the resisting wind and rain, brought plenty of them in with him.

"He'll not bite you," she said to the half-drowned man. "Just wants to make friends."

It had not occurred to her to be afraid till she saw the stranger lock the door and put the key in his pocket. Then he shot the bolt.

"Who else is here?" he demanded in a husky voice, taking in at a glance the one room of the cabin.

The eyes he turned back on her through the drippings that trickled from his pulled-down slouch-hat made her hesitate, as she answered:

"Nobody—not now."

"Not *now?*" he repeated, as if to get her meaning. "Oh!" he exclaimed, as his gaze lighted on the coffee-pot and egg-shells, and, taking in the slippers and pajamas, traveled to the rumpled bed. "You mean somebody *was* here and has just gone to work. I know they change shifts over at the Bonnie Bell about this time. Is that it?"

"Yes," she answered, falling into the lie intuitively.

Past him, through the little window, she could see the light coming down the side of the mountain. It was still very small. Of course, it had the storm to fight—but oh, why didn't it hurry?

"Then," the man was saying, "we're not apt to be disturbed for some eight hours? Am I right?"

And again she lied:

"Yes."

He removed his hat and shook the drippings into the wood-box; then, unbuttoning his khaki coat, threw back its collar and turned down the collar of the double-breasted blue flannel shirt underneath, the flying moisture sizzling against the tiny stove.

"Then, for mercy's sake, fix me up something to eat!" he said. "I'm starved!"

He dropped into the chair before the fire, and let his head fall between his hands, as if able to hold up no longer.

As she pushed back some sewing things on the table to make room for the dishes, she watched the nervous fingers digging in the thick, unkempt hair. They belonged to the hands of a working man, but one who had been estranged from soap and water for some time, excepting what the rain furnished. What she could see of the face told the same story, and needed shaving, besides. The steam-emitting khaki clothes looked as if he slept in them.

He dragged a chair to the table and started eating before she was ready for him—munching bread till she got the ham and eggs to his plate, and then hurrying them down his throat, with great swallows of coffee, which he drew, with a swishing sound, through his mustache.

"I don't want to harm you, ma'am," he said, gulping down a final chunk of bread and slipping back his chair; "but I want to get a couple of hours' sleep before daylight. All you've got to do is keep quiet. It wouldn't do you any good hollering, anyhow, in this storm—even if your neighbors weren't so far away; and whoever comes in that door, I'll blow his brains out!"

He reached around to his hip-pocket and drew from it a six-shooter. The frightened woman knew he wasn't only talking.

She watched him stagger toward the bed she had so recently vacated and tumble into it, wet clothing, boots, and all.

"Better turn down the light," he drowsily ordered, adjusting his hand over the gun on the coverlet. "Same as you had it before it attracted me this way. It might attract somebody else. Better turn it out altogether."

Hardly done, before his snores vied with the outside elements.

Noiselessly Phil Martin's wife tiptoed to the door and drew back the bolt; but the lock was locked for keeps.

Then she turned to the little window. It was in a side wall of the cabin, at right angles with the one containing the door. If it was large enough to admit her, she would have to climb over the snoring man to get to it; and even then she would be obliged to lift the sash and break through the screen tacked on from the outside.

One of the muddy yellow boots slipping to the floor startled her, but the snores didn't miss a beat.

The firelight revealed the figure on the bed, lying on its back, the slipped boot dragging on the floor. Should he sit up suddenly, he would be facing the door, and she could well believe that he would keep his word about the gun.

Across him she could see the light coming down the mountain. How it was growing! Her lips moved in prayer as she watched it—a desperate prayer that its bearer might stumble and turn an ankle, or even break an arm. It would be better than having his brains blown out in his own doorway!

Should she risk her life and scream when he got nearer? Willingly, willingly; but that would only hurry him on, not drive him back. Then she prayed again.

And all this time the light was getting nearer and larger!

It could not have been more than a block away when something brought her gaze back to her surroundings. The room about her was quite dark. The fire had almost died out!

A new terror seized her. She groped her way to the wood-box, and stooped to get some fuel to replenish the dying fire, when she felt the little dog settling himself on her skirts.

She put out a hand to pat him, thankful for his nearness, but it stopped in the middle of the caress as a drop of moisture fell on the back of it.

Even in the dark the natural instinct was to look up to see where the water came from. A sudden flash of lightning revealed a crescent-shaped opening, like a new moon—a thin slice of the stovepipe hole.

Then it was dark again. On the heels of the thunder-clap that followed, she could hear the outside chimney, which some merciful wind had blown off, go clattering over the roof and off it, to join the other tin things rolling down Golden Street.

With a sudden inspiration she snatched the dog to her, and hunted around in the wood-box for the empty egg-crate. She remembered throwing it there.

Then she remembered her sewing-basket on the table, and blindly made her way to it, knocking over the lately used cup in its saucer when she got there.

Frightened, she paused for developments; but the noise it made was such a slight one compared to the surrounding bedlam that it caused no perceptible difference in the snores issuing from the bed.

The sewing-basket located, she fingered around in it for a piece of blue tailor's chalk which she always kept there. When she found it, she unlocked the cardboard strips of the egg-crate and selected one. Then she seated herself at the table. While the dog, cuddled in her left arm, affectionately licked her neck where it rose out of the wrapper, with her right hand she blindly traced what ought to read:

Don't come unarmed. Bring help.

She folded the strip of cardboard and refolded it, and, wrapping the little bunch in her pocket-handkerchief, tied it securely to Monk's leather collar.

They both trembled as she climbed up on the chair, feeling along the still warm stovepipe till she came to the crescent-shaped opening.

With a handful of her wrapper she shoved the pipe further aside. Taking the shivering dog in her two hands, she reached up and tried to force him through the enlarged stovepipe hole. His head once out, he slipped from her hands so quickly that she almost lost her balance.

She knew that Monk had seen his master and recognized him.

Once out, it was an easy thing for him to run along the roof and down the side of the hill into which it was built.

When she could recover her breath, she pushed the pipe back in place and descended to firmer footing.

The light was so near that she almost screamed! She held her breath when she saw it approach the ground, as if its bearer was stooping—to pat the dog, for instance. Then her heart came up in her throat and stuck there while she waited for it to move on again.

When it did, it took another direction. It went down-town.

"Thank God!" she breathed.

She began to feel cold. She drew her wrapper about her and huddled, with her feet tucked up under her, in the big armchair before the dead fire.

Once the man on the bed stirred and mumbled something incoherent, but his words died away in gurgles as his big snore again filled the dark room.

She waited—she knew not for what. Even if the man woke, he would never guess what she had done. He might think she had fallen asleep and let the fire die out. Even if he knew that the wind blew the chimney off and the rain put it out, it would make no difference.

She got up and looked across him again, but all that she could see was the streaky light from down-town. If there was anything on its way to her, it was lost in those streaks.

Returning to the chair, a drowsiness came over her. She wasn't anxious about Phil any more. She was even wishing that the man on the bed would finish his sleep and go. She was so tired—and the cabin wasn't a cabin any more—it was a boat. She liked the rocking—and the splashing of the waves on its sides—

A sudden crash brought her to, as the door burst in and a flash of light revealed the gun in the hand of the man on the bed. She uttered a piercing scream which almost drowned the report that followed!

But it came through the little window; and the extended arm dropped helpless while the gun clattered to the floor.

Men came from everywhere.

"So it's you, Buck Hennessy, is it?" said Casey, the sheriff; snapping the bracelets on the wounded man's wrists. "Sorry we couldn't let you finish your sleep, but they want you right bad over at Goldfield for holding up Jim Breen, paymaster of the Gold Bar, and putting him out of business. Maybe you'll be able to tell them what you did with the two sacks of currency you got away with—you see, the miners would like their pay. Been hiding around in our nice hills here about three days now, haven't you, and thought you'd get over to Beatty and catch that train in the morning? Not this trip, Buck! Just walk on ahead of me. Make room for him, gentlemen!"

When the cabin was cleared of the crowd, made up mostly of men from the Seventy-seven saloon, where Phil Martin found them killing the lonely hours of the wet night with poker, roulette, faro, craps, and a few other innocent amusements, the big oilskin-coated miner put his arms around his little wife and let her cry on his shoulder.

"Poor little girlie!" he crooned, patting the heaving form in the soot-streaked wrapper. "You've had a night of it!"

As he tried to tell her about the five hundred dollars' reward that was coming to her, the little dog was bouncing around them, yelping and barking for attention.

"You, too, Monk," he said, picking him up from the floor and holding the little black bundle tenderly against his face. "You'll get a nice gold collar!"

MRS. PROTHEROE

Booth Tarkington

When Alonzo Rawson took his seat as the Senator from Stackpole in the upper branch of the General Assembly of the State, an expression of pleasure and of greatness appeared to be permanently imprinted upon his countenance. He felt that if he had not quite arrived at all which he meant to make his own, at least he had emerged upon the arena where he was to win it, and he looked about him for a few other strong spirits with whom to construct a focus of power which should control the Senate. The young man had not long to look, for within a week after the beginning of the session these others showed themselves to his view, rising above the general level of mediocrity and timidity, party leaders and chiefs of factions, men who were on their feet continually, speaking half a dozen times a day, freely and loudly. To these, and that house at large, he felt it necessary to introduce himself by a speech which must prove him one of the elect, and he awaited impatiently an opening.

Alonzo had no timidity himself. He was not one of those who first try their voices on motions to adjourn, written in form and handed out to novices by presiding officers and leaders. He was too conscious of his own gifts, and he had been "accustomed to speaking" ever since his days in the Stackpole City Seminary. He was under the impression, also, that his appearance alone would command attention from his colleagues and the gallery. He was tall; his hair was long, with a rich waviness, rippling over both brow and collar, and he had, by years of endeavor, succeeded in molding his features to present an aspect of stern and thoughtful majesty whenever he "spoke."

The opportunity to show his fellows that new greatness was among them was delayed not overlong, and Senator Rawson arose, long and bony in his best clothes, to address the Senate with a huge voice in denunciation of the

"Sunday Baseball Bill," then upon second reading. The classical references, which, as a born orator, he felt it necessary to introduce, were received with acclamations which the gavel of the Lieutenant-Governor had no power to still.

"What led to the De-cline and Fall of the Roman Empire?" he exclaimed. "I await an answer from the advocates of this *de-* generate measure! I *demand* an answer from them! Let me hear from them on *that* subject! Why don't they speak up? They can't give one. Not because they ain't familiar with history— no, sir! That's not the reason! It's because they *daren't,* because their answer would have to go on record *against* 'em! Don't any of you try to raise it against me that I ain't speaking to the point, for I tell you that when you encourage Sunday Baseball, or any kind of Sabbath-breakin' on Sunday you're tryin' to start the State on the downward path that beset Rome! *I'll* tell you what ruined it. The Roman Empire started out to be the greatest nation on earth, and they had a good start, too, just like the United States has got to-day. Then what happened to 'em? Why, them old ancient fellers got more interested in athletic games and gladiatorial combats and racing and all kinds of outdoor sports, and bettin' on 'em, than they were in oratory, or literature, or charitable institutions and good works of all kinds. At first they were moderate and the country was prosperous. But six days in the week wouldn't content 'em, and they went at it all the time, so that at last they gave up the seventh day to their sports, the way this bill wants *us* to do, and from that time on the result was *de*-generacy and *de*-gradation! You better remember *that* lesson, my friends, and don't try to sink this State to the level of Rome!"

When Alonzo Rawson wiped his dampened brow, and dropped into his chair, he was satisfied to the core of his heart with the effect of his maiden effort. There was not one eye in the place that was not fixed upon him and shining with surprise and delight, while the kindly Lieutenant-Governor, his face very red, rapped for order. The young Senator across the aisle leaned over and shook Alonzo's hand excitedly.

"That was beautiful, Senator Rawson!" he whispered. "I'm *for* the bill, but I can respect a masterly opponent."

"I thank you, Senator Truslow," Alonzo returned graciously. "I am glad to have your good opinion, Senator."

"You have it, Senator," said Truslow enthusiastically. "I hope you intend to speak often."

"I do, Senator. I intend to make myself heard," the other answered gravely, "upon all questions of moment."

"You will fill a great place among us, Senator!"

Then Alonzo Rawson wondered if he had not underestimated his neighbor across the aisle; he had formed an opinion of Truslow as one of small account and no power, for he had observed that, although this was Truslow's second term, he had not once demanded recognition nor attempted to take part in a debate. Instead, he seemed to spend most of his time frittering over some desk work, though now and then he walked up and down the aisles talking in a low voice to various Senators. How such a man could have been elected at all, Alonzo failed to understand. Also, Truslow was physically inconsequent, in his colleague's estimation—"a little, insignificant, dudish kind of a man," he had thought; one whom he would have darkly suspected of cigarettes had he not been dumfounded to behold Truslow smoking an old black pipe in the lobby. The Senator from Stackpole had looked over the other's clothes with a disapproval that amounted to bitterness. Truslow's attire reminded him of pictures in New York magazines, or the dress of boys newly home from college, he didn't know which, but he did know that it was contemptible. Consequently, after receiving the young man's congratulations, Alonzo was conscious of the keenest surprise at his own feeling that there might be something in him after all.

He decided to look him over again, more carefully to take the measure of one who had shown himself so frankly an admirer. Waiting, therefore, a few moments until he felt sure that Truslow's gaze had ceased to rest upon himself, he turned to bend a surreptitious but piercing scrutiny upon his neighbor. His glance, however, sweeping across Truslow's shoulder toward the face, suddenly encountered another pair of eyes beyond, so intently fixed upon himself that he started. The clash was like two searchlights meeting— and the glorious brown eyes that shot into Alonzo's were not the eyes of Truslow.

Truslow's desk was upon the outer aisle, and along the wall were placed comfortable leather chairs and settees, originally intended for the use of members of the upper house, but nearly always occupied by their wives and daughters, or "lady-lobbyists," or other women spectators.

Leaning back with extraordinary grace, in the chair nearest Truslow, sat the handsomest woman Alonzo had ever seen in his life. Her long coat of soft gray fur was unrecognizable to him in connection with any familiar breed of squirrel; her broad flat hat of the same fur was wound with a gray veil, underneath which her heavy brown hair seemed to exhale a mysterious glow, and never, not even in a lithograph, had he seen features so regular or a skin so clear! And to look into her eyes seemed to Alonzo like diving deep into clear water and turning to stare up at the light.

His own eyes fell first. In the breathless awkwardness that beset him they seemed to stumble shamefully down to his desk, like a country boy getting back to his seat after a thrashing on the teacher's platform. For the lady's gaze, profoundly liquid as it was, had not been friendly.

Alonzo Rawson had neither the habit of petty analysis, nor the inclination toward it; yet there arose within him a wonder at his own emotion, at its strangeness and the violent reaction of it. A moment ago his soul had been steeped in satisfaction over the figure he had cut with his speech and the extreme enthusiasm which had been accorded it—an extraordinarily pleasant feeling: suddenly this was gone, and in its place he found himself almost choking with a dazed sense of having been scathed, and at the same time understood in a way in which he did not understand himself. And yet—he and this most unusual lady had been so mutually conscious of each other in their mysterious interchange that he felt almost acquainted with her. Why, then, should his head be hot with resentment? Nobody had *said* anything to him!

He seized upon the fattest of the expensive books supplied to him by the State, opened it with emphasis and began not to read it, with abysmal abstraction, tinglingly alert to the circumstance that Truslow was holding a low-toned but lively conversation with the unknown. Her laugh came to him, at once musical, quiet, and of a quality which irritated him into saying bitterly to himself that he guessed there was just as much refinement in Stackpole as there was in the Capital City, and just as many old families! The clerk calling his vote upon the "Baseball Bill" at that moment, he roared "No!" in a tone which was profane. It seemed to him that he was avenging himself upon somebody for something and it gave him a great deal of satisfaction.

He returned immediately to his imitation of Archimedes, only relaxing the intensity of his attention to the text (which blurred into jargon before his fixed gaze) when he heard that light laugh again. He pursed his lips, looked up at the ceiling as if slightly puzzled by some profound question beyond the reach of womankind; solved it almost immediately, and, setting his hand to pen and paper, wrote the capital letter "O" several hundred times on note paper furnished by the State. So oblivious was he, apparently, to everything but the question of statecraft which occupied him that he did not even look up when the morning's session was adjourned and the law-makers began to pass noisily out, until Truslow stretched an arm across the aisle and touched him upon the shoulder.

"In a moment, Senator!" answered Alonzo in his deepest chest tones. He made it a very short moment, in deed, for he had a wild, breath-taking suspicion of what was coming.

"I want you to meet Mrs. Protheroe, Senator," said Truslow, rising, as Rawson, after folding his writings with infinite care, placed them in his breast pocket.

"I am pleased to make your acquaintance, ma'am," Alonzo said in a loud, firm voice, as he got to his feet, though the place grew vague about him when the lady stretched a charming, slender, gloved hand to him across Truslow's desk. He gave it several solemn shakes.

"We shouldn't have disturbed you, perhaps?" she asked, smiling radiantly upon him. "You were at some important work, I'm afraid."

He met her eyes again, and their beauty and the thoughtful kindliness of them fairly took his breath. "I am the chairman, ma'am," he replied, swallowing, "of the committee on drains and dikes."

"I knew it was something of great moment," she said gravely, "but I was anxious to tell you that I was interested in your speech."

A few minutes later, without knowing how he had got his hat and coat from the cloak-room, Alonzo Rawson found himself walking slowly through the marble vistas of the State-house to the great outer doors with the lady and

Truslow. They were talking inconsequently of the weather, and of various legislators, but Alonzo did not know it. He vaguely formed replies to her questions, and he hardly realized what the questions were; he was too stirringly conscious of the rich quiet of her voice and of the caress of the gray fur of her cloak when the back of his hand touched it—rather accidentally—now and then, as they moved on together.

It was a cold, quick air to which they emerged, and Alonzo, daring to look at her, found that she had pulled the veil down over her face, the color of which, in the keen wind, was like that of June roses seen through morning mists. At the curb a long, low, rakish black automobile was in waiting, the driver a mere indistinguishable cylinder of fur.

Truslow, opening the little door of the tonneau, offered his hand to the lady. "Come over to the club, Senator, and lunch with me," he said. "Mrs. Protheroe won't mind dropping us there on her way."

That was an eerie ride for Alonzo, whose feet were falling upon strange places. His pulses jumped and his eyes swam with tears of unlawful speed, but his big ungloved hand tingled not with the cold so much as with the touch of that divine gray fur upon his little finger.

"You intend to make many speeches, Mr. Truslow tells me," he heard the rich voice saying.

"Yes, ma'am," he summoned himself to answer. "I expect I will. Yes, ma'am." He paused, and then repeated, "Yes, ma'am."

She looked at him for a moment. "But you will do some work, too, won't you?" she asked slowly.

Her intention in this passed by Alonzo at the time. "Yes, ma'am," he answered. "The committee work interests me greatly, especially drains and dikes."

"I have heard," she said, as if searching his opinion, "that almost as much is accomplished in the committee-rooms as on the floor? There—and in the lobby and in the hotels and clubs?"

"I don't have much to do with that!" he returned quickly. "I guess none of them lobbyists will get much out of me! I even sent back all their railroad tickets. They needn't come near me!"

After a pause which she may have filled with unexpressed admiration, she ventured, almost timidly: "Do you remember that it was said that Napoleon once attributed the secret of his power over other men to one quality?"

"I am an admirer of Napoleon," returned the Senator from Stackpole. "I admire all great men."

"He said that he held men by his reserve."

"It can be done," observed Alonzo, and stopped, feeling that it was more reserved to add nothing to the sentence.

"But I suppose that such a policy," she smiled upon him inquiringly, "wouldn't have helped him much with women?"

"No," he agreed immediately. "My opinion is that a man ought to tell a *good* woman everything. What is more sacred than—"

The car, turning a corner much too quickly, performed a gymnastic squirm about an unexpected street-car and the speech ended in a gasp, as Alonzo, not of his own volition, half rose and pressed his cheek closely against hers. Instantaneous as it was, his heart leaped violently, but not with fear. Could all the things of his life that had seemed beautiful have been compressed into one instant it would not have brought him even the suggestion of the wild shock of joy of that one, wherein he knew the glamourous perfume of Mrs. Protheroe's brown hair and felt her cold cheek firm against his, with only the gray veil between.

"I'm afraid this driver of mine will kill me some day," she said, laughing and composedly straightening her hat. "Do you care for big machines?"

"Yes, ma'am," he answered huskily. "I haven't been in many."

"Then I'll take you again," said Mrs. Protheroe. "If you like I'll come down to the State-house and take you out for a run in the country."

"When?" said the lost young man, staring at her with his mouth open. "When?"

"Saturday afternoon if you like. I'll be there at two."

They were in front of the club and Truslow had already jumped out. Mrs. Protheroe gave him her hand and they exchanged a glance significant of something more than a friendly good-by. Indeed, one might have hazarded that there was something almost businesslike about it. The confused Senator from Stackpole, climbing out reluctantly, observed it not, nor could he have understood, even if he had seen, that delicate signal which passed between his two companions.

When he was upon the ground, Mrs. Protheroe extended her hand without speaking, but her lips formed the word "Saturday." Then she was carried away quickly, while Alonzo, his heart hammering, stood looking after her, born into a strange world, the touch of the gray fur upon his little finger, the odor of her hair faintly about him, one side of his face red, the other pale.

"To-day is Wednesday," he said, half aloud.

"Come on, Senator." Truslow took his arm and turned him toward the club doors.

The other looked upon his new friend vaguely. "Why, I forgot to thank her for the ride," he said.

"You'll have other chances, Senator," Truslow assured him. Mrs. Protheroe has a hobby for studying politics and she expects to come down often. She has plenty of time—she's a widow, you know."

"I hope you didn't think," exclaimed Alonzo indignantly, "that I thought she was a married woman!"

After lunch they walked back to the State-house together, Truslow regarding his thoughtful companion with sidelong whimsicalness. Mrs. Protheroe's question, suggestive of a difference between work and speechmaking, had recurred to Alonzo, and he had determined to make himself felt, off the floor as well as upon it. He set to this with a fine energy that afternoon in his committee-room, and the Senator from Stackpole knew his subject. On drains and dikes he had no equal. He spoke convincingly to his colleagues of the committee upon every bill that was before them, and he compelled their humblest respect. He went earnestly at it, indeed, and sat very late that night in his room at a nearby boarding-house, studying bills, trying to keep his mind upon them and not to think of his strange morning and of Saturday. Finally his neighbor in the next room, Senator Ezra Trumbull, long abed, was awakened by his praying and groaned slightly. Trumbull meant to speak to Rawson about his prayers, for Trumbull was an early one to bed and they woke him every night. The partition was flimsy and Alonzo addressed his Maker in the loud voice of those accustomed to talking across wide out-of-door spaces. Trumbull considered it especially unnecessary in the city; though, as a citizen of a county which loved but little his neighbor's district, he felt that in Stackpole there was good reason for a person to shout his prayers at the top of his voice and even then have small chance to carry through the distance. Still, it was a delicate matter to mention, and he put it off from day to day.

Thursday passed slowly for Alonzo Rawson, nor was his voice lifted in debate. There was little but routine: and the main interest of the chamber was in the lobbying that was being done upon the "Sunday Baseball Bill," which had passed to its third reading and would come up for final disposition within a fortnight. This was the measure which Alonzo had set his heart upon defeating. It was a simple enough bill: it provided, in substance, that baseball might be played on Sunday by professionals in the State capital, which was proud of its league team. Naturally, it was denounced by clergymen, and deputations of ministers and committees from women's religious societies were constantly arriving at the State-house to protest against its passage. The Senator from Stackpole reassured all of these with whom he talked, and was one of their staunchest allies and supporters. He was active in leading the wavering among his colleagues, or even the inimical, out to meet and face the deputations. It was in this occupation that he was engaged, on Friday afternoon, when he received a shock.

A committee of women from a church society was waiting in the corridor, and he had rounded up a reluctant half-dozen senators and led them forth to be interrogated as to their intentions regarding the bill. The committee and the lawmakers soon distributed themselves into little argumentative clumps, and Alonzo found himself in the centre of these, with one of the ladies who had unfortunately—but, in her enthusiasm, without misgivings—begun a reproachful appeal to an advocate of the bill whose name was Goldstein.

"Senator Goldstein," she exclaimed, "I could not believe it when I heard that you were in favor of this measure! I have heard my husband speak in the highest terms of your old father. May I ask you what *he* thinks of it? If you voted for the desecration of Sunday by a low baseball game, could you dare go home and face that good old man?"

"Yes, madam," said Goldstein mildly; "we are *both* Jews."

A low laugh rippled out from near-by, and Alonzo, turning almost violently, beheld his lady of the furs. She was leaning back against a broad pilaster, her hands sweeping the same big coat behind her, her face turned toward him, but her eyes, sparklingly delighted, resting upon Goldstein.

Under the broad fur hat she made a picture as engaging, to Alonzo Rawson, as it was bewitching. She appeared not to see him, to be quite unconscious of him—and he believed it. Truslow and five or six members of both houses were about her, and they all seemed to be bending eagerly toward her. Alonzo was furious with her.

Her laugh lingered upon the air for a moment, then her glance swept round the other way, omitting the Senator from Stackpole, who, immediately putting into practice a reserve which would have astonished Napoleon, swung about and quitted the deputation without a word of farewell or explanation. He turned into the cloak-room and paced the floor for three minutes with a malevolence which awed the colored attendants into not brushing his coat; but, when he returned to the corridor, cautious inquiries addressed to the tobacconist elicited the information that the handsome lady with Senator Truslow had departed.

Truslow himself had not gone. He was lounging in his seat when Alonzo returned and was genially talkative. The latter refrained from replying in kind, not altogether out of reserve, but more because of a dim suspicion (which rose within him the third time Truslow called him "Senator" in one sentence) that his first opinion of the young man as a light-minded person might have been correct.

There was no session the following afternoon, but Alonzo watched the street from the windows of his committee-room, which overlooked the splendid breadth of stone steps leading down from the great doors to the pavement. There were some big bookcases in the room, whose glass doors served as mirrors in which he more and more sternly regarded the soft image of an entirely new gray satin tie, while the conviction grew within him that (arguing from her behavior of the previous day) she would not come, and that the Stackpole girls were nobler by far at heart than many who might wear a king's-ransom's-worth of jewels round their throats at the opera-house in a large city. This sentiment was heartily confirmed by the clock when it marked half-past two. He faced the bookcase doors and struck his breast, his open hand falling across the gray tie with tragic violence; after which, turning for the last time to the windows, he uttered a loud exclamation and, laying hands upon an ulster and a gray felt hat, each as new as the satin tie, ran hurriedly from the room. The black automobile was waiting.

"I thought it possible you might see me from a window," said Mrs. Protheroe as he opened the little door.

"I was just coming out," he returned, gasping for breath. "I thought—from yesterday—you'd probably forgotten."

"Why 'from yesterday'?" she asked.

"I thought—I thought—" He faltered to a stop as the full glorious sense of her presence overcame him. She wore the same veil.

"You thought I did not see you yesterday in the corridor?"

"I thought you might have acted more—more—"

"More cordially?"

"Well, he said, looking down at his hands, "more like you knew we'd been introduced."

At that she sat silent, looking away from him, and he, daring a quick glance at her, found that he might let his eyes remain upon her face. That was a dangerous place for eyes to rest, yet Alonzo Rawson was anxious for the risk. The car flew along the even asphalt on its way to the country like a wild goose on a long slant of wind, and, with his foolish fury melted inexplicably into honey, Alonzo looked at her—and looked at her—till he would have given an arm for another quick corner and a street-car to send his cheek against that veiled, cold cheek of hers again. It was not until they reached the alternate vacant lots and bleak Queen Anne cottages of the city's ragged edge that she broke the silence.

"You were talking to some one else," she said almost inaudibly.

"Yes, ma'am, Goldstein, but—"

"Oh, no!" She turned toward him, lifting her hand. "You were quite the lion among ladies."

"I don't know what you mean, Mrs. Protheroe," he said, truthfully.

"What were you talking to all those women about?"

"It was about the 'Sunday Baseball Bill.' "

"Ah! The bill you attacked in your speech last Wednesday?"

"Yes, ma'am."

"I hear you haven't made any speeches since then," she said indifferently.

"No, ma'am," he answered gently. "I kind of got the idea that I'd better lay low for a while, at first, and get in some quiet, hard work."

"I understand. You are a man of intensely reserved nature."

"With men," said Alonzo, "I am. With ladies I am not so much so. I think a good woman ought to be told—"

"But you are interested," she interrupted, "in defeating that bill?"

"Yes, ma'am," he returned. "It is an iniquitous measure."

"Why?"

"Mrs. Protheroe!" he exclaimed, taken aback. "I thought all the ladies were against it. My own mother wrote to me from Stackpole that she'd rather see me in my grave than votin' for such a bill, and I'd rather see myself there!"

"But are you sure that you understand it?"

"I only know it desecrates the Sabbath. That's enough for me!"

She leaned toward him and his breath came quickly.

"No. You're wrong," she said, and rested the tips of her fingers upon his sleeve.

"I don't understand why—why you say that," he faltered. "It sounds kind of—surprising to me—"

"Listen," she said. Perhaps Mr. Truslow told you that I am studying such things. I do not want to be an idle woman; I want to be of use to the world, even if it must be only in small ways."

"I think that is a noble ambition!" he exclaimed. "I think all good women ought—" "Wait," she interrupted gently. "Now, that bill is a worthy one, though it astonishes you to hear me say so. Perhaps you don't understand the conditions. Sunday is the laboring man's only day of recreation—and what recreation is he offered?"

"He ought to go to church," said Alonzo promptly.

"But the fact is that he doesn't—not often—not at *all* in the afternoon. Wouldn't it be well to give him some wholesome way of employing his Sunday afternoons? This bill provides for just that, and it keeps him away from drinking, too, for it forbids the sale of liquor on the grounds."

"Yes, I know," said Alonzo plaintively. "But it ain't *right!* I was raised to respect the Sabbath and—"

"Ah, that's what you should do! You think I could believe in anything that wouldn't make it better and more sacred?"

"Oh, no, ma'am!" he cried reproachfully. "It's only that I don't see—"

"I am telling you." She lifted her veil and let him have the full dazzle of her beauty. "Do you know that many thousands of laboring people spend their Sundays drinking and carousing about the low country road-houses because the game is played at such places on Sunday? They go there because they never get a chance to see it played in the city. And don't you understand that there would be no Sunday liquor trade, no workingmen poisoning themselves every seventh day in the low groggeries, as hundreds of them do now, if they had something to see that would interest them?—something as wholesome and fine as this sport would be, under the conditions of this bill; something to keep them in the open air, something to bring a little gayety into their dull lives!" Her voice had grown louder and it shook a little, with a rising emotion, though its sweetness was only the more poignant. "Oh, my dear Senator, she cried, "don't you *see* how wrong you are? Don't you want to *help* these poor people?"

Her fingers, which had tightened upon his sleeve, relaxed and she leaned back, pulling the veil down over her face as if wishing to conceal from him that her lips trembled slightly; then resting her arm upon the leather cushions, she turned her head away from him, staring fixedly into the gaunt beech woods lining the country road along which they were now coursing. For a time she heard nothing from him, and the only sound was the monotonous chug of the machine.

"I suppose you think it rather shocking to hear a woman talking practically of such commonplace things," she said at last, in a cold voice, just loud enough to be heard.

"No, ma'am," he said huskily.

"Then what *do* you think?" she cried, turning toward him again with a quick, imperious gesture.

"I think I'd better go back to Stackpole," he answered very slowly, "and resign my job. I don't see as I've got any business in the Legislature."

"I don't understand you."

He shook his head mournfully. "It's a simple enough matter. I've studied out a good many bills and talked 'em over and I've picked up some influence and—"

"I know you have," she interrupted eagerly. "Mr. Truslow says that the members of your drains-and-dikes committee follow your vote on every bill."

"Yes, ma'am," said Alonzo Rawson meekly, "but I expect they oughtn't to. I've had a lesson this afternoon."

"You mean to say—"

"I mean that I didn't know what I was doing about that baseball bill. I was just pig-headedly goin' ahead against it, not knowing nothing about the conditions, and it took a lady to show me what they were. I would have done a wrong thing if you hadn't stopped me."

"You mean," she cried, her splendid eyes widening with excitement and delight; "you mean that you—that you—"

"I mean that I will vote for the bill!" He struck his clinched fist upon his knee. "I come to the Legislature to do *right!*"

"You will, ah, you *will* do right in this!" Mrs. Protheroe thrust up her veil again and her face was flushed and radiant with triumph. "And you'll work, and you'll make a speech for the bill?"

At this the righteous exaltation began rather abruptly to simmer down in the soul of Alonzo Rawson. He saw the consequences of too violently reversing, and knew how difficult they might be to face.

"Well, not—not exactly," he said weakly. "I expect our best plan would be for me to lay kind of low and not say any more about the bill at all. Of course, I'll quit workin' against it; and on the roll-call I'll edge close up to the clerk and say 'Aye' so that only him'll hear me. That's done every day—and I— well, I don't just exactly like to come out too publicly for it, after my speech and all I've done against it."

She looked at him sharply for a short second, and then offered him her hand and said: "Let's shake hands *now* on the vote. Think what a triumph it is for me to know that I helped to show you the right."

"Yes, ma'am," he answered confusedly, too much occupied with shaking her hand to know what he said. She spoke one word in an undertone to the driver and the machine took the very shortest way back to the city.

After this excursion several days passed before Mrs. Protheroe came to the State-house again. Rawson was bending over the desk of Senator Josephus Battle, the white-bearded leader of the opposition to the "Sunday Baseball Bill," and was explaining to him the intricacies of a certain drainage measure, when Battle, whose attention had wandered, plucked his sleeve and whispered:

"If you want to see a mighty pretty woman that's doin' no good here, look behind you, over there in the chair by the big fireplace at the back of the room."

Alonzo looked.

It was she whose counterpart had been in his dream's eye every moment of the dragging days which had been vacant of her living presence. A number of his colleagues were hanging over her almost idiotically; her face was gay and her voice came to his ears, as he turned, with the accent of her cadenced laughter running through her talk like a chime of tiny bells flitting through a strain of music.

"This is the third time she's been here," said Battle, rubbing his beard the wrong way. "She's lobbyin' for that infernal Sabbath-Desecration bill, but we'll beat her, my son."

"Have you made her acquaintance, Senator?" asked Alonzo stiffly.

"No, sir, and I don't want to. But I knew her father—the slickest old beat and the smoothest talker that ever waltzed up the pike. She married rich; her husband left her a lot of real estate around here, but she spends most of her time away. Whatever struck her to come down and lobby for that bill I don't know—yet—but I will! Truslow's helping her to help himself; he's got stock in the company that runs the baseball team, but what she's up to—well, I'll bet there's a nigger in the woodpile *some*where!"

"I expect there's a lot of talk like that!" said Alonzo, red with anger, and taking up his papers abruptly.

"Yes, *sir!*" said Battle emphatically, utterly misunderstanding the other's tone and manner. "Don't you worry, my son. We'll kill that venomous bill right here in this chamber! We'll kill it so dead that it won't make one flop after the axe hits it. You and me and some others'll tend to *that!* Let her work that pretty face and those eyes of hers all she wants to! I'm keepin' a little lookout, too—and I'll—"

He broke off, for the angry and perturbed Alonzo had left him and gone to his own desk. Battle, slightly surprised, rubbed his beard the wrong way and sauntered out to the lobby to muse over a cigar. Alonzo, loathing Battle with a great loathing, formed bitter phrases concerning that vicious-minded old gentleman, while for a moment he affected to be setting his desk in order. Then he walked slowly up the aisle, conscious of a roaring in his ears (though not aware how red they were) as he approached the semicircle about her.

He paused within three feet of her in a sudden panic of timidity, and then, to his consternation, she looked him squarely in the face, over the shoulders of two of the group, and the only sign of recognition that she exhibited was a slight frown of unmistakable repulsion, which appeared between her handsome eyebrows.

It was very swift; only Alonzo saw it; the others had no eyes for anything but her, and were not aware of his presence behind them, for she did not even pause in what she was saying.

Alonzo walked slowly away with the wormwood in his heart. He had not grown up among the young people of Stackpole without similar experiences, but it had been his youthful boast that no girl had ever "stopped speaking" to him without reason, or "cut a dance" with him and afterward found opportunity to repeat the indignity.

"What have I *done* to *her?*" was perhaps the hottest cry of his bruised soul, for the mystery was as great as the sting of it.

It was no balm upon that sting to see her pass him at the top of the outer steps, half an hour later, on the arm of that one of his colleagues who had been called the "best-dressed man in the Legislature." She swept by him without a sign, laughing that same laugh at some sally of her escort, and they got into the black automobile together and were whirled away and out of sight by the impassive bundle of furs who manipulated the wheel.

For the rest of that afternoon and the whole of that night no man, woman, or child heard the voice of Alonzo Rawson, for he spoke to none. He came not to the evening meal, nor was he seen by any who had his acquaintance. He entered his room at about midnight, and Trumbull was awakened by his neighbor's overturning a chair. No match was struck, however, and Trumbull was relieved to think that the Senator from Stackpole intended going directly to bed without troubling to light the gas, and that his prayers would soon be over. Such was not the case, for no other sound came from the room, nor were Alonzo's prayers uttered that night, though the unhappy statesman in the next apartment could not get to sleep for several hours on account of his nervous expectancy of them.

After this, as the day approached upon which hung the fate of the bill which Mr. Josephus Battle was fighting, Mrs. Protheroe came to the Senate Chamber nearly every morning and afternoon. Not once did she appear to be conscious of Alonzo Rawson's presence, nor once did he allow his eyes to delay upon her, though it can not be truthfully said that he did not always know when she came, when she left, and with whom she stood or sat or talked. He evaded all mention or discussion of the bill or of Mrs. Protheroe; avoided Truslow (who, strangely enough, was avoiding *him)* and, spending upon drains and dikes all the energy that he could manage to concentrate, burned the midnight oil and rubbed salt into his wounds to such marked effect that by the evening of the Governor's Reception—upon the morning following which the mooted bill was to come up—he offered an impression so haggard and worn that an actor might have studied him for a make-up as a young statesman going into a decline.

Nevertheless he dressed with great care and bitterness, and placed the fragrant blossom of a geranium—taken from a plant belonging to his landlady—in the lapel of his long coat before he set out.

And yet, when he came down the Governor's broad stairs, and wandered through the big rooms, with the glare of lights above him and the shouting of the guests ringing in his ears, a sense of emptiness beset him; the crowded place seemed vacant and without meaning. Even the noise sounded hollow and remote—and why had he bothered about the geranium? He hated her and would never look at her again—but why was she not there?

By and by, he found himself standing against a wall, where he had been pushed by the press of people.

He was wondering drearily what he was to do with a clean plate and a napkin which a courteous negro had handed him, half an hour earlier, when he felt a quick jerk at his sleeve. It was Truslow, who had worked his way along the wall, and who now, standing on tiptoe, spoke rapidly but cautiously, close to his ear.

"Senator, be quick," he said sharply, at the same time alert to see that they were unobserved. "Mrs. Protheroe wants to speak to you at once. You'll find her near the big palms under the stairway in the hall."

He was gone—he had wormed his way half across the room—before the other, in his simple amazement, could answer. When Alonzo at last found a word, it was only a monosyllable, which, with his accompanying action, left a matron of years, who was at that moment being pressed fondly to his side, in a state of mind almost as dumfounded as his own. *"Here!"* was all he said as he pressed the plate and napkin into her hand and departed forcibly for the hall, leaving a spectacular wreckage of trains behind him.

The upward flight of the stairway left a space underneath, upon which, as it was screened (save for a narrow entrance) by a thicket of palms, the crowd had not encroached. Here were placed a divan and a couple of chairs; there was shade from the glare of gas, and the light was dim and cool. Mrs. Protheroe had risen from the divan when Alonzo entered this grotto, and stood waiting for him.

He stopped in the green entrance-way with a quick exclamation.

She did not seem the same woman who had put such slights upon him, this tall, white vision of silk, with the summery scarf falling from her shoulders. His great wrath melted at the sight of her; the pain of his racked pride, which had been so hot in his breast, gave way to a species of fear. She seemed not a human being, but a white spirit of beauty and goodness who stood before him, extending two fine arms to him in long, white gloves.

She left him to his trance for a moment, then seized both his hands in hers and cried to him in her rapturous, low voice: "Ah, Senator, you have come! I *knew* you understood!"

"Yes ma'am," he whispered chokily.

She drew him to one of the chairs and sank gracefully down upon the divan near him.

"Mr. Truslow was so afraid you wouldn't," she went on rapidly, "but I was sure. You see I didn't want anybody to suspect that I had any influence with you. I didn't want them to know, even, that I'd talked to you. It all came to me after the first day that we met. You see I've believed in you, in your power and in your reserve, from the first. I want all that you do to seem to come from yourself and not from me or any one else. Oh, I *believe* in great, strong men who stand upon their own feet and conquer the world for themselves! That's *your* way, Senator Rawson. So, you see, as they think I'm lobbying for the bill, I wanted them to believe that your speech for it to-morrow comes from your own great, strong mind and heart and your sense of right, and not from any suggestion of mine."

"My speech!" he stammered.

"Oh, I know," she cried; "I know you think I don't believe much in speeches, and I don't ordinarily, but a few simple, straightforward and vigorous words from you, to-morrow, may carry the bill through. You've made such *progress,* you've been so *reserved,* that you'll carry great weight—and there are three votes of the drains-and-dikes that are against us now, but will follow yours absolutely. Do you think I would have 'cut' *you* if it hadn't been *best?*"

"But I—"

"Oh, I know you didn't actually promise me to speak, that day. But I knew you would when the time came! I knew that a man of power goes over *all* obstacles, once his sense of *right* is aroused! I *knew*— I never doubted it, that once *you* felt a thing to be right you would strike for it, with all your great strength—at all costs—at all—"

"I can't—I—I—can't!" he whispered nervously. "Don't you see—don't you see—I—"

She leaned toward him, lifting her face close to his. She was so near him that the faint odor of her hair came to him again, and once more the unfortunate Senator from Stackpole risked a meeting of his eyes with hers, and saw the light shining far down in their depths.

At this moment the shadow of a portly man who was stroking his beard the wrong way projected itself upon them from the narrow, green entrance to the grotto. Neither of them perceived it.

Senator Josephus Battle passed on, but when Alonzo Rawson emerged, a few moments later, he was pledged to utter a few simple, straightforward, and vigorous words in favor of the bill. And—let the shame fall upon the head of the scribe who tells it—he had kissed Mrs. Protheroe!

The fight upon the "Sunday Baseball Bill" the next morning was the warmest of that part of the session, though for a while the reporters were disappointed. They were waiting for Senator Battle, who was famous among them for the vituperative vigor of his attacks and for the kind of personalities which made valuable copy. And yet, until the debate was almost over, he contented himself with going quietly up and down the aisles, whispering to the occupants of the desks, and writing and sending a multitude of notes to his colleagues. Meanwhile, the orators upon both sides harangued their fellows, the lobby, the unpolitical audience, and the patient presiding officer to no effect, so far as votes went. The general impression was that it would be close.

Alonzo Rawson sat bent over his desk, his eyes fixed with gentle steadiness upon Mrs. Protheroe, who occupied the chair wherein he had first seen her. A senator of the opposition was finishing his denunciation, when she turned and nodded almost imperceptibly to the young man.

He gave her one last look of pathetic tenderness and rose.

"The Senator from Stackpole!"

"I want," Alonzo began, in his big voice—"I want to say a few simple, straightforward but vigorous words about this bill. You may remember I spoke against it on its second reading—"

"You did *that!*" shouted Senator Battle suddenly.

"I want to say now," the Senator from Stackpole continued, "that at that time I hadn't studied the subject sufficiently. "I didn't know the conditions of the case, nor the facts, but since then a great light has broke in upon me—"

"I should say it had! I saw it break!" was Senator Battle's second violent interruption.

When order was restored, Alonzo, who had become very pale, summoned his voice again. "I think we'd ought to take into consideration that Sunday is the working-man's only day of recreation and not drive him into low groggeries, but give him a chance in the open air to indulge his love of wholesome sport—"

"Such as the ancient Romans enjoyed!" interposed Battle vindictively.

"No, sir!" Alonzo wheeled upon him, stung to the quick. "Such a sport as free-born Americans and *only* free-born Americans can play in this wide world—the American game of baseball, in which no other nation of the *Earth* is our equal!"

This was a point scored and the cheering lasted two minutes. Then the orator resumed:

"I say: 'Give the working-man a chance!' Is his life a happy one? You know it ain't! Give him his one day. *Don't* spoil it for him with your laws—he's only got one! I'm not goin' to take up any more of your time, but if there's anybody here who thinks my well-considered opinion worth following I say: *'Vote for this bill.'* It is right and virtuous and ennobling, and it ought to be passed! I say: *'Vote for it.'* "

The reporters decided that the Senator from Stackpole had "wakened things up." The gavel rapped a long time before the chamber quieted down, and when it did, Josephus Battle was on his feet and had obtained the recognition of the chair.

"I wish to say, right here," he began, with a rasping leisureliness, "that I hope no member of this honored body will take my remarks as personal or unparliamentary—*but*"— he raised a big forefinger and shook it with menace at the presiding officer at the same time suddenly lifting his voice to an unprintable shriek—"I say to *you,* sir, that the song of the siren has been *heard* in the land, and the call of Delilah has been answered! When the Senator from Stackpole rose in his chamber, less than three weeks ago, and denounced this iniquitous measure, I heard him with pleasure—we *all* heard him with pleasure—*and* respect! In spite of his youth and the poor quality of his expression, *we* listened to him. *We* knew he was sincere! What has caused the change in him? What *has,* I ask? I shall not tell you, upon this floor, but I've taken mighty good care to let most of you know, during the morning, either by word of mouth or by *note* of hand! Especially those of you of the drains-and-dikes and others who might follow this young Samson, whose locks have been shore! *I've* told you all about that, and more—*I've* told you the *inside* history of some *facts* about the bill that I will not make public, because I am too confident of our strength to defeat this devilish measure, and prefer to let our vote speak our opinion of it! Let me not detain you longer. *I* thank you!"

Long before he had finished, the Senator from Stackpole was being held down in his chair by Truslow and several senators whose seats were adjacent; and the vote was taken amid an uproar of shouting and confusion. When the clerk managed to proclaim the result over all other noises, the bill was shown to be defeated and "killed," by a majority of five votes.

A few minutes later, Alonzo Rawson, his neckwear disordered and his face white with rage, stumbled out of the great doors upon the trail of Battle, who had quietly hurried away to his hotel for lunch as soon as he had voted.

The black automobile was vanishing round a corner. Truslow stood upon the edge of the pavement staring after it ruefully:

"Where is Mrs. Protheroe?" gasped the Senator from Stackpole.

"She's gone," said the other.

"Gone where?"

"Gone back to Paris. She sails day after to-morrow. She just had time enough to catch her train for New York after waiting to hear how the vote went. She told me to tell you good-by, and that she was sorry. Don't stare at me, Rawson! I guess we're in the same boat!— Where are you going?" he finished abruptly.

Alonzo swung by him and started across the street. "To find Battle!" the hoarse answer came back.

The conquering Josephus was leaning meditatively upon the counter of the cigar-stand of his hotel when Alonzo found him. He took one look at the latter's face and backed to the wall, tightening his grasp upon the heavy-headed ebony cane it was his habit to carry, a habit upon which he now congratulated himself.

But his precautions were needless. Alonzo stopped out of reaching distance.

"You tell me," he said in a breaking voice; you tell me what you meant about Delilah and sirens and Samsons and inside facts! You tell me!"

"You wild ass of the prairies," said Battle, "I saw you last night behind them pa'ms! But don't you think I told it—or ever will! I just passed the word around that she'd argued you into her way of thinkin', same as she had a good many others. And as for the rest of it, I found out where the nigger in the woodpile was, and I handed that out, too. Don't you take it hard, my son, but I told you her husband left her a good deal of land around here. She owns the ground that they use for the baseball park, and her lease would be worth considerable more if they could have got the right to play on Sunday!"

Senator Trumbull sat up straight, in bed, that night, and, for the first time during his martyrdom, listened with no impatience to the prayer which fell upon his ears.

"O Lord Almighty," through the flimsy partition came the voice of Alonzo Rawson, quaveringly, but with growing strength: "Aid Thou me to see my way more clear! I find it hard to tell right from wrong, and I find myself beset with tangled wires. O God, I feel that I am ignorant, and fall into many devices. These are strange paths wherein Thou hast set my feet, but I feel that through Thy help, and through great anguish, I am learning!"

IN EACH OTHER'S SHOES

George Parsons Lathrop

I

John Crombie had taken a room at the new apartment building, The Lorne; having advanced so far in his experience of New York as to be aware that if he could once establish himself in a house associated by name with foreign places and titles his chance of securing "position" would be greatly increased. He did not, however, take his meals in the expensive café of that establishment, finding it more economical to go to an outlandish little French restaurant, some distance away, which had been nicknamed among those of his acquaintance who resorted to it "The Fried Cat." This designation, based on a supposed resemblance to the name of the proprietor, Fricat, was also believed to have value as a sarcasm.

It was with no pleasant sensations, therefore, that Crombie, waking on a gray and drizzling morning of November, remembered that he must hie him to "The Fried Cat" for an early breakfast. He was in a hurry that day; he had a great deal to do. His room was very small and dark; he bounced up and dressed himself, in an obscure sort of way, surreptitiously opening the door and reaching vaguely for his shoes, which stood just outside, ready blacked. Nor did it add to his comfort to know that the shoes were very defective as to their soles, and would admit the water freely from the accumulated puddles of the sidewalks. In fact, he had been ashamed to expose their bad condition to the porter when he put them out every night, as he was forced to do, since they were his only pair. Drawing them on hastily, in order to conceal his mortification from even his own mind, he sallied forth; and though at the moment of putting them on a dim sense of something unfamiliar crossed his mind, it was not until he reached "The Fried Cat" that he became fully aware that he had carried off some one else's shoes. He turned up the soles, privately, underneath the low-hanging tablecloth, and by a brief examination convinced himself that the gaiters did not belong to him. The test was simple: his feet were unaccountably dry, and there were none of those breaks in the lower surface of their leather covering which he had so often been obliged to contemplate.

He saw at once that the porter of The Lorne had made a mistake, and must have deposited at another apartment his own very insufficient foot-gear; but there was no chance now to remedy the confusion. Crombie had barely time to reach the office where he was employed.

On an ordinary occasion he would perhaps have gone back to The Lorne and effected an honorable exchange. This particular day, however, was by no means an ordinary occasion. Crombie had made up his mind to take a momentous step; and it was therefore essential that he should appear at his desk exactly on time.

He was a clerk in an important engraving company. For several years he had occupied that post, without any opportunity having presented itself for a promotion. At the best, even should he rise, what could he expect? To be cashier, perhaps, or possibly, under exceptional circumstances, a confidential private secretary. This prospect did not satisfy him; he was determined to strike for something higher.

It will naturally be inferred that he was ambitious. I am not in a position to deny this; but all I can be certain of is, that he was in love—which is often about the same thing.

Several times at The Lorne he had met in the hallways or in the elevator a young lady, who was in no small degree beautiful, and charmed him still more by her generous presence, which conveyed the idea of a harmonious and lovely character. She had light hair and blue eyes, but these outward attributes were joined with a serenity and poise of manner that indicated greater stability than is attributed, as a rule, to individuals of her type.

Once he happened to arrive at the main entrance just as this vision of beauty emerged to take her place in a coupé which was waiting by the curbstone. She dropped her card-case upon the sidewalk, and Crombie's heart throbbed with delight as he picked it up, gave it to her, and received her smiling thanks for his little service. Another time, as he was descending in the elevator, a door opposite the shaft, on the second floor, stood open, and he caught a glimpse of the apartment to which it gave access. The room was finished in soft tints, and was full of upholstery and hangings that lent it a dim golden atmosphere. In the middle of it stood the young girl, clad in the palest blue, above which her hair shone like a golden cloud on some dim evening sky.

Slight occurrences of this sort had affected him. He learned that she was the daughter of Littimer, the rich, widowed banker: her name was Blanche.

II

In these new, stout shoes that did not belong to him Crombie trod with a buoyancy and assurance strongly in contrast with the limp and half-hearted pace to which his old, shabby gaiters had formerly inclined him. He rattled down the stairs of the elevated station with an alacrity almost bumptious; and the sharp, confident step that announced his entrance into the company's office made the other clerks quite ashamed of their own want of spirit.

He worked at his desk until noon; but when the bells of Trinity rang twelve in solemn music over the busy streets, he dropped his pen, walked with a decisive air the length of the room, and, opening a door at the other end, presented himself before Mr. Blatchford, the treasurer, who was also an influential director. "Crombie, eh? Well, what is it?"

"I want to speak with you a moment, sir."

"Anything important? I'm busy."

"Yes, sir; quite important—to me. Possibly it may be to you."

"Fire away, then; but cut it short." Mr. Blatchford's dense, well-combed gray side whiskers were directed toward the young man in an aggressive way, as if they had been some sort of weapon.

Crombie nonchalantly settled himself in a chair, at ease.

"I am tired of being a clerk," he said. "I'm going to be a director in this company."

"I guess you're going to be an inmate of a lunatic asylum," Mr. Blatchford remarked with astonished cheerfulness.

"That seems as unlikely to me as the other thing does to you," said Crombie.

Hereupon Mr. Blatchford became sarcastically deferential. "And just about when do you propose to become a director?" he asked.

"In the course of a month. The election, I believe, takes place in December."

"Quite right," said his senior, whose urbanity was meant to be crushing. "Meanwhile, you will need leisure to attend to this little matter. Suppose I oblige you by saying that the company has no further need of your services?"

"Suppose you do. What then?"

Mr. Blatchford gave way to his anger. "What then? Why, then you would have to go; that's all. You would be thrown out of employment. You would have to live on your principal, as long as there was any; and afterward you would be obliged to find some other work, or beg, or borrow, or—"

"That's enough," said Crombie, rising with dignity.

"No, it isn't," the treasurer declared, "for you don't seem to understand even now. I discharge you, Mr. Crombie, on the company's behalf, and you may leave this office at once."

Crombie bowed and went out. "I'm going to be a director, all the same," he told Mr. Blatchford before he closed the door. Then he collected the few articles that belonged to him from his desk, and departed, a free man. He had his future to himself; or else he had no future worth speaking of; he wasn't sure which. Nevertheless, he felt quite happy. Such a result as this had

183

seemed to him, in the prospect, hardly possible; but now that it had arrived he was not discomfited. Unbounded courage seemed to rise from the stout soles of the alien boots, percolating through his whole system. He was surprised at himself. He had intended to use more diplomacy with Mr. Blatchford, and it was no joke to him to lose his place. But instead of feeling despondent, or going at once in search of new employment, he cheerfully went about making calls on several gentlemen who, he thought, might be induced to aid in his ambitious project. His manner was that of a person sure of his powers and enjoying a well-earned leisure. It had its effect. Two or three stockholders of the company joined in agreeing with him that improved methods could be introduced into its management, and that it would be a good thing to have in the board, say, two young, fresh, active men—of whom Crombie, by reason of his experience and training, should be one.

"I own a little stock," said the deposed clerk, who had taken the precaution to obtain a couple of shares by great effort in saving. "Besides, not having any other engrossing interests at present, I could give my whole attention to the company's affairs."

"Quite so," said the merchant whom he was addressing, comfortably. "We must see if we can get together a majority; no time to be lost, you know."

"No, sir. I shall go right to work; and perhaps you will speak to some of your friends, and give me some names."

"Certainly. Come in again pretty soon; will you?"

Crombie saw that he had a good foundation to build upon already. Blatchford was not popular, even among the other directors; and sundry stockholders, as well as people having business with the company, had conceived a strong dislike of him on account of his overbearing manners. Therefore it would not be hard to enlist sympathy for a movement obnoxious to him. But it was imperative that the self-nominated candidate should acquire more of the stock; and to do this capital must be had. Crombie did not see quite how it was to be got; he had no sufficient influence with the bankers.

The afternoon was nearly spent, and he trudged uptown, thinking of the ways and means. But though the problem was far from solved, he still continued in a state of extraordinary buoyancy. Those shoes, those shoes! He was so much impressed by their comfort and the service they had done him in making a good appearance that he resolved to get a new pair of his own. He stopped and bought them; then kept on toward The Lorne, carrying his purchase under his arm without embarrassment.

On regaining his modest apartment he sent for the boot-boy, and inquired the whereabouts of his missing shoes.

"Couldn't tell you, sir," said the servant. "Pretty near all the men's boots in the house has gone out, you see, and they'll only be coming back just about now. I'll look out for 'em, sir, and nab 'em as soon as they show up."

"All right. Whose are these that I've been wearing?"

The boy took them, turned them over, and examined them with the eye of a connoisseur in every part. "Them? I should say, sir, them was Mr. Littimer's."

Crombie blushed with mortification. Of all the dwellers in the Lorne, this was the very one with whom it was the most embarrassing to have such a complication occur; and yet, strange inconsistency! he had been longing for any accident, no matter how absurd or fantastic, that could bring him some chance of an acquaintance with Blanche.

"Take these boots, dry them right away, and give 'em a shine. Then carry them up to Mr. Littimer's rooms." He gave the boy a quarter: he was becoming reckless.

Now that he had embarked upon a new career, he perceived the impropriety of a future director in the Engraving Company going to dine at "The Fried Cat," and so resolved to take his dinner in the gorgeous café of The Lorne. While he was waiting for the proper moment to descend thither, he could not get the shoe question out of his mind. Surely, the boot-boy could not have been so idiotic as to have left that ancient, broken-down pair at Littimer's threshold! And yet it was possible. Crombie felt another flush of humility upon his cheeks. Then he wandered off into reverie upon the multifarious errands of all the pairs of boots and shoes that had gone forth from the great apartment house that day.

Breaking off from these idle fancies at length, he went down to the café; and there he had the pleasure of dining at a table not far from Blanche Littimer. But, to his surprise, she was alone. Her father did not appear during the meal.

III

The fact was that the awful possibility, mere conjecture of which had frightened Crombie, had occurred. Littimer had received the young man's shoes in place of his own.

They happened to fit him moderately well; so that he likewise, did not notice the exchange until he had started for his office. He believed in walking the entire distance, no matter what the weather and to this practice he made rare exceptions. But he had not progressed very far before he became annoyed by an unaccustomed intrusion of dampness that threatened him with a cold. He looked down, carefully surveyed the artificial casing of his extremities, and decided to hail the first unoccupied coupé he should meet. It was some time before he found one; and when finally he took his seat in the luxurious little bank parlor at Broad Street, his feet were quite wet.

His surprise at this occurrence was doubled when, on taking off the shoes and scrutinizing them more closely, he ascertained that they were the work of his usual maker. What had happened to him? Was he dreaming? It seemed to him that he had gone back many years; that he was a poor young man again, entering upon his first struggle for a foothold in the crowded, selfish, unhome-like metropolis. He remembered the day when *he* had worn shoes like these.

He sent out for an assortment of new ones, from which, with unnecessary lavishness, he chose and kept three or four pairs. All the rest of the day, nevertheless, those sorry Congress boots of Crombie's, which he had directed his office-boy to place beside the soft-coal fire, for drying, faced him with a sort of haunting look. However much he might be occupied with weightier matters, he could not keep his eyes from straying in that direction; and when-ever they rested on that battered "right" and that way-worn "left," turned up in that mute, appealing repose and uselessness at the fender, his thoughts recurred to his early years of trial and poverty. Ah! how greatly he had changed since then! On some accounts he could almost wish that he were poor again. But when he remembered Blanche, he was glad, for her sake, that he was rich.

But if for her sake, why not for others? Perhaps he had been rather selfish, not only about Blanche, but toward her. His conscience began to reproach him. Had he made for her a large life? Since her mother's premature death, had he instilled into her sympathies, tastes, companionships that would make her existence the richer? Had he not kept her too much to himself? On the other hand, he had gratified all her material wants; she could wear what she pleased, she could go where she chose, she had acquaintances of a sort be-coming to the daughter of a wealthy man. Yet there was something lacking. What did she know about old, used-up boots and all that pertains to them? What did she know about indigence, real privation, and brave endurance, such as a hundred thousand fellow-creatures all around her were undergoing?

Somehow it dawned upon the old banker that if she knew about all these things and had some share in them, albeit only through sympathy and help-ing, she might be happier, more truly a woman, than she was now.

As he sat alone, in revery, he actually heaved a deep sigh. A sigh is often as happy a deliverance as a laugh, in this world of sorrows. It was the first that had escaped Littimer in years. Let us say that it was a breathing space, which gave him time for reflection; it marked the turning of a leaf; it was the beginning of a new chapter in his life. Before he left the bank he locked the door of the private parlor, and was alone for two or three minutes. The office boy was greatly puzzled the next morning, when he found all the new pairs of shoes ranged intact in the adjoining cupboard. The old ones were missing.

Littimer had gone away in them, furtively. He was ashamed of his own impulse.

This time he resolutely remained afoot instead of hiring a carriage. He despatched a messenger to Blanche, saying that sudden business would pre-vent his returning to dinner, and continued indefinitely on his way—whither? As to that he was by no means certain; he knew only that he must get out of the beaten track, out of the ruts. For an hour or two he must cease to be Littimer, the prosperous moneyed man, and must tread once more the obscure paths through which he had made his way to fortune. He could hardly have explained the prompting which he obeyed.

As it chanced, he passed by "The Fried Cat"; and, dingy though the place was, he felt an irresistible desire to enter it. Seating himself, he ordered the regular dinner of the day. The light was dim; the tablecloth was dirty; the attendance was irregular and distracted. Littimer took one sip of the sour wine—which had a flavor resembling vinegar and carmine ink in equal parts —and left the further contents of his bottle untasted. The soup, the stew, and the faded roast that were set before him, he could scarcely swallow; but a small cup of coffee at the end of the repast came in very palatably.

In default of prandial attractions, Littimer tried to occupy himself by looking at the people around him. The omnifarious assembly included pale, primwhiskered young clerks; shabby, lonely, sallow young women, whose sallowness and shabbiness stamped them with the mark of integrity; other females whose specious splendor was not nearly so reassuring; old men, broken-down men, middle-aged men of every description.

"Some of them," Littimer reflected, "are no worse than I am. But are any of them really any better?"

He could not convince himself that they were; yet his sympathies, somehow, went out toward this motley crowd. It appeared to him very foolish that he should sympathize, but he could not help it. "And, after all," was the next thought that came to him, "are we to give pity to people, or withhold it, simply because they are better or worse than ourselves? No; there is something more in it than that."

Leaving "The Fried Cat" abruptly, he betook himself to an acquaintance who, he knew, was very active in charities—a man who worked practically, and gave time to the work.

"Do you visit any of your distress cases tonight?" he asked.

"Yes, I shall make a few calls," answered the man of charity. "Would you like to go along?"

"Very much."

So the two started out together. The places they went to were of various kinds, and revealed a considerable diversity of misfortune. Sometimes they entered tenement houses of the most wretched character; but in other instances they went to small and cheap but decent lodgings over the shops on West Side avenues, or even penetrated into boarding-houses of such good appearance that the banker was surprised to find his friend's mission carrying him thither. All the cases, however, had been studied, and were vouched for; and several were those of young men and women having employment, but temporarily disabled, and without friends who could help them.

"You do well to help these beginners, at critical times," said the banker, with satisfaction.

It was almost the same as if he were receiving relief himself. Who knows? Perhaps he was; but to the outward eye it appeared merely that, with his friend's sanction, he was dispensing money and offers of good-will to the needy. What a strange freak it was, though, in Littimer! He kept on with the work until quite late in the evening, regardless of the risk he ran by continuing out-of-doors when so ill shod.

IV

Having waited a reasonable length of time after dinner, Crombie again left his room, resolved to make a call upon Mr. Littimer, on the plea of apologizing for having marched away with his shoes.

He would not run the risk, by sending his card, of being denied as a stranger; so, notwithstanding much hesitation and tremor, he approached the door which he had once seen standing open, and knocked. A voice which he now heard for the second time in his life, but which was so sweet and crept so naturally into the centre of his heart that the thought of it seemed always to have been there, answered: "Come in." And he did come in.

"Is Mr. Lit—is your father at home?" It seemed to bring him a little nearer to her to say "your father."

Blanche had risen from the chair where she was reading, and looked very much surprised. "Oh," she exclaimed, with girlish simplicity, "I thought it was the waiter! N-no; he hasn't come home yet."

"I beg pardon. Then perhaps I'd better call later." Crombie made a feeble movement toward withdrawal.

"Did you want to see him on business? Who shall I tell him?"

"Mr. Crombie, please. It's nothing very important."

"Oh," said Blanche, with a little blush at her own deception, "haven't I seen you in the house before? Are you staying here?"

She remembered distinctly the incident of the card-case, and how very nice she had thought him, both on that occasion and every time she had seen him. But as for him, his heart sank at the vague impersonality with which she seemed to regard him.

"Yes, I'm here, and can easily come in again."

"I expect my father almost any moment," she said. "Would you like to wait?"

What an absurd question, to one in his frame of mind! "Well, really, it is such a very small matter," he began, examining his hat attentively. Then he glanced up at her again and smiled: "I only wanted to—to make an apology."

"An apology!" echoed Blanche, becoming rather more distant. "Oh, dear! I'm very sorry, I'm sure. I didn't know there'd been any trouble." She began to look anxious, and turned her eyes upon the smouldering fire in the grate. So this was to be the end of her pleasant, cheerful reveries about this nice young man. And the reveries had been more frequent than she had been aware of until now.

"There has been no trouble," he assured her, eagerly. "Just a little mistake that occurred; and, in fact, I was hardly responsible for it."

Blanche's eyes began to twinkle with a new and amusing interpretation. "Ah!" she cried, "are you the gentleman who—" Then she stopped short.

Crombie was placed in an unexpected embarrassment. How could he possibly drag into his conversation with this lovely young creature so commonplace and vulgar a subject as shoe-leather! Ignoring her unfinished question, he asked: "Do you know, Miss Littimer, whether the—a—one of the servants here has brought up anything for your father—that is, a parcel, a—"

"A pair of shoes?" Blanche broke in, her eyes dancing, while her lips parted in a smile.

"Yes, yes; that's what I meant."

"They came up just after dinner," Blanche returned. "Then you *are* the gentleman."

"I'm afraid I am," Crombie owned, and they both laughed.

Blanche quietly, and with no apparent intention, resumed her chair; and this time Crombie took a seat without waiting to be invited again. Thus they fell to talking in the friendliest way.

"I can't imagine what has become of papa," said Blanche. "He sent word, in the most mysterious manner, that he had an engagement; and it is so unusual! Perhaps it's something about the new house he's building—up-town, you know. Dear me! it does make so much trouble, and I don't believe I shall like it half as well as these little, cosey rooms."

The little, cosey rooms were as the abode of giants compared with Crombie's contracted quarters; but he drew comfort from what she said, thinking how such sentiments might make it possible to win even so unattainable an heiress into some modest home of his own.

"You don't know till you try it," he replied. "Just think of having a place all to yourself, belonging to you."

Blanche lifted her eyebrows, and a little sigh escaped her. She was reflecting, perhaps, that a place all to herself would be rather lonely.

"You have never met my father?" she asked.

"No. I have seen him."

"Well, I think you will like him when you know him."

"I don't doubt it!" Crombie exclaimed with fervor, worshiping the very furniture that surrounded Blanche.

"I hope we may become better acquainted."

"Only I think, Mr. Crombie, he will owe *you* an apology now."

"Why?"

"For keeping your shoes out so late."

"*My* shoes!" said the young man, in surprise.

"Why, yes. Didn't you know they came to him? The porter said so."

Crombie grew red with the sense of his disgrace in having his poverty-stricken boots come to the knowledge of the banker. Really, his mortification

was so great that the accident seemed to him to put an end to all his hopes of
further relations with Blanche and her father.

"Oh, I assure you," he said rising, "that makes no difference at all! I'm
sorry I mentioned the matter. Pray tell Mr. Littimer not to think of it. I—I
believe I'd better go now.

Blanche rose too, and Crombie was on the point of bowing a good-night,
when the door opened, and a weary figure presented itself on the threshold;
the figure of a short man with a spare face, and whiskers in which gray
mingled with the sandy tint. He had a pinched, half-growling expression, was
draped in a light, draggled overcoat, and carried an umbrella, the ribs of
which hung loose around the stick.

"There's papa this moment!" cried Blanche.

Crombie perceived that escape was impossible, and, in a few words, the
reason of his presence there was made known to the old gentleman.

Littimer examined the visitor swiftly, from head to foot—especially the
foot. He advanced to the fire, toasted first one and then the other of the damp
gaiters he had on, and at length broke out, in a tone bordering on reproach:
"So you are the owner, are you? Then my sympathy has all been wasted!
Why, I supposed, from the condition of these machines that I've been lugging
around with me half the day that you must be in the greatest distress. And, lo
and behold! I find you a young fellow in prime health, spruce and trim, doing
well, and perfectly happy."

"I can't help that, sir," retorted Crombie, nettled, but speaking with respect. "I confess I was very happy until a moment or two ago."

"What do you mean by that?" the other demanded, with half-yielding
pugnacity. "Till I came in—is that the idea?"

"Oh, papa!" said Blanche, softly.

"Well, honey-bee, what's the matter?" her father asked, trying to be gruff.
"Can't I say what I like, here?" But he surrendered at once by adding: "You
may be sure I don't want to offend any one. Sit down, Mr. Crombie, and wait
just a few moments while I go into the other room and rejuvenate my hoofs,
so to speak—for I fear I've made a donkey of myself."

He disappeared into an adjoining room with Blanche, who there informed
him artlessly of Crombie's consideration and attentiveness in restoring the
errant shoes. When they came back Littimer insisted upon having the young
man remain a little longer and drink a glass of port with him. Before taking
his departure, however, Crombie, who felt free to speak since Blanche had
retired, made a brief statement in satisfaction of conscience.

"You hinted," he said, "that you judged me to be doing well. I don't want
to leave you with a false impression. The truth is, I am not doing well. I have
no money to speak of, and to-day I lost the position on which I depended."

"You don't tell me!" Littimer's newly roused charitable impulses came to
the fore. "Why, now you begin to be really interesting, Mr. Crombie."

"Thanks," said Crombie; "I'm not ambitious to interest people in that way,
I told you only because I thought it fair."

"Don't be touchy, my dear sir," answered the banker. "I meant what I said. Come, let's see what can be done. Have you any scheme in view?"

"Yes, I have," said Crombie, with decision.

Littimer gave a grunt. He was afraid of people with schemes, and was disappointed with the young man's want of helplessness. Dependence would have been an easier thing to deal with.

"Well," said he, "we must talk it over. Come and see me at the bank to-morrow. You know the address."

V

The next day Crombie called at the bank; but Littimer was not there. He was not very well, it was said; had not come down-town. Crombie did what he could toward organizing his fight for a directorship, and then returned to The Lorne, where he punctually inquired after Mr. Littimer's health, and learned that the banker's ardor in making the rounds among distressed people the night before had been followed by reaction into a bad cold, with some threat of pneumonia. Blanche was plainly anxious. The attack lasted three or four days, and Crombie, though the affair of the directorship was pressing for attention, could not forbear to remain as near as possible to Blanche, offering every aid within his power, so far as he might without overstepping the lines of his very recent acquaintance. But the Littimers did not, according to his observation, number any very intimate companions in their circle, or at least had not many friends who would be assiduous in such an emergency. Perhaps their friends were too busy with social engagements. Consequently, he saw a good deal of Blanche, and became to her an object of reliance.

Well, it was simply one of those things that happen only in fairy tales or in romances—or in real life. Littimer recovered without any serious illness, and, after a brief conference with Crombie, entered heartily into the young man's campaign. Crombie showed him just what combinations could be formed, how success could be achieved, and what lucrative results might be made to ensue. He conquered by figures and by lucid common-sense. Littimer agreed to buy a number of shares in the Engraving Company, which he happened to know could be purchased, and to advance Crombie a good sum with which to procure a portion of the same lot. But before this agreement could be consummated, Crombie, with his usual frankness, said to the banker:

"I will conceal nothing from you, Mr. Littimer. I fell in love with Blanche before I knew her, and if this venture of mine succeeds, I shall ask her to become my wife."

"Let us attend to business," said Littimer, severely. "Sentiment can take care of itself."

Their manoeuvre went on so vigorously that Blatchford became alarmed, and sent an ambassador to arrange a compromise; but by this time Crombie had determined to oust Blatchford himself and elect an entirely new set of men, to compose more than half the Board, and so control everything. He succeeded.

But Littimer did not forget the charitable enthusiasm which had been awakened by a circumstance on the surface so trivial as the mistake of a boot-boy. He did not desist from his interest in aiding disabled or unfortunate people who could really be aided. Some time after Crombie had achieved his triumph in the Engraving Company, and had repaid Littimer's loan, he was admitted to a share in the banking business; and eventually the head of the house was able to give a great deal of attention to perfecting his benevolent plans.

When the details of their wedding were under discussion, Crombie said to Blanche: "Oughtn't we to have an old shoe thrown after the carriage as we drive away?"

She smiled; looked him full in the eyes with a peculiar tenderness in which there was a bright, delicious sparkle of humor. "No; old shoes are much too useful to be wasted that way."

Somehow she had possessed herself of that particular, providential pair; and, though I don't want anybody to laugh at my two friends, I must risk saying that I suspect Mrs. Crombie of preserving it somewhere to this day, in the big new house up-town.

THE POLITE HORSE

Henry Beach Needham

Oh! Ascot Heath's a pleasant spot
All on a Gold-Cup day;
You'd have your work cut out, I wot,
To find a scene so gay. . . .

You try your fortune in The Ring;
Mostlike you have to pay.
No matter! Still a fling's a fling
On Ascot Gold-Cup day

        —Truth.

Jimmie Hatton was desperately homesick. His home, or what had been his home, was in Brooklyn, and in that section of the far-flung borough distinguished as Flatbush. He was domiciled in London. After his bacon and eggs and coffee of a morning, two minutes' walk brought him to the hub of the universe—Piccadilly Circus.

For Brooklyn thoroughfares, therefore, Jimmie Hatton had substituted on his neighborhood map high-sounding streets like Duke, Regent, Jermyn—where he lived—and Piccadilly. But a public highway by a less flossy name—Flatbush Avenue—may sound as sweet, even sweeter. Yes, Jimmie was all-fired homesick.

The distance from Piccadilly to New York is considerably greater than from Flatbush to London. From Jimmie's point of view this distance New Yorkward was not linear or nautical, but monetary.

In language more forlorn, he was far from home, and he was broke. Not dead broke—worse than that!

Across from his "digs," as he called his rooms, was the headquarters of the

193

organization which found a way for stranded Americans to navigate the Atlantic westward. But what to many an unhappy soul was God's lend-a-hand society, was to Jimmie Hatton nothing less than a scourge. Several times he had vowed to change his abode, all on account of this reminder of home and of King's County.

You see, Jimmie could pay his passage back. That's why his trial balance approximated a state more embittering than bankruptcy. He could go back—come back—but again among his old pals he would be forced to find a job in order, not alone to live as he had become accustomed to live, but, more important, to hold up his end. And the only business he knew had been cut from under him by that—"animated feather duster," as he delineated the governor who had "tied the can to racing in New York State."

Jimmie Hatton followed the horses.

In his carefree youth Jimmie was an exercise boy at Sheepshead Bay. His ambition was to be a jock, but nature defeated this aim. Jimmie ate himself out of the saddle!

Carrying weight for youth, he became a bookmaker's advance agent, otherwise a tout. But a tout he did not forever remain. He participated in several "killings," and reaching man's estate was heralded far and wide in the "pink uns" as Plunger Hatton. This title he retained against all bookmakers until his forced exile to England.

There were times before his expatriation when he was reported to be flattened out financially; other times when he was classed with the plungers of Wall Street. Never once, as a record of fact, had he been clean busted. Unlike most turf ventures he had salted away a tidy little sum in gilt-edged electric-lighting bonds. These he had purchased 'way below par, thanks to a tip from his pal at city hall, Dan Foss, and the securities were now quoted at double the figure he had paid for the coupon engraving. Every quarter Jimmie received $312.50, or annually $1,250—an amount representing interest at five per cent on the face value of the bonds.

In London, Jimmie Hatton could subsist on this income, if worse overtook worse, and make faces at the wolf. But not in little old America. It took real money, he told himself, to live comfortably at home. Jimmie hadn't it, and Jimmie had no sure thing in sight.

All he required was fifty thousand dollars. A mere bag o' shells, he dubbed it; a sum an office boy in Wall Street might peel off any bull movement. Fifty thousand dollars! Dan Foss had written to say that he could buy Jimmie a cozy freehold on the bright side of Comfort Street, U. S. A., for that trifling amount. Thus wrote Dan:

> Racing may be dead, but we've found a game what leaves it at the post. That's city contracting! You can't lose, and what you make —say, it's shameful. Can grab you off a nice interest in our company for fifty thousand. From Mike Doolan's estate—you've heard poor Mike died in a sanitarium. Couldn't stand prosperity.

Let me know bout the interest quick. Sure to be snapped up. Take care of yourself.

It was kind of Dan—oh, very kind! Perhaps some other friend would give him a chance to buy Mr. Rockefeller out. He was always getting good things offered him, was Jimmie.

And he possessed exactly one hundred pounds sterling to his name. Five hundred dollars in God's own currency! Which wasn't much for a "plunger." The bonds?—of course, but Jimmie would as soon have thought of hocking his mother's wedding ring, which he wore on his little finger, as to gamble with his "life insurance against manual labor." Not Jimmie Hatton.

But he did want that interest in the Invincible Contracting Company. And his chances of copping it were equal in any "book" to that of a 100-to-1 shot in a race with an odds-on favorite.

Wearily he turned to the racing page of the *St. James Gazette,* to ascertain what "The Judge" had to offer for explanation why Sunfire had been beaten the day before for the Coronation Cup.

Sunfire had lost Jimmie fifty quid. And he had spent a lot of time and mental effort figuring the horse a safe winner. In Sunfire's first important race of the season—the Newmarket Handicap for three-year-olds and upward—the big chestnut's defeat was excusable. He had got off to a bad start, but even so had come with a splendid rush in the stretch, and Thistleton had beaten him scarcely half a length.

Sunfire's losing in the Longleat Plate at Salisbury, as Jimmie doped it out, was attributed to ivory-headed riding. Allis, the jock, had waited too long before making his run on Sunfire. At that Thistleton was a lucky winner, having no more than a neck to spare.

Thistleton had given Sunfire two pounds at Newmarket and four pounds in the Longleat Plate, but in the Coronation Cup at Epsom he had to concede ten pounds to his rival. This had decided Jimmie. Thistleton couldn't carry the added weight and beat Sunfire—two hundred and fifty dollars of Jimmie's money said so.

But again Thistleton had won—nosed out Sunfire. Jimmie could think of no "alibi" for the chestnut three-year-old, unless he was too straight in the shoulder for coming down the hill before Tattenham Corner.

It could hardly be the distance, for Sunfire had run as well at Newmarket for a mile and a quarter as at Salisbury for the straight mile, proving himself a good sticker. The Coronation Cup was but two furlongs farther—over the Derby course of a mile and a half. Jimmie was stumped. Could The Judge evolve an excuse, he wondered, and read:

> Sunfire put up a good fight for the Coronation Cup, but couldn't quite do it against the redoubtable Thistleton. Three times these three-year-olds have met this season, and though each race has

been fought gamely to the finish, thrice Thistleton has been the victor.

For the Gold Cup at Ascot, Thistleton will surely start favorite with Sunfire next in demand. If Thistleton for any reason were scratched—he has been worked hard, by the bye—Sunfire should rule favorite. With his rival a nonstarter, Sunfire would represent no end of a good sporting chance. In that event my tip would be to back the chestnut three-year-old.

Thoughtfully Jimmie read over the outgiving of The Judge:

If Thistleton . . . were scratched . . . Sunfire would represent no end of a good sporting chance.

"I wonder," whispered Jimmie to his own judgment, carefully folding up the paper for future reference.

In his mind's vision he recalled Sunfire as he had looked him over in the paddock at Epsom the day before. A magnificent chestnut, every inch a racing machine! Jimmie had liked his head, he had liked his hocks, as he liked his eye. Above all he had liked Sunfire's high-bred air—something more, even, than manners and conformation. A courtly, an estimable, and withal "a deferential horse," Jimmie had thought.

A deferential horse!

II

Jimmie Hatton strolled into the Somerset next afternoon, and after "looking 'em over" as the summery procession of swell dames in filmy attire floated in to tea, visited the comfortable bar overlooking the Embankment. Immediately he was hailed by a group of American business men—London "entertainers" for their companies—and Americans not actively engaged in business.

There was Wilson Bayne, who had succeeded in giving a "bad" Yankee trust a good name in London town. Bayne had tons of personality and carloads of tact, everybody said so.

Seated next to him was H. Portner Cabot, formerly of Boston, who looked out for the shoe-machinery trust. Five years in London had made him quite human.

Colonel Rogers was there. The colonel was a perpetual promoter who never landed, yet who was never without expense money in some new promotion.

Of course Bobbie Marsh was present. Bobbie, according to Lanson, of the *Sun,* represented the American spending habit abroad.

To a man they liked Jimmie Hatton—liked him because they believed him thoroughly honest. "Squarest plunger in New York or London," any one of the group would have said.

"Hel-lo, Jimmie!" sang out Bayne. "Come join the ancient order of highbinders. Gentlemen, allow me—James Hatton, who is slowly but surely eliminating the British bookie from the scheme of things. Aren't you, Jimmie?"

"Slowly—yes," agreed Hatton. "There are a few left."

"You talk like a disappointed backer of Sunfire," Colonel Rogers observed.

"Beefy, take Mr. Hatton's order!" directed H. Portner Cabot.

"What will you have, sir?" asked Beefy, the wise waiter of the Somerset bar.

"Cigar, thank you—small, but strong."

The cigar fetched, lighted, and Jimmie Hatton smoking contentedly—his contribution to the general conviviality—Wilson Bayne made an announcement. Before making it he laid great stress on its importance.

"We've hit on a new name for Sunfire," he said.

"What's the matter with his moniker in Ruff's Guide?" asked Jimmie innocently.

"He was overlooked in the birthday honors," put in Cabot. "We must supply the deficiency."

"Y' see," explained Bayne, "for the third time this season Sunfire has dumped our coin in the stretch, when the race was as good as won by the sorrel devil."

"Chestnut," corrected Jimmie, who was becoming interested.

"Yellow—that's his real color," growled Colonel Rogers.

"Go on, Wilson," urged Bobbie Marsh.

"Henceforth and in the hereafter," Bayne resumed, "Sunfire is to be—The Polite Horse!"

"Lay you a quid you don't get it," said Colonel Rogers.

"I don't—you win, colonel," answered Jimmie cheerfully.

"Sunfire always finishes second to Thistleton, doesn't he?" asked Bayne.

"So far," agreed Jimmie.

"Why?" asked Bobbie Marsh, acting the interlocutor.

"Because he's too *polite* to beat the other horse," explained Bayne.

"Says to Thistleton—'After you, my dear Alphonse!' " the colonel interpreted.

"Wherefore—The Polite Horse," concluded Cabot.

"I s-e-e," said Jimmie.

Then as quickly as he could, without appearing to do so, Jimmie Hatton changed the conversation.

III

On the Saturday before Ascot, Thistleton, the popular favorite for the Gold Cup, broke down. His trainer sent him over the full course, and while the three-year-old showed no actual lameness at the finish, he pulled up very leg weary. The afternoon papers announced that Thistleton had been scratched by his owner, Lord Hardwicke. And without exception every racing authority, including The Judge, picked Sunfire to win the big race. So generally was the chestnut preferred that it was reasonably certain he would rule an even-money favorite. In three big events Sunfire had run second—twice a very close second—to Thistleton. What horse was there to beat the chestnut three-year-old? Not an expert would hazard a tip on any other thoroughbred to outrun Sunfire.

Jimmie Hatton experienced a most trying Sunday. He figured and he doped —he shut his eyes and called loudly upon his common sense.

Was he to back Sunfire and rely upon The Polite Horse to recoup his season's losses?

Jimmie didn't know—couldn't determine. Tired out, head weary, he went to bed, more homesick than ever for Brooklyn.

Monday morning brought no relief. In truth, his condition of mind became one of more acute desperation. There was a week-end cable from Dan Foss, who urged Jimmie most emphatically to buy the Doolan interest in the contracting company. The urgency of an immediate decision was underscored— "in four days." That meant, Jimmie supposed, until Thursday—the day of the Gold Cup. Then the chance would be gone. "Only fifty thousand to be comfortable all your life among your pals," concluded Dan.

Only fifty thousand!

"Ha!" Jimmie was homesick enough to cry, viewed it as a bitter joke.

He endeavored to dismiss it from his thoughts, but couldn't. It simply wouldn't be dismissed! The opportunity Dan Foss presented joined hands, so to say, with Jimmie's hunch on the Gold Cup—not his dope, but his hunch. Remember that.

Vainly James Hatton sought an avenue of escape. He tried logic with himself. Failed. He tried persuasion. Failed again. Then he asserted his authority —authority of sense over sentiment, of mind over disaster. Failed dismally. Upon which Jimmie called himself every variety of fool he could think of, and then coupled with "fool" an assortment of derogatory and shameful modifying epithets from his rich vocabulary. All to no purpose. He gave it up.

But he fought every step of the way to the safety-deposit vaults, where, dominated by Opportunity and Hunch, he removed from safekeeping the electric-lighting bonds—his insurance against manual labor—and with the precious securities in his pocket, visited the office of Wilson Bayne. Jimmie had done no bank borrowing in London, and required help.

Bayne knew the bonds well, and said offhand that he could arrange a loan in a couple of hours' time.

"How much do you want to raise?" he asked.

"The limit!—all the securities will stand," replied Jimmie hurriedly. Then cursed himself to himself once more.

"Believe I can get you the equivalent for twenty-five thousand dollars."

"Fine!" Jimmie said it without enthusiasm, as he might have said "Fudge!"

"How do you want the money?"

"In five and ten-pound notes."

Wilson Bayne glanced curiously from the bonds to the countenance of James Hatton, then said:

"Right-o, Jimmie. Meet me at the Somerset bar, two o'clock, and I'll have your money."

"Two o'clock, Somerset," repeated Jimmie, and arose to go.

"Say—none of my business," confessed Bayne—"but if it's no secret, what's your game, Jimmie?"

"No secret, simply this: As a backer of horses I've been losing pretty regular this season. So I'm going to turn bookmaker."

"Bookmaker?" questioned Bayne incredulously. "You are? For good?"

"That depends—how I make out. See you at the Somerset. Thanks for your trouble. So long."

It was never the rôle of wisdom, Jimmie believed, to appear too eager. Restraint was a top-weight virtue. Therefore he sauntered into the Somerset bar fifteen minutes after two. Wilson Bayne, who had arrived before time, was at the large round table, about which Beefy was moving quietly, taking orders.

"Sorry to be late," apologized Jimmie, "but—"

"Aw right, Jimmie," broke in Bayne. "Here's your money." Bayne handed him a small bundle of snow-white Bank of England notes, which are never reissued, therefore always clean and non-germ-bearing. "Better count it."

Jimmie counted the notes—indifferently, it appeared to the little group; rolled them up, slipped a rubber band about the roll, and stuffed it into the pocket of his trousers. Then he took a cigar from Beefy, pierced the end with a cutter he had in his pocket, calmly lighted the dark panetela, and began to smoke in silence. Everybody at the table had been looking at him the while, but apparently Jimmie hadn't realized it—or been moved by it.

H. Portner Cabot, formerly of Boston, was the first to speak.

"We understand from Bayne—"

"You said it wasn't any secret," interrupted Bayne.

"Course," agreed Jimmie.

"—that you are intending to make a 'book' hereafter," finished Cabot.

Jimmie nodded. Then added, with a pleasing smile: "At your service, gentlemen."

"Reckon you wouldn't want us for clients on the Gold Cup," said Colonel Rogers.

"Why not?" asked Jimmie. "Your money's as good as anybody's—better, I'd say."

"But we're all plunging on the same horse—on the horse you probably fancy," explained Bobbie Marsh. "We're out to get even."

"So?" murmured Jimmie. "Before you name the horse I'll say now I'll cover your money."

"On Sunfire—will you?" asked Bayne eagerly.

"Sure!" Jimmie spoke lightly. "On Sunfire or any horse in the Gold Cup."

"What odds?" inquired Colonel Rogers.

"What's your notion of odds?" countered Jimmie.

"Y' ought to give us seven to five at least, I reckon," responded the colonel.

"Not James Hatton. Even money," announced Jimmie decidedly.

"Even money on a horse that hasn't won this year?" whined the colonel.

"Even money on the horse that's run second in three of the big events this season—second to Thistleton, the winner in all three races, who's scratched!" Jimmie gave a positive jerk to his head which bore conviction.

"That's fair enough, commented Wilson Bayne. "Go you five hundred quid Sunfire wins."

"You're on!—five hundred quid," said Jimmie, making a memorandum in his pocket notebook.

"Go you the same," said H. Portner Cabot.

"Five hundred quid," said Jimmie, writing the bet down.

"Me, too—the same," piped Bobbie Marsh.

Jimmie agreed. "Five hundred quid," he wrote in his book.

"I'm game," insisted Colonel Rogers. "I'll bet you five hundred quid, even money, Sunfire wins the Gold Cup."

"You're on, colonel!—five hundred quid Sunfire wins the Gold Cup."

Jimmie wrote; then, closing his notebook, suggested:

"Suppose we meet here Friday—say at one o'clock—and make settlements?"

"Suits me. Right-o! Friday at one. Day after the race," came tumbling the answers of Sunfire's four backers.

"Beefy!"

"Yes, sir," responded the wise waiter of the Somerset bar.

"Another round," ordered Jimmie Hatton.

"Very good, sir," replied Beefy.

If The Polite Horse won the Gold Cup, Jimmie Hatton already stood to lose approximately ten thousand dollars.

So much the American invaders in the Somerset bar understood. And when Jimmie had departed, they lamented his headlong plunge to ruin. For they liked him—he was square, always on the level, and never a sponger.

"Good sort—Jimmie Hatton," began Bobbie Marsh. "Too bad to trim him."

"Reckon it's his own fault," said Colonel Rogers. "He offered to bet before we named the horse."

"Know he did," admitted Marsh, "but, all the samey, we're backing a certain winner."

"Nothing certain in a horse race," cautioned Wilson Bayne.

"Usually not," conceded H. Portner Cabot. "But when a horse has Sunfire's record—three seconds to the same winner, and that winner scratched—why, it's as sure a thing as one will ever get in a gamble."

"Right you are," agreed Bayne.

"What's got into Jimmie, d'you suppose?" asked Marsh.

James Hatton, turned bookmaker, was inconspicuously but properly dressed for the notable occasion. He wore dark steel-gray trousers, dull black morning coat and waistcoat, rich but quiet necktie with plain snow-white linen, and a well-ironed silk hat. And he wasn't accoutered with field glasses. Naturally good looking and modest, he might have been mistaken for a gentleman—using the misused term in its English significance—and not likely spotted as a bookie.

"No turf plunger lived who didn't come a cropper sooner or later," argued the colonel. "Jimmie Hatton's tumble is long past due."

"He's lasted better than any of them," Bayne reminded the others.

"Nevertheless, I hate to be one to kick him into the 'broke' class," insisted Marsh.

"Course you do—*you* have a pipe line to a trust treasury," growled Colonel Rogers. "Some of us have to rustle to keep out of that broke class. I'm one, I don't mind saying."

IV

Ascot Heath, you should know, is the royal race course, situate but a few miles from Windsor Castle.

Derby Day at Epsom Downs represents one end of the social ladder, Gold Cup Day at Ascot the other. At the Derby all England unbends, everybody fraternizes. Ascot is much more starchy. The royal procession makes of Gold Cup Day *the* outdoor event on the social calendar. With it there's nothing anywhere to compare, unless it be the Sunday of the Grand Prix at Longchamps. One for England, the other for France constitute the summer "opening" for society. Thenceforth fashion is a copy cat.

As on Gold cup Day appearances count for much, it is high time to describe the figure cut by Jimmie Hatton. He didn't display, as critics of racing might have expected, white spats, checked trousers, speaking waistcoat, wide braid on his morning coat, a diamond or two, or a pearl-gray top hat with a black band, to which odd headgear the king had extended royal sanction.

Jimmie steered clear of "the ring," otherwise Tattersall's, until after the first race. Thus he was a quiescent onlooker at the arrival of the king and queen.

Every one English was on tiptoe of circumspect excitement as the hour drew near for the royal entry. All loyal eyes were turned in the direction of the Windsor Road to the Heath, when, out of the heat mist, the cavalcade burst into view—outriders, postilions, high-stepping horses, the royal equipage, and then the carriages bearing the favored guests of their majesties.

The semi-state procession approached the assemblage of waiting racegoers at a rattling gait, the powerful bays attached to the carriages—four to the royal conveyance—all of a lather. Reaching the stands the pace slowed down almost to a walk, and the cortège moved majestically along the course.

In the royal equipage was a bearded man of commonplace visage and demeanor, and a self-conscious woman of more commanding mien. The attendant carriages were filled with royalty or titled personages of less degree, none of them below the rank of earl and countess, however. They seemed to feel the weight of their hereditary responsibility, socially speaking, for, one and all, their countenances were very austere. When the royal inclosure was reached, the king and queen alighted and proceeded to the pavilion, followed by their haughty guests.

With the outriders and postilions in gorgeous liveries, heavily ornamented in gold, with the pagoda-shaped parasols of queens—the consort of the ex-king of the republic of Portugal, humorously called *Queen* Augusta, was in the party—with the art sunshades of duchesses and of countesses, the royal procession was spectacular, if not really impressive. But Jimmie Hatton was unmoved.

"Like a circus, but not near so classy as the grand entry at Barnum & Bailey's," he mumbled to himself.

Jimmie left the "gayly dressed throng" for the bustle and jostle of the ring. It was business now—riches or ruin.

In the betting ring Jimmie Hatton began craftily to take bets on Sunfire. If backers asked what price he would lay against any other horse entered for the Gold Cup, he would invariably reply:

"I've laid my book against him, sir; I can't offer you a fair price." He was out to wager a small fortune that The Polite Horse wouldn't win. Nothing else doing.

As soon as he had bet an amount equal to fifteen thousand dollars, which, with the ten thousand wagered at the Somerset, amounted to twenty-five thousand dollars—all the money he had in the world, or could raise on security—he started to leave the ring. But at that moment Wilson Bayne brought up Lord Witherby, introduced Jimmie to him, and said that his lordship wanted to back Sunfire. Somewhat awed by the hearty handclasp of a real lord, and anxious to oblige, before he realized it Jimmie had accepted a wager of four hundred quid—two thousand dollars.

Then there was an unaccountable rush to his book. Those who favored Sunfire seemed afraid lest they might not get their money on. Jimmie was carried off his feet by the onslaught. When he could fight his way out of the betting ring, and in a corner of the lawn consult his betting book, he found, to his horror, that he had wagered fully ten thousand dollars more than he had!

If Sunfire won he would be obligated to pay *thirty-five thousand dollars,* and all he possessed to his name was a hundred quid above twenty-five thousand American dollars. Incidentally—what a word to use!—he would lose his electric-lighting bonds, his insurance against manual labor. Realization of his dire predicament gave him the same unhappy feeling at the pit of his stomach that one gets when an express elevator drops ten stories without notice to passengers.

He didn't permit himself to think that possibly he might have thirty-five thousand clear after redeeming his precious bonds. Not for one fleeting second. Although never before a quitter, James Hatton was in a dark-blue funk. It was partly because he faced ruin. It was even more because he was so acutely homesick, and home appeared to be receding all too rapidly. If a good fairy, at the moment, had offered to transport him to Brooklyn, and set him down in Flatbush, free of debt and with one hundred dollars in his pocket, Jimmie Hatton, plunger, would have transferred his bets in a moment. Yes, he was ready to quit.

The race for the Gold Cup, two miles and four furlongs, starts at the cup post above the grand stand, and the course is once around to the winning post, which is at the boundary between the royal inclosure and the paddock. Therefore, in the running of the classic event, the horses twice pass in front of the lawn, Tattersall's, and the royal inclosure. The time is under four minutes and a half; so Jimmie prepared for four and a half hours of misery!

His intention was to try to find standing room in the grand stand. But nearing the entrance to the elevated structure something queer happened to his legs. They seemed to cave under him, and he sank down on the steps of the stand—not the lower step, for he contrived to totter to a place which gave him a circumscribed view over the heads of the conclave on the lawn.

There was a tedious, nerve-lashing delay at the cup post, caused by two or three vicious brutes which insisted on making trouble for over thirty well-behaved starters. At last a shout announced that they were off!

As they flashed by the grand stand Jimmie furtively took a look. In the lead was Destiny, an outsider, bent on running her legs off. Next came Amner, twenty-five-to-one-shot, and then Lie-abed, second choice in the betting. Sunfire was fourth, excellently positioned and running easily. Jolly Miller, another outsider, was fifth, and close behind ran his majesty's horse, Longspear.

"The favorite goes well," remarked a swell who stood near the steps within range of Jimmie's hearing.

"What pretty colors!" exclaimed the doll-faced creature with the swell; "violet jacket, light-green cap. Wish I'd backed those colors—Sunfire will win!"

Jimmie groaned and covered his face with his hands. Over four hours more of agony!

"Not four hours—four minutes," whispered Common Sense.

"Will drag like four hours," urged Cruel Fate.

"Four minutes and you will know whether you have won," said Common Sense.

"Four hours on the grid, and you'll see you're ruined," insisted Cruel Fate.

"For God's sake, have it over!" moaned Jimmie.

The scourging suspense was frightful. Yet he felt in his heart there was no hope.

A faint murmur, like the droning of idling insects, was wafted down the course and hummed in Jimmie's ear. Gradually this murmur, the common voice of the crowd, increased, grew in volume, until it developed into a medley of sound, incoherent but expressive of vital significance—proclaiming the finish of a most important race. The fascination of this sound no one could deny. The phlegmatic English were roused by it to the pitch of downright enthusiasm. It was astonishing how such a vast concourse of people could be whipped into near madness by the struggle of less than half a dozen thoroughbreds—for to this number the contest for the Gold Cup was now reduced after two miles and more of grueling pace.

A terrific roar disclosed that the favorite was well to the front, running shoulder to shoulder with Jolly Miller, a rank outsider certain to wither in the finish. Already Lie-abed was beaten, slipping back at every stride.

"Sunfire! Sunfire!" was the cry of victory from the lungs of thousands, backers of the chestnut three-year-old.

All was over, thought Jimmie, and glad he was for the relief. It's uncertainty that kills.

As the pick of England's thoroughbreds, fighting for the Gold Cup, nostrils distended and showing red, every ounce of stamina put forth in the final effort, boomed down the stretch toward the winning post, the shout of "Sunfire! Sunfire!" continued. But suddenly a new cry went up.

A jockey wearing the purple, gold and scarlet colors dear to all loyal Britons, made a rush on a powerful black thoroughbred. As Jolly Miller tired, Longspear challenged Sunfire for the lead. Instantly the cry:

"The king wins! The king wins!"

Jimmie couldn't believe it—wouldn't believe it. From other race meetings he understood full well that always there was a conspicuous following for his majesty's entry. Always a contingent too ready to acclaim the king a winner. Many a time—doubtless this time—the cry of victory for the royal stables proved to be premature. So Jimmie goaded himself to remember. His hopes shouldn't rise, to sink again into despair.

Neck and neck the chestnut and the black, shaking off pursuers, raced for the winning post. On and on they fought, Sunfire and Longspear. It was a gallant struggle, and for a brief second promised a dead heat. Valiantly his majesty's horse endeavored to respond to the royal jockey's whip and command. But he couldn't forge ahead. Loyal subjects realized that their choice of winner was hardly to be justified. There was an appreciable diminution in the cry "The king wins!" Jimmie was among the first to sense it, and once more his heart sank, express elevator-like.

Sunfire was running beautifully. The grand chestnut to all appearances possessed sure reserve power.

With a last burst of speed the favorite would now win the Gold Cup. Scarcely one in a thousand thought otherwise. Again the shout:

"Sunfire! Sunfire wins!"

Then, to the amazement of everybody, to the consternation of his legion of backers, Sunfire, the favorite, after glancing at the black thoroughbred racing at his side, faltered! Or was it rather a voluntary slowing down on the part of The Polite Horse—true deference of a loyal animal, born and bred in England, to his majesty?

However it was, Jimmie Hatton, who had lacked the nerve to raise his eyes to the winning post as the victor's number was hoisted into view, found himself thrilled by the air played by the band.

Off came the hats of the male multitude to the strains of "God Save the King." Off came Jimmie's hat, and he stood bareheaded with tears of joy coursing down his cheek. It was the sweetest tune he'd ever heard. To Jimmie's ear—"America."

From Waterloo James Hatton, reformed bookmaker and man of large affairs, went directly to the cable office, and sent this message to his pal, Dan Foss:

Cinch me Doolan interest your company. Cabling five thousand deposit. Sailing Saturday, *Lauretania.* Meet me Sandy Hook with tug and brass band. Sure am coming back.

JIMMIE.

V

Not to appear anxious at all, Jimmie Hatton was half an hour late at the Somerset bar next day. The backers of Sunfire were all there, with the exception of Colonel Rogers. After Bayne, Cabot, and Marsh had paid up, Bayne delivered a message to the bookmaker pro tem.

"Here's two hundred and fifty quid from the colonel. He sends word he'll pay you the other two-fifty soon as he possibly can. Poor old codger is flat broke, I guess. You'll have to give him a little time, Jimmie, or else his friends must chip in and settle for him."

For a moment Jimmie said nothing, then inquired:

"Who hit on the moniker for Sunfire?"

"What—The Polite Horse?" asked Bobbie Marsh.

Jimmie nodded.

"The colonel," answered Bayne.

"Then I owe him a fat commission," said Jimmie. "I think two-fifty quid would be about right. It was the colonel gave me my tip."

"What tip?"—in unison.

"The Polite Horse—that he would *not* win," said Jimmie.

"What *do* you mean?"—chorus.

" 'After you, my dear Alphonse!' " Jimmie smiled.

"We may be dull—guess we are," said Bayne, "and I guess you're bright, Jimmie—the way you cleaned up on the Gold Cup. Admitting all this, please explain."

"All right," agreed Jimmie. "The start's in Brooklyn—h-o-m-e." He rolled the word on his tongue; it was sweet, indeed. "There was a piebald nag used to haul a milk wagon through my street—Flatbush Avenue. Knew ev'ry customer, he did. Would stop at the right door, and the moment the driver showed his mug would move off toward the next customer's. Had the route down cold."

H. Portner Cabot shot Jimmie a look, which was as to say: "How very irrelevant this nonsense." But Jimmie, unheeding, continued his story:

"One day—great day in Brooklyn—all the Knight Templars in the United States paraded—marched through Flatbush. A lot of the sachems, or whatever you call 'em, had to ride. Gee, but there was a scramble for mounts! Every horse that didn't have to pos-i-*tive*-ly do his regular work was drafted. Among 'em the milk-wagon horse! He'd finished his route in time for the parade.

"Well, when the procession turned into Flatbush Avenue near my house, one plumed knight found himself stalled—standing still right in front of my door! The milkhorse stopped just where he was accustomed to stop. He had the habit!"

"What's this to do with yesterday's race?" asked Bobbie Marsh peevishly.

"You think it's got nothing to do with the Gold Cup. I think it's got everything to do with it. Listen:

"When you fellows told me in this here bar that you were going to call Sunfire The Polite Horse, you took it as a joke. *That's where you lost.* I took it seriously. *That's where I won.*"

"I may be dense," interposed Wilson Bayne—regarded as the cleverest American business man in London—"but I don't see yet."

"You may be," chuckled Jimmie, "but you will see. Wait!

"I thought and thought about your little joke.—The Polite Horse," Jimmie went on. "Thought how Sunfire in ev'ry race this season had run second—been beaten by Thistleton. And ev'ry time I thought about it, the remark of Colonel Rogers popped into my head—'After you, my dear Alphonse!' "

"Come to the point, come to the point," urged Cabot.

"Presently," said Jimmie. "But let me tell you that deliberation ain't a bad thing. It won me all of thirty-five thousand dollars, deliberation did!

"You see," resumed Jimmie, "it wasn't altogether that Sunfire ran second —didn't win. It was that *he didn't want to win.* The Polite Horse—'After you, my dear Alphonse!' That's what my hunch told me. Sunfire was used to running second—letting the other horse beat him. Didn't know no better. It was habit, habit—like turning into my door was habit with the nag on the milk wagon.

"I says to myself, says I: 'Makes no difference what horse is at his withers in the stretch, Sunfire wouldn't win. He always finished right behind another horse—he always will! Just like the wheel horse on a coach. He wouldn't think of being leader. So The Polite Horse wouldn't think of passing the winning post first. Otherwise you fellows would never have called the beast The Polite Horse.

"That's all," concluded Jimmie Hatton.

"You're some guesser," admitted Bobbie Marsh.

"Jimmie's a mind reader from Boston," observed Wilson Bayne.

"No—a psychologist from Cambridge," corrected H. Portner Cabot.

"Just a dopester *of* Flatbush." Jimmie grinned, and beckoned to Beefy.

THE DUEL

Nikolai Teleshov

It was early morning—

Vladimir Kladunov, a tall, graceful young man, twenty-two years of age, almost boyish in appearance, with a handsome face and thick, fair curls, dressed in the uniform of an officer and in long riding boots, minus overcoat and cap, stood upon a meadow covered with new-fallen snow, and gazed at another officer, a tall, red-faced, mustached man, who faced him at a distance of thirty paces, and was slowly lifting his hand in which he held a revolver, and aimed it straight at Vladimir.

With his arms crossed over his breast and also holding in one hand a revolver, Kladunov, almost with indifference, awaited the shot of his opponent. His handsome, young face, though a little paler than usual, was alight with courage, and wore a scornful smile. His dangerous position, and the merciless determination of his adversary, the strenuous attention of the seconds who silently stood at one side, and the imminence of death, made the moment one of terrible intensity—mysterious, almost solemn. A question of honor was to be decided. Every one felt the importance of the question; the less they understood what they were doing, the deeper seemed the solemnity of the moment.

A shot was fired; a shiver ran through all. Vladimir threw his hands about, bent his knees, and fell. He lay upon the snow, shot through the head, his hands apart, his hair, face, and even the snow around his head covered with blood. The seconds ran toward him and lifted him; the doctor certified his death, and the question of honor was solved. It only remained to announce the news to the regiment and to inform, as tenderly and carefully as possible, the mother, who was now left alone in the world, for the boy that had been killed was her only son. Before the duel no one had given her even a thought;

but now they all became very thoughtful. All knew and loved her, and recognized the fact that she must be prepared by degrees for the terrible news. At last Ivan Golubenko was chosen as most fit to tell the mother, and smooth out matters as much as possible.

Pelageia Petrovna had just risen, and was preparing her morning tea when Ivan Golubenko, gloomy and confused, entered the room.

"Just in time for tea, Ivan Ivanovich!" amiably exclaimed the old lady, rising to meet her guest. "You have surely called to see Vladimir!"

"No, I—in passing by—" Golubenko stammered abashed.

"You will have to excuse him, he is still asleep. He walked up and down his room the whole of last night, and I told the servant not to wake him, as it is a —holy day. But probably you came on urgent business?"

"No, I only stepped in for a moment in passing—"

"If you wish to see him, I will give the order to wake him up."

"No, no, do not trouble yourself!"

But Pelageia Petrovna, believing that he had called to see her son on some business or other, left the room, murmuring to herself.

Golubenko walked excitedly to and fro, wringing his hands, not knowing how to tell her the terrible news. The decisive moment was quickly approaching, but he lost control of himself, was frightened, and cursed fate that had so mixed him up with the whole business.

"Now! How can a body trust you young people!" good-naturedly exclaimed Pelageia to her guest, reentering the room. "Here I have been taking care not to make the least noise with the cups and saucers, and asking you not to wake my boy, and he has long ago departed without leaving a trace! But why do you not take a seat, Ivan Ivanovich, and have a cup of tea? You have been neglecting us terribly lately!"

She smiled as with a secret joy, and added in a low voice:

"And we have had so much news during that time!—Vladimir surely could not keep it. He must have told you all about it by this; for he is very straightforward and open-hearted, my Vladimir. I was thinking last night, in my sinful thoughts: 'Well, when my Vladimir paces the room the whole night— that means that he is dreaming of Lenochka!' That is always the case with him: if he paces the room the whole night, he will surely leave to-morrow— Ah, Ivan Ivanovich, I only ask the Lord to send me this joy in my old age. What more does an old woman need? I have but one desire, one joy—and it seems to me I shall have nothing more to pray for after Vladimir and Lenochka are married. So joyful and happy it would make me!—I do not need anything besides Vladimir; there is nothing dearer to me than his happiness."

The old lady became so affected that she had to wipe away the tears which came to her eyes.

"Do you remember," she continued, "things did not go well in the beginning—either between the two or on account of the money—You young officers are not even allowed to marry without bonds—Well, now everything has been arranged; I have obtained the necessary five thousand rubles for Vladimir, and they could go to the altar even to-morrow! Yes, and Lenochka has written such a lovely letter to me—My heart is rejoicing!"

Continuing to speak, Pelageia Petrovna took a letter out of her pocket, which she showed to Golubenko, and then put back again.

"She is such a dear girl! And so good!"

Ivan Golubenko, listening to her talk, sat as if on red-hot coals. He wanted to interrupt her flow of words, to tell her that everything was at an end, that her Vladimir was dead, and that in one short hour nothing would remain to her of all her bright hopes; but he listened to her and kept silent. Looking upon her good, gentle face, he felt a convulsive gripping in his throat.

"But why are you looking so gloomy to-day?" the old lady at last asked. "Why, your face looks as black as night!"

Ivan wanted to say "Yes! And yours will be the same when I tell you!" but instead of telling her anything, he turned his head away, and began to twirl his mustaches.

Pelageia Petrovna did not notice it, and, wholly absorbed in her own thoughts, continued:

"I have a greeting for you. Lenochka writes that I should give Ivan Ivanovich her regards, and should compel him to come with Vladimir and pay her a visit—You know yourself how she likes you, Ivan Ivanovich!—No, it seems I am not able to keep it to myself. I must show you the letter. Just see for yourself how loving and sweet it is."

And Pelageia Petrovna again took out the package of letters from her pocket, took from it a thin letter-sheet, closely written, and unfolded it before Ivan Golubenko, whose face had become still gloomier, and he tried to push away with his hand the extended note, but Pelageia Petrovna had already started to read:

> "DEAR PELAGEIA PETROVNA—When will the time arrive when I will be able to address you, not as above, but as my dear, sweet mother! I am anxiously awaiting the time, and hope so much that it will soon come that even now I do not want to call you otherwise than mama—"

Pelageia Petrovna lifted her head, and, ceasing to read, looked at Golubenko with eyes suffused with tears.

"You see, Ivan Ivanovich." she added; but seeing that Golubenko was biting his mustaches, and that his eyes too were moist, she rose, placed a trembling hand upon his hair, and quietly kissed him on the forehead. "Thank you, Ivan Ivanovich," she whispered, greatly moved. "I always thought that you and Vladimir were more like brothers than like simple friends—Forgive me—I am so very happy, God be thanked!"

Tears streamed down her cheeks, and Ivan Golubenko was so disturbed and confused that he could only catch in his own her cold, bony hand and cover it with kisses; tears were suffocating him, and he could not utter a word, but in this outburst of motherly love he felt such a terrible reproach to himself that he would have preferred to be lying himself upon the field, shot through the head, than to hear himself praised for his friendship by this woman who would in half an hour find out the whole truth; what would she then think of him? Did not he, the friend, the almost brother, stand quietly by when a revolver was pointed at Vladimir? Did not this brother himself measure the space between the two antagonists and load the revolvers? All this he did himself, did consciously; and now this friend and brother silently sat there without having even the courage to fulfil his duty.

He was afraid; at this moment he despised himself, but could not prevail upon himself to say even one word. His soul was oppressed by a strange lack of harmony; he felt sick at heart and stifling. And in the meanwhile time flew —he knew it, and the more he knew it the less had he the courage to deprive Pelageia Petrovna of her few last happy moments. What should he say to her? How should he prepare her? Ivan Golubenko lost his head entirely.

He had had already time enough to curse in his thoughts all duels, all quarrels, every kind of heroism, and all kinds of so-called questions of honor, and he at last rose from his seat ready to confess or to run away. Silently and quickly he caught the hand of Pelageia Petrovna, and stooping over it to touch it with his lips, thus hid his face, over which a torrent of tears suddenly streamed down; impetuously, without another thought, he ran out into the corridor, snatching his great coat, and then out of the house without having said a word.

Pelageia Petrovna looked after him with astonishment, and thought:

"He also must be in love, poor fellow—Well, that is their young sorrow—before happiness!" . . .

And she soon forgot him, absorbed in her dreams of the happiness which seemed to her so inviolable and entire.

THE HANGING AT LA PIROCHE

Alexandre Dumas, fils

Do you know La Piroche?

No. No more do I. So I shall not abuse my privilege as an author by giving you a description; especially since, between you and me be it said, they are very tiresome, those descriptions. Unless it be a question of the virgin forests of America, as in Cooper, or of Meschaccbé, as in Chateaubriand, that is to say, countries that are not close at hand, and about which the imagination, to obtain a clear vision of the details, must be assisted by those poetical voyagers who have visited them, in general descriptions are not of much consequence except to be skipped by the reader. Literature has this advantage over painting, sculpture, and music; the threefold advantage of being able to paint by itself a picture in a single word, to carve a statue in one phrase, to mold a melody on one page; it must not abuse itself of that privilege, and one should leave to the special arts a little of their own prerogative. I own, then, for my part, and for lack of better advice, that when I find that I have to describe a country which every one has seen, or every one could see, if it be near, if it does not differ from our own, I prefer to leave to my reader the pleasure of recalling it if he has seen it, or of imagining it if he does not yet know it. The reader likes well enough to be left to do his share of the work he is reading. This flatters him and makes him believe that he is capable of doing the rest. Indeed, it is an excellent thing to flatter your reader. Moreover, the whole world in reality knows what the sea is like—a plain, a forest, a blue sky, an effect of sun, an effect of the moon, or an effect of storm. Of what use to dwell upon it? It would be far better to trace a landscape in one stroke of the brush like Rubens or Delacroix: this should be said without comparison and keep the whole value of your palette for the figures you wish to reanimate. When one blackens with descriptions page after page of paper, one doesn't give the reader an impression equal to that experienced by the most artless bourgeois who walks through the Bois de Vincennes on a soft April day, or by an unlettered girl who strolls in June, on the arm of her fiancé, at eleven o'clock at night through the shady vistas of the woods of Romainville or the park of Enghien. We all have in our minds and hearts a gallery of landscapes made from memory, and which serves as background for all the stories of the world. There is but one word to use—day or night, winter or spring, calm or storm, wood or plain—to evoke at once a most finished landscape. So I have only to tell you this: that at the moment when the story I am about to tell you begins it is noon, that it is May, that the highway we are going to enter is bordered on the right with furze bushes, on the left by the sea; you know at once all that I have not told you; that is to say, that the bushes are green, that the sea is murmuring, that the sky is blue, that the sun is warm, and that there is dust on the road.

I have only to add that this highway that winds along the coast of Brittany runs from La Poterie to La Piroche; that Piroche is a village about which I know nothing, but which must be more or less like all villages, that we are in the middle of the fifteenth century, in 1418, and that two men, one older than the other, one the father of the other, both peasants, are following the highway mounted on two nags trotting along comfortably enough for two nags under the weight of two peasants.

"Shall we get there in time?" said the son.

"Yes, it is not to take place until two o'clock," replied the father, "and the sun marks but a quarter after noon."

"Oh, but I am curious to see that!"

"I can well believe it."

"So he will be hanged in the armor that he stole?"

"Yes."

"How the devil did he get the idea of stealing armor?"

"It's not the idea that is hard to get—"

"It's the armor," interrupted the boy, who wanted his share in making a part of that joke.

"And that, too, he didn't get."

"Was it fine armor?"

"Splendid, they say, all shining with gold."

"And did they catch him as he was carrying it away?"

"Yes, you know as well as I do that armor like that never goes astray without raising a great outcry; it can't escape its proper owner all by itself."

"So, then, it was of iron?"

"They woke up in the château at the noise they heard."

"And did they arrest the man?"

"Not at once; they began by being afraid."

"Of course, it's always that way that people who have been robbed begin when they are in the presence of thieves; otherwise there would be no object in being a thief."

"No, nor any pleasant excitement in being robbed! But those brave folks had no idea that it was an affair of robbery."

"Of what, then?"

"Of a ghost. That wretched, most vigorous fellow was carrying the armor in front of him, holding his head at the height of the loins of said armor so effectively that he acquired gigantic proportions in the corridor where he passed. Add to this a clattering noise which the rascal made behind him, and you will appreciate the fright of the valets. But, unfortunately for him, he woke up the Seigneur of La Piroche, he who has fear of neither the dead nor the living, who easily, and all by himself, arrested the thief and handed him over, bound, to his well-deserved justice."

"And his well-deserved justice?"

"The condemned man is to be hanged clothed in the armor."

"Why that clause in the sentence?"

"Because the Seigneur of La Piroche is not only a brave captain, but a man of common sense and of spirit, who wished to draw from this just condemnation an example for others and an advantage for himself. Why, don't you know that whatever touches a hanged man becomes a talisman for him who possesses it? So the Seigneur of La Piroche has ordered that the thief should be hanged dressed in his armor, so as to reclaim it when the man is dead and have a talisman to wear during our next wars."

"That is very ingenious."

"I should think so."

"Let's make haste, for I am so anxious to see the poor man hanged."

"We have plenty of time! We must not wear our beasts out. We are not going to stop at La Piroche; we will have to go on a league farther, and then return to La Poterie."

"Yes, but our beasts will rest for five or six hours, for we do not return until evening."

The father and son continued on their way, talking, and half an hour later they reached La Piroche.

As the father had said, they arrived on time. Have fathers always the privilege of being right?

There was an immense concourse of people on the great square in front of the château, for it was there that the scaffold had been erected, a splendid gallows, in faith, of sound oak, not very high, it is true, since it was intended for a wretched, obscure criminal, but high enough, nevertheless, for death to do its work between earth and the end of the rope which was swinging in the fresh sea breeze like an eel hanging by its tail.

The condemned man was certain of having a beautiful view at the moment of death, for he was to die with his face turned toward the ocean. If this view could be any consolation to him, so much the better, but, for my part, I doubt it.

And all the while the sea was blue, and from time to time between the azure of the sky and that of the sea floated a white cloud, like an angel on its way to heaven, but whose long robes still trailed upon the earth it was quitting.

The two companions approached as near as possible to the scaffold, so as to miss nothing that was going on, and, like all the rest, they waited, having this advantage over the others, that they were mounted on two nags and could see better with less fatigue.

They had not long to wait.

At a quarter of two the gates of the château opened, and the condemned man appeared, preceded by the guards of the Seigneur of La Piroche and followed by the executioner.

The thief was dressed in the stolen armor and was mounted reversed on the bare back of a jackass. He rode with vizor down and head lowered. They had tied his hands behind his back, and if they wish for our opinion in the matter we have no hesitation in saying that, judging by his position, in default of his face, which could not be seen, he ought to have been very ill at ease, and indulging at that moment in very sad reflections.

They conducted him to the side of the scaffold, and a moving picture hardly pleasant for him began to silhouette itself against the blue sky. The hangman set his ladder against the scaffold, and the chaplain of the Seigneur of La Piroche, mounted on a prepared platform, delivered the sentence of justice.

The condemned man did not move. One might have said that he had given the spectators the slip by dying before he was hanged.

They called to him to descend from his ass and deliver himself to the hangman.

He did not move. We understand his hesitation.

Then the hangman took him by the elbows, lifted him off the ass, and set him upright on the ground.

Fine fellow, that hangman!

When we say that he set him upright, we do not lie. But we would lie in saying that he remained as they placed him. He had in two minutes jumped two-thirds of the alphabet; that is to say, in vulgar parlance, that instead of standing straight like an I, he became zigzag like a Z.

During this time the chaplain finished reading the sentence.

"Have you any request to make?" he asked of the culprit.

"Yes," replied the unfortunate, in a voice sad and low.

"What do you ask?"

"I ask for pardon."

I do not know if the word "farceur" was invented in those days, but then or never was the time to invent it and to speak it.

The Seigneur of La Piroche shrugged his shoulders and ordered the executioner to do his duty.

The latter made ready to mount the ladder leaning against the gibbet, which, impassive, was about to draw with extended arm the soul out of a body, and he attempted to make the condemned mount in front of him, but it was not an easy thing to do. One does not know, in general, what obstacles those condemned to death will put in the way of their dying.

The hangman and the man there had the air of passing civilities one to another. It was a question of who should go first.

The hangman, to make him mount on his ladder, returned to the method he employed in making him descend from his ass. He seized him around the middle of his body, balanced him on the third rung of the ladder, and began to push him up from beneath.

"Bravo!" cried the crowd.

He ought to have mounted well.

Then the executioner adroitly slipped the running noose, which adorned the end of the rope, around the neck of the culprit, and, giving the latter a vigorous kick in the back, he flung him out into space, which strongly resembled Eternity.

An immense clamor greeted this looked-for dénouement, and a shudder passed through the crowd. Whatever may be the crime he has committed, the man who dies is always at the moment greater than those who watch him die.

The hanged man swung for three or four minutes at the end of his rope, as he had a right to do, danced, wriggled, then hung motionless and rigid.

The Z had become an I again.

They gazed a while longer on the culprit, whose gilded armor glistened in the sun, then the spectators divided themselves, little by little, into groups, and went their way home, chatting about the event.

"Pooh! a horrid thing is death!" said the son of the peasant, as he continued his journey with his father.

"In good faith, to hang one for not having succeeded in stealing a piece of armor, that's expensive. What do you think?"

" 'I wonder, I do, what they would have done to him if he had really stolen the armor?"

"They would not have done anything to him, for if he had really stolen the armor he would have been able to escape from the château. Then, possibly, he would not have returned to be arrested."

"Yet he is punished more for a crime that he has not committed than he would have been if he had committed the crime!"

"But he had the intention of committing it."

"And the intention was accounted as a fact—"

"That is perfectly just."

"But it isn't pretty to look at."

And since they found themselves on rising ground, the two companions turned to contemplate for the last time the silhouette of the unfortunate.

Twenty minutes later they entered the little town where, save the mark! they were to receive certain moneys, and which they were to leave that evening in order to accomplish the return home that same night.

On the morrow, at break of day, the guards sallied out from the château of La Piroche for the purpose of taking down the corpse of the hanging man, from which they intended to recover the armor of the Seigneur, but they discovered something which they had been far from anticipating, that is to say, the gibbet was there, as always, but the hanged man was not there.

The two guards rubbed their eyes, believing themselves to be dreaming, but the thing was very real. No more hanged man, and naturally no more armor.

And what was extraordinary, the rope was neither broken nor cut, but just in the condition it was before receiving the condemned.

The two guards ran to announce this news to the Seigneur of La Piroche. He was not willing to believe it, and proceeded to assure himself of the truth of the facts. So puissant a seigneur was he that he was convinced the hanged man would reappear for him there; but he saw what all the rest had seen.

What had become of the dead? For the condemned had certainly died the day before, before the eyes of the whole village.

Had another thief profited by the night to get possession of the armor that covered the corpse?

Possibly—but in taking the armor he would naturally leave the corpse, for which he had no use.

Had the friends or relations of the culprit wished to give him Christian burial?

Nothing impossible in that if it were not for the fact that the culprit had neither friends nor relations, and that people who had had religious sentiments like that would have taken the culprit and left the armor. That, then, was no longer to be thought of. What should one believe, then?

The Seigneur of La Piroche was in despair. He was all for his armor. He made promise of a reward of ten gold *écus* to any one who should deliver to him the thief, dressed as he was in dying.

They ransacked the houses; they found nothing.

No one presented himself.

They caused a sage of the town of Rennes to be sent for, and they propounded this question to him:

"In what way does a dead man who has been hanged manage to free himself from the rope that holds him in the air by the neck?"

The sage demanded eight days to ponder over the question, at the termination of which he replied:

"He can not do it."

Then they propounded this second question:

"A thief, unsuccessful in stealing while alive, and having been condemned to death for stealing, can he steal after his death?"

The sage replied:

"Yes."

He was asked how it could be done. He replied that he knew nothing about it.

He was the greatest sage of his time.

They sent him home and contented themselves with believing, for those were the days of witchcraft, that the thief was a wizard.

Then they said masses to exorcise that evil spirit, which was without doubt taking his revenge upon the Seigneur who had ordered his death and upon those who had come to see him die.

A month passed in fruitless search.

The gibbet still stood there as always, humiliated, gloomy, and discredited. Never had a gibbet committed such a breach of confidence.

The Seigneur of La Piroche continued to clamor for his armor from man, God, and the devil.

Nothing.

At last he was beginning, without a doubt, to make the best of this strange event, and of the loss which had been the result, when one morning, as he was waking, he heard a great commotion on the square where the execution had taken place. He was making ready to inform himself of what was passing when his chaplain entered the room.

"Monseigneur," said he, "do you know what has happened?"

"No, but I am going to ask."

"I can tell you, I can."

"What is it, then?"

"A miracle from heaven!"

"Really!"

"The hanged man—"

"Well?"

"He is there!"

"Where?"

"On the scaffold."

"Hanging?"

"Yes, Monseigneur."

"In his armor?"

"In your armor."

"True, for it *is* mine. And is he dead?"

"Absolutely dead—only—"

"Only what?"

"Did he have spurs on when they hanged him?"

"No."

"Well, Monseigneur, he has them, and in place of having the casque on his head, he has placed it with great care at the foot of the gibbet, and left his head hanging uncovered."

"Let us see, Mr. Chaplain, let us see, straight off!"

The Seigneur of La Piroche ran to the square crowded with the curious. The neck of the hanged man had passed again into the running noose, the corpse was there at the end of the rope, and the armor was there on the corpse.

It was astounding. So they proclaimed it a miracle.

"He has repented," said one, "and has come to hang himself over again."
"He has been there all the time," said another; "only we did not see him."
"But why has he got spurs?" asked a third.

"No doubt, because he has come from afar and wished to return in a hurry."

"I know well, for my part, that far or near, I would not have needed to put on spurs, for I would not have come back."

And they laughed, and they stared at the ugly face the dead man made.

As for the Seigneur of La Piroche, he thought of nothing but of making sure that the thief was quite dead, and of securing his armor.

They cut down the corpse and stripped it; then, once despoiled, they hung it up again, and the ravens investigated so thoroughly that at the end of two days it was all jagged, at the end of eight days it had only the appearance of a rag, and at the end of fifteen days it had no longer the appearance of anything at all; or, if it did resemble anything, it was only those impossible hanged men we used to make pictures of on the first page of our text-book, and below which we wrote the amphibious quatrain, half Latin, half French:

> *Aspice* Pierrot pendu,
> *Qui nunc librum* n'a pas rendu,
> *Si hunc librum reddidisset:*
> Pierrot pendu *non-faisset.*[1]

But what had the hanged man been doing during his month of absence? How did it happen that he escaped, and, having escaped, that he hanged himself again?

We will give below the three versions which have been presented to us.

A magician, a pupil of Merlin, declared that if at the moment of dying the culprit has had the will to disappear and the ability to absorb his body into his will, the will being an immaterial thing, invisible, and impalpable, the body, which finds itself absorbed by it, and consequently hidden in it, becomes by that means also impalpable, immaterial, and invisible, and that if the body of a thief has reappeared at the end of a month, and at the end of a rope, it is because at that supreme moment his will, troubled by his conscience, has not had sufficient force for eternal absorption.

This may not be a good version, but it is one.

The theologians affirm that the culprit did succeed in vanishing, but that, pursued by remorse and being in haste to reconcile himself with God, he could not endure the life longer than one month, and, full of repentance, came to execute upon himself that justice which he had escaped the first time.

---

[1]Behold Pierrot suspendered,
Who has not his Latin rendered.
But 'twas otherwisely fated:
Pierrot was the one translated.

That, perhaps, is not the true version, but it is always Christian logic, and as a Christian we will not dismiss it altogether.

Finally, they declared that our two peasants in returning home that evening, and passing close to the gibbet, heard lamentations, a rattling, and something like a prayer; that they piously crossed themselves and demanded what was the matter; that they received no reply, but the lamentations continued, and it seemed to them that they came from the corpse that was above their heads. Then they took the ladder that the hangman had left at the foot of the scaffold, rested it against the arm of the gibbet, and the son, having mounted to the level of the condemned, said to him:

"Is it you who are making these complaints, poor man?"

The condemned gathered all his strength together and said:

"Yes."

"Then you are still alive?"

"Yes."

"You repent of your crime?"

"Yes."

"Then I will loosen you, and since the Evangelist commands us to give succor to those who suffer, and that you suffer, I am going to succor you and bring you to life in order to bring you to good. God prefers a soul that repents to a corpse that expiates."

Then the father and the son cut down the dying man, and saw how it was that he still lived. The rope, instead of tightening about the neck of the thief, had tightened at the base of the casque so effectually that the culprit was suspended but not strangled, and, occupying with his head a kind of vantage-point in the interior of the casque, he was able to breathe and to keep alive up to the time our two companions passed by.

The latter took him down and carried him home with them, where they gave him into the care of the mother and the young daughter.

But he who has stolen will steal.

There were but two things to steal at the peasant's, for the money he had brought back with him was not in his house. These two things were his horse and his daughter, a fair-haired girl of sixteen.

The ex-hanged decided to steal both the one and the other, for he was covetous of the horse and had fallen in love with the daughter.

So one night he saddled the horse, buckled on the spurs to make him ride faster, and went to take the young girl while she was asleep, and lift her up on to the crupper.

But the girl awoke and cried out.

The father and the son came running up. The thief tried to escape, but he was too late. The young girl told about the attempt of the hanged man; and the father and the son, seeing well that no repentance was to be expected from such a man, resolved to execute justice upon him, but more effectually than the Seigneur of La Piroche had allowed himself to do it. They bound the thief to the horse which he had saddled himself, led him to the square of La

Piroche, and strung him up there where he had been hanged, but placed his casque on the ground to make sure that he should not vanish again; then they returned home quietly.

There is the third version. I do not know why I believe it to be the most probable, and that you would do well, like me, to give it preference over the other two.

As for the Seigneur of La Piroche, as soon as he had secured a real talisman, he went happily off to the wars, where he was the first to be killed.

A WORK OF ART
THE STORY OF A GIFT

Anton Chekhov

Alexander Smirnoff, the only son of his mother, holding in his hand some object carefully wrapped in a newspaper, an angelic smile on his youthful face, entered the consulting-room of Dr. Koshelkoff.

"Ah, dear youth!" exclaimed the doctor, "how are you? What is the good news?"

Confused and excited, the young man replied:

"Doctor, my mother is sending her regards—I am her only son, you know —You saved my life. Your skill—We hardly know how to thank you!"

"Say no more, dear boy!" said the doctor, beaming with delight. "I have only done my duty. Anybody else would have done the same."

"I am the only son of my mother. We are poor, and, of course, can not repay you for your labors as you have deserved—and we feel it deeply. At the same time my mother—I am her only son, doctor—my mother humbly begs you to accept as a token of our gratitude a little statuette she values very highly. It is a piece of antique bronze, and a rare work of art."

"My good fellow—" commenced the physician.

"No, doctor, you must not refuse," continued Alexander, unfolding his parcel. "You will deeply offend mother and myself, too. It is a little beauty. A rare antique. We have kept it in memory of father, who was a dealer in antique bronzes. My mother and myself continue the business."

Finally the youth succeeded in freeing his present from its wrappings, and placed it on the table with an air of great solemnity. It was a moderately tall candelabrum of antique bronze and of artistic workmanship. It represented two female figures somewhat scantily attired, and bearing an air of frivolity to describe which I have neither the required daring nor the temperament.

223

The figures smiled coquettishly, and looked as if they were ready to jump on the floor and to engage in some wild frolic, were they not restrained by the task of supporting the candle holder.

The doctor regarded his present for a few moments in silence, then scratched his head and coughed irresolutely.

"A beautiful article, to be sure," he finally said. "But you know—what shall I say? Why, it is hardly the thing, you know. Talk of *déshabille!* This is beyond the bounds of propriety. The devil!"

"W-w-why?"

"Now, how could I put a thing like that on my table? It will corrupt my residence."

"Doctor, you surprise me," answered Alexander, with an offended tone. "What queer views of art! This is a work of art! Look at it! What beauty, what delicacy of workmanship! It fills the soul with joy merely to look at it; it brings tears to one's eyes. Observe the movement, the atmosphere, the expression!"

"I fully appreciate it, my boy," interrupted the physician. "But you know I am a man of family. I have children. A mother-in-law. Ladies call here."

"Of course, if you look at it from the point of view of the common herd, you might regard it in a different light. But I beg of you, rise above the mob. Your refusal would hurt the feelings of my mother and of myself. I am her only son. You saved my life. We are asking you to accept something we hold very dear. I only deplore the fact that we have no companion piece to it."

"Thank you, dear fellow, and thank your mother. I see that I can not reason with you. But you should have thought of my children, you know, and the ladies. But I fear you will not listen to arguments."

"No use arguing, doctor," replied the grateful patient, made happy by the implied acceptance. "You put it right here, next to the Japanese vase. What a pity I have not the pair. What a pity!"

When his caller departed the doctor thoughtfully regarded his unwelcome present. He scratched his head and pondered.

"It is an exquisite thing, without doubt. It would be a pity to throw it into the street. It is quite impossible to leave it here, though. What a dilemma to be in. To whom could I give it? How to get rid of it?"

Finally he bethought himself of Ukhoff, a dear friend of his school days, and a rising lawyer, who had just successfully represented him in some trifling case.

"Good," said the doctor. "As a friend he refused to charge me a fee, and it is perfectly proper that I should make him a present. Besides, he is a single man and tremendously sporty."

Losing no time, the doctor carefully wrapped up the candlestick and drove to Ukhoff.

"There, old chap," he said to the lawyer, whom he happily found at home; "there I have come to thank you for that little favor. You refused to charge me a fee, but you must accept this present in token of my gratitude. Look—what a beauty!"

On seeing the present the attorney was transported with delight.

"This beats everything!" he fairly howled. "Hang it all, what inventive genius! Exquisite, immense. Where did you get such a little gem?"

Having expressed his delight, the lawyer anxiously looked at his friend and said:

"But you know, you must not leave this thing here. I can not accept it."

"Why?" gasped the doctor.

"You know my mother calls here, clients, too. Why, I would not dare to look my servants in the face. Take it away."

"Never! You must not refuse," exclaimed the physician with the energy of despair. "Look at the workmanship! Look at the expression! I will not listen to any refusals. I will feel insulted."

With these words the doctor hurried out of the house.

"A white elephant," the lawyer mumbled sadly, while the doctor, rubbing his hands with glee, drove home with an expression of relief.

The attorney studied his present at length and wondered what to do with it.

"It is simply delicious, but I can not keep it. It would be vandalism to throw it away, and the only thing to do is to give it away. But to whom?

"I have it now," he fairly shouted. "The very thing, and how appropriate. I will take it to Shashkin, the comedian. The rascal is a connoisseur in such things. And this is the night of his jubilee."

In the evening the candelabrum, carefully wrapped, was taken to Shashkin's dressing-room by a messenger boy. The whole evening that dressing-room was besieged by a crowd of men who came to view the present. An incessant roar of delight was kept up within, sounding like the joyous neighing of many horses. Whenever an actress approached the door leading to the sanctum, and curiously knocked, Shashkin's hoarse voice was heard in reply:

"No, my dear, you can't come in, I am not fully dressed."

After the performance Shashkin shrugged his shoulders and said:

"What on earth shall I do with this disreputable thing? My landlady would not tolerate it in the house. Here actresses call to see me. This is not a photograph, you can't hide it in the drawer."

The hair-dresser listened sympathetically while arranging the comedian's hair.

"Why don't you sell it?" he finally asked the actor. "A neighbor of mine, an old lady, deals in such things, and she will pay you a good price for it. An old woman by the name of Smirnoff, the whole town knows her."

Shashkin obeyed.

Two days later Dr. Koshelkoff sat peacefully in his study, enjoying his pipe and thinking of things medical, when suddenly the door of his room flew open, and Alexander Smirnoff burst upon his sight. His face beamed with joy, he fairly shone, and his whole body breathed inexpressible content.

In his hands he held an object wrapped in a newspaper.

"Doctor," he began breathlessly, "imagine my joy! What good fortune! Luckily for you my mother has succeeded in obtaining a companion piece to your candelabrum. You now have the pair complete. Mother is so happy. I am her only son, you know. You saved my life."

Trembling with joy and with excess of gratitude, young Smirnoff placed the candelabrum before the doctor. The physician opened his mouth, attempted to say something, but the power of speech failed him—and he said nothing.

THE BIT OF STRING

Guy de Maupassant

Along all the roads leading to Goderville the peasants and their wives were going toward the town, for it was market-day. The men walked at an easy pace, the whole body thrown ahead at each movement of the long, crooked legs, men deformed by rude labor, by guiding the plow, which at once forces the right shoulder upward and twists the waist; by reaping, which spreads the knees, for solid footing; by all the patient and painful toil of the country. Their blue blouses, glossy with starch, as though varnished, ornamented at the neck and wrists by a simple pattern in white, swelled out round their bony chests, like captive balloons from which heads, arms, and legs were protruding.

Some were leading by a cord a cow or calf, and their wives behind the animals were hastening their pace by the strokes of branches stripped of their leaves. The women carried on their arms great baskets, out of which hung, here and there, heads of chickens or ducks. They walked with shorter steps than their husbands, and at a more rapid pace, spare, erect and wrapped in scant shawls pinned across their flat chests, their heads enveloped in white linen drawn closely over the hair and surmounted by a bonnet.

Now a pleasure wagon passed at a jerky pony trot, shaking fantastically two men seated side by side, and a woman at the back of the vehicle, holding on to its sides to soften the hard jolts.

In the square of Goderville was a crowd—a jam of mingled human beings and beasts. The horns of cattle, the high hats of the rich farmers and the head-dresses of the women, emerged from the surface of the assembly; and discordant voices, clamorous, bawling, kept up a continuous and savage bable, overtopped now and then by a shout from the robust lungs of a merry countryman, or the lowing of a cow attached to the wall of a house. All this mass was redolent of the stable and soilure, of milk, of hay, of sweat, and diffused that rank, penetrating odor, human and bestial, peculiar to people of the fields.

Master Hauchecorne of Bréauté had just arrived at Goderville, and was going toward the square when he saw on the ground a bit of string. Master Hauchecorne, economist, like every true Norman, thought that anything might be of use worth picking up, and he bent down painfully, for he suffered from rheumatism. He took up the piece of string, and was winding it carefully, when he noticed Malandin, the harness-maker, watching him from his doorway. The two men had long ago had a quarrel about a halter, and both being vindictive, had remained unfriendly. Hauchecorne was seized with a kind of shame, at thus being seen by his enemy picking a bit of twine out of the mud. He quickly hid his prize under his blouse, then in his breeches pocket; then he pretended to search the ground again for something which he did not find, and he went off toward the market, his head in advance, bent double by his infirmities.

He was forthwith lost in the noisy, shuffling crowd everywhere in motion from innumerable buyings and sellings. The peasants examined the cows, went away, came back, hesitated, always fearful of being outwitted, never daring to decide, peering into the face of the vender, endlessly searching to discover the ruse in the man and the fault in the beast.

The women, putting their great baskets down at their feet, had drawn out their fowls, which were lying on the ground, legs bound, eyes wild, combs scarlet. They listened to offers, held to their prices unmoved, their faces inscrutable; or suddenly deciding to accept an offer, cried out to the would-be purchaser slowly moving away:

"Agreed, Master Hutine; I will give it at your price."

Then little by little the square emptied, and the Angelus sounding noon, those who lived too far to go home dispersed in the various public houses.

At Jourdain's the great dining-room was full of feasters, as the vast court was full of vehicles of every pedigree—carts, gigs, tilburies, pleasure vans, carioles innumerable, yellow with mud, mended, out of order, lifting to heaven their shafts, like two arms, or nosing the ground, rear in the air.

Opposite the tables of diners the great chimney-piece, full of bright flame, threw a lively warmth on the backs of the row at the right. Three spits were turning, weighted with chickens, pigeons, and legs of mutton, and a delectable odor of roast flesh and of juice streaming over its golden brown skin, escaped from the hearth, put every one in gay humor, and made mouths water. All the aristocracy of the plow dined there with Master Jourdain, innkeeper and horsedealer, a shrewd fellow, who had his dollars.

The platters were passed and emptied as were the tankards of yellow cider. Each one talked of his affairs, his purchases, his sales. The harvest was discussed. The weather was good for grass, but a little sharp for grain.

All at once the drum sounded in the court before the house. All save a few indifferent fellows were quickly on their feet, and running to the door or the windows, their mouths full, their napkins in their hands.

When he had finished his roulade the public crier held forth in a jerky voice, cutting his phrases at the wrong place:

"It is made known to the inhabitants of Goderville and in general to all— the people present at market, that there was lost this morning, on the Benzeville road between—nine and ten o'clock, a wallet containing five hundred francs and important papers. You are asked to return—it to the town hall, without delay, or to the house of Master Fortuné Houlebrèque, of Manneville. There will be twenty francs reward."

Then the crier went on. One heard once more far off the muffled beating of his drum, and his voice enfeebled by the distance. Then they all began to talk of the event, estimating Master Houlebrèque's chances of finding or not finding his wallet.

And the meal went on.

They were finishing their coffee when the chief of police appeared at the door.

"Where is Master Hauchecorne of Bréauté?" he asked.

Hauchecorne, seated at the farther end of the table, replied:

"I'm here."

The chief proceeded:

"Master Hauchecorne, will you have the kindness to accompany me to the town hall? The mayor wishes to speak with you."

The countryman, surprised and disquieted, emptied at a draft his little glass of rum, arose, and, still more bent than in the morning, for the first movement after each relaxation was particularly difficult, he set out, repeating:

"I'm here, I'm here."

And he followed the chief.

The mayor was waiting for him, seated in his fauteuil. He was the notary of the vicinity, a big, solemn man, of pompous phrases.

"Master Hauchecorne," said he, "you were seen to pick up, on the Benzeville road, this morning, the wallet lost by Master Holebrèque, of Manneville."

The peasant, astonished, looked at the mayor, frightened already, without knowing why, by this suspicion which had fallen on him.

"What! what! I picked up the wallet?"

"Yes; you yourself."

"Word of honor, I didn't even know of it."

"You were seen."

"Seen? What? Who saw me?"

"Monsieur Malandin, the harness-maker."

Then the old man remembered, understood, reddened with anger.

"He saw meh, th' lout? He saw meh pick up that string! See here, m'sieu mayor," and feeling in the bottom of his pocket, he drew out the bit of cord.

But the mayor, incredulous, shook his head.

"You won't make me believe, Master Hauchecorne, that Malandin, who is a man worthy of credence, took that thread for a wallet."

The peasant, furious, raised his hand, spit, to attest his innocence, and declared:

"Yet it's the truth of God, the sacred truth, m'sieu mayor. On my soul and my salvation, I repeat it."

The mayor continued:

"After picking up the object you went on searching in the mud a long time to see if some piece of money mightn't have escaped you."

The old man gasped with indignation and fear.

"May one tell—may one tell lies like that to injure an honest man? May one say—"

His protest was vain. He was not believed. He was confronted with Monsieur Malandin, who repeated and sustained his former affirmation. For an hour the two men hurled insults at each other. Hauchecorne was searched, at his demand, and nothing was found on him. Finally the mayor, greatly perplexed, sent him away, warning him that he should inform the council and await orders.

The news spread. When he came out of the town hall the old man was surrounded and questioned with a curiosity serious or mocking, but with no ill-will in it.

He began to recount the story of the string, but no one believed him—they only laughed.

He went on, stopped by everybody, stopping his acquaintances, beginning anew his tale and his protestations, turning his pockets inside out to prove that he had nothing.

"Move on, old quibbler," they said to him.

And he became angry, exasperated, feverish, sick at heart, at not being believed. He did not know what to do, but told his story over and over.

Night came. It was time to go home. He set out with three of his neighbors, to whom he pointed out the place where he had picked up the bit of cord, and all the way home he talked of his adventure. In the evening he made a circuit of the village of Bréauté to tell it to everybody. He met only incredulity. He was ill all night from his trouble.

The next day, toward one o'clock in the afternoon, Marius Paumelle, a farm hand, of Ymanville, returned the wallet and its contents to Monsieur Houlebrèque, of Manneville. The man stated, in effect, that he had found the wallet in the road, but not knowing how to read, had taken it home to his employer.

The news spread all about. Master Hauchecorne was told of it. He at once set out again on his travels, and began to narrate his story, completed by the dénouement. He was triumphant.

"It's not the thing 'at grieved me most, you understand," he said, "but it's the lie. Nothing harms you like being charged with a lie."

All day long he talked of his adventure. He told it on the streets to men passing, in the taverns to men drinking, after church the next Sunday. He stopped strangers to tell it to them. Now he was tranquil, yet something half disturbed him, without his knowing exactly what. People had an amused air as they listened to him. They did not appear convinced. He thought he detected whispers behind his back.

Tuesday of the following week he betook himself to the market of Goderville, driven there by the need of exploiting his case. Malandin, standing in his doorway, began to laugh when he saw him passing. Why? He accosted a farmer of Criquetot, who did not let him finish, but giving him a blow in the pit of the stomach, cried in his face:

"Go your way, humbug!"

Master Hauchecorne was dumfounded, and more and more ill at ease. Why had he been called a humbug?

When he was seated at table in Jourdain's inn he again began to explain the affair. A jockey of Montivilliers cried to him:

"Come, come, old croaker, I know about your string!"

Hauchecorne stammered:

"But since it is found—the wallet?"

The other answered:

"Hold your tongue, father. One finds, another returns. I know nothing about it, but I implicate you."

The peasant was left choking. He understood at last. He was accused of having returned the wallet through an accomplice. He tried to protest. The whole table began to laugh. He could not finish his dinner, and went out in the midst of mockeries.

He returned home, ashamed and disgraced, strangling with rage and confusion, so much the more overwhelmed, in that he was capable, with his Norman duplicity, of doing the very thing of which he was accused, and even boasting of it as a good stroke. Confusedly he saw his innocence impossible to prove, his chicanery being well known, and he felt himself cut to the heart by the injustice of the suspicion.

Then he commenced again to recount his adventure, lengthening each day his story, adding each time new reasonings, more energetic protestations, more solemn oaths, which he invented and arranged in his hours of solitude, his mind occupied solely with the story of the string. He was believed the less in proportion to the complication of his defense and the subtlety of his argument.

"That's the reasoning of a liar," they said behind his back.

He felt it, spent himself, wore his life out in useless efforts. He wasted away visibly. Wags now made him tell "the string" for their amusement, as one makes a soldier who has fought recount his battle. His mind, harassed and unsettled, grew feeble.

Toward the end of December he took to his bed. He died early in January, and in the delirium of his agony he attested his innocence, repeating:

"A little string . . . a little string . . . wait, here it is, m'sieu mayor!"

A Scandal in
Bohemia

Arthur Conan Doyle

I

To Sherlock Holmes she is always *the* woman. I have seldom heard him
mention her under any other name. In his eyes she eclipses and predominates
the whole of her sex. It was not that he felt any emotion akin to love for Irene
Adler. All emotions, and that one particularly, were abhorrent to his cold,
precise, but admirably balanced mind. He was, I take it, the most perfect
reasoning and observing machine that the world has seen; but as a lover, he
would have placed himself in a false position. He never spoke of the softer
passions, save with a gibe and a sneer. They were admirable things for the
observer—excellent for drawing the veil from men's motives and actions. But
for the trained reasoner to admit such intrusions into his own delicate and
finely adjusted temperament was to introduce a distracting factor which
might throw a doubt upon all his mental results. Grit in a sensitive instrument, or a crack in one of his own high-power lenses, would not be more
disturbing than a strong emotion in a nature such as his. And yet there was
but one woman to him, and that woman was the late Irene Adler, of dubious
and questionable memory.

I had seen little of Holmes lately. My marriage had drifted us away from
each other. My own complete happiness, and the home-centered interests
which rise up around the man who first finds himself master of his own
establishment, were sufficient to absorb all my attention; while Holmes, who
loathed every form of society with his whole Bohemian soul, remained in our
lodgings in Baker Street, buried among his old books, and alternating from

week to week between cocaine and ambition, the drowsiness of the drug, and the fierce energy of his own keen nature. He was still, as ever, deeply attracted by the study of crime, and occupied his immense faculties and extraordinary powers of observation in following out those clews, and clearing up those mysteries, which had been abandoned as hopeless by the official police. From time to time I heard some vague account of his doings; of his summons to Odessa in the case of the Trepoff murder, of his clearing up of the singular tragedy of the Atkinson brothers at Trincomalee, and finally of the mission which he had accomplished so delicately and successfully for the reigning family of Holland. Beyond these signs of his activity, however, which I merely shared with all the readers of the daily press, I knew little of my former friend and companion.

One night—it was on the 20th of March, 1888—I was returning from a journey to a patient (for I had now returned to civil practice), when my way led me through Baker Street. As I passed the well-remembered door, which must always be associated in my mind with my wooing, and with the dark incidents of the Study in Scarlet, I was seized with a keen desire to see Holmes again, and to know how he was employing his extraordinary powers. His rooms were brilliantly lighted, and even as I looked up, I saw his tall, spare figure pass twice in a dark silhouette against the blind. He was pacing the room swiftly, eagerly, with his head sunk upon his chest, and his hands clasped behind him. To me, who knew his every mood and habit, his attitude and manner told their own story. He was at work again. He had risen out of his drug-created dreams, and was hot upon the scent of some new problem. I rang the bell, and was shown up to the chamber which had formerly been in part my own.

His manner was not effusive. It seldom was; but he was glad, I think, to see me. With hardly a word spoken, but with a kindly eye, he waved me to an armchair, threw across his case of cigars, and indicated a spirit case and a gasogene in the corner. Then he stood before the fire, and looked me over in his singular introspective fashion.

"Wedlock suits you," he remarked. "I think, Watson, that you have put on seven and a half pounds since I saw you."

"Seven," I answered.

"Indeed, I should have thought a little more. Just a trifle more, I fancy, Watson. And in practice again, I observe. You did not tell me that you intended to go into harness."

"Then how do you know?"

"I see it, I deduce it. How do I know that you have been getting yourself very wet lately, and that you have a most clumsy and careless servant girl?"

"My dear Holmes," said I, "this is too much. You would certainly have been burned had you lived a few centuries ago. It is true that I had a country walk on Thursday and came home in a dreadful mess; but as I have changed my clothes, I can't imagine how you deduce it. As to Mary Jane, she is incorrigible, and my wife has given her notice; but there again I fail to see how you work it out."

He chuckled to himself and rubbed his long, nervous hands together.

"It is simplicity itself," said he; "my eyes tell me that on the inside of your left shoe, just where the firelight strikes it, the leather is scored by six almost parallel cuts. Obviously they have been caused by some one who has very carelessly scraped round the edges of the sole in order to remove crusted mud from it. Hence, you see, my double deduction that you had been out in vile weather, and that you had a particularly malignant boot-slicking specimen of the London slavery. As to your practice, if a gentleman walks into my rooms, smelling of iodoform, with a black mark of nitrate of silver upon his right forefinger, and a bulge on the side of his top-hat to show where he has secreted his stethoscope, I must be dull indeed if I do not pronounce him to be an active member of the medical profession."

I could not help laughing at the ease with which he explained his process of deduction. "When I hear you give your reasons," I remarked, "the thing always appears to me so ridiculously simple that I could easily do it myself, though at each successive instance of your reasoning I am baffled, until you explain your process. And yet, I believe that my eyes are as good as yours."

"Quite so," he answered, lighting a cigarette, and throwing himself down into an armchair. "You see, but you do not observe. The distinction is clear. For example, you have frequently seen the steps which lead up from the hall to this room."

"Frequently."

"How often?"

"Well, some hundreds of times."

"Then how many are there?"

"How many? I don't know?"

"Quite so! You have not observed. And yet you have seen. That is just my point. Now, I know there are seventeen steps, because I have both seen and observed. By the way, since you are interested in these little problems, and since you are good enough to chronicle one or two of my trifling experiences, you may be interested in this." He threw over a sheet of thick pink-tinted note-paper which had been lying open upon the table. "It came by the last post," said he. "Read it aloud."

The note was undated, and without either signature or address.

"There will call upon you to-night, at 7:45 o'clock," it said, "a gentleman who desires to consult you upon a matter of the deepest moment. Your recent services to one of the royal houses of Europe have shown that you are one who may safely be trusted with matters which are of an importance which can hardly be exaggerated. This account of you we have from all quarters received. Be in your chamber, then, at that hour, and do not take it amiss if your visitor wears a mask."

"This is indeed a mystery," I remarked. "What do you imagine that it means?"

"I have no data yet. It is a capital mistake to theorize before one has data. Insensibly one begins to twist facts to suit theories, instead of theories to suit facts. But the note itself—what do you deduce from it?"

I carefully examined the writing, and the paper upon which it was written.

"The man who wrote it was presumably well to do," I remarked, endeavoring to imitate my companion's processes. "Such paper could not be bought under half a crown a packet. It is peculiarly strong and stiff."

"Peculiar—that is the very word," said Holmes. "It is not an English paper at all. Hold it up to the light."

I did so, and saw a large E with a small g, a P and a large G with a small t woven into the texture of the paper.

"What do you make of that?" asked Holmes.

"The name of the maker, no doubt; or his monogram, rather."

"Not at all. The G with the small t stands for 'Gesellschaft,' which is the German for 'Company.' It is a customary contraction like our 'Co.' P, of course, stands for 'Papier.' Now for the Eg. Let us glance at our 'Continental Gazetteer.' " He took down a heavy brown volume from his shelves. "Eglow, Eglonitz—here we are, Egria. It is in a German-speaking country—in Bohemia, not far from Carlsbad. 'Remarkable as being the scene of the death of Wallenstein, and for its numerous glass factories and paper mills.' Ha! ha! my boy, what do you make of that?" His eyes sparkled, and he sent up a great blue triumphant cloud from his cigarette.

"The paper was made in Bohemia," I said.

"Precisely. And the man who wrote the note is a German. Do you note the peculiar construction of the sentence—'This account of you we have from all quarters received?' A Frenchman or Russian could not have written that. It is the German who is so uncourteous to his verbs. It only remains therefore, to discover what is wanted by this German who writes upon Bohemian paper, and prefers wearing a mask to showing his face. And here he comes, if I am not mistaken, to resolve all our doubts."

As he spoke there was the sharp sound of horses' hoofs and grating wheels against the curb, followed by a sharp pull at the bell. Holmes whistled.

"A pair, by the sound," said he. "Yes," he continued, glancing out of the window. "A nice little brougham and a pair of beauties. A hundred and fifty guineas apiece. There's money in this case, Watson, if there is nothing else."

"I think I had better go, Holmes."

"Not a bit, doctor. Stay where you are. I am lost without my Boswell. And this promises to be interesting. It would be a pity to miss it."

"But your client—"

"Never mind him. I may want your help, and so may he. Here he comes. Sit down in that arm chair, doctor, and give us your best attention."

A slow and heavy step, which had been heard upon the stairs and in the passage, paused immediately outside the door. Then there was a loud and authoritative tap.

"Come in!" said Holmes.

A man entered who could hardly have been less than six feet six inches in height, with the chest and limbs of a Hercules. His dress was rich with a richness which would, in England, be looked upon as akin to bad taste. Heavy bands of astrakan were slashed across the sleeves and front of his double-breasted coat, while the deep-blue cloak which was thrown over his shoulders was lined with flame-colored silk, and secured at the neck with a brooch which consisted of a single flaming beryl. Boots which extended halfway up his calves, and which were trimmed at the tops with rich brown fur, completed the impression of barbaric opulence which was suggested by his whole appearance. He carried a broad-brimmed hat in his hand, while he wore across the upper part of his face, extending down past the cheek bones, a black visard-mask, which he had apparently adjusted that very moment, for his hand was still raised to it as he entered. From the lower part of the face he appeared to be a man of strong character, with a thick, hanging lip, and a long, straight chin, suggestive of resolution pushed to the length of obstinacy.

"You had my note?" he asked, with a deep, harsh voice and a strongly marked German accent. "I told you that I would call." He looked from one to the other of us, as if uncertain which to address.

"Pray take a seat," said Holmes. "This is my friend and colleague, Dr. Watson, who is occasionally good enough to help me in my cases. Whom have I the honor to address?"

"You may address me as the Count von Kramm, a Bohemian nobleman. I understand that this gentleman, your friend, is a man of honor and discretion, whom I may trust with a matter of the most extreme importance. If not, I should much prefer to communicate with you alone."

I rose to go, but Holmes caught me by the wrist and pushed me back into my chair. "It is both, or none," said he. "You may say before this gentleman anything which you may say to me."

The count shrugged his broad shoulders. "Then I must begin," said he, "by binding you both to absolute secrecy for two years, at the end of that time the matter will be of no importance. At present it is not too much to say that it is of such weight that it may have an influence upon European history."

"I promise," said Holmes.

"And I."

"You will excuse this mask," continued our strange visitor. "The august person who employs me wishes his agent to be unknown to you, and I may confess at once that the title by which I have just called myself is not exactly my own."

"I was aware of it," said Holmes dryly.

"The circumstances are of great delicacy, and every precaution has to be taken to quench what might grow to be an immense scandal, and seriously compromise one of the reigning families of Europe. To speak plainly, the matter implicates the great House of Ormstein, hereditary kings of Bohemia."

"I was also aware of that," murmured Holmes, settling himself down in his armchair, and closing his eyes.

Our visitor glanced with some apparent surprise at the languid, lounging figure of the man who had been, no doubt, depicted to him as the most incisive reasoner and most energetic agent in Europe. Holmes slowly reopened his eyes and looked impatiently at his gigantic client.

"If your majesty would condescend to state your case," he remarked, "I should be better able to advise you."

The man sprung from his chair, and paced up and down the room in uncontrollable agitation. Then, with a gesture of desperation, he tore the mask from his face and hurled it upon the ground.

"You are right," he cried, "I am the king. Why should I attempt to conceal it?"

"Why, indeed?" murmured Holmes. "Your majesty had not spoken before I was aware that I was addressing Wilhelm Gottsreich Sigismond von Ormstein, Grand Duke of Cassel-Felstein, and hereditary King of Bohemia."

"But you can understand," said our strange visitor, sitting down once more and passing his hand over his high, white forehead, "you can understand that I am not accustomed to doing such business in my own person. Yet the matter was so delicate that I could not confide it to an agent without putting myself in his power. I have come incognito from Prague for the purpose of consulting you."

"Then, pray consult," said Holmes, shutting his eyes once more.

"The facts are briefly these: Some five years ago, during a lengthy visit to Warsaw, I made the acquaintance of the well-known adventuress Irene Adler. The name is no doubt familiar to you."

"Kindly look her up in my index, doctor," murmured Holmes, without opening his eyes. For many years he had adopted a system for docketing all paragraphs concerning men and things, so that it was difficult to name a subject or a person on which he could not at once furnish information. In this case I found her biography sandwiched in between that of a Hebrew rabbi and that of a staff-commander who had written a monogram upon the deep-sea fishes.

"Let me see!" said Holmes. "Hum! Born in New Jersey in the year 1858. Contralto—hum! La Scala—hum! Prima-donna Imperial Opera of Warsaw—yes! Retired from operatic stage—ha! Living in London—quite so! Your majesty, as I understand, became entangled with this young person, wrote her some compromising letters, and is now desirous of getting those letters back."

"Precisely so. But how—"

"Was there a secret marriage?"

"None."

"No legal papers or certificates?"

"None."

"Then I fail to follow your majesty. If this young person should produce her letters for blackmailing or other purposes, how is she to prove their authenticity?"

"There is the writing."

"Pooh, pooh! Forgery."

"My private note-paper."

"Stolen."

"My own seal."

"Imitated."

"My photograph."

"Bought."

"We were both in the photograph."

"Oh, dear! That is very bad. Your majesty has indeed committed an indiscretion."

"I was mad—insane."

"You have compromised yourself seriously."

"I was only crown prince then. I was young. I am but thirty now."

"It must be recovered."

"We have tried and failed."

"Your majesty must pay. It must be bought."

"She will not sell."

"Stolen, then."

"Five attempts have been made. Twice burglars in my pay ransacked her house. Once we diverted her luggage when she traveled. Twice she has been waylaid. There has been no result."

"No sign of it?"

"Absolutely none."

Holmes laughed. "It is quite a pretty little problem," said he.

"But a very serious one to me," returned the king reproachfully.

"Very, indeed. And what does she propose to do with the photograph?"

"To ruin me."

"But how?"

"I am about to be married."

"So I have heard."

"To Clotilde Lothman von Saxe-Meiningen, second daughter of the King of Scandinavia. You may know the strict principles of her family. She is herself the very soul of delicacy. A shadow of a doubt as to my conduct would bring the matter to an end."

"And Irene Adler?"

"Threatens to send them the photograph. And she will do it. I know that she will do it. You do not know her, but she has a soul of steel. She has the face of the most beautiful of women and the mind of the most resolute of men. Rather than I should marry another woman, there are no lengths to which she would not go—none."

"You are sure that she has not sent it yet?"

"I am sure."

"And why?"

"Because she has said that she would send it on the day when the betrothal was publicly proclaimed. That will be next Monday."

"Oh, then we have three days yet," said Holmes, with a yawn. "That is very fortunate, as I have one or two matters of importance to look into just at present. Your majesty will, of course, stay in London for the present?"

"Certainly. You will find me at the Langham, under the name of the Count von Kramm."

"Then I shall drop you a line to let you know how we progress."

"Pray do so; I shall be all anxiety."

"Then, as to money?"

"You have *carte blanche.*"

"Absolutely?"

"I tell you that I would give one of the provinces of my kingdom to have that photograph."

"And for present expenses?"

The king took a heavy chamois leather bag from under his cloak, and laid it on the table.

"There are three hundred pounds in gold, and seven hundred in notes," he said.

Holmes scribbled a receipt upon a sheet of his note-book, and handed it to him.

"And mademoiselle's address?" he asked.

"Is Briony Lodge, Serpentine Avenue, St. John's Wood."

Holmes took a note of it. "One other question," said he thoughtfully. "Was the photograph a cabinet?"

"It was."

"Then, good-night, your majesty, and I trust that we shall soon have some good news for you. And good-night, Watson," he added, as the wheels of the royal brougham rolled down the street. "If you will be good enough to call tomorrow afternoon, at three o'clock, I should like to chat this little matter over with you."

II

At three o'clock precisely I was at Baker Street, but Holmes had not yet returned. The landlady informed me that he had left the house shortly after eight o'clock in the morning. I sat down beside the fire, however, with the intention of awaiting him, however long he might be. I was already deeply interested in his inquiry, for, though it was surrounded by none of the grim and strange features which were associated with the two crimes which I have already recorded, still, the nature of the case and the exalted station of his client gave it a character of its own. Indeed, apart from the nature of the investigation which my friend had on hand, there was something in his masterly grasp of a situation, and his keen, incisive reasoning, which made it a pleasure to me to study his system of work, and to follow the quick, subtle methods by which he disentangled the most inextricable mysteries. So accustomed was I to his invariable success that the very possibility of his failing had ceased to enter into my head.

It was close upon four before the door opened, and a drunken-looking groom, ill-kempt and side-whiskered, with an inflamed face and disreputable clothes, walked into the room. Accustomed as I was to my friend's amazing powers in the use of disguises, I had to look three times before I was certain that it was indeed he. With a nod he vanished into the bedroom, whence he emerged in five minutes tweed-suited and respectable, as of old. Putting his hand into his pockets, he stretched out his legs in front of the fire, and laughed heartily for some minutes.

"Well, really!" he cried, and then he choked, and laughed again until he was obliged to lie back, limp and helpless, in the chair.

"What is it?"

"It's quite too funny. I am sure you could never guess how I employed my morning, or what I ended by doing."

"I can't imagine. I suppose that you have been watching the habits, and, perhaps, the house of Miss Irene Adler."

"Quite so, but the sequel was rather unusual. I will tell you, however. I left the house a little after eight o'clock this morning in the character of a groom out of work. There is a wonderful sympathy and freemasonry among horsy men. Be one of them, and you will know all that there is to know. I soon found Briony Lodge. It is a bijou villa, with a garden at the back, but built out in front right up to the road, two stories. Chubb lock to the door. Large sitting-room on the right side, well furnished, with long windows almost to the floor, and those preposterous English window-fasteners which a child could open. Behind there was nothing remarkable, save that the passage window could be reached from the top of the coach house. I walked round it and examined it closely from every point of view, but without noting anything else of interest.

I then lounged down the street, and found, as I expected, that there was a mews in a lane which runs down by one wall of the garden. I lent the hostlers a hand in rubbing down their horses, and I received in exchange twopence, a glass of half-and-half, two fills of shag tobacco, and as much information as I could desire about Miss Adler, to say nothing of half a dozen other people in the neighborhood, in whom I was not in the least interested, but whose biographies I was compelled to listen to."

"And what of Irene Adler?" I asked.

"Oh, she has turned all the men's heads down in that part. She is the daintiest thing under a bonnet on this planet. So say the Serpentine Mews, to a man. She lives quietly, sings at concerts, drives out at five every day, and returns at seven sharp for dinner. Seldom goes out at other times, except when she sings. Has only one male visitor, but a good deal of him. He is dark, handsome, and dashing; never calls less than once a day, and often twice. He is a Mr. Godfrey Norton of the Inner Temple. See the advantages of a cabman as a confidant. They had driven him home a dozen times from Serpentine Mews, and knew all about him. When I had listened to all that they had to tell, I began to walk up and down near Briony Lodge once more, and to think over my plan of campaign.

This Godfrey Norton was evidently an important factor in the matter. He was a lawyer. That sounded ominous. What was the relation between them, and what the object of his repeated visits? Was she his client, his friend, or his mistress? If the former, she had probably transferred the photograph to his keeping. If the latter, it was less likely. On the issue of this question depended whether I should continue my work at Briony Lodge, or turn my attention to the gentleman's chambers in the Temple. It was a delicate point, and it widened the field of my inquiry. I fear that I bore you with these details, but I have to let you see my little difficulties, if you are to understand the situation."

"I am following you closely," I answered.

"I was still balancing the matter in my mind, when a hansom cab drove up to Briony Lodge, and a gentleman sprung out. He was a remarkably handsome man, dark, aquiline, and mustached—evidently the man of whom I had heard. He appeared to be in a great hurry, shouted to the cabman to wait, and brushed past the maid, who opened the door, with the air of a man who was thoroughly at home.

He was in the house about half an hour, and I could catch glimpses of him in the windows of the sitting room, pacing up and down, talking excitedly and waving his arms. Of her I could see nothing. Presently he emerged, looking even more flurried than before. As he stepped up to the cab, he pulled a gold watch from his pocket and looked at it earnestly. 'Drive like the devil!' he shouted, 'first to Gross & Hankey's in Regent Street, and then to the Church of St. Monica in the Edgeware Road. Half a guinea if you do it in twenty minutes!'

Away they went, and I was just wondering whether I should not do well to follow them, when up the lane came a neat little landau, the coachman with his coat only half buttoned, and his tie under his ear, while all the tags of his harness were sticking out of the buckles. It hadn't pulled up before she shot out of the hall door and into it. I only caught a glimpse of her at the moment, but she was a lovely woman, with a face that a man might die for.

'The Church of St. Monica, John,' she cried; 'and half a sovereign if you reach it in twenty minutes.'

This was quite too good to lose, Watson. I was just balancing whether I should run for it, or whether I should perch behind her landau, when a cab came through the street. The driver looked twice at such a shabby fare; but I jumped in before he could object. 'The Church of St. Monica,' said I, 'and half a sovereign if you reach it in twenty minutes.' It was 11:35, and of course it was clear enough what was in the wind.

My cabby drove fast. I don't think I ever drove faster, but the others were there before us. The cab and landau with their steaming horses were in front of the door when I arrived. I paid the man, and hurried into the church. There was not a soul there save the two whom I had followed, and a surpliced clergyman, who seemed to be expostulating with them. They were all three standing in a knot in front of the altar. I lounged up the side aisle like any other idler who has dropped into a church. Suddenly, to my surprise, the three at the altar faced round to me, and Godfrey Norton came running as hard as he could toward me.

'Thank God!' he cried. 'You'll do. Come! Come!'

'What then?' I asked.

'Come, man, come; only three minutes, or it won't be legal.'

"I was half-dragged up to the altar, and, before I knew where I was, I found myself mumbling responses which were whispered in my ear, and vouching for things of which I knew nothing, and generally assisting in the secure tying up of Irene Adler, spinster, to Godfrey Norton, bachelor. It was all done in an instant, and there was the gentleman thanking me on the one side and the lady on the other, while the clergyman beamed on me in front. It was the most preposterous position in which I ever found myself in my life, and it was the thought of it that started me laughing just now. It seems that there had been some informality about their license; that the clergyman absolutely refused to marry them without a witness of some sort, and that my lucky appearance saved the bridegroom from having to sally out into the streets in search of a best man. The bride gave me a sovereign, and I mean to wear it on my watch chain in memory of the occasion."

"This is a very unexpected turn of affairs," said I; "and what then?"

"Well, I found my plans very seriously menaced. It looked as if the pair might take an immediate departure, and so necessitate very prompt and energetic measures on my part. At the church door, however, they separated, he driving back to the Temple, and she to her own house. 'I shall drive out in the park at five as usual,' she said, as she left him. I heard no more. They drove away in different directions and I went off to make my own arrangements."

"Which are?"

"Some cold beef and a glass of beer," he answered, ringing the bell. "I have been too busy to think of food, and I am likely to be busier still this evening. By the way, doctor, I shall want your co-operation."

"I shall be delighted."

"You don't mind breaking the law?"

"Not in the least."

"Nor running a chance of arrest?"

"Not in a good cause."

"Oh, the cause is excellent!"

"Then I am your man."

"I was sure that I might rely on you."

"But what is it you wish?"

"When Mrs. Turner has brought in the tray I will make it clear to you. Now," he said, as he turned hungrily on the simple fare that our landlady had provided, "I must discuss it while I eat, for I have not much time. It is nearly five now. In two hours we must be on the scene of action. Miss Irene, or madame, rather, returns from her drive at seven. We must be at Briony Lodge to meet her."

"And what then?"

"You must leave that to me. I have already arranged what is to occur. There is only one point on which I must insist. You must not interfere, come what may. You understand?"

"I am to be neutral?"

"To do nothing whatever. There will probably be some small unpleasantness. Do not join in it. It will end in my being conveyed into the house. Four or five minutes afterward the sitting-room window will open. You are to station yourself close to that open window."

"Yes."

"You are to watch me, for I will be visible to you."

"Yes."

"And when I raise my hand—so—you will throw into the room what I give you to throw, and will, at the same time, raise the cry of fire. You quite follow me?"

"Entirely."

"It is nothing very formidable," he said, taking a long, cigar-shaped roll from his pocket. It is an ordinary plumber's smoke-rocket, fitted with a cap at either end, to make it self-lighting. Your task is confined to that. When you raise your cry of fire, it will be taken up by quite a number of people. You may then walk to the end of the street, and I will rejoin you in ten minutes. I hope that I have made myself clear?"

"I am to remain neutral, to get near the window, to watch you, and, at the signal, to throw in this object, then to raise the cry of fire, and to wait you at the corner of the street."

"Precisely."

"Then you may entirely rely on me."

"That is excellent. I think, perhaps, it is almost time that I prepared for the new rôle I have to play."

He disappeared into his bedroom, and returned in a few minutes in the character of an amiable and simple-minded Nonconformist clergyman. His broad, black hat, his baggy trousers, his white tie, his sympathetic smile, and general look of peering and benevolent curiosity were such as Mr. John Hare alone could have equaled. It was not merely that Holmes changed his costume. His expression, his manner, his very soul seemed to vary with every fresh part that he assumed. The stage lost a fine actor, even as science lost an acute reasoner, when he became a specialist in crime.

It was 6:15 when we left Baker Street, and it still wanted ten minutes to the hour when we found ourselves in Serpentine Avenue. It was already dusk, and the lamps were just being lighted as we paced up and down in front of Briony Lodge, waiting for the coming of its occupant. The house was just such as I had pictured it from Sherlock Holmes' succinct description, but the locality appeared to be less private than I expected. On the contrary, for a small street in a quiet neighborhood, it was remarkably animated. There was a group of shabbily dressed men smoking and laughing in a corner, a scissors-grinder with his wheel, two guardsmen who were flirting with a nurse girl, and several well-dressed young men who were lounging up and down with cigars in their mouths.

"You see," remarked Holmes, as we paced to and fro in front of the house, "this marriage rather simplifies matters. The photograph becomes a double-edged weapon now. The chances are that she would be as averse to its being seen by Mr. Godfrey Norton as our client is to its coming to the eyes of his princess. Now the question is—where are we to find the photograph?"

"Where, indeed?"

"It is most unlikely that she carries it about with her. It is cabinet size. Too large for easy concealment about a woman's dress. She knows that the king is capable of having her waylaid and searched. Two attempts of the sort have already been made. We may take it, then, that she does not carry it about with her."

"Where, then?"

"Her banker or her lawyer. There is that double possibility. But I am inclined to think neither. Women are naturally secretive, and they like to do their own secreting. Why should she hand it over to any one else? She could trust her own guardianship, but she could not tell what indirect or political influence might be brought to bear upon a business man. Besides, remember that she had resolved to use it within a few days. It must be where she can lay her hands upon it. It must be in her own house."

"But it has twice been burglarized."

"Pshaw! They did not know how to look."

"But how will you look?"

"I will not look."

"What then?"

"I will get her to show me."

"But she will refuse."

"She will not be able to. But I hear the rumble of wheels. It is her carriage. Now carry out my orders to the letter."

As he spoke, the gleam of the side-lights of a carriage came round the curve of the avenue. It was a smart little landau which rattled up to the door of Briony Lodge. As it pulled up one of the loafing men at the corner dashed forward to open the door in the hope of earning a copper, but was elbowed away by another loafer who had rushed up with the same intention. A fierce quarrel broke out, which was increased by the two guardsmen, who took sides with one of the loungers, and by the scissors-grinder, who was equally hot upon the other side. A blow was struck, and in an instant the lady, who had stepped from her carriage, was the centre of a little knot of struggling men who struck savagely at each other with their fists and sticks. Holmes dashed into the crowd to protect the lady; but, just as he reached her, he gave a cry and dropped to the ground, with the blood running freely down his face. At his fall the guardsmen took to their heels in one direction and the loungers in the other, while a number of better dressed people who had watched the scuffle without taking part in it crowded in to help the lady and to attend to the injured man. Irene Adler, as I will still call her, had hurried up the steps; but she stood at the top, with her superb figure outlined against the lights of the hall, looking back into the street.

"Is the poor gentleman much hurt?" she asked.

"He is dead," cried several voices.

"No, no, there's life in him," shouted another. "But he'll be gone before you can get him to the hospital."

"He's a brave fellow," said a woman. "They would have had the lady's purse and watch if it hadn't been for him. They were a gang, and a rough one, too. Ah! he's breathing now."

"He can't lie in the street. May we bring him in, marm?"

"Surely. Bring him into the sitting room. There is a comfortable sofa. This way, please." Slowly and solemnly he was borne into Briony Lodge, and laid out in the principal room, while I still observed the proceedings from my post by the window. The lamps had been lighted, but the blinds had not been drawn, so that I could see Holmes as he lay upon the couch. I do not know whether he was seized with compunction at that moment for the part he was playing, but I know that I never felt more heartily ashamed of myself in my life when I saw the beautiful creature against whom I was conspiring, or the grace and kindliness with which she waited upon the injured man. And yet it would be the blackest treachery to Holmes to draw back now from the part which he had intrusted to me. I hardened my heart, and took the smoke-rocket from under my ulster. After all, I thought, we are not injuring her. We are but preventing her from injuring another.

Holmes had sat upon the couch, and I saw him motion like a man who is in need of air. A maid rushed across and threw open the window. At the same instant I saw him raise his hand, and at the signal I tossed my rocket into the room with a cry of "Fire!" The word was no sooner out of my mouth than the whole crowd of spectators, well dressed and ill—gentlemen, hostlers, and servant-maids—joined in a general shriek of "Fire!" Thick clouds of smoke curled through the room, and out at the open window. I caught a glimpse of rushing figures, and a moment later the voice of Holmes from within assuring them that it was a false alarm. Slipping through the shouting crowd, I made my way to the corner of the street, and in ten minutes was rejoiced to find my friend's arm in mine, and to get away from the scene of uproar. He walked swiftly and in silence for some few minutes, until we had turned down one of the quiet streets which led toward the Edgware Road.

"You did it very nicely, doctor," he remarked. "Nothing could have been better. It is all right."

"You have the photograph?"

"I know where it is."

"And how did you find out?"

"She showed me, as I told you that she would."

"I am still in the dark."

"I do not wish to make a mystery," said he, laughing. "The matter was perfectly simple. You, of course, saw that every one in the street was an accomplice. They were all engaged for the evening."

"I guessed as much."

"Then, when the row broke out, I had a little moist red paint in the palm of my hand. I rushed forward, fell down, clapped my hand to my face, and became a piteous spectacle. It is an old trick."

"That also I could fathom."

"Then they carried me in. She was bound to have me in. What else could she do? And into her sitting room, which was the very room which I suspected. It lay between that and her bedroom, and I was determined to see which. They laid me on a couch, I motioned for air, they were compelled to open the window, and you had your chance."

"How did that help you?"

"It was all important. When a woman thinks that her house is on fire, her instinct is at once to rush to the thing which she values most. It is a perfectly overpowering impulse, and I have more than once taken advantage of it. In the case of the Darlington Substitution Scandal it was of use to me, and also in the Arnsworth Castle business. A married woman grabs at her baby—an unmarried one reaches for her jewel-box. Now it was clear to me that our lady of to-day had nothing in the house more precious to her than what we are in quest of. She would rush to secure it. The alarm of fire was admirably done. The smoke and shouting were enough to shake nerves of steel. She responded beautifully. The photograph is in a recess behind a sliding panel just above the right bell-pull. She was there in an instant, and I caught a glimpse of it as she half drew it out. When I cried out that it was a false alarm, she replaced it, glanced at the rocket, rushed from the room, and I have not seen her since. I rose, and, making my excuses, escaped from the house. I hesitated whether to attempt to secure the photograph at once; but the coachman had come in, and as he was watching me narrowly, it seemed safer to wait. A little overprecipitance may ruin all."

"And now?" I asked.

"Our quest is practically finished. I shall call with the king to-morrow, and with you, if you care to come with us. We will be shown into the sitting-room to wait for the lady, but it is probable that when she comes she may find neither us nor the photograph. It might be a satisfaction to his majesty to regain it with his own hands."

"And when will you call?"

"At eight in the morning. She will not be up, so that we shall have a clear field. Besides, we must be prompt, for this marriage may mean a complete change in her life and habits. I must wire to the king without delay."

We had reached Baker Street, and had stopped at the door. He was searching his pockets for the key, when some one passing said:

"Good-night, Mister Sherlock Holmes."

There were several people on the pavement at the time, but the greeting
appeared to come from a slim youth in an ulster who had hurried by.

"I've heard that voice before," said Holmes, staring down the dimly lighted
street. "Now, I wonder who the deuce that could have been?"

III

I slept at Baker Street that night, and we were engaged upon our toast and
coffee in the morning when the King of Bohemia rushed into the room.

"You have really got it?" he cried, grasping Sherlock Holmes by either
shoulder, and looking eagerly into his face.

"Not yet."

"But you have hopes?"

"I have hopes."

"Then come. I am all impatience to be gone."

"We must have a cab."

"No, my brougham is waiting."

"Then that will simplify matters." We descended, and started off once more
for Briony Lodge.

"Irene Adler is married," remarked Holmes.

"Married! When?"

"Yesterday."

"But to whom?"

"To an English lawyer named Norton."

"But she could not love him."

"I am in hopes that she does."

"And why in hopes?"

"Because it would spare your majesty all fear of future annoyance. If the
lady loves her husband, she does not love your majesty. If she does not love
your majesty, there is no reason why she should interfere with your majesty's
plan."

"It is true. And yet—Well, I wish she had been of my own station. What a
queen she would have made!" He relapsed into a moody silence, which was
not broken until we drew up in Serpentine Avenue.

The door of Briony Lodge was open, and an elderly woman stood upon the
steps. She watched us with a sardonic eye as we stepped from the brougham.

"Mr. Sherlock Holmes, I believe?" said she.

"I am Mr. Holmes," answered my companion, looking at her with a questioning and rather startled gaze.

"Indeed! My mistress told me that you were likely to call. She left this morning, with her husband, by the 5:15 train from Charing Cross, for the Continent."

"What!" Sherlock Holmes staggered back, white with chagrin and surprise. "Do you mean that she has left England?"

"Never to return."

"And the papers?" asked the king hoarsely. "All is lost!"

"We shall see." He pushed past the servant, and rushed into the drawing room, followed by the king and myself. The furniture was scattered about in every direction, with dismantled shelves, and open drawers, as if the lady had hurriedly ransacked them before her flight. Holmes rushed at the bell-pull, tore back a small sliding shutter, and plunging in his hand, pulled out a photograph and a letter. The photograph was of Irene Adler herself in evening dress; the letter was superscribed to "Sherlock Holmes, Esq. To be left till called for." My friend tore it open, and we all three read it together. It was dated at midnight of the preceding night, and ran in this way:

MY DEAR MR. SHERLOCK HOLMES: You really did it very well. You took me in completely. Until after the alarm of the fire, I had not a suspicion. But then, when I found how I had betrayed myself, I began to think. I had been warned against you months ago. I had been told that if the king employed an agent, it would certainly be you. And your address had been given me. Yet, with all this, you made me reveal what you wanted to know. Even after I became suspicious, I found it hard to think evil of such a dear, kind old clergyman. But, you know, I have been trained as an actress myself. Male costume is nothing new to me. I often take advantage of the freedom which it gives. I sent John, the coachman, to watch you, ran upstairs, got into my walking clothes, as I call them, and came down just as you departed.

"Well, I followed you to the door, and so made sure that I was really an object of interest to the celebrated Mr. Sherlock Holmes. Then I, rather imprudently, wished you good-night, and started for the Temple to see my husband.

"We both thought the best resource was flight, when pursued by so formidable an antagonist; so you will find the nest empty when you call to-morrow. As to the photograph, your client may rest in peace. I love and am loved by a better man than he. The king may do what he will without hindrance from one whom he has cruelly wronged. I keep it only to safeguard myself, and preserve a weapon which will always secure me from any steps which he might take in the future. I leave a photograph which he might care to possess; and I remain, dear Mr. Sherlock Holmes, very truly yours,

"IRENE NORTON, *née* ADLER"

"What a woman—oh, what a woman!" cried the King of Bohemia, when we had all three read this epistle. "Did I not tell you how quick and resolute she was? Would she not have made an admirable queen? Is it not a pity that she was not on my level?"

"From what I have seen of the lady, she seems, indeed, to be on a very different level to your majesty," said Holmes coldly. "I am sorry that I have not been able to bring your majesty's business to a more successful conclusion."

"On the contrary, my dear sir," cried the king, "nothing could be more successful. I know that her word is inviolate. The photograph is now as safe as if it were in the fire."

"I am glad to hear your majesty say so."

"I am immensely indebted to you. Pray tell me in what way I can reward you. This ring—" He slipped an emerald snake ring from his finger, and held it out upon the palm of his hand.

"Your majesty has something which I should value even more highly," said Holmes.

"You have but to name it."

"This photograph!"

The king stared at him in amazement.

"Irene's photograph!" he cried. "Certainly, if you wish it."

"I thank your majesty. Then there is no more to be done in the matter. I have the honor to wish you a very good morning." He bowed and turning away without observing the hand which the king had stretched out to him, he set off in my company for his chambers.

And that was how a great scandal threatened to affect the kingdom of Bohemia, and how the best plans of Mr. Sherlock Holmes were beaten by a woman's wit. He used to make merry over the cleverness of women, but I have not heard him do it of late. And when he speaks of Irene Adler, or when he refers to her photograph, it is always under the honorable title of *the* woman.

LOVE AND BREAD

Jean August Strindberg

When young Gustaf Falk, the assistant councilor, made his ceremonial proposal for Louise's hand to her father, the old gentleman's first question was: "How much are you earning?"

"Not more than a hundred kroner a month. But Louise—"

"Never mind the rest," interrupted Falk's prospective father-in-law; "you don't earn enough."

"Oh, but Louise and I love each other so dearly! We are so sure of one another."

"Very likely. However, let me ask you: is twelve hundred a year the sum total of your resources?"

"We first became acquainted at Lidingö."

"Do you make anything beside your government salary?" persisted Louise's parent.

"Well, yes, I think we shall have sufficient. And then, you see, our mutual affection—"

"Yes, exactly; but let's have a few figures."

"Oh," said the enthusiastic suitor, "I can get enough by doing extra work!"

"What sort of work? And how much?"

"I can give lessons in French, and also translate. And then I can get some proofreading."

"How much translation?" queried the elder, pencil in hand.

"I can't say exactly, but at present I am translating a French book at the rate of ten kroner per folio."

"How many folios are there altogether?"

"About a couple of dozen, I should say."

"Very well. Put this at two hundred and fifty kroner. Now, how much else?"

"Oh, I don't know. It's a little uncertain."

"What, you are not certain, and you intend to marry? You seem to have queer notions of marriage, young man! Do you realize that there will be children, and that you will have to feed and clothe them, and bring them up?"

"But," objected Falk, "the children may not come so very soon. And we love each other so dearly, that—"

"That the arrival of children may be prophesied quite safely." Then, relenting, Louise's father went on:

"I suppose you are both set on marrying, and I don't doubt but what you are really fond of each other. So it seems as though I should have to give my consent after all. Only make good use of the time that you are engaged to Louise by trying to increase your income."

Young Falk flushed with joy at this sanction, and demonstratively kissed the old man's hand. Heavens, how happy he was—and his Louise, too! How proud they felt the first time they went out walking together arm in arm, and how everybody noticed the radiant happiness of the engaged couple!

In the evenings he came to see her, bringing with him the proof-sheets he had undertaken to correct. This made a good impression on papa, and earned the industrious young man a kiss from his betrothed. But one evening they went to the theatre for a change, and drove home in a cab, the cost of that evening's entertainment amounting to ten kroner. Then, on a few other evenings, instead of giving the lessons, he called at the young lady's house to take her for a little walk.

As the day set for the wedding drew near, they had to think about making the necessary purchases to furnish their flat. They bought two handsome beds of real walnut, with substantial spring mattresses and soft eiderdown quilts. Louise must have a blue quilt, as her hair was blond. They, of course, also paid a visit to the house-furnishers', where they selected a lamp with a red shade, a pretty porcelain statuette of Venus, a complete table service with knives, forks, and fine glassware. In picking out the kitchen utensils they were benefited by mama's advice and aid. It was a busy time for the assistant councilor—rushing about to find a house, looking after the workmen, seeing that all the furniture was got together, writing out checks, and what not.

Meanwhile it was perfectly natural that Gustaf could earn nothing extra. But when they were once married he would easily make it up. They intended to be most economical—only a couple of rooms to start with. Anyhow, you could furnish a small apartment better than a large one. So they took a first-floor apartment at six hundred kroner, consisting of two rooms, kitchen, and larder. At first Louise said she would prefer three rooms on the top landing. But what did it matter, after all, so long as they sincerely loved each other?

At last the rooms were furnished. The sleeping chamber was like a small sanctuary, the beds standing side by side like chariots taking their course along life's journey. The blue quilts, the snowy sheets, and the pillow-spreads embroidered with the young people's initials amorously intertwined, all had a bright and cheerful appearance. There was a tall, elegant screen for the use of Louise, whose piano—costing twelve hundred kroner—stood in the other chamber, which served as sitting-room, dining-room, and study, in one. Here, too, stood a large walnut writing-desk and dining-table, with chairs to match; a large gilt-framed mirror, a sofa, and a bookcase added to the general air of comfort and coziness.

The marriage ceremony took place on a Saturday night, and late on Sunday morning the happy young couple was still asleep. Gustaf rose first. Although the bright light of day was peering in through the shutters, he did not open them, but lit the red-shaded lamp, which threw a mysterious rosy glow over the porcelain Venus. The pretty young wife lay there languid and content; she had slept well, and had not been awakened—as it was Sunday—by the rumbling of early market wagons. Now the church bells were ringing joyfully, as if to celebrate the creation of man and woman.

Louise turned over, while Gustaf retired behind the screen to put on a few things. He went out into the kitchen to order lunch. How dazzlingly the new copper and tin utensils gleamed and glistened! And all was his own—his and hers. He told the cook to go to the neighboring restaurant, and request that the lunch be sent in. The proprietor knew about it; he had received full instructions the day before. All he needed now was a reminder that the moment had come.

The bridegroom thereupon returns to the bedchamber and taps softly: "May I come in?"

A little scream is heard. Then: "No, dearest; just wait a minute!"

Gustaf lays the table himself. By the time the lunch arrives from the restaurant, the new plates and cutlery and glasses are set out on the fresh, white linen cloth. The bridal bouquet lies beside Louise's place. As she enters the room in her embroidered morning wrapper, she is greeted by the sunbeams. She still feels a little tired, so he makes her take an armchair, and wheels it to the table. A drop or two of liqueur enlivens her; a mouthful of caviar stimulates her appetite. Fancy what mama would say if she saw her daughter drinking spirits! But that's the advantage of being married, you know; then you can do whatever you please.

The young husband waits most attentively upon his fair bride. What a pleasure, too! Of course he has had good luncheons before, in his bachelor days; but what comfort or satisfaction had he ever derived from them? None. Thus he reflects while consuming a plate of oysters and a glass of beer. What numbskulls they are, those bachelors, not to marry! And how selfish! Why, there ought to be a tax on them, as on dogs. Louise is not quite so severe, urging gently and sweetly that perhaps the poor fellows who elect the single state are subjects of pity. No doubt if they could afford to marry, they would —she thinks. Gustaf feels a slight pang at his heart. Surely happiness is not to be measured by money. No, no; but, but—Well, never mind, there will soon be lots of work, and then everything will run smoothly. For the present there is this delicious roast partridge with cranberry sauce to be considered, and the Burgundy. These luxuries, together with some fine artichokes, cause the young wife a moment's alarm, and she timidly asks Gustaf if they can afford living on such a scale. But Gustaf pours more wine into the glass of his little Louise, reassuring her and softening those groundless fears. "One day is not every day," he says; "and people ought to enjoy life when they can. Ah, how beautiful life is!"

At six o'clock an elegant carriage, with two horses, pulls up before the door, and the bridal pair take a drive. Louise is charmed as they roll along through the park, reclining there so comfortably, while they meet acquaintances on foot, who bow to them in obvious astonishment and envy. The assistant councilor has made a good match, they must think; he has chosen a girl with money. And they, poor souls, have to walk. How much pleasanter to ride, without effort, leaning against these soft cushions! It is symbolical of agreeable married life.

The first month was one of unceasing enjoyment—balls, parties, dinners, suppers, theatres. Still, the time they spent at home was really the best of all! It was a delightful sensation to carry Louise off home, from her parents, at night, when they would do as they pleased under their own roof. Arriving at the flat, they would make a little supper, and then they would sit comfortably, chatting until a late hour. Gustaf was all for economy—the theory of it, that is to say. One day the young bride and housekeeper tried smoked salmon with boiled potatoes. How she relished it, too! But Gustaf demurred, and when smoked salmon day came round again he invested in a brace of partridges. These he bought at the market for a kroner, exulting over the splendid bargain, of which Louise did not approve. She had once bought a pair for less money. Besides, to eat game was extravagant. However, it would not do to disagree with her husband about such a trifling matter.

After a couple of months more Louise Falk became strangely indisposed. Had she caught cold? Or had she perchance been poisoned by the metal kitchen utensils? The doctor who was called in merely laughed, and said it was all right—a queer diagnosis, to be sure, when the young lady was seriously ailing. Perhaps there was arsenic in the wall-paper. Falk took some to a chemist, biding him make a careful analysis. The chemist's report stated the wall-paper to be quite free from any harmful substance.

His wife's sickness not abating, Gustaf began to investigate on his own account, his studies in a medical book resulting in a certainty as to her ailment. She took warm foot-baths, and in a month's time her state was declared entirely promising. This was sudden—sooner than they had expected; yet how lovely to be papa and mama! Of course the child would be a boy—no doubt of that; and one must think of a name to give him. Meanwhile, though, Louise took her husband aside, and reminded him that since their marriage he had earned nothing to supplement his salary, which had proved far from sufficient. Well, it was true they had lived rather high, but now a change should be made, and everything would be satisfactory.

Next day the assistant councilor went to see his good friend the barrister, with a request that he indorse a promissory note. This would allow him to borrow the money that would be needed to meet certain unavoidable forth-coming expenses—as Falk made clear to his friend. "Yes," agreed the man of law, "marrying and raising a family is an expensive business. I have never been able to afford it."

Falk felt too much ashamed to press his request, and when he returned home, empty-handed, was greeted with the news that two strangers had been to the house, and had asked for him. They must be lieutenants in the army, thought Gustaf, friends belonging to the garrison of Fort Vaxholm. No, he was told, they could not have been lieutenants; they were much older-looking men. Ah, then they were two fellows he used to know in Upsala; they had probably heard of his marriage, and had come to look him up. Only the servant said they were not from Upsala, but were Stockholmers, and carried sticks. Mysterious—very; but no doubt they would come back.

Then the young husband went marketing again. He bought strawberries—at a bargain, of course.

"Just fancy," he triumphantly exclaimed to his housewife, "a pint of these large strawberries for a kroner and a half, at this time of year!"

"Oh, but Gustaf dear, we can't afford that sort of thing!"

"Never mind, darling; I have arranged for some extra work."

"But what about our debts?"

"Debts? Why, I'm going to make a big loan, and pay them all off at once that way."

"Ah," objected Louise, "but won't this simply mean a new debt?"

"No matter if it does. It will be a respite, you know. But why discuss such unpleasant things? What capital strawberries, eh, dear? And don't you think a glass of sherry would go well now after the strawberries?"

Upon which the servant was sent out for a bottle of sherry—the best, naturally.

When Falk's wife awoke from her afternoon nap on the sofa that day, she apologetically reverted to the subject of debt. She hoped he would not be angry at what she had to say. Angry? No, of course not. What was it? Did she want some money for the house? Louise explained:

"The grocer has not been paid, the butcher has threatened us, and the livery-stable man also insists on having his bill settled."

"Is that all?" replied the assistant councilor. "They shall be paid at once—to-morrow—every farthing. But let's think of something else. How would you like to go out for a little drive to the park? You'd rather not take a carriage? All right, then, there's the tramway; that will take us to the park."

So they went to the park, and they had dinner in a private room at the Alhambra Restaurant. It was great fun, too, because the people in the general dining-room thought they were a frisky young pair of lovers. This idea amused Gustaf, though Louise seemed a trifle depressed, especially when she saw the bill. They could have had a good deal at home for that amount.

The months go by, and now arises the need for actual preparation—a cradle, infant's clothing, and so forth.

Falk has no easy time raising the money. The livery-stable man and the grocer refuse further credit, for they, too, have families to feed. What shocking materialism!

At length the eventful day arrives. Gustaf must secure a nurse, and even while holding his new-born daughter in his arms is called out to pacify his creditors. The fresh responsibilities weigh heavily upon him; he almost breaks down under the strain. He succeeds, it is true, in getting some translation to do, but how can he perform the work when at every touch and turn he is obliged to run errands? In this frame of mind he appeals to his father-in-law for help. The old gentleman receives him coldly:

"I will help you this once, but not again. I have little enough myself, and you are not my only child."

Delicacies must be provided for the mother, chicken and expensive wine. And the nurse has to be paid.

Fortunately, Falk's wife is soon on her feet again. She is like a girl once more, with a slender figure. Her pallor is quite becoming. Louise's father talks seriously to his son-in-law, however:

"Now, no more children, if you please, unless you want to be ruined."

For a brief space the junior Falk family continued to live on love and increasing debts. But one day bankruptcy knocked at the door. The seizure of the household effects was threatened. Then the old man came and took away Louise and her child, and as they rode off in a cab he made the bitter reflection that he had lent his girl to a young man, who had given her back after a year, dishonored. Louise would willingly have stayed with Gustaf, but there was nothing more to subsist upon. He remained behind, looking on while the bailiffs—those men with the sticks—denuded the flat of everything, furniture, bedding, crockery, cutlery, kitchen utensils, until it was stripped bare.

Now began real life for Gustaf. He managed to get a position as proofreader on a newspaper which was published in the morning, so that he had to work at his desk for several hours each night. As he had not actually been declared a bankrupt, he was allowed to keep his place in the government service, although he could hope for no more promotion. His father-in-law made the concession of letting him see his wife and child on Sundays, but he was never permitted to be alone with them. When he left, in the evening, to go to the newspaper office, they would accompany him to the gate, and he would depart in utter humiliation of soul. It might take him perhaps twenty years to pay off all his obligations. And then—yes, what then? Could he then support his wife and child? No, probably not. If, in the mean time, his father-in-law should die, they would be left without a home. So he must be thankful even to the hard-hearted old man who had so cruelly separated them.

Ah, yes, human life itself is indeed hard and cruel! The beasts of the field find maintenance easily enough, while of all created beings man alone must toil and spin. It is a shame, yes, it is a crying shame, that in this life everybody is not provided with gratuitous partridges and strawberries.

THE SUICIDE CLUB

STORY OF THE YOUNG MAN WITH THE CREAM TARTS

Robert Louis Stevenson

During his residence in London, the accomplished Prince Florizel of Bohemia gained the affection of all classes by the seduction of his manner and by a well-considered generosity. He was a remarkable man even by what was known of him; and that was but a small part of what he actually did. Although of a placid temper in ordinary circumstances, and accustomed to take the world with as much philosophy as any plowman, the Prince of Bohemia was not without a taste for ways of life more adventurous and eccentric than that to which he was destined by his birth. Now and then, when he fell into a low humor, when there was no laughable play to witness in any of the London theatres, and when the season of the year was unsuitable to those field sports in which he excelled all competitors, he would summon his confidant and Master of the Horse, Colonel Geraldine, and bid him prepare himself against an evening ramble. The Master of the Horse was a young officer of a brave and even temerarious disposition. He greeted the news with delight, and hastened to make ready. Long practise and a varied acquaintance of life had given him a singular facility in disguise; he could adapt not only his face and bearing, but his voice and almost his thoughts, to those of any rank, character, or nation; and in this way he diverted attention from the Prince, and sometimes gained admission for the pair into strange societies. The civil authorities were never taken into the secret of these adventures; the imperturbable courage of the one and the ready invention and chivalrous devotion of the other had brought them through a score of dangerous passes; and they grew in confidence as time went on.

One evening in March they were driven by a sharp fall of sleet into an

Oyster Bar in the immediate neighborhood of Leicester Square. Colonel Geraldine was dressed and painted to represent a person connected with the Press in reduced circumstances; while the Prince had, as usual, travestied his appearance by the addition of false whiskers and a pair of large adhesive eyebrows. These lent him a shaggy and weather-beaten air, which, for one of his urbanity, formed the most impenetrable disguise. Thus equipped, the commander and his satellite sipped their brandy and soda in security.

The bar was full of guests, both male and female; but though more than one of these offered to fall into talk with our adventurers, none of them promised to grow interesting upon a nearer acquaintance. There was nothing present but the lees of London and the commonplace of disrespectability; and the Prince had already fallen to yawning, and was beginning to grow weary of the whole excursion, when the swing doors were pushed violently open, and a young man, followed by a couple of commissionaires, entered the bar. Each of the commissionaires carried a large dish of cream tarts under a cover, which they at once removed; and the young man made the round of the company, and pressed these confections upon every one's acceptance with an exaggerated courtesy. Sometimes his offer was laughingly accepted; sometimes it was firmly, or even harshly, rejected. In these latter cases the newcomer always ate the tart himself, with some more or less humorous commentary.

At last he accosted Prince Florizel.

"Sir," said he, with a profound obeisance, proffering the tart at the same time between his thumb and forefinger, "will you so far honor an entire stranger? I can answer for the quality of the pastry, having eaten two dozen and three of them myself since five o'clock."

"I am in the habit," replied the Prince, "of looking not so much to the nature of a gift as to the spirit in which it is offered."

"The spirit, sir," returned the young man, with another bow, "is one of mockery."

"Mockery?" repeated Florizel. "And whom do you propose to mock?"

"I am not here to expound my philosophy," replied the other, "but to distribute these cream tarts. If I mention that I heartily include myself in the ridicule of the transaction, I hope you will consider honor satisfied and condescend. If not, you will constrain me to eat my twenty-eighth, and I own to being weary of the exercise."

"You touch me," said the Prince, "and I have all the will in the world to rescue you from this dilemma, but upon one condition. If my friend and I eat your cakes—for which we have neither of us any natural inclination—we shall expect you to join us at supper by way of recompense."

The young man seemed to reflect.

"I have still several dozen upon hand," he said at last; "and that will make it necessary for me to visit several more bars before my great affair is concluded. This will take some time; and if you are hungry—"

The Prince interrupted him with a polite gesture.

"My friend and I will accompany you," he said: "for we have already a deep interest in your very agreeable mode of passing an evening. And now that the preliminaries of peace are settled, allow me to sign the treaty for both."

And the Prince swallowed the tart with the best grace imaginable.

"It is delicious," said he.

"I perceive you are a connoisseur," replied the young man.

Colonel Geraldine likewise did honor to the pastry; and every one in that bar having now either accepted or refused his delicacies, the young man with the cream tarts led the way to another and similar establishment. The two commissionaires, who seemed to have grown accustomed to their absurd employment, followed immediately after; and the Prince and the Colonel brought up the rear, arm in arm, and smiling to each other as they went. In this order the company visited two other taverns, where scenes were enacted of a like nature to that already described—some refusing, some accepting, the favors of this vagabond hospitality, and the young man himself eating each rejected tart.

On leaving the third saloon the young man counted his store. There were but nine remaining, three in one tray and six in the other.

"Gentlemen," said he, addressing himself to his two new followers, "I am unwilling to delay your supper. I am positively sure you must be hungry. I feel that I owe you a special consideration. And on this great day for me, when I am closing a career of folly by my most conspicuously silly action, I wish to behave handsomely to all who give me countenance. Gentlemen, you shall wait no longer. Although my constitution is shattered by previous excesses, at the risk of my life I liquidate the suspensory condition."

With these words he crushed the nine remaining tarts into his mouth, and swallowed them at a single movement each. Then, turning to the commissionaires, he gave them a couple of sovereigns.

"I have to thank you," said he, "for your extraordinary patience."

And he dismissed them with a bow apiece. For some seconds he stood looking at the purse from which he had just paid his assistants, then, with a laugh, he tossed it into the middle of the street, and signified his readiness for supper.

In a small French restaurant in Soho, which had enjoyed an exaggerated reputation for some little while, but had already begun to be forgotten, and in a private room up two pair of stairs, the three companions made a very elegant supper, and drank three or four bottles of champagne, talking the while upon indifferent subjects. The young man was fluent and gay, but he laughed louder than was natural in a person of polite breeding; his hands trembled violently, and the voice took sudden and surprising inflections, which seemed to be independent of his will. The dessert had been cleared away, and all three had lighted their cigars, when the Prince addressed him in these words:—

"You will, I am sure, pardon my curiosity. What I have seen of you has greatly pleased but even more puzzled me. And though I should be loath to seem indiscreet, I must tell you that my friend and I are persons very well worthy to be entrusted with a secret. We have many of our own, which we are continually revealing to improper ears. And if, as I suppose, your story is a silly one, you need have no delicacy with us, who are two of the silliest men in England. My name is Godall, Theophilus Godall; my friend is Major Alfred Hammersmith—or at least, such is the name by which he chooses to be known. We pass our lives entirely in the search for extravagant adventures; and there is no extravagance with which we are not capable of sympathy."

"I like you, Mr. Godall," returned the young man; "you inspire me with a natural confidence; and I have not the slightest objection to our friend, the Major; whom I take to be a nobleman in masquerade. At least, I am sure he is no soldier."

The Colonel smiled at this compliment to the perfection of his art; and the young man went on in a more animated manner.

"There is every reason why I should not tell you my story. Perhaps that is just the reason why I am going to do so. At least, you seem so well prepared to hear a tale of silliness that I can not find it in my heart to disappoint you. My name, in spite of your example, I shall keep to myself. My age is not essential to the narrative. I am descended from my ancestors by ordinary generation, and from them I inherited the very eligible human tenement which I still occupy and a fortune of three hundred pounds a year. I suppose they also handed on to me a hare-brain humor, which it has been my chief delight to indulge. I received a good education. I can play the violin nearly well enough to earn money in the orchestra of a penny gaff, but not quite. The same remark applies to the flute and the French horn. I learned enough of whist to lose about a hundred a year at that scientific game. My acquaintance with French was sufficient to enable me to squander money in Paris with almost the same facility as in London. In short, I am a person full of manly accomplishments. I have had every sort of adventure, including a duel about nothing. Only two months ago I met a young lady exactly suited to my taste in mind and body; I found my heart melt; I saw that I had come upon my fate at last, and was in the way to fall in love. But when I came to reckon up what remained to me of my capital, I found it amounted to something less than four hundred pounds! I ask you fairly—can a man who respects himself fall in love on four hundred pounds? I concluded, certainly not; left the presence of my charmer, and slightly accelerating my usual rate of expenditure, came this morning to my last eighty pounds. This I divided into two equal parts; forty I reserved for a particular purpose; the remaining forty I was to dissipate before the night. I have passed a very entertaining day, and played many farces besides that of the cream tarts which procured me the advantage of your acquaintance; for I was determined, as I told you, to bring a foolish career to a still more foolish conclusion; and when you saw me throw my purse into the street, the forty pounds were at an end. Now you know me as well as I know myself: a fool, but consistent in his folly; and, as I will ask you to believe, neither a whimperer nor a coward."

From the whole tone of the young man's statement it was plain that he harbored very bitter and contemptuous thoughts about himself. His auditors were led to imagine that his love affair was nearer his heart than he admitted, and that he had a design on his own life. The farce of the cream tarts began to have very much the air of a tragedy in disguise.

"Why, is this not odd," broke out Geraldine, giving a look to Prince Florizel, "that we three fellows should have met by the merest accident in so large a wilderness as London, and should be so nearly in the same condition?"

"How?" cried the young man. "Are you, too, ruined? Is this supper a folly like my cream tarts? Has the devil brought three of his own together for a last carouse?"

"The devil, depend upon it, can sometimes do a very gentlemanly thing," returned Prince Florizel; "and I am so much touched by this coincidence, that, although we are not entirely in the same case, I am going to put an end to the disparity. Let your heroic treatment of the last cream tarts be my example."

So saying, the Prince drew out his purse and took from it a small bundle of bank-notes.

"You see, I was a week or so behind you, but I mean to catch you up and come neck and neck into the winning-post," he continued. "This," laying one of the notes upon the table, "will suffice for the bill. As for the rest—"

He tossed them into the fire, and they went up the chimney in a single blaze.

The young man tried to catch his arm, but as the table was between them his interference came too late.

"Unhappy man," he cried, "you should not have burned them all! You should have kept forty pounds."

"Forty pounds!" repeated the Prince. "Why, in Heaven's name, forty pounds?"

"Why not eighty?" cried the Colonel; "for to my certain knowledge there must have been a hundred in the bundle."

"It was only forty pounds he needed," said the young man gloomily. "But without them there is no admission. The rule is strict. Forty pounds for each. Accursed life, where a man can not even die without money!"

The Prince and the Colonel exchanged glances.

"Explain yourself," said the latter. "I have still a pocket-book tolerably well lined, and I need not say how readily I would share my wealth with Godall. But I must know to what end: you must certainly tell us what you mean."

The young man seemed to awaken; he looked uneasily from one to the other, and his face flushed deeply.

"You are not fooling me?" he asked. "You are indeed ruined men like me?"

"Indeed, I am for my part," replied the Colonel.

"And for mine," said the Prince, "I have given you proof. Who but a ruined man would throw his notes into the fire? The action speaks for itself."

"A ruined man—yes," returned the other suspiciously, "or else a millionaire."

"Enough, sir," said the Prince; "I have said so, and I am not accustomed to have my word remain in doubt."

"Ruined?" said the young man. "Are you ruined, like me? Are you, after a life of indulgence, come to such a pass that you can only indulge yourself in one thing more? Are you"—he kept lowering his voice as he went on—"are you going to give yourself that last indulgence! Are you going to avoid the consequences of your folly by the one infallible and easy path? Are you going to give the slip to the sheriff's officers of conscience by the one open door?"

Suddenly he broke off and attempted to laugh.

"Here is your health!" he cried, emptying his glass, "and good night to you, my merry ruined men."

Colonel Geraldine caught him by the arm as he was about to rise.

"You lack confidence in us," he said, "and you are wrong. To all your questions I make answer in the affirmative. But I am not so timid, and can speak the Queen's English plainly. We too, like yourself, have had enough of life, and are determined to die. Sooner or later, alone or together, we mean to seek out death and beard him where he lies ready. Since we have met you, and your case is more pressing, let it be to-night—and at once—and, if you will, all three together. Such a penniless trio," he cried, "should go arm in arm into the hall of Pluto, and give each other some countenance among the shades!"

Geraldine had hit exactly on the manners and intonations that became the part he was playing. The Prince himself was disturbed, and looked over at his confidant with a shade of doubt. As for the young man, the flush came back darkly into his cheek, and his eyes threw out a spark of light.

"You are the men for me!" he cried, with an almost terrible gaiety. "Shake hands upon the bargain!" (his hand was cold and wet). "You little know in what a company you will begin the march! You little know in what a happy moment for yourselves you partook of my cream tarts! I am only a unit, but I am a unit in an army. I know Death's private door. I am one of his familiars, and can show you into eternity without ceremony and yet without scandal."

They called upon him eagerly to explain his meaning.

"Can you muster eighty pounds between you?" he demanded.

Geraldine ostentatiously consulted his pocketbook, and replied in the affirmative.

"Fortunate beings!" cried the young man. "Forty pounds is the entry money of the Suicide Club."

"The Suicide Club," said the Prince, "why, what the devil is that?"

"Listen," said the young man; "this is the age of conveniences, and I have to tell you of the last perfection of the sort. We have affairs in different places;

and hence railways were invented. Railways separated us infallibly from our friends; and so telegraphs were made that we might communicate speedily at great distances. Even in hotels we have lifts to spare us a climb of some hundred steps. Now, we know that life is only a stage to play the fool upon as long as the part amuses us. There was one more convenience lacking to modern comfort; a decent, easy way to quit that stage; the back stairs to liberty; or, as I said this moment, Death's private door. This, my two fellow-rebels, is supplied by the Suicide Club. Do not suppose that you and I are alone, or even exceptional, in the highly reasonable desire that we profess. A large number of our fellowmen, who have grown heartily sick of the performance in which they are expected to join daily and all their lives long, are only kept from flight by one or two considerations. Some have families who would be shocked, or even blamed, if the matter became public; others have a weakness at heart and recoil from the circumstances of death. That is, to some extent, my own experience. I can not put a pistol to my head and draw the trigger; for something stronger than myself withholds the act; and although I loathe life, I have not strength enough in my body to take hold of death and be done with it. For such as I, and for all who desire to be out of the coil without posthumous scandal, the Suicide Club has been inaugurated. How this has been managed, what is its history, or what may be its ramifications in other lands, I am myself uninformed; and what I know of its constitution, I am not at liberty to communicate to you. To this extent, however, I am at your service. If you are truly tired of life, I will introduce you to-night to a meeting; and if not to-night, at least some time within the week, you will be easily relieved of your existences. It is now (consulting his watch) eleven; by half-past, at latest, we must leave this place; so that you have half an hour before you to consider my proposal. It is more serious than a cream tart," he added, with a smile; "and I suspect more palatable."

"More serious, certainly," returned Colonel Geraldine; "and as it is so much more so, will you allow me five minutes' speech in private with my friend, Mr. Godall?"

"It is only fair," answered the young man. "If you will permit, I will retire."

"You will be very obliging," said the Colonel.

As soon as the two were alone—"What," said Prince Florizel, "is the use of this confabulation, Geraldine? I see you are flurried, whereas my mind is very tranquilly made up. I will see the end of this."

"Your Highness," said the Colonel turning pale; "let me ask you to consider the importance of your life, not only to your friends, but to the public interest. 'If not to-night,' said this madman; but supposing that to-night some irreparable disaster were to overtake your Highness's person, what, let me ask you, what would be my despair, and what the concern and disaster of a great nation?"

"I will see the end of this," repeated the Prince in his most deliberate tones; "and have the kindness, Colonel Geraldine, to remember and respect your word of honor as a gentleman. Under no circumstances, recollect, nor without my special authority, are you to betray the incognito under which I choose to go abroad. These were my commands, which I now reiterate. And now," he added, "let me ask you to call for the bill."

Colonel Geraldine bowed in submission; but he had a very white face as he summoned the young man of the cream tarts, and issued his directions to the waiter. The Prince preserved his undisturbed demeanor, and described a Palais Royal farce to the young suicide with great humor and gusto. He avoided the Colonel's appealing looks without ostentation, and selected another cheroot with more than usual care. Indeed, he was now the only man of the party who kept any command over his nerves.

The bill was discharged, the Prince giving the whole change of the note to the astonished waiter; and the three drove off in a four wheeler. They were not long upon the way before the cab stopped at the entrance to a rather dark court. Here all descended.

After Geraldine had paid the fare, the young man turned, and addressed Prince Florizel as follows:

"It is still time, Mr. Godall, to make good your escape into thraldom. And for you too, Major Hammersmith. Reflect well before you take another step; and if your hearts say no—here are the crossroads."

"Lead on, sir," said the Prince. "I am not the man to go back from a thing once said."

"Your coolness does me good," replied their guide. "I have never seen any one so unmoved at this conjuncture; and yet you are not the first whom I have escorted to this door. More than one of my friends has preceded me, where I knew I must shortly follow. But this is of no interest to you. Wait me here for only a few moments; I shall return as soon as I have arranged the preliminaries of your introduction."

And with that the young man, waving his hand to his companions, turned into the court, entered a doorway and disappeared.

"Of all our follies," said Colonel Geraldine in a low voice, "this is the wildest and most dangerous."

"I perfectly believe so," returned the Prince.

"We have still," pursued the Colonel, "a moment to ourselves. Let me beseech your Highness to profit by the opportunity and retire. The consequences of this step are so dark, and may be so grave, that I feel myself justified in pushing a little farther than usual the liberty which your Highness is so condescending as to allow me in private."

"Am I to understand that Colonel Geraldine is afraid?" asked his Highness, taking his cheroot from his lips, and looking keenly into the other's face.

"My fear is certainly not personal," replied the other proudly; "of that your Highness may rest well assured."

"I had supposed as much," returned the Prince, with undisturbed good-humor; "but I was unwilling to remind you of the difference in our stations.

No more—no more," he added, seeing Geraldine about to apologize, "you stand excused."

And he smoked placidly, leaning against a railing, until the young man returned.

"Well," he asked, "has our reception been arranged?"

"Follow me," was the reply. "The President will see you in the cabinet. And let me warn you to be frank in your answers. I have stood your guarantee; but the club requires a searching inquiry before admission; for the indiscretion of a single member would lead to the dispersion of the whole society forever."

The Prince and Geraldine put their heads together for a moment. "Bear me out in this," said the one; and "bear me out in that," said the other; and by boldly taking up the characters of men with whom both were acquainted, they had come to an agreement in a twinkling, and were ready to follow their guide into the President's cabinet.

There were no formidable obstacles to pass. The outer door stood open; the door of the cabinet was ajar; and there, in a small but very high apartment, the young man left them once more.

"He will be here immediately," he said with a nod, as he disappeared.

Voices were audible in the cabinet through the folding doors which formed one end; and now and then the noise of a champagne cork, followed by a burst of laughter, intervened among the sounds of conversation. A single tall window looked out upon the river and the embankment; and by the disposition of the lights they judged themselves not far from Charing Cross station. The furniture was scanty, and the coverings worn to the thread; and there was nothing movable except a hand-bell in the center of a round table, and the hats and coats of a considerable party hung round the wall on pegs.

"What sort of a den is this?" said Geraldine.

"That is what I have come to see," replied the Prince. "If they keep live devils on the premises, the thing may grow amusing."

Just then the folding door was opened no more than necessary for the passage of a human body; and there entered at the same moment a louder buzz of talk, and the redoubtable President of the Suicide Club. The President was a man of fifty or upward; large and rambling in his gait, with shaggy side-whiskers, a bald top to his head, and a veiled gray eye, which now and then emitted a twinkle. His mouth, which embraced a large cigar, he kept continually screwing round and round and from side to side, as he looked sagaciously and coldly at the strangers. He was dressed in light tweeds, with his neck very open, in a striped shirt collar; and carried a minute book under one arm.

"Good evening," said he, after he had closed the door behind him. "I am told you wish to speak with me."

"We have a desire, sir, to join the Suicide Club," replied the Colonel.

The President rolled his cigar about in his mouth.

"What is that?" he said abruptly.

"Pardon me," returned the Colonel, "but I believe you are the person best qualified to give us information on that point."

"I?" cried the President. "A Suicide Club? Come, come! this is a frolic for All Fools' Day. I can make allowances for gentlemen who get merry in the liquor; but let there be an end to this."

"Call your Club what you will," said the Colonel, "you have some company behind these doors, and we insist on joining it."

"Sir," returned the President, curtly, "you have made a mistake. This is a private house, and you must leave it instantly."

The Prince had remained quietly in his seat throughout this little colloquy; but now, when the Colonel looked over to him, as much as to say, "Take your answer and come away, for God's sake!" he drew his cheroot from his mouth, and spoke:

"I have come here," said he, "upon the invitation of a friend of yours. He has doubtless informed you of my intention in thus intruding on your party. Let me remind you that a person in my circumstances has exceedingly little to bind him, and is not at all likely to tolerate much rudeness. I am a very quiet man, as a usual thing; but, my dear sir, you are either going to oblige me in the little matter of which you are aware, or you shall very bitterly repent that you ever admitted me to your ante-chamber."

The President laughed aloud.

"That is the way to speak," said he. "You are a man who is a man. You know the way to my heart, and can do what you like with me. Will you," he continued, addressing Geraldine, "will you step aside for a few minutes? I shall finish first with your companion, and some of the club's formalities require to be fulfilled in private."

With these words he opened the door of a small closet, into which he shut the Colonel.

"I believe in you," he said to Florizel, as soon as they were alone; "but are you sure of your friend?"

"Not so sure as I am of myself, though he has more cogent reasons," answered Florizel, "but sure enough to bring him here without alarm. He has had enough to cure the most tenacious man of life. He was cashiered the other day for cheating at cards."

"A good reason, I daresay," replied the President; "at least, we have another in the same case, and I feel sure of him. Have you also been in the Service, may I ask?"

"I have," was the reply; "but I was too lazy, I left it early."

"What is your reason for being tired of life?" pursued the President.

"The same, as near as I can make out," answered the Prince; "unadulterated laziness."

The President started. "D—n it," said he, "you must have something better than that."

"I have no more money," added Florizel. "That is also a vexation, without doubt. It brings my sense of idleness to an acute point."

The President rolled his cigar round in his mouth for some seconds, directing his gaze straight into the eyes of this unusual neophyte; but the Prince supported his scrutiny with unabashed good temper.

"If I had not a deal of experience," said the President at last, "I should turn you off. But I know the world; and this much any way, that the most frivolous excuses for a suicide are often the toughest to stand by. And when I downright like a man, as I do you, sir, I would rather strain the regulation than deny him."

The Prince and the Colonel, one after the other, were subjected to a long and particular interrogatory: the Prince alone; but Geraldine in the presence of the Prince, so that the President might observe the countenance of the one while the other was being warmly cross-examined. The result was satisfactory; and the President, after having booked a few details of each case, produced a form of oath to be accepted. Nothing could be conceived more passive than the obedience promised, or more stringent than the terms by which the juror bound himself. The man who forfeited a pledge so awful could scarcely have a rag of honor or any of the consolations of religion left to him. Florizel signed the document, but not without a shudder; the Colonel followed his example with an air of great depression. Then the President received the entry money; and without more ado, introduced the two friends into the smoking-room of the Suicide Club.

The smoking-room of the Suicide Club was the same height as the cabinet into which it opened, but much larger, and papered from top to bottom with an imitation of oak wainscot. A large and cheerful fire and a number of gas-jets illuminated the company. The Prince and his follower made the number up to eighteen. Most of the party were smoking, and drinking champagne; a feverish hilarity reigned, with sudden and rather ghastly pauses.

"Is this a full meeting?" asked the Prince.

"Middling," said the President. "By the way," he added, "if you have any money, it is usual to offer some champagne. It keeps up a good spirit, and is one of my own little perquisites."

"Hammersmith," said Florizel, "I may leave the champagne to you."

And with that he turned away and began to go round among the guests. Accustomed to play the host in the highest circles, he charmed and dominated all whom he approached; there was something at once winning and authoritative in his address; and his extraordinary coolness gave him yet another distinction in this half maniacal society. As he went from one to another he kept both his eyes and ears open, and soon began to gain a general idea of the people among whom he found himself. As in all other places of resort, one type predominated: people in the prime of youth, with every show of intelligence and sensibility in their appearance, but with little promise of strength or the quality that makes success. Few were much above thirty, and not a few were still in their teens. They stood, leaning on tables and shifting on their feet; sometimes they smoked extraordinarily fast, and sometimes they let their cigars go out; some talked well, but the conversation of others was plainly the result of nervous tension, and was equally without wit or purport. As each new bottle of champagne was opened, there was a manifest improvement in gaiety. Only two were seated—one in a chair in the recess of the window, with his head hanging and his hands plunged deep into his trouser pockets, pale, visibly moist with perspiration, saying never a word, a very wreck of soul and body; the other sat on the divan close by the chimney, and attracted notice by a trenchant dissimilarity from all the rest. He was probably upward of forty, but he looked fully ten years older; and Florizel thought he had never seen a man more naturally hideous, nor one more ravaged by disease and ruinous excitements. He was no more than skin and bone, was partly paralyzed, and wore spectacles of such unusual power, that his eyes appeared through the glasses greatly magnified and distorted in shape. Except the Prince and the President, he was the only person in the room who preserved the composure of ordinary life.

There was little decency among the members of the club. Some boasted of the disgraceful actions, the consequences of which had reduced them to seek refuge in death; and the others listened without disapproval. There was a tacit understanding against moral judgments; and whoever passed the club doors enjoyed already some of the immunities of the tomb. They drank to each other's memories, and to those of notable suicides in the past. They compared and developed their different views of death—some declaring that it was no more than blackness and cessation; others full of a hope that that very night they should be scaling the stars and commercing with the mighty dead.

"To the eternal memory of Baron Trenck, the type of suicides," cried one. "He went out of a small cell into a smaller, that he might come forth again to freedom."

"For my part," said a second, "I wish no more than a bandage for my eyes and cotton for my ears. Only they have no cotton thick enough in this world."

A third was for reading the mysteries of life in a future state; and a fourth professed that he would never have joined the club, if he had not been induced to believe in Mr. Darwin.

"I could not bear," said this remarkable suicide, "to be descended from an ape."

Altogether, the Prince was disappointed by the bearing and conversation of the members.

"It does not seem to me," he thought, "a matter for so much disturbance. If a man has made up his mind to kill himself, let him do it, in God's name, like a gentleman. This flutter and big talk is out of place."

In the meanwhile Colonel Geraldine was a prey to the blackest apprehensions; the club and its rules were still a mystery, and he looked round the room for some one who should be able to set his mind at rest. In this survey his eye lighted on the paralytic person with the strong spectacles; and seeing him so exceedingly tranquil, he besought the President, who was going in and out of the room under a pressure of business, to present him to the gentleman on the divan.

The functionary explained the needlessness of all such formalities within the club, but nevertheless presented Mr. Hammersmith to Mr. Malthus.

Mr. Malthus looked at the Colonel curiously, and then requested him to take a seat upon his right.

"You are a newcomer," he said, "and wish information? You have come to the proper source. It is two years since I first visited this charming club."

The Colonel breathed again. If Mr. Malthus had frequented the place for two years there could be little danger for the Prince in a single evening. But Geraldine was none the less astonished, and began to suspect a mystification.

"What!" cried he, "two years! I thought—but indeed I see I have been made the subject of a pleasantry."

"By no means," replied Mr. Malthus mildly. "My case is peculiar. I am not, properly speaking, a suicide at all; but, as it were, an honorary member. I rarely visit the club twice in two months. My infirmity and the kindness of the President have procured me these little immunities, for which besides I pay at an advanced rate. Even as it is my luck has been extraordinary."

"I am afraid," said the Colonel, "that I must ask you to be more explicit. You must remember that I am still most imperfectly acquainted with the rules of the club."

"An ordinary member who comes here in search of death like yourself," replied the paralytic, "returns every evening until fortune favors him. He can, even if he is penniless, get board and lodging from the President: very fair, I believe, and clean, although, of course, not luxurious; that could hardly be, considering the exiguity (if I may so express myself) of the subscription. And then the President's company is a delicacy in itself."

"Indeed!" cried Geraldine, "he had not greatly prepossessed me."

"Ah!" said Mr. Malthus, "you do not know the man: the drollest fellow! What stories! What cynicism! He knows life to admiration and, between ourselves, is probably the most corrupt rogue in Christendom."

"And he also," asked the Colonel, "is a permanency—like yourself, if I may say so without offense?"

"Indeed, he is a permanency in a very different sense from me," replied Mr. Malthus. "I have been graciously spared, but I must go at last. Now he never plays. He shuffles and deals for the club, and makes the necessary arrangements. That man, my dear Mr. Hammersmith, is the very soul of ingenuity. For three years he has pursued in London his useful and, I think I may add, his artistic calling; and not so much as a whisper of suspicion has been once aroused. I believe him myself to be inspired. You doubtless remember the celebrated case, six months ago, of the gentleman who was accidentally poisoned in a chemist's shop? That was one of the least rich, one of the least racy, of his notions; but then, how simple! and how safe!"

"You astound me," said the Colonel. "Was that unfortunate gentleman one of the—" He was about to say "victims"; but bethinking himself in time, he substituted—"members of the club?"

In the same flash of thought, it occurred to him that Mr. Malthus himself had not at all spoken in the tone of one who is in love with death; and he added hurriedly:

"But I perceive I am still in the dark. You speak of shuffling and dealing; pray for what end? And since you seem rather unwilling to die than otherwise, I must own that I can not conceive what brings you here at all."

"You say truly that you are in the dark," replied Mr. Malthus with more animation. "Why, my dear sir, this club is the temple of intoxication. If my enfeebled health could support the excitement more often, you may depend upon it I should be more often here. It requires all the sense of duty engendered by a long habit of ill-health and careful regimen, to keep me from excess in this, which is, I may say, my last dissipation. I have tried them all, sir," he went on, laying his hand on Geraldine's arm, "all without exception, and I declare to you, upon my honor, there is not one of them that has not been grossly and untruthfully overrated. People trifle with love. Now, I deny that love is a strong passion. Fear is the strong passion; it is with fear that you must trifle, if you wish to taste the intense joys of living. Envy me—envy me, sir," he added with a chuckle, "I am a coward!"

Geraldine could scarcely repress a movement of repulsion for this deplorable wretch; but he commanded himself with an effort, and continued his inquiries.

"How, sir," he asked, "is the excitement so artfully prolonged? and where is there any element of uncertainty?"

"I must tell you how the victim for every evening is selected," returned Mr. Malthus; "and not only the victim, but another member, who is to be the instrument in the club's hands, and death's high priest of that occasion."

"Good God!" said the Colonel, "do they then kill each other?"

"The trouble of suicide is removed in that way," returned Malthus with a nod.

"Merciful Heavens!" ejaculated the Colonel, "and may you—may I—may the—my friend, I mean—may any of us be pitched upon this evening as the slayer of another man's body and immortal spirit? Can such things be possible among men born of women? Oh, infamy of infamies!"

He was about to rise in his horror, when he caught the Prince's eye. It was fixed upon him from across the room with a frowning and angry stare. And in a moment Geraldine recovered his composure.

"After all," he added, "why not? And since you say the game is interesting, *vogue la galère*—I follow the club!"

Mr. Malthus had keenly enjoyed the Colonel's amazement and disgust. He had the vanity of wickedness; and it pleased him to see another man give way to a generous movement, while he felt himself, in his entire corruption, superior to such emotions.

"You now, after your first moment of surprise," said he, "are in a position to appreciate the delights of our society. You can see how it combines the excitement of a gaming-table, a duel, and a Roman amphitheater. The Pagans did well enough; I cordially admire the refinement of their minds; but it has been reserved for a Christian country to attain this extreme, this quintessence, this absolute of poignancy. You will understand how vapid are all amusements to a man who has acquired a taste for this one. The game we play," he continued, "is one of extreme simplicity. A full pack—but I perceive you are about to see the thing in progress. Will you lend me the help of your arm? I am unfortunately paralyzed."

Indeed, just as Mr. Malthus was beginning his description, another pair of folding-doors was thrown open, and the whole club began to pass, not without some hurry, into the adjoining room. It was similar in every respect to the one from which it was entered, but somewhat differently furnished. The centre was occupied by a long green table, at which the President sat shuffling a pack of cards with great particularity. Even with the stick and the Colonel's arm, Mr. Malthus walked with so much difficulty that every one was seated before this pair and the Prince, who had waited for them, entered the apartment; and, in consequence, the three took seats close together at the lower end of the board.

"It is a pack of fifty-two," whispered Mr. Malthus. "Watch for the ace of spades, which is the sign of death, and the ace of clubs, which designates the official of the night. Happy, happy young men!" he added. "You have good eyes, and can follow the game. Alas! I can not tell an ace from a deuce across the table."

And he proceeded to equip himself with a second pair of spectacles.

"I must at least watch the faces," he explained.

The Colonel rapidly informed his friend of all that he had learned from the honorary member, and of the horrible alternative that lay before them. The Prince was conscious of a deadly chill and a contraction about his heart; he swallowed with difficulty, and looked from side to side like a man in a maze.

"One bold stroke," whispered the Colonel, "and we may still escape."

But the suggestion recalled the Prince's spirits.

"Silence!" said he. "Let me see that you can play like a gentleman for any stake, however serious."

And he looked about him, once more to all appearance at his ease, although his heart beat thickly, and he was conscious of an unpleasant heat in his bosom. The members were all very quiet and intent; every one was pale, but none so pale as Mr. Malthus. His eyes protruded; his head kept nodding involuntarily upon his spine; his hands found their way, one after the other, to his mouth, where they made clutches at his tremulous and ashen lips. It was plain that the honorary member enjoyed his membership on very startling terms.

"Attention, gentlemen!" said the President.

And he began slowly dealing the cards about the table in the reverse direction, pausing until each man had shown his card. Nearly every one hesitated; and sometimes you would see a player's fingers stumble more than once before he could turn over the momentous slip of pasteboard. As the Prince's turn drew nearer, he was conscious of a growing and almost suffocating excitement; but he had somewhat of the gambler's nature, and recognized almost with astonishment that there was a degree of pleasure in his sensations. The nine of clubs fell to his lot; the three of spades was dealt to Geraldine; and the queen of hearts to Mr. Malthus, who was unable to suppress a sob of relief. The young man of the cream tarts almost immediately afterward turned over the ace of clubs, and remained frozen with horror, the card still resting on his finger; he had not come there to kill, but to be killed; and the Prince, in his generous sympathy with his position, almost forgot the peril that still hung over himself and his friend.

The deal was coming round again, and still Death's card had not come out. The players held their respiration, and only breathed by gasps. The Prince received another club; Geraldine had a diamond; but when Mr. Malthus turned up his card a horrible noise, like that of something breaking, issued from his mouth; and he rose from his seat and sat down again, with no sign of his paralysis. It was the ace of spades. The honorary member had trifled once too often with his terrors.

Conversation broke out again almost at once. The players relaxed their rigid attitudes, and began to rise from the table and stroll back by twos and threes into the smoking-room. The President stretched his arms and yawned, like a man who had finished his day's work. But Mr. Malthus sat in his place, with his head in his hands, and his hands upon the table, drunk and motionless—a thing stricken down.

The Prince and Geraldine made their escape at once. In the cold night air their horror of what they had witnessed was redoubled.

"Alas!" cried the Prince, "to be bound by an oath in such a matter! to allow this wholesale trade in murder to be continued with profit and impunity! If I but dared to forfeit my pledge!"

"That is impossible for your Highness," replied the Colonel, whose honor is the honor of Bohemia. "But I dare, and may with propriety, forfeit mine."

"Geraldine," said the Prince, "if your honor suffers in any of the adventures into which you follow me, not only will I never pardon you, but—what I believe will much more sensibly affect you—I should never forgive myself."

"I receive your Highness's commands," replied the Colonel. "Shall we go from this accursed spot?"

"Yes," said the Prince. "Call a cab in Heaven's name, and let me try to forget in slumber the memory of this night's disgrace."

But it was notable that he carefully read the name of the court before he left it.

The next morning, as soon as the Prince was stirring, Colonel Geraldine brought him a daily newspaper, with the following paragraph marked:

MELANCHOLY ACCIDENT.—This morning, about two o'clock, Mr. Bartholomew Malthus, of 16 Chepstow Place, Westbourne Grove, on his way home from a party at a friend's house, fell over the upper parapet in Trafalgar Square, fracturing his skull and breaking a leg and an arm. Death was instantaneous. Mr. Malthus, accompanied by a friend, was engaged in looking for a cab at the time of the unfortunate occurrence. As Mr. Malthus was paralytic, it is thought that his fall may have been occasioned by another seizure. The unhappy gentleman was well known in the most respectable circles, and his loss will be widely and deeply deplored.

"If ever a soul went straight to Hell," said Geraldine solemnly, "it was that paralytic man's."

The Prince buried his face in his hands, and remained silent.

"I am almost rejoiced," continued the Colonel, "to know that he is dead. But for our young man of the cream tarts I confess my heart bleeds."

"Geraldine," said the Prince, raising his face, "that unhappy lad was last night as innocent as you and I; and this morning the guilt of blood is on his soul. When I think of the President, my heart grows sick within me. I do not know how it shall be done, but I shall have that scoundrel at my mercy as there is a God in Heaven. What an experience, what a lesson, was that game of cards!"

"One," said the Colonel, "never to be repeated."

The Prince remained so long without replying that Geraldine grew alarmed.

"You can not mean to return," he said. "You have suffered too much and seen too much horror already. The duties of your high position forbid the repetition of the hazard."

"There is much in what you say," replied Prince Florizel, "and I am not altogether pleased with my own determination. Alas! in the clothes of the greatest potentate, what is there but a man? I never felt my weakness more acutely than now, Geraldine, but it is stronger than I. Can I cease to interest myself in the fortunes of the unhappy young man who supped with us some hours ago? Can I leave the President to follow his nefarious career unwatched? Can I begin an adventure so entrancing, and not follow it to an end? No, Geraldine; you ask of the Prince more than the man is able to perform. To-night, once more, we take our places at the table of the Suicide Club."

Colonel Geraldine fell upon his knees.

"Will your Highness take my life?" he cried. "It is his—his freely; but do not, oh, do not! let him ask me to countenance so terrible a risk."

"Colonel Geraldine," replied the Prince, with some haughtiness of manner, "your life is absolutely your own. I only looked for obedience; and when that is unwillingly rendered, I shall look for that no longer. I add one word: your importunity in this affair has been sufficent."

The Master of the Horse regained his feet at once. "Your Highness," he said, "may I be excused in my attendance this afternoon? I dare not, as an honorable man, venture a second time into that fatal house until I have perfectly ordered my affairs. Your Highness shall meet, I promise him, with no more opposition from the most devoted and grateful of his servants."

"My dear Geraldine," returned Prince Florizel, "I always regret when you oblige me to remember my rank. Dispose of your day as you think fit, but be here before eleven in the same disguise."

The club, on this second evening, was not so fully attended; and when Geraldine and the Prince arrived, there were not above half a dozen persons in the smoking-room. His Highness took the President aside and congratulated him warmly on the demise of Mr. Malthus.

"I like," he said, "to meet with capacity, and certainly find much of it in you. Your profession is of a very delicate nature, but I see you are well qualified to conduct it with success and secrecy."

The President was somewhat affected by these compliments from one of his Highness's superior bearing. He acknowledged them almost with humility.

"Poor Malthy!" he added, "I shall hardly know the club without him. The most of my patrons are boys, sir, and poetical boys, who are not much company for me. Not but what Malthy had some poetry, too; but it was of a kind that I could understand."

"I can readily imagine you should find yourself in sympathy with Mr. Malthus," returned the Prince. "He struck me as a man of a very original disposition."

The young man of the cream tarts was in the room, but painfully depressed and silent. His late companions sought in vain to lead him into conversation.

"How bitterly I wish," he cried, "that I had never brought you to this infamous abode! Begone, while you are clean-handed. If you could have heard the old man scream as he fell, and the noise of his bones upon the pavement! Wish me, if you have any kindness to so fallen a being—wish the ace of spades for me, to-night!"

A few more members dropped in as the evening went on, but the club did not muster more than the devil's dozen when they took their places at the table. The Prince was again conscious of a certain joy in his alarms; but he was astonished to see Geraldine so much more self-possessed than on the night before.

"It is extraordinary," thought the Prince, "that a will, made or unmade, should so greatly influence a young man's spirit."

"Attention, gentlemen!" said the President, and he began to deal.

Three times the cards went all around the table, and neither of the marked cards had yet fallen from his hand. The excitement as he began the fourth distribution was overwhelming. There were just cards enough to go once more entirely round. The Prince, who sat second from the dealer's left, would receive, in the reverse mode of dealing practised at the club, the second last card. The third player picked up a black ace—it was the ace of clubs. The next received a diamond, the next a heart, and so on; but the ace of spades was still undelivered. At last Geraldine, who sat upon the Prince's left, turned his card; it was an ace, but the ace of hearts.

When Prince Florizel saw his fate upon the table in front of him, his heart stood still. He was a brave man, but the sweat poured off his face. There were exactly fifty chances out of a hundred that he was doomed. He reversed the card; it was the ace of spades. A loud roaring filled his brain, and the table swam before his eyes. He heard the player on his right break into a fit of laughter that sounded between mirth and disappointment; he saw the company rapidly dispersing, but his mind was full of other thoughts. He recognized how foolish, how criminal, had been his conduct. In perfect health, in the prime of his years, the heir to a throne, he had gambled away his future and that of a brave and loyal country. "God," he cried, "God forgive me!" And with that, the confusion of his senses passed away, and he regained his self-possession in a moment.

To his surprise Geraldine had disappeared. There was no one in the card-room but his destined butcher consulting with the President, and the young man of the cream tarts, who slipped up to the Prince and whispered in his ear:

"I would give a million, if I had it, for your luck."

His Highness could not help reflecting, as the young man departed, that he would have sold his opportunity for a much more moderate sum.

The whispered conference now came to an end. The holder of the ace of clubs left the room with a look of intelligence, and the President, approaching the unfortunate Prince, proffered him his hand.

"I am pleased to have met you, sir," said he, "and pleased to have been in a position to do you this trifling service. At least, you can not complain of delay. On the second evening—what a stroke of luck!"

The Prince endeavored in vain to articulate something in response, but his mouth was dry and his tongue seemed paralyzed.

"You feel a little sickish?" asked the President, with some show of solicitude. "Most gentlemen do. Will you take a little brandy?"

The Prince signified in the affirmative, and the other immediately poured some of the spirit into a tumbler.

"Poor old Malthy!" ejaculated the President, as the Prince drained the glass. "He drank near upon a pint, and little enough good it seemed to do him!"

"I am more amenable to treatment," said the Prince, a good deal revived. "I am my own man again at once, as you perceive. And so, let me ask you, what are my directions?"

"You will proceed along the Strand in the direction of the City, and on the left-hand pavement, until you meet the gentleman who has just left the room. He will continue your instructions, and him you will have the kindness to obey; the authority of the club is vested in his person for the night. And now," added the President, "I wish you a pleasant walk."

Florizel acknowledged the salutation rather awkwardly, and took his leave. He passed through the smoking-room, where the bulk of the players were still consuming champagne, some of which he had himself ordered and paid for; and he was surprised to find himself cursing them in his heart. He put on his hat and great-coat in the cabinet, and selected his umbrella from a corner. The familiarity of these acts, and the thought that he was about them for the last time, betrayed him into a fit of laughter which sounded unpleasantly in his own ears. He conceived a reluctance to leave the cabinet, and turned instead to the window. The sight of the lamps and the darkness recalled him to himself.

"Come, come, I must be a man," he thought, "and tear myself away."

At the corner of Box Court three men fell upon Prince Florizel and he was unceremoniously thrust into a carriage, which at once drove rapidly away. There was already an occupant.

"Will your Highness pardon my zeal?" said a well-known voice.

The Prince threw himself upon the Colonel's neck in a passion of relief.

"How can I ever thank you?" he cried. "And how was this effected?"

Although he had been willing to march upon his doom, he was overjoyed to yield to friendly violence, and return once more to life and hope.

"You can thank me effectually enough," replied the Colonel, "by avoiding all such dangers in the future. And as for your second question, all has been managed by the simplest means. I arranged this afternoon with a celebrated detective. Secrecy has been promised and paid for. Your own servants have been principally engaged in the affair. The house in Box Court has been surrounded since nightfall, and this, which is one of your own carriages, has been awaiting you for nearly an hour."

"And the miserable creature who was to have slain me—what of him?" inquired the Prince.

"He was pinioned as he left the club," replied the Colonel, "and now awaits your sentence at the Palace, where he will soon be joined by his accomplices."

"Geraldine," said the Prince, "you have saved me against my explicit orders, and you have done well. I owe you not only my life, but a lesson; and I should be unworthy of my rank if I did not show myself grateful to my teacher. Let it be yours to choose the manner."

There was a pause, during which the carriage continued to speed through the streets, and the two men were each buried in his own reflections. The silence was broken by Colonel Geraldine.

"Your Highness," said he, "has by this time a considerable body of prisoners. There is at least one criminal among the number to whom justice should be dealt. Our oath forbids us all recourse to law; and discretion would forbid it equally if the oath were loosened. May I inquire your Highness's intention?"

"It is decided," answered Florizel; "the President must fall in duel. It only remains to choose his adversary."

"Your Highness has permitted me to name my own recompense," said the Colonel. "Will he permit me to ask the appointment of my brother? It is an honorable post, but I dare assure your Highness that the lad will acquit himself with credit."

"You ask me an ungracious favor," said the Prince, "but I must refuse you nothing."

The Colonel kissed his hand with the greatest affection; and at that moment the carriage rolled under the archway of the Prince's splendid residence.

An hour after, Florizel in his official robes, and covered with all the orders of Bohemia, received the members of the Suicide Club.

"Foolish and wicked men," said he, "as many of you as have been driven into this strait by the lack of fortune shall receive employment and remuneration from my officers. Those who suffer under a sense of guilt must have recourse to a higher and more generous Potentate than I. I feel pity for all of you, deeper than you can imagine; to-morrow you shall tell me your stories; and as you answer more frankly, I shall be the more able to remedy your misfortunes. As for you," he added, turning to the President, "I should only offend a person of your parts by any offer of assistance; but I have instead a piece of diversion to propose to you. Here," laying his hand on the shoulder of Colonel Geraldine's young brother, "is an officer of mine who desires to make a little tour upon the Continent; and I ask you, as a favor, to accompany him on this excursion. Do you," he went on, changing his tone, "do you shoot well with the pistol? Because you may have need of that accomplishment. When two men go traveling together, it is best to be prepared for all. Let me add that, if by any chance you should lose young Mr. Geraldine upon the way, I shall always have another member of my household to place at your disposal; and I am known, Mr. President, to have long eyesight, and as long an arm."

With these words, said with much sternness, the Prince concluded his address. Next morning the members of the club were suitably provided for by his munificence, and the President set forth upon his travels, under the supervision of Mr. Geraldine, and a pair of faithful and adroit lackeys, well trained in the Prince's household. Not content with this, discreet agents were put in possession of the house of Box Court, and all letters of visitors for the Suicide Club or its officials were to be examined by Prince Florizel in person.

BOLESS

—⚜—

Maxim Gorki

An acquaintance of mine once told me the following story:

While still a student at Moscow I happened to be living alongside one of those—well, she was a Polish woman, Teresa by name. A tall, powerfully built brunette with heavy, bushy eyebrows, and a large, coarse, vulgar face, as if carved out with an ax—the animal gleam of her eyes, the deep bass voice, the gait and manners of a cabman, and her immense strength like that of a market-woman, inspired me with an inexpressible horror. I lived in the garret of the house, and her room was opposite mine. I never opened my door when I knew that she was in. But this, of course, happened very rarely. Sometimes I chanced to meet her on the landing, staircase, or in the yard, and she would look at me with a smile which seemed to me cynical and rapacious. Occasionally I saw her in her cups, with bleary eyes, her hair and clothes in disorder and with a particularly loathsome smile. On such occasions she would meet my eye with an impudent stare and say:

"How are you, Pan Student?"

And her stupid laugh would increase my dislike for her still more. I would have liked nothing better than to change my quarters in order to get rid of her proximity, but my room was so nice, and the view from my window was so fine, the street below so quiet and peaceful, that I concluded to endure it.

One morning after I had dressed and was sprawling on the cot, trying to invent some sort of an excuse for not attending my classes, the door of my room suddenly opened, and the disgusting bass voice of the Polish woman sounded from the threshold:

"Good morning, Pan Student!"

"What is it you wish?" I asked her. I saw she looked confused and had in her face a kind of pleading expression, something unusual with her.

281

"You see, Pan Student, I came to beg you to do me a great favor. Don't refuse me, please!"

Lying there on my cot I thought that it was just some pretext or other to make my further acquaintance. Take care, my boy!

"You see, I have to send a letter to my native country," she continued in a supplicating, low, tremulous voice.

"Well," I thought, "the devil take you. If you wish I will write it for you." And springing to my feet I sat down to the table, took some paper and said: "Well, come nearer; sit down and dictate."

She came over; sat down cautiously on the edge of the chair and looked at me in rather a guilty way.

"To whom shall I write?"

"To Boleslav Kapshat, in the town Sventsiani, on the Warsaw railroad."

"Well, what shall I write? Speak."

"My dearest Boless, my heart's delight, my beloved. May the Mother of God protect you! My golden heart, why have you not written for so long a time to your sorrowing dove, Teresa—"

I could hardly keep from laughing. A sorrowing dove, indeed! Almost six feet tall, with the fists of a prize-fighter, and a face so black that it seemed as if the "dove" had been sweeping chimneys all her life and had never thoroughly washed herself. But I somehow kept my face straight and asked:

"Who is this Bolesst?"

"Boless, Pan Student," she replied seemingly offended because of my mis-pronouncing the name. "He is my affianced."

"Affianced!"

"And why are you so astonished? Can not I, a girl, have an affianced?"

She—a girl! well, this beats everything I ever heard. Oh, well, who can tell about such matters! Everything is possible in this world.

"And have you been long engaged?"

"The sixth year."

"Oh, oh!" I thought and then said aloud: "Well, go ahead with your letter."

And I must confess—so tender and loving was this message—that I would have willingly exchanged places with this Boless had the fair correspondent been any one else but Teresa.

"I thank you from my inmost soul for your favor, Pan Student," Teresa said, bowing low. "Can I in any way be of service to you?"

"No, thank you."

"But maybe the Pan's shirts or trousers need mending?"

This made me quite angry. I felt that this mastodon in petticoats was making the blood mount to my cheeks, and I told her quite sharply that her services were not required; and she departed.

Two weeks or so passed. One evening I was sitting at my window, softly whistling and thinking hard how to get away from myself. I felt very bored. The weather was as nasty as it could be. To go out that evening was out of the question, and having nothing better to do I began from sheer ennui a course of self-analysis. This proved dull enough work, but there was nothing else to do. Suddenly the door opened, thank God! Some one was coming to see me.

"Are you very busy just now, Pan Student?"

"Teresa! H'm—" I thought I would have preferred any one at all to her. Then I said aloud.

"No, what is it you want now?"

"I wish to ask the Pan Student to write me another letter."

"Very well. Is it again to Boless you wish me to write?"

"No, this time I want you to write a letter from Boless to me."

"Wha-at?"

"I beg your pardon, Pan Student. How stupid of me! It is not for me, this letter, but for a friend of mine, a man acquaintance; he has a fiancée. Her name is like mine, Teresa. He does not know how to write, so I want the Pan Student to write for him a letter to that Teresa—"

I looked at her. She seemed very confused and frightened, and her fingers trembled. And though I failed at first to understand what was the matter with her I at last understood.

"Look here, my lady," I said to her. "You have been telling me a pack of lies. There are no Bolesses nor Teresas among your acquaintances. It is only a pretext for coming in here. I tell you outright that there is no use of coming sneaking around me, as I do not wish to have anything to do with you. Do you understand?"

She grew very red in the face and I saw that she was strangely frightened and confused, and moved her lips so oddly, wishing to say something, without being able to say it. And somehow I began to think that I had misjudged her a little. There was something behind all this. But what?

"Pan Student," she suddenly began, but broke off, and turning toward the door walked out of the room.

I remained with a very unpleasant feeling in my heart. I heard her shut her own door with a bang; evidently the poor girl was very angry—I thought the matter over and decided to go in to her and induce her to return; I would write her the letter she wished.

I entered her room. She was sitting at the table with her head pressed in her hands.

"Teresa," I said, "will you listen to me a moment?"

Whenever I come to this turn of the story I always feel very awkward and embarrassed. But let us return to my narrative. Seeing that she did not reply I repeated:

"Listen to me, my girl—"

She sprang to her feet, came close up to me, with eyes flashing, and placing her two hands on my shoulders she began to whisper, or rather to hum in her deep bass voice:

"Look you here, Pan Student. What of it, what of it if there is no Boless? And what if there is no Teresa? What difference does it make to you? Is it so hard for you to draw a few lines on the paper! Oh, you! And I thought you such a good fellow, such a nice fair-haired little boy. Yes, it is true—there is no Boless, and there is no Teresa, there is only me! Well, what of it?"

"Allow me," I said greatly disconcerted by this reception. "What is it you are saying? Is there no Boless?"

"Yes, there is none. But what of it?"

"And no Teresa either?"

"No, no Teresa either; that is, yes, I am her."

I could not understand a word. I stared straight into her eyes, trying to determine which of us two had lost our reason. And she returned once more to the table, rummaged for some time in the drawer, and coming back to me said in an offended tone:

"Here is the letter you wrote for me, take it back. You do not wish to write me a second one anyway. Others will probably be kinder than you and would do so."

I recognized the letter she held out to me as the one I wrote for her to Boless. Humph!

"Look here, Teresa," I said to her. "Will you please explain to me what it all means? Why do you ask people to write letters for you when you do not find it necessary even to post them?"

"Post them? Where to?"

"Why, to this Boless, of course."

"But he does not exist!"

I really could not understand a word. There was nothing left for me to do but to spit and walk out of the room. But she explained herself.

"Well, what of it?" she began in an offended voice. "He does not exist. He does not, so," and she extended her hands as if she could not herself clearly understand why he did not exist in reality. "But I want him to. Am I not as much of a human being as the others? Of course I—I know— But it does no harm to any one, that I am writing to him—"

"Allow me—to whom?"

"To Boless, of course."

"But he does not exist."

"Oh, Mother of God! What if he does not exist? He does not; still to me he does. And Teresa—this is myself, and he replies to my letters, and I write to him again."

I understood. I felt so sick at heart, so ashamed of myself to know that alongside of me, only three paces removed, lived a human being who had no one in the whole world to love and sympathize with her, and that this being had to invent a friend for herself.

"Here you have written a letter from me to Boless, and I gave it to another to read, and when I hear it read it really begins to seem to me as if there is a Boless. And then I ask that a letter be written from Boless to Teresa—that is to me. And when such a letter is written and is read to me then I am almost entirely convinced that there is a Boless, and that makes my life easier."

"Yes, the devil take it all," continued my acquaintance. To make a long story short I began from that time on to write with the greatest punctuality twice a week letters to Boless and vice versa. I wrote splendid replies to her. She used to listen to my reading of those epistles and to weep in her bass voice. In return for this she used to mend my clothes and darn my socks.

Three months later she was thrown into prison for some reason or other and by now she must surely be dead.

My acquaintance blew the ashes from his cigarette, looked thoughtfully at the sky, and concluded:

Y-e-s, the more a human being has drunk of the cup of bitterness the more ardently he longs for sweetness. And we, enveloped in our wornout virtues and gazing at each other through the haze of self-sufficiency and convinced of our righteousness, fail to understand it.

And the whole affair turns out very stupid, and very cruel. Fallen people we say—but who and what are those fallen ones? First of all they are human beings of the very same bone and blood, of the very same flesh and nerves as ourselves. We have been told the very same thing for whole ages, day in and day out. And we listen and—and the devil alone knows how stupid it all is! In reality we, too, are but fallen people and more deeply fallen too, probably— into the abyss of self-sufficiency, convinced of our own sinlessness and superiority, the superiority of our own nerves and brains over the nerves and brains of those who are only less crafty than we are, and who can not, as we can, feign a goodness they do not possess—but enough of this. It is all so old and stale—so old and stale indeed that one is ashamed to speak of it—

THE MUMMY'S FOOT

Théophile Gautier

I had entered, in an idle mood, the shop of one of those curiosity-venders, who are called *marchands de bric-à-brac* in that Parisian *argot* which is so perfectly unintelligible elsewhere in France.

You have doubtless glanced occasionally through the windows of some of these shops, which have become so numerous now that it is fashionable to buy antiquated furniture, and that every petty stockbroker thinks he must have his *chambre au moyen âge*.

There is one thing there which clings alike to the shop of the dealer in old iron, the wareroom of the tapestry-maker, the laboratory of the chemist, and the studio of the painter—in all those gloomy dens where a furtive daylight filters in through the window-shutters the most manifestly ancient thing is dust;—the cobwebs are more authentic than the guimp laces; and the old pear-tree furniture on exhibition is actually younger than the mahogany which arrived but yesterday from America.

The warehouse of my bric-à-brac dealer was a veritable Capharnaum; all ages and all nations seemed to have made their rendezvous there; an Etruscan lamp of red clay stood upon a Boule cabinet, with ebony panels, brightly striped by lines of inlaid brass; a duchess of the court of Louis XV nonchalantly extended her fawn-like feet under a massive table of the time of Louis XIII, with heavy spiral supports of oak, and carven designs of Chimeras and foliage intermingled.

Upon the denticulated shelves of several side-boards glittered immense Japanese dishes with red and blue designs relieved by gilded hatching; side by side with enameled works by Bernard Palissy, representing serpents, frogs, and lizards in relief.

From disemboweled cabinets escaped cascades of silver-lustrous Chinese silks and waves of tinsel, which an oblique sunbeam shot through with luminous beads; while portraits of every era, in frames more or less tarnished, smiled through their yellow varnish.

The striped breastplate of a damascened suit of Milanese armor glittered in one corner; Loves and Nymphs of porcelain; Chinese grotesques, vases of *céladon* and crackle-ware; Saxon and old Sèvres cups encumbered the shelves and nooks of the department.

The dealer followed me closely through the tortuous way contrived between the piles of furniture; warding off with his hand the hazardous sweep of my coat-skirts; watching my elbows with the uneasy attention of an antiquarian and a usurer.

It was a singular face, that of the merchant—an immense skull, polished like a knee, and surrounded by a thin aureole of white hair, which brought out the clear salmon tint of his complexion all the more strikingly, lent him a false aspect of patriarchal *bonhomie,* counteracted, however, by the scintillation of two little yellow eyes which trembled in their orbits like two louis-d'or upon quicksilver. The curve of his nose presented an aquiline silhouette, which suggested the Oriental or Jewish type. His hands—thin, slender, full of nerves which projected like strings upon the finger-board of a violin, and armed with claws like those on the terminations of bats' wings—shook with senile trembling; but those convulsively agitated hands became firmer than steel pincers or lobsters' claws when they lifted any precious article—an onyx cup, a Venetian glass, or a dish of Bohemian crystal. This strange old man had an aspect so thoroughly rabbinical and cabalistic that he would have been burnt on the mere testimony of his face three centuries ago.

"Will you not buy something from me to-day, sir? Here is a Malay kreese with a blade undulating like flame: look at those grooves contrived for the blood to run along, those teeth set backward so as to tear out the entrails in withdrawing the weapon—it is a fine character of ferocious arm, and will look well in your collection: this two-handed sword is very beautiful—it is the work of Josepe de la Hera; and this *coliche-marde,* with its fenestrated guard —what a superb specimen of handicraft!"

"No; I have quite enough weapons and instruments of carnage;—I want a small figure, something which will suit me as a paper-weight; for I can not endure those trumpery bronzes which the stationers sell, and which may be found on everybody's desk."

The old gnome foraged among his ancient wares, and finally arranged before me some antique bronzes—so-called, at least; fragments of malachite; little Hindu or Chinese idols—a kind of poussah-toys in jade-stone, representing the incarnations of Brahma or Vishnu, and wonderfully appropriate to the very undivine office of holding papers and letters in place.

I was hesitating between a porcelain dragon, all constellated with warts— its mouth formidable with bristling tusks and ranges of teeth—and an abominable little Mexican fetish, representing the god Vitziliputzili *au naturel;*

when I caught sight of a charming foot, which I at first took for a fragment of some antique Venus.

It had those beautiful ruddy and tawny tints that lend to Florentine bronze that warm, living look so much preferable to the gray-green aspect of common bronzes, which might easily be mistaken for statues in a state of putrefaction: satiny gleams played over its rounded forms, doubtless polished by the amorous kisses of twenty centuries; for it seemed a Corinthian bronze, a work of the best era of art—perhaps molded by Lysippus himself.

"That foot will be my choice," I said to the merchant, who regarded me with an ironical and saturnine air, and held out the object desired that I might examine it more fully.

I was surprised at its lightness; it was not a foot of metal, but in sooth a foot of flesh—an embalmed foot—a mummy's foot: on examining it still more closely the very grain of the skin, and the almost imperceptible lines impressed upon it by the texture of the bandages, became perceptible. The toes were slender and delicate, and terminated by perfectly formed nails, pure and transparent as agates; the great toe, slightly separated from the rest, afforded a happy contrast, in the antique style, to the position of the other toes, and lent it an aerial lightness—the grace of a bird's foot;—the sole, scarcely streaked by a few almost imperceptible cross lines, afforded evidence that it had never touched the bare ground, and had only come in contact with the finest matting of Nile rushes, and the softest carpets of panther skin.

"Ha, ha!—you want the foot of the Princess Hermonthis"—exclaimed the merchant, with a strange giggle, fixing his owlish eyes upon me—"ha, ha, ha! —for a paper-weight!—an original idea!—artistic idea! Old Pharaoh would certainly have been surprised had some one told him that the foot of his adored daughter would be used for a paper-weight after he had had a mountain of granite hollowed out as a receptacle for the triple coffin, painted and gilded—covered with hieroglyphics and beautiful paintings of the Judgment of Souls"—continued the queer little merchant, half audibly, as though talking to himself!

"How much will you charge me for this mummy fragment?"

"Ah, the highest price I can get; for it is a superb piece: if I had the match of it you could not have it for less than five hundred francs;—the daughter of a Pharaoh! nothing is more rare."

"Assuredly that is not a common article; but, still, how much do you want? In the first place, let me warn you that all my wealth consists of just five louis: I can buy anything that costs five louis, but nothing dearer;—you might search my vest pockets and most secret drawers without even finding one poor five-franc piece more."

"Five louis for the foot of the Princess Hermonthis! that is very little, very little indeed; 'tis an authentic foot," muttered the merchant, shaking his head, and imparting a peculiar rotary motion to his eyes. "Well, take it, and I will give you the bandages into the bargain," he added, wrapping the foot in an ancient damask rag—"very fine! real damask!—Indian damask which has never been redyed; it is strong, and yet it is soft," he mumbled, stroking the frayed tissue with his fingers, through the trade-acquired habit which moved him to praise even an object of so little value that he himself deemed it only worth the giving away.

He poured the gold coins into a sort of medieval alms-purse hanging at his belt, repeating:

"The foot of the Princess Hermonthis, to be used for a paper-weight!"

Then turning his phosphorescent eyes upon me, he exclaimed in a voice strident as the crying of a cat which has swallowed a fish-bone:

"Old Pharoah will not be well pleased: he loved his daughter—the dear man!"

"You speak as if you were a contemporary of his: you are old enough, goodness knows! but you do not date back to the Pyramids of Egypt," I answered, laughingly, from the threshold.

I went home, delighted with my acquisition.

With the idea of putting it to profitable use as soon as possible, I placed the foot of the divine Princess Hermonthis upon a heap of papers scribbled over with verses, in themselves an undecipherable mosaic work of erasures; articles freshly begun; letters forgotten, and posted in the table drawer instead of the letter-box—an error to which absent-minded people are peculiarly liable. The effect was charming, bizarre, and romantic.

Well satisfied with this embellishment, I went out with the gravity and pride becoming one who feels that he has the ineffable advantage over all the passers-by whom he elbows, of possessing a piece of the Princess Hermonthis, daughter of Pharaoh.

I looked upon all who did not possess, like myself, a paper-weight so authentically Egyptian, as very ridiculous people; and it seemed to me that the proper occupation of every sensible man should consist in the mere fact of having a mummy's foot upon his desk.

Happily I met some friends, whose presence distracted me in my infatuation with this new acquisition: I went to dinner with them; for I could not very well have dined with myself.

When I came back that evening, with my brain slightly confused by a few glasses of wine, a vague whiff of Oriental perfume delicately titillated my olfactory nerves: the heat of the room had warmed the natron, bitumen, and myrrh in which the *paraschistes,* who cut open the bodies of the dead, had bathed the corpse of the princess;—it was a perfume at once sweet and penetrating—a perfume that four thousand years had not been able to dissipate.

The Dream of Egypt was Eternity: her odors have the solidity of granite, and endure as long.

I soon drank deeply from the black cup of sleep: for a few hours all remained opaque to me; Oblivion and Nothingness inundated me with their sombre waves.

Yet light gradually dawned upon the darkness of my mind: dreams commenced to touch me softly in their silent flight.

The eyes of my soul were opened; and I beheld my chamber as it actually was: I might have believed myself awake, but for a vague consciousness which assured me that I slept, and that something fantastic was about to take place.

The odor of the myrrh had augmented in intensity: and I felt a slight headache, which I very naturally attributed to several glasses of champagne that we had drunk to the unknown gods and our future fortunes.

I peered through my room with a feeling of expectation which I saw nothing to justify: every article of furniture was in its proper place; the lamp, softly shaded by its globe of ground crystal, burned upon its bracket; the water-color sketches shone under their Bohemian glass; the curtains hung down languidly; everything wore an aspect of tranquil slumber.

After a few moments, however, all this calm interior appeared to become disturbed; the woodwork cracked stealthily; the ash-covered log suddenly emitted a jet of blue flame; and the disks of the pateras seemed like great metallic eyes, watching, like myself, for the things which were about to happen.

My eyes accidentally fell upon the desk where I had placed the foot of the Princess Hermonthis.

Instead of remaining quiet—as behooved a foot which had been embalmed for four thousand years—it commenced to act in a nervous manner; contracted itself, and leaped over the papers like a startled frog;—one would have imagined that it had suddenly been brought into contact with a galvanic battery: I could distinctly hear the dry sound made by its little heel, hard as the hoof of a gazel.

I became rather discontented with my acquisition, inasmuch as I wished my paper-weights to be of a sedentary disposition, and thought it very unnatural that feet should walk about without legs; and I commenced to experience a feeling closely akin to fear.

Suddenly I saw the folds of my bed-curtain stir; and heard a bumping sound, like that caused by some person hopping on one foot across the floor.

I must confess I became alternately hot and cold; that I felt a strange wind chill my back; and that my suddenly-rising hair caused my nightcap to execute a leap of several yards.

The bed-curtain opened, and I beheld the strangest figure imaginable before me.

It was a young girl of a very deep coffee-brown complexion, like the bayadere Amani, and possessing the purest Egyptian type of perfect beauty; her eyes were almond-shaped and oblique, with eyebrows so black that they seemed blue; her nose was exquisitely chiseled, almost Greek in its delicacy of outline; and she might indeed have been taken for a Corinthian statue of bronze, but for the prominence of her cheek-bones and the slightly African fulness of her lips, which compelled one to recognize her as belonging beyond all doubt to the hieroglyphic race which dwelt upon the banks of the Nile.

Her arms, slender and spindle-shaped, like those of very young girls, were encircled by a peculiar kind of metal bands, and bracelets of glass beads; her hair was all twisted into little cords; and she wore upon her bosom a little idol figure of green paste, bearing a whip with seven lashes, which proved it to be an image of Isis: her brow was adorned with a shining plate of gold; and a few traces of paint relieved the coppery tint of her cheeks.

As for her costume, it was very odd indeed.

Fancy a *pagne* or skirt all formed of little strips of material bedizened with red and black hieroglyphics, stiffened with bitumen, and apparently belonging to freshly unbandaged mummy.

In one of those sudden flights of thought so common in dreams I heard the hoarse falsetto of the *bric-à-brac* dealer, repeating like a monotonous refrain, the phrase he had uttered in his shop with so enigmatical an intonation:

"Old Pharaoh will not be well pleased: he loved his daughter, the dear man!"

One strange circumstance, which was not at all calculated to restore my equanimity, was that the apparition had but one foot; the other was broken off at the ankle!

She approached the table where the foot was starting and fidgeting about more than ever; and there supported herself upon the edge of the desk. I saw her eyes fill with pearly-gleaming tears.

Although she had not as yet spoken, I fully comprehended the thoughts which agitated her: she looked at her foot—for it was indeed her own—with an exquisitely graceful expression of coquettish sadness; but the foot leaped and ran hither and thither, as though impelled on steel springs.

Twice or thrice she extended her hand to seize it, but could not succeed.

Then commenced between the Princess Hermonthis and her foot—which appeared to be endowed with a special life of its own—a very fantastic dialogue in a most ancient Coptic tongue, such as might have been spoken thirty centuries ago in the syrinxes of the land of Ser: luckily I understood Coptic perfectly well that night.

The Princess Hermonthis cried, in a voice sweet and vibrant as the tones of a crystal bell:

"Well, my dear little foot, you always flee from me; yet I always took good care of you. I bathed you with perfumed water in a bowl of alabaster; I smoothed your heel with pumice-stone mixed with palm oil; your nails were cut with golden scissors and polished with a hippopotamus tooth; I was careful to select *tatbebs* for you, painted and embroidered and turned up at the toes, which were the envy of all the young girls in Egypt: you wore on your great toe rings bearing the device of the sacred Scarabaeus; and you supported one of the lightest bodies that a lazy foot could sustain.

The foot replied in a pouting and chagrined tone:

"You know well that I do not belong to myself any longer. I have been bought and paid for: the old merchant knew what he was about: he bore you a grudge for having refused to espouse him. This is an ill turn which he has done you. The Arab who violated your royal coffin in the subterranean pits of the necropolis of Thebes was sent thither by him: he desired to prevent you from being present at the reunion of the shadowy nations in the cities below. Have you five pieces of gold for my ransom?"

"Alas, no!—my jewels, my rings, my purses of gold and silver, were all stolen from me," answered the Princess Hermonthis, with a sob.

"Princess," I then exclaimed, "I never retained anybody's foot unjustly;—even though you have not got the five louis which it cost me, I present it to you gladly: I should feel unutterably wretched to think that I were the cause of so amiable a person as the Princess Hermonthis being lame."

I delivered this discourse in a royally gallant, troubadour tone which must have astonished the beautiful Egyptian girl.

She turned a look of deepest gratitude upon me; and her eyes shone with bluish gleams of light.

She took her foot—which surrendered itself willingly this time—like a woman about to put on her little shoe; and adjusted it to her leg with much skill.

This operation over, she took a few steps about the room, as though to assure herself that she was really no longer lame.

"Ah, how pleased my father will be!—he who was so unhappy because of my mutilation; and who from the moment of my birth, set a whole nation at work to hollow me out a tomb so deep that he might preserve me intact until that last day, when souls must be weighed in the balance of Amenthi! Come with me to my father!—he will receive you kindly; for you have given me back my foot."

I thought this proposition natural enough. I arrayed myself in a dressing-gown of large-flowered pattern, which lent me a very Pharaonic aspect; hurriedly put on a pair of Turkish slippers, and informed the Princess Hermonthis that I was ready to follow her.

Before starting, Hermonthis took from her neck the little idol of green paste, and laid it on the scattered sheets of paper which covered the table.

"It is only fair," she observed, smilingly, "that I should replace your paper-weight."

She gave me her hand, which felt soft and cold, like the skin of a serpent; and we departed.

We passed for some time with the velocity of an arrow through a fluid and grayish expanse, in which half-formed silhouettes flitted swiftly by us, to right and left.

For an instant we saw only sky and sea.

A few moments later obelisks commenced to tower in the distance: pylons and vast flights of steps guarded by sphinxes became clearly outlined against the horizon.

We had reached our destination.

The princess conducted me to a mountain of rose-colored granite, in the face of which appeared an opening so narrow and low that it would have been difficult to distinguish it from the fissures in the rock, had not its location been marked by two stelae wrought with sculptures.

Hermonthis kindled a torch, and led the way before me.

We traversed corridors hewn through the living rock: their walls, covered with hieroglyphics and paintings of allegorical processions, might well have occupied thousands of arms for thousands of years in their formation;—these corridors, of interminable length, opened into square chambers, in the midst of which pits had been contrived, through which we descended by cramp-irons or spiral stairways;—these pits again conducted us into other chambers, opening into other corridors, likewise decorated with painted sparrow-hawks, serpents coiled in circles, the symbols of the *tau* and *pedum*—prodigious works of art which no living eye can ever examine—interminable legends of granite which only the dead have time to read through all eternity.

At last we found ourselves in a hall so vast, so enormous, so immeasurable, that the eye could not reach its limits; files of monstrous columns stretched far out of sight on every side, between which twinkled livid stars of yellowish flame;—points of light which revealed further depths incalculable in the darkness beyond.

The Princess Hermonthis still held my hand, and graciously saluted the mummies of her acquaintance.

My eyes became accustomed to the dim twilight; and objects became discernible.

I beheld the kings of the subterranean races seated upon thrones—grand old men, though dry, withered, wrinkled like parchment, and blackened with naptha and bitumen—all wearing *pshents* of gold, and breastplates and gorgets glittering with precious stones; their eyes immovably fixed like the eyes of sphinxes, and their long beards whitened by the snow of centuries. Behind them stood their peoples, in the stiff and constrained posture enjoined by Egyptian art, all eternally preserving the attitude prescribed by the hieratic code. Behind these nations, the cats, ibises, and crocodiles cotemporary with them—rendered monstrous of aspect by their swathing bands—mewed, flapped their wings, or extended their jaws in a saurian giggle.

All the Pharaohs were there—Cheops, Chephrenes, Psammetichus, Sesostris, Amenotaph—all the dark rulers of the pyramids and syrinxes:—on yet higher thrones sat Chronos and Xisouthros—who was contemporary with the deluge; and Tubal Cain, who reigned before it.

The beard of King Xisouthros had grown seven times around the granite table, upon which he leaned, lost in deep reverie—and buried in dreams.

Further back, through a dusty cloud, I beheld dimly the seventy-two Preadamite Kings, with their seventy-two peoples—forever passed away.

After permitting me to gaze upon this bewildering spectacle a few moments, the Princess Hermonthis presented me to her father Pharaoh, who favored me with a most gracious nod.

"I have found my foot again!—I have found my foot!" cried the princess, clapping her little hands together with every sign of frantic joy: "it was this gentleman who restored it to me."

The races of Kemi, the races of Nahasi—all the black, bronzed, and copper-colored nations repeated in chorus:

"The Princess Hermonthis has found her foot again!"

Even Xisouthros himself was visibly affected.

He raised his heavy eyelids, stroked his mustache with his fingers, and turned upon me a glance weighty with centuries.

"By Oms, the dog of Hell, and Tmei, daughter of the Sun and of Truth! this is a brave and worthy lad!" exclaimed Pharaoh, pointing to me with his sceptre which was terminated with a lotus-flower.

"What recompense do you desire?"

Filled with that daring inspired by dreams in which nothing seems impossible, I asked him for the hand of the Princess Hermonthis;—the hand seemed to me a very proper antithetic recompense for the foot.

Pharaoh opened wide his great eyes of glass in astonishment at my witty request.

"What country do you come from? and what is your age?"

"I am a Frenchman; and I am twenty-seven years old, venerable Pharaoh."

"—Twenty-seven years old! and he wishes to espouse the Princess Hermonthis, who is thirty centuries old!"—cried out at once all the Thrones and all the Circles of Nations.

Only Hermonthis herself did not seem to think my request unreasonable.

"If you were even only two thousand years old," replied the ancient King, "I would willingly give you the Princess; but the disproportion is too great; and, besides, we must give our daughters husbands who will last well: you do not know how to preserve yourselves any longer; even those who died only fifteen centuries ago are already no more than a handful of dust;—behold! my flesh is solid as basalt; my bones are bars of steel!

"I will be present on the last day of the world, with the same body and the same features which I had during my lifetime: my daughter Hermonthis will last longer than a statue of bronze.

"Then the last particles of your dust will have been scattered abroad by the winds; and even Isis herself, who was able to find the atoms of Osiris, would scarce be able to recompose your being.

"See how vigorous I yet remain, and how mighty is my grasp," he added, shaking my hand in the English fashion with a strength that buried my rings in the flesh of my fingers.

He squeezed me so hard that I awoke, and found my friend Alfred shaking me by the arm to make me get up.

"O you everlasting sleeper!—must I have you carried out into the middle of the street, and fireworks exploded in your ears? It is after noon; don't you recollect your promise to take me with you to see M. Aguado's Spanish pictures?"

"God! I forgot all, all about it," I answered, dressing myself hurriedly; "we will go there at once; I have the permit lying there on my desk."

I started to find it;—but fancy my astonishment when I beheld, instead of the mummy's foot I had purchased the evening before, the little green paste idol left in its place by the Princess Hermonthis!

THE END OF CANDIA

Gabriele d'Annunzio

I

Three days after the Easter banquet, which was traditionally a great occasion in the Lamonica household, both in its lavishness and in the number of its guests, Donna Cristina Lamonica was counting the table linen and silver service, and replacing them one by one, methodically, in drawer and cupboard, in readiness for future banquets.

As usual, she had with her, to help in the task, the chambermaid, Maria Bisaccia, and the laundress, Candida Marcanda, familiarly known as Candia. The huge hampers, filled with fine linen, stood in a row upon the floor. The silver platters and other table service gleamed brightly from the sideboard—massive vessels, somewhat crudely wrought by rustic silversmiths, and of more or less liturgical design, like all the plate which rich provincial families hand down from generation to generation. A fresh fragrance of soapy water pervaded the room.

From the hampers Candia took tablecloths, napkins, and towels; she made the mistress take note that each piece was intact, and then passed them over to Maria, who laid them away in the drawers, while the mistress sprinkled lavender between them and entered the numbers in a book. Candia was a tall, lean, angular woman of fifty, with back somewhat bent from the habitual attitude of her calling, with arms of unusual length, and the head of a bird of prey mounted on a turtle's neck. Maria Bisaccia was a native of Ortona, a trifle stout, with a fresh complexion and the clearest of eyes; she had a soft fashion of speech, and the light, leisurely touch of one whose hands were almost always busy over cakes and sirups, pastry and preserves. Donna Cristina, also an Ortonese, and educated in a Benedictine convent, was of small

297

stature, with a somewhat too generous expanse of bosom, a face overstrewn with freckles, a large, long nose, poor teeth, and handsome eyes cast downward in a way that made one think of a priest in woman's clothing.

The three women were performing their task with the utmost care, giving up to it the greater part of the afternoon. All at once, just as Candia was leaving with the empty baskets, Donna Cristina, in the course of counting the small silver, found that a spoon was missing.

"Maria! Maria!" she cried, in utter dismay, "count these! There's a spoon missing! Count them yourself!"

"But how could it? That's impossible, Signora!" replied Maria, "let me have a look." And she in turn began to count the small pieces, telling off the numbers aloud, while Donna Cristina looked on, shaking her head. The silver gave forth a clear, ringing sound.

"Well, it's a fact!" Maria exclaimed at last, with a gesture of despair; "what's to be done about it!"

She herself was safe from all suspicion. For fifteen years she had given proofs of her fidelity and honesty in this very household. She had come from Ortona together with Donna Cristina at the time of the wedding, almost as though she were a part of the marriage settlement; and from the first she had acquired a certain authority in the house, through the indulgence of her mistress. She was full of religious superstitions, devoted to the saint and the belfry of her birthplace, and possessed of great shrewdness. She and her mistress had formed a sort of offensive alliance against Pescara and all pertaining to it, and more particularly against the saint of the Pescarese. She never missed a chance to talk of her native town, to vaunt its beauty and its riches, the splendor of its basilica, the treasures of San Tommaso, the magnificence of its religious ceremonies, as compared with the poverty of San Cetteo, that possessed only one single little silver cross.

Donna Cristina said:

"Take a good look in there."

Maria left the room to extend the search. She explored every nook and corner of the kitchen and the balcony, but in vain. She came back empty-handed.

"It isn't there! It isn't there!"

Then the two together tried to think, to make conjectures, to ransack their memories. They went out upon the balcony that communicated with the court, the balcony back of the laundry, to make one last research. As they talked together in loud tones, women's heads began to appear at the windows of the surrounding houses.

"What has happened, Donna Cristina? Tell us about it."

Donna Cristina and Maria related the occurrence with many words and many gestures.

"Lord, Lord! Then there have been thieves here?"

In a moment the report of the theft had spread through the neighborhood, through all Pescara. Men and women fell to discussing, to imagining who could have been the thief. By the time the news had reached the most distant houses of Sant' Agostino, it had gathered volume; it was no longer a question of a mere spoon, but of all the silver plate in the house of Lamonica.

Now, since the weather was fine and roses were beginning to bloom upon the balcony, and a pair of linnets were singing in their cage, the women lingered at their windows, for the pleasure of gossiping across the grateful warmth of the outdoor air. Female heads continued to appear from behind the pots of sweet basil, and a chatter arose that must have rejoiced the cats upon the housetops.

Clasping her hands, Donna Cristina asked: "Who could it have been?"

Donna Isabella Sertale, nicknamed the Polecat, who had the lithe and stealthy movements of a beast of prey, asked in a strident voice: "Who did you have with you, Donna Cristina? It seems to me that I saw Candia on her way—"

"Ahah!" exclaimed Donna Felicetta Margasanta, nicknamed the Magpie because of her continuous garrulity. "Ahah!" repeated the other gossips.— "And you hadn't thought of it?"—"And you never noticed?"—"And you don't know about Candia?"—"We can tell you about Candia!"—"Indeed we can!"—"Oh, yes, we can tell you about her!"

"She washes clothes well, there is no denying it. She is the best laundress in Pescara, there's no question about it. But the trouble with her is that she is too light-fingered—didn't you know that, my dear?"

"She got a couple of towels from me once."—"And a napkin from me."— "And a night-gown from me."—"And three pairs of stockings from me."— "And a new petticoat from me."—"And I never got them back again."— "Nor I."—"Nor I."

"But I didn't discharge her. Whom could I get? Silvestra?"

"Oh! oh!"

"Angelantonia? The African?"

"Each one worse than the other!"

"We must put up with it."

"But it's a spoon this time!"

"That's a little too much!"

"Don't you let it pass, Donna Cristina, don't you let it pass!"

"Let it pass, or not let it pass!" burst forth Maria Bisaccia, who, in spite of her placid and benign appearance, never let an opportunity pass for displaying her superiority over her fellow servants. "That is for us to decide, Donna Isabella, that is for us to decide!"

And the chatter continued to flow back and forth from windows to balcony. And the accusation spread from lip to lip throughout the whole countryside.

II

The following morning, Candia Marcanda already had her arms in a tubful of clothes, when the village constable, Biagio Pesce, nicknamed the Little Corporal, appeared at her door.

"His Honor, the mayor, wants you up at his office right away," he told the laundress.

"What's that?" demanded Candia, wrinkling her brows into a frown, yet without interrupting the task before her.

"His Honor, the mayor, wants you up at his office, right away."

"Wants me? What does he want me for?" Candia demanded rather sharply, for she was at a loss to understand this unexpected summons, and it turned her as stubborn as a horse balking at a shadow.

"I can't tell you what for," replied the Little Corporal, "those were my orders."

"What were your orders?" From an obstinacy that was natural to her, she would not cease from asking questions. She could not convince herself that it was a reality. "The mayor wants me? What for? What have I done, I should like to know? I'm not going. I haven't done anything."

The Little Corporal, losing his temper, answered: "Oh, you won't go, won't you? We'll see about that!" and he went off, muttering, with his hand upon the hilt of the ancient sword he wore.

Meanwhile there were others along the narrow street who had overheard the conversation and came out upon their doorsteps, where they could watch Candia vigorously working her arms up and down in the tubful of clothes. And since they knew about the silver spoon, they laughed meaningly and interchanged ambiguous phrases, which Candia could not understand. But this laughter and these phrases awoke a vague forboding in the woman's mind. And this forboding gathered strength when the Little Corporal reappeared, accompanied by another officer.

"Step lively," said the Little Corporal peremptorily.

Candia wiped her arms, without replying, and went with them. In the public square, people stopped to look. One of her enemies, Rosa Panura, called out from the door of her shop, with a hateful laugh: "Drop your stolen bone!"

The laundress, dazed by this persecution for which she could find no reason, was at a loss for a reply.

Before the mayor's office a group of curious idlers had gathered to watch her as she went in. Candia, in an access of anger, mounted the steps in a rush and burst into the mayor's presence, breathlessly demanding: "Well, what is it you want of me?"

Don Silla, a man of peaceful proclivities, was for the moment perturbed by the laundress's strident tones, and cast a glance at the two faithful custodians of his official dignity. Then, taking a pinch of tobacco from his horn snuffbox, he said to her: "My daughter, be seated."

But Candia remained standing. Her beak-like nose was inflated with anger, and her wrinkled cheeks quivered curiously. "Tell me, Don Silla."

"You went yesterday to take back the wash to Donna Cristina Lamonica?"

"Well, and what of it? What of it? Was there anything missing? All of it counted, piece by piece—and not a thing missing. What's the matter with it now?"

"Wait a moment, my daughter! In the same room there was the table silver—"

Candia, comprehending, turned like an angry hawk, about to swoop upon its prey. Her thin lips twitched convulsively.

"The silver was in the room, and Donna Cristina found that a spoon was missing. Do you understand, my daughter? Could you have taken it—by mistake?"

Candia jumped like a grasshopper before the injustice of this accusation. As a matter of fact she had stolen nothing.

"Oh, it was I, was it? I? Who says so? Who saw me? I am astonished at you, Don Silla! I am astonished at you! I, a thief? I? I?"

And there was no end to her indignation. She was all the more keenly stung by the unjust charge, because she knew herself to be capable of the action they attributed to her.

"Then it was you who took it?" interrupted Don Silla, prudently sinking back into the depths of his spacious judicial chair.

"I am astonished at you!" snarled the woman once more, waving her long arms around as though they had been two sticks.

"Very well, you may go. We will see about it."

Candia went out without a salutation, blindly bumping into the doorpost. She had turned fairly green; she was beside herself. As she set foot in the street and saw the crowd which had gathered, she realized that already public opinion was against her; that no one was going to believe in her innocence. Nevertheless, she began to utter a vociferous denial. The crowd continued to laugh as it dispersed. Full of fury, she returned home, and hopelessly began to weep upon her doorstep.

Don Donato Brandimarte, who lived next door, said mockingly: "Cry louder, cry louder! There are people passing by!"

Since there were heaps of clothing still waiting for the suds, she finally calmed herself, bared her arms, and resumed her task. As she worked, she thought out her denials, elaborated a whole system of defense, sought out in her shrewd woman's brain an ingenious method of establishing her innocence; racking her brain for specious subtleties, she had recourse to every trick of rustic dialectic to construct a line of reasoning that would convince the most incredulous.

Then, when her day's work was ended, she went out, deciding to go first to see Donna Cristina.

Donna Cristina was not to be seen. It was Maria Bisaccia who listened to Candia's flood of words, shaking her head but answering nothing, and withdrawing in dignified silence.

Next, Candia made the circuit of all her clients. To each in turn she related the occurrence, to each she unfolded her defense, continually adding some new argument, amplifying her words, growing constantly more excited, more desperate, in the face of incredulity and distrust. And all in vain; she felt that from now on there was no further defense possible. A sort of blind hopelessness took possession of her—what more was there to do? What more was there to say?

III

Meanwhile Donna Cristina Lamonica gave orders to send for Cinigia, a woman of the people, who practised magic and empirical medicine with considerable success. Cinigia had several times before discovered stolen goods; and it was said that she was secretly in league with the thieves.

"Find that spoon for me," Donna Cristina told her, "and you shall have a big reward."

"Very well," Cinigia replied; "twenty-four hours are all I need."

And twenty-four hours later she brought back her answer; the spoon was to be found in a hole in the courtyard, near the well.

Donna Cristina and Maria descended to the courtyard, made search, and, to their great amazement, found the spoon.

Swiftly the news spread throughout Pescara.

Then triumphantly Candia Marcanda went the rounds of all the streets. She seemed to have grown taller; she held her head erect; she smiled, looking every one straight in the eye, as if to say, "I told you so! I told you so!"

The people in the shops, seeing her pass by, would murmur something and then break forth into a significantly sneering laugh. Filippo La Selvi, who sat drinking a glass of liqueur brandy in the Café d'Ange, called Candia in.

"Another glass for Candia, the same as mine!"

The woman, who was fond of strong spirits, pursed up her lips covetously.

"You certainly deserve it, there's no denying that!" added Filippo La Selvi.

An idle crowd had gathered in front of the café. They all had the spirit of mischief in their faces. While the woman drank, Filippo La Selvi turned and addressed his audience:

"Say, she knew how to work it, didn't she? Isn't she the foxy one?" and he slapped the laundress familiarly upon her bony shoulder.

The crowd laughed. A little dwarf, called Magnafave, or "Big Beans," weak-minded and stuttering, joined the forefinger of his right hand to that of his left, and striking a grotesque attitude and dwelling upon each syllable, said:

"Ca—ca—ca—Candia—Ci—ci—Cinigia!" and he continued to make gestures and to stammer forth vulgar witticisms, all implying that Candia and Cinigia were in league together. His spectators indulged in contortions of merriment.

For a moment Candia sat there bewildered, with the glass still in her hand. Then in a flash she understood—they did not believe in her innocence. They accused her of having brought back the silver spoon secretly, by agreement with the sorceress, to save herself further trouble.

An access of blind anger came upon her. Speechless with passion, she flung herself upon the weakest of them, upon the little hunchback, in a hurricane of blows and scratches. And the crowd, at the sight of this struggle, formed a circle and jeered at them in cruel glee, as at a fight between two animals, and egged on the two combatants with voice and gesture.

Big Beans, badly scared by her unexpected violence, tried to escape, hopping about like a little ape; and held fast by the laundress's terrible arms, whirled round and round with increasing velocity, like a stone in a sling, until at last he fell violently upon his face.

Some of the men hastened to pick him up. Candia withdrew in the midst of hisses, shut herself within her house, and flung herself across her bed, sobbing and gnawing her fingers, in the keenness of her suffering. The new accusation cut her deeper than the first, and all the more that she knew herself capable of such a subterfuge. How was she to clear herself now? How was she to establish the truth? She grew hopeless as she realized that she could not allege in defense any material difficulties that might have interfered with carrying out the deception. Access to the courtyard was perfectly simple; a door, that was never fastened, opened from the ground floor of the main stairway; people came and went freely through that door, to remove the garbage, or for other causes. So it was impossible for her to close the lips of her accusers by saying, "How could I have got in?" The means of successfully carrying out such a plan were many and easy.

Candia proceeded to conjure up new arguments to convince them; she sharpened up her wits; she invented three, four, five different cases to prove that the spoon never could have been found in that hole in the courtyard; she split hairs with marvelous ingenuity. Next she took to making the rounds of the shops and the houses, seeking in very possible way to overcome the people's incredulity. They listened to her, greatly entertained by her captious reasoning; and they would end by saying, "Oh, it's all right!"

But there was a certain tone in their voice that left Candia annihilated. So, then, all her trouble was for nothing! No one would believe her! Yet with marvelous persistence she would return to the attack, spending whole nights in thinking out new arguments. And little by little, under this continued strain, her mind gave way; she could no longer follow any sustained thought but that of the silver spoon.

Neglecting her work, she had sunk to a state of actual want. When she went down to the river bank, under the iron bridge, where the other washwomen congregated, she would sometimes let slip from between her fingers the garments that the current swept away forever. And she would talk continually, unweariedly, of the one single subject. In order not to hear her, the young laundresses would begin to sing, and would mock her with the improvised rimes of their songs. And she meanwhile would shout and gesticulate like a crazy woman.

No one could give her work any longer. Out of pity, some of her former employers would send her food. Little by little she fell into the habit of begging, and wandered through the streets, bowed over, unkempt, and all in rags. The street urchins would tag behind her, shouting: "Tell us the story of the spoon," 'cause we never heard it, Auntie Candia!"

She would stop strangers sometimes as they passed by, to tell them the story and to argue out her defense. Young fellows would sometimes send for her, and pay her a copper to tell it all over, two, three, or four times; they would raise up difficulties against her arguments; they would hear her all the way through, and then at last stab her with a final word. She would shake her head, and go on her way; she found companionship among other beggars and would reason with them endlessly, indefatigably, invincibly. Her chosen friend was a deaf woman, whose skin was a mass of angry blotches, and who limped on one leg.

In the winter of 1874 she was at last stricken with serious illness. The woman with the blotches cared for her. Donna Cristina Lamonica sent her a cordial and a scuttle of coals.

The sick woman, lying on her pallet, still raved of the silver spoon. She would raise herself on her elbow and struggle to wave her arm, to give emphasis to her fevered arguments.

And at the last, when her staring eyes already seemed overspread with a veil of troubled waters that rose from within, Candia gasped forth:

"It wasn't I, madam—because you see—the spoon—"

THE CLOAK

Nikolai Gogol

In the department of—but it is better not to mention the department. There is nothing more irritable than departments, regiments, courts of justice, and, in a word, every branch of public service. Each individual attached to them nowadays thinks all society insulted in his person. Quite recently a complaint was received from a justice of the peace, in which he plainly demonstrated that all the imperial institutions were going to the dogs, and that the Czar's sacred name was being taken in vain; and in proof he appended to the complaint a romance, in which the justice of the peace is made to appear about once in every ten lines, and sometimes in a drunken condition. Therefore, in order to avoid all unpleasantness, it will be better to designate the department in question as a certain department.

So, in a certain department there was a certain official—not a very high one, it must be allowed—short of stature, somewhat pock-marked, red-haired, and short-sighted, with a bald forehead, wrinkled cheeks, and a complexion of the kind known as sanguine. The St. Petersburg climate was responsible for this. As for his official status, he was what is called a perpetual titular councilor, over which some writers make merry and crack their jokes, obeying the praiseworthy custom of attacking those who can not bite back.

His family name was Bashmatchkin. This name is evidently derived from *bashmak* (shoe); but when, at what time, and in what manner, is not known. His father and grandfather, and all the Bashmatchkins, always wore boots, which only had new heels two or three times a year. His name was Akakiy Akakievitch. It may strike the reader as rather singular and far-fetched; but he may rest assured that it was by no means far-fetched, and that the circumstances were such that it would have been impossible to give him any other.

This was how it came about.

Akakiy Akakievitch was born, if my memory fails me not, in the evening on the 23d of March. His mother, the wife of a Government official, and a very fine woman, made all due arrangements for having the child baptized. She was lying on the bed opposite the door; on her right stood the godfather, Ivan Ivanovitch Eroshkin, a most estimable man, who served as presiding officer of the senate; and the godmother, Anna Semenovna Byelobrushkova, the wife of an officer of the quarter, and a woman of rare virtues. They offered the mother her choice of three names, Mokiya, Sossiya, or that the child should be called after the martyr Khozdazat. "No," said the good woman, "all those names are poor." In order to please her, they opened the calendar at another place; three more names appeared, Triphiliy, Dula, and Varakhasiy. "This is a judgment," said the old woman. "What names! I truly never heard the like. Varadat or Varukh might have been borne, but not Triphiliy and Varakhasiy!" They turned to another page and found Pavsikakhiy and Vakhtisiy. "Now I see," said the old woman, "that it is plainly fate. And since such is the case, it will be better to name him after his father. His father's name was Akakiy, so let his son's be Akakiy too." In this manner he became Akakiy Akakievitch. They christened the child, whereat he wept, and made a grimace, as though he foresaw that he was to be a titular councilor.

In this manner did it all come about. We have mentioned it in order that the reader might see for himself that it was a case of necessity, and that it was utterly impossible to give him any other name. When and how he entered the department, and who appointed him, no one could remember. However much the directors and chiefs of all kinds were changed, he was always to be seen in the same place, the same attitude, the same occupation; so that it was afterward affirmed that he had been born in undress uniform with a bald head.

No respect was shown him in the department. The porter not only did not rise from his seat when he passed, but never even glanced at him, any more than if a fly had flown through the reception-room. His superiors treated him in coolly despotic fashion. Some subchief would thrust a paper under his nose without so much as saying "Copy," or "Here's a nice, interesting affair," or anything else agreeable, as is customary among well-bred officials. And he took it, looking only at the paper, and not observing who handed it to him, or whether he had the right to do so; simply took it, and set about copying it.

The young officials laughed at and made fun of him, so far as their official wit permitted; told in his presence various stories concocted about him, and about his landlady, an old woman of seventy; declared that she beat him; asked when the wedding was to be; and strewed bits of paper over his head, calling them snow. But Akakiy Akakievitch answered not a word, any more than if there had been no one there besides himself. It even had no effect upon his work: amid all these annoyances he never made a single mistake in a letter. But if the joking became wholly unbearable, as when they jogged his hand, and prevented his attending to his work, he would exclaim, "Leave me

alone! Why do you insult me?" And there was something strange in the
words and the voice in which they were uttered. There was in it something
which moved to pity; so much that one young man, a newcomer, who, taking
pattern by the others, had permitted himself to make sport of Akakiy, suddenly stopped short, as though all about him had undergone a transformation
and presented itself in a different aspect. Some unseen force repelled him from
the comrades whose acquaintance he had made, on the supposition that they
were well-bred and polite men. Long afterward, in his gayest moments, there
recurred to his mind the little official with the bald forehead, with his heart-
rending words, "Leave me alone! Why do you insult me?" In these moving
words, other words resounded—"I am thy brother." And the young man
covered his face with his hand; and many a time afterward, in the course of
his life, shuddered at seeing how much inhumanity there is in man, how
much savage coarseness is concealed beneath delicate, refined worldliness,
and even, O God! in that man whom the world acknowledges as honorable
and noble.

It would be difficult to find another man who lived so entirely for his
duties. It is not enough to say that Akakiy labored with zeal: no, he labored
with love. In his copying he found a varied and agreeable employment. Enjoyment was written on his face: some letters were even favorites with him,
and when he encountered these he smiled, winked, and worked with his lips,
till it seemed as though each letter might be read in his face, as his pen traced
it. If his pay had been in proportion to his zeal, he would, perhaps, to his
great surprise, have been made even a councilor of state. But he worked, as
his companions, the wits, put it, like a horse in a mill.

Moreover, it is impossible to say that no attention was paid to him. One
director, being a kindly man, and desirous of rewarding him for his long
service, ordered him to be given something more important than mere copying. So he was ordered to make a report of an already concluded affair to
another department; the duty consisting simply in changing the heading and
altering a few words from the first to the third person. This caused him so
much toil that he broke into a perspiration, rubbed his forehead, and finally
said: "No, give me rather something to copy." After that they let him copy on
forever.

Outside this copying, it appeared that nothing existed for him. He gave no
thought to his clothes; his undress uniform was not green, but a sort of rusty-
meal color. The collar was low, so that his neck, in spite of the fact that it was
not long, seemed inordinately so as it emerged from it, like the necks of those
plaster cats which wag their heads and are carried about upon the heads of
scores of image sellers. And something was always sticking to his uniform,
either a bit of hay or some trifle. Moreover, he had a peculiar knack, as he
walked along the street, of arriving beneath a window just as all sorts of
rubbish was being flung out of it; hence he always bore about on his hat
scraps of melon rinds and other such articles. Never once in his life did he
give heed to what was going on every day in the street; while it is well known

that his young brother officials train the range of their glances till they can see when any one's trouser-straps come undone upon the opposite sidewalk, which always brings a malicious smile to their faces. But Akakiy Akakievitch saw in all things the clean, even strokes of his written lines; and only when a horse thrust his nose, from some unknown quarter, over his shoulder, and sent a whole gust of wind down his neck from his nostrils, did he observe that he was not in the middle of a page, but in the middle of the street.

On reaching home he sat down at once at the table, supped his cabbage-soup up quickly, and swallowed a bit of beef with onions, never noticing their taste, and gulping down everything with flies and anything else which the Lord happened to send at the moment. His stomach filled, he rose from the table and copied papers which he had brought home. If there happened to be none, he took copies for himself, for his own gratification, especially if the document was noteworthy, not on account of its style, but of its being addressed to some distinguished person.

Even at the hour when the gray St. Petersburg sky had quite disappeared, and all the official world had eaten or dined, each as he could, in accordance with the salary he received and his own fancy; when all were resting from the departmental jar of pens, running to and fro from their own and other people's indispensable occupations, and from all the work that an uneasy man makes willingly for himself, rather than what is necessary; when officials hasten to dedicate to pleasure the time which is left to them, one bolder than the rest going to the theatre; another into the street, looking under all the bonnets; another wasting his evening in compliments to some pretty girl, the star of a small official circle; another—and this is the common case of all—visiting his comrades on the fourth or third floor, in two small rooms with an anteroom or kitchen, and some pretensions to fashion, such as a lamp or some other trifle, which has cost many a sacrifice of dinner or pleasure trip; in a word, at the hour when all officials disperse among the contracted quarters of their friends, to play whist as they sip their tea from glasses with a kopek's worth of sugar, smoke long pipes, relate at times some bits of gossip which a Russian man can never, under any circumstances, refrain from, and, when there is nothing else to talk of, repeat eternal anecdotes about the commandant to whom they had sent word that the tails of the horses on the Falconet Monument had been cut off, when all strive to divert themselves, Akakiy Akakievitch indulged in no kind of diversion. No one could ever say that he had seen him at any kind of evening party. Having written to his heart's content, he lay down to sleep, smiling at the thought of the coming day—of what God might send him to copy on the morrow.

Thus flowed on the peaceful life of the man, who, with a salary of four hundred rubles, understood how to be content with his lot; and thus it would have continued to flow on, perhaps, to extreme old age were it not that there are various ills strewn along the path of life for titular councilors as well as for private, actual, court, and every other species of councilor, even for those who never give any advice or take any themselves.

There exists in St. Petersburg a powerful foe of all who receive a salary of four hundred rubles a year, or thereabouts. This foe is no other than the northern cold, although it is said to be very healthy. At nine o'clock in the morning, at the very hour when the streets are filled with men bound for the various official departments, it begins to bestow such powerful and piercing nips on all noses impartially that the poor officials really do not know what to do with them. At an hour when the foreheads of even those who occupy exalted positions ache with the cold, and tears start to their eyes, the poor titular councilors are sometimes quite unprotected. Their only salvation lies in traversing as quickly as possible, in their thin little cloaks, five or six streets, and then warming their feet in the porter's room, and so thawing all their talents and qualifications for official service which had become frozen on the way.

Akakiy Akakievitch had felt for some time that his back and shoulders suffered with peculiar poignancy in spite of the fact that he tried to traverse the distance with all possible speed. He began finally to wonder whether the fault did not lie in his cloak. He examined it thoroughly at home, and discovered that in two places, namely, on the back and shoulders, it had become thin as gauze; the cloth was worn to such a degree that he could see through it, and the lining had fallen into pieces. You must know that Akakiy Akakievitch's cloak served as an object of ridicule to the officials; they even refused it the noble name of cloak, and called it a cape. In fact, it was of singular make; its collar diminishing year by year, but serving to patch its other parts. The patching did not exhibit great skill on the part of the tailor, and was, in fact, baggy and ugly. Seeing how the matter stood, Akakiy Akakievitch decided that it would be necessary to take the cloak to Petrovitch, the tailor, who lived somewhere on the fourth floor, up a dark staircase, and who, in spite of his having but one eye, and pock-marks all over his face, busied himself in repairing the trousers and coats of officials and others; that is to say, when he was sober, and not nursing some other scheme in his head.

It is not necessary to say much about this tailor; but, as it is the custom to have the character of each personage in a novel clearly defined, there is no help for it, so here is Petrovitch the tailor. At first he was called only Grigoriy, and was some gentleman's serf; he commenced calling himself Petrovitch from the time when he received his free papers, and further began to drink heavily on all holidays, at first on the great ones, and then on all church festivals without discrimination, wherever a cross stood in the calendar. On this point he was faithful to ancestral custom; and when quarreling with his wife he called her a low female and a German. As we have mentioned his wife, it will be necessary to say a word or two about her. Unfortunately, little is known of her beyond the fact that Petrovitch has a wife, who wears a cap and a dress, but can not lay claim to beauty; at least, no one but the soldiers of the guard even looked under her cap when they met her.

Ascending the staircase which led to Petrovitch's room—which staircase was all soaked with dish-water and reeked with the smell of spirits which affects the eyes, and is an inevitable adjunct to all dark stairways in St. Petersburg houses—ascending the stairs, Akakiy Akakievitch pondered how much Petrovitch would ask, and mentally resolved not to give more than two rubles. The door was open; for the mistress, in cooking some fish, had raised such a smoke in the kitchen that not even the beetles were visible. Akakiy Akakievitch passed through the kitchen unperceived, even by the housewife, and at length reached a room where he beheld Petrovitch seated on a large unpainted table, with his legs tucked under him like a Turkish pasha. His feet were bare, after the fashion of tailors as they sit at work; and the first thing which caught the eye was his thumb, with a deformed nail thick and strong as a turtle's shell. About Petrovitch's neck hung a skein of silk and thread, and upon his knees lay some old garment. He had been trying unsuccessfully for three minutes to thread his needle, and was enraged at the darkness and even at the thread, growling in a low voice, "It won't go through, the barbarian! You pricked me, you rascal!"

Akakiy Akakievitch was vexed at arriving at the precise moment when Petrovitch was angry; he liked to order something of Petrovitch when the latter was a little downhearted, or, as his wife expressed it, "when he had settled himself with brandy, the one-eyed devil!" Under such circumstances, Petrovitch generally came down in his price very readily, and even bowed and returned thanks. Afterward, to be sure, his wife would come, complaining that her husband was drunk, and so had fixed the price too low; but if only a ten-kopek piece were added, then the matter was settled. But now it appeared that Petrovitch was in a sober condition, and therefore rough, taciturn, and inclined to demand, Satan only knows what price. Akakiy Akakievitch felt this, and would gladly have beat a retreat; but he was in for it. Petrovitch screwed up his one eye very intently at him; and Akakiy Akakievitch involuntarily said: "How do you do, Petrovitch?"

"I wish you a good-morning, sir," said Petrovitch, squinting at Akakiy Akakievitch's hands, to see what sort of booty he had brought.

"Ah! I—to you, Petrovitch, this—" It must be known that Akakiy Akakievitch expressed himself chiefly by prepositions, adverbs, and scraps of phrases which had no meaning whatever. If the matter was a very difficult one, he had a habit of never completing his sentences; so that frequently, having begun a phrase with the words, "This, in fact, is quite—" he forgot to go on, thinking that he had already finished it.

"What is it?" asked Petrovitch, and with his one eye scanned Akakievitch's whole uniform from the collar down to the cuffs, the back, the tails, and the button-holes, all of which were well known to him, since they were his own handiwork. Such is the habit of tailors; it is the first thing they do on meeting one.

"But I, here, this—Petrovitch—a cloak, cloth—here you see, everywhere, in different places, it is quite strong—it is a little dusty, and looks old, but it is new, only here in one place it is a little—on the back, and here on one of the shoulders, it is a little worn, yes, here on this shoulder it is a little—do you see? that is all. And a little work—"

Petrovitch took the cloak, spread it out, to begin with, on the table, looked hard at it, shook his head, reached out his hand to the window-sill for his snuff-box, adorned with the portrait of some general, though what general is unknown, for the place where the face should have been had been rubbed through by the finger, and a square bit of paper had been pasted over it. Having taken a pinch of snuff, Petrovitch held up the cloak, and inspected it against the light, and again shook his head. Then he turned it, lining upward, and shook his head once more. After which he again lifted the general-adorned lid with its bit of pasted paper, and, having stuffed his nose with snuff, closed and put away the snuff-box, and said finally, "No, it is impossible to mend it; it's a wretched garment!"

Akakiy Akakievitch's heart sank at these words.

"Why is it impossible, Petrovitch?" he said, almost in the pleading voice of a child; "all that ails it is that it is worn at the shoulders. You must have some pieces—"

"Yes, patches could be found, patches are easily found," said Petrovitch, "but there's nothing to sew them to. The thing is completely rotten; if you put a needle to it—see, it will give way."

"Let it give way, and you can put on another patch at once."

"But there is nothing to put the patches on to; there's no use in strengthening it; it is too far gone. It's lucky that it's cloth; for, if the wind were to blow, it would fly away."

"Well, strengthen it again. How this, in fact."

"No," said Petrovitch decisively, "there is nothing to be done with it. It's a thoroughly bad job. You'd better, when the cold winter comes on, make yourself some gaiters out of it, because stockings are not warm. The Germans invented them in order to make more money." Petrovitch loved, on all occasions, to have a fling at the Germans. "But it is plain you must have a new cloak."

At the word "new," all grew dark before Akakiy Akakievitch's eyes and everything in the room began to whirl round. The only thing he saw clearly was the general with the paper face on the lid of Petrovitch's snuff-box. "A new one?" said he, as if still in a dream: "why, I have no money for that."

"Yes, a new one," said Petrovitch, with barbarous composure.

"Well, if came to a new one, how it?"

"You mean how much would it cost?"

"Yes."

"Well, you would have to lay out a hundred and fifty or more," said Petrovitch, and pursed up his lips significantly. He liked to produce powerful effects, liked to stun utterly and suddenly and then to glance sidewise to see what face the stunned person would put on the matter.

"A hundred and fifty rubles for a cloak!" shrieked poor Akakiy

Akakievitch, perhaps for the first time in his life, for his voice had always been distinguished for softness.

"Yes, sir," said Petrovitch, "for any kind of cloak. If you have a marten fur on the collar, or a silk-lined hood, it will mount up to two hundred."

"Petrovitch, please," said Akakiy Akakievitch in a beseeching tone, not hearing, and not trying to hear, Petrovitch's words, and disregarding all his "effects," "some repairs, in order that it may wear yet a little longer."

"No, it would only be a waste of time and money," said Petrovitch; and Akakiy Akakievitch went away after these words, utterly discouraged. But Petrovitch stood for some time after his departure, with significantly compressed lips, and without betaking himself to his work, satisfied that he would not be dropped, and an artistic tailor employed.

Akakiy Akakievitch went out into the street as if in a dream. "Such an affair!" he said to himself: "I did not think it had come to—" and then after a pause he added: "Well, so it is! see what it has come to at last! and I never imagined that it was so!" Then followed a long silence, after which he exclaimed: "Well, so it is! see what already—nothing unexpected that it would be nothing—what a strange circumstance!" So saying, instead of going home, he went in exactly the opposite direction without himself suspecting it. On the way a chimney-sweep bumped up against him and blackened his shoulder, and a whole hatful of rubbish landed on him from the top of a house which was building. He did not notice it; and only when he ran against a watchman, who, having planted his halberd beside him, was shaking some snuff from his box into his horny hand, did he recover himself a little, and that because the watchman said, "Why are you poking yourself into a man's very face? Haven't you the pavement?" This caused him to look about him, and turn toward home.

There only he finally began to collect his thoughts and to survey his position in its clear and actual light, and to argue with himself, sensibly and frankly, as with a reasonable friend, with whom one can discuss private and personal matters. "No," said Akakiy Akakievitch, "it is impossible to reason with Petrovitch now; he is that—evidently his wife has been beating him. I'd better go to him on Sunday morning; after Saturday night he will be a little cross-eyed and sleepy, for he will want to get drunk, and his wife won't give him any money; and at such a time a ten-kopek piece in his hand will—he will become more fit to reason with, and then the cloak, and that—" Thus argued Akakiy Akakievitch with himself, regained his courage, and waited until the first Sunday, when, seeing from afar that Petrovitch's wife had left the house, he went straight to him.

Petrovitch's eye was, indeed, very much askew after Saturday: his head drooped and he was very sleepy; but for all that, as soon as he knew what it was a question of, it seemed as though Satan jogged his memory. "Impossible," said he; "please to order a new one." Thereupon Akakiy Akakievitch handed over the ten-kopek piece. "Thank you, sir; I will drink your good health," said Petrovitch; "but as for the cloak, don't trouble yourself about it;

it is good for nothing. I will make you a capital new one, so let us settle about it now."

Akakiy Akakievitch was still for mending it; but Petrovitch would not hear of it, and said: "I shall certainly have to make you a new one, and you may depend upon it that I shall do my best. It may even be, as the fashion goes, that the collar can be fastened by silver hooks under a flap."

Then Akakiy Akakievitch saw that it was impossible to get along without a new cloak, and his spirit sank utterly. How, in fact, was it to be done? Where was the money to come from? He might, to be sure, depend, in part, upon his present at Christmas; but that money had long been allotted beforehand. He must have some new trousers, and pay a debt of long standing to the shoe-maker for putting new tops to his old boots, and he must order three shirts from the seamstress, and a couple of pieces of linen. In short, all his money must be spent; and even if the director should be so kind as to order him to receive forty-five rubles instead of forty, or even fifty, it would be a mere nothing, a mere drop in the ocean toward the funds necessary for a cloak; although he knew that Petrovitch was often wrong-headed enough to blurt out some outrageous price, so that even his own wife could not refrain from exclaiming, "Have you lost your senses, you fool?" At one time he would not work at any price, and now it was quite likely that he had named a higher sum than the cloak would cost.

But although he knew that Petrovitch would undertake to make a cloak for eighty rubles, still, where was he to get the eighty rubles from? He might possibly manage half; yes, half might be procured, but where was the other half to come from? But the reader must first be told where the first half came from. Akakiy Akakievitch had a habit of putting, for every ruble he spent, a kopek into a small box, fastened with lock and key, and with a slit in the top for the reception of money. At the end of every half-year he counted over the heap of coppers, and changed it for silver. This he had done for a long time, and in the course of years the sum had mounted up to over forty rubles. Thus he had one-half on hand; but where was he to find the other half? where was he to get another forty rubles from? Akakiy Akakievitch thought and thought, and decided that it would be necessary to curtail his ordinary expenses for the space of one year at least—to dispense with tea in the evening, to burn no candles, and, if there was anything which he must do, to go into his landlady's room and work by her light. When he went into the street he must walk as lightly as he could, and as cautiously, upon the stones, almost upon tiptoe, in order not to wear his heels down in too short a time; he must give the laundress as little to wash as possible; and, in order not to wear out his clothes, he must take them off as soon as he got home, and wear only his cotton dressing-gown, which had been long and carefully saved.

To tell the truth, it was a little hard for him at first to accustom himself to these deprivations; but he got used to them at length, after a fashion, and all went smoothly. He even got used to being hungry in the evening, but he made up for it by treating himself, so to say, in spirit, by bearing ever in mind the idea of his future cloak. From that time forth his existence seemed to become, in some way, fuller, as if he were married, or as if some other man lived in him, as if, in fact, he were not alone, and some pleasant friend had consented to travel along life's path with him, the friend being no other than the cloak, with thick wadding and a strong lining incapable of wearing out. He became more lively, and even his character grew firmer, like that of a man who has made up his mind and set himself a goal. From his face and gait, doubt and indecision, all hesitating and wavering traits, disappeared of themselves. Fire gleamed in his eyes, and occasionally the boldest and most daring ideas flitted through his mind; why not, for instance, have marten fur on the collar? The thought of this almost made him absent-minded. Once, in copying a letter, he nearly made a mistake, so that he exclaimed almost aloud, "Ugh!" and crossed himself. Once in the course of every month he had a conference with Petrovitch on the subject of the cloak, where it would be better to buy the cloth, and the color, and the price. He always returned home satisfied, though troubled, reflecting that the time would come at last when it could all be bought, and then the cloak made.

The affair progressed more briskly than he had expected. Far beyond all his hopes, the director awarded neither forty nor forty-five rubles for Akakiy Akakievitch's share, but sixty. Whether he suspected that Akakiy Akakievitch needed a cloak, or whether it was merely chance; at all events, twenty extra rubles were by this means provided. This circumstance hastened matters. Two or three months more of hunger and Akakiy Akakievitch had accumulated about eighty rubles. His heart, generally so quiet, began to throb. On the first possible day he went shopping in company with Petrovitch. They bought some very good cloth, and at a reasonable rate too, for they had been considering the matter for six months, and rarely let a month pass without their visiting the shops to inquire prices. Petrovitch himself said that no better cloth could be had. For lining, they selected a cotton stuff, but so firm and thick that Petrovitch declared it to be better than silk, and even prettier and more glossy. They did not buy the marten fur because it was, in fact, dear, but in its stead they picked out the very best of cat-skin which could be found in the shop, and which might, indeed, be taken for marten at a distance.

Petrovitch worked at the cloak two whole weeks, for there was a great deal of quilting; otherwise it would have been finished sooner. He charged twelve rubles for the job; it could not possibly have been done for less. It was all sewed with silk, in small, double seams; and Petrovitch went over each seam afterward with his own teeth.

It was—it is difficult to say precisely on what day, but probably the most glorious one in Akakiy Akakievitch's life, when Petrovitch at length brought home the cloak. He brought it in the morning, before the hour when it was necessary to start for the department. Never did a cloak arrive so exactly in the nick of time, for the severe cold had set in, and it seemed to threaten to increase. Petrovitch brought the cloak himself as befits a good tailor. On his countenance was a significant expression, such as Akakiy Akakievitch had never beheld there. He seemed fully sensible that he had done no small deed, and crossed a gulf separating tailors who only put in linings and execute repairs from those who make new things. He took the cloak out of the pocket-handkerchief in which he had brought it. The handkerchief was fresh from the laundress, and he put it in his pocket for use. Taking out the cloak, he gazed proudly at it, held it up with both hands, and flung it skilfully over the shoulders of Akakiy Akakievitch. Then he pulled it and fitted it down behind with his hand, and he draped it around Akakiy Akakievitch without buttoning it. Akakiy Akakievitch, like an experienced man, wished to try the sleeves. Petrovitch helped him on with them, and it turned out that the sleeves were satisfactory also. In short, the cloak appeared to be perfect and most seasonable. Petrovitch did not neglect to observe that it was only because he lived in a narrow street, and had no signboard, and had known Akakiy Akakievitch so long, that he had made it so cheaply; but that if he had been in business on the Nevsky Prospect he would have charged seventy-five rubles for the making alone. Akakiy Akakievitch did not care to argue this point with Petrovitch. He paid him, thanked him, and set out at once in his new cloak for the department. Petrovitch followed him, and, pausing in the street, gazed long at the cloak in the distance, after which he went to one side expressly to run through a crooked alley and emerge again into the street beyond to gaze once more upon the cloak from another point, namely, directly in front.

Meantime Akakiy Akakievitch went on in holiday mood. He was conscious, every second of the time, that he had a new cloak on his shoulders; and several times he laughed with internal satisfaction. In fact, there were two advantages, one was its warmth, the other its beauty. He saw nothing of the road, but suddenly found himself at the department. He took off his cloak in the anteroom, looked it over carefully, and confided it to the especial care of the attendant. It is impossible to say precisely how it was that every one in the department knew at once that Akakiy Akakievitch had a new cloak, and that the "cape" no longer existed. All rushed at the same moment into the anteroom, to inspect it. They congratulated him and said pleasant things to him, so that he began at first to smile and then to grow ashamed. When all surrounded him and said that the new cloak must be "christened," and that he must give a whole evening at least to this, Akakiy Akakievitch lost his head completely, and did not know where he stood, what to answer, or how to get out of it. He stood blushing all over for several minutes, and was on the point of assuring them with great simplicity that it was not a new cloak, that it was so and so, that it was in fact the old "cape."

At length one of the officials, a subchief probably, in order to show that he was not at all proud, and on good terms with his inferiors, said: "So be it, only I will give the party instead of Akakiy Akakievitch; I invite you all to tea with me to-night; it happens quite à propos, as it is my name-day." The officials naturally at once offered the subchief their congratulations, and accepted the invitation with pleasure. Akakiy Akakievitch would have declined, but all declared that it was discourteous, that it was simply a sin and a shame, and that he could not possibly refuse. Besides, the notion became pleasant to him when he recollected that he should thereby have a chance of wearing his new cloak in the evening also.

That whole day was truly a most triumphant festival day for Akakiy Akakievitch. He returned home in the most happy frame of mind, took off his cloak, and hung it carefully on the wall, admiring afresh the cloth and the lining. Then he brought out his old, worn-out cloak for comparison. He looked at it and laughed, so vast was the difference. And long after dinner he laughed again when the condition of the "cape" recurred to his mind. He dined cheerfully, and after dinner wrote nothing, but took his ease for a while on the bed, until it got dark. Then he dressed himself leisurely, put on his cloak, and stepped out into the street. Where the host lived, unfortunately, we can not say; our memory begins to fail us badly; and the houses and streets in St. Petersburg have become so mixed up in our head that it is very difficult to get anything out of it again in proper form. This much is certain, that the official lived in the best part of the city; and, therefore, it must have been anything but near to Akakiy Akakievitch's residence. Akakiy Akakievitch was first obliged to traverse a kind of wilderness of deserted, dimly lighted streets; but in proportion as he approached the official's quarter of the city the streets became more lively, more populous, and more brilliantly illuminated. Pedestrians began to appear; handsomely dressed ladies were more frequently encountered; the men had otter-skin collars to their coats; peasant wagoners, with their gratelike sledges stuck over with brass-headed nails, became rarer; while, on the other hand, more and more drivers in red velvet caps, lacquered sledges, and bear-skin coats began to appear, and carriages with rich ham-mer-cloths flew swiftly through the streets, their wheels crunching the snow. Akakiy Akakievitch gazed upon all this as upon a novel sight. He had not been in the streets during the evening for years. He halted out of curiosity before a shop-window, to look at a picture representing a handsome woman, who had thrown off her shoe, thereby baring her whole foot in a very pretty way; while behind her the head of a man with whiskers and a handsome mustache peeped through the doorway of another room. Akakiy Akakievitch shook his head and laughed, and then went on his way. Why did he laugh? Either because he had met with a thing utterly unknown, but for which every one cherishes, nevertheless, some sort of feeling; or else he thought, like many officials, as follows: "Well, those French! What is to be said? If they do go in anything of that sort, why—" But possibly he did not think at all.

Akakiy Akakievitch at length reached the house in which the subchief lodged. The subchief lived in fine style; the staircase was lit by a lamp, his apartment being on the second floor. On entering the vestibule, Akakiy Akakievitch beheld a whole row of goloshes on the floor. Among them, in the centre of the room, stood a samovar, or tea-urn, humming and emitting clouds of steam. On the walls hung all sorts of coats and cloaks, among which there were even some with beaver collars or velvet facings. Beyond, the buzz of conversation was audible, and became clear and loud when the servant came out with a trayful of empty glasses, cream-jugs, and sugar-bowls. It was evident that the officials had arrived long before, and had already finished their first glass of tea.

Akakiy Akakievitch, having hung up his own cloak, entered the inner room. Before him all at once appeared lights, officials, pipes, and cardtables; and he was bewildered by a sound of rapid conversation rising from all the tables, and the noise of moving chairs. He halted very awkwardly in the middle of the room, wondering what he ought to do. But they had seen him. They received him with a shout, and all thronged at once into the anteroom, and there took another look at his cloak. Akakiy Akakievitch, although somewhat confused, was frank-hearted, and could not refrain from rejoicing when he saw how they praised his cloak. Then, of course, they all dropped him and his cloak, and returned, as was proper, to the tables set out for whist.

All this, the noise, the talk, and the throng of people was rather overwhelming to Akakiy Akakievitch. He simply did not know where he stood, or where to put his hands, his feet, and his whole body. Finally he sat down by the players, looked at the cards, gazed at the face of one and another, and after a while began to gape, and to feel that it was wearisome, the more so as the hour was already long past when he usually went to bed. He wanted to take leave of the host; but they would not let him go, saying that he must not fail to drink a glass of champagne, in honor of his new garment. In the course of an hour, supper, consisting of vegetables, salad, cold veal, pastry, confectioner's pies, and champagne, was served. They made Akakiy Akakievitch drink two glasses of champagne, after which he felt things grow livelier.

Still, he could not forget that it was twelve o'clock, and that he should have been at home long ago. In order that the host might not think of some excuse for detaining him, he stole out of the room quickly, sought out, in the anteroom, his cloak, which, to his sorrow, he found lying on the floor, brushed it, picked off every speck upon it, put it on his shoulders, and descended the stairs to the street.

In the street all was still bright. Some petty shops, those permanent clubs of servants and all sorts of folks, were open. Others were shut, but, nevertheless, showed a streak of light the whole length of the door-crack, indicating that they were not yet free of company, and that probably some domestics, male and female, were finishing their stories and conversations, while leaving their masters in complete ignorance as to their whereabouts. Akakiy Akakievitch went on in a happy frame of mind: he even started to run, without knowing why, after some lady, who flew past like a flash of lightning. But he stopped short, and went on very quietly as before, wondering why he had quickened his pace. Soon there spread before him those deserted streets, which are not cheerful in the daytime, to say nothing of the evening. Now they were even more dim and lonely: the lanterns began to grow rarer, oil, evidently, had been less liberally supplied. Then came wooden houses and fences: not a soul anywhere; only the snow sparkled in the streets and mournfully veiled the low-roofed cabins with their closed shutters. He approached the spot where the street crossed a vast square with houses barely visible on its farther side, a square which seemed a fearful desert.

Afar, a tiny spark glimmered from some watchman's box, which seemed to stand on the edge of the world. Akakiy Akakievitch's cheerfulness diminished at this point in a marked degree. He entered the square, not without an involuntary sensation of fear, as though his heart warned him of some evil. He glanced back and on both sides, it was like a sea about him. "No, it is better not to look," he thought, and went on, closing his eyes. When he opened them, to see whether he was near the end of the square, he suddenly beheld, standing just before his very nose, some bearded individuals of precisely what sort he could not make out. All grew dark before his eyes, and his heart throbbed.

"But, of course, the cloak is mine!" said one of them in a loud voice, seizing hold of his collar. Akakiy Akakievitch was about to shout "watch" when the second man thrust a fist about the size of a man's head into his mouth, muttering, "Now scream!"

Akakiy Akakievitch felt them strip off his cloak and give him a push with a knee; he fell headlong upon the snow, and felt no more. In a few minutes he recovered consciousness, and rose to his feet; but no one was there. He felt that it was cold in the square and that his cloak was gone; he began to shout, but his voice did not appear to reach to the outskirts of the square. In despair, but without ceasing to shout, he started at a run across the square, straight toward the watch-box, beside which stood the watchman, leaning on his halberd, and apparently curious to know what kind of a customer was running toward him and shouting. Akakiy Akakievitch ran up to him, and began in a sobbing voice to shout that he was asleep and attended to nothing, and did not see when a man was robbed. The watchman replied that he had seen two men stop him in the middle of the square, but supposed that they were friends of his; and that, instead of scolding vainly, he had better go to the police on the morrow, so that they might make a search for whoever had stolen the cloak.

Akakiy Akakievitch ran home in complete disorder; his hair, which grew very thinly upon his temples and the back of his head, wholly disordered; his body, arms, and legs covered with snow. The old woman, who was mistress of his lodgings, on hearing a terrible knocking, sprang hastily from her bed, and, with only one shoe on, ran to open the door, pressing the sleeve of her chemise to her bosom out of modesty; but when she had opened it she fell back on beholding Akakiy Akakievitch in such a state. When he told her about the affair she clasped her hands, and said that he must go straight to the district chief of police, for his subordinate would turn up his nose, promise well, and drop the matter there. The very best thing to do, therefore, would be to go to the district chief, whom she knew, because Finnish Anna, her former cook, was now nurse at his house. She often saw him passing the house; and he was at church every Sunday, praying, but at the same time gazing cheerfully at everybody; so that he must be a good man, judging from all appearances. Having listened to this opinion, Akakiy Akakievitch betook himself sadly to his room; and how he spent the night there any one who can put himself in another's place may readily imagine.

Early in the morning he presented himself at the district chief's; but was told that this official was asleep. He went again at ten and was again informed that he was asleep; at eleven, and they said, "The superintendent is not at home;" at dinner time, and the clerks in the anteroom would not admit him on any terms, and insisted upon knowing his business. So that at last, for once in his life, Akakiy Akakievitch felt an inclination to show some spirit, and said curtly that he must see the chief in person; that they ought not to presume to refuse him entrance; that he came from the department of justice, and that when he complained of them, they would see.

The clerks dared make no reply to this, and one of them went to call the chief, who listened to the strange story of the theft of the coat. Instead of directing his attention to the principal points of the matter, he began to question Akakiy Akakievitch: Why was he going home so late? Was he in the habit of doing so, or had he been to some disorderly house? So that Akakiy Akakievitch got thoroughly confused, and left him without knowing whether the affair of his cloak was in proper train or not.

All that day, for the first time in his life, he never went near the department. The next day he made his appearance, very pale, and in his old cape, which had become even more shabby. The news of the robbery of the cloak touched many; although there were some officials present who never lost an opportunity, even such a one as the present, of ridiculing Akakiy Akakievitch. They decided to make a collection for him on the spot, but the officials had already spent a great deal in subscribing for the director's portrait, and for some book, at the suggestion of the head of that division, who was a friend of the author; and so the sum was trifling.

One of them, moved by pity, resolved to help Akakiy Akakievitch with some good advice at least, and told him that he ought not to go to the police, for although it might happen that a police officer, wishing to win the approval of his superiors, might hunt up the cloak by some means, still his cloak would remain in the possession of the police if he did not offer legal proof that it belonged to him. The best thing for him, therefore, would be to apply to a certain prominent personage; since this prominent personage, by entering into relations with the proper persons, could greatly expedite the matter.

As there was nothing else to be done, Akakiy Akakievitch decided to go to the prominent personage. What was the exact official position of the prominent personage remains unknown to this day. The reader must know that the prominent personage had but recently become a prominent personage, having up to that time been only an insignificant person. Moreover, his present position was not considered prominent in comparison with others still more so. But there is always a circle of people to whom what is insignificant in the eyes of others is important enough. Moreover, he strove to increase his importance by sundry devices; for instance, he managed to have the inferior officials meet him on the staircase when he entered upon his service; no one was to presume to come directly to him, but the strictest etiquette must be observed; the collegiate recorder must make a report to the government secretary, the government secretary to the titular councilor, or whatever other man was proper, and all business must come before him in this manner. In Holy Russia all is thus contaminated with the love of imitation; every man imitates and copies his superior. They even say that a certain titular councilor, when promoted to the head of some small separate room, immediately partitioned off a private room for himself, called it the audience chamber, and posted at the door a lackey with red collar and braid, who grasped the handle of the door and opened to all comers; though the audience chamber would hardly hold an ordinary writing table.

The manners and customs of the prominent personage were grand and imposing, but rather exaggerated. The main foundation of his system was strictness. "Strictness, strictness, and always strictness!" he generally said; and at the last word he looked significantly into the face of the person to whom he spoke. But there was no necessity for this, for the half-score of subordinates, who formed the entire force of the office, were properly afraid; on catching sight of him afar off, they left their work, and waited, drawn up in line, until he had passed through the room. His ordinary converse with his inferiors smacked of sternness, and consisted chiefly of three phrases: "How dare you?" "Do you know whom you are speaking to?" "Do you realize who stands before you?"

Otherwise he was a very kind-hearted man, good to his comrades, and ready to oblige; but the rank of general threw him completely off his balance. On receiving any one of that rank he became confused, lost his way, as it were, and never knew what to do. If he chanced to be among his equals, he was still a very nice kind of man, a very good fellow in many respects, and not stupid; but the very moment that he found himself in the society of people but one rank lower than himself, he became silent; and his situation aroused sympathy, the more so as he felt himself that he might have been making an incomparably better use of his time. In his eyes there was sometimes visible a desire to join some interesting conversation or group; but he was kept back by the thought, "Would it not be a very great condescension on his part? Would it not be familiar? and would he not thereby lose his importance?" And in consequence of such reflections he always remained in the same dumb state, uttering from time to time a few monosyllabic sounds, and thereby earning the name of the most wearisome of men.

To this prominent personage, Akakiy Akakievitch presented himself, and this at the most unfavorable time for himself, though opportune for the prominent personage. The prominent personage was in his cabinet, conversing very gaily with an old acquaintance and companion of his childhood, whom he had not seen for several years, and who had just arrived, when it was announced to him that a person named Bashmatchkin had come. He asked abruptly: "Who is he?" "Some official," he was informed. "Ah, he can wait! this is no time for him to call," said the important man.

It must be remarked here that the important man lied outrageously: he had said all he had to say to his friend long before; and the conversation had been interspersed for some time with very long pauses, during which they merely slapped each other on the leg, and said: "You think so, Ivan Abramovitch?" "Just so, Stephan Varlamovitch!" Nevertheless, he ordered that the official should be kept waiting, in order to show his friend, a man who had not been in the service for a long time, but had lived at home in the country, how long officials had to wait in his anteroom.

At length, having talked himself completely out, and more than that, having had his fill of pauses, and smoked a cigar in a very comfortable armchair with reclining back, he suddenly seemed to recollect, and said to the secretary, who stood by the door with papers of reports, "So it seems that there is a tchinovnik waiting to see me. Tell him that he may come in." On perceiving Akakiy Akakievitch's modest mien and his worn undress uniform, he turned abruptly to him and said: "What do you want?" in a curt, hard voice, which he had practised in his room in private, and before the looking-glass, for a whole week before being raised to his present rank.

Akakiy Akakievitch, who was already imbued with a due amount of fear, became somewhat confused; and, as well as his tongue would permit, explained, with a rather more frequent addition than usual of the word "that," that his cloak was quite new and had been stolen in the most inhuman manner; that he had applied to him in order that he might, in some way, by his intermediation—that he might enter into correspondence with the chief of police, and find the cloak.

For some inexplicable reason this conduct seemed familiar to the prominent personage. "What, my dear sir!" he said abruptly, "are you not acquainted with etiquette? Where have you come from? Don't you know how such matters are managed? You should first have entered a complaint about this at the court below: it would have gone to the head of the department, then to the chief of the division, then it would have been handed over to the secretary, and the secretary would have given it to me."

"But, your excellency," said Akakiy Akakievitch, trying to collect his small handful of wits, and conscious at the same time that he was perspiring terribly, "I, your excellency, presumed to trouble you because secretaries— are an untrustworthy race."

"What, what, what!" said the important personage. "Where did you get such courage? Where did you get such ideas? What impudence toward their chiefs and superiors has spread among the young generation!" The prominent personage apparently had not observed that Akakiy Akakievitch was already in the neighborhood of fifty. If he could be called a young man, it must have been in comparison with some one who was seventy. "Do you know to whom you speak? Do you realize who stands before you? Do you realize it? do you realize it? I ask you!" Then he stamped his foot and raised his voice to such a pitch that it would have frightened even a different man from Akakiy Akakievitch.

Akakiy Akakievitch's senses failed him; he staggered, trembled in every limb, and, if the porters had not run in to support him, would have fallen to the floor. They carried him out insensible. But the prominent personage, gratified that the effect should have surpassed his expectations, and quite intoxicated with the thought that his word could even deprive a man of his senses, glanced sidewise at his friend in order to see how he looked upon this, and perceived, not without satisfaction, that his friend was in a most uneasy frame of mind, and even beginning, on his part, to feel a trifle frightened.

Akakiy Akakievitch could not remember how he descended the stairs, and got into the street. He felt neither his hands nor feet. Never in his life had he been so rated by any high official, let alone a strange one. He went staggering on through the snowstorm, which was blowing in the streets, with his mouth wide open, the wind, in St. Petersburg fashion, darted upon him from all quarters, and down every cross street. In a twinkling it had blown a quinsy into his throat, and he reached home unable to utter a word. His throat was swollen, and he lay down on his bed. So powerful is sometimes a good scolding!

The next day a violent fever showed itself. Thanks to the generous assistance of the St. Petersburg climate, the malady progressed more rapidly than could have been expected; and when the doctor arrived, he found, on feeling the sick man's pulse, that there was nothing to be done, except to prescribe a fomentation, so that the patient might not be left entirely without the beneficent aid of medicine; but at the same time he predicted his end in thirty-six hours. After this he turned to the landlady, and said: "And as for you, don't waste your time on him: order his pine coffin now, for an oak one will be too expensive for him." Did Akakiy Akakievitch hear these fatal words? and if he heard them, did they produce any overwhelming effect upon him? Did he lament the bitterness of his life? We know not, for he continued in a delirious condition. Visions incessantly appeared to him each stranger than the other. Now he saw Petrovitch and ordered him to make a cloak with some traps for robbers who seemed to him to be always under the bed; and cried every moment to the landlady to pull one of them from under his coverlet. Then he inquired why his old mantle hung before him when he had a new cloak. Next he fancied that he was standing before the prominent person listening to a thorough setting-down and saying: "Forgive me, your excellency!" but at last he began to curse, uttering the most horrible words, so that his aged landlady crossed herself, never in her life having heard anything of the kind from him, the more so, as those words followed directly after the words "your excellency." Later on he talked utter nonsense, of which nothing could be made: all that was evident being that his incoherent words and thoughts hovered ever about one thing, his cloak.

At length poor Akakiy Akakievitch breathed his last. They sealed up neither his room nor his effects, because, in the first place, there were no heirs, and, in the second, there was very little to inherit beyond a bundle of goose-quills, a quire of white official paper, three pairs of socks, two or three buttons which had burst off his trousers, and the mantle already known to the reader. To whom all this fell, God knows. I confess that the person who told me this tale took no interest in the matter. They carried Akakiy Akakievitch out, and buried him.

And St. Petersburg was left without Akakiy Akakievitch, as though he had never lived there. A being disappeared, who was protected by none, dear to none, interesting to none, and who never even attracted to himself the attention of those students of human nature, who omit no opportunity of thrusting a pin through a common fly, and examining it under the microscope. A being who bore meekly the jibes of the department, and went to his grave without having done one unusual deed, but to whom, nevertheless, at the close of his life, appeared a bright visitant in the form of a cloak, which momentarily cheered his poor life, and upon whom, thereafter, an intolerable misfortune descended, just as it descends upon the heads of the mighty of this world!

Several days after his death, the porter was sent from the department to his lodgings with an order for him to present himself there immediately; the chief commanding it. But the porter had to return unsuccessful, with the answer that he could not come; and to the question, "Why?" replied, "Well, because he is dead! he was buried four days ago." In this manner did they hear of Akakiy Akakievitch's death at the department; and the next day a new official sat in his place, with a handwriting by no means so upright, but more inclined and slanting.

But who could have imagined that this was not really the end of Akakiy Akakievitch, that he was destined to raise a commotion after death, as if in compensation for his utterly insignificant life? But so it happened, and our poor story unexpectedly gains a fantastic ending.

A rumor suddenly spread through St. Petersburg that a dead man had taken to appearing on the Kalinkin Bridge and its vicinity, at night, in the form of a tchinovnik seeking a stolen cloak, and that, under the pretext of its being the stolen cloak, he dragged, without regard to rank or calling, every one's cloak from his shoulders, be it catskin, beaver, fox, bear, sable; in a word, every sort of fur and skin which men adopted for their covering. One of the department officials saw the dead man with his own eyes, and immediately recognized in him Akakiy Akakievitch. This, however, inspired him with such terror that he ran off with all his might, and therefore did not scan the dead man closely, but only saw how the latter threatened him from afar with his finger. Constant complaints poured in from all quarters, of those who were exposed to the danger of a cold, on account of the frequent dragging off of their cloaks.

Arrangements were made by the police to catch the corpse, alive or dead, at any cost, and punish him as an example to others, in the most severe manner. In this they nearly succeeded; for a watchman, on guard in Kirushkin Alley, caught the corpse by the collar on the very scene of his evil deeds, when attempting to pull off the frieze cloak of a retired musician. Having seized him by the collar, he summoned, with a shout, two of his comrades, whom he enjoined to hold him fast, while he himself felt for a moment in his boot, in order to draw out his snuff-box, and refresh his frozen nose. But the snuff was of a sort which even a corpse could not endure. The watchman, having closed his right nostril with his finger, had no sooner succeeded in holding half a handful up to the left than the corpse sneezed so violently that he completely filled the eyes of all three. While they raised their hands to wipe them, the dead man vanished completely, so that they positively did not know whether they had actually had him in their grip at all. Thereafter the watchmen conceived such a terror of dead men that they were afraid even to seize the living, and only screamed from a distance: "Hey, there! go your way!" So the dead tchinovnik began to appear, even beyond the Kalinkin Bridge, causing no little terror to all timid people.

But we have totally neglected that certain prominent personage, who may really be considered as the cause of the fantastic turn taken by this true history. First of all, justice compels us to say that after the departure of poor, annihilated Akakiy Akakievitch, he felt something like remorse. Suffering was unpleasant to him, for his heart was accessible to many good impulses, in spite of the fact that his rank often prevented his showing his true self. As soon as his friend had left his cabinet he began to think about poor Akakiy Akakievitch. And from that day forth poor Akakiy Akakievitch, who could not bear up under an official reprimand, recurred to his mind almost every day. The thought troubled him to such an extent that a week later he even resolved to send an official to him, to learn whether he really could assist him; and when it was reported to him that Akakiy Akakievitch had died suddenly of fever, he was startled, harkened to the reproaches of his conscience, and was out of sorts for the whole day.

Wishing to divert his mind in some way, and drive away the disagreeable impression, he set out that evening for one of his friends' houses, where he found quite a large party assembled. What was better, nearly every one was of the same rank as himself, so that he need not feel in the least constrained. This had a marvelous effect upon his mental state. He grew expansive, made himself agreeable in conversation, in short, he passed a delightful evening. After supper he drank a couple of glasses of champagne—not a bad recipe for cheerfulness, as every one knows. The champagne inclined him to various adventures; and he determined not to return home, but to go and see a certain well-known lady, of German extraction, Karolina Ivanovna, a lady, it appears, with whom he was on a very friendly footing.

It must be mentioned that the prominent personage was no longer a young man, but a good husband, and respected father of a family. Two sons, one of whom was already in the service; and a good-looking, sixteen-year-old daughter, with a rather *retroussé* but pretty little nose, came every morning to kiss his hand, and say: *"Bon jour,* papa." His wife, a still fresh and good-looking woman, first gave him her hand to kiss, and then, reversing the procedure, kissed his. But the prominent personage, though perfectly satisfied in his domestic relations, considered it stylish to have a friend in another quarter of the city. This friend was scarcely prettier or younger than his wife; but there are such puzzles in the world, and it is not our place to judge them. So the important personage descended the stairs, stepped into his sledge, said to the coachman, "To Karolina Ivanovna's," and, wrapping himself luxuriously in his warm cloak, found himself in that delightful frame of mind than which a Russian can conceive nothing better, namely, when you think of nothing yourself, yet when the thoughts creep into your mind of their own accord, each more agreeable than the other, giving you no trouble either to drive them away or seek them. Fully satisfied, he recalled all the gay features of the evening just passed, and all the *mots* which had made the little circle laugh. Many of them he repeated in a low voice, and found them quite as funny as before; so it is not surprising that he should laugh heartily at them. Occasionally, however, he was interrupted by gusts of wind, which, coming suddenly, God knows whence or why, cut his face, drove masses of snow into it, filled out his cloak-collar like a sail, or suddenly blew it over his head with supernatural force, and thus caused him constant trouble to disentangle himself.

Suddenly the important personage felt some one clutch him firmly by the collar. Turning round, he perceived a man of short stature, in an old, worn uniform, and recognized, not without terror, Akakiy Akakievitch. The official's face was white as snow, and looked just like a corpse's. But the horror of the important personage transcended all bounds when he saw the dead man's mouth open, and, with a terrible odor of the grave, give vent to the following remarks: "Ah, here you are at last! I have you, that—by the collar! I need your cloak; you took no trouble about mine, but reprimanded me; so now give up your own."

The pallid prominent personage almost died of fright. Brave as he was in the office and in the presence of inferiors generally, and although, at the sight of his manly form and appearance, every one said, "Ugh! how much character he has!" at this crisis, he, like many possessed of a heroic exterior, experienced such terror that, not without cause, he began to fear an attack of illness. He flung his cloak hastily from his shoulders and shouted to his coachman in an unnatural voice: "Home at full speed." The coachman, hearing the tone which is generally employed at critical moments, and even accompanied by something much more tangible, drew his head down between his shoulders in case of an emergency, flourished his whip, and flew on like an arrow. In a little more than six minutes the prominent personage was at the entrance of his own house. Pale, thoroughly scared, and cloakless, he went home instead of to Karolina Ivanovna's, reached his room somehow or other, and passed the night in the direst distress; so that the next morning over their tea his daughter said: "You are very pale to-day, papa." But papa remained silent, and said not a word to any one of what had happened to him, where he had been, or where he had intended to go.

This occurrence made a deep impression upon him. He even began to say:

"How dare you? do you realize who stands before you?" less frequently to the under-officials, and, if he did utter the words, it was only after first having learned the bearings of the matter. But the most noteworthy point was that from that day forward the apparition of the dead tchinovnik ceased to be seen. Evidently the prominent personage's cloak just fitted his shoulders; at all events, no more instances of his dragging cloaks from people's shoulders were heard of. But many active and apprehensive persons could by no means reassure themselves, and asserted that the dead tchinovnik still showed himself in distant parts of the city.

In fact, one watchman in Kolomna saw with his own eyes the apparition come from behind a house. But being rather weak of body, he dared not arrest him, but followed him in the dark, until, at length, the apparition looked round, paused, and inquired: "What do you want?" at the same time showing such a fist as is never seen on living men. The watchman said: "It's of no consequence," and turned back instantly. But the apparition was much too tall, wore huge mustaches, and, directing its steps apparently toward the Obukhoff Bridge, disappeared in the darkness of the night.

RAILROAD AND CHURCHYARD

Björnstjerne Björnson

I

Knud Aakre belonged to an old family in the parish, where it had always been renowned for its intelligence and its devotion to the public welfare. His father had worked his way up to the priesthood, but had died early, and as the widow came from a peasant stock the children were brought up as peasants. Knud had, therefore, received only the education afforded by the public schools of his day; but his father's library had early inspired him with a love of knowledge. This was further stimulated by his friend Henrik Wergeland, who frequently visited him, sent him books, seeds, and much valuable counsel. Following some of the latter, Knud early founded a club, which in the beginning had a very miscellaneous object, for instance: "to give the members practise in debating and to study the constitution," but which later was turned into a practical agricultural society for the entire bailiwick. According to Wergeland's advice, he also founded a parish library, giving his father's books as its first endowment. A suggestion from the same quarter led him to start a Sunday-school on his gard, for those who might wish to learn writing, arithmetic, and history. All this drew attention to him, so that he was elected member of the parish board of supervisors, of which he soon became chairman. In this capacity he took a deep interest in the schools, which he brought into a remarkably good condition.

Knud Aakre was a short man, brisk in his movements, with small, restless eyes and very disorderly hair. He had large lips, which were in constant motion, and a row of splendid teeth which always seemed to be working with them, for they glistened while his words were snapped out, crisp and clear, crackling like sparks from a great fire.

Foremost among the many he had helped to gain an education was his neighbor Lars Högstad. Lars was not much younger than Knud, but he had developed more slowly. Knud liked to talk about what he read and thought, and he found in Lars, whose manner was quiet and grave, a good listener, who by degrees grew to be a man of excellent judgment. The relations between them soon became such that Knud was never willing to take any important step without first consulting Lars Högstad, and the matter on hand was thus likely to gain some practical amendment. So Knud drew his neighbor into the board of supervisors, and gradually into everything in which he himself took part. They always drove together to the meetings of the board, where Lars never spoke; but on the way back and forth Knud learned his opinions. The two were looked upon as inseparable.

One fine autumn day the board of supervisors convened to consider, among other things, a proposal from the bailiff to sell the parish grain magazine and with the proceeds establish a small savings-bank. Knud Aakre, the chairman, would undoubtedly have approved this measure had he relied on his unbiased judgment. But he was prejudiced, partly because the proposal came from the bailiff, whom Wergeland did not like, and who was consequently no favorite of Knud's either, and partly because the grain magazine had been built by his influential paternal grandfather and by him presented to the parish. Indeed, Knud was rather inclined to view the proposition as a personal insult, therefore he had not spoken of it to any one, not even to Lars, and the latter never entered on a topic that had not first been set afloat by some one else.

As chairman, Knud Aakre read the proposal without adding any comments; but, as was his wont, his eyes sought Lars, who usually sat or stood a little aside, holding a straw between his teeth—he always had one when he took part in a conversation; he either used it as a toothpick or he let it hang loosely in one corner of his mouth, turning it more rapidly or more slowly, according to the mood he was in. To his surprise Knud saw that the straw was moving very fast.

"Do you think we should agree to this?" he asked.

Lars answered dryly:

"Yes, I do."

The whole board, feeling that Knud held quite a different opinion, looked in astonishment at Lars, but the latter said no more, nor was he further questioned. Knud turned to another matter, as though nothing had transpired. Not until the close of the meeting did he resume the subject, and then asked, with apparent indifference, if it would not be well to send the proposal back to the bailiff for further consideration, as it certainly did not meet the views of the people, for the parish valued the grain magazine. No one replied. Knud asked whether he should enter the resolution in the register, the measure did not seem to be a wise one.

"Against one vote," added Lars. "Against two," cried another, promptly. "Against three," came from a third; and before the chairman could realize what was taking place, a majority had voted in favor of the proposal.

Knud was so surprised that he forgot to offer any opposition. He recorded the proceedings, and read, in a low voice: "The measure is recommended— adjourned."

His face was fiery red as he rose and put up the minute-book; but he determined to bring forward the question once more at the meeting of the representatives. Out in the yard, he put his horse to the wagon, and Lars came and took his seat at his side. They discussed various topics on their way home, but not the one they had nearest at heart.

The next day Knud's wife sought Lars's wife to inquire if there was anything wrong between the two men, for Knud had acted so strangely when he came home. A short distance above the gard buildings she met Lars's wife, who was on her way to ask the same question, for her husband, too, had been out of sorts the day before. Lars's wife was a quiet, bashful person, somewhat cowed, not by harsh words, but by silence, for Lars never spoke to her unless she had done something amiss, or he feared that she might do wrong. Knud Aakre's wife, on the other hand, talked more with her husband, and particularly about the board, for lately it had taken his thoughts, work, and affection away from her and the children. She was as jealous of it as of a woman; she wept at night over the board and quarreled with her husband about it during the day. But for that very reason she could say nothing about it now when for once he had returned home unhappy; for she immediately became more wretched than he, and for her life she could not rest until she had discovered what was the matter. Consequently, when Lars's wife could not give her the desired information, she had to go out in the parish to seek it. Here she obtained it, and of course was at once of her husband's opinion; she found Lars incomprehensible, not to say wicked. When, however, she let her husband perceive this, she felt that as yet there was no breach between Lars and him; and, that, on the contrary, he clung warmly to him.

The representatives met. Lars Högstad drove over to Aakre in the morning; Knud came out of the house and took his seat beside him. They exchanged the usual greetings, spoke perhaps rather less than was their wont on the way, and not of the proposal. All the members of the board were present; some, too, had found their way in as spectators, which Knud did not like, for it showed that there was a stir in town about the matter. Lars was armed with his straw, and he stood by the stove warming himself, for the autumn was beginning to be cold. The chairman read the proposal, in a subdued, cautious manner, remarking when he was through that it must be remembered this came from the bailiff, who was not apt to be very felicitous in his proposals. The building, it was well known, was a gift, and it was not usual to part with gifts, especially when there was no need of doing so.

Lars, who never before had spoken at the meetings, now took the floor, to the astonishment of all. His voice trembled, but whether it did so out of regard for Knud, or from anxiety lest his own cause should be lost, shall remain unsaid. But his arguments were good and clear, and full of a logic and confidence which had scarcely been heard at these meetings before. And when he had gone over all the ground, he added, in conclusion:

"What does it matter if the proposal does come from the bailiff? This affects the question as little as who erected the building, or in what way it came into the public possession."

Knud Aakre had grown very red in the face (he blushed easily), and he shifted uneasily from side to side, as was his wont when he was impatient, but none the less did he exert himself to be circumspect and to speak in a low voice. There were savings-banks enough in the country, he thought, and quite near at hand, he might almost say *too* near. But if, after all, it was deemed expedient to have one, there were surely other ways of reaching it than those leading over the gifts of the dead and the love of the living. His voice was a little unsteady when he said this, but quickly recovered as he proceeded to speak of the grain magazine in itself, and to show what its advantages were.

Lars answered him thoroughly on the last point, and then added:

"However, one thing and another lead me to doubt whether this parish is managed for the sake of the living or the dead; furthermore, whether it is the love and hatred of a single family which controls matters here, or the good of the whole." Knud answered quickly: "I do not know whether he who has just spoken has been least benefited by his family—both by the dead and by him who now lives."

The first shot was aimed at the fact that Knud's powerful grandfather had saved the gard for Lars's paternal grandfather, when the latter, on his part, was absent on a little excursion to the penitentiary.

The straw which long had been in brisk motion suddenly became still.

"It is not my way to keep talking everywhere about myself and my family," said Lars, then turned again with calm superiority to the subject under discussion, briefly reviewing all the points with one definite object. Knud had to admit to himself that he had never viewed the matter from such a broad standpoint; involuntarily he raised his eyes and looked at Lars, who stood before him, tall, heavily built, with clearness on the vigorous brow and in the deep eyes. The lips were tightly compressed, the straw still played in the corner of his mouth; all the surrounding lines indicated vigor. He kept his hands behind him, and stood rigidly erect, while his voice was as deep and as hollow as if it proceeded from the depths of the earth. For the first time in his life Knud saw him as he was, and in his inmost soul he was afraid of him; for this man must always have been his superior. He had taken all Knud himself knew and could impart; he had rejected the tares and kept what produced this strong, hidden growth.

He had been fostered and loved by Knud, but had now become a giant who hated Knud deeply, terribly. Knud could not explain to himself why, but as he looked at Lars he instinctively felt this to be so, and all else becoming swallowed up in this thought he started up, exclaiming:

"But Lars! Lars! what in Heaven's name is the matter with you?" His agitation overcame him—"you, whom I have—you who have—"

Powerless to utter another word, he sat down; but in his effort to gain the mastery over the emotion he deemed Lars unworthy of seeing, he brought his fist down with violence on the table, while his eyes flashed beneath his stiff, disorderly hair, which always hung over them. Lars acted as if he had not been interrupted, and turning toward the others he asked if this was to be the decisive blow; for if such were the case there was no need for further remarks.

This calmness was more than Knud could endure.

"What is it that has come among us?" cried he. "We who have, until to-day, been actuated by love and zeal alone, are now stirred up against each other, as though goaded on by some evil spirit," and he cast a fiery glance at Lars, who replied:

"It must be you yourself who bring in this spirit, Knud; for I have kept strictly to the matter before us. But you never can see the advantage of anything you do not want yourself; now we shall learn what becomes of the love and the zeal when once this matter is decided as we wish."

"Have I then illy served the interests of the parish?"

There was no reply. This grieved Knud, and he continued: "I really did persuade myself that I had accomplished various things—various things which have been of advantage to the parish; but perhaps I have deceived myself."

He was again overcome by his feelings; for his was a fiery nature, ever variable in its moods, and the breach with Lars pained him so deeply that he could scarcely control himself. Lars answered:

"Yes, I know you appropriate the credit for all that is done here, and if one should judge by the amount of speaking at these meetings, you certainly have accomplished the most."

"Is that the way of it?" shouted Knud, looking sharply at Lars. "Is it you who deserve the entire honor?"

"Since we must finally talk about ourselves," said Lars, "I am free to admit that every question has been carefully considered by both of us before it was introduced here."

Here little Knud Aakre regained his ready speech:

"Take the honor, in God's name; I am able to live without it; there are other things harder to lose!"

Involuntarily Lars evaded his gaze, but said, as he set the straw in very rapid motion:

"If I were to express *my* opinion, I should say that there is not very much to take credit for. No doubt the priest and the schoolmasters are content with what has been done; but certainly the common people say that up to the present time the taxes of this parish have grown heavier and heavier."

Here arose a murmur in the crowd, and the people grew very restless. Lars continued:

"Finally, to-day we have a matter brought before us that might make the parish some little amends for all it has paid out; this is perhaps the reason why it encounters such opposition. This is a question which concerns the parish; it's for the good of all; it is our duty to guard it from becoming a mere family matter."

People exchanged glances, and spoke in half-audible tones; one of them remarked, as he rose to go for his dinner-pail, that these were the truest words he had heard in these meetings for many years. Now all rose from their seats, the conversation became general, and Knud Aakre, who alone remained sitting, felt that all was lost, fearfully lost, and made no further effort to save it. The truth was, he possessed something of the temperament attributed to Frenchmen: he was very good at a first, second, or even third attack, but poor at self-defense, for his sensibilities overwhelmed his thoughts. He was unable to comprehend this, nor could he sit still any longer, and so resigning his place to the vice-chairman, he left. The others could not refrain from a smile.

He had come to the meeting in company with Lars, but went home alone, although the way was long. It was a cold autumn day, the forest was jagged and bare, the meadow gray-yellow, frost was beginning here and there to remain on the roadside. Disappointment is a terrible companion. Knud felt so small, so desolate, as he walked along; but Lars appeared everywhere before him, towering up to the sky, in the dusk of the evening, like a giant. It vexed him to think it was his own fault that this had been the decisive battle; he had staked too much on one single little issue. But surprise, pain, anger, had mastered him; they still burned, tingled, moaned, and stormed within him. He heard the rumbling of cart-wheels behind him; it was Lars driving his superb horse past him, in a brisk trot, making the hard road resound like distant thunder. Knud watched the broad-shouldered form that sat erect in the cart, while the horse, eager for home, sped onward, without any effort on the part of Lars, who merely gave him a loose rein. It was but a picture of this man's power: he was driving onward to the goal! Knud felt himself cast out of his cart, to stagger on alone in the chill autumn air.

In his home at Aakre, Knud's wife was waiting for him. She knew that a battle was inevitable; she had never in her life trusted Lars, and now she was positively afraid of him. It had been no comfort to her that he and her husband had driven away together; it would not have consoled her had they returned in the same way. But darkness had fallen and they had not come. She stood in the doorway, gazing out on the road in front of the house; she walked down the hill and back again, but no cart appeared.

Finally she hears a rattling on the hard road, her heart throbs as the wheels go round, she clings to the casement, peering out into the night; the cart draws near; only one is in it; she recognizes Lars, who sees and recognizes her, but drives past without stopping. Now she became thoroughly alarmed. Her limbs gave way under her, she tottered in and sank down on the bench by the window. The children gathered anxiously about her, the youngest one asked for papa; she never spoke with them except of him. He had such a noble disposition, and this was what made her love him; but now his heart was not with his family, it was engrossed in all sorts of business which brought him only unhappiness, and so they were all unhappy.

If only no misfortune had befallen him! Knud was so hot-tempered. Why had Lars come home alone? Why did he not stop? Should she run after him, or down the road after her husband? She was in an agony of distress, and the children pressed around her, asking what was the matter. But this she would not tell them, so rising she said they must eat supper alone, then got everything ready and helped them. All the while she kept glancing out on the road. He did not come. She undressed the children and put them to bed, and the youngest repeated the evening prayer while she bowed over him. She herself prayed with such fervor in the words which the infant lips so soothingly uttered that she did not heed the steps outside.

Knud stood upon the threshold, gazing at his little company at prayer. The mother drew herself up; all the children shouted: "Papa!" but he seated himself at once, and said, softly: "Oh, let him say it once more!"

The mother turned again to the bedside, that he, meanwhile, should not see her face, for it would have seemed like intruding on his grief before he felt the need of revealing it. The little one folded its hands over its breast, all the rest did likewise, and it repeated:

> "I, a little child, pray Heaven
> That my sins may be forgiven;
> With time, I'll larger, wiser grow,
> And my father and mother joy shall know,
> If only Thou, dearest, dearest Lord,
> Will help me to keep Thy precious word!
> And now to our Heavenly Father's merciful keeping
> Our souls let us trust while we're sleeping."

What peace now fell upon the room! Not a minute had elapsed ere all the children were sleeping as in the arms of God; but the mother moved softly away and placed supper before the father, who was, however, unable to eat. But after he had gone to bed, he said:

"Henceforth I shall be at home."

And his wife lay at his side trembling with joy which she dared not betray; and she thanked God for all that had happened, for whatever it might be it had resulted in good!

II

In the course of a year Lars had become chairman of the parish board of supervisors, president of the savings-bank, and leading commissioner in the court of reconciliation; in short, he held every office to which his election had been possible. In the board of supervisors for the amt (county) he was silent during the first year, but the second year he created the same sensation when he spoke as in the parish board; for here, too, coming forward in opposition to him who had previously been the guiding power, he became victorious over the entire rank and file, and was from that time himself the leader. From this his path led him to the storthing (parliament), where his fame had preceded him, and where consequently there was no lack of challenges. But here, although steady and firm, he always remained retiring. He did not care for power, except where he was well known, nor would he risk leadership at home by a possible defeat abroad.

For he had a pleasant life at home. When he stood by the church wall on Sundays, and the congregation walked slowly past, saluting him and stealing side glances at him, and one after another paused in order to exchange a few words with him—then truly it might be said that he controlled the entire parish with a straw, for of course this hung in the corner of his mouth.

He deserved his honors. The road leading to the church, he had opened; the new church they were standing beside, he had built; this and much more was the fruit of the savings-bank which he had founded and now managed himself. For its resources were further made fruitful, and the parish was constantly held up as an example to all others of self-management and good order.

Knud Aakre had entirely withdrawn from the field, although at first he attended a few of the meetings of the board, because he had promised himself that he would continue to offer his services, even if it were not altogether pleasing to his pride. In the first proposal he had made he became so greatly perplexed by Lars, who insisted upon having it represented in all its details, that, somewhat hurt, he said: "When Columbus discovered America he did not have it divided into parishes and deaneries: this came gradually;" whereupon Lars, in his reply, compared the discovery of America with Knud's proposal—it so happened that this treated of stable improvements—and afterward Knud was known by no other name in the board than "Discovery of America." So Knud thought that as his usefulness had ceased, so too had his obligations to work, and he refused to accept further reelections.

But he continued to be industrious; and in order that he might still have a field for usefulness, he enlarged his Sunday-school, and placed it, by means of small contributions from the attendants, in communication with the mission cause, of which he soon became the centre and leader in his own and the surrounding counties. Thereupon Lars Högstad remarked, that if ever Knud undertook to collect money for any purpose, he must know beforehand that it was to do good thousands of miles from home.

There was, be it observed, no more strife between them. To be sure, they no longer associated with each other, but they bowed and spoke when they met.

Knud always felt a little pain at the mere thought of Lars, but strove to suppress it, and persuade himself that matters could not have been otherwise. At a large wedding-party, many years afterward, where both were present and both were in good spirits, Knud mounted a chair and proposed a toast for the chairman of the parish board, and the first representative their amt had sent to the storthing! He spoke until he became deeply moved, and, as usual, expressed himself in an exceedingly handsome way. Every one thought it was honorably done, and Lars came up to him, and his gaze was unsteady as he said that, for much of what he knew and was, he was indebted to him.

At the next election of the board of supervisors Knud was again made chairman!

But had Lars Högstad foreseen what now followed, he would certainly not have used his influence for this. "Every event happens in its own time," says an old proverb, and just as Knud Aakre again entered the board, the best men of the parish were threatened with ruin, as the result of a speculation craze which had long been raging, but which now first began to demand its victims. It was said that Lars Högstad was the cause of this great disaster, for he had taught the parish to speculate. This penny fever had originated in the parish board of supervisors, for the board itself was the greatest speculator of all. Every one down to the laboring youth of twenty years desired in his transactions to make ten dollars out of one; a beginning of extreme avarice in the efforts to hoard, was followed by an excessive extravagance, and as all minds were bent only on money, there had at the same time developed a spirit of suspicion, of intolerance, of caviling, which resulted in lawsuits and hatred. This also was due to the example of the board, it was said, for among the first things Lars had done as chairman was to sue the venerable old priest for holding doubtful titles. The priest had lost, but had also immediately resigned. At that time some had praised, some censured this suit; but it had proved a bad example. Now came the consequences of Lars's management, in the form of loss to every single man of property in the parish, consequently public opinion underwent a sharp change! The opposing force, too, soon found a leader, for Knud Aakre had come into the board, introduced by Lars.

The struggle began forthwith. All those youths to whom Knud in his time had given instructions, were now grown up and were the most enlightened men in the parish, thoroughly at home in all its transactions and public affairs. It was against these men that Lars now had to contend, and they had borne him a grudge from their childhood up. When of an evening after one of these stormy proceedings he stood on the steps in front of his house, gazing over the parish, he could hear a sound as of distant rumbling thunder rising toward him from the large gards, now lying in the storm. He knew that the day they met their ruin, the savings-bank and himself would be overthrown, and all his long efforts would culminate in imprecations on his own head.

In these days of conflict and despair, a party of railroad commissioners, who were to survey the route for a new road, made their appearance one evening at Högstad, the first gard at the entrance to the parish. In the course of conversation during the evening, Lars learned that there was a question whether the road should run through this valley or another parallel to it.

Like a flash of lightning it darted through his mind that if he could succeed in having it laid here, all property would rise in value, and not only would he himself be saved but his fame would be transmitted to the latest posterity! He could not sleep that night, for his eyes were dazzled by a glowing light, and sometimes he could even hear the sound of the cars. The next day he went himself with the commissioners while they examined the locality; his horse took them, and to his gard they returned. The next day they drove through the other valley; he was still with them, and he drove them back again to his house. They found a brilliant illumination at Högstad; the first men of the parish had been invited to be present at a magnificent party given in honor of the commissioners; it lasted until morning. But to no avail, for the nearer they came to a final issue, the more plainly it appeared that the road could not pass through this locality without undue expense. The entrance to the valley lay through a narrow gorge, and just as it swung into the parish, the swollen river swung in also, so that the railroad would either have to take the same curve along the mountain that the highway now made, thus running at a needlessly high altitude and crossing the river twice, or it would have to run straight forward, and thus through the old, now unused churchyard. Now the church had but recently been removed, and it was not long since the last burial had taken place there.

If it only depended on a bit of old churchyard, thought Lars, whether or not this great blessing came into the parish, then he must use his name and his energy for the removal of this obstacle! He at once set forth on a visit to the priest and the dean, and furthermore to the diocese council; he talked and he negotiated, for he was armed with all possible facts concerning the immense advantage of the railroad on one hand, and the sentiments of the parish on the other, and actually succeeded in winning all parties. It was promised him that by a removal of part of the bodies to the new churchyard the objections might be set aside, and the royal permission obtained for the churchyard to be taken for the line of railroad. It was told him that nothing was now needed but for him to set the question afloat in the board of supervisors.

The parish had grown as excited as himself: the spirit of speculation which for many years had been the only one prevailing in the parish, now became madly jubilant. There was nothing spoken or thought of but Lars's journey and its possible results. When he returned with the most magnificent promises, they made much of him; songs were sung in his praise; indeed, if at that time the largest gards had gone to destruction, one after another, no one would have paid any attention to it: the speculation craze had given way to the railroad craze.

The board of supervisors assembled: there was presented for approval a respectful petition, that the old churchyard might be appropriated as the route of the railroad. This was unanimously adopted; there was even mention of giving Lars a vote of thanks and a coffee-pot in the form of a locomotive. But it was finally thought best to wait until the whole plan was carried into execution. The petition came back from the diocese council, with a demand for a list of all bodies that would have to be removed. The priest made out such a list, but instead of sending it direct, he had his own reasons for sending it through the parish board. One of the members carried it to the next meeting. Here it fell to the lot of Lars, as chairman to open the envelope and read the list.

Now it chanced that the first body to be disinterred was that of Lars's own grandfather! A little shudder ran through the assembly! Lars himself was startled, but nevertheless continued to read. Then it furthermore chanced that the second body was that of Knud Aakre's grandfather, for these two men had died within a short time of each other. Knud Aakre sprang from his seat; Lars paused; everyone looked up in consternation, for old Knud Aakre had been the benefactor of the parish and its best beloved man, time out of mind. There was a dead silence, which lasted for some minutes. At last Lars cleared his throat and went on reading. But the further he proceeded the worse the matter grew; for the nearer they came to their own time, the dearer were the dead. When he had finished, Knud Aakre asked quietly whether the others did not agree with him in thinking that the air about them was filled with spirits. It was just beginning to grow dark in the room, and although they were mature men, sitting in numbers together, they could not refrain from feeling alarmed. Lars produced a bundle of matches from his pocket and struck a light, dryly remarking that this was no more than they knew before.

"Yes, it is," said Knud, pacing the floor, "it is more than I knew before. Now I begin to think that even railroads can be purchased too dearly."

These words sent a quiver through the audience, and, observing that they had better further consider the matter, Knud made a motion to that effect.

In the excitement which had prevailed, he said, the benefit likely to be derived from the road had been overestimated. Even if the railroad did not pass through this parish, there would have to be stations at both ends of the valley; true, it would always be a little more troublesome to drive to them than to a station right in our midst, yet the difficulty would not be so very great that it would be necessary because of it to violate the repose of the dead.

Knud was one of those who when his thoughts were once in rapid motion could present the most convincing arguments; a moment before what he now said had not occurred to his mind, nevertheless it struck home to all. Lars felt the danger of his position, and concluding that it was best to be cautious, apparently acquiesced in Knud's proposition to reconsider. Such emotions are always worse in the beginning, he thought; it is wisest to temporize with them.

But he had miscalculated. In ever-increasing waves the dread of touching the dead of their own families swept over the inhabitants of the parish; what none of them had thought of as long as the matter existed merely in the abstract, now became a serious question when it was brought home to themselves. The women especially were excited, and the road near the courthouse was black with people the day of the next meeting. It was a warm summer day, the windows were removed, and there were as many without the house as within. All felt that a battle was to be fought.

Lars came driving up with his handsome horse, and was greeted by all; he looked calmly and confidently around, not seeming to be surprised at anything. He took a seat near the window, found his straw, and a suspicion of a smile played over his keen face as he saw Knud Aakre rise to his feet to act as spokesman for all the dead in the old Högstad churchyard.

But Knud Aakre did not begin with the churchyard. He began with an accurate exposition of how greatly the profits likely to accrue from having the railroad run through the parish had been overestimated in all this turmoil. He had positive proofs for every statement he made; he had calculated the distance of each gard from the nearest station. Finally he asked:

"Why has there been so much ado about this railroad, if not in behalf of the parish?"

This he could easily explain to them. There were those who had occasioned so great a disturbance that a still greater one was required to conceal it. Moreover, there were those who in the first outburst of excitement could sell their gards and belongings to strangers who were foolish enough to purchase. It was a shameful speculation which not only the living but the dead must serve to promote!

The effect of his address was very considerable. But Lars had once for all resolved to preserve his composure let come what would. He replied, therefore, with a smile, that he had been under the impression that Knud himself was eager for the railroad, and certainly no one would accuse him of having any knowledge of speculation. (Here followed a little laugh.) Knud had not evinced the slightest objection to the removal of the bodies of common people for the sake of the railroad; but when his own grandfather's body was in question then it suddenly affected the welfare of the whole community! He said no more, but looked with a faint smile at Knud, as did also several others. Meanwhile, Knud Aakre surprised both him and them by replying:

"I confess it; I did not comprehend the matter until it touched my own family feelings; it is possible that this may be a shame, but it would have been a far greater one not to have realized it at last—as is the case with Lars! Never," he concluded, "could this raillery have been more out of place; for to people with common decency the whole affair is revolting."

"This feeling is something that has come up quite recently," replied Lars; "we may, therefore, hope that it will soon pass over again. May it not perhaps help the matter a little to think what the priest, dean, diocese council, engineers, and government will all say if we first unanimously set the ball in motion, then come and beg to have it stopped? If we first are jubilant and sing songs, then weep and deliver funeral orations? If they do not say that we have gone mad in this parish, they must at all events say that we have acted rather strangely of late."

"Yes, God knows, they may well think so!" replied Knud. "We have, in-deed, acted very strangely of late, and it is high time for us to mend our ways. Things have come to a serious pass when we can each disinter his own grand-father to make way for a railroad; when we can disturb the resting-place of the dead in order that our own burdens may the more easily be carried. For is not this rooting in our churchyard in order to make it yield us food the same thing? What is buried there in the name of Jesus, we take up in Moloch's name—this is but little better than eating the bones of our ancestors."

"Such is the course of nature," said Lars, dryly.

"Yes, of plants and of animals."

"And are not we animals?"

"We are, but also the children of the living God, who have buried our dead in faith in Him: it is He who shall rouse them and not we."

"Oh, you are talking idly! Are we not obliged to have the graves dug up at any rate, when their turn comes? What harm if it happen now?"

"I will tell you. What was born of them still draws the breath of life; what they built up yet remains; what they loved, taught, and suffered for, lives about us and within us; and should we not allow them to rest in peace?"

"Your warmth shows me that you are thinking of your own grandfather again," replied Lars, "and I must say it seems to me high time the parish should be rid of *him.* He monopolized too much space while he lived; and so it is scarcely worth while to have him lie in the way now that he is dead. Should his corpse prevent a blessing to this parish that would extend through a hundred generations, we may truly say that of all who have been born here, *he* has done us the greatest harm."

Knud Aakre tossed back his disorderly hair, his eyes flashed, his whole person looked like a bent steel spring.

"How much of a blessing what you are speaking about may be, I have already shown. It has the same character as all the other blessings with which you have supplied the parish, namely, a doubtful one. It is true, you have provided us with a new church, but you have also filled it with a new spirit— and it is not that of love. True, you have furnished us with new roads, but also with new roads to destruction, as is now plainly manifest in the misfortunes of many. True, you have diminished our public taxes, but you have increased our private ones; lawsuits, promissory notes, and bankruptcies are no fruitful gifts to a community. And *you* dare to dishonor in his grave the man whom the whole parish blesses? You dare assert that he lies in our way; ay, no doubt he does lie in your way, this is plain enough now, for his grave will be the cause of your downfall! The spirit which has reigned over you, and until to-day over us all, was not born to rule but to enter into servitude. The church-yard will surely be allowed to remain in peace; but to-day it shall have one grave added to it, namely, that of your popularity, which is now to be buried there."

Lars Högstad rose, white as a sheet; his lips parted, but he was unable to utter a word, and the straw fell. After a few vain efforts to find and recover his powers of speech, he burst forth like a volcano with:

"And so these are the thanks I get for all my toil and drudgery! If such a woman-preacher is to be allowed to rule—why, then, may the devil be your chairman if ever I set my foot here again! I have kept things together until this day, and after me your trash will fall into a thousand pieces, but let it tumble down now—here is the register!" And he flung it on the table. "Shame on such an assembly of old women and brats!" Here he struck the table with great violence. "Shame on the whole parish that it can see a man rewarded as I am now."

He brought down his fist once more with such force that the great court-house table shook, and the inkstand with its entire contents tumbled to the floor, marking for all future generations the spot where Lars Högstad fell in spite of all his prudence, his long rule, and his patience.

He rushed to the door and in a few moments had left the place. The entire assembly remained motionless; for the might of his voice and of his wrath had frightened them, until Knud Aakre, remembering the taunt he had received at the time of *his* fall, with beaming countenance and imitating Lars's voice, exclaimed:

"Is *this* to be the decisive blow in the matter?"

The whole assembly burst into peals of merriment at these words! The solemn meeting ended in laughter, talk, and high glee; only a few left the place, those remaining behind called for drink to add to their food, and a night of thunder succeeded a day of lightning. Every one felt as happy and independent as of yore, ere the commanding spirit of Lars had cowed their souls into dumb obedience. They drank toasts to their freedom; they sang, indeed, finally they danced, Knud Aakre and the vice-chairman taking the lead and all the rest following, while boys and girls joined in, and the young folks outside shouted "Hurrah!" for such a jollification they had never before seen!

III

Lars moved about in the large rooms at Högstad without speaking a word. His wife, who loved him, but always in fear and trembling, dared not come into his presence. The management of the gard and of the house might be carried on as best it could, while on the other hand there kept growing a multitude of letters, which passed back and forth between Högstad and the parish, and Högstad and the post-office; for Lars had claims against the parish board, and these not being satisfied he prosecuted; against the savings-bank, which were also unsatisfied, and so resulted in another suit. He took offense at expressions in the letters he received and went to law again, now against the chairman of the parish board, now against the president of the savings-bank. At the same time there were dreadful articles in the newspapers, which report attributed to him, and which were the cause of great dissension in the parish, inciting neighbor against neighbor. Sometimes he was absent whole weeks, no one knew where, and when he returned he lived as secluded as before. At church he had not been seen after the great scene at the representatives' meeting.

Then one Saturday evening the priest brought tidings that the railroad was to run through the parish after all, and across the old churchyard! It struck like lightning into every home. The unanimous opposition of the parish board had been in vain, Lars Högstad's influence had been stronger. This was the meaning of his journeys, this was his work! Involuntary admiration of the man and his stubborn persistence tended to suppress the dissatisfaction of the people at their own defeat, and the more they discussed the matter the more reconciled they became; for a fact accomplished always contains within itself reasons why it is so, which gradually force themselves upon us after there is no longer possibility of change. The people assembled about the church the next day, and they could not help laughing as they met one another. And just as the whole congregation, young and old, men and women, ay, even children, were all talking about Lars Högstad, his ability, his rigorous will, his immense influence, he himself with his whole household came driving up in four conveyances, one after the other. It was two years since his last visit there! He alighted and passed through the crowd, while all, as by one impulse, unhesitatingly greeted him, but he did not deign to bestow a glance on either side, nor to return a single salutation. His little wife, pale as death, followed him. Inside of the church the astonishment grew to such a pitch that as one after another caught sight of him they stopped singing and only stared at him. Knud Aakre, who sat in his pew in front of Lars, noticed that there was something the matter, and as he saw nothing remarkable in front of him, he turned round. He saw Lars bowed over his hymn-book, searching for the place.

He had not seen him since that evening at the meeting, and such a complete change he had not believed possible. For this was no victor! The thin, soft hair was thinner than ever, the face was haggard and emaciated, the eyes hollow and bloodshot, the giant neck had dwindled into wrinkles and cords. Knud comprehended at a glance what this man had gone through; he was seized with a feeling of strong sympathy, indeed, he felt something of the old love stirring within his breast. He prayed for Lars to his God, and made a resolute vow that he would seek him after service; but Lars had started on ahead. Knud resolved to call on him that evening. His wife, however, held him back.

"Lars is one of those," said she, "who can scarcely bear a debt of gratitude: keep away from him until he has an opportunity to do you some favor, and then perhaps he will come to you!"

But he did not come. He appeared now and then at church, but nowhere else, and he associated with no one. On the other hand, he now devoted himself to his gard and other business with the passionate zeal of one who had determined to make amends in one year for the neglect of many; and, indeed, there were those who said that this was imperative.

Railroad operations in the valley began very soon. As the line was to go directly past Lars's gard, he tore down the portion of his house that faced the road, in order to build a large and handsome balcony, for he was determined that his gard should attract attention. This work was just being done when the temporary rails for the conveyance of gravel and timber to the road were laid and a small locomotive was sent to the spot. It was a beautiful autumn evening that the first gravel car was to pass over the road. Lars stood on his front steps, to hear the first signal and to see the first column of smoke; all the people of the gard were gathered about him. He gazed over the parish, illumined by the setting sun, and he felt that he would be remembered as long as a train should come roaring through this fertile valley. A sense of forgiveness glided into his soul. He looked toward the churchyard, a part of which still remained, with crosses bowed down to the ground, but a part of it was now the railroad. He was just endeavoring to define his own feeling when the first signal whistled, and presently the train came slowly working its way along, attended by a cloud of smoke, mingled with sparks, for the locomotive was fed with pine wood. The wind blew toward the house so that those standing without were soon enveloped in a dense smoke, but as this cleared away Lars saw the train working its way down through the valley like a strong will.

He was content, and entered his house like one who has come from a long day's work. The image of his grandfather stood before him at this moment. This grandfather had raised the family from poverty to prosperity; true, a portion of his honor as a citizen was consumed in the act, but he had advanced nevertheless! His faults were the prevailing ones of his time: they were based on the uncertain boundary lines of the moral conceptions of his day. Every age has its uncertain moral distinctions and its victims.

Honor be to him in his grave, for he had suffered and toiled! Peace be with him! It must be good to rest in the end. But he was not allowed to rest because of his grandson's vast ambition; his ashes were thrown up with the stones and the gravel. Nonsense! he would only smile at his grandson's work.

Amid thoughts like these Lars had undressed and gone to bed. Once more his grandfather's image glided before him. It was sterner now than the first time. Weariness enfeebles us, and Lars began to reproach himself. But he defended himself also. What did his grandfather want? Surely he ought to be satisfied now, for the family honor was proclaimed in loud tones above his grave. Who else had such a monument? And yet what is this? These two monstrous eyes of fire and this hissing, roaring sound belong no longer to the locomotive, for they turn away from the railroad track. And from the churchyard straight toward the house comes an immense procession. The eyes of fire are his grandfather's, and the long line of followers are all the dead. The train advances steadily toward the gard, roaring, crackling, flashing. The windows blaze in the reflection of the dead men's eyes. Lars made a mighty effort to control himself, for this was a dream, unquestionably.

There, now I am awake. Come on, poor ghosts!

And lo! they really did come from the churchyard, overthrowing road, rails, locomotive, and train, so that these fell with a mighty crash to the ground, and the green sod appeared in their stead, dotted with graves and crosses as before. Like mighty champions they advanced, and the hymn, "Let the dead repose in peace!" preceded them. Lars knew it; for through all these years it had been sighing within his soul, and now it had become his requiem; for this was death and death's visions. The cold sweat started out over his whole body, for nearer and nearer—and behold, on the window pane! there they are now, and he heard some one speak his name. Overpowered with dread he struggled to scream; for he was being strangled, a cold hand was clenching his throat, and he regained his voice in an agonized "Help me!" and awoke. The window had been broken in from the outside; the pieces flew all about his head. He sprang up. A man stood at the window, surrounded by smoke and flames.

"The gard is on fire, Lars! We will help you out!" It was Knud Aakre.

When Lars regained his consciousness, he was lying outside in a bleak wind, which chilled his limbs. There was not a soul with him; he saw the flaming gard to the left; around him his cattle were grazing and making their voices heard; the sheep were huddled together in a frightened flock; the household goods were scattered about, and when he looked again he saw some one sitting on a knoll close by, weeping. It was his wife. He called her by name. She started.

"The Lord Jesus be praised that you are alive!" cried she, coming forward and seating herself, or rather throwing herself down in front of him. "O God! O God! We surely have had enough of this railroad now!"

"The railroad?" asked he, but ere the words had escaped his lips a clear comprehension of the case passed like a shudder over him; for, of course, sparks from the locomotive that had fallen among the shavings of the new side wall had been the cause of the fire. Lars sat there brooding in silence; his wife, not daring to utter another word, began to search for his clothes. He accepted her attentions in silence, but as she knelt before him to cover his feet, he laid his hand on her head. Falling forward she buried her face in his lap and wept aloud. Many eyed her curiously. But Lars understood her and said: "You are the only friend I have."

Even though it had cost the gard to hear these words, it mattered not to her; she felt so happy that she gained courage, and rising up and looking humbly into her husband's face, she said:

"Because there is no one else who understands you."

Then a hard heart melted, and tears rolled down the man's cheeks as he clung to his wife's hand.

Now he talked to her as to his own soul. Now too she opened her mind to him. They also talked about how all this had happened, or rather he listened while she told about it. Knud Aakre had been the first to see the fire, had roused his people, sent the girls out over his parish, while he had hastened himself with men and horses to the scene of the conflagration, where all were sleeping. He had engineered the extinguishing of the flames and the rescuing of the household goods, and had himself dragged Lars from the burning room, and carried him to the left side of the house from whence the wind was blowing and had laid him out here in the churchyard.

And while they were talking of this, some one came driving rapidly up the road and turned into the churchyard, where he alighted. It was Knud, who had been home after his church-cart—the one in which they had so many times ridden together to and from the meetings of the parish board. Now he requested Lars to get in and ride home with him. They grasped each other by the hand, the one sitting, the other standing.

"Come with me now," said Knud.

Without a word of reply, Lars rose. Side by side they walked to the cart. Lars was helped in; Knud sat down beside him. What they talked about as they drove along, or afterward in the little chamber at Aakre, where they remained until late in the morning, has never been known. But from that day they were inseparable as before.

As soon as misfortune overtakes a man, every one learns what he is worth. And so the parish undertook to rebuild Lars Högstad's houses, and to make them larger and handsomer than any others in the valley. He was reelected chairman, but with Knud Aakre at his side; he never again failed to take counsel of Knud's intelligence and heart—and from that day forth nothing went to ruin.

THE SIRE DE MALÉTROIT'S DOOR

Robert Louis Stevenson

Denis de Beaulieu was not yet two-and-twenty, but he counted himself a grown man, and a very accomplished cavalier into the bargain. Lads were early formed in that rough, warfaring epoch; and when one has been in a pitched battle and a dozen raids, has killed one's man in an honorable fashion, and knows a thing or two of strategy and mankind, a certain swagger in the gait is surely to be pardoned. He had put up his horse with due care, and supped with due deliberation; and then, in a very agreeable frame of mind, went out to pay a visit in the gray of the evening. It was not a very wise proceeding on the young man's part. He would have done better to remain beside the fire or go decently to bed. For the town was full of the troops of Burgundy and England under a mixed command; and though Denis was there on safe-conduct, his safe-conduct was like to serve him little on a chance encounter.

It was September, 1429; the weather had fallen sharp; a flighty piping wind, laden with showers, beat about the township; and the dead leaves ran riot along the street. Here and there a window was already lighted up; and the noise of men-at-arms making merry over supper within, came forth in fits and was swallowed up and carried away by the wind. The night fell swiftly; the flag of England, fluttering on the spire-top, grew ever fainter and fainter against the flying clouds—a black speck like a swallow in the tumultuous, leaden chaos of the sky. As the night fell the wind rose, and began to hoot under archways and roar amid the tree-tops in the valley below the town.

Denis de Beaulieu walked fast and was soon knocking at his friend's door; but though he promised himself to stay only a little while and make an early return, his welcome was so pleasant, and he found so much to delay him, that it was already long past midnight before he said good-by upon the threshold. The wind had fallen again in the meanwhile; the night was as black as the grave; not a star, nor a glimmer of moonshine, slipped through the canopy of cloud. Denis was ill-acquainted with the intricate lanes of Chateau Landon; even by daylight he had found some trouble in picking his way; and in this absolute darkness he soon lost it altogether. He was certain of one thing only —to keep mounting the hill; for his friend's house lay at the lower end, or tail, of Chateau Landon, while the inn was up at the head, under the great church spire. With this clue to go upon he stumbled and groped forward, now breathing more freely in open places where there was a good slice of sky overhead, now feeling along the wall in stifling closes. It is an eery and mysterious position to be thus submerged in opaque blackness in an almost unknown town. The silence is terrifying in its possibilities. The touch of cold window bars to the exploring hand startles the man like the touch of a toad; the inequalities of the pavement shake his heart into his mouth; a piece of denser darkness threatens an ambuscade or a chasm in the pathway; and where the air is brighter, the houses put on strange and bewildering appearances, as if to lead him farther from his way. For Denis, who had to regain his inn without attracting notice, there was real danger as well as mere discomfort in the walk; and he went warily and boldly at once, and at every corner paused to make an observation.

He had been for some time threading a lane so narrow that he could touch a wall with either hand when it began to open out and go sharply downward. Plainly this lay no longer in the direction of his inn; but the hope of a little more light tempted him forward to reconnoiter. The lane ended in a terrace with a bartizan wall, which gave an outlook between high houses, as out of an embrasure, into the valley lying dark and formless several hundred feet below. Denis looked down, and could discern a few tree-tops waving and a single speck of brightness where the river ran across a weir. The weather was clearing up, and the sky had lightened, so as to show the outline of the heavier clouds and the dark margin of the hills. By the uncertain glimmer, the house on his left hand should be a place of some pretensions; it was surmounted by several pinnacles and turret-tops; the round stern of a chapel, with a fringe of flying buttresses, projected boldly from the main block; and the door was sheltered under a deep porch carved with figures and overhung by two long gargoyles. The windows of the chapel gleamed through their intricate tracery with a light as of many tapers, and threw out the buttresses and the peaked roof in a more intense blackness against the sky. It was plainly the hotel of some great family of the neighborhood; and as it reminded Denis of a town house of his own at Bourges, he stood for some time gazing up at it and mentally gaging the skill of the architects and the consideration of the two families.

There seemed to be no issue to the terrace but the lane by which he had reached it; he could only retrace his steps, but he gained some notion of his whereabouts, and hoped by this means to hit the main thoroughfare and speedily regain the inn. He was reckoning without that chapter of accidents which was to make this night memorable above all others in his career; for he had not gone back above a hundred yards before he saw a light coming to meet him, and heard loud voices speaking together in the echoing narrows of the lane. It was a party of men-at-arms going the night round with torches. Denis assured himself that they had all been making free with the wine-bowl, and were in no mood to be particular about safe-conducts or the niceties of chivalrous war. It was as like as not that they would kill him like a dog and leave him where he fell. The situation was inspiriting but nervous. Their own torches would conceal him from sight, he reflected; and he hoped that they would drown the noise of his footsteps with their own empty voices. If he were but fleet and silent, he might evade their notice altogether.

Unfortunately, as he turned to beat a retreat, his foot rolled upon a pebble; he fell against the wall with an ejaculation, and his sword rang loudly on the stones. Two or three voices demanded who went there—some in French, some in English; but Denis made no reply, and ran the faster down the lane. Once upon the terrace, he paused to look back. They still kept calling after him, and just then began to double the pace in pursuit, with a considerable clank of armor, and great tossing of the torchlight to and fro in the narrow jaws of the passage.

Denis cast a look around and darted into the porch. There he might escape observation, or—if that were too much to expect—was in a capital posture whether for parley or defense. So thinking, he drew his sword and tried to set his back against the door. To his surprise, it yielded behind his weight; and though he turned in a moment, continued to swing back on oiled and noise-less hinges, until it stood wide open on a black interior. When things fall out opportunely for the person concerned, he is not apt to be critical about the how or why, his own immediate personal convenience seeming a sufficient reason for the strangest oddities and revolutions in our sublunary things; and so Denis, without a moment's hesitation, stepped within and partly closed the door behind him to conceal his place of refuge. Nothing was further from his thoughts than to close it altogether; but for some inexplicable reason—perhaps by a spring or a weight—the ponderous mass of oak whipped itself out of his fingers and clanked to, with a formidable rumble and a noise like the falling of an automatic bar.

The round, at that very moment, debouched upon the terrace and proceeded to summon him with shouts and curses. He heard them ferreting in the dark corners; the stock of a lance even rattled along the outer surface of the door behind which he stood; but these gentlemen were in too high a humor to be long delayed, and soon made off down a corkscrew pathway which had escaped Denis's observation, and passed out of sight and hearing along the battlements of the town.

Denis breathed again. He gave them a few minutes' grace for fear of accidents, and then groped about for some means of opening the door and slipping forth again. The inner surface was quite smooth, not a handle, not a molding, not a projection of any sort. He got his finger-nails round the edges and pulled, but the mass was immovable. He shook it, it was as firm as a rock. Denis de Beaulieu frowned and gave vent to a little noiseless whistle. What ailed the door? he wondered. Why was it open? How came it to shut so easily and so effectually after him? There was something obscure and underhand about all this, that was little to the young man's fancy. It looked like a snare, and yet who could suppose a snare in such a quiet by-street, and in a house of so prosperous and even noble an exterior? And yet—snare or no snare, intentionally or unintentionally—here he was, prettily trapped; and for the life of him he could see no way out of it again. The darkness began to weigh upon him. He gave ear; all was silent without, but within and close by he seemed to catch a faint sighing, a faint sobbing rustle, a little stealthy creak—as though many persons were at his side, holding themselves quite still, and governing even their respiration with the extreme of slyness. The idea went to his vitals with a shock, and he faced about suddenly as if to defend his life. Then, for the first time, he became aware of a light about the level of his eyes and at some distance in the interior of the house—a vertical thread of light, widening toward the bottom, such as might escape between two wings of arras over a doorway. To see anything was a relief to Denis; it was like a piece of solid ground to a man laboring in a morass; his mind seized upon it with avidity; and he stood staring at it and trying to piece together some logical conception of his surroundings. Plainly there was a flight of steps ascending from his own level to that of this illuminated doorway; and indeed he thought he could make out another thread of light, as fine as a needle, and as faint as phosphorescence, which might very well be reflected along the polished wood of a handrail. Since he had begun to suspect that he was not alone, his heart had continued to beat with smothering violence, and an intolerable desire for action of any sort had possessed itself of his spirit. He was in deadly peril, he believed. What could be more natural than to mount the staircase, lift the curtain, and confront his difficulty at once? At least he would be dealing with something tangible; at least he would be no longer in the dark. He stepped slowly forward with outstretched hands, until his foot struck the bottom step; then he rapidly scaled the stairs, stood for a moment to compose his expression, lifted the arras and went in.

He found himself in a large apartment of polished stone. There were three doors; one on each of three sides; all similarly curtained with tapestry. The fourth side was occupied by two large windows and a great stone chimney-piece, carved with the arms of the Malétroits. Denis recognized the bearings, and was gratified to find himself in such good hands. The room was strongly illuminated; but it contained little furniture except a heavy table and a chair or two, the hearth was innocent of fire, and the pavement was but sparsely strewn with rushes clearly many days old.

On a high chair beside the chimney, and directly facing Denis as he entered, sat a little old gentleman in a fur tippet. He sat with his legs crossed and his hands folded, and a cup of spiced wine stood by his elbow on a bracket on the wall. His countenance had a strongly masculine cast; not properly human, but such as we see in the bull, the goat, or the domestic boar; something equivocal and wheedling, something greedy, brutal, and dangerous. The upper lip was inordinately full, as though swollen by a blow or a toothache; and the smile, the peaked eyebrows, and the small, strong eyes were quaintly and almost comically evil in expression. Beautiful white hair hung straight all round his head, like a saint's, and fell in a single curl upon the tippet. His beard and mustache were the pink of venerable sweetness. Age, probably in consequence of inordinate precautions, had left no mark upon his hands; and the Malétroit hand was famous. It would be difficult to imagine anything at once so fleshy and so delicate in design; the taper, sensual fingers, were like those of one of Leonardo's women; the fork of the thumb made a dimpled protuberance when closed; the nails were perfectly shaped, and of a dead, surprising whiteness. It rendered his aspect tenfold more redoubtable, that a man with hands like these should keep them devoutly folded like a virgin martyr—that a man with so intent and startling an expression of face should sit patiently on his seat and contemplate people with an unwinking stare, like a god, or a god's statue. His quiescence seemed ironical and treacherous, it fitted so poorly with his looks.

Such was Alain, Sire de Malétroit.

Denis and he looked silently at each other for a second or two.

"Pray step in," said the Sire de Malétroit. "I have been expecting you all the evening."

He had not risen but he accompanied his words with a smile and a slight but courteous inclination of the head. Partly from the smile, partly from the strange musical murmur with which the Sire prefaced his observation, Denis felt a strong shudder of disgust go through his marrow. And what with disgust and honest confusion of mind, he could scarcely get words together in reply.

"I fear," he said, "that this is a double accident. I am not the person you suppose me. It seems you were looking for a visit; but for my part, nothing was further from my thoughts—nothing could be more contrary to my wishes —than this intrusion."

"Well, well," replied the old gentleman indulgently, "here you are, which is the main point. Seat yourself, my friend, and put yourself entirely at your ease. We shall arrange our little affairs presently."

Denis perceived that the matter was still complicated with some misconception, and he hastened to continue his explanations.

"Your door . . ." he began.

"About my door?" asked the other raising his peaked eyebrows. "A little piece of ingenuity." And he shrugged his shoulders. "A hospitable fancy! By your own account, you were not desirous of making my acquaintance. We old people look for such reluctance now and then; when it touches our honor, we cast about until we find some way of overcoming it. You arrive uninvited, but believe me, very welcome."

"You persist in error, sir," said Denis. "There can be no question between you and me. I am a stranger in this countryside. My name is Denis, damoiseau de Beaulieu. If you see me in your house, it is only—"

"My young friend," interrupted the other, "you will permit me to have my own ideas on that subject. They probably differ from yours at the present moment," he added with a leer, "but time will show which of us is in the right."

Denis was convinced he had to do with a lunatic. He seated himself with a shrug, content to wait the upshot; and a pause ensued, during which he thought he could distinguish a hurried gabbling as of prayer from behind the arras immediately opposite him. Sometimes there seemed to be but one person engaged, sometimes two; and the vehemence of the voice, low as it was, seemed to indicate either great haste or an agony of spirit. It occurred to him that this piece of tapestry covered the entrance to the chapel he had noticed from without.

The old gentleman meanwhile surveyed Denis from head to foot with a smile, and from time to time emitted little noises like a bird or a mouse, which seemed to indicate a high degree of satisfaction. This state of matters became rapidly insupportable; and Denis, to put an end to it, remarked politely that the wind had gone down.

The old gentleman fell into a fit of silent laughter, so prolonged and violent that he became quite red in the face. Denis got upon his feet at once, and put on his hat with a flourish.

"Sir," he said, "if you are in your wits, you have affronted me grossly. If you are out of them, I flatter myself I can find better employment for my brains than to talk with lunatics. My conscience is clear; you have made a fool of me from the first moment; you have refused to hear my explanations; and now there is no power under God will make me stay here any longer; and if I can not make my way out in a more decent fashion, I will hack your door in pieces with my sword."

The Sire de Malétroit raised his right hand and wagged it at Denis with the fore and little fingers extended.

"My dear nephew," he said, "sit down."

"Nephew!" retorted Denis, "you lie in your throat"; and he snapped his fingers in his face.

"Sit down, you rogue!" cried the old gentleman, in a sudden, harsh voice, like the barking of a dog. "Do you fancy," he went on, "that when I had made my little contrivance for the door I had stopped short with that? If you prefer to be bound hand and foot till your bones ache, rise and try to go away. If you choose to remain a free young buck, agreeably conversing with an old gentleman—why, sit where you are in peace, and God be with you."

"Do you mean I am a prisoner?" demanded Denis.

"I state the facts," replied the other. "I would rather leave the conclusion to yourself."

Denis sat down again. Externally he managed to keep pretty calm, but within, he was now boiling with anger, now chilled with apprehension. He no longer felt convinced that he was dealing with a madman. And if the old gentlemen was sane, what, in God's name, had he to look for? What absurd or tragical adventure had befallen him? What countenance was he to assume?

While he was thus unpleasantly reflecting, the arras that overhung the chapel door was raised, and a tall priest in his robes came forth and, giving a long, keen stare at Denis, said something in an undertone to Sire de Malétroit.

"She is in a better frame of spirit?" asked the latter.

"She is more resigned, messire," replied the priest.

"Now the Lord help her, she is hard to please!" sneered the old gentleman. "A likely stripling—not ill-born—and of her own choosing, too? Why, what more would the jade have?"

"The situation is not usual for a young damsel," said the other, "and somewhat trying to her blushes."

"She should have thought of that before she began the dance. It was none of my choosing, God knows that: but since she is in it, by our Lady, she shall carry it to the end." And then addressing Denis, "Monsieur de Beaulieu," he asked, "may I present you to my niece? She has been waiting your arrival, I may say, with even greater impatience than myself."

Denis had resigned himself with a good grace—all he desired was to know the worst of it as speedily as possible; so he rose at once, and bowed in acquiescence. The Sire de Malétroit followed his example and limped, with the assistance of the chaplain's arm, toward the chapel door. The priest pulled aside the arras, and all three entered. The building had considerable architectural pretensions. A light groining sprang from six stout columns, and hung down in two rich pendants from the center of the vault. The place terminated behind the altar in a round end, embossed and honeycombed with a superfluity of ornament in relief, and pierced by many little windows shaped like stars, trefoils, or wheels. These windows were imperfectly glazed, so that the night air circulated freely in the chapel. The tapers, of which there must have been half a hundred burning on the altar, were unmercifully blown about; and the light went through many different phases of brilliancy and semieclipse. On the steps in front of the altar knelt a young girl richly attired as a bride. A chill settled over Denis as he observed her costume; he fought with desperate energy against the conclusion that was being thrust upon his mind; it could not—it should not—be as he feared.

"Blanche," said the Sire, in his most flute-like tones, "I have brought a friend to see you, my little girl; turn round and give him your pretty hand. It is good to be devout; but it is necessary to be polite, my niece."

The girl rose to her feet and turned toward the newcomers. She moved all of a piece; and shame and exhaustion were expressed in every line of her fresh young body; and she held her head down and kept her eyes upon the pavement, as she came slowly forward. In the course of her advance, her eyes fell upon Denis de Beaulieu's feet—feet of which he was justly vain, be it remarked, and wore in the most elegant accouterment even while traveling. She paused—started, as if his yellow boots had conveyed some shocking meaning —and glanced suddenly up into the wearer's countenance. Their eyes met; shame gave place to horror and terror in her looks; the blood left her lips; with a piercing scream she covered her face with her hands and sank upon the chapel floor.

"That is not the man!" she cried. "My uncle, that is not the man!"

The Sire de Malétroit chirped agreeably. "Of course not," he said, "I expected as much. It was so unfortunate you could not remember his name."

"Indeed," she cried, "indeed, I have never seen this person till this moment —I have never so much as set eyes upon him—I never wish to see him again. Sir," she said, turning to Denis, "if you are a gentleman, you will bear me out. Have I ever seen you—have you ever seen me—before this accursed hour?"

"To speak for myself, I have never had that pleasure," answered the young man. "This is the first time, messire, that I have met with your engaging niece."

The old gentleman shrugged his shoulders.

"I am distressed to hear it," he said. "But it is never too late to begin. I had little more acquaintance with my own late lady ere I married her; which proves," he added, with a grimace, "that these impromptu marriages may often produce an excellent understanding in the long run. As the bridegroom is to have a voice in the matter, I will give him two hours to make up for lost time before we proceed with the ceremony." And he turned toward the door, followed by the clergyman.

The girl was on her feet in a moment. "My uncle, you can not be in earnest," she said. "I declare before God I will stab myself rather than be forced on that young man. The heart rises at it; God forbids such marriages; you dishonor your white hair. Oh, my uncle, pity me! There is not a woman in all the world but would prefer death to such a nuptial. Is it possible," she added, faltering—"is it possible that you do not believe me—that you still think this"—and she pointed at Denis with a tremor of anger and contempt— "that you still think *this* to be the man?"

"Frankly," said the old gentleman, pausing on the threshold, "I do. But let me explain to you once for all, Blanche de Malétroit, my way of thinking about this affair. When you took it into your head to dishonor my family and the name that I have borne, in peace and war, for more than three-score years, you forfeited, not only the right to question my designs, but that of looking me in the face. If your father had been alive, he would have spat on you and turned you out of doors. His was the hand of iron. You may bless your God you have only to deal with the hand of velvet, mademoiselle. It was my duty to get you married without delay. Out of pure good-will, I have tried to find your own gallant for you. And I believe I have succeeded. But before God and all the holy angels, Blanche de Malétroit, if I have not, I care not one jackstraw. So let me recommend you to be polite to our young friend: for upon my word, your next groom may be less appetizing."

And with that he went out, with the chaplain at his heels; and the arras fell behind the pair.

The girl turned upon Denis with flashing eyes.

"And what, sir," she demanded, "may be the meaning of all this?"

"God knows," returned Denis, gloomily. "I am a prisoner in this house, which seems full of mad people. More I know not; and nothing do I understand."

"And pray how came you here?" she asked.

He told her as briefly as he could. "For the rest," he added, "perhaps you will follow my example, and tell me the answer to all these riddles, and what, in God's name, is like to be the end of it."

She stood silent for a little, and he could see her lips tremble and her tearless eyes burn with a feverish luster. Then she pressed her forehead in both hands.

"Alas, how my head aches!" she said wearily—"to say nothing of my poor heart! But it is due to you to know my story, unmaidenly as it must seem. I am called Blanche de Malétroit; I have been without father or mother for—oh! for as long as I can recollect, and indeed I have been most unhappy all my life. Three months ago a young captain began to stand near me every day in church. I could see that I pleased him; I am much to blame, but I was so glad that any one should love me; and when he passed me a letter, I took it home with me and read it with great pleasure. Since that time he has written many. He was so anxious to speak with me, poor fellow! and kept asking me to leave the door open some evening that we might have two words upon the stair. For he knew how much my uncle trusted me." She gave something like a sob at that, and it was a moment before she could go on. "My uncle is a hard man, but he is very shrewd," she said at last. "He has performed many feats in war, and was a great person at court, and much trusted by Queen Isabeau in old days. How he came to suspect me I can not tell; but it is hard to keep anything from his knowledge; and this morning, as we came from mass, he took my hand into his, forced it open, and read my little billet, walking by my side all the while. When he finished, he gave it back to me with great politeness. It contained another request to have the door left open; and this has been the ruin of us all. My uncle kept me strictly in my room until evening, and then ordered me to dress myself as you see me—a hard mockery for a young girl, do you not think so? I suppose, when he could not prevail with me to tell him the young captain's name, he must have laid a trap for him: into which, alas! you have fallen in the anger of God. I looked for much confusion; for how could I tell whether he was willing to take me for his wife on these sharp terms? He might have been trifling with me from the first; or I might have made myself too cheap in his eyes. But truly I had not looked for such a shameful punishment as this! I could not think that God would let a girl be so disgraced before a young man. And now I tell you all; and I can scarcely hope that you will not despise me."

Denis made her a respectful inclination.

"Madam," he said, "you have honored me by your confidence. It remains for me to prove that I am not unworthy of the honor. Is Messire de Malétroit at hand?"

"I believe he is writing in the salle without," she answered.

"May I lead you thither, madam?" asked Denis, offering his hand with his most courtly bearing.

She accepted it; and the pair passed out of the chapel, Blanche in a very drooping and shamefaced condition, but Denis strutting and ruffling in the consciousness of a mission, and the boyish certainty of accomplishing it with honor.

The Sire de Malétroit rose to meet them with an ironical obeisance.

"Sir," said Denis, with the grandest possible air," I believe I am to have some say in the matter of this marriage; and let me tell you at once, I will be no party to forcing the inclination of this young lady. Had it been freely offered to me, I should have been proud to accept her hand, for I perceive she is as good as she is beautiful; but as things are, I have now the honor, messire, of refusing."

Blanche looked at him with gratitude in her eyes; but the old gentleman only smiled and smiled, until his smile grew positively sickening to Denis.

"I am afraid," he said, "Monsieur de Beaulieu, that you do not perfectly understand the choice I have offered you. Follow me, I beseech you, to this window." And he led the way to one of the large windows which stood open on the night. "You observe," he went on, "there is an iron ring in the upper masonry, and reeved through that, a very efficacious rope. Now, mark my words: if you should find your disinclination to my niece's person insurmountable, I shall have you hanged out of this window before sunrise. I shall only proceed to such an extremity with the greatest regret, you may believe me. For it is not at all your death that I desire, but my niece's establishment in life. At the same time, it must come to that if you prove obstinate. Your family, Monsieur de Beaulieu, is very well in its way; but if you sprang from Charlemagne, you should not refuse the hand of a Malétroit with impunity— not if she had been as common as the Paris road—not if she were as hideous as the gargoyle over my door. Neither my niece nor you, nor my own private feelings, move me at all in this matter. The honor of my house has been compromised; I believe you to be the guilty person, at least you are now in the secret; and you can hardly wonder if I request you to wipe out the stain. If you will not, your blood be on your own head! It will be no great satisfaction to me to have your interesting relics kicking their heels in the breeze below my windows, but half a loaf is better than no bread, and if I can not cure the dishonor, I shall at least stop the scandal."

There was a pause.

"I believe there are other ways of settling such imbroglios among gentlemen," said Denis. "You wear a sword, and I hear you have used it with distinction."

The Sire de Malétroit made a signal to the chaplain, who crossed the room with long silent strides and raised the arras over the third of the three doors. It was only a moment before he let it fall again; but Denis had time to see a dusky passage full of armed men.

"When I was a little younger, I should have been delighted to honor you, Monsieur de Beaulieu," said Sire Alain; "but I am now too old. Faithful retainers are the sinews of age, and I must employ the strength I have. This is one of the hardest things to swallow as a man grows up in years; but with a little patience, even this becomes habitual. You and the lady seem to prefer the salle for what remains of your two hours; and as I have no desire to cross your preference, I shall resign it to your use with all the pleasure in the world. No haste!" he added, holding up his hand, as he saw a dangerous look come into Denis de Beaulieu's face. "If your mind revolt against hanging, it will be time enough two hours hence to throw yourself out of the window or upon the pikes of my retainers. Two hours of life are always two hours. A great many things may turn up in even as little a while as that. And, besides, if I understand her appearance, my niece has something to say to you. You will not disfigure your last hours by a want of politeness to a lady?"

Denis looked at Blanche, and she made him an imploring gesture.

It is likely that the old gentleman was hugely pleased at this symptom of an understanding; for he smiled on both, and added sweetly: "If you will give me your word of honor, Monsieur de Beaulieu, to await my return at the end of the two hours before attempting anything desperate, I shall withdraw my retainers, and let you speak in greater privacy with mademoiselle."

Denis again glanced at the girl, who seemed to beseech him to agree.

"I give you my word of honor," he said.

Messire de Malétroit bowed, and proceeded to limp about the apartment, clearing his throat the while with that odd musical chirp which had already grown so irritating in the ears of Denis de Beaulieu. He first possessed himself of some papers which lay upon the table; then he went to the mouth of the passage and appeared to give an order to the men behind the arras; and lastly he hobbled out through the door by which Denis had come in, turning upon the threshold to address a last smiling bow to the young couple, and followed by the chaplain with a hand-lamp.

No sooner were they alone than Blanche advanced toward Denis with her hands extended. Her face was flushed and excited, and her eyes shone with tears.

"You shall not die!" she cried, "you shall marry me after all."

"You seem to think, madam," replied Denis, "that I stand much in fear of death."

"Oh, no, no," she said, "I see you are no poltroon. It is for my own sake—I could not bear to have you slain for such a scruple."

"I am afraid," returned Denis, "that you underrate the difficulty, madam. What you may be too generous to refuse, I may be too proud to accept. In a moment of noble feeling toward me, you forget what you perhaps owe to others."

He had the decency to keep his eyes on the floor as he said this, and after he had finished, so as not to spy upon her confusion. She stood silent for a moment, then walked suddenly away, and falling on her uncle's chair, fairly burst out sobbing. Denis was in the acme of embarrassment. He looked round, as if to seek for inspiration, and seeing a stool, plumped down upon it for something to do. There he sat playing with the guard of his rapier, and wishing himself dead a thousand times over, and buried in the nastiest kitchen-heap in France. His eyes wandered round the apartment, but found nothing to arrest them. There were such wide spaces between the furniture, the light fell so badly and cheerlessly over all, the dark outside air looked in so coldly through the windows, that he thought he had never seen a church so vast, nor a tomb so melancholy. The regular sobs of Blanche de Malétroit measured out the time like the ticking of a clock. He read the device upon the shield over and over again, until his eyes became obscured; he stared into shadowy corners until he imagined they were swarming with horrible animals; and every now and again he awoke with a start, to remember that his last two hours were running, and death was on the march.

Oftener and oftener, as the time went on, did his glance settle on the girl herself. Her face was bowed forward and covered with her hands, and she was shaken at intervals by the convulsive hiccup of grief. Even thus she was not an unpleasant object to dwell upon, so plump and yet so fine, with a warm brown skin, and the most beautiful hair, Denis thought, in the whole world of womankind. Her hands were like her uncle's: but they were more in place at the end of her young arms, and looked infinitely soft and caressing. He remembered how her blue eyes had shone upon him, full of anger, pity, and innocence. And the more he dwelt on her perfections, the uglier death looked, and the more deeply was he smitten with penitence at her continued tears. Now he felt that no man could have the courage to leave a world which contained so beautiful a creature; and now he would have given forty minutes of his last hour to have unsaid his cruel speech.

Suddenly a hoarse and ragged peal of cockcrow rose to their ears from the dark valley below the windows. And this shattering noise in the silence of all around was like a light in a dark place, and shook them both out of their reflections.

"Alas, can I do nothing to help you?" she said, looking up.

"Madame," replied Denis, with a fine irrelevancy, "if I have said anything to wound you, believe me, it was for your own sake and not for mine."

She thanked him with a tearful look.

"I feel your position cruelly," he went on. "The world has been bitter hard on you. Your uncle is a disgrace to mankind. Believe me, madame, there is no young gentleman in all France but would be glad of my opportunity, to die in doing you a momentary service."

"I know already that you can be very brave and generous," she answered. "What I *want* to know is whether I can serve you—now or afterward," she added, with a quaver.

"Most certainly," he answered with a smile. "Let me sit beside you as if I were a friend, instead of a foolish intruder; try to forget how awkwardly we are placed to one another; make my last moments go pleasantly: and you will do me the chief service possible."

"You are very gallant," she added, with a yet deeper sadness . . . "very gallant . . . and it somehow pains me. But draw nearer, if you please; and if you find anything to say to me, you will at least make certain of a very friendly listener. Ah! Monsieur de Beaulieu," she broke forth—"ah! Monsieur de Beaulieu, how can I look you in the face?" And she fell to weeping again with a renewed effusion.

"Madame," said Denis, taking her hand in both of his, "reflect on the little time I have before me, and the great bitterness into which I am cast by the sight of your distress. Spare me, in my last moments, the spectacle of what I can not cure even with the sacrifice of my life."

"I am very selfish," answered Blanche. "I will be braver, Monsieur de Beaulieu, for your sake. But think if I can do you no kindness in the future— if you have no friends to whom I could carry your adieus. Charge me as heavily as you can; every burden will lighten, by so little, the invaluable gratitude I owe you. Put it in my power to do something more for you than weep."

"My mother is married again, and has a young family to care for. My brother Guichard will inherit my fiefs; and if I am not in error, that will content him amply for my death. Life is a little vapor that passeth away, as we are told by those in holy orders. When a man is in a fair way and sees all life open in front of him, he seems to himself to make a very important figure in the world. His horse whinnies to him; the trumpets blow and the girls look out of the window as he rides into town before his company; he receives many assurances of trust and regard—sometimes by express in a letter—sometimes face to face, with persons of great consequence falling on his neck. It is not wonderful if his head is turned for a time. But once he is dead, were he as brave as Hercules or as wise as Solomon, he is soon forgotten. It is not ten years since my father fell, with many other knights around him, in a very fierce encounter, and I do not think that any one of them, nor so much as the name of the fight, is now remembered. No, no, madame, the nearer you come to it, you see that death is a dark and dusty corner, where a man gets into his tomb and has the door shut after him till the judgment day. I have few friends just now, and once I am dead I shall have none."

"Ah, Monsieur de Beaulieu!" she exclaimed, "you forget Blanche de Malé-troit."

You have a sweet nature, madam, and you are pleased to estimate a little service far beyond its worth."

"It is not that," she answered. "You mistake me if you think I am easily touched by my own concerns. I say so, because you are the noblest man I have ever met; because I recognize in you a spirit that would have made even a common person famous in the land."

"And yet here I die in a mousetrap—with no more noise about it than my own squeaking," answered he.

A look of pain crossed her face, and she was silent for a little while. Then a light came into her eyes, and with a smile she spoke again.

"I can not have my champion think meanly of himself. Any one who gives his life for another will be met in Paradise by all the heralds and angels of the Lord God. And you have no such cause to hang your head. For . . . Pray, do you think me beautiful?" she asked, with a deep flush.

"Indeed, madam, I do," he said.

"I am glad of that," she answered heartily. "Do you think there are many men in France who have been asked in marriage by a beautiful maiden—with her own lips—and who have refused her to her face? I know you men would half despise such a triumph; but believe me, we women know more of what is precious in love. There is nothing that should set a person higher in his own esteem; and we women would prize nothing more dearly."

"You are very good," he said; "but you can not make me forget that I was asked in pity and not for love."

"I am not so sure of that," she replied, holding down her head. "Hear me to an end, Monsieur de Beaulieu. I know how you must despise me; I feel you are right to do so; I am too poor a creature to occupy one thought of your mind, although, alas! you must die for me this morning. But when I asked you to marry me, indeed, and indeed, it was because I respected and admired you, and loved you with my whole soul, from the very moment that you took my part against my uncle. If you had seen yourself, and how noble you looked, you would pity rather than despise me. And now," she went on, hurriedly checking him with her hand, "although I have laid aside all reserve and told you so much, remember that I know your sentiments toward me already. I would not, believe me, being nobly born, weary you with importunities into consent. I too have a pride of my own; and I declare before the holy mother of God, if you should now go back from your word already given, I would no more marry you than I would marry my uncle's groom."

Denis smiled a little bitterly.

"It is a small love," he said, "that shies at a little pride."

She made no answer, although she probably had her own thoughts.

"Come hither to the window," he said with a sigh. "Here is the dawn."

And indeed the dawn was already beginning. The hollow of the sky was full of essential daylight, colorless and clean; and the valley underneath was flooded with a gray reflection. A few thin vapors clung in the coves of the forest or lay along the winding course of the river. The scene disengaged a surprising effect of stillness, which was hardly interrupted when the cocks began once more to crow among the steadings. Perhaps the same fellow who had made so horrid a clangor in the darkness not half an hour before, now sent up the merriest cheer to greet the coming day. A little wind went bustling and eddying among the tree-tops underneath the windows. And still the daylight kept flooding insensibly out of the east, which was soon to grow incandescent and cast up that red-hot cannon-ball, the rising sun.

Denis looked out over all this with a bit of a shiver. He had taken her hand, and retained it in his almost unconsciously.

"Has the day begun already?" she said; and then, illogically enough: "the night has been so long! Alas! what shall we say to my uncle when he returns?"

"What you will," said Denis, and he pressed her fingers in his.

She was silent.

"Blanche," he said, with a swift, uncertain, passionate utterance, "you have seen whether I fear death. You must know well enough that I would as gladly leap out of that window into the empty air as to lay a finger on you without your free and full consent. But if you care for me at all do not let me lose my life in a misapprehension; for I love you better than the whole world; and though I will die for you blithely, it would be like all the joys of Paradise to live on and spend my life in your service."

As he stopped speaking, a bell began to ring loudly in the interior of the house; and a clatter of armor in the corridor showed that the retainers were returning to their post, and the two hours were at an end.

"After all that you have heard?" she whispered, leaning toward him with her lips and eyes.

"I have heard nothing," he replied.

"The captain's name was Florimond de Champdivers," she said in his ear.

"I did not hear it," he answered, taking her supple body in his arms, and covered her wet face with kisses.

A melodious chirping was audible behind, followed by a beautiful chuckle, and the voice of Messire de Malétroit wished his new nephew a good morning.

THE THIEF

————— ❧⚮❧ —————

Fyodor Dostoevsky

One morning, just as I was about to leave for my place of employment, Agrafena (my cook, laundress, and housekeeper all in one person) entered my room, and, to my great astonishment, started a conversation.

She was a quiet, simple-minded woman, who during the whole six years of her stay with me had never spoken more than two or three words daily, and that in reference to my dinner—at least, I had never heard her.

"I have come to you, sir," she suddenly began, "about the renting out of the little spare room."

"What spare room?"

"The one that is near the kitchen, of course; which should it be?"

"Why?"

"Why do people generally take lodgers? Because."

"But who will take it?"

"Who will take it! A lodger, of course! Who should take it?"

"But there is hardly room in there, mother mine, for a bed; it will be too cramped. How can one live in it?"

"But why live in it! He only wants a place to sleep in; he will live on the window-seat."

"What window-seat?"

"How is that? What window-seat? As if you did not know! The one in the hall. He will sit on it and sew, or do something else. But maybe he will sit on a chair; he has a chair of his own—and a table also, and everything."

"But who is he?"

"A nice, worldly-wise man. I will cook for him and will charge him only three rubles in silver a month for room and board—"

At last, after long endeavor, I found out that some elderly man had talked

Agrafena into taking him into the kitchen as lodger. When Agrafena once got a thing into her head that thing had to be done; otherwise I knew I would have no peace. On those occasions when things did go against her wishes, she immediately fell into a sort of brooding, became exceedingly melancholy, and continued in that state for two or three weeks. During this time the food was invariably spoiled, the linen was missing, the floors unscrubbed; in a word, a lot of unpleasant things happened. I had long ago become aware of the fact that this woman of very few words was incapable of forming a decision, or of coming to any conclusion based on her own thoughts; and yet when it happened that by some means there had formed in her weak brain a sort of idea or wish to undertake a thing, to refuse her permission to carry out this idea or wish meant simply to kill her morally for some time. And so, acting in the sole interest of my peace of mind, I immediately agreed to this new proposition of hers.

"Has he at least the necessary papers, a passport, or anything of the kind?"

"How then? Of course he has. A fine man like him—who has seen the world—He promised to pay three rubles a month."

On the very next day the new lodger appeared in my modest bachelor quarters; but I did not feel annoyed in the least—on the contrary, in a way I was glad of it. I live a very solitary, hermit-like life. I have almost no acquaintance and seldom go out. Having led the existence of a moor-cock for ten years, I was naturally used to solitude. But ten, fifteen years or more of the same seclusion in company with a person like Agrafena, and in the same bachelor dwelling, was indeed a joyless prospect. Therefore, the presence of another quiet, unobtrusive man in the house was, under these circumstances, a real blessing.

Agrafena had spoken the truth: the lodger was a man who had seen much in his life. From his passport it appeared that he was a retired soldier, which I noticed even before I looked at the passport.

As soon as I glanced at him in fact.

Astafi Ivanich, my lodger, belonged to the better sort of soldiers, another thing I noticed as soon as I saw him. We liked each other from the first, and our life flowed on peacefully and comfortably. The best thing was that Astafi Ivanich could at times tell a good story, incidents of his own life. In the general tediousness of my humdrum existence, such a narrator was a veritable treasure. Once he told me a story which has made a lasting impression upon me; but first the incident which led to the story.

Once I happened to be left alone in the house, Astafi and Agrafena having gone out on business. Suddenly I heard some one enter, and I felt that it must be a stranger; I went out into the corridor and found a man of short stature, and notwithstanding the cold weather, dressed very thinly and without an overcoat.

"What is it you want?"

"The Government clerk Alexandrov? Does he live here?"

"There is no one here by that name, little brother; good day."

"The porter told me he lived here," said the visitor, cautiously retreating toward the door.

"Go on, go on, little brother; be off!"

Soon after dinner the next day, when Astafi brought in my coat, which he had repaired for me, I once more heard a strange step in the corridor. I opened the door.

The visitor of the day before, calmly and before my very eyes, took my short coat from the rack, put it under his arm, and ran out.

Agrafena, who had all the time been looking at him in open-mouthed surprise through the kitchen door, was seemingly unable to stir from her place and rescue the coat. But Astafi Ivanich rushed after the rascal, and, out of breath and panting, returned empty-handed. The man had vanished as if the earth had swallowed him.

"It is too bad, really, Astafi Ivanich," I said. "It is well that I have my cloak left. Otherwise the scoundrel would have put me out of service altogether."

But Astafi seemed so much affected by what had happened that as I gazed at him I forgot all about the theft. He could not regain his composure, and every once in a while threw down the work which occupied him, and began once more to recount how it had all happened, where he had been standing, while only two steps away my coat had been stolen before his very eyes, and how he could not even catch the thief. Then once more he resumed his work, only to throw it away again, and I saw him go down to the porter, tell him what had happened, and reproach him with not taking sufficient care of the house, that such a theft could be perpetrated in it. When he returned he began to upbraid Agrafena. Then he again resumed his work, muttering to himself for a long time—how this is the way it all was—how he stood here, and I there, and how before our very eyes, no farther than two steps away, the coat was taken off its hanger, and so on. In a word, Astafi Ivanich, though he knew how to do certain things, worried a great deal over trifles.

"We have been fooled, Astafi Ivanich," I said to him that evening, handing him a glass of tea, and hoping from sheer ennui to call forth the story of the lost coat again, which by dint of much repetition had begun to sound extremely comical.

"Yes, we were fooled, sir. It angers me very much, though the loss is not mine, and I think there is nothing so despicably low in this world as a thief. They steal what you buy by working in the sweat of your brow—Your time and labor— The loathsome creature! It sickens me to talk of it—pfui! It makes me angry to think of it. How is it, sir, that you do not seem to be at all sorry about it?"

"To be sure, Astafi Ivanich, one would much sooner see his things burn up than see a thief take them. It is exasperating—"

"Yes, it is annoying to have anything stolen from you. But of course there are thieves and thieves—I, for instance, met an honest thief through an accident."

"How is that? An honest thief? How can a thief be honest, Astafi Ivanich?"

"You speak truth, sir. A thief can not be an honest man. There never was such. I only wanted to say that he was an honest man, it seems to me, even though he stole. I was very sorry for him."

"And how did it happen, Astafi Ivanich?"

"It happened just two years ago. I was serving as house steward at the time, and the baron whom I served expected shortly to leave for his estate, so that I knew I would soon be out of a job, and then God only knew how I would be able to get along; and just then it was that I happened to meet in a tavern a poor forlorn creature, Emelian by name. Once upon a time he had served somewhere or other, but had been driven out of service on account of tippling. Such an unworthy creature as he was! He wore whatever came along. At times I even wondered if he wore a shirt under his shabby cloak; everything he could put his hands on was sold for drink. But he was not a rowdy. Oh, no; he was of a sweet, gentle nature, very kind and tender to every one; he never asked for anything, was, if anything, too conscientious—Well, you could see without asking when the poor fellow was dying for a drink, and of course you treated him to one. Well, we became friendly, that is, he attached himself to me like a little dog—you go this way, he follows—and all this after our very first meeting.

"Of course he remained with me that night; his passport was in order and the man seemed all right. On the second night also. On the third he did not leave the house, sitting on the window-seat of the corridor the whole day, and of course he remained over that night too. Well, I thought, just see how he has forced himself upon you. You have to give him to eat and to drink and to shelter him. All a poor man needs is some one to sponge upon him. I soon found out that once before he had attached himself to a man just as he had now attached himself to me; they drank together, but the other one soon died of some deep-seated sorrow. I thought and thought: What shall I do with him? Drive him out—my conscience would not allow it—I felt very sorry for him: he was such a wretched, forlorn creature, terrible! And so dumb he did not ask for anything, only sat quietly and looked you straight in the eyes, just like a faithful little dog. That is how drink can ruin a man. And I thought to myself: Well, suppose I say to him: 'Get out of here, Emelian; you have nothing to do in here, you come to the wrong person; I will soon have nothing to eat myself, so how do you expect me to feed *you?*' And I tried to imagine what he would do after I'd told him all this. And I could see how he would look at me for a long time after he had heard me, without understanding a word; how at last he would understand what I was driving at, and, rising from the window-seat, take his little bundle—I see it before me now—a red-checked little bundle full of holes, in which he kept God knows what, and which he carted along with him wherever he went; how he would brush and fix up his worn cloak a little, so that it would look a bit more decent and not show so much the holes and patches—he was a man of very fine feelings!

How he would have opened the door afterward and would have gone forth with tears in his eyes.

"Well, should a man be allowed to perish altogether? I all at once felt heartily sorry for him; but at the same time I thought: And what about me, am I any better off? And I said to myself: Well, Emelian, you will not feast overlong at my expense; soon I shall have to move from here myself, and then you will not find me again. Well, sir, my baron soon left for his estate with all his household, telling me before he went that he was very well satisfied with my services, and would gladly employ me again on his return to the capital. A fine man my baron was, but he died the same year.

Well, after I had escorted my baron and his family a little way, I took my things and the little money I had saved up, and went to live with an old woman I knew, who rented out a corner of the room she occupied by herself. She used to be a nurse in some well-to-do family, and now, in her old age, they had pensioned her off. Well, I thought to myself, now it is good-by to you, Emelian, dear man, you will not find me now! And what do you think, sir? When I returned in the evening—I had paid a visit to an acquaintance of mine—whom should I see but Emelian sitting quietly upon my trunk with his red-checked bundle by his side. He was wrapped up in his poor little cloak, and was awaiting my home-coming. He must have been quite lonesome, because he had borrowed a prayer-book of the old woman and held it upside down. He had found me after all! My hands fell helplessly at my sides. Well, I thought, there is nothing to be done, why did I not drive him away first off? And I only asked him: "Have you taken your passport along, Emelian?" Then I sat down, sir, and began to turn the matter over in my mind: Well, could he, a roving man, be much in my way? And after I had considered it well, I decided that he would not, and besides, he would be of very little expense to me. Of course, he would have to be fed, but what does that amount to? Some bread in the morning and, to make it a little more appetizing, a little onion or so. For the midday meal again some bread and onion, and for the evening again onion and bread, and some kvass, and, if some cabbage-soup should happen to come our way, then we could both fill up to the throat. I ate little, and Emelian, who was a drinking man, surely ate almost nothing: all he wanted was vodka. He would be the undoing of me with his drinking; but at the same time I felt a curious feeling creep over me. It seemed as if life would be a burden to me if Emelian went away. And so I decided then and there to be his father-benefactor. I would put him on his legs, I thought, save him from perishing, and gradually wean him from drink. Just you wait, I thought. Stay with me, Emelian, but stand pat now. Obey the word of command!

Well, I thought to myself, I will begin by teaching him some work, but not at once; let him first enjoy himself a bit, and I will in the mean while look around and discover what he finds easiest, and would be capable of doing, because you must know, sir, a man must have a calling and a capacity for a certain work to be able to do it properly. And I began stealthily to observe him. And a hard subject he was, that Emelian! At first I tried to get at him with a kind word. Thus and thus I would speak to him: "Emelian, you had better take more care of yourself and try to fix yourself up a little."

"Give up drinking. Just look at yourself, man, you are all ragged, your cloak looks more like a sieve than anything else. It is not nice. It is about time for you to come to your senses and know when you have had enough."

"He listened to me, my Emelian did, with lowered head; he had already reached that state, poor fellow, when the drink affected his tongue and he could not utter a sensible word. You talk to him about cucumbers, and he answers beans. He listened, listened to me for a long time, and then he would sigh deeply.

"What are you sighing for, Emelian?" I ask him.

"Oh, it is nothing, Astafi Ivanich, do not worry. Only what I saw to-day, Astafi Ivanich—two women fighting about a basket of huckleberries that one of them had upset by accident."

"Well, what of that?"

"And the woman whose berries were scattered snatched a like basket of huckleberries from the other woman's hand, and not only threw them on the ground, but stamped all over them."

"Well, but what of that, Emelian?"

"Ech!" I think to myself, "Emelian! You have lost your poor wits through the cursed drink!"

"And again," Emelian says, "a baron lost a bill on the Gorokhova Street— or was it on the Sadova? A muzhik saw him drop it, and says, "My luck," but here another one interfered and says, "No, it is my luck! I saw it first. . . .""

"Well, Emelian?"

"And the two muzhiks started a fight, Astafi Ivanich, and the upshot was that a policeman came, picked up the money, handed it back to the baron, and threatened to put the muzhiks under lock for raising a disturbance."

"But what of that? What is there wonderful or edifying in that, Emelian?"

"Well, nothing, but the people laughed, Astafi Ivanich."

"E-ch, Emelian! What have the people to do with it?" I said. "You have sold your immortal soul for a copper. But do you know what I will tell you, Emelian?"

"What, Astafi Ivanich?"

"You'd better take up some work, really you should. I am telling you for the hundredth time that you should have pity on yourself!"

"But what shall I do, Astafi Ivanich? I do not know where to begin and no one would employ me, Astafi Ivanich."

"That is why they drove you out of service, Emelian; it is all on account of drink!"

"And to-day," said Emelian, "they called Vlass the barkeeper into the office."

"What did they call him for, Emelian?" I asked.

"I don't know why, Astafi Ivanich. I suppose it was needed, so they called him."

"Ech," I thought to myself, "no good will come of either of us, Emelian! It is for our sins that God is punishing us!"

"Well, what could a body do with such a man, sir!"

"But he was sly, the fellow was, I tell you! He listened to me, listened, and at last it seems it began to tire him, and as quick as he would notice that I was growing angry he would take his cloak and slip out—and that was the last to be seen of him! He would not show up the whole day, and only in the evening would he return, as drunk as a lord. Who treated him to drinks, or where he got the money for it, God only knows; not from me, surely! . . .

"Well," I say to him, "Emelian, you will have to give up drink, do you hear? you will have to give it up! The next time you return tipsy, you will have to sleep on the stairs. I'll not let you in!"

"After this Emelian kept to the house for two days; on the third he once more sneaked out. I wait and wait for him; he does not come! I must confess that I was kind of frightened; besides, I felt terribly sorry for him. What had I done to the poor devil! I thought. I must have frightened him off. Where could he have gone to now, the wretched creature? Great God, he may perish yet! The night passed and he did not return. In the morning I went out into the hall, and he was lying there with his head on the lower step, almost stiff with cold.

"What is the matter with you, Emelian? The Lord save you! Why are you here?"

"But you know, Astafi Ivanich," he replied, "you were angry with me the other day; I aggravated you, and you promised to make me sleep in the hall, and I—so I—did not dare—to come in—and lay down here."

"It would be better for you, Emelian," I said, filled with anger and pity, "to find a better employment than needlessly watching the stairs!"

"But what other employment, Astafi Ivanich?"

"Well, wretched creature that you are," here anger had flamed up in me, "if you would try to learn the tailoring art. Just look at the cloak you are wearing! Not only is it full of holes, but you are sweeping the stairs with it! You should at least take a needle and mend it a little, so it would look more decent. E-ch, a wretched tippler you are, and nothing more!"

"Well, sir! What do you think! He did take the needle—I had told him only for fun, and there he got scared and actually took the needle. He threw off his cloak and began to put the thread through; well, it was easy to see what would come of it; his eyes began to fill and reddened, his hands trembled! He pushed and pushed the thread—could not get it through: he wetted it, rolled it between his fingers, smoothed it out, but it would not—go! He flung it from him and looked at me.

"Well, Emelian!" I said, "you served me right! If people had seen it I would have died with shame! I only told you all this for fun, and because I was angry with you. Never mind sewing; may the Lord keep you from sin! You need not do anything, only keep out of mischief, and do not sleep on the stairs and put me to shame thereby!"

"But what shall I do, Astafi Ivanich; I know myself that I am always tipsy and unfit for anything! I only make you, my be—benefactor, angry for nothing."

"And suddenly his bluish lips began to tremble, and a tear rolled down his unshaven, pale cheek, then another and another one, and he broke into a very flood of tears, my Emelian. Father in Heaven! I felt as if some one had cut me over the heart with a knife.

"E-ch you, sensitive man; why, I never thought! And who *could* have thought such a thing! No, I'd better give you up altogether, Emelian; do as you please."

"Well, sir, what else is there to tell! But the whole thing is so insignificant and unimportant, it is really not worth while wasting words about it; for instance, you, sir, would not give two broken groschen for it; but I, I would give much, if I had much, that this thing had never happened! I owned, sir, a pair of breeches, blue, in checks, a first-class article, the devil take them—a rich landowner who came here on business ordered them from me, but refused afterward to take them, saying that they were too tight, and left them with me.

"Well, I thought, the cloth is of first-rate quality! I can get five rubles for them in the old-clothes market-place, and, if not, I can cut a fine pair of pantaloons out of them for some St. Petersburg gent, and have a piece left over for a vest for myself. Everything counts with a poor man! And Emelian was at that time in sore straits. I saw that he had given up drinking, first one day, then a second, and a third, and looked so downhearted and sad.

"Well, I thought, it is either that the poor fellow lacks the necessary coin or maybe he has entered on the right path, and has at last listened to good sense.

"Well, to make a long story short, an important holiday came just at that time, and I went to vespers. When I came back I saw Emelian sitting on the window-seat as drunk as a lord. Eh! I thought, so that is what you are about! And I go to my trunk to get out something I needed. I look! The breeches are not there. I rummage about in this place and that place: gone! Well, after I had searched all over and saw that they were missing for fair, I felt as if something had gone through me! I went after the old woman—as to Emelian, though there was evidence against him in his being drunk, I somehow never thought of him!

"No," says my old woman; "the good Lord keep you, gentleman, what do I need breeches for? can I wear them? I myself missed a skirt the other day. I know nothing at all about it."

"Well," I asked, "has any one called here?"

"No one called," she said. "I was in all the time; your friend here went out for a short while and then came back; here he sits! Why don't you ask him?"

"Did you happen, for some reason or other, Emelian, to take the breeches out of the trunk? The ones, you remember, which were made for the landowner?"

"No," he says, "I have not taken them, Astafi Ivanich."

"What *could* have happened to them?" Again I began to search, but nothing came of it! And Emelian sat and swayed to and fro on the window-seat.

"I was on my knees before the open trunk, just in front of him. Suddenly I threw a sidelong glance at him. Ech, I thought, and felt very hot round the heart, and my face grew very red. Suddenly my eyes encountered Emelian's.

"No," he says, "Astafi Ivanich. You perhaps think that I—you know what I mean—but I have not taken them."

"But where have they gone, Emelian?"

"No," he says, "Astafi Ivanich, I have not seen them at all."

"Well, then, you think they simply went and got lost by themselves, Emelian?"

"Maybe they did, Astafi Ivanich."

"After this I would not waste another word on him. I rose from my knees, locked the trunk, and after I had lighted the lamp I sat down to work. I was remaking a vest for a government clerk, who lived on the floor below. But I was terribly rattled, just the same. It would have been much easier to bear, I thought, if all my wardrobe had burned to ashes. Emelian, it seems, felt that I was deeply angered. It is always so, sir, when a man is guilty; he always feels beforehand when trouble approaches, as a bird feels the coming storm.

"And do you know, Astafi Ivanich," he suddenly began, "the leach married the coachman's widow to-day."

I just looked at him; but, it seems, looked at him so angrily that he understood: I saw him rise from his seat, approach the bed, and begin to rummage in it, continually repeating: "Where could they have gone, vanished, as if the devil had taken them!"

I waited to see what was coming; I saw that my Emelian had crawled under the bed. I could contain myself no longer.

"Look here," I said. "What makes you crawl under the bed?"

"I am looking for the breeches, Astafi Ivanich," said Emelian from under the bed. "Maybe they got here somehow or other."

"But what makes you, sir (in my anger I addressed him as if he was—somebody), what makes you trouble yourself on account of such a plain man as I am; dirtying your knees for nothing!"

"But, Astafi Ivanich—I did not mean anything—I only thought maybe if we look for them here we may find them yet."

"Mm! Just listen to me a moment, Emelian!"

"What, Astafi Ivanich?"

"Have you not simply stolen them from me like a rascally thief, serving me so for my bread and salt?" I said to him, beside myself with wrath at the sight of him crawling under the bed for something he knew was not there.

"No, Astafi Ivanich." For a long time he remained lying flat under the bed. Suddenly he crawled out and stood before me—I seem to see him even now—as terrible a sight as sin itself.

"No," he says to me in a trembling voice, shivering through all his body and pointing to his breast with his finger, so that all at once I became scared and could not move from my seat on the window. "I have not taken your breeches, Astafi Ivanich."

"Well," I answered, "Emelian, forgive me if in my foolishness I have accused you wrongfully. As to the breeches, let them go hang; we will get along without them. We have our hands, thank God, we will not have to steal, and now, too, we will not have to sponge on another poor man; we will earn our living."

Emelian listened to me and remained standing before me for some time, then he sat down and sat motionless the whole evening; when I lay down to sleep he was still sitting in the same place.

In the morning, when I awoke, I found him sleeping on the bare floor, wrapped up in his cloak; he felt his humiliation so strongly that he had no heart to go and lie down on the bed.

Well, sir, from that day on I conceived a terrible dislike for the man; that is, rather, I hated him the first few days, feeling as if, for instance, my own son had robbed me and given me deadly offense. Ech, I thought, Emelian, Emelian! And Emelian, my dear sir, had gone on a two weeks' spree. Drunk to bestiality from morning till night. And during the whole two weeks he had not uttered a word. I suppose he was consumed the whole time by a deep-seated grief, or else he was trying in this way to make an end to himself. At last he gave up drinking. I suppose he had no longer the wherewithal to buy vodka—had drunk up every copeck—and he once more took up his old place on the window-seat. I remember that he sat there for three whole days without a word; suddenly I see him weep; sits there and cries, but what crying! The tears come from his eyes in showers, drip, drip, as if he did not know that he was shedding them. It is very painful, sir, to see a grown man weep, all the more when the man is of advanced years, like Emelian, and cries from grief and a sorrowful heart.

"What ails you, Emelian?" I say to him.

He starts and shivers. This was the first time I had spoken to him since that eventful day.

"It is nothing—Astafi Ivanich."

"God keep you, Emelian; never you mind it all. Let bygones be bygones. Don't take it to heart so, man!" I felt very sorry for him.

"It is only that—that I would like to do something—some kind of work, Astafi Ivanich."

"But what kind of work, Emelian?"

"Oh, any kind. Maybe I will go into some kind of service, as before. I have already been at my former employer's asking. It will not do for me, Astafi Ivanich, to use you any longer. I, Astafi Ivanich, will perhaps obtain some employment, and then I will pay you for everything, food and all."

"Don't, Emelian, don't. Well, let us say you committed a sin; well, it is over! The devil take it all! Let us live as before—as if nothing had happened!"

"You, Astafi Ivanich, you are probably hinting about *that*. But I have not taken your breeches."

"Well, just as you please, Emelian!"

"No, Astafi Ivanich, evidently I can not live with you longer. You will excuse me, Astafi Ivanich."

"But God be with you, Emelian," I said to him; "who is it that is offending you or driving you out of the house? Is it I who am doing it?"

"No, but it is unseemly for me to misuse your hospitality any longer, Astafi Ivanich; 'twill be better to go."

I saw that he had in truth risen from his place and donned his ragged cloak —he felt offended, the man did, and had gotten it into his head to leave, and —basta.

"But where are you going, Emelian? Listen to sense: what are you? Where will you go?"

"No, it is best so, Astafi Ivanich, do not try to keep me back," and he once more broke into tears; "let me be, Astafi Ivanich, you are no longer what you used to be."

"Why am I not? I am just the same. But you will perish when left alone— like a foolish little child, Emelian."

"No, Astafi Ivanich. Lately, before you leave the house, you have taken to locking your trunk, and I, Astafi Ivanich, see it and weep—No, it is better you should let me go, Astafi Ivanich, and forgive me if I have offended you in any way during the time we have lived together."

Well, sir! And so he did go away. I waited a day and thought: Oh, he will be back toward evening. But a day passes, then another, and he does not return. On the third—he does not return. I grew frightened, and a terrible sadness gripped at my heart. I stopped eating and drinking, and lay whole nights without closing my eyes. The man had wholly disarmed me! On the fourth day I went to look for him; I looked in all the taverns and pot-houses in the vicinity, and asked if any one had seen him. No, Emelian had wholly disappeared! Maybe he has done away with his miserable existence, I thought. Maybe, when in his cups, he has perished like a dog, somewhere under a fence. I came home half dead with fatigue and despair, and decided to go out the next day again to look for him, cursing myself bitterly for letting the foolish, helpless man go away from me. But at dawn of the fifth day (it was a holiday) I heard the door creak. And whom should I see but Emelian! But in what a state! His face was bluish and his hair was full of mud, as if he had slept in the street; and he had grown thin, the poor fellow had, as thin as a rail. He took off his poor cloak, sat down on my trunk, and began to look at me. Well, sir, I was overjoyed, but at the same time felt a greater sadness than ever pulling at my heart-strings. This is how it was, sir: I felt that if a thing like that had happened to me, that is—I would sooner have perished like a dog, but would not have returned. And Emelian did. Well, naturally, it is hard to see a man in such a state. I began to coddle and to comfort him in every way.

"Well," I said, "Emelian, I am very glad you have returned; if you had not come so soon, you would not have found me in, as I intended to go hunting for you. Have you had anything to eat?"

"I have eaten, Astafi Ivanich."

"I doubt it. Well, here is some cabbage soup—left over from yesterday; a nice soup with some meat in it—not the meagre kind. And here you have some bread and a little onion. Go ahead and eat; it will do you good."

I served it to him; and immediately realized that he must have been starving for the last three days—such an appetite as he showed! So it was hunger that had driven him back to me. Looking at the poor fellow, I was deeply touched, and decided to run into the nearby dram-shop. I will get him some vodka, I thought, to liven him up a bit and make peace with him. It is enough. I have nothing against the poor devil any longer. And so I brought the vodka and said to him: "Here, Emelian, let us drink to each other's health in honor of the holiday. Come, take a drink. It will do you good."

He stretched out his hand, greedily stretched it out, you know, and stopped; then, after a while, he lifted the glass, carried it to his mouth, spilling the liquor on his sleeve; at last he did carry it to his mouth, but immediately put it back on the table.

"Well, why don't you drink, Emelian?"

"But no, I'll not, Astafi Ivanich."

"You'll not drink it!"

"But I, Astafi Ivanich, I think—I'll not drink any more, Astafi Ivanich."

"Is it for good you have decided to give it up, Emelian, or only for to-day?"

He did not reply, and after a while I saw him lean his head on his hand, and I asked him: "Are you not feeling well, Emelian?"

"Yes, pretty well, Astafi Ivanich."

I made him go to bed, and saw that he was truly in a bad way. His head was burning hot and he was shivering with ague. I sat by him the whole day; toward evening he grew worse. I prepared a meal for him of kvass, butter, and some onion, and threw in it a few bits of bread, and said to him: "Go ahead and take some food; maybe you will feel better!"

But he only shook his head: "No, Astafi Ivanich, I shall not have any dinner to-day."

I had some tea prepared for him, giving a lot of trouble to the poor old woman from whom I rented a part of the room—but he would not take even a little tea.

Well, I thought to myself, it is a bad case. On the third morning, I went to see the doctor, an acquaintance of mine, Dr. Kostopravov, who had treated me when I still lived in my last place. The doctor came, examined the poor fellow, and only said: "There was no need of sending for me, he is already too far gone, but you can give him some powders which I will prescribe."

Well, I didn't give him the powders at all, as I understood that the doctor was only doing it for form's sake; and in the mean while came the fifth day.

He lay dying before me, sir. I sat on the window-seat with some work I had on hand lying on my lap. The old woman was raking the stove. We were all silent, and my heart was breaking over this poor, shiftless creature, as if he were my own son whom I was losing. I knew that Emelian was gazing at me all the time; I noticed for the earliest morning that he longed to tell me something, but seemingly dared not. At last I looked at him, and saw that he did not take his eyes from me, but that whenever his eyes met mine, he immediately lowered his own.

"Astafi Ivanich!"

"What, Emelian?"

"What if my cloak should be carried over to the old clothes market, would they give much for it, Astafi Ivanich?"

"Well," I said, "I do not know for certain, but three rubles they would probably give for it, Emelian." I said it only to comfort the simple-minded creature; in reality they would have laughed in my face for even thinking to sell such a miserable, ragged thing.

"And I thought that they might give a little more, Astafi Ivanich. It is made of cloth, so how is it that they would not wish to pay more than three rubles for it?"

"Well, Emelian, if you wish to sell it, then of course you may ask more for it at first."

Emelian was silent for a moment, then he once more called to me.

"Astafi Ivanich!"

"What is it, Emelian?"

"You will sell the cloak after I am no more; no need of burying me in it, I can well get along without it; it is worth something, and may come handy to you."

Here I felt such a painful gripping at my heart as I can not even express, sir. I saw that the sadness of approaching death had already come upon the man. Again we were silent for some time. About an hour passed in this way. I looked at him again and saw that he was still gazing at me, and when his eyes met mine he immediately lowered his.

"Would you like a drink of cold water?" I asked him.

"Give me some, and may God repay you, Astafi Ivanich."

"Would you like anything else, Emelian?"

"No, Astafi Ivanich, I do not want anything, but I—"

"What?"

"You know that—"

"What is it you want, Emelian?"

"The breeches—You know—It was I who took them—Astafi Ivanich—"

"Well," I said, "the great God will forgive you, Emelian, poor, unfortunate fellow that you are! Depart in peace."

And I had to turn away my head for a moment because grief for the poor devil took my breath away and the tears came in torrents from my eyes.

"Astafi Ivanich!—"

I looked at him, saw that he wished to tell me something more, tried to raise himself, and was moving his lips—He reddened and looked at me— Suddenly I saw that he began to grow paler and paler; in a moment he fell with his head thrown back, breathed once, and gave his soul into God's keeping."

THE BEAUTY SPOT

Alfred de Musset

I

In 1756, when Louis XV, wearied with the quarrels between the magistrature and the grand council, about the "two sous tax," determined upon holding a special *lit de justice,* the members of Parliament resigned. Sixteen of these resignations were accepted, and as many exiles decreed. "But," said Madame de Pompadour to one of the presidents, "could you calmly stand by and see a handful of men resist the authority of the King of France? Would you not have a very bad opinion of such a policy? Throw off the cloak of petty pretense, M. le President, and you will see the situation just as I see it myself."

It was not only the exiles that had to pay the penalty of their want of compliance, but also their relatives and friends. The violation of mail-secrets was one of the King's amusements. To relieve the monotony of his other pleasures, it pleased him to hear his favorite read all the curious things that were to be found in his subjects' private correspondence. Of course, under the fallacious pretext of doing his own detective work, he reaped a large harvest of enjoyment from the thousand little intrigues which thus passed under his eyes; but whoever was connected, whether closely or in a remote degree, with the leaders of the factions, was almost invariably ruined.

Every one knows that Louis XV, with all his manifold weaknesses, had one, and only one, strong point: he was inexorable.

One evening, as he sat before the fire with his feet on the mantelpiece, melancholy as was his wont, the marquise, looking through a packet of letters, suddenly burst into a laugh and shrugged her shoulders. The King wished to know what was the matter.

"Why, I have found here," answered she, "a letter, without a grain of common sense in it, but a very touching thing for all that—quite pitiable in fact."

"Whose is the signature?" said the King.

"There is none, it is a love-letter."

"And what is the address?"

"That is just the point. It is addressed to Mademoiselle d'Annebault, the niece of my good friend, Madame d'Estrades. Apparently it has been put in among these papers on purpose for me to see."

"And what is there in it?" the King persisted.

"Why, I tell you it is all about love. There is mention also of Vauvert and of Neauflette. Are there any gentlemen in those parts? Does your Majesty know of any?"

The King always prided himself upon knowing France by heart, that is, the nobility of France. The etiquette of his court, which he had studied thoroughly, was not more familiar to him than the armorial bearings of his realm. Not a very wide range of learning; still nothing beyond it did he reckon worthy the study; and it was a point of vanity with him, the social hierarchy being, in his eyes, something like the marble staircase of his palace; he must set foot on it as sole lord and master. After having pondered a few moments, he knitted his brow, as though struck by an unwelcome remembrance; then, with a sign to the marquise to read, he threw himself back in his easy chair, saying with a smile:

"Read on—she is a pretty girl."

Madame de Pompadour assumed her sweetest tone of raillery and began to read a long letter, which, from beginning to end, was one rhapsody of love.

"Just see," said the writer, "how the fates persecute me! At first everything seemed to work for the fulfilment of my wishes, and you yourself, my sweet one, had you not given me reason to hope for happiness? I must, however, renounce this heavenly dream, and that for no fault of mine. Is it not an excess of cruelty to have let me catch a glimpse of paradise, only to dash me into the abyss? When some unfortunate wretch is doomed to death, do they take a barbarous pleasure in placing before his eyes all that would make him love life and regret leaving it? Such is, however, my fate: I have no other refuge, no other hope, than the tomb, for, in my dire misfortune, I can no longer dream of winning your hand. When fate smiled on me, all my hopes were that you should be mine; to-day, a poor man, I should abhor myself if I dared still to think of such blessedness, and, now that I can no longer make you happy, though dying of love for you, I forbid you to love me—"

The Marquise smiled at these last words.

"Madame," said the King, "this is an honorable man. But what prevents him from marrying his lady-love?"

"Permit me, sire, to continue."

"—This overwhelming injustice from the best of kings surprises me. You know that my father asked for me a commission as cornet or ensign in the

Guards, and that on this appointment depended the happiness of my life, since it would give me the right to offer myself to you. The Duc de Biron proposed my name; but the King rejected me in a manner the memory of which is very bitter to me. If my father has his own way of looking at things (admitting that it is a wrong one) must I suffer for it? My devotion to the King is as true, as unbounded, as my love for you. How gladly would I give proof of both these sentiments, could I but draw the sword! Assuredly I feel deeply distressed at my request being refused; but that I should be thus disgraced without good reason is a thing opposed to the well-known kindness of his Majesty."

"Aha!" said the King, "I am becoming interested."

"—If you knew how very dull we are! Ah! my friend! This estate of Neauflette, this country-house of Vauvert, these wooded glades!—I wander about them all day long. I have forbidden a rake to be used; the sacrilegious gardener came yesterday with his iron-shod besom. He was about to touch the sand. But the trace of your steps, lighter than the wind, was not effaced. The prints of your little feet and of your red satin heels were still upon the path; they seemed to walk before me, as I followed your beautiful image, and that charming fantom took shape at times as though it were treading in the fugitive prints. It was there, while conversing with you by the flower-beds, that it was granted me to know you, to appreciate you. A brilliant education joined to the spirit of an angel, the dignity of a queen with the grace of a nymph, thoughts worthy of Leibnitz expressed in language so simple, Plato's bee on the lips of Diana, all this enfolded me as in a veil of adoration. And, during those delicious moments, the darling flowers were blooming about us, I inhaled their breath while listening to you, in their perfume your memory lived. They droop their heads now; they present to me the semblance of death!"

"This is all Rousseau and water," said the King. "Why do you read such stuff to me?"

"Because your Majesty commanded me to do so, for the sake of Mademoiselle d'Annebault's beautiful eyes."

"It is true, she has beautiful eyes."

"—And when I return from these walks, I find my father alone, in the great drawing-room, near the lighted candle, leaning on his elbow, amid the faded gildings which cover our moldy wainscot. It is with pain that he sees me enter. My grief disturbs his. Athénaïs! At the back of that drawing-room, near the window, is the harpsichord over which flitted those sweet fingers that my lips have touched but once—once, while yours opened softly to harmonies of celestial music—opened with such dainty art that your songs were but a smile. How happy are they—Rameau, Lulli, Duni, and so many more! Yes, yes, you love them—they are in your memory—their breath has passed through your lips. I too seat myself at that harpsichord, I strive to play one of those airs that you love;—how cold, how monotonous they seem to me! I leave them and listen to their dying accents while the echo loses itself

beneath that lugubrious vault. My father turns to me and sees me distressed
—what can he do? Some boudoir gossip, some report from the servants' hall
has closed upon us the gates that lead into the world. He sees me young,
ardent, full of life, asking only to live in this world, he is my father, and can
do nothing for me."

"One would think," said the King, "that this fellow was starting for the
hunt, and that his falcon had been killed on his wrist. Against whom is he
inveighing, may I ask?"

"—It is quite true," continued the Marquise, reading in a lower tone. "It is
quite true that we are near neighbors, and distant relatives, of the Abbé
Chauvelin. . . ."

"That is what it is, is it?" said Louis XV, yawning. "Another nephew of the
enquêtes et requêtes. My Parliament abuses my bounty; it really has too large
a family."

"But if it is only a *distant* relative!"

"Enough; all these people are good for nothing. This Abbé Chauvelin is a
Jansenist; not a bad sort of fellow, in his way; but he has dared to resign.
Please throw the letter into the fire, and let me hear no more about it."

II

If these last words of the King were not exactly a death-warrant, they were
something like a refusal of permission to live. What could a young man
without fortune do, in 1756, whose King would not hear his name mentioned? He might have looked for a clerkship, or tried to turn philosopher, or
poet, perhaps; but without official dedication, the trade was worth nothing.

And besides, such was not, by any means, the vocation of the Chevalier
Vauvert, who had written, with tears, the letter which made the King laugh.
At this very moment, alone with his father, in the old château of Neauflette,
his look was desperate and gloomy, even to frenzy, as he paced to and fro.

"I must go to Versailles," he said.

"And what will you do there?"

"I know not; but what am I doing here?"

"You keep me company. It certainly can not be very amusing for you, and
I will not in any way seek to detain you. But do you forget that your mother
is dead?"

"No, sir. I promised her to consecrate to you the life that you gave me. I
will come back, but I must go. I really can not stay in this place any longer."

"And why, if I may ask?"

"My desperate love is the only reason. I love Mademoiselle d'Annebault
madly."

"But you know that it is useless. It is only Molière who contrives successful matches without dowries. Do you forget too the disfavor with which I am regarded?"

"Ah! sir, that disfavor! Might I be allowed, without deviating from the profound respect I owe you, to ask what caused it? We do not belong to the Parliament. We pay the tax; we do not order it. If the Parliament stints the King's purse, it is his affair, not ours. Why should M. l'Abbé Chauvelin drag us into his ruin?"

"Monsieur l'Abbé Chauvelin acts as an honest man. He refuses to approve the 'dixième' tax because he is disgusted at the prodigality of the court. Nothing of this kind would have taken place in the days of Madame de Chateauroux! She was beautiful, at least, that woman, and did not cost us anything, not even what she so generously gave. She was sovereign mistress, and declared that she would be satisfied if the King did not send her to rot in some dungeon when he should be pleased to withdraw his good graces from her. But this Étioles, this le Normand, this insatiable Poisson!"

"What does it matter?"

"What does it matter! say you? More than you think. Do you know that now, at this very time, while the King is plundering us, the fortune of this grisette is incalculable? She began by contriving to get an annuity of a hundred and eighty thousand livres—but that was a mere bagatelle, it counts for nothing now; you can form no idea of the startling sums that the King showers upon her; three months of the year can not pass without her picking up, as though by chance, some five or six hundred thousand livres—yesterday out of the salt-tax, to-day out of the increase in the appropriation for the Royal mews. Although she has her own quarters in the royal residences, she buys La Selle, Cressy, Aulnay, Brimborion, Marigny, Saint-Remy, Bellevue, and a number of other estates—mansions in Paris, in Fontainebleau, Versailles, Compiègne—without counting secret hoards in all the banks of Europe, to be used in case of her own disgrace or a demise of the crown. And who pays for all this, if you please?"

"That I do not know, sir, but, certainly, not I."

"It *is* you, as well as everybody else. It is France, it is the people who toil and moil, who riot in the streets, who insult the statue of Pigalle. But Parliament will endure it no longer, it will have no more new imposts. As long as there was question of defraying the cost of the war, our last crown was ready; we had no thought of bargaining. The victorious King could see clearly that he was beloved by the whole kingdom, still more so when he was at the point of death. Then all dissensions, all faction, all ill-feeling ceased. All France knelt before the sick-bed of the King, and prayed for him. But if we pay, without counting, for his soldiers and his doctors, we will no longer pay for his mistresses; we have other things to do with our money than to support Madame de Pompadour."

"I do not defend her, sir. I could not pretend to say either that she was in the wrong or in the right. I have never seen her."

"Doubtless; and you would not be sorry to see her—is it not so?—in order

to have an opinion on the subject? For, at your age, the head judges through
the eyes. Try it then, if the fancy takes you. But the satisfaction will be denied
you."

"Why, sir?"

"Because such an attempt is pure folly; because this marquise is as invisible
in her little boudoir at Brimborion as the Grand Turk in his seraglio; because
every door will be shut in your face. What are you going to do? Attempt an
impossibility? Court fortune like an adventurer?"

"By no means, but like a lover. I do not intend to supplicate, sir, but to
protest against an injustice. I had a well-founded hope, almost a promise,
from M. de Biron; I was on the eve of possessing the object of my love, and
this love is not unreasonable; you have not disapproved of it. Let me venture,
then, to plead my own cause. Whether I shall appeal to the King or to
Madame de Pompadour I know not, but I wish to set out."

"You do not know what the court is, and you wish to present yourself
there."

"I may perhaps be the more easily received for the very reason that I am
unknown there."

"You unknown, Chevalier. What are you thinking about? With such a
name as yours! We are gentlemen of an old stock, Monsieur; you could not be
unknown."

"Well, then, the King will listen to me."

"He will not even hear you. You see Versailles in your dreams, and you will
think yourself there when your postilion stops his horses at the city gates.
Suppose you get as far as the antechamber—the gallery, the Oeil de Boeuf;
perhaps there may be nothing between his Majesty and yourself but the thickness of a door; there will still be an abyss for you to cross. You will look about
you, you will seek expedients, protection, and you will find nothing. We are
relatives of M. de Chauvelin, and how do you think the King takes vengeance
on such as we? The rack for Damiens, exile for the Parliament, but for us a
word is enough, or, worse still—silence. Do you know what the silence of the
King is, when, instead of replying to you, he mutely stares at you, as he
passes, and annihilates you? After the Grève, and the Bastille, this is a degree
of torture which, though less cruel in appearance, leaves its mark as plainly as
the hand of the executioner. The condemned man, it is true, remains free, but
he must no longer think of approaching woman or courtier, drawing-room,
abbey, or barrack. As he moves about every door closes upon him, every one
who is anybody turns away, and thus he walks this way and that, in an
invisible prison."

"But I will so bestir myself in my prison that I shall get out of it."

"No more than any one else! The son of M. de Meynières was no more to
blame than you. Like you, he had received promises, he entertained most
legitimate hopes. His father, a devoted subject of his Majesty, an upright man
if there is one in the kingdom, repulsed by his sovereign, bowed his gray head
before the *grisette,* not in prayer, but in ardent pleading. Do you know what

she replied? Here are her very words, which M. de Meynières sends me in a letter: 'The King is the master, he does not deem it appropriate to signify his displeasure to you personally; he is content to make you aware of it by depriving your son of a calling. To punish you otherwise would be to begin an unpleasantness, and he wishes for none; we must respect his will. I pity you, however; I realize your troubles. I have been a mother; I know what it must cost you to leave your son without a profession!' This is how the creature expresses herself; and you wish to put yourself at her feet!"

"They say they are charming, sir."

"Of course they say so. She is not pretty, and the King does not love her, as every one knows. He yields, he bends before this woman. She *must* have something else than that wooden head of hers to maintain her strange power."

"But they say she has so much wit."

"And no heart!—Much to her credit, no doubt."

"No heart! She who knows so well how to declaim the lines of Voltaire, how to sing the music of Rousseau! She who plays Alzire and Colette! No heart. Oh, that can not be! I will never believe it."

"Go then and see, since you wish it. I advise, I do not command, but you will only be at the expense of a useless journey.—You love this D'Annebault young lady very much then?"

"More than my life."

"*Alors,* be off!"

III

It has been said that journeys injure love, because they distract the mind; it has also been said that they strengthen love, because they give one time to dream over it. The chevalier was too young to make such nice distinctions. Weary of the carriage, when half-way on his journey, he had taken a saddle-hack and thus arrived toward five o'clock in the evening at the "Sun" Inn—a sign then out of fashion, since it dated back to the time of Louis XIV.

There was, at Versailles, an old priest who had been rector of a church near Neauflette; the chevalier knew him and loved him. This curé, poor and simple himself, had a nephew, who held a benefice, a court abbé, who might therefore be useful. So the chevalier went to this nephew who—man of importance as he was—his chin ensconced in his "rabat," received the newcomer civilly, and condescended to listen to his request.

"Come!" said he, "you arrive at a fortunate moment. This is to be an opera-night at the court, some sort of fête or other. I am not going, because I am sulking so as to get something out of the marquise; but here I happen to have a note from the Duc d'Aumont; I asked for it for some one else, but never mind, you can have it. Go to the fête; you have not yet been presented, it is true, but, for this entertainment, that is not necessary. Try to be in the King's way when he goes into the little *foyer*. One look, and your fortune is made."

The chevalier thanked the abbé, and, worn out by a disturbed night and a day on horse-back, he made his toilet at the inn in that negligent manner which so well becomes a lover. A maidservant, whose experience had been decidedly limited, dressed his wig as best she could, covering his spangled coat with powder. Thus he turned his steps toward his luck with the hopeful courage of twenty summers.

The night was falling when he arrived at the château. He timidly advanced to the gate and asked his way of a sentry. He was shown the grand staircase. There he was informed by the tall Swiss that the opera had just commenced, and that the King, that is to say, everybody, was in the hall.

"If Monsieur le Marquis will cross the court," added the doorkeeper (he conferred the title of "Marquis" at a venture), "he will be at the play in an instant. If he prefers to go through the apartments—"

The chevalier was not acquainted with the palace. Curiosity prompted him, at first, to reply that he would cross the apartments; then, as a lackey offered to follow as a guide, an impulse of vanity made him add that he needed no escort. He, therefore, went forward alone, but not without a certain emotion of timidity.

Versailles was resplendent with light. From the ground-floor to the roof there glittered and blazed lustres, chandeliers, gilded furniture, marbles. With the exception of the Queen's apartments, the doors were everywhere thrown open. As the chevalier walked on he was struck with an astonishment and an admiration better imagined than described, for the wonder of the spectacle that offered itself to his gaze was not only the beauty, the sparkle of the display itself, but the absolute solitude which surrounded him in this enchanted wilderness.

To find one's self alone in a vast enclosure, be it temple, cloister, or castle, produces a strange, even a weird feeling. The movement—whatever it be— seems to weigh upon the solitary individual; its walls gaze at him! its echoes are listening to him; the noise of his steps breaks in upon a silence so deep that he is impressed by an involuntary fear and dares not advance without a feeling akin to awe. Such were the chevalier's first impressions, but curiosity soon got the upper hand and drew him on. The candelabra of the Gallery of Mirrors, looking into the polished surfaces, saw their flames redoubled in them. Every one knows what countless thousands of cherubs, nymphs, and shepherdesses disport themselves on the panelings, flutter about on the ceilings, and seem to encircle the entire palace as with an immense garland. Here, vast halls, with canopies of velvet shot with gold and chairs of state still impressed with the stiff majesty of the "great King"; there, creased and disordered ottomans, chairs in confusion around a card-table; a neverending succession of empty salons, where all this magnificence shone out the more that it seemed entirely useless. At intervals were half-concealed doors opening

upon corridors that extended as far as the eye could reach, a thousand stair-
cases, a thousand passages crossing each other as in a labyrinth; colonnades,
raised platforms built for giants, boudoirs ensconced in corners like children's
hiding-places, an enormous painting of Vanloo near a mantel of porphyry; a
forgotten patch-box, lying beside a piece of grotesque Chinese workmanship;
here a crushing grandeur, there an effeminate grace; and everywhere, in the
midst of luxury, of prodigality, and of indolence, a thousand intoxicating
odors, strange and diverse, mingle perfumes of flowers and women, an ener-
vating warmth, the very material and sensible atmosphere of pleasure itself.

To be in such a place, amid such marvels, at twenty, and to be there alone,
is surely quite sufficient cause for temporary intoxication. The chevalier advanced at haphazard, as in a dream.

"A very palace of fairies," he murmured, and, indeed, he seemed to behold,
unfolding itself before him, one of those tales in which wandering knights
discover enchanted castles. Were they indeed mortal creatures that inhabited
this matchless abode? Were they real women who came and sat on these
chairs and whose graceful outlines had left on those cushions that slight
impress, so suggestive, even yet, of indolence? Who knows but that, behind
those thick curtains, at the end of some long dazzling gallery, there may
perhaps soon appear a princess asleep for the last hundred years, a fairy in
hoops, an Armida in spangles, or some court hamadryad that shall issue forth
from this marble column, or burst from out of that gilded panel?

Bewildered, almost overpowered, at the sight of all these novel objects, the
young chevalier, in order the better to indulge his reverie, had thrown himself
on a sofa, and would doubtless have forgotten himself there for some time
had he not remembered that he was in love. What, at this hour, was Mademoiselle d'Annebault, his beloved, doing—left behind in her old château?

"Athénaïs!" he exclaimed suddenly, "why do I thus waste my time here? Is
my mind wandering? Great heavens! Where am I? And what is going on
within me?"

He soon rose and continued his travels through this *terra incognita,* and of
course lost his way. Two or three lackeys, speaking in a low voice, stood
before him at the end of a gallery. He walked toward them and asked how he
should find his way to the play.

"If M. le Marquis," he was answered (the same title being still benevolently
granted him), "will give himself the trouble to go down that staircase and
follow the gallery on the right, he will find at the end of it three steps going
up; he will then turn to the left, go through the Diana salon, that of Apollo,
that of the Muses, and that of Spring; he will go down six steps more, then,
leaving the Guards' Hall on his right and crossing over to the Ministers'
staircase, he will not fail to meet there other ushers who will show him the
way."

"Much obliged," said the chevalier, "with such excellent instruction, it will
certainly be my fault if I do not find my way."

He set off again boldly, constantly stopping, however, in spite of himself, to look from side to side, then once more remembering his love. At last, at the end of a full quarter of an hour, he once more found, as he had been told, a group of lackeys.

"M. le Marquis is mistaken," they informed him; "it is through the other wing of the château that he should have gone, but nothing is easier for him than to retrace his steps. M. le Marquis has but to go down this staircase, then he will cross the salon of the Nymphs, that of Summer, that of—"

"I thank you," said the chevalier, proceeding on his way. "How foolish I am," he thought, "to go on asking people in this fashion like a rustic. I am making myself ridiculous to no purpose, and even supposing—though it is not likely—that they are not laughing at me, of what use is their list of names, and the pompous sobriquets of these salons, not one of which I know?"

He made up his mind to go straight before him as far as possible. "For," after all," said he to himself, "this palace is very beautiful and prodigiously vast, but it is not boundless, and, were it three times as large as our rabbit enclosure, I must at last reach the end of it."

But it is not easy in Versailles to walk on for a long time in one direction, and this rustic comparison of the royal dwelling to a rabbit enclosure doubtless displeased the nymphs of the place, for they at once set about leading the poor lover astray more than ever, and, doubtless, to punish him, took pleasure in making him retrace his steps over and over again, constantly bringing him back to the same place, like a countryman lost in a thicket of quickset; thus did they shut him in in this Cretan labyrinth of marble and gold.

In the "Antiquities of Rome," by Piranesi, there is a series of engravings which the artist calls "his dreams," and which are supposed to reproduce his own visions during a fit of delirious fever. These engravings represent vast Gothic halls; on the flagstones are strewn all sorts of engines and machines, wheels, cables, pulleys, levers, catapults, the expression of enormous power and formidable resistance. Along the walls you perceive a staircase, and upon this staircase, climbing, not without trouble, Piranesi himself. Follow the steps a little higher and they suddenly come to an end before an abyss. Whatever has happened to poor Piranesi, you think that he has, at any rate, reached the end of his labors, for he can not take another step without falling; but lift your eyes and you will see a second staircase rising in the air, and upon these stairs Piranesi again, again on the brink of a precipice.

Look now still higher, and another staircase still rises before you, and again poor Piranesi continuing his ascent, and so on, until the everlasting staircase and the everlasting Piranesi disappear together in the skies; that is to say, in the border of the engraving.

This allegory, offspring of a nightmare, represents with a high degree of accuracy the tedium of useless labor and the species of vertigo which is brought on by impatience. The chevalier, wandering incessantly from salon to salon and from gallery to gallery, was at last seized with a fit of downright exasperation.

"Parbleu," said he, "but this is cruel! After having been so charmed, so enraptured, so enthralled, to find myself alone in this cursed palace." (It was no longer a palace of fairies!) "I shall never be able to get out of it! A plague upon the infatuation which inspired me with the idea of entering this place, like Prince Fortunatus with his boots of solid gold, instead of simply getting the first lackey I came across to take me to the play at once!"

The chevalier experienced this tardy feeling of repentance for his rashness at a moment when, like Piranesi, he was half-way up a staircase, on a landing between three doors. Behind the middle one, he thought he heard a murmur so sweet, so light, so voluptuous, that he could not help listening. At the very instant when he was tremblingly advancing with the indiscreet intention of eavesdropping, this door swung open. A breath of air, balmy with a thousand perfumes, a torrent of light that rendered the very mirrors of the gallery lustreless struck him so suddenly that he perforce stepped back.

"Does Monsieur le Marquis wish to enter?" asked the usher who had opened the door.

"I wish to go to the play," replied the chevalier.

"It is just this moment over."

At the same time, a bevy of beautiful ladies, their complexions delicately tinted with white and carmine, escorted by lords, old and young, who led them, not by the arm, nor by the hand, but by the tips of their fingers, began filing out from the Palace Theatre, taking care to walk sidewise, in order not to disarrange their hoops.

All of these brilliant people spoke in a low voice, with an air half grave, half gay, a mixture of awe and respect.

"What can this be?" said the Chevalier, not guessing that chance had luckily brought him to the little *foyer.*

"The King is about to pass," replied the usher.

There is a kind of intrepidity, which hesitates at nothing; it comes but too easily, it is the courage of vulgar people. Our young provincial, although he was reasonably brave, did not possess this faculty. At the mere words, "The King is about to pass," he stood motionless and almost terror-stricken.

King Louis XV, who when out hunting would ride on horseback a dozen leagues with ease, was, in other respects, as is known, royally indolent. He boasted, not without reason, that he was the first gentleman of France, and his mistresses used to tell him, not without truth, that he was the best built and the most handsome. It was something to remember to see him leave his chair, and deign to walk in person. When he crossed the *foyer,* with one arm laid, or rather stretched, on the shoulder of Monsieur d'Argenson, while his red heel glided over the polished floor (he had made his laziness the fashion), all whisperings ceased; the courtiers lowered their heads, not daring to bow outright, and the fine ladies, gently bending their knees within the depths of their immense furbelows, ventured that coquettish good-night which our grandmothers called a courtesy, and which our century has replaced by the brutal English shake of the hand.

But the King paid attention to nothing, and saw only what pleased him.

Alfieri, perhaps, was there, and it is he who thus describes, in his memoirs, his presentation at Versailles:

"I well knew that the king never spoke to strangers who were not of striking appearance; all the same I could not brook the impassible and frowning demeanor of Louis XV. He scanned from head to foot the man who was being presented to him, and it looked as if he received no impression by so doing. It seems to me, however, that if one were to say to a giant, 'Here is an ant I present to you,' he would smile on looking at it, or perhaps say, 'Oh! what a little creature.' "

The taciturn monarch thus passed among these flowers of feminine loveliness, and all this court, alone in spite of the crowd. It did not require of the chevalier much reflection to understand that he had nothing to hope from the King, and that the recital of his love would obtain no success in that quarter.

"Unfortunate that I am!" thought he. "My father was but too well informed when he told me that within two steps of the king I should see an abyss between him and me. Were I to venture to ask for an audience, who would be my patron? Who would present me? There he is—the absolute master, who can by a word change my destiny, assure my fortune, fulfil my desires. He is there before me; were I to stretch out my hand I could touch his embroidered coat—and I feel myself farther from him than if I were still buried in the depths of my native province! Oh! If I could only speak to him! Only approach him! Who will come to my help?"

While the chevalier was in this unhappy state of mind he saw entering with an air of the utmost grace and delicacy a young and attractive woman, clad very simply in a white gown, without diamonds or embroideries and with a single rose in her hair. She gave her hand to a lord *tout à l'ambre,* as Voltaire expresses it, and spoke softly to him behind her fan. Now chance willed it that, in chatting, laughing, and gesticulating, this fan should slip from her and fall beneath a chair, immediately in front of the chevalier. He at once hurried to pick it up, and as in doing so he had set one knee on the floor, the young lady appeared to him so charming that he presented her the fan without rising. She stopped, smiled, and passed on, thanking him with a slight movement of the head, but at the look she had given the chevalier he felt his heart beat without knowing why. He was right. This young lady was *la petite d'Etioles,* as the malcontents still called her, while others in speaking of her said "la Marquise" in that reverent tone in which one says "The Queen."

IV

"She will protect me! She will come to my rescue! Ah! how truly the abbé spoke when he said that one look might decide my life. Yes, those eyes, so soft and gentle, that little mouth, both merry and sweet, that little foot almost hidden under the *pompon*—Yes, here is my good fairy!"

Thus thought the chevalier, almost aloud, as he returned to the inn. Whence came this sudden hope? Did his youth alone speak, or had the eyes of the marquise told a tale?

He passed the greater part of the night writing to Mademoiselle d'Annebault such a letter as we heard read by Madame de Pompadour to her lord.

To reproduce this letter would be a vain task. Excepting idiots, lovers alone find no monotony in repeating the same thing over and over again.

At daybreak the chevalier went out and began roaming about, carrying his dreams through the streets. It did not occur to him to have recourse once more to the protecting abbé, and it would not be easy to tell the reason which prevented his doing so. It was like a blending of timidity and audacity, of false shame and romantic honor. And, indeed, what would the abbé have replied to him, if he had told his story of the night before? "You had the unique good fortune to pick up this fan; did you know how to profit by it? What did the marquise say to you?"

"Nothing."

"You should have spoken to her."

"I was confused; I had lost my head."

"That was wrong; one must know how to seize an opportunity; but this can be repaired. Would you like me to present you to Monsieur So-and-so, one of my friends; or perhaps to Madame Such-a-one? That would be still better. We will try and secure for you access to this marquise who frightened you so, and then"—and so forth.

Now the chevalier little relished anything of this kind. It seemed to him that, in telling his adventure, he would, so to speak, soil and mar it. He said to himself that chance had done for him something unheard of, incredible, and that it should remain a secret between himself and Fortune. To confide this secret to the first comer was, to his thinking, to rob it of its value, and to show himself unworthy of it. "I went alone yesterday to the castle at Versailles," thought he, "I can surely go alone to Trianon?" This was, at the time, the abode of the favorite.

Such a way of thinking might, and even should, appear extravagant to calculating minds, who neglect no detail, and leave as little as possible to chance; but colder mortals, if they were ever young, and not everybody is so, even in youth, have known that strange sentiment, both weak and bold, dangerous and seductive, which drags us to our fate. One feels one's self blind, and wishes to be so; one does not know where one is going and yet walks on. The charm of the thing consists in this recklessness and this very ignorance; it is the pleasure of the artist in his dreams, of the lover spending the night beneath the windows of his mistress; it is instinct of the soldier; it is, above all, that of the gamester.

The chevalier, almost without knowing it, had thus taken his way to Trianon. Without being very *paré*, as they said in those days, he lacked neither elegance nor that indescribable air which forbids a chance lackey, meeting one, from daring to ask where one is going. It was, therefore, not difficult for him, thanks to information he had obtained at the inn, to reach the gate of the château—if one can so call that marble *bonbonnière,* which has seen so many pleasures and pains in bygone days. Unfortunately, the gate was closed, and a stout Swiss wearing a plain coat was walking about, his hands behind his back, in the inner avenue, like a person who is not expecting any one.

"The King is here!" said the chevalier to himself, "or else the marquise is away. Evidently, when the doors are closed, and valets stroll about, the masters are either shut in or gone out."

What was to be done? Full as he had been, a moment earlier, of courage and confidence, he now felt, all at once, confused and disappointed. The mere thought, "The King is here!" alone gave him more alarm than those few words, on the night before: "The King is about to pass!" For then he was but facing the unknown, and now he knew that icy stare, that implacable, impassible majesty.

"Ah! Bon Dieu! What a figure I should cut if I were to be so mad as to try and penetrate this garden, and find myself face to face with this superb monarch, sipping his coffee beside a rivulet."

At once the sinister shadow of the Bastille seemed to fall before the poor lover; instead of the charming image that he had retained of the marquise and her smile, he saw dungeons, cells, black bread, questionable water; he knew the story of Latude, thirty years an inmate of the Bastille. Little by little his hope seemed to be taking to itself wings.

"And yet," he again said to himself, "I am doing no harm, nor the King either. I protest against an injustice; but I never wrote or sang scurrilous songs. I was so well received at Versailles yesterday, and the lackeys were so polite. What am I afraid of? Of committing a blunder? I shall make many more which will repair this one."

He approached the gate and touched it with his finger. It was not quite closed. He opened it, and resolutely entered.

The gatekeeper turned round with a look of annoyance.

"What are you looking for? Where are you going?"

"I am going to Madame de Pompadour."

"Have you an audience?"

"Yes."

"Where is your letter?"

He was no longer the "marquis" of the night before, and, this time, there was no Duc d'Aumont. The chevalier lowered his eyes sadly, and noticed that his white stockings and Rhinestone buckles were covered with dust. He had made the mistake of coming on foot, in a region where no one walked. The gatekeeper also bent his eyes, and scanned him, not from head to foot, but from foot to head. The dress seemed neat enough, but the hat was rather askew, and the hair lacked powder.

"You have no letter. What do you wish?"

"I wish to speak to Madame de Pompadour."

"Really! And you think this is the way it is done?"

"I know nothing about it. Is the King here?"

"Perhaps. Go about your business and leave me alone."

The chevalier did not wish to lose his temper, but, in spite of himself, this insolence made him turn pale.

"I sometimes have told a lackey to go away," he replied, "but a lackey never said so to me."

"Lackey! I a lackey?" exclaimed the enraged gatekeeper.

"Lackey, doorkeeper, valet, or menial, I care not, and it matters little."

The gatekeeper made a step toward the chevalier with clenched fists and face aflame. The chevalier, brought to himself by the appearance of a threat, lifted the handle of his sword slightly.

"Take care, fellow," said he, "I am a gentleman, and it would cost me but thirty-six livres to put a boor like you under ground."

"If you are a nobleman, monsieur, I belong to the King; I am only doing my duty; so do not think—"

At this moment the flourish of a hunting-horn sounding from the Bois de Satory was heard afar, and lost itself in the echo. The chevalier allowed his sword to drop into its scabbard, no longer thinking of the interrupted quarrel.

"I declare," said he, "it is the King starting for the hunt! Why did you not tell me that before?"

"That has nothing to do with me, nor with you either."

"Listen to me, my good man. The King is not here; I have no letter, I have no audience. Here is some money for you; let me in."

He drew from his pocket several pieces of gold. The gatekeeper scanned him anew with a superb contempt.

"What is that?" said he, disdainfully. "Is it thus you seek to penetrate into a royal dwelling? Instead of making you go out, take care I don't lock you in."

"*You*—you valet!" said the chevalier, getting angry again and once more seizing his sword.

"Yes, I," repeated the big man. But during this conversation, in which the historian regrets to have compromised his hero, thick clouds had darkened the sky; a storm was brewing. A flash of lightning burst forth, followed by a violent peal of thunder, and the rain began to fall heavily. The chevalier, who still held his gold, saw a drop of water on his dusty shoe as large as a crown piece.

"Peste!" said he, "let us find shelter. It would never do to get wet."

He turned nimbly toward the den of Cerberus, or, if you please, the gate-keeper's lodge.

Once in there, he threw himself unceremoniously into the big armchair of the gatekeeper himself.

"Heavens! How you annoy me!" said he, "and how unfortunate I am! You take me for a conspirator, and you do not understand that I have in my pocket a petition for his Majesty! If I am from the country, you are nothing but a dolt."

The gatekeeper, for answer, went to a corner to fetch his halberd, and remained standing thus with the weapon in his fist.

"When are you going away?" he cried out in a stentorian voice.

The quarrel, in turn forgotten and taken up again, seemed this time to be becoming quite serious, and already the gatekeeper's two big hands trembled strangely on his pike;—what was to happen? I do not know. But, suddenly turning his head—"Ah!" said the chevalier, "who comes here?"

A young page mounted on a splendid horse (not an English one;—at that time thin legs were not the fashion) came up at full speed. The road was soaked with rain; the gate was but half open. There was a pause; the keeper advanced and opened the gate. The page spurred his horse, which had stopped for the space of an instant; it tried to resume its gait, but missed its footing, and, slipping on the damp ground, fell.

It is very awkward, almost dangerous, to raise a fallen horse. A riding-whip is of no use. The kicking of the beast, which is doing its best, is extremely disagreeable, especially when one's own leg is caught under the saddle.

The chevalier, however, came to the rescue without thinking of these inconveniences, and set about it so cleverly that the horse was soon raised and the rider freed. But the latter was covered with mud and could scarcely limp along.

Carried as well as might be to the gatekeeper's lodge and seated in his turn in the big armchair, "Sir," said he to the chevalier, "you are certainly a nobleman. You have rendered me a great service, but you can render me a still greater one. Here is a message from the King for Madame la Marquise, and this message is very urgent, as you see, since my horse and I, in order to go faster, almost broke our necks. You understand that, wounded as I am, with a lame leg, I could not deliver this paper. I should have, in order to do so, to be carried myself. Will you go there in my stead?"

At the same time he drew from his pocket a large envelope ornamented with gilt arabesques and fastened with the royal seal.

"Very willingly, sir," replied the chevalier, taking the envelope.

And, nimble and light as a feather, he set out at a run and on the tips of his toes.

V

When the chevalier arrived at the château he found another doorkeeper in front of the peristyle:

"By the King's order," said the young man, who this time no longer feared halberds, and, showing his letter, he passed gaily between half a dozen lackeys.

A tall usher, planted in the middle of the vestibule, seeing the order and the royal seal, gravely inclined himself, like a poplar bent by the wind—then, smiling, he touched with one of his bony fingers the corner of a piece of paneling.

A little swinging door, masked by tapestry, at once opened as if of its own accord. The bony man made an obsequious sign, the chevalier entered, and the tapestry, which had been drawn apart, fell softly behind him.

A silent valet introduced him into a drawing-room, then into a corridor, in which there were two or three closed doors, then at last into a second drawing-room, and begged him to wait a moment.

"Am I here again in the château of Versailles?" the chevalier asked himself. "Are we going to begin another game of hide-and-seek?"

Trianon was, at that time, neither what it is now nor what it had been. It has been said that Madame de Maintenon had made of Versailles an oratory, and Madame de Pompadour a boudoir. It has also been said of Trianon that *ce petit château de porcelaine* was the boudoir of Madame de Montespan. Be that as it may, concerning these boudoirs, it appears that Louis XV put them everywhere. This or that gallery, which his ancestor walked majestically, was then divided oddly into an infinity of apartments. There were some of every color, and the King went fluttering about in all these gardens of silk and velvet.

"Do you think my little furnished apartments are in good taste?" he one day asked the beautiful Comtesse de Sérrant.

"No," said she, "I would have them in blue."

As blue was the King's color, this answer flattered him.

At their next meeting, Madame de Sérrant found the salon upholstered in blue, as she had wished it.

That in which the chevalier now found himself alone was neither blue nor pink, it was all mirrors. We know how much a pretty woman with a lovely figure gains by letting her image repeat itself in a thousand aspects. She bewilders, she envelops, so to speak, him whom she desires to please. To whatever side he turns, he sees her. How can he avoid being charmed? He must either take to flight or own himself conquered.

The chevalier looked at the garden, too. There, behind, the bushes and labyrinths, the statues and the marble vases, that pastoral style which the marquise was about to introduce, and which, later on, Madame Du Barry and Marie Antoinette were to push to such a high degree of perfection, was beginning to show itself. Already there appeared the rural fantasies where the *blasé* conceits were disappearing. Already the puffing tritons, the grave goddesses, and the learned nymphs, the busts with flowing wigs, frozen with horror in their wealth of verdure, beheld an English garden rise from the ground, amid the wondering trees. Little lawns, little streams, little bridges, were soon to dethrone Olympus to replace it by a dairy, strange parody of nature, which the English copy without understanding—very child's play, for the nonce the pastime of an indolent master who tried in vain to escape the ennui of Versailles while remaining at Versailles itself.

But the chevalier was too charmed, too enraptured at finding himself there for a critical thought to present itself to his mind. He was, on the contrary, ready to admire everything, and was indeed admiring, twirling his missive between his fingers as a rustic does his hat, when a pretty waiting-maid opened the door, and said to him softly:

"Come, monsieur."

He had followed her, and after having once more passed through several corridors which were more or less mysterious, she ushered him into a large apartment where the shutters were half-closed. Here she stopped and seemed to listen.

"Still at hide-and-seek!" said the chevalier to himself. However, at the end of a few moments, yet another door opened, and another waiting-maid, who seemed to be even prettier than the first, repeated to him in the same tone the same words:

"Come, monsieur."

If he had been the victim of one kind of emotion at Versailles, he was subject to another, and still deeper feeling now, for he stood on the threshold of the temple in which the divinity dwelt. He advanced with a palpitating heart. A soft light, slightly veiled by thin, gauze curtains, succeeded obscurity; a delicious perfume, almost imperceptible, pervaded the air around him; the waiting-maid timidly drew back the corner of a silk portière, and, at the end of a large chamber furnished with elegant simplicity, he beheld the lady of the fan—the all-powerful marquise.

She was alone, seated before a table, wrapped in a dressing gown, her head resting on her hand, and, seemingly, deeply preoccupied. On seeing the chevalier enter, she rose with a sudden and apparently involuntary movement.

"You come on behalf of the King?"

The chevalier might have answered, but he could think of nothing better than to bow profoundly while presenting to the marquise the letter which he brought her. She took it, or rather seized upon it, with extreme eagerness. Her hands trembled on the envelope as she broke the seal.

This letter, written by the King's hand, was rather long. She devoured it at first, so to speak, with a glance, then she read it greedily, with profound attention, with wrinkled brow and tightened lips. She was not beautiful thus, and no longer resembled the magic apparition of the *petit foyer*. When she reached the end, she seemed to reflect. Little by little her face, which had turned pale, assumed a faint color (at this hour she did not wear rouge), and not only did she regain that graceful air which habitually belonged to her, but a gleam of real beauty illumined her delicate features; one might have taken her cheeks for two rose-leaves. She heaved a sigh, allowed the letter to fall upon the table, and, turning toward the chevalier, said, with the most charming smile:

"I kept you waiting, monsieur, but I was not yet dressed, and, indeed, am hardly so even now. That is why I was forced to get you to come through the private rooms, for I am almost as much besieged here as though I were at home. I would like to answer the King's note. Would it be too much trouble to you to do an errand for me?"

This time he *must* speak; the chevalier had had time to regain a little courage:

"Alas! madame," said he, sadly, "you confer a great favor on me, but, unfortunately, I can not profit by it."

"Why not?"

"I have not the honor to belong to his Majesty."

"How, then, did you come here?"

"By chance; I met on my way a page who had been thrown and who begged me—"

"How 'thrown'?" repeated the marquise, bursting out laughing. She seemed so happy at this moment that gaiety came to her without an effort.

"Yes, madame, he fell from his horse at the gate. I luckily found myself there to help him to rise, and, as his dress was very much disordered, he begged me to take charge of his message."

"And by what chance did you find yourself there?"

"Madame, it was because I had a petition to present to his Majesty."

"His Majesty lives at Versailles."

"Yes, but you live here."

"Oh! So it is you who wished to entrust me with a message."

"Madame, I beg you to believe—"

"Do not trouble yourself, you are not the first. But why do you address yourself to me? I am but a woman—like any other."

As she uttered these words with a somewhat ironical air, the marquise threw a triumphant look upon the letter she had just read.

"Madame," continued the chevalier, "I have always heard that men exercise power, and that women—"

"Guide it, eh? Well, monsieur, there is a queen of France."

"I know it, madame; that is how it happened that I found myself *here* this morning."

The marquise was more than accustomed to such compliments, though they were generally made in a whisper; but, in the present circumstances, this appeared to be quite singularly gratifying to her.

"And on what faith," said she, "on what assurance, did you believe yourself able to penetrate as far as this? For you did not count, I suppose, upon a horse's falling on the way."

"Madame, I believed—I hoped—"

"What did you hope?"

"I hoped that chance—might make—"

"Chance again! Chance is apparently one of your friends; but I warn you that if you have no other, it is a sad recommendation."

Perhaps offended Chance wished to avenge herself for this irreverence, for the chevalier, whom these few questions had more and more troubled, suddenly perceived, on the corner of the table, the identical fan that he had picked up the night before. He took it, and, as on the night before, presented it to the marquise, bending the knee before her.

"Here, madame," he said to her, "is the only friend that could plead for me—"

The marquise seemed at first astonished, and hesitated a moment, looking now at the fan, now at the chevalier.

"Ah! you are right," she said at last, "it is you, monsieur! I recognize you. It is you whom I saw yesterday, after the play, as I went by with M. de Richelieu. I let my fan drop, and you 'found yourself there,' as you were saying."

"Yes, madame."

"And very gallantly, as a true chevalier, you returned it to me. I did not thank you, but I was sure all the same, that he who knows how to pick up a fan with such grace would also know, at the right time, how to pick up the glove. And we are not ill-pleased at that, we women."

"And it is but too true, madame; for, on reaching here just now, I almost had a duel with the gatekeeper."

"Mercy on us!" said the marquise, once more seized with a fit of gaiety. "With the gatekeeper! And what about?"

"He would not let me come in."

"That would have been a pity! But who are you, monsieur? And what is your request?"

"Madame, I am called the Chevalier de Vauvert. M. de Biron had asked in my behalf for a cornetcy in the Guards."

"Oh! I remember now. You come from Neauflette; you are in love with Mademoiselle d'Annebault—"

"Madame, who could have told you?"

"Oh! I warn you that I am much to be feared. When memory fails me, I guess. You are a relative of the Abbé de Chauvelin, and were refused on that account; is not that so? Where is your petition?"

"Here it is, madame; but indeed I can not understand—"

"Why need you understand? Rise and lay your paper on the table. I am going to answer the King's letter; you will take him, at the same time, your request and my letter."

"But, madame, I thought I had mentioned to you—"

"You will go. You entered here on the business of the King, is not that true? Well, then, you will enter there in the business of the Marquise de Pompadour, lady of the palace to the Queen."

The chevalier bowed without a word, seized with a sort of stupefaction. The world had long known how much talk, how many ruses and intrigues, the favorite had brought to bear, and what obstinacy she had shown to obtain this title, which in reality brought her nothing but a cruel affront from the Dauphin. She had longed for it for ten years; she willed it, and she had succeeded. So M. de Vauvert, whom she did not know, although she knew of his love, pleased her as a bearer of happy news.

Immovable, standing behind her, the chevalier watched the marquise as she wrote, first, with all her heart—with passion—then with reflection, stopping, passing her hand under her little nose, delicate as amber. She grew impatient: the presence of a witness disturbed her. At last she made up her mind and drew her pen through something; it must be owned that after all it was but a rough draft.

Opposite the chevalier, on the other side of the table, there glittered a fine Venetian mirror. This timid messenger hardly dared raise his eyes. It would, however, have been difficult not to see in this mirror, over the head of the marquise, the anxious and charming face of the new lady of the palace.

"How pretty she is!" thought he; "it is a pity that I am in love with somebody else; but Athénaïs is more beautiful, and moreover it would be on my part such a horrible disloyalty."

"What are you talking about?" said the marquise. The chevalier, as was his wont, had thought aloud without knowing it. "What are you saying?"

"I, madame? I am waiting."

"There; that is done," the marquise went on, taking another sheet of paper; but at the slight movement she had made in turning around the dressing-gown had slipped on her shoulder.

Fashion is a strange thing. Our grandmothers thought nothing of going to court in immense robes exposing almost the entire bosom, and it was by no means considered indecent; but they carefully hid the back of their necks, which the fine ladies of to-day expose so freely in the balcony of the opera. This is a newly invented beauty.

On the frail, white, dainty shoulder of Madame de Pompadour there was a little black mark that looked like a fly floating in milk. The chevalier, serious as a giddy boy who is trying to keep his countenance, looked at the mark, and the marquise, holding her pen in the air, looked at the chevalier in the mirror.

In that mirror a rapid glance was exchanged, which meant to say on the one side, "You are charming," and on the other, "I am not sorry for it."

However, the marquise readjusted her dressing-gown.

"You are looking at my beauty spot?"

"I am not looking, madame; I see and I admire."

"Here is my letter; take it to the King with your petition."

"But, madame—"

"Well?"

"His Majesty is hunting; I have just heard the horn in the wood of Satory."

"That is true. I did not think of it. Well, to-morrow. The day after; it matters little. No, immediately. Go. You will give that to Lebel. Good-by, monsieur. Try and remember the beauty spot you have just seen; the King alone in the whole kingdom has seen it; and as for your friend, Chance, tell her, I beg of you, to take care and not chatter to herself so loud, as she did just now. Farewell, chevalier."

She touched a little bell, then, lifting a flood of laces upon her sleeve, held out to the young man her bare arm. He once more bent low, and with the tips of his lips scarcely brushed the rosy nails of the marquise. She saw no impoliteness in it—far from it—but, perhaps, a little too much modesty.

At once the little waiting-maids reappeared (the big ones were not yet up), and, standing behind them, like a steeple in the middle of a flock of sheep, the bony man, still smiling, was pointing the way.

VI

Alone, ensconced in an old armchair in the back of his little room at the sign of "the Sun," the chevalier waited the next day, then the next, and no news!

"Singular woman! Gentle and imperious, good and bad, the most frivolous of women, and the most obstinate! She has forgotten me. What misery! She is right;—she is all-powerful, and I am nothing."

He had risen, and was walking about the room.

"Nothing!—no, I am but a poor devil. How truly my father spoke! The marquise was mocking me; that is all; while I was looking at her, it was only the reflection in that mirror, and in my eyes, of her own charms—which are, certainly, incomparable—that made her look so pleased! Yes, her eyes are small, but what grace! And Latour, before Diderot, has taken the dust from a butterfly's wing to paint her portrait. She is not very tall, but her figure is perfectly exquisite. Ah! Mademoiselle d'Annebault! Ah! my beloved friend, is it possible that I, too, should forget?"

Two or three sharp raps at the door awoke him from his grief.

"Who is there?"

The bony man, clad all in black, with a splendid pair of silk stockings, which simulated calves that were lacking, entered, and made a deep bow.

"This evening, Monsieur le Chevalier, there is to be a masked ball at the court, and Madame la Marquise sends me to say that you are invited."

"That is enough, monsieur. Many thanks."

As soon as the bony man had retired, the chevalier ran to the bell; the same maid-servant who, three days before, had done her best to be of service to him, assisted him to put on the same spangled coat, striving to acquit herself even better than before.

And then the young man took his way toward the palace, invited this time, and more quiet outwardly, but more anxious and less bold than when he had made his first steps in that, to him, still unknown world.

VII

Bewildered, almost as much as on the former occasion, by all the splendors of Versailles, which this evening was not empty, the chevalier walked in the great gallery, looking on every side and doing all he could to learn why he was there; but nobody seemed to think of accosting him. At the end of an hour he became wearied and was about to leave, when two masks, exactly alike, seated on a bench, stopped him on his way. One of them took aim at him with her finger as if with a pistol; the other rose and went to him:

"It appears, monsieur," said the mask, carelessly taking his arm, "that you are on very good terms with our marquise."

"I beg your pardon, madame, but of whom are you speaking?"

"You know well enough."

"Not the least in the world."

"Oh! but indeed you do."

"Not at all."

"All the court knows it."

"I do not belong to the court."

"You are playing the child. I tell you it is well known!"

"That may be, madame, but I am ignorant of it."

"You are not ignorant, however, of the fact that the day before yesterday a page fell from his horse at the gate of Trianon. Were you not there by chance?"

"Yes, madame."

"Did you not help him to rise?"

"Yes, madame."

"And did not you enter the château?"

"Certainly."

"And was not a paper given to you?"

"Yes, madame."

"And did you not take it to the King?"

"Assuredly."

"The King was not at Trianon; he was hunting; the marquise was alone—is not that so?"

"Yes, madame."

"She had just risen; she was scarcely clad, excepting, as it is rumored, in a wide dressing-gown."

"People whom one can not prevent from speaking tell all that runs through their heads."

"That is all well enough, but it appears that there passed between your eyes and hers a look which did not offend her."

"What do you mean by that, madame?"

"That you did not displease her."

"I know nothing about that, and I should be distressed that such sweet and rare good-will, which I did not expect, and which touched me to the bottom of my heart, should give occasion to any idle speeches."

"You take fire too quickly, chevalier; one would think that you were chal-
lenging the whole court; you would never succeed in killing so many people."

"But, madame, if the page fell, and if I carried his message—allow me to
ask why I am interrogated."

The mask pressed his arm and said to him:

"Listen, monsieur."

"As much as you please, madame."

"This is what we are thinking about now: The King no longer loves the
marquise, and nobody believes that he ever loved her. She has just committed
an imprudence; she has set the whole Parliament against her with her "two
sous" tax, and to-day she dares attack a far greater power—the Society of
Jesuits. She will fail, but she has weapons, and, before perishing, she will
defend herself."

"Well, madame, what can I do?"

"I will tell you. M. de Choiseul has half quarreled with M. de Bernis;
neither of them is sure what it is he would like to attempt. Bernis is going
away; Choiseul will take his place. A word from you can decide it."

"In what way, madame, pray?"

"By allowing your story of the other day to be told."

"What earthly connection can there be between my visit, the Jesuits, and
the Parliament?"

"Write me one word and the marquise is lost. And do not doubt that the
warmest interest, the most complete gratitude—"

"I humbly beg your pardon again, madame, but what you are asking of me
would be an act of cowardice."

"Is there any honor in politics?"

"I know nothing of all that. Madame de Pompadour let her fan fall before
me; I picked it up; I gave it back to her; she thanked me; she permitted me
with that peculiar grace of hers to thank her in my turn."

"A truce to ceremonies: time flies; my name is the Countess d'Estrades;
you love Mademoiselle d'Annebault, my niece; do not say no, it is useless.
You are seeking a cornetcy; you shall have it to-morrow, and if you care for
Athénaïs you will soon be my nephew."

"Ah! madame, what excess of goodness!"

"But you must speak."

"No, madame."

"I have been told that you love that little girl."

"As much as it is possible to love; but if ever my love is to declare itself in
her presence my honor must also be there."

"You are very obstinate, chevalier! Is that your final reply?"

"It is the last, as it was the first."

"You refuse to enter the Guards? You refuse the hand of my niece?"

"Yes, madame, if that be the price."

Madame d'Estrades cast upon the chevalier a piercing look, full of curiosity; then seeing in his face no sign of hesitation she slowly walked away, losing herself in the crowd.

The chevalier, unable to make anything of this singular adventure, went and sat down in a corner of the gallery.

"What does that woman mean to do?" said he to himself. "She must be a little mad. She wishes to upset the state by means of a silly calumny, and she proposes to me that in order to merit the hand of her niece I should dishonor myself. But Athénaïs would no longer care for me, or, if she lent herself to such an intrigue, I would no longer care for her. What! Strive to harm this good marquise, to defame her, to blacken her character. Never! no, never!"

Always intent upon his own thoughts, the chevalier very probably would have risen and spoken aloud, but just then a small rosy finger touched him on the shoulder.

He raised his eyes and saw before him the pair of masks who had stopped him.

"You do not wish to help us a little then?" said one of the masks, disguising her voice. But although the two costumes were exactly alike, and all seemed calculated to mislead, the chevalier was not deceived. Neither the look nor the tone was the same.

"Will you answer, sir?"

"No, madame."

"Will you write."

"Neither will I write."

"It is true that you are obstinate. Good-night, lieutenant."

"What do you say, madame?"

"There is your commission and your marriage contract." And she threw the fan to him.

It was the one which the chevalier had already twice picked up. The little cupids of Boucher sported on the parchment of the gilded mother-of-pearl masterpiece. There was no longer any doubt; it was the fan of Madame de Pompadour.

"Heavens! Marquise, is it possible?"

"Very possible," said she, raising the little piece of black veil on her chin.

"I know, madame, how to answer—"

"It is not necessary. You are a loyal gentleman, and we shall see each other again, for we are to be in the same house. The King has placed you in the 'cornette blanche.' Remember that for a petitioner there is no greater eloquence than to know how to be silent if need be—"

"And forgive us," added she, laughing as she ran away, "if before bestowing upon you our niece's hand, we thought it expedient to find out your true worth."

THE LONG EXILE

―――――――❧❦❧―――――――

Leo Tolstoy

"God sees the truth, but bides his time."

Once upon a time there lived in the city of Vladímir a young merchant named Aksénof. He had two shops and a house. Aksénof himself had a ruddy complexion and curly hair; he was a very jolly fellow and a good singer. When he was young he used to drink too much, and when he was tipsy he was turbulent; but after his marriage he ceased drinking, and only occasionally had a spree.

One time in summer Aksénof was going to Nízhni to the great Fair. As he was about to bid his family good-by, his wife said to him:

"Iván Dmítrievitch, do not go to-day; I had a dream, and dreamed that some misfortune befell you."

Aksénof laughed at her, and said: "You are always afraid that I shall go on a spree at the Fair."

His wife said: "I myself know not what I am afraid of, but I had such a strange dream: you seemed to be coming home from town, and you took off your hat, and I looked, and your head was all gray."

Aksénof laughed. "That means good luck. See, I am going now. I will bring you some rich remembrances."

And he bade his family farewell and set off.

When he had gone half his journey, he fell in with a merchant of his acquaintance, and the two stopped together at the same tavern for the night. They took tea together, and went to sleep in two adjoining rooms.

Aksénof did not care to sleep long; he awoke in the middle of the night, and in order that he might get a good start while it was cool he aroused his driver and bade him harness up, went down into the smoky hut, settled his account with the landlord, and started on his way.

After he had driven forty versts, he again stopped to get something to eat; he rested in the vestibule of the inn, and when it was noon, he went to the doorstep and ordered the samovár got ready; then he took out his guitar and began to play.

Suddenly a troïka with a bell dashed up to the inn, and from the equipage leaped an official with two soldiers; he comes directly up to Aksénof and asks: "Who are you? Where did you come from?"

Aksénof answers without hesitation, and asks him if he would not have a glass of tea with him.

But the official keeps on with his questions: "Where did you spend last night? Were you alone or with a merchant? Have you seen the merchant this morning? Why did you leave so early this morning?"

Aksénof wondered why he was questioned so closely; but he told everything just as it was, and he asks. "Why do you ask me so many questions? I am not a thief or a murderer. I am on my own business; there is nothing to question me about."

Then the official called up the soldiers, and said: "I am the police inspector, and I have made these inquiries of you because the merchant with whom you spent last night has been stabbed. Show me your things, and you men search him."

They went into the tavern, brought in the trunk and bag, and began to open and search them. Suddenly the police inspector pulled out from the bag a knife, and demanded: "Whose knife is this?"

Aksénof looked and saw a knife covered with blood taken from his bag, and he was frightened.

"And whose blood is that on the knife?"

Aksénof tried to answer, but he could not articulate his words:

"I—I—don't—know—I—That knife—it is—not mine—"

Then the police inspector said: "This morning the merchant was found stabbed to death in his bed. No one except you could have done it. The tavern was locked on the inside, and there was no one in the tavern except yourself. And here is the bloody knife in your bag, and your guilt is evident in your face. Tell me how you killed him and how much money you took from him."

Aksénof swore that he had not done it, that he had not seen the merchant after he had drunken tea with him, that the only money that he had with him —eight thousand rubles—was his own, and that the knife was not his.

But his voice trembled, his face was pale, and he was all quivering with fright, like a guilty person.

The police inspector called the soldiers, commanded them to bind Aksénof and take him to the wagon.

When they took him to the wagon with his feet tied, Aksénof crossed himself and burst into tears.

They confiscated Aksénof's possessions and his money, and took him to the next city and threw him into prison.

They sent to Vladímir to make inquiries about Aksénof's character, and all the merchants and citizens of Vladímir declared that Aksénof, when he was young, used to drink and was wild, but that now he was a worthy man. Then he was brought up for judgment. He was sentenced for having killed the merchant and for having robbed him of twenty thousand rubles.

Aksénof's wife was dumfounded by the event, and did not know what to think. Her children were still small, and there was one at the breast. She took them all with her and journeyed to the city where her husband was imprisoned.

At first they would not grant her admittance, but afterward she got permission from the chief, and was taken to her husband.

When she saw him in his prison garb, in chains together with murderers, she fell to the floor, and it was a long time before she recovered from her swoon. Then she placed her children around her, sat down amid them, and began to tell him about their domestic affairs, and to ask him about everything that had happened to him.

He told her the whole story.

She asked: "What is to be the result of it?"

He said: "We must petition the Czar. It is impossible that an innocent man should be condemned."

The wife said that she already sent in a petition to the Czar, but that the petition had not been granted. Aksénof said nothing, but was evidently very much downcast.

Then his wife said: "You see the dream that I had, when I dreamed that you had become gray-headed, meant something, after all. Already your hair has begun to turn gray with trouble. You ought to have stayed at home that time." And she began to tear her hair, and said: "Ványa, my dearest husband, tell your wife the truth: Did you commit that crime or not?"

Aksénof said: "So you, too, have no faith in me!" And he wrung his hands and wept.

Then a soldier came and said that it was time for the wife and children to go. And Aksénof for the last time bade farewell to his family.

When his wife was gone, Aksénof began to think over all that they had said. When he remembered that his wife had also distrusted him, and had asked him if he had murdered the merchant, he said to himself: "It is evident that no one but God can know the truth of the matter, and He is the only one to ask for mercy, and He is the only one from whom to expect it."

And from that time Aksénof ceased to send in petitions, ceased to hope, and only prayed to God. Aksénof was sentenced to be knouted, and then to exile with hard labor. And so it was done.

He was flogged with the knout, and then, when the wounds from the knout were healed, he was sent with other exiles to Siberia.

Aksénof lived twenty-six years in the mines. The hair on his head had become white as snow, and his beard had grown long, thin, and gray. All his gaiety had vanished.

He was bent, his gait was slow, he spoke little, he never laughed, and he spent much of his time in prayer.

Aksénof had learned while in prison to make boots, and with the money that he earned he bought the "Book of Martyrs," and used to read it when it was light enough in prison, and on holidays he would go to the prison church, read the Gospels, and sing in the choir, for his voice was still strong and good.

The authorities liked Aksénof for his submissiveness, and his prison associates respected him and called him "Grandfather" and the "man of God." Whenever they had petitions to be presented, Aksénof was always chosen to carry them to the authorities; and when quarrels arose among the prisoners, they always came to Aksénof as umpire.

Aksénof never received any letters from home, and he knew not whether his wife and children were alive.

One time some new convicts came to the prison. In the evening all the old convicts gathered around the newcomers, and began to ply them with questions as to the cities or villages from which this one or that had come, and what their crimes were.

At this time Aksénof was sitting on his bunk, near the strangers, and, with bowed head, was listening to what was said.

One of the new convicts was a tall, healthy looking old man of sixty years, with a close-cropped gray beard. He was telling why he had been arrested. He said:

"And so, brothers, I was sent here for nothing. I unharnessed a horse from a postboy's sledge, and they caught me in it, and insisted that I was stealing it. 'But,' says I, 'I only wanted to go a little faster, so I whipped up the horse. And besides, the driver was a friend of mine. It's all right,' says I. 'No,' say they; 'you were stealing it.' But they did not know what and where I had stolen. I have done things which long ago would have sent me here, but I was not found out; and now they have sent me here without any justice in it. But what's the use of grumbling? I have been in Siberia before. They did not keep me here very long though—"

"Where did you come from?" asked one of the convicts.

"Well, we came from the city of Vladímir; we are citizens of that place. My name is Makár, and my father's name was Semyón."

Aksénof raised his head and asked:

"Tell me, Semyónitch, have you ever heard of the Aksénofs, merchants in Vladímir city? Are they alive?"

"Indeed, I heard of them! They are rich merchants, though their father is in Siberia. It seems he was just like any of the rest of us sinners. And now tell me, Grandfather, what you were sent here for?"

Aksénof did not like to speak of his misfortune; he sighed, and said:

"Twenty-six years ago I was condemned to hard labor on account of my sins."

Makár Semyónof said:

"But what was your crime?"

Aksénof replied: "I must, therefore, have deserved this."

But he would not tell or give any further particulars; the other convicts, however, related why Aksénof had been sent to Siberia. They told how on the road some one had killed a merchant, and put the knife into Aksénof's luggage, and how he had been unjustly punished for this.

When Makár heard this, he glanced at Aksénof, clasped his hands round his knees, and said:

"Well, now, that's wonderful! You have been growing old, Grandfather!"

They began to ask him what he thought was wonderful, and where he had seen Aksénof. But Makár did not answer; he only repeated:

"A miracle, boys! how wonderful that we should meet again!"

And when he said these words, it came over Aksénof that perhaps this man might know who it was that had killed the merchant. And he said:

"Did you ever hear of that crime, Semyónitch, or did you ever see me before?"

"Of course I heard of it! The country was full of it. But it happened a long time ago. And I have forgotten what I heard," said Makár.

"Perhaps you heard who killed the merchant?" asked Aksénof.

Makár laughed, and said:

"Why, of course the man who had the knife in his bag killed him. If any one put the knife in your things and was not caught doing it—it would have been impossible. For how could they have put the knife in your bag? Was it not standing close by your head? And you would have heard it, wouldn't you?"

As soon as Aksénof heard these words he felt convinced that this was the very man who had killed the merchant.

He stood up and walked away. All that night he was unable to sleep. Deep melancholy came upon him, and he began to call back the past in his imagination.

He imagined his wife as she had been when for the last time she had come to see him in the prison. She seemed to stand before him exactly as though she were alive, and he saw her face and her eyes, and he seemed to hear her words and her laugh.

Then his imagination brought up his children before him; one a little boy in a little fur coat, and the other on his mother's breast.

And he imagined himself as he was at that time, young and happy. He remembered how he had sat on the steps of the tavern when they arrested him, and how his soul was full of joy as he played on his guitar.

And he remembered the place of execution where they had knouted him, and the knoutsman, and the people standing around, and the chains and the convicts, and all his twenty-six years of prison life, and he remembered his old age. And such melancholy came upon Aksénof that he was tempted to put an end to himself.

"And all on account of this criminal!" said Aksénof to himself.

And then he began to feel such anger against Makár Semyónof that he almost fell upon him, and was crazy with desire to pay off the load of vengeance. He repeated prayers all night, but could not recover his calm. When day came he walked by Makár and did not look at him.

Thus passed two weeks. Aksénof was not able to sleep, and such melancholy had come over him that he did not know what to do.

One time during the night, as he happened to be passing through the prison, he saw that the soil was disturbed under one of the bunks. He stopped to examine it. Suddenly Makár crept from under the bunk and looked at Aksénof with a startled face.

Aksénof was about to pass on so as not to see him, but Makár seized his arm, and told him how he had been digging a passage under the wall, and how every day he carried the dirt out in his bootlegs and emptied it in the street when they went out to work. He said:

"If you only keep quiet, old man, I will get you out too. But if you tell on me, they will flog me; but afterward I will make it hot for you. I will kill you."

When Aksénof saw his enemy, he trembled all over with rage, twitched away his arm, and said: "I have no reason to make my escape, and to kill me would do no harm; you killed me long ago. But as to telling on you or not, I shall do as God sees fit to have me."

On the next day, when they took the convicts out to work, the soldiers discovered where Makár had been digging in the ground; they began to make a search, and found the hole. The chief came into the prison and asked every one, "Who was digging that hole?"

All denied it. Those who knew did not name Makár, because they were aware that he would be flogged half to death for such an attempt.

Then the chief came to Aksénof. He knew that Aksénof was a truthful man, and he said: "Old man, you are truthful; tell me before God who did this."

Makár was standing near, in great excitement, and did not dare to look at Aksénof.

Aksénof's hands and lips trembled, and it was some time before he could speak a word. He said to himself: "If I shield him—But why should I forgive him when he has been my ruin? Let him suffer for my sufferings! But shall I tell on him? They will surely flog him? But what difference does it make what I think of him? Will it be any the easier for me?"

Once more the chief demanded:

"Well, old man, tell the truth! Who dug the hole?"

Aksénof glanced at Makár, and then said:

"I can not tell, your Honor. God does not bid me tell. I will not tell. Do with me as you please; I am in your power."

In spite of all the chief's efforts, Aksénof would say nothing more. And so they failed to find out who dug the hole.

On the next night as Aksénof was lying on his bunk, and almost asleep, he heard some one come along and sit down at his feet.

He peered through the darkness and saw that it was Makár.

Aksénof asked:

"What do you wish of me? What are you doing here?"

Makár remained silent. Aksénof arose, and said:

"What do you want? Go away, or else I will call the guard."

Makár went up close to Aksénof and said in a whisper:

"Iván Dmítritch, forgive me!"

Aksénof said: "What have I to forgive you?"

"It was I who killed the merchant and put the knife in your bag. And I was going to kill you too, but there was a noise in the yard; I thrust the knife in your bag, and slipped out of the window."

Aksénof said nothing, and he did not know what to say. Makár got down from the bunk, knelt on the ground, and said:

"Iván Dmítritch, forgive me, forgive me for Christ's sake. I will confess that I killed the merchant—they will pardon you. You will be able to go home." Aksénof said:

"It is easy for you to say that, but how could I endure it? Where should I go now? My wife is dead! my children have forgotten me. I have nowhere to go."

Makár did not rise; he beat his head on the ground, and said:

"Iván Dmítritch, forgive me! When they flogged me with the knout, it was easier to bear than it is now to look at you. And you had pity on me after all this—you did not tell on me. Forgive me for Christ's sake! Forgive me though I am a cursed villain!"

And the man began to sob.

When Aksénof heard Makár Semyónof sobbing, he himself burst into tears, and said:

"God will forgive you; maybe I am a hundred times worse than you are!"

And suddenly he felt a wonderful peace in his soul. And he ceased to mourn for his home, and had no desire to leave the prison, but only thought of his last hour.

Makár would not listen to Aksénof, and confessed his crime.

When they came to let Aksénof go home, he was dead.